A Garland Series

The
Flowering of the Novel

Representative Mid-Eighteenth Century Fiction
1740-1775

A Collection of 121 Titles

The Virtuous Villager

Chevalier de Mouhy

Garland Publishing, Inc., New York & London

1975

———

Bibliographical note:

Part I of this facsimile has been made from
a copy in the Newberry Library
(Case.Y.1565.M862)
and Part II from a copy in the Yale
University Library (Hfd29.59f)

———

Library of Congress Cataloging in Publication Data

Mouhy, Charles de Fieux, chevalier de, 1701-1784.
    The virtuous villager.

    (The Flowering of the novel)
    Translation of La paysanne parvenue.
    Reprint of the 1742 ed. published by F. Cogan, London.
    I. Title. II. Title: Virgin's victory.
III. Series.
PZ3.M8596Vi3 ₍PQ2013.M65₎   843'.5   74-34593
ISBN 0-8240-1106-6

Printed in the United States of America

THE
VIRTUOUS VILLAGER,
OR
VIRGIN'S VICTORY:
BEING

The MEMOIRS of a very GREAT
LADY at the Court of *France*.

Written by HERSELF.

In which the Artifices of defigning Men are fully
detected and expofed; and the Calamities they
bring on credulous believing Woman, are particularly related.

Tranflated from the Original, by the Author of
La Belle Affemblée.

In TWO VOLUMES.

VOL. I.

In vain are mufty Morals taught in Schools,
By rigid Teachers, and as rigid Rules,
Where Virtue with a frowning Afpect ftands,
And frights the Pupil from her rough Commands:
But charming Woman can true Converts make,
We love the Precept for the Teacher's fake;
Virtue in them appears fo bright, fo gay,
We bear with Tranfport, and with Pride obey.

LONDON:
Printed for FRANCIS COGAN, at the *Middle-Temple-Gate.*

MDCCXLII.

TO

Mrs. CRAWLEY.

MADAM,

A WORK chiefly intended to inculcate the Principles of Virtue, can no where so justly hope Protection, as from a Lady, whose Patronage will give a dou-

ble

ble Weight, to all the amiable Precepts contained in it, by being herself so shining an Example.

Paternal Tenderness——filial Duty and Affection——the Obligations of disinterested Friendship——true Generosity——Benevolence——a soft Commiseration for Distress, and the strictest Piety, can with no shew of Probability be carried to a more sublime Pitch than in the following little History, and I am very certain are Qualifications too dear to you, not to afford you

you Satisfaction in feeing them difplayed, with all the Advantages they can receive, from the Pen of a Lady, whofe Wit and Eloquence render her, at this Day, one of the greateft Ornaments of the *French* Court.

The noble Authoref has doubtlef done her part, and as I have taken the utmoft Care that none of her Beauties fhall fuffer by being put into an *Englifh* Drefs, I flatter myfelf, Madam, with obtaining your pardon, for the liberty I take in laying my

Endeavours

Endeavours at your Feet, and telling you in this publick manner, that I am with the most perfect Respect and Submission,

MADAM,

Your most humble, and

most devoted Servant,

ELIZA HAYWOOD.

PREFACE.

A *Translation of* la Payſan Parvenu, *from the* French *of the Chevalier* Mouhi, *having already appeared, we think it highly neceſſary to inform the* Publick, *that the following Sheets, tho' they contain much the ſame Facts are not tranſlated from the ſame Original, but from the real Manuſcript of the Marchioneſs de* L——V——; *it is certain that Lady committed her Papers*

to

to the Chevalier, with a Defign to have
them printed, and the Letters he has inferted, were doubtlefs wrote by her to him
for that purpofe ; but fome Accidents re-
tarding the Publication for feveral Months
many of them were miflaid, and the Marchionefs being at that time at a confiderable diflance from Paris, he was obliged to make up the Deficiency by the help
of his Memory, and where that failed by
his Invention; fo that in many places, there
is a wide Difference between what fhe intended for the World, and what he has
prefented to it.

It was from Madame de Melicourt,
whofe Hiflory has no inconfiderable Share
in thefe Volumes, and who is ftill no lefs dear
to the admirable Authorefs, than the Reader will find fhe was at the time they were
wrote,

wrote, that an English *Lady of Quality, now in* Paris, *procured the Copy of these interesting Memoirs, and also Permission to send it over to a Person, who she is pleased to think qualified to do it justice, both as to the Spirit and Expression.*

This we believe sufficient to clear us from any sinister Views in what we have done; but least there should be any so scrupulously just as to imagine a second Translation, a kind of Invasion on the Property of the first, we beg leave to assure the Publick, that this was begun long before the Country-Maid *was advertised, tho' laid aside for some time, on the account of a severe Indisposition, and afterwards on hearing it was doing by another hand; nor probably would ever have been resumed, but on the Instances of the Lady above mentioned,*

mentioned, and to rescue the Characters
of those noble Persons, whose Elegance of
Stile, as well as Sentiments, Wit and Spirit, are most miserably impaired through-
out the whole Translation from Mouhi.
For the Truth of this we appeal to the
Readers of it. Since it would be preposterous to quote particular Passages from
a Work where all alike is dull and spirit-
less, as indeed all Translations will be
where without any Considerations of the
different Idioms of Languages, or any Endeavour, or perhaps Capacity of entring
into the Soul of the Author, a slavish
Adherence to the Letter only is observed.

THE

THE

VIRTUOUS VILLAGER,

OR,

VIRGIN's VICTORY.

T is not without great Difficulty, that Persons raised from the lowest to the most elevated Station, consent to mention the mean Original from which they sprung : I do not pretend to distinguish from what Principle this Vanity is derived ; but whatever it be, I confess, I feel a secret Repugnance in doing it, which I ought to be more ashamed of than the Cause ; and tho' Reason and Religion have taught me to despise this Prejudice, I cannot accustom myself to remember, with the Ease I could wish to do, that the Marchioness *de L.——— V———* who holds so high a Rank in the present World, was once no more than plain *Jeanetta*, the Daughter of *John B———*, a poor Cleaver of Wood, in the Forest of *Fountainbleau.*

VOL. I.   B   From

From this mean Source, however, I derive my Being; he was Head Gardener to the Count *de N*————, my Mother waited on Madam la Counteſs, and found ſomewhat in him which inſpired her with a Paſſion, which not all the Remonſtrances of her Lady (to whom ſhe was extremely dear) could over-power. In fine ſhe married him, ſo was oblig'd to ſhare his Fortune ; which, though mean at the firſt, became ſtill worſe, by both being diſcharg'd from the Family on Account of this Marriage, which was look'd upon as very diſproportionable, my Mother being of a much better Deſcent, as well as Education.

My Father afterwards took a little Cottage in a Hamlet near the Caſtle, and for the Subſiſtance of his Family was reduced to work in the Foreſt, in the manner I have already related. But what Toils ! What Scarcities cannot be chearfully ſuſtain'd for the Sake of an Object for whom we have a ſincere Affection !————My Father underwent with Pleaſure thoſe Labours he was uſed but to direct ; and my Mother regretted not the Loſs of thoſe Delicacies to which ſhe had been accuſtomed————Love ſoftned every Care————made every Burthen light, and happy in each other they ſeem'd to wiſh for nothing more.

I was the firſt Fruit of their Marriage, and my Birth ſo far from cieating any Diſquiet, ſeem'd to them to be a Preſage of better Fortune ; how right theſe Conjectures were the Sequel of my Adventures will determine.

My Mother, who had ſome time before I was born been reſtor'd to the good Graces of the Counteſs, ſo far as to be permitted to attend her frequently at the Caſtle, from whence ſhe never return'd without ſome Preſent, had now a Confirmation that her Ladyſhip ſtill retain'd great Part of the Affection ſhe formerly had for her, by her offering to hold me at the Font, and giving me that Name, which muſt remain with me in all Alterations of Fortune.

The Counteſs choſe for her Partner in the Honour ſhe did us the Marquis *De L*———— *V*————, who lived in the Neighbourhood, and was extremely intimate with her

her————My Baptifm was folemniz'd with a Pomp more befitting the Condition of the illuftrious Goffips, than that of the Perfon to whom they did this Honour; and our Family experienced the Sweets of it, by the Prefents ufual on fuch Occafions.

The firft Years of my Infancy pafs'd over without any thing remarkable; but as foon as I was of an Age capable of liftning to Inftruction, my Mother was always giving me Leffons of that Referve, which Perfons of my Sex ought to obferve to thofe of the other: She often told me that Virtue and Difcretion might be the Portion of all Conditions, and to give a greater Weight to her Precepts, related to me many Examples of young Maids, who from a low Degree, had been raifed to Greatnefs, by a ftrict Adherence to the Rules fhe laid down for my Behaviour; and of others who had fallen into extreme Mifery and Infamy, by fwerving from them. Living feveral Years with the Countefs, and attending her to Court, and in many Parties of Pleafures, had given her a great Knowledge of the World, and furnifh'd her with a Variety of Hiftories of this Sort; and to do her Juftice, fhe knew fo well how to embellifh them in the Recital, that they were not only an agreeable Amufement to me at that Time, but alfo made fuch an Impreffion on my Mind, as was not eafy to be eraced, and were of infinite Service to me, in the various Accidents that afterwards befell me.

As I had never known a better State, I repined not at, nor indeed was fenfible of the Mifery of ours, and the only Trouble I felt was at the Murmurings of a Brother and Sifter I had, who, tho' younger than myfelf, were obliged to affift my Father in his Work, while I was kept at Home with my Mother in lefs painful Employments; the greateft Part of my Labours being to carry them their Dinner. This partial Diftinction as they termed it, occafioned fuch bitter Complaints, that my Father fometimes could not refrain taking Part in them; and feldom a Day pafs'd in which my Mother had not fome frefh Motive to lament that rude and clownifh manner, which People are apt to contract in

fuch

such mean Occupations ; and she frequently said it seem'd to her, as if the Toils of the Body had an Influence on the Mind, and render'd it incapable of any refined or or elevated Ideas.

As there was, however, some Regard paid to my Mother, the Fury of their Resentment fell upon me, which grew more grievous to me, as my Notions became every Day more delicate ; and here was my first Opportunity of exerting that Patience and Resignation to the Divine Will, which had been instill'd into me from my most early Years. But notwithstanding all the Precepts which had been given me, and the constant Admonitions my Ears were perpetually filled with, to cast all my Cares on that Supreme Being, who could alone relieve them ; I have since found, and set it down as a Maxim, on recollecting what Sentiments I had at that Time, that Vanity is inseparable from Youth. I remember very well, that when I came to be about the Age of Thirteen, I resented every little Insult with a kind of Disdain of those that offer'd it ; and would often tell them they used me in that manner, only because they knew no better. The Truth is, I then began to grow fond of myself, and to imagine I had something extraordinary about me : Every body said I was pretty———— one prais'd my Eyes————another my Mouth————some my Complexion————and others the fine turn of my Neck————in fine, every Part had its Admirers, and I easily believed all I heard to my Advantage ; but what most contributed to advance the good Opinion I now entertain'd of myself was this.

I was sent one Day to the Castle with some Cream for the Countess : I had always Admission to her Toilet, and a Gentleman happening to be with her at that Time, she presented me to him as her God-Daughter. ————He finding something in me agreeable to his Taste, I suppose, cry'd out several times, Heavens ! how lovely she is !———— What a Set of Features are there !————What a Skin————what Eyes !————O Madam ! What will not those Eyes be capable of when animated with tender Sentiments !————He was running

ning on in this manner, when the Countess interrupted him; saying good Monsieur don't teach her these Things ———Vanity is too soon learned———go, go, *Jeanetta*, continued she, you must not regard what Monsieur says———he talks in this manner to every body. This put me into a great Confusion, I blush'd and obey'd, after paying my Obedience in the best manner I could, and, indeed, was glad when I was out of the Room.

As on my setting down to write these Memoirs of myself, I intended them as a kind of Mirror, wherein my Sex might view themselves, and perceive by what swift Degrees Errors, if not timely repelled, gain Entrance into the Heart, it would not answer the good End I aim'd at, to conceal any of those Weaknesses, which want of thinking justly made me guilty of: I therefore frankly own, that what this gay Monsieur had said to me in the Countess's Chamber, had a great Impression on me.———I was elevated beyond Measure at his Praises———I forgot not the least Word, but was vex'd I could not comprehend the meaning of one Expression:———I was never from the Glass, when my Mother's Absence gave me an Opportunity, and cry'd to myself, *What is it that my Eyes will be capable of doing, when animated with tender Sentiments?*———I wanted impatiently to know what those tender Sentiments were, that I might try the Effect of them in my Eyes; and the simple manner in which I reasoned on this Subject, has since been matter of Diversion to me, when unbent from Reflections of a more solid Nature. ———Not the most perfect Innocence is exempt from some Share of Vanity———we Women seem to be born with a desire of Admiration———to wish to be thought beautiful is in a manner inherent to our Composition———whoever praises us is sure of pleasing us, tho' otherwise not worthy our Regard; and it is only Time, Reason, and Experience can convince us, that to be loved only by those we love, is all can make us truly happy, and that the Perfections of the *Mind*, are infinitely preferable to those of the *Body*.

Some

Some few Days after I had sufficient matter to gratify this, at that Time, only Passion of my young Heart: As I was returning from the Forest where I had carried some Refreshment to my Father, I perceived a Company of Horsemen coming towards me; so drew off to the Roadside, the better to observe them as they pass'd. I had never seen the King, but had heard great Talk of him, and as I knew he was in those Parts, was in hopes he was among this Troop, and I might satisfy my Curiosity. The Picture I had drawn of him in my Mind, from the Admiration and Love with which I had always heard him mentioned, was all shining like the Sun, and so far distinguishable from the rest of Mankind, that I doubted not but I should know him in the midst of his Attendants———When they came near, I look'd earnestly for such a Figure as my Fancy had formed; but the whole Company being all of the most Grand Appearance, I found I had deceiv'd myself, and growing quite impatient, seeing most of them were past, I ran hastily up to one of them; crying aloud, Sir, I beseech you shew me the King.———I never saw him in my Life.——— That I will, my pretty Maid, answer'd the Person I address'd, who was extremely handsome; that is he ———which, Sir, cry'd I ?—Give me your Hand, rejoined he, and pointing with it, there, said he, is the King on the White Horse.———Yes, yes, cryed I again, that is the King for certain———Good God, how charming he is ! How happy should I be, if he did not ride so fast !—O dear, he is gone already !———He could not help smiling at my Exclamations ; but as I afterwards found had all this Time been considering me with the utmost Attention.———How lovely, said he, is this Simplicity, how preferable to all the Arts our Court-Ladies put in practice !———Where do you live, my little Dear, cry'd he ?———in that Village, Sir, replied I, pointing to it.———Will you give me leave to come and see you there ? Resumed he.———If it depended on me, Sir, answered I, your Visit would not be unwelcome ; but I am not my own Mistress.———As for that, said he, leave it to me———I shall contrive Means

without

without occasioning you any Blame. He had scarce
ended these Words, when another fine Gentleman comes
galloping back to him, crying, the King calls for you
Marquis.———His Majesty muſt know what Buſineſs
this pretty Maid has with you ; and what was the Motive of that Surprize ſhe teſtified in ſo pleaſant a Manner, as we paſs'd by———her Beauty and Innocence have
intereſted the whole Court. I do not wonder at it, ſaid
the Marquis, you ſee how handſome ſhe is———her
native Lovelineſs exceeds any thing I ever ſaw———
for my Part I think, ſhe not only merits the Notice our
Royal Maſter has taken of her; but alſo that he
ſhould confer greater Favours on her ; and it ſhall not
be my Fault, if ſhe has not reaſon to think this Adventure very fortunate for her. Nor mine, rejoin'd the
other, looking on me in a Faſhion which I then was far
from comprehending, where does ſhe live ?———She is
ſurprizingly beautiful ———I am deſperately in love
with her. At theſe Words he offer'd to alight, which
put me into ſuch a Conſternation, that without taking
any leave, or thanking the Marquis for his Civilities,
I ran as faſt as I could toward our Village : Stay ! Stay,
pretty Maid ! Cry'd the Marquis, no body intends you
any harm. ———He added ſomewhat more, but I
made too much haſte to hear him ; never looking back
till I was almoſt at our own Door. I then turn'd about,
and ſaw only one Chevalier at the Place I ran from,
which I ſoon after diſtinguiſh'd to be the Marquis ; the
other I ſuppoſe being gone back after the King. I went
in, full of what had paſs'd, and when recovered from
the little Terror I had been in, was highly delighted
with the Compliments I had received ———My Mother had too much Penetration not to perceive, I was
more than ordinarily taken up with ſomething, and
would needs know what it was, nor did I ſcruple to
make her an exaơt Recital.

I excuſe your Curioſity, ſaid ſhe as ſoon as I had ended, for his Sake who occaſion'd it ; but I would have
you be more reſerved for the future : It was not a Fault
to addreſs yourſelf to the Marquis, becauſe, perhaps, it

was

was the only Means you had of finding out the King;
but remember you ought never to suffer yourself to be
dazzled with Pomp and Equipage————you have spoke
of this Affair, and described the Person and Gallantry of
the Marquis, with a Warmth not becoming a Maid
of your Age and Rank.————Ah! *Jeanetta*————
Jeanetta, you must have no Eyes, nor Ears, for Persons of his high Character————the Complaisance they
assume————the tender Looks they put on————the
Praises they give you, are but so many Flatteries, and
Snares laid to entrap your Innocence, and draw you into Mischiefs, from which if ever you are able to disin-
tangle yourself, it cannot be done without great Difficulty
and bitter Heart-achings. I'll tell you, continued she,
an Accident that happened in this Village, soon after we
came to settle in it, which will shew you what Miseries
are naturally the Consequence of Vanity and Credulity.

The *History* of CHARLOTTA.

SHE was the only Daughter of a Person, whose sole
Subsistance was a large Orchard on the Skirts of this
Hamlet, which notwithstanding he so well cultivated,
that the Profits brought him in sufficient to maintain his
Family in a decent Manner.————The ordinary Fruit he
disposed of to those who sold it again, and the fine Sort
he either sent his Daughter with, or carry'd himself to
the Houses of the Nobility : Every body blamed him
for sending the young *Charlotta* on such Errands, which
cou'd not fail of laying her under dangerous Temptations ;
but the great Prices she always got, made him deaf to
any Remonstrances on that score.

She

She was extremely beautiful, well shaped, and had something in her Air far above her Degree; these Perfections added to the sweetest Temper in the World, made her beloved by all that knew her; and mean as she was, several advantagious Matches were proposed to her; but she refused all Offers of that kind, and testified so great an Aversion to Marriage, that as well to gratify her Inclination to a single Life, as to encrease his own Gains by the Favours she daily received at those Houses where she carry'd Fruit; he did not great greatly press her to change her Condition, for some Years; but at last beginning to reflect, that if Providence should take him from her, it would be a melancholy thing to leave her unsettled in the World; and a very wealthy Person at that Time happening to make his Addresses, he omitted nothing to prevail with her, to receive him as a Man she could approve of for a Partner for Life: But young *Charlotta* was not to be moved, either by the Assiduities of her Lover, or the Admonitions of her Father; and when urged by him, seemed to have such an Abhorrence to obey him in this Point, that he could not resolve to lay any Constraint on the Inclinations of a Child, who in all things else was the most dutiful Creature that ever was.

Her Resolution being known, deterr'd many others from offering themselves, and she was more free than she had been from any Importunities, than which she desired nothing more; and I have heard her say a thousand times, that she did not believe Heaven had ever created a Man capable of inspiring her with a Wish of being his.

But alas, *Jeanetta*, continued my Mother with a Sigh, how little do we know ourselves in this Point; the fatal Time at last arrived, when the hitherto insensible *Charlotta* became the Victim of a Passion she before despised.

Going one Day to *Fountainbleau* to sell Fruit, she heard some body call to her from a Window: On this she went to House, and was met at the Door by a Servant, who carry'd her into an Apartment magnificently

furnish'd.

furnish'd. A Gentleman of a graceful Appearance was sitting in an easy Chair, and as soon as he saw her, come in, pretty Maid, said he, let's see your Fruit, it should be fair if like yourself. As for that, Sir, answered she, I don't pretend to any Fairness; but as to my Fruit, there is none more nice in the whole Kingdom. With these Words she uncover'd her Basket, and began to set it forth to all the Advantage she could, not observing the Person she was before, nor that instead of looking on the Fruit, he was all the time considering her with the utmost Attention.

This Nobleman, who was no less a Person than the Duke De——, was about Twenty-four Years of Age, a handsome Man, and full of amorous Inclinations, for the Gratification of which, he entirely dedicated a certain Part of his Income; but had a high Notion of Honour, and never made use of any Treachery to gain his Ends himself, though he wink'd at it in *Dupin* his Valet de Chambre, who mangaged all these Affairs for him, and scrupled nothing to accomplish them.

The innocent Charms of *Charlotta* soon made a Conquest of his Heart: He look'd on her with Eyes, which spoke the utmost Passion —— how lovely, cry'd he, is every thing about you!——Who could imagine such Beauty was the Produce of a Cottage! ——I never saw any thing so perfectly agreeable! ——O! Sir, said she, you fine Gentlemen take a Pleasure in diverting yourselves with such poor Girls as myself, who you know can't make any Reply to such Compliments. No, pretty Creature, interrupted the Duke, I scorn to say any thing I don't think, and if you were acquainted with my Character, you would know that I was the sincerest Man on Earth; but since you don't believe me, I have done. Poor *Charlotta's* Vanity had made her pleased with the Praises given her by this Nobleman, and though she would have conceal'd it, it was not in her power. I don't pretend to say, Sir, resumed she, that I have any reason to think you mean any harm: Not in the least, replied the Duke, unwilling to fright her from coming again, no body wishes
you

you better—I only think you are very pretty and very innocent, and ought to be encouraged; so will buy all the Fruit you have, and shall be glad if you bring me more another time. With these Words he made her a little Bow and went out of the Room, ordering his Valet de Chambre to take care of her. *Dupin* knew very well what he was to do : he treated her with great Respect, made her breakfast in the Larder, paid her double the Worth of her Fruit, and under the Pretence of enquiring where it grew, learn'd her Place of Abode: He made her Promise to come again, and magnified his Master's Honour and Generosity, in such a manner, that she came away highly satisfied with her new Customer, and determined to go again in a short Time.

Her Father was pleas'd with the advantageous Market she had made that Day, and the Prospect of selling his Fruit upon the same Terms for the future, made him send her to Town two Days after: She did not fail going to the Duke's, and had immediate Admittance to him ; his Behaviour was extremely tender, but offer'd not the least Freedom unbecoming Modesty, so she returned more satisfied and more elated than before.

The third Time she went, the Duke seeing her from the Window, opened the Door to her himself, and being an extreme handsome Man and dress'd to the utmost Advantage, *Charlotta* took but too much notice of him ; and he too well skilled in the Language of the Eyes, easily perceived the Impression he had made.

You seem surprized, my pretty Maid, said he, to see me come to the Door myself; but all my Servants are out of the way ——— they often serve me thus ———they know I don't know how to chide, and impose upon my Good-nature ;———but come in, continued he, we'll chat a little till some of them return. In speaking this he led her into a Parlour, furnished and adorned in the most rich and elegant manner. *Charlotta's* Eyes were perfectly dazzled with the Splendor of every thing she saw, and could not help crying out, Heavens ! What a fine Place ! Yes, my sweet One, replied the Duke, I think it so now you are in it.———

Sit

Sit down, and lay aside your Basket.———I'll have it
so, continued he, finding she made a Difficulty, I am an
utter Enemy to all Ceremony. With this he gently forced
her on a Chair, and placing himself very near her ; my
Valet de Chambre, said he, informs me you live at
N———,the next Time I pass that Way, I'll call and
eat some Cream with you ; I am a great Lover of it,
and shall think it doubly delicious, when it comes
from your Hand. She made no other Answer to these
Words, than a low Bow, nor, indeed, had she the
Power, her Spirits were in so great an Agitation : He
seeing her Confusion went on, I'll tell you a Secret, added he, from the first Moment I cast my Eyes upon
your Face, my Heart became entirely devoted to you,
I have neither thought, nor dreamt of any thing but
you———in fine, I love you, and if I could obtain
a return of Affection, should look on myself as the
happiest of Mankind.———Speak, my Angel, ———
pursued he, taking her Hand, may I hope to be so
blest ? What can I say, my Lord, answer'd she, in a
Voice faultering with Confusion ? This is the first time
I ever heard such things. ———I wish I knew whether I ought to take such Speeches as Favours, or the
contrary ; but the Simplicity of a Country Life———
that lovely Simplicity, cry'd he, interrupting her, gives
the greatest Lustre to your Charms——— how adorable
would some Ladies be that I know, were they as ignorant of their Perfections as you are———and yet that
very Ignorance renders me unhappy———you don't
understand me———you cannot comprehend what 'tis
I feel for you———O ! how wretched must I be, if
you grow not more sensible of my Passion———dearest
———loveliest.———sweetest Creature———all this Time
he grasped her Hand between his, kiss'd it with Vehemence, and sometimes wetted it with his Tears. The
Addresses that *Charlotta* had hitherto received, had been
in so different a manner, that she was quite confounded
at this : She doubted not, however, if it was sincere, and
imagin'd he was overwhelm'd with Affliction ; Vanity
and Inclination conspired to subdue her Heart ; and to

be

be loved to such a Degree by a Man of his Quality seemed so great an honour, that she knew not how to refuse him any thing, though ashamed to grant———— the Perplexity of her Thoughts pervented her from speaking or withdrawing her Hand, which at last he took Courage to put into his Bosom————feel, charming Maid, the Condition of my Heart————how it flutters as it would burst my Breast————— Yes, it will burst and I shall die before your Eyes, if you consent not to reward my Passion.————O! Heaven forbid! cry'd the believing Maid, 'twere better I had ne'er been born————could I have foreseen this, I never would have come into your House. No, that I cannot wish, reply'd he, you kill me, indeed, yet the Wounds you give are such as I would not be without————even Death from you is welcome————how much more then would Life be————yes, you must let me live, and live the happiest of Mortals————with these Words he attempted to take her in his Arms.————This really frighted her, she rose hastily up, and told him she now found it was time to leave him.————She gave with these Words a sudden Spring toward the Door; but he no less nimble and equally agitated by his Desires, as she by her Fears, got between her and it, and cry'd out————you must not go, my Angel————you are Mistress here, and shall command me in every thing ———— I'll do whatever you require————I'll make a Settlement on you, shall put you on the Level with Quality, and if ever you are dispos'd to marry, will give you a Fortune.——I am too young and unexperienced, reply'd she, to know how to judge of such offers————therefore, for Heaven's sake let me go. She fell a weeping bitterly while she spoke this, and the Duke with all his Eloquence had much ado to pacify her, till *Dupin* coming in put an end to her Apprehensions, and the Duke convinced this was not the way to bring her to his Purpose, and that he had gone too far, suffered her to depart.

But notwithstanding the Repulse she had given him, she return'd Home with a Disquiet of Mind of which Love was the Source: The Pressures of so great and so

handsome

handsome a Man had their Effect; her Heart was ensnared, and in a small Time she languished for another Interview; though, no longer ignorant of his Designs, she had too much Virtue, to put herself again into his power. But this Constraint on her Inclinations was of Prejudice to her Health, she grew pale, pensive, and was not the same Creature she had been, as we all took notice of.

Several Days pass'd over without her hearing any thing from the Duke, and her Inquietudes encreas'd to such a Degree, that she began almost to repent the Severity of her Behaviour; she fancied she might have listened to him, yet still have preserv'd her Innocence, and wish'd some Chance might throw her in his way, without her seeming to desire it. In this Disposition, so favourable to his Wishes, did she continue till her ill Genius brought about the Completion of Desires, so fatal to her in the End.

The Duke came to the Village, and enquiring after a Man, whose Daughter came to Town with Fruit sometimes, was soon directed to his House.————The Gardener was transported, that so great a Man vouchsafed to honour his Orchard with his Presence, and waited on him through all the Walks of it, shewing the Variety of Fruits he had, and entertaining him with the Methods, by which he brought such and such a Tree to Perfection.

While the Father was thus taken up with the Duke; the subtle Valet de Chambre took the Opportunity of talking to the Daughter: He made use of all his Artifice to seduce her to *Fountainbleau*, and gratify his Master's Passion.

He magnified the Birth, Riches, and Person of the Duke, described the Advantages attending an Amour with a Man of his Rank and uncommon Generosity; but *Charlotta*'s Modesty not suffering her to hear with Patience any Arguments on that Head, he changed his manner of Discourse, and assumed the Appearance of Virtue to draw her into Vice.————I only say, resumed the crafty Purveyor of his Master's Pleasures, that a Woman might think herself extremely happy to be the Duke's Mistress; but the Love he has for you is of a

d i f f e r e n t

different kind ; in fine, pretty *Charlotta*, said he, it is your own Fault if you are not his Wife. The very mention of the Word Wife, made her Heart spring with Joy ; but concealing it as well as she was able.——O ! I cannot think of that, answer'd she, there is too great an Inequality between us————there is so, indeed, resumed he, yet it may be brought about————'tis true the Duke is not wholly determined ; but if you will come into the Measures I propose, I know him well enough to promise you Success.————But, added he, you must consider how great he is, and how mean you are, and not expect to be address'd in the Fashion of great Ladies————you must rather humour him, and appear grateful for the Honour he does you————what tho' he was a little free with you, you should not have refrained coming————the more he sees you, the more will his Passion encrease ; and such a Prospect of Advantage ought not to be neglected for a foolish Punctilio. By such like crafty Insinuations he stagger'd her Resolution ; Love and Ambition prevail'd, and she promised to come the next Day to Town, to see, as he told her, that there was no ill Design harbour'd against her Virtue.

As soon as they came Home, *Dupin* acquainted the Duke with the Progress he had made, and represented to him, that if he hoped to compass his Designs, it was absolutely necessary, he should veil them under an honourable Pretence.

The Duke, though given to some Excesses, had a great Sense of Honour, as I have before observed, and was angry that *Dupin* had made any such Promises to *Charlotta*————what said he, though I love the Girl to Distraction, I value my own Character yet more———— nor will enter into Engagements with her, which I mean not to perform————much less could all her Innocence tempt me to marry her————there is nothing can excuse such preposterous Matches.————I never should be weak enough to follow the Example of Monsieur———— who in order to gratify his Passion, was guilty of a thousand Extravagancies, and then to crown the Folly married

ried his own Servant.———Some say her Virtue and Discretion merited that Honour; but I should never have forgiven the Artifices she made use of to gain her Ends.———Another also of my Acquaintance married a Baker's Daughter after he had debauch'd her.—She got in League with his Valet de Chambre, he acted the Part of an Apparition, and at dead of Night threatened him with eternal Perdition, if he did not attone the Wrong he had done her by marrying her the next Day: The Gentleman was afraid of Spirits, and the Plot succeeded.——— The Count of———is still less to be pitied, who by an Accident owing his Life to a poor Girl married her, to save the Payment of 2000 Crowns that he had promised her.———I could enumerate many such ridiculous Instances; but *Dupin* be assured I shall never add to the Number; so take your own Measures for to bring *Charlotta* to my Arms.———I confess myself possess'd of the most vehement desire of possessing her; but remember that I will neither make nor keep any Promise inconsistent with my Quality.

Dupin would fain have persuaded him, however, to talk in an ambiguous manner to *Charlotta* when she came ; but all he could bring him to was not to contradict what he had said to her. This Wretch had therefore a hard Task of it ; but so it will be when Servants endeavour to render themselves useful to their Masters, only by promoting their Vices.

When *Charlotta* came he entertain'd her a long Time before she went into the Duke, and at last succeeded so well in his wicked Arguments, that she really believ'd their was the strongest Probability of her becoming a Dutchess: In orde to which she was not to insist on being made so, but to leave every thing to the Duke's Love and Generosity.

The Conversation the Duke had with her, flatter'd the Hopes *Dupin* had inspired her with : He treated her with Respect, took no Liberties unbecoming Modesty to grant, and only told her he loved her without mentioning what End he propos'd by it. So that now believing *Dupin* had been sincere in his Advice, she agreed to pass

a

a Week at *Fountainbleau*, on Condition her Father would give his Confent. The Bufinefs was foon brought about, a Meffage was contrived, as from the Duke's Mother to the Gardener, defiring him to fend his Daughter to her for a few Days; the old Man, far from any Guile himfelf, fufpected not the Artifice, and was tranfported with the Honour done him.

A fine Apartment was hired for her Reception, and Cloaths and Jewels provided to adorn her; fo that fhe thought herfelf a Dutchefs indeed: Dazzled with the Splendor of every Thing about her, and indulged in all the Luxuries of Life; fhe look'd back on her Village with Contempt and Loathing: The Duke vifited her twice or thrice every Day, her Paffion for him every Day was heightned by his Converfation; and though he faid not one Word of marrying her, *Dupin* had fo fully prevail'd on her, to believe the fureft Way to make him do fo, was to depend entirely on his Honour, that fhe never urged him on that Article; and on his taking the Advantage of a foft Moment at laft, he obtain'd that from her, which ought to have been yielded only to a Hufband.

Every Day fhe expected the Effect of the Promifes made her by *Dupin*, and while this hope remain'd was perfectly happy; but Time flipping away, and fhe finding herfelf with Child, thefe Golden Dreams began to vanifh, and fhe awoke to real Mifery; when taking the Liberty to mention to the Duke what had been faid to her by *Dupin*, he utterly difown'd it all; and told her he had never given him any Commiffion to act in that manner. She raved, tore her Hair, was ready to lay violent Hands on herfelf; but he was little moved, his Paffion was fated, and he defired nothing more than to get rid of her————not but he pitied her; and to alleviate her Sorrows offer'd to give her 3000 Crowns for a Provifion for her Child and Self, on Condition fhe would make no Noife of the Affair————this drove her to Extremes————fhe told him fhe defpifed his Money———— that fhe yielded on the Affurances given her by a Perfon, who fhe knew was acquainted with his moft fecret

Thoughts

Thoughts——and vowed to proclaim the Injustice had been done her to all the World.——This so much incensed the Duke, that he left her without even bidding her Farewel ; and his Birth and Employment demanding his Attendance on the King, went directly to *Paris*, where the Court then was.

Before his Departure he consulted with *Dupin* what was best to be done, to prevent her Desperation from being of Prejudice to his Character ; and that crafty Villain having already contrived the Means, entreated him to take no farther care about it, for he would undertake to manage the Affair so as she should be no trouble to him. ——This young Nobleman was an Enemy to Consideration on any thing, which he look'd upon so much beneath him as *Charlotta*; therefore proceeded on his Journey, leaving *Dupin* behind him to make good his Word.

This Monster, for he deserves no other Name, pursued my Mother, no sooner saw his Lord was gone than he went to *Charlotta*'s Apartment : He found her in bitter Agonies, and bewailing her Misfortune in Terms, that would have melted any Heart but his. At the Sight of him, her Lamentations were mingled with Reproaches and Exclamations on his Perfidy. He listened to her with a composed Countenance, and when she had rail'd herself almost out of Breath : Well, beautiful *Charlotta*, said he, I would not interrupt you, because the going too hastily from the Extreme of one Passion to another, might be fatal ; but now I see you more in a Condition to receive the News I bring you, permit me to wish you Joy of the great Fortune you are going to receive—— What! Do you insult me too, cry'd she ? Far be it from me, answer'd he ; no, Madam, the Duke has made the Trial he intended————had you accepted of the 3000 Crowns he offered, he never would have seen you more ; but as you refused it with so noble an Air, and regarded nothing without the Possession of his Person in an honourable Way, he finds you worthy of being what you wish to be, and in a few Days will make you his Wife. The natural Vanity of *Charlotta* made her think what

he

he told her was feasible; but being willing to be more confirm'd, where is he, said she, if he designs to make me happy, why does he not come and let me hear the blessed Tidings from his own Mouth? He would have done so, reply'd he, but a special Mandate from the King oblig'd him to quit *Fountainbleau* in less than two Hours after he came from your Apartment———the Messenger waited his return from you, and his Hurry was so great, that he had only time to order me to bring you this Message from his ever faithful Heart; and to do all in my power to divert you till he comes back, which will be in a very short Time.

If what you tell me be sincere, reply'd *Charlotta*, I shall have Cause to blush at having injur'd you, in suspecting your Veracity;———but, added she, you know best if it will be in my power to make you Amends. ———*Dupin* made no other Answer to these Words than a low Bow; then proceeded to acquaint her how the Duke had commanded him to prepare every thing necessary for their Nuptials as soon as he return'd, and, added he, if there be any thing particular to be observed, I shall be proud to receive your Directions.

No, said *Charlotta* with an Air of Grandeur, I shall follow the Example of my Lord Duke, and leave the Care of what is to be done to you. After this he left the Room laughing within himself at the stately Behaviour she assumed. The Truth is, she so firmly believed she was going to be a Woman of Quality, that, like most rais'd above their Hopes, she somewhat over-acted her Part.

After this he waited on her in the most obsequious manner every Day to know her Commands, and on her asking him from time to time what Progress he had made in executing the Duke's Commands, and how, and where the Ceremony of their Marriage was to be perform'd? Who were to be present, and whether privately or with Pomp? To all which Questions he found such Answers as satisfied her Vanity.

For ten Days *Charlotta* indulg'd herself in an Ideal Happiness—she thought of nothing, but how well she should look lolling in a Coach and Six, with her Laoquies before

fore and behind in rich Liveries; and how the Populace would admire her as she pass'd; but at the Expiration of that Time, *Dupin* presents her with a Letter, which he said he had just receiv'd, enclosed in one to himself, from the Duke. She hastily open'd it, and found it contain'd, as near as I can remember, these Words:

To my dear and most adorable Charlotta.

I WON'T trouble you with the Concern I was in, that I could not myself be the Messenger of the News, which was what you so much wish'd to hear———— *Dupin* has doubtless inform'd you————I thought I had done with making Tryals of your Love; but there is one to come which it was not possible for me to forsee. ————The King has commanded me to *D*————on a particular Affair, and I know not how long I may be detain'd; as I am impatient till I do Justice to your Virtue, I beg you will meet me there, under the Conduct of the faithful *Dupin*, who has my Commands to make both the Voyage and Journey, as little fatiguing to you as possible.————Farewel, my Charmer, your Guardian Angel protect you, and bring you safe once more into the Arms of him, who never can be but

Yours,

The Duke De N————,

It must be confess'd such a Letter join'd to what *Dupin* had told her, the Homage he had paid her since the Duke's Departure, and the fine Things he daily bought for her, were enough to deceive a young Woman of more Penetration.————She made not the least Hesitation; and when the time arriv'd that all things were ready for their Departure, left *Fountainbleau* with a Chearfulness befitting her suppos'd Condition.

They travelled in a handsome manner to the Port where she was to embark, and a Vessel being ready, they immediately went on board.

Charlotta

Charlotta was scarce seated in her Cabbin before *Dupin* counterfeiting the utmost Vexation, cry'd out, what has bewitch'd me————I am certainly mad————I have left a Box of Writings behind me in the Inn, that are of the utmost Consequence.————I durst not look the Duke in the Face without them————I am undone if they cannot put off the Boat, that I may go back for them————with these Words he ran up on the Deck; and soon after, on her enquiring for him, the Sailors told her he was gone on shore.

As she had not the least Suspicion, she gave herself no trouble about it, till Night coming on, and no *Dupin* returning, she began to be under Apprehensions that he was detain'd by some cross Accident, which might retard her Voyage: She laid herself down, however, on the Bed prepared for her, and, perhaps, dreamt not of the wretched Condition she was in; but what became of her, when early in the Morning she found by the Motion of the Ship that it was under Sail; she call'd for the Captain, and demanded the Reason of his weighing Anchor before *Dupin* came back. Because, answer'd the surly Fellow, I had not a Mind to wait till Doomsday.————Such a Reply, and Looks so different in all their Faces, from those she had been received with on her coming on board, had Reason to alarm her.———— She went on Deck, and complain'd of this Usage to one, and to another, on which some sneer'd as in Derision, and others shook their Heads; but none vouchsafed to give her any Satisfaction, till the Mate, more humane than the rest, said to her, I find you are insensible of your Condition.————You expected the Monsieur who brought you hither would have returned, but he has deceived you, he never intended it. — He contracted only for your Passage; so since Things are as they are, 'tis best for you to be as easy as you can. Horror and Amazement then seiz'd the Soul of this unhappy Creature.————She found she was betray'd, and wanting to know the Particulars of her Misfortune, asked him many Questions, which he had not in his power to answer; all he could inform her of was, that *Dupin* had agreed with the Captain
tain

tain to take her to *St. Lucia*, whether the Ship was bound; and to leave her there without any regard to the Entreaties she might make. To *St. Lucia* ! cry'd *Charlotta*, it cannot be———what shall I do there——my Business is at *D*——I tell you that you are deceived, resumed he, for what Reason I don't pretend to say. ———Though I can guess pretty near the Matter too, I believe.—I suppose Monsieur has made you some Promises he don't mean to keep, and so takes this Method to send you out of the Way———but you need not be disheartened, you'll live well enough when you come to *St. Lucia.* O Heaven! said she, but why do I call on Heaven——— Heaven has abandon'd me,——— this World is Hell and Men are the Fiends———she could no more———Rage and Grief stopp'd the Passage of her Words, and at last deprived her of Breath———she fell motionless at the Feet of those who stood gaping at her Despair———they threw Water on her Face, and endeavour'd in their rude way to bring her to herself; but when she recover'd, it was but to burst into Exclamations.———The Captain bid his Men take her into the Cabbin and leave her to herself; saying her standing there hinder'd the working of the Ship———on this some of them took hold of her, and were about to force her down the Stairs ; but she sprung from them, and crying out, I will not go where they would have me.———Tell *Dupin* and his villainous Master, that my Ruin was not worth half the Pains they have taken. She had no sooner ended these Words, than casting her Eyes wildly round, she flung herself over the side of the Ship, and was immediately swallowed up by the Waves.

My Mother could not refrain weeping, while she repeated this sad Catastrophe of *Charlotta*'s Fate, nor was I less moved at hearing it. O Heaven! cryed I, what could the ungrateful Duke and his wicked Valet de Chambre think of themselves, for such an Action ?

I'll tell you Child, resumed she ; some time past over without any News of the unhappy *Charlotta* ; her Father was like a Man distracted———he soon found she
had

had never been at the Dutchefs de N———s, he fought her far and near, but *Dupin* had taken fuch care to keep all things fecret, that no Intelligence could be had, till about two Years after as near as I can remember, the Duke happening to be again in thefe Parts, *Dupin* who ftill lived with him, was fuddenly feized with an unaccountable kind of Frenzy.—he raved on *Charlotta*—talk'd to her, as if fhe had been prefent————Cry'd out———— it was not my Fault that you threw yourfelf overboard— I did not advife you to that, tho' I did to leave your Father——With fuch like Exclamations did he run about the Country——tearing his Cloaths————and terrifying all he met with his Wildnefs. He was at length feized, and proper Remedies being applied he returned to fome Degree of Reafon, but it was but by Intervals, in fome of which he confeffed not only to the Prieft, but many more Witneffes, that he had fent *Charlotta* away in the Manner I have related, and that on the Return of the Ship, having been informed what her Defpair had made her guilty of, he had ever fince been haunted with her Spirit————Sleeping, or waking, faid he, fhe is ever before my Eyes————there————there fhe ftands would he frequently cry out, and then fall again into his former Ravings, in one of which Fits he died.

Whither this miferable Wretch really faw any thing, or confcious Guilt made him imagine he did fo, has been the Occafion of much Difpute, but the dreadful way in which he perifh'd, was fhocking to the whole Country.—'Twas rumour'd alfo that the Duke was much difturbed, 'tis certain he grew very melancholly, but there needed not an Apparition to remind him that the Ruin of an innocent Perfon is a Crime, which not all the Fafhionablenefs of it can excufe————The Deaths of *Charlotta* and *Dupin* were but too fad Demonftrations of this Truth; and tho' he was far from contriving, or even knowing till it was too late, the Means which *Dupin* made ufe of to eafe him of the Importunities of the poor undone *Charlotta*, yet by permitting him to put in practice what Methods he thought proper to feduce

her,

her, and afterwards leaving her to his Difpofal, he could not but think himfelf guilty, and confequently muft feel the moft ftinging Remorfe.

Juft as my Mother had concluded this melancholly Narrative, a Neighbour came in to fee us, and prevented the Remarks fhe would otherwife have made upon it, as was her Cuftom whenever fhe related any thing to me, fhe defired I fhould keep in Mind ; and this perhaps was the Caufe, together with the Heedleffnefs of my Humour, that it made not an immediate Impreffion on me, tho' in a very fhort Time after, it came ftrong upon my Thoughts, and I began to think there was a Poffibility of its being applicable to myfelf.

Three Days were paft fince my accofting the Marquis in the Foreft ——I was ftill taken up with that Adventure——I forgot not that he had promifed to contrive a Way to fee me, and thinking nothing lefs than that he would break his Word, imagined he was coming on every little Noife I heard, and prefently the Colour flufh'd into my Face, my Heart flutter'd, a Thrilling ran thro' all my Veins, and I was in a manner quite out of myfelf.

The fourth Day convinced me I had not been deceived in my Expectations : I was at Mattins when the Sound of Horfes from without made every body turn their eyes to the Church-Door——My Curiofity was at leaft equal to the reft, and immediately I faw the Marquis himfelf enter, and with an Air fo grand, fo noble, fo enchanting, that all I had conceived of an Angel was fhort of what I now in reality beheld—— The whole Congregation appear'd furprized and charm'd ; I found myfelf feized with fomewhat, to which I then knew not how to give a Name ———— a Confufion——a Hurry of Spirits————an Alarm which was painful and pleafing to me at the fame Time.——He foon diftinguifhed me from the Croud————his Eyes met mine, and ignorant as I was, I thought had fomewhat in them, that feemed to confirm what he had faid to me in the Foreft.

The

The Marks of Diſtinction that appear'd about him, had no leſs Influence on the Curate than Congregation—he preſently ſent to invite him into the Choir————an eaſy Chair was brought for him, and the Place cleared of all the Country-People. This gave me an infinite Satisfaction, and I think I could not have been much more elevated, had all theſe Honours been paid to my-ſelf————its certain I was all the Time of Maſs, in a Situation which it is impoſſible to deſcribe, and never had ſaid my Prayers with ſo little Devotion.

Divine Service was no ſooner over, than the Marquis retired, but ſtopping in the middle of the Church, and fixing his Eyes on me whiſpered ſomething to a Perſon who walk'd near him, and who alſo look'd earneſtly up-on me; then raiſing his Voice as he went out, ſtay in this Village, ſaid he, till my Retinue arrives: I ſhall dine at the Caſtle, and in the Afternoon ſee what Diver-ſion the Field affords.

It pleaſed me to hear how he intended to diſpoſe of himſelf, but was equally concerned at his Departure, tho' I knew not the Cauſe I was ſo————I had not Power to take my Eyes off him till he took Horſe, and when he did ſo, he made me a low Bow————the Girls who were with me look'd one upon another————ſee, ſaid one of them, how complaiſant theſe Courtiers are——when does any of our young Men take ſuch Notice of us!—Aye, but cries another, did you mind how hand-ſome he is————one would ſwear his very Eyes could ſpeak————I ſaid nothing to all this, but my Heart ſpoke a thouſand Admirations————as we were walking on, the Perſon to whom the Marquis had whiſper'd, and who we found afterwards was his Gentleman, min-gled with my Companions; how do you paſs your Time here on *Sundays*, ſaid he, do you dance, or walk in the Woods? for theſe I ſuppoſe are all the Diverſions this Place affords. Sometimes one, and ſometimes another, anſwer'd ſhe he addreſſed to, but continued ſhe one would take you to have been born in the Country, you know the Cuſtoms of it ſo well. You are right, replyed he, notwithſtanding theſe fine Cloaths, I am country-born as you are, but since I have had the Honour to serve my Lord Marquis, I have a perfect Aversion for all Places but *Paris*——O! there is nothing like a Town Life, especially with such a noble Gentleman as my Master—— I look upon my Fortune as good as made, for he has promised to do handsomely for me, and he never breaks his Word———he is all Sincerity, Courtesy and Discretion———we find few like him now a Days—— He seems to be such a one indeed, rejoyn'd the Girl. Ah, if you did but know him, said he———but I am very much concerned about him of late, within these few Days he has been strangely melancholly and thoughtful, what the Meaning is I know not, but he is never out of the Saddle, yesterday did we ride about the Woods here from Morning to Night——I should be very sorry if any thing should have made him take a Dislike to *Paris*; but somewhat more than ordinary I am sure has happened, to make him love Solitude so well, who used to be never out of Company.

All this Time he never spoke one Syllable to me, but as we came pretty near Home, I perceived he had a Paper in his Hand, which, by a Sign he made, I imagin'd was intended for me, I resolved to try at least, and let fall my Handkerchief, which he presently took up, and had the Dexterity to slip the Letter with it into my Hand, unperceived by any of my Companions. By the Manner in which I received this Billet, any body would think it had not been the first by a great many, yet so ingenious does Love make his Votaries, tho' I then little suspected myself to be such, that poor innocent simple Country-Girl, as I then was, I acted the same Part a Woman bred in Town, and accustomed to Intrigue would have done.

On my opening my Letter, I was terribly at a Loss for the Contents———my Mother, indeed, had taught me to read Print, but Manuscript was not intelligible to me——I knew not what to do in this Case, at first I thought of shewing it to a Schoolmaster that lived in the Village, but he was acquainted with my Father, and I durst not hazard his betraying me.——At last I found

out

out an Expedient, which I can never remember without laughing, and for a Girl of my Age and bringing up, had in it somewhat surprizing enough.

Among the Number of those who pretended to admire me was one *Collin* the Son of a Wood-Merchant, for whom my Father work'd: He was a young Fellow who had nothing disagreeable in his Person, and was distinguished by his Wealth above most of his Condition; to add to this, his Behaviour, tho' far from polite, was less rustick than the greatest Part of our Villagers—— Such as he was, however, the Regard he testifyed for me, drew on me the Envy of all the young Girls in the Neighbourhood, and I had not been a little pleased at the Preference he gave me, tho' since I had seen the Marquis I neither took Pride nor Pleasure in his Addresses; and having found there was something in me worthy of being taken Notice of by the great World, began to think I should be guilty of an Injustice to myself, if I permitted (any farther than my Circumstances oblig'd me) the Society of these Clods of Earth, as I now call'd them.————O the Vanity of a flatter'd Girl!————What ridiculous Ideas rise in the youthful Brain before Reason, or to speak more properly, Experience convinces us we are not what they would make us believe they think us————but to return.

It was this very *Colin* I pitch'd upon to read to me, and to answer, if Occasion required, the Marquis's Letter: an Opportunity soon offer'd: He came to bring me some fine Flowers, I being at that time passionately fond of Nosegays, which I accepted of then with more Civility than I had done for some Days past: He was quite transported to see a Smile upon my Face: How charming you look to-day, *Jeanetta*, said he, your Eyes are killing bright.————O! what a Shape! pursued he, taking me round the Waist. Forbear, cry'd I, pushing him from me, cannot you be satisfied with speaking to me; but your Hands must also be employ'd————you spoil'd me one Apron last *Sunday*, and I suppose you intend to serve this the same way. I was to blame, indeed, answer'd he, he who breaks the Glasses ought to pay for them.——

I

will make you a Present of an Apron, the next time I go to Town, I'll be sure to buy one for you. That's not what I concern myself about at present, said I, you must do a Favour for me. I'll do you Fifty, cry'd he, and shall be proud you will command me. Well then, said I, we'll take a Turn in that Grove yonder, and I can tell you the Business without being interrupted; how happy am I, said *Colin*, ah! *Jeanetta*! indeed, I love you, and I begin to hope you will make me some return————if it were once come to that————you'd see what I would do ————'Tis true you have no Portion, but no matter————'tis not Money that makes People happy————you are as fair as Alablaster; have Eyes as piercing as a Mouse, and are as strait as a Pine, that is Portion enough————my Father, indeed, may not happen to think as I do; but what if he does not, he shall hear Reason, or I'll leave him and go to the Army, as many a young Man has done, that has been cross'd in Love. All this, said I, is nothing to my present Business: Will you promise me to keep a Secret, and to ask no Questions? Ay, you don't know me, I find, reply'd he, do you think I cannot keep a Secret————why I have kept an hundred in my time ————witness the other Day————you must understand, I catch'd *Matthew*'s Wife and fat *George* very close together in a Corner————she made me promise not to tell her Husband————there would be fine doings if I could not keep a Secret. For that reason, said I, I have made Choice of you in this Affair————a Friend of mine has receiv'd a Letter; but as she can't read, nor I neither, she desired me to ask you to examine the Contents, and get an Answer wrote, in Case it should require one. Well, well, that's soon done, cry'd *Colin*, taking it out of my Hand; but, hark you, *Jeanetta*, is it from the Gentleman in Red, that I saw talking with two or three of you before your Door? Yes, answer'd I, that's well, resumed he, for to tell you the Truth, I was a little ruffled to see such a Spark among you; but since 'tis not you, I don't care who else he loves. No, no, said I, he never spoke a single Word to me; that

I

I am fenfible of, anfwer'd *Colin*, for I was not far off, and watch'd him pretty narrowly————but let's fee what he fays here.————He then read as follows :

To the Fair Maid of the Foreſt.

THIS is the only Means by which I can acquaint my charming Creature, how deep an Impreſſion her Beauty and Innocence has made on me————the firſt Moment I beheld you, my Heart was entirely devoted to you ; and in hopes of a ſecond Interview at the ſame Place, have been almoſt continually on Horſeback———— at laſt I bethought me of your Pariſh Church, and come to pay my Adoration to my earthly Deity.————I ſhall not ſpeak to you at preſent, but will find an Opportunity for it, ſo as the Motive may not be ſuſpeſted. All that I beg is, that you will not oppoſe what I ſhall here-after contrive for your Advantage, and to ſhew, which 'tis impoſſible for Words to do, how very much I love you, *Yours.*

It cannot be doubted but that I liſtened to what he read with the greateſt Attention : Indeed, it ſeem'd as if my whole Soul was collected in my Ears, and ſo fear-ful was I of forgetting, or miſtaking the leaſt Word, that I made him repeat the whole Letter over and over ; and the oftner I heard it, the more my Satisfaction en-creas'd : *Colin* obſerved it in my Eyes, and took notice of it to me ; but I turned it off ſaying, I am thinking how happy this Girl is to have ſuch a Perſon in love with her———— he ſeems to be ſincere in what he writes, and I think ſhe ought to encourage his Ad-dreſſes. Aye, certainly, anſwer'd he, Coquettry and Overcoyneſs ſpoils many a good Match————'tis a ſilly thing for a Maid to play faſt and looſe, as one may call it, with a young Man————there is nothing like telling one's mind at once.———— But then I ſpeak only of our honeſt Country Lads, for as for the Town Blades, a Maiden had need be careful of the main Chance.

That's true, answer'd I, and being weary of this Talk, left him under Pretence of acquainting the Girl with the Contents of her Letter; but, indeed, to indulge myself with running over the tender things in it.

————I got to a retired Corner and threw myself on the Grass, where I fell into one of those Resveries which are so properly called the Day Dreams of a Mind in Love.————I had heard of several Country Maids, whose Beauty had raised them to great Fortunes; and the Praises had been given me, made me imagine there required not a Miracle to render me as happy as I could wish. I therefore resolv'd to answer the Marquis's Letter; but the shame of owning I could not write gave me some Disquiet: The desire I had of continuing a Correspondence with him, however, overcame all Obstacles, and when I had stay'd long enough for *Colin* to believe, I had been talking to this supposed Friend, I returned to him, and carried Pen, Ink, and Paper with me.

Come *Colin*, said I, we have no time to lose————she will have the Letter answer'd immediately, and has given me Directions how she will have it done.—He then took the Paper out of my Hand, and we both sitting down at the Foot of a Tree, he made a Desk of his Hat, and then ask'd me what he should say————why says I, she would have you tell him that——

She is not so vain as to imagine he can be so much in love with her as he pretends, that in spite of her mean Education, she is not insensible of the great Disproportion there is between them, nor of the Difficulties that would attend the Passion he seems desirous to create in her; but yet she could wish, tho' she can give no Reason for it, that he were sincere in what he says———— that she has never been taught to write, and is oblig'd to have recourse to a Friend to answer his Letter; but will not run any such Hazards any more for fear of a Discovery.————

I will write no such thing, cry'd *Colin*, interrupting me————why so, said I, because, reply'd he, then you'll have no farther Occasion for me ————Pish, resumed I, she will have it so————therefore, don't

be

be a Fool, but write on——we may be surpriz'd else,
before we have made an End.

He comply'd at last, and concluded the Epistle with
a grateful Acknowledgment for the Kindness express'd in
that, to which this was an Answer.

I put the Letter into my Bosom, and to recompence
Colin for the Trouble I had given him permitted him to
go Home with me. I knew also that my Mother would
be very well pleased to see me so accompanied——for she
had a view in encouraging his Addresses, and desired nothing more than that his Father should be of the same
Mind.

The little Inclination I had to be with him, however, made me glad when the time of Vespers arrived;
and I went to Church, not without some hope, that I
should there have an Opportunity of delivering it, which
happened accordingly. I had not been there three Minutes before the Marquis's Valet de Chambre came and
knelt just behind me——my Heart exulted with a
secret Joy, even at the sight of him, and Love inspired
me with the dexterity to slip my Paper into his Hand
unseen by any who were present.

When Prayers were over I saw no more of him; but
I return'd Home no less proud of my own Conduct in
this Intrigue, than with the Intrigue itself.——I fancied I was now capable of bringing any thing to pass
I went about, and that my Wit was not inferior to any
of my Sex—the Truth is, I was an apt Scholar in the
School of Love, and soon became a Proficient in its
most abstruse Lessons.

My Father being come from his Work, we were going to sit down to Supper, when the Marquis's Valet de
Chambre, accompanied by the Mayor and Curate,
came into our House. I trembled at the sight of them,
and thought of nothing but being discover'd, happy was
it for me that the surprize of seeing such Visitors, prevented either my Father or Mother from taking notice
of my Countenance at that time. Have not you a
Daughter, said the Valet to my Father, that goes sometimes to the Forest to carry Refreshment to the Work-

men?

men? Yes, Monsieur, reply'd he, here she is ⸻
Come forward *Jeanetta*, pursued he, how have you
merited the Honour of such good Company? ⸻
The Confusion I was then in was too visible; but was
look'd upon only as the Effect of my Bashfulness. Don't
be alarm'd, fair Maid, said the Valet, neither these
Gentlemen nor myself come with any design to your
Prejudice; and tho' my Master the Marquis *De L*⸻
V⸻, has an Order from the King concerning you,
we have nothing to inform you of, that will not be perfectly agreeable⸻therefore, I beg, Madam, you
will compose yourself. *Jeanetta*'s, at your Service, interrupted my Father, we have no Gentlewomen in our
Family; if you have not at present, said the Curate
gravely, you don't know but you may have. But let
that pass, and thank Monsieur for the Pains he has taken
to find your Daughter. We have been all round the
Village⸻we went to *John Le Moyn*'s your Gos-
sip⸻then to *James Rouss*⸻and to *Thomas* at the
Vine, not knowing but it might be some of their Daughters, without once thinking of you⸻but it seems
we are right at last, and I am very glad of it.

I was going to acquaint you, said the Valet de Chambre, that my Lord Marquis commanded me to make
Enquiry for a Girl, who was in the Road between this
Village and the Forest last *Wednesday*, when the King
pass'd that way. The Cause of it is this: My Lord
gave his Majesty an Account of the extraordinary Surprize she was seized with at sight of his Royal Person:
And he was so well pleased with the sweet Simplicity he
describ'd, that he has sent a Gratuity by him.⸻
I know not how much, but imagine it must be something worthy both of the Donor's Bounty, and the Person's Greatness who is to be the Messenger⸻but
you will see in a short time⸻I will go and acquaint him that you are the Person⸻he will be
here himself.

O! by no Means, cry'd my Mother, transported at
what she heard⸻that would be too great a trouble

ble———I will take her to wait upon him———alas! we
have not a Place to receive such a Person.

The Curate and Mayor approv'd of what she said;
but that not suiting with the Marquis's design, the Valet
de Chambre readily answer'd, that such a Respect would
be improper in this Affair. My Lord, said he, is entrusted with the Execution of the King's Order, and will
not swerve the least Tittle from his Instructions.———I'll
let him know I have succeeded in my Enquiry, which
he will be very glad to hear, as he is a Man whose
chief Delight is in Acts of Generosity.

With these Words he left us, followed by the Mayor
and Curate, the latter of whom, overjoy'd to be concern'd in any Affair where the King's Name was mention'd, stroak'd me over the Face, crying, be a good
Girl, *Jeanetta*, and God will raise you Friends.

My Parents were both of them in a perfect Extasy at
what had happen'd.———Scarce could they speak, the
Joy so unexpected an Honour had overwhelm'd them
with————the Neighbours, seeing who came in had
been upon the Watch, came in, and in their Fashion congratulated us on this Occasion, tho' I could see they
envy'd it thro' all their Compliments. As to my Brother and Sister who never lov'd me, they ill so disguised
their Discontent, that my Father perceiv'd it, and chid
them pretty severely. As he did not want Sense he
began to see into the little Jealousies of their Tempers,
and was determined to give henceforward less Ear than
he had done to their Complaints. The Girl has been always lucky from her Birth, said he to the Neighbours;
and, indeed, she is good-natur'd enough, and modest,
and I hope with God's Grace, and the reverend Father's good Advice, she may come to something in
me.

While my Father was talking to these People, I had
Opportunity to make my little Reflections on this Adventure: I had not so little Penetration as not to see
it was owing to my Letter to the Marquis, and no
more than a Pretence for seeing me often without Suspicion; and, perhaps, with a View of doing something for

me, which, however, vain as I was, I durft not yet indulge the Hope of. The Idea of it would notwithstanding all my Efforts rife in my Mind, and I have catch'd myfelf at faying, how happy would be my addreffing this charming Marquis, if he fhould one Day make me his Wife; but then I repell'd this, as it then appear'd even to me, wild and prefumptuous Notion, and I reflected that if all this Pains fhould be taken to feduce me, how wretched I fhould be———*Charlotta*'s unhappy Fate came now into my Head, with all the previous Circumftances which brought on her Undoing; and I made that Moment a firm Refolution within myfelf to be more wary, and whatever Temptations fhould arife, never to fwerve from the Paths of Virtue; but as often as I found my Heart giving way to Weaknefs to call in the Affiftance of that unerring Guide.——— Thank Heaven which has enabled me to do it, I have ever fince conftantly adhered to this Maxim. and it is to that alone I am indebted for the good Fortune I enjoy.

I was in the midft of thefe Cogitations when they faid the Marquis was coming—the Countefs *De N*———my Godmother was with him, and they were followed by a great deal of Company, who happened to be that Day at the Caftle. He had to'd them what happened on my feeing the King. and the Prefent his Majefty had order'd me by his Hand; but carefully conceal'd the Tendernefs he in that Inftant had taken for me, and which put him on defcribing my loyal Tranfports, in fuch interefting Terms, as laid his Majefty under a kind of Obligation to make me fome Acknowledgment———all the illuftrious Company were charm'd with his Recital, and begg'd leave to be Witneffes in what manner I would behave on this Occafion. The Countefs then told them I was her God-daughter; and the Marquis *De L———V*———Father to the young Nobleman then prefent was my Godfather———which Difcovery gave him a fecret Pleafure, and was afterwards a good Pretence for giving me fo many Tokens of his Love and Generofity, under his Father's Name.

As the Company drew near we all advanced to meet them, and the Countess no sooner saw me, than she cry'd out, come hither, my dear *Jeanetta*; I am over-joy'd that you begin so early to experience good For-tune——don't be asham'd, continued she, we know you have had no other Education than such a Village af-fords——then turning to the Marquis, how do you like my God-daughter, my Lord, said she, she is quite un-polish'd as yet; but with a little modelling she may make a tollerable Figure enough. Indeed, Madam, replied the Marquis, I think her perfectly agreeable, and that she wants but a very little Instruction to render her as accomplish'd, as your Ladyship could wish.

After this every one had something to say in my Praise ——one extoll'd my Beauty——one my Shape—— the Neatness of my Country Habit pleas'd another—— in fine, they all seem'd to vie who should commend me most——As much as it delighted me to hear such fine Things said of me, I was now so over-whelm'd with Confusion, that I could not lift up my Eyes, which my Father perceiving, said they but jested with their humble Servant, that I was infinitely obliged for the Honour they did; but he hoped I knew my Unworthiness too well, to imagine I merited any Part of this Goodness. My Mother added something to the same Purpose; while I stood all the time with my Head down, as though I wanted a Prop for my Chin, and I believe a Person capable of receiving them in the most elegant manner, could not have given them half the Satisfaction that my aukward Behaviour did on this Occa-sion.

The Marquis pitied me from his Heart, as he has since told me, and advancing toward me with the same Respect, as he would have approach'd a Dutchess; lovely Maid, said he, the King has commanded me to present you with this Purse of *Louis d'Ors*, as a small Compli-ment for the Pleasure you testified at him, an Account of which happening to be given him. I am extremely glad his Majesty employ'd me on this Occasion, as Ma-dam la Countess informs me, my Father was your God-

father,

father, and I doubt not but he will be highly satisfied when I relate this Adventure to him.

I am very certain he will, answer'd the Countess; but *Jeanetta*, pursued she, what Acknowledgments do you make to my Lord Marquis for all the Trouble he has given himself about you? I then curtsied very low, and thanked him, but in so low and faultring a Voice, that I believe no body knew what I said, nor, indeed, could I well tell myself, so great was my Agitation at that Time.

Poor Thing, cry'd my God-mother, she is quite daunted, yet I cannot forbear adding a little to her Confusion——observe now——this she spoke in a half Whisper to the Marquis; but so as I heard it——then turning to me, well *Jeanetta*, continued she, let us know what you will do with all this Money? my Lord here tells me there are 30 *Louis d'Ors* in that Purse—I shall be glad to hear what Use you will put it to?

Since you are pleas'd to command me, Madam, reply'd I, I think the best Use I can put it to is to give it my Mother. That's well said, cry'd the Countess. How, interrupted the Marquis hastily, will you reserve nothing for yourself. I don't want any Thing, my Lord, answer'd I, not having Courage to look him in the Face, I shall only desire she will have me taught to write, that I may be able to let her know my Thoughts, if ever I should be separated from her.

This Nobleman was charm'd with my Answer, which he comprended the meaning of perfectly well by the Letter that *Colin* wrote for me——Ah! Madam! cry'd he to the Countess, what can be more Praise-worthy than this Desire of Improvement! How barbarous would it be to neglect cultivating a Mind, which seems to want nothing but Care to render it as sparkling as her Eyes —— I am of your Mind, Marquis, answer'd she, and I think I will do something too for the King to be inform'd of. She spoke these Words laughing, and then turning to me, *Jeanetta*, said she, should you like to live with me?————If you should, I'll take you Home with me this very Evening, and you shall learn to write, and every thing else you can desire.——What do you
say

say——are you willing to go? On this I turned my Eyes on my Mother, and said, I beg you will instruct me in what manner I shall answer the great Goodness of her Ladyship; for I shall always be directed by you.

It is not to be doubted, but both my Parents looked on such an Offer as the greatest Honour and Happiness could befall me, and accepted it with Joy and Humility——well then, said the Countess, from this Moment I take Charge of her, and will endeavour to make her worthy of the Notice his Majesty has taken of her—— Come, *Jeanetta*, continued she, bid your Friends adieu, and follow me; with these Words she turned away, and all the Company followed her.

Here I felt the force of Nature, not the Honour done me, not all the Elegancies of Life I was going to partake of, and which my Heart was fond of, not even the Hope of seeing the Marquis often, could over-power the tender Sorrows of parting from my Mother and Family, I fell upon her Bosom and wept bitterly; but my Father chid this Folly, as he term'd it in me, and told me I rather ought to rejoice, and thank Providence for having provided for me in so unexpected a Manner, and so far beyond all their Hopes. I was sensible of the Reasonableness of what he said, and composed myself as well as possible to follow the Countess, who was already gone a good Distance——my Mother left me not till we were near; nor then without charging me to keep in mind the Lessons she had given me, and which she said, she foresaw I should have Occasion for——I put into her Hands the Purse I had received from the Marquis, and she told me she would buy with Part of the Money a handsome Garment for me, and some other Necessaries, and send them after me to the Castle.

The Marquis during the time of my taking leave had frequently look'd back, and no sooner saw I was alone than he retired a few Paces to join me.——How happy am I, beautiful *Jeanetta*, said he, to have this Opportunity of speaking to you, and to hope that I shall frequently renew that Satisfaction.————I wish you could be sensible of what I have suffer'd since I saw you

in

in the Foreſt, and the many Stratagems I have form'd for ſeeing you, before I could find any befitting my Character or yours, to put in practice.

I am as ſenſible, my Lord, reply'd I, of all your Goodneſs, as I am of my own Unworthineſs; and if I do not thank you as I ought, impute it to my want of Capacity, and the Converſation I have hitherto had, which being only with Perſons of my own Station, may very well render me confuſed when about to talk with one of yours. But I hope when I have been ſome time with my God-mother, I ſhall know how to behave better.

You have a great deal of Wit, anſwer'd the Marquis, and I doubt not but a very little Education will make you as bright a Woman, as any I know ———— but above all Things, my dear *Jeanetta*, I would have you learn to diſtinguiſh between thoſe who may pretend to be your Friends, and thoſe who really are ſuch.————I am very ſure none are more of the number of the latter than myſelf, yet I do not wiſh you ſhould believe me without Proofs ————You are beautiful, and will every Day become more ſo————the Counteſs keeps a World of Company————you will not be long without Admirers; but, *Jeanetta*, few Men of my Age think as I do————they may be ſincere when they ſay they love you; but the End they propoſe will not be for your Honour————if you liſten to their Addreſſes, you loſe me for ever.————I have not time at preſent to explain what I mean; but a little knowledge of the World, and the Paſſions of Mankind, will let you into part of it———— in the mean while, I would adviſe you to omit nothing which may endear you to the Counteſs: She is a very valuable Woman; and, making ſome few Exceptions, is a Pattern for you to imitate. You ſee, continued he, I do not treat you as a Child. ————Pardon me, however, that I take upon me to give you Leſſons; but the great ſhare I muſt bear in every thing that concerns you, makes me look forward into your Affairs.————One thing, purſued he, I had almoſt forgot, the Counteſs has a Daughter, who wanting your Charms will be jealous

lous of the Admiration you will excite————she has
also a Son, a fine Gentleman ; but his Notions with regard to your Sex, are altogether different from mine ; I
dare say, however, he will be as little able to resist your
Beauty as myself————he will have continual Opportunities of seeing you, and, perhaps, you will love him
————if that should happen, what will become of me!

I know not, said I, what Love is : I have never been
acquainted with any Trouble but when I saw my Father or Mother in Affliction, or my Brother and Sister
were peevish with me————nothing but your Generosity towards me could————O! no more, cry'd he,
of my Generosity, I cannot bear you should give that
name to such trifling Marks of my ever faithful Love
and Friendship————you know me not as yet, *Jeanetta,*
when you do you will be sensible I can know no Happiness, but in Opportunities of testifying how much I
love you.

Bless me! interrupted I smiling, you are always talking to me of this same Love.————I beseech your
Lordship say no more of it, till I know what it is, and
whether a Maid ought to listen to it. I will teach you
what it is, reply'd he ; no, no, my Lord, said I, my
Mother has always told me, 'twas dangerous to listen to
Men on that Subject ; and that all they said upon it was
only to impose upon us. And I dare answer the Countess is of the same Mind.

Take care, reply'd he, eagerly, that you do not let
her suspect any thing of the Passion I have for you————
she is a Lady tenacious of her power of pleasing ;————
but I shall tell you more of that hereafter————this,
however, may suffice ; she would prevent my seeing
you, and on that Blessing my Life depends. Ah!
then, cry'd I, it must be a Crime, or you would not be
so careful to conceal it. No, my dearest *Jeanetta,* I
assure you it is far from being so, answer'd he, have
more Confidence in me————you never will have reason to repent it.

I was about to reply, when the Countess turning about
and seeing us together, call'd to me ; upon our coming

up to her. How now, *Jeanetta*, said she, what Subject is the Marquis entertaining you with ?————Not Love, I hope !————Remember you mult set a guard upon your Ears whenever the Word is mention'd, it carries with it a kind of Poifon that is fometimes fatal.

I aſſure your Ladyſhip, anſwer'd I, I am entirely ignorant of any ſuch thing: My Lord Marquis has been diverting himſelf, with enquiring how we of the Village amuſe ourſelves, when we are not at Work, and I have given him the beſt Account I can.

It is very true, ſaid he, this pretty Creature has given ſo natural a Deſcription of their Rural Pleaſures, that I think them preferrable to thoſe of the Town. The Counteſs fell a laughing, and began to rally him on his new Taſte; and the reſt of the Company having all ſomething to ſay on the ſame Head, the Converſation became general, till without perceiving it we arrived at the Caſtle.

The Counteſs was no ſooner in her Apartment, than ſhe call'd for Madamoiſelle *Du Pare:* She had formerly been her Woman ; but of late Years had no other Employment than to controul her Ladyſhip, as well as the reſt of the Family: This Favourite was upwards of Fifty, was pale, lean, and very much wrinkled, of a wheedling Behaviour ; till by ſeeming to think as the Perſon who entruſted her, ſhe got into the bottom of their Secrets, and then became a perfect Tyrant.————Money alone could humanize her, and any Fault was excuſeable when ſhe was a gainer by it————it was to this formal antiquated thing that I was given in Charge. I put my God-daughter wholly under your Care, ſaid the Counteſs, ſhe is good-natur'd, and no Fool————all her Misfortune is want of Education, which I don't doubt but ſhe will ſoon advance in by your Direction ————I can tell you, purſued ſhe, that ſhe has been taken Notice of by the King, and his Majeſty has juſt now ſent her Thirty *Lewis D'Ors* by the Hands of the young Marquis *De L————V————*. Thirty *Lewis D'Ors!* cry'd Madamoiſelle *Du Pare*, a very pretty Preſent upon my Word————and what has ſhe done with them.

Her

Her Duty and Affection to her Parents, reply'd her Ladyship, has prevail'd with her to give them all to her
Mother. Foolish enough, said the old *Abigail* with a
Frown, could not I have them laid by for her.———How
does she know what she may want—sure I could have
taken care of such a Sum for her. That's true, resum'd
the Countess, but we'll think no more of it———I
would have you get her taught to write in the first Place;
and as soon as she is a little Mistress of her Pen, I'll
take her to *Versailles*, and she shall return the King
Thanks in her own Hand-writing———who knows but
it may engage him to continue his Bounty to her.
Right, Madam, cry'd my new Governess, that's an
excellent Thought in your Ladyship. All this time
I never spoke one Word; but my Heart beat, I trembled, and already regretted my Change of Situation,
and wish'd myself again at the Village in my Father's
homely Cottage. After some farther Discourse about
it, Mademoiselle *Du Pare* seized on me as her Prey,
and ever after watch'd all my Motions.

The Marquis stay'd some time at the Castle, and was
continually seeking an Opportunity of speaking to me;
but all his Diligence was ineffectual, so close did Mademoiselle *Du Pare* keep to me; I was always with her,
or in the Countess's Bed-chamber, where I was learning
to embroider: I often met his Eyes, and as by Degrees
I learnt their Language, read in them how uneasy this
Restraint was to him. I cannot say but I had a secret
Pleasure in this Mark of his Affection, and I was so taken up with the sweet Reflection, that I never consider'd
whether the indulging it were a Fault———indeed, I
look'd on the Tenderness I already had for him, as Gratitude only for the Favours he had done me, and imagin'd not that the gentle Heat which then warm'd my
Bosom, would one Day burst out in a Flame. The Satisfaction I took in seeing him, made me not over attentive to any thing else, tho' I soon found there
were some Tempers in the Family, which it very much
behoved me to study and guard against.

Mademoiselle

Mademoiselle *D'Elbieux* the Countess's Daughter was one of those: She was then about fifteen Years of Age; but except a good Complection had not one thing about her that could be call'd beautiful.————Her Eyes were large indeed, but dull and heavy, and tho' she wanted not Wit, had the least Appearance of it in her Countenance that ever I saw.————Her Voice and manner of Deportment to those whose good Opinion she desir'd, was such as made her pass well condition'd; but under this shew of Softness was conceal'd an implacable Rancour, Envy and Malice. The Favours I receiv'd from her Mother while I was at the Castle, would have made me omit this Character, if it had been possible for me to have proceeded in my Story without doing it; as she had so great a Hand in bringing on many of my future Troubles————therefore all I can do is to soften the Touches, when I shall have cause to mention either her Cruelty or her Infidelity. My little Experience did not hinder me from perceiving the Discontent she conceiv'd at my coming to the Castle; where every one else receiv'd me with Demonstrations of liking, till her sullen, and, indeed, insolent Behaviour, diminish'd the good Opinion they at first had of me.

The Chevalier her Brother was in the opposite Extreme; he lik'd me but too well, as I easily saw from the first Moment of my Arrival————my Youth, my mean Birth, my Ignorance of the World, made him look on me as an easy Conquest; and my Innocence and Beauty, as an agreeable Amusement to pass the Time with, while he stay'd in the Country. How different, indeed, was his way of thinking from that of the Marquis————the *one* all Tender, Generous and Faithful————the *other* Vain-glorious, Self-interested and Fierce; yet like his Sister, had he the Art of dissembling his bad Qualities; and the Usage I afterwards had from them both, convinced me, that one ought never to build an Opinion upon the first Impression, nor contract any Friendship with Persons, from whom one has not previous Proofs of Sincerity and Honour.

I

I did not, however, so much as I ought to have done, study the Characters of the Persons I was among—— the charming Marquis was under the same Roof with me, and I had leisure to contemplate on only him ; but now the time arrived for his Departure, which he could not protract without giving Suspicion of the motive of his Stay ; and I now first experienc'd, that there were Thorns attending the Roses of even the most innocent Affection, by the Fears I was in, that he would go without being able to find any Opportunity of speaking to me.

But the Anxiety, as he since told me, he was in on the same Account, at last, assisted his Invention in finding out the Means————the Evening of the Day before that prefixed for his leaving the Castle, there happened to be a great deal of Company in the Countess's Chamber, I was there at my Work as usual————they proposed Play, the Marquis made one ; but pretending he did not understand the Game, prevail'd on the Countess to hold his Cards————she readily undertook the Commission, and every one drawing near the Table thro' their eagerness of Play————Mademoiselle *Du Pare*, and I were soon left by ourselves. The Marquis soon after quitted the Gamesters, and after a little Chat, ask'd my Governess why she did not play, and offer'd her a *Lewis D'Or* to venture with, telling her she should go Halves with him in whatever she won: She gladly accepted the Proposal, and left us together : as soon as he found her Back turn'd, dearest *Jeanetta*, said he, how long sought for, and how precious is this Opportunity of speaking to you ! But as it must be short, and I go hence To-morrow, let me not leave you without knowing if I have any Interest in your Heart.————Heaven can only tell when I shall be able to see you again, and yet the hope of it soon is all the Consolation I have. He spoke this with such a Tenderness, that I could not forbear Sighing :————What means that Sigh, cry'd he fondly, am I so happy as to have made any Impression on you————speak, my Angel————continued he, assure my Bliss, and let the sweet Reflection that my Idea is present

sent with you, enable me to bear with some Patience the Pains of Absence. Ah! my Lord! reply'd I, do not press me any farther I beseech you——whenever you are near me, or speak to me, I am not myself—— what do you aim at——what do you expect from me——why do you endeavour to engage a young Maid of my Condition——I know very well the Respect that is due to you, and the Obligations I have to you; but were you ten times greater than you are, and I more beholden, I would not listen to any thing in prejudice of my Virtue. May it be ever sacred, cry'd he, and no prophane Wretch ever attempt its Violation. ——No, *Jeanetta*, *Jeanetta*, added he, my Affections are pure as your own Virgin Thoughts——the whole of my Desires is to be loved by you.——Bless me, said I, I think the Gentlemen can talk of nothing else ——I suppose it is the Fashion among People of Quality.——I never heard so much of Love since I was born, as in the eight Days I have been here. How! cry'd the Marquis in a kind of perplex'd Sur- prize, I was never happy enough to mention mine till this Moment. Is your Lordship the only Person I see here, answer'd I, without considering the Folly I was guilty of? all the other Gentlemen that visit the Countess, say much the same things to me as you do; but above all the Chevalier *D'Elbieux* persecutes me continually. O! Heaven! interrupted he, is the Che- valier *D'Elbieux* in love with you? I know not that ——answer'd I; but if one ought to believe a Man when he says he is in love, he has told me so too often for me to doubt it. And what Answer have you given him? said the Marquis hastily. The Conversations we have had together on that Head, said I, were so little pleasing to me, that I gave them no Place in my Me- mory——all I know is, that I should not be sorry if he were no less desirous of entertaining me, than Made- moiselle his Sister seems to be, and that I might be eas'd of his Importunities. May I depend on your Sincerity in this Point, lovely *Jeanetta?* resumed he, do you not feel a secret Pleasure when he talks to you?——

No, indeed, interrupted I, with the most perfect Simplicity, one Word from you dwells more upon me than an hundred from him.

I had no sooner utter'd these Words, than the Marquis appear'd all Extasy———his Eyes sparkled with brighter and fiercer Fires———a glowing Red cover'd all his Face, and he cry'd out———O! happy! happy! that I am———if what you say be real, I would not change Conditions with a Monarch———Repeat——— repeat, my lovely Maid, the blissful Sound———this soft Confession has given me a new Life———methinks, I breathe another Air———I'm in Heaven.——— Never had I been more surprized than at that Instant, ———I knew not what he meant, and thought him mad ———Heavens! cry'd I, what have I said———what is it that transports you?———Have I spoke any thing I ought not———no, no, rejoin'd he hastily, speak ever thus———if your Heart dictated these charming Words! O! do not contradict it———never—never shall you have cause to repent the Tenderness you have for me. My Heart has said nothing, cry'd I, with a good deal of Vivacity: if I have let fall any Words without knowing the meaning, you ought not to turn them to my Disadvantage. How, said the Marquis with a visible Change in all his Air, am I to go from you overwhelm'd with Grief and Dispair!———your Heart has said nothing, *Jeanetta*———'tis well; to another, perhaps, it will speak———I have no more to do but to die, since I have incurr'd your Hatred.

He spoke these last Words with an Accent which pierc'd me to the Soul!———my God, said I, how unhappy am I, not to be able to express myself in a manner to be understood———it was not my Intention to offend———but, my Lord, you should not talk to one, who has not yet arriv'd at Sense enough to answer you ———when I become more polite, as this is the Place to make me so, I will say nothing that shall displease you. ———He could not forbear smiling at my Simplicity, which I perceiving, well, said I, what a strange thing is this! You were just now ready to weep, and now I have

made

made I suppose, some fresh Blunder you laugh at me——
'tis best for me to be silent for the future.

After these Words, which I could not pronounce without Peevishness, I turned my Eyes upon my Work,
nor would be prevail'd upon by all the tender things he
said, either to look up or speak.

Finding every thing ineffectual at last, he ceas'd, and
I imagining he was turn'd away, lifted up my Eyes
hastily to see what was become of him; but cast them
down immediately with a good deal of Confusion, finding him standing in the same Posture he had been in,
and looking stedfastly upon me.————You then resolve
my Death, said he, since you will neither speak to me
nor look upon me——cruel Creature!——Farewel for
ever.——

The word *Cruel* picqued me, I thought the Marquis
very unjust to accuse me of so base a thing, but how
little I understood his meaning in it, will best be shewn
in the childish Answer I made him————No, my
Lord, said I, I don't deserve such Reproach——I am
not, nor ever was *Cruel* to any thing——I never saw
a Lamb killed without weeping————and when my
Brother and Sister have fallen upon me, I would not so
much as defend myself for fear I should hurt them——
how then can I be call'd *Cruel*?————I went on still
repeating the word *Cruel*, and as Love makes us look
with favourable Eyes on every Thing, the Marquis was
so pleased with my ingenuous Simplicity, that he would
not interrupt me. But perceiving I had done, I ask
your pardon, my dearest *Jeanetta*, said he, the Word
Cruel in a Lover's Mouth implies not being ill-natured,
but being insensible of the Passion he aims to inspire——
if you should prove so to me, I cannot blame you for
it, tho' I should lament my own hard Fate————I
should die, *Jeanetta*, but ought not to complain——
I hope, however, more Comfort from your Compassion ;
and as there is no Time to be lost, permit me to tell you,
that I will send my Valet de Chambre twice a Week,
with a pretended Compliment to the Countess, but in
reality to hear News of you————He will find Means

to speak to you, and will bring your Answers back, which will in some Degree soften the Asperity of Absence————Besides I shall take all Opportunities possible to come down here————at present I will press you no farther for the knowledge how I stand in your good Wishes, since you seem so averse to declare your self on that Point; however I shall be able to form some Judgment of it, by the Progress you shall make in learning to write, and I flatter myself I then find you will at least not hate me because I love you————He was proceeding to say something more but my Governess came to us, she had won four *Lewis d'Ors* and ran to offer the Marquis his Share; no Madamoiselle, said he, putting back her Hand, I desire you will keep them your self————they may be lucky another time———— when I return to *Versailles*, I will play for you, and try if you are as fortunate in deep Play as you have been here. I do not desire in Return you will take Care of this Girl; but if I hear you do so, will promise you shall find your Account in it hereafter————this was taking her on the weak Side, especially as she knew the Liberality of the Marquis, and how punctual he was in keeping his Word. You need not doubt, my Lord, answered she, for I love her as my own Child, and will be no less watchful over her.————I am not to learn that our young Chevalier has a Design upon her, but God forbid he should succeed——no, no, I shall keep so strict an Eye upon him, that he shall not so much as speak to her but when I am by————I know him well enough, and he also knows me, he dares not affront me; just as she had left off speaking, the Company rose from Table, the Bank was broke, and the Countess came to acquaint the Marquis with his Loss, which he seemed little concern'd at. Soon after they all adjourn'd to the Garden, and I remain'd with only Madamoiselle *Du Parc*, whose Change of Behaviour to me, made me see the good Effects of the Marquis's Civilities, for so she call'd the Money and the Promises she had received from him; and indeed from this time

forward

forward she used me with the greatest Tenderness imaginable.

When the Marquis, and all the other Company departed, the Chevalier *D'Elbieux* had Leisure to prosecute the unhappy Passion he had entertain'd for me, and was so diligent in following me wherever I went, that the whole Family perceived it, and the Countess being inform'd of it, reprimanded him accordingly; but her Words, far from having the Effect she expected, served but to encrease his Desires, as it afterwards prov'd; though for the present he seem'd, as he promis'd he would do, to have banish'd me entirely from his Thoughts: He neither spoke to me, nor endeavour'd to find any Opportunity of accosting me, and when any one offer'd without his seeking it, he scarce vouchsafed a Look towards me; but I too soon found this Change of Behaviour was only Dissimulation, and that nothing is more dangerous than Constraint in a Heart, not under the Direction of Virtue.

As to my Treatment from the rest of the Family it was different: The Countess herself was extremely kind and condescending, but not all my Assiduities could engage Mademoiselle *d'Elbieux* to behave to me with the least Good-nature: I know not whether the Devoirs paid me by the Marquis had inspired me with a certain Indignity to Affronts, or that I really had it in my Nature; but I confess I found a World of Difficulty in submitting to a Person of her haughty Carriage; though had she used me with any Degree of Affability, I should have thought nothing too much to oblige her. I often wept when alone, and the Absence of the Marquis, perhaps, contributed not a little to the calling forth my Tears.——Every little rebuff I met with made me remember his Tenderness and Politeness, and set all his Virtues in the most amiable Light.——In fine, I loved him, and was now no longer ignorant I did so——at first I would have imputed my Inquietudes to some other source; but it was in vain for me to go about to deceive myself in this Point, tho' I was lucky enough to deceive others for a good while.

During

During the Abfence of the Marquis I apply'd clofely to Writing, and profited fo well by my Inftructions, that I foon knew how to join my Letters; the firft Ufe I made of my Proficiency, was to fcribble a whole Sheet of Paper, and took an extreme, tho' innocent Pleafure, in teftifying to my Lover, that I had not forgot what he faid to me on that Account: This I gave, with a great Charge to *Dubois*, the Marquis's Valet de Chambre, who was then come to the Caftle on the Errand mentioned to me by the Marquis, and he affured me, he would give it into his Mafter's own Hand, who he knew would be highly delighted with it.————He then enquired concerning the Behaviour of the Chevalier, I doubted not but he was commiffion'd to do fo, and gave him a faithful Account of every thing.

How happy did I now think myfelf in the Confideration my dear Marquis had for me, and how many bewitching Ideas ran through my Mind, and render'd me incapable of feeing the Thorns, that muft neceffarily attend the prefent Rofes of my flatter'd Paffion————but reciprocal, faithful Love, would be too much of Heaven for Mortals to enjoy, if permanent————but, alas, 'tis fleeting, or fo chequer'd with crofs Accidents, that convinces us no perfect Happinefs is to be found below.

I had contracted a very great Intimacy with a young Woman at the Caftle, call'd Mademoifelle *Catherina*; fhe was Neice to my Governefs, and perfectly acquainted with all her good and bad Qualities, which fhe did not fcruple to fpeak impartially of to me: She had an Infinity of Good-nature, a great deal of Wit, and a liberal Education, and I was very much indebted to the Pains fhe took with me, that I fo foon fhook off the Rufticity of a Country Life. Her Age as well as Experience was fuperior to mine; but that did not hinder us from being infeparable Companions: the Evening after *Dubois* went away, this Friend, myfelf and Governefs, went to take a little walk in a Wood adjacent to the Caftle. Mademoifelle *Du Pare* had a Book in her Hand, on which fhe feeming attentive, we had the Opportunity of retiring fome Diftance from her. Our

Conversation accidently turn'd on the Countess, and I expressing some surprize that she could live so long without seeing her Husband, whom she had left at *Versailles*, and had never been once at the Castle the whole Summer; she inform'd me, that for many Years they had been on very indifferent Terms together, that he never came into the Country till she left it; nor she to Town without being certain he was absent, and that this was the only Point in which they agreed. Good God, said I, is it possible for married People to live separate from each other——we never hear of any such thing in our Village, what can be the Occasion of it?———Love and Jealousy, reply'd Mademoiselle *Catherina*; Monsieur does not approve that his Wife should have Admirers, and Madam cannot live without them. What do Women admit of Courtship after they are married? cry'd I. Yes, my dear *Jeanetta*, said she, I know it is not right; but it is very common, especially at *Paris* ———Interest makes more Marriages than Inclination, and where there is no Sympathy of Minds, there can be no Conformity to Rules——yet this vile Custom daily gains ground, and will prevail above Reason.—The Husband enjoys himself with his Mistresses, the Wife consoles with her Gallants; and tho' they live together in the same House, seldom see each others Faces, and these are reckon'd among the happiest Couples; for there are Husbands less obliging, who expect an exact Adherence to Duty in their Wives, while themselves riot in all the Excesses of Libertinism, and if she expostulates, or refuses to comply, the House becomes a perfect Babel of Confusion————nothing is to be heard but Quarrels and Complaints, and an eternal Separation is the best that can befal them ———Some again agree never to disturb each others Pleasures, and if there can be any true Felicity without Virtue, these partake it, because under no Restraint. Some too without being under any Engagement elsewhere, are quite indifferent to each other; and the Age is not without Examples of some, who having liv'd a long time together in a State of Disagreement, have at last found out Charms in

each

each other, which have brought them to a perfect Reconciliation; but this happens very rarely, and I dare answer will never be the Case of our Lord and Lady.
———Your God-mother, indeed, has the Character of a virtuous Woman, but she affects the Air of a Coquette; she loves to be thought amiable, and to amuse herself with the Addresses of Persons who make a Figure in the World.———Some People are of that unhappy Temper, that they cannot be easy without it———she is of that Number, and nothing can be more dull and spleenatic than her Ladyship has been these three Months, that she has been in the Country,———'tis but since the young Marquis *De L*———*V*———paid his Devoirs, that she has been once in a gay Humour———indeed, some Days before his Departure, he appear'd so very much enamour'd, and behav'd toward her with such Assiduity and Tenderness, as might have render'd a Person less desirous of attracting, vain of her Conquest.———

She said something more, but I was incapable of hearing it———touch'd to the Heart with a Passion I never before had any Notion of, the Force overwhelm'd at once my unguarded Faculties, and I fainted away on the Grass where we were sitting.———*Catherina* soon brought me to myself, and her Aunt seeing what had happen'd to me, came hastily up, and I was led between them to the Castle, where they put me immediately to Bed, and persuaded me to endeavour to Sleep, as being the best Remedy for my Disorder; I pretended to be of the same Opinion in order to be left alone, and when I was, gave a loose to all the Horrors that in that dreadful Moment had Possession of my Mind.

Ah! wretched Creature that I am, cry'd I to myself, to have suffer'd a Passion so fatal to my Repose, ever to gain Entrance into my Heart———why, cruel Marquis, did you take Pleasure in deceiving a poor Girl, whose only guard was Innocence?———Could you not love the Countess without my Ruin?———I attempted not to gain your Affection? O! why did you take such Pains to inspire me with a Tenderness, which can afford you no Satisfaction.———O! *Charlotta*———

Charlotta

Charlotta————I now feel your Pains, when you found yourself abandon'd by all that was dear to you.————

In this manner did I exclaim, and the Story of that unhappy Maid, coming now fresh again into my Mind, I drew Parallels between her Case and mine, and when I consider'd the Catastrophe of hers, cry'd the same might have been mine, but for the Goodness of an all directing Providence.

The Agitations of my Mind would have been too violent to sustain, had they not found vent in Tears, which at last bringing a Heaviness on my Eyes made me fall into a Slumber: I awoke the next Morning much refresh'd, and those excellent Lessons given me by my Mother to submit all to Heaven, render'd me more composed, and I found Consolation in the Thought, that as the Marquis was false, so early a Discovery of his Perfidy was the greatest Happiness could befal me.

As I was coming out of my Chamber, I met the Chevalier *D'Elbieux*; I come, said he, to enquire of your Health, they tell me you were indispos'd last Night; but I see no Remains of it, in your Countenance this Morning. So much the worse, reply'd I, for I am still very ill. Will you give me leave to prescribe for you, resumed he, I am the best Physician in the World, and if you put your Confidence in me will engage a perfect Cure; with these Words he took hold of my Hand, and press'd it very hard, let me go, Monsieur, said I, I will put Confidence in no Man in the World.————O! cry'd he, you are in Ill-humour this Morning————there is a Man in the World that merits you should regard him with more Complaisance.—Ha! is there not—in speaking these Words, he put on an Air which denoted he meant no other than himself; and this Vanity, join'd to the Dislike I before had to him, render'd him so contemptible, that I could not help discovering it in my Eyes; but he was so far from being daunted at it, as a Person who truly lov'd would have been, that he catch'd me forcibly in his Arms, and cry'd, come, come, I must teach you to be less scornful.————I gave a great Shriek, and struggled to disengage myself.————

Mademoiselle

Mademoiselle *Du Pare* heard and come running to my Assistance, on which he let me go. Fie, Monsieur, said she, is this the Respect you pay to your Mother's Commands?————I dont know how her Ladyship may resent it; but I am sure, I will not suffer such a Behaviour to a young Girl committed to my Care. With this she push'd him out of the Room, and shut the Door with Vehemence against him. He said not a Word in answer to her, but I then thought I could see Malice and Fury in his Eyes, and afterwards proved I had not been deceived in my Conjectures.

You did well to cry out, said my Governess as soon as we were alone, you see how I managed him————a boisterous Creature————I shall be glad when he is gone, and that will be in a short Time, as his Mother informs me————they say he has a great deal of Wit, if his Pride would give him leave to moderate his Passions; but for my Part there is a certain sullen Cast with his Eyes, that I never liked————he always looks, according to my Judgment, as if he were meditating some Mischief.

After some further Discourse on the same Subject we went to the Countess's Apartment, where to my great surprize we found the Marquis; as I had not heard of his Arrival, I was not prepar'd for this Encounter, and I believe had gone out of the Room had not Resentment and Shame detain'd me.

As soon as he perceived me he ran hastily toward me, crying, my dear *Jeanetta*, how do you do? Heavens! added he, as he approach'd me nearer, how she is alter'd ————what can be the meaning of this————what has befallen you since I was here?————with these words he took my Hand, but I snatch'd it hastily away, and at the same time gave him a look full of Indignation. I saw he was amazed at my Behaviour, but he endeavour'd to stifle it————the Girl is feverish, Madam, said he, turning to the Countess, has she been indisposed? a little, my Lord replyed she, last Night, but Mademoiselle *Du Pare* says 'twill go off again. I shall be glad to find her not mistaken, resumed he, but in my opinion she is now very ill. On this, the Countess call'd me to her, and

having

having felt my Pulse, found it enough disorder'd to think the Marquis was in the right———she has a little Fever indeed, said she, order a Physician to be sent for, Mademoiselle, and let her be put to Bed and taken care of.

The Marquis's Eyes were never off me, he hoped to have discover'd by mine, as he afterwards told me, the Cause of that Chagrin, which had render'd me so unlike what I was when he left me, but I gave him as little time for Examination as possible, and as soon as the Countess had given the Charge concerning me to Mademoiselle *Du Pare*, made a low Curtesy and withdrew.

I went to Bed disordered enough indeed both in Mind and Body—the sight of the Marquis—the Charms I still saw in him———the Certainty I thought I had that his Mind was far unworthy of his lovely Person, threw me into Agonies, which made so sensible a Revolution in me, that in a few Hours I fell in good earnest into a burning Fever, which still encreasing, I became quite delirious the next Day.

The Extremity of my Distemper made me wholly incapable of knowing what pass'd, so that I am indebted to Mademoiselle *Catherina*, who never left my Chamber, for this part of my History. The Countess, on being inform'd of my Condition, was very much concern'd, and commanded that nothing should be omitted for my Recovery, but came not to visit me, her Ladyship being one of those who dread the Sick, and not even her own Children in that Condition would have expected to see her. Nor am I at all surpriz'd at it, for since my living in the World, I have known People carry their Apprehensions to such an Extravagance, as not to bear the Conversation of any one who has visited the Sick. It was well for the Marquis that she was not of this Number; for hearing of the Danger I was in, he ran like one bereft of Reason to my Chamber, and his Love and Fears for me making him imagine me yet worse than I was, he was no longer the Master of his Actions; he threw himself on the Floor by the Bed-side, and broke forth into such passionate Exclamations, that my Governess and her Neice, who luckily were the only Persons in the Room, soon perceived how

dear

dear I was to him.　Nor did he seem desirous to make them think otherwise, when a little recover'd from the first Emotions of his Grief———'tis in vain for me, said he, to go about to conceal the Interest I take in this dear Girl's Recovery———my Life depends upon it———while he spoke he drew out a Purse, and putting it into Mademoiselle *Du Pare*'s Hand, there are, pursued he, an hundred *Lewis D'Ors*, I beg your acceptance of them———but if you can save this dear, this only Jewel of my Soul, my Acknowledgments to you shall be as unlimited as my Joy ———then turning to *Catherina*, who was weeping by me, and plucking a Ring off his Finger, be pleased to wear this Diamond as a Reward for your kind Care.——— I see you love this charming Maid, and that's enough to make you forever dear to me.———The regard———the Adoration I have for her is not to be express'd———not to be conceiv'd———ye Heavens, who know the Purity of my Intentions, restore her to me———Ah, *Jeanetta*——— *Jeanetta*! you hear me not———O that the giving up my own Life could preserve yours———Look upon me, my Cherubim; see to what a Condition I am reduced———He could no more, they told me for Tears; and when the Torrent ceas'd———good God! said he, what can have brought on this dreadful Change!———I left her in perfect Health———O how she burns———her Eyes are open, yet she sees me not.———

His Valet coming that Moment to the Chamber-door to receive his Orders———go, said he, take post immediately ———fly, and bring hither Monsieur de *N*———Heavens, how miserable am I———his Expressions were accompanied with so sincere a Grief, that neither my Governess nor her Neice could refrain weeping.

My God-mother soon after sent her Page to desire his Company below Stairs—Mademoiselle *Du Pare* entreated him to conceal his Trouble, and to leave the Castle the next Day———you will not, said she, be able to command yourself if you remain here any time———the Countess has discerning Eyes, she will discover the Secret of your Love, the consequence of which will be, that *Jeanetta* will be sent home, and the World be left at liberty to

censure

censure as they please the Cause——go therefore, my Lord, pursued she, your Presence here can be of no manner of service to the dear Girl——depend upon it, I will omit nothing that may be conducive to her Recovery, nor do I despair of it——she has Youth, and a good Constitution on her side. By this and the like Arguments he was at last prevail'd on: after kissing my Hands with Agonies too great for utterance he retired, and the next Day took his leave of the Countess, to whom he was oblig'd to invent an Excuse for his Daparture, so much sooner than she expected on his Arrival.

On his Journey he met *Dubois* and Monsieur de *N——* the Physician, to whom he strenuously recommended the care of his Patient, and beg'd him not to quit me till he had made a perfect Cure. *Dubois* had also Orders not to return to him, till he could bring him the News of my Recovery.

The great care that was taken of me, join'd to the Skill of the Physician, put me out of Danger in about fifteen Days——the Recital which *Catherina* made me of what had pass'd, contributed not a little to my Recovery:—the Despair which the Marquis testifyed, gave me the highest Contentment, and I scrupled not, when I found he had made no Secret of his Passion, to discover the Cause that had brought me even to the Gates of Death: they blamed my Jealousy, and convinced me how unjust it was, by telling me, that his Love for the Countess was but an Expedient to be near me without Suspicion. I confess'd to them how great a progress Love had made in my Heart, but at the same Time assured them, that it should never influence me so far as to lay myself liable to the Mischiefs poor *Charlotta*, whose Story they had heard from me, was involved in.

Mademoiselle *Du Pare* embraced me with the utmost Tenderness, and applauded my Resolution: she assured me she would contribute all in her power to confirm me in them, and preserve my Virtue from all the Dangers that might threaten it. The Presents her Niece and self had receiv'd from the Marquis had made a great Impression

preſſion on them; they drew from his Behaviour a Preſage of Conſequences happy for them, as well as for me: Every thing conſpir'd to flatter me; we talk'd of nothing all Day but my Lover, I every Day heard News of him, and ſuch agreeable Entertainments diſſipated all my Apprehenſions, and by ſwift Degrees reſtor'd me to my former Strength.

I had nothing now to diſconcert me, but the Chevalier *D'Elbieux*, who came ten times a Day into my Chamber; I was vex'd at his Importunities, but durſt not be rude to him, as I was under ſuch Obligations to his Mother: Mademoiſelle *Du Parc*, however, made me more eaſy, by promiſing ſhe would take care he never ſhould have any Opportunity to treat me with more Freedom, than was becoming me to allow.————I dreaded his Preſence notwithſtanding, tho' I knew not why, for he now pretended his former Fires were quite extinguiſh'd in the more laudable ones of Friendſhip, and Admiration of my Virtue————it ſeem'd as if I had a Foreboding of what was ſhortly to enſue, and to which I owe all the Series of Troubles, which ſo long delay'd my Happineſs.

In the mean time the Marquis, to whom my Governeſs without letting me know it, had given an Account of the Occaſion of my Illneſs, wrote me a long Letter to entreat my Pardon for his having been the innocent Occaſion————it was full of the moſt tender Aſſurances of an everlaſting Fidelity————and the moſt ſolemn Vows, that he would one Day give me an undeniable Proof of it.————He alſo wrote, that he would be at the Caſtle the next Day, to prevent my being ſurpriz'd at ſeeing him unexpectedly.

To be able to judge of my Satisfaction one muſt love like me, and have a Lover ſuch as the Marquis.———— I read the dear Billet a thouſand and a thouſand times, and laid it carefully by, as a Teſtimony of the moſt tender Paſſion that ever was.

The Counteſs was overjoy'd at my Recovery————, the Chevalier appear'd ſo too; but kept himſelf within the Bounds of that Moderation, which might be expected

from

from a virtuous Friendship.————I now began to have
a sincere one for him, and to check all Apprehensions
of his being otherwise than what he seem'd————this
Change in him being what I most earnestly wish'd, I
now thought myself very happy.   The following Day
after my Letter, which was that in which I expected
the Marquis, I appear'd more than ordinarily sprightly :
My Governess seeing me so well establish'd, propos'd a
Walk, as believing the Air would be of Service to me :
She mention'd it at the Countess's Table, where I had
the Honour of sitting since my Recovery, to the great
Mortification of Mademoiselle *D'Elbieux :* The Physi-
cian, who still attended me, approved of my taking the
Air, and it was agreed we should go toward Evening.

After Dinner *Catherina* whisper'd me, that this
Walk was a Contrivance of her Aunt's to meet the Marquis, that he might have the Pleasure of congratulating
my Recovery, in a less restrain'd manner than he could have
done before Persons who were not in the Secret ; I took
this extremely kind, and was under no Scruples of meeting my Lover, having with me a Confidante of Mademoiselle *Du Parc*'s Character ; for tho' I knew she was
greatly govern'd by Interest, yet I knew also that she
would not for any view be guilty of a base Action.———
Her Neice, who was Sincerity itself, having told me
those things which might justly be call'd Faults, made
me acquainted also with her good Qualities.

The Heat of the Day being over, I went out accompany'd only by my Governess and *Catherina* ; we took the
Road which we knew the Marquis must pass, it was in
the middle of a Wood ; and after we had walk'd about
half an Hour, we sat down on a little Bank at the Foot
of some Trees, in sight of the Road ; but we had not
been there above ten or twelve Minutes, before we heard
a Whistle a little distance from us.————I was startled,
but Mademoiselle *Du Parc* and *Catherina* laugh'd at me,
and told me I had no Occasion to be frighted————
there could be no danger of any thing in that Place ; and
that the Whistle I had heard, was, perhaps, Children,
who were diverting themselves in calling the Birds.   A
                                                    second

second Whistle, however, was immediately given from another Quarter, and which seem'd to answer the first, and the next Moment we heard the Noise of Horses: I turn'd about hastily and gave a loud Cry, seeing four Men vizarded, and riding full Gallop towards us. Neither of my Companions had time to utter a Syllable, much less to quit the Place————we were seized in an Instant by three of these Ruffians, while the fourth was left to take Care of the Horses————they put Handkerchiefs in our Mouths to prevent our crying out, and dragg'd us to a By-place surrounded with a Coppice, where they bound Mademoiselle *Du Parc* and her Neice, and left them tied to two Trees.————I was carry'd still farther into a kind of Grotto, and left alone with one of the Men who seem'd to be the principal; and who on his throwing off his Vizard, I discover'd to be the Chevalier *D'Elbieux*.————O! what was my Surprize————what Millions of horrid Ideas did in one Instant croud into my Mind————since nothing but Violence, said he, can prevail on you,————'tis fit you should be used according to your own Fashion. These Words were accompany'd with suitable Actions————as I was not bound, and the Danger I was in giving me uncommon Strength, I defended myself for some time; the Handkerchief also falling out of my Mouth, I made the Forest echo with my Shrieks————but notwithstanding all my Resistance, I must have fallen a Victim to the brutal Passion of this Monster, had not Heaven took Compassion on my Innocence———— the Sound of a Horse coming toward us oblig'd him to desist————he turn'd to look whence it proceeded, and the Imprecations he utter'd on seeing a Man coming to my Assistance, were almost as shocking to me as the Force he offer'd.————Determining not to lose his Prey if he could avoid it, he flew to fetch his Pistols from the Holsters of his Saddle.————I took the Opportunity and ran as fast as I could, and it is not to be doubted, but on such an Occasion, Fear gave Wings to my Feet.————I was soon at a great Distance from the Place; but the Noise of their Fighting reach'd my

Ears

Ears————the Report of their Pistols eechoing through every quarter of the Forest, was very terrible.———— Here my Strength fail'd me————Fear and Fatigue overcame me————I could go no farther, and fell without Sense or Motion at the Foot of a Tree.

The End of the FIRST PART.

T H E

THE

VIRTUOUS VILLAGER,

OR,

VIRGIN's VICTORY.

PART. II.

HE Night was far advanc'd, when I recover'd from my Swoon: A cold Dew hung upon my Face: My Limbs seem'd numb'd, and it was with the utmost Difficulty I rose from my uneasy Bed. Darkness in itself is dreadful when alone, but the Solitude I was in had something in it more terrible than can be exprefs'd ————the Screaming of Owls————the Howling of Wolves————the hollow Murmurings of the Winds ruftling through the Trees————the uncertain Glimmerings of a few fcatter'd Stars, which ferv'd to give no other Light than juft to fhew the Horrors of every thing around, and render Night more fhocking, might well have ftruck a damp to a Heart more couragious than

mine

mine.————What will become of me, said I to myfelf?————where am I?————whether fhall I go?
————how efcape the Fate that purfues me?————
trembling and ignorant what Road I ought to take, I
wander'd without knowing where————my Fears not only augmented every Danger, but created more————
fometimes I ran with all the Speed I could————fometimes ftood ftill————a Bat but brufh'd me with its
Wings, I thought myfelf loft————a Stump of a
Tree catch'd my Gown, I imagin'd the Ravifher had
feiz'd me, and cry'd out————a low hung Bough hit
me on the Face, and I fell down, more with the force
of Apprehenfion than the Blow.————I had been fo
fcar'd with thefe imaginary Mifchiefs, that the real one
which foon enfued had lefs Effect upon me—as I was profecuting my diftracted Progrefs, I felt the Ground fink
under me, and I fell into a Pit; it either could not be
very deep, or I was very fortunate in my Fall, for I
found myfelf in a fitting Pofture at the Bottom, without
having receiv'd the leaft Hurt.

What new Alarms invaded me in fo unexpected a Situation, may eafily be conceiv'd: I gather'd myfelf all in
a Heap, and wrapping my Gown about me gave a loofe
to Tears and to Complainings, till Sleep at laft had pity
on my Wretchednefs, and clos'd my watry Eyes in fweet
Forgetfulnefs and Death of Care.

The Dawn of Day had begun to pierce the Obfcurity
of the Wood————and the Birds with their chearful
Notes welcom'd the Return of the Father of Light,
when I awoke, and ftarted in a Fright, which had more
real Foundation than all that had preceded it. A Wolf,
which Fear reprefented to me ten times larger than he
was, lay clofe by me————our Fortunes were a like,
he could not fcape the Snare laid for him, and all ftrong
and furious as he was, was as unable to help himfelf as
I was————fo terrible a Sight made me not doubt
but my laft Hour was come; and fet myfelf to pray
with all my might.————I look'd on thefe Misfortunes
as a Punifhment, Heaven inflicted on me, for having
too much indulg'd my Inclinations for the Marquis; and
                                                    made

made a solemn Promise, that if I were preserved from the
devouring Jaws of this fierce Animal, I would avoid all
Opportunities of seeing him for the future, and devote
myself wholly to the Love of God and his Divine In-
spirations.

We never pray with so much Fervor as in times of
Danger, nor is any thing so great a Consolation to us:
At least I found it so; for after finishing my Devotion,
I felt myself much more composed, the Horror of my
Situation diminish'd; and as before I durst not cast
my Eyes towards my formidable Neighbour, I could
now look him in the Face. He seem'd also chang'd
from what he was by Nature ———— his Countenance
so far from fierce had something of Pity moving in it
———— he view'd his Prison round, as tho' to find out
some way of escaping, then cast his Eyes to the Top
with an Earnestness; Instinct informing him that was
the Place where he descended———— he walk'd slowly
backward and forward, and every Step he took I trembled, and thought he was coming to devour me————
on a sudden he seem'd to listen to some Noise, then
changing his Place, crept hastily under my Gown————
I was now in such a Terror that I could do nothing but
lift my Eyes to Heaven————when a new, and as it
might have prov'd, more dangerous Apparition struck
my Sight————it was a Man just going to fire a Gun
into the Pit.————Ah! cry'd I, pity me, spare me,
and pity me!————Ha! return'd he, looking into the
the Pit, what have we here ———— 'tis well you spoke
————I should have made fine Work else————what
do you do here————and how happen'd it, that you
and the Wolf have made but one Bed————for God's
sake, reply'd I, a little consoled at these Words; save
me, and I'll satisfy your Curiosity————save you!————
Ay, that I will gladly, said he; but you must stay a
little. I can't get you out without help————I'll fetch
one of my Companions who is not far off————in the
mean time fear nothing————the Beast will do you no
hurt; when a Wolf is once taken he is as harmless as
a Sheep. With these Words he left the Place, but in a

Moment after return'd with him he mention'd——one of them jump'd down into the Pit, and lifted me up as well he could, and the other took hold of my Hands and drew me out. The first thing I did was to prostrate myself on the Earth, and thank Heaven for having deliver'd me from so great a Danger.

While I was taken up with discharging this Duty, my Deliverer dispatch'd the unfortunate Wolf, and afterwards coming up me; one of them cry'd out! O God! what do I see——look, *Christopher*——what a Chance is this——'tis *Jeanetta*——this drew my Eyes upon him, and to my great Amazement found him to be *Colin*, the Woodmonger's Son, my first Lover, of whom I spoke in the beginning of these Memoirs.

I could not help sending forth a Cry of Astonishment? what is it you, *Colin*, said I?——and is it you, *Jednetta*, cry'd he, whom we gave over for lost?—— my first Emotions were the Effect of that Joy, which naturally arises from the sight of Persons we have been acquainted with in our Childhood; but on Reflection it went off, and an Aversion succeeded, the Reason of which may be easily guess'd.

I had promised to give them an Account how I fell into the Danger from which they had deliver'd me; but when I found they were of our own Village, I judg'd it improper to relate the whole of the Affair; so only said, that flying from some rude Men, I hid myself in the Wood, and happening to lose my Way, as I was returning to the Castle it grew dark, and I fell into the Pit where he found me.

I am glad, reply'd *Colin*, that you have escap'd so great a Danger, and that I had a Hand in it—— tho' all things consider'd, you don't much deserve it from me.——Ah! *Jeanetta*! I am very much troubled at what I have heard——indeed, I never thought your going to live at the Castle would turn to any good Account——and so I find it.

Pray what do you find, cry'd I, you are a great judge I suppose. I spoke this with such an Air of mingled Pride and Peevishness, that he stared at me some time

before

before he anfwer'd; but when he did, it was in thefe
Terms, what do I find, refumed he, I find enough I
think————why they tell me, that that fame Marquis,
who brought you the Money from the King, is in love
with you; but that's nothing to the Purpofe————you
may remember what pafs'd between us the Day I wrote
the Love-Letter, I was as good as my Word————I
told you, I would bring the old Man to give his Confent
for me to marry you————and fo I did————my
Friend, *Chriftopher*, here, and I, made him believe,
you were to have every Year the fame Sum, as that
which made fuch a Noife in the Village————fo he
told me I might e'en do as I lik'd————it was but
Yefterday I had brought the Matter to bear, and I ran
this Morning to acquaint you with it————but you
were gone, and I found all things in an Uproar————
rare Work you have made, indeed.

What Work, faid I haftily, what do you mean *Colin?* My Danger over, the Adventures of the Evening
came into my Mind, I trembled for the Marquis, and
was cruelly alarm'd for the Confequences of the Chevalier's rafh Proceeding, what News, purfued I, have you
heard at the Caftle————what do they fay————has any
thing happen'd.————I afk'd all thefe Queftions in
almoft the fame Breath, and my Emotions were fo great,
that *Colin*, who wanted not good Senfe, tho' he exprefs'd
himfelf in a plain Country manner, eafily perceiv'd my
Concern in my Countenance. O! you would know
all at once, anfwer'd he;————they fay that the Chevalier *D'Elbieux*, has run away with you————that
he has not been feen fince he fought with that Devil of
a Marquis; who I think is rightly ferv'd, for going
about to corrupt honeft Maids.————How ferved,
cry'd I, impatiently, what has befallen him?————
Ah! *Jeanetic*————*Jeanetta!* refum'd he, how you
betray yourfelf————do you think I don't fee how fearful you are for him; but, I'll punifh you————I'll
tell you no more.

Be dumb for ever then, cry'd I, with the utmoft
Spite, *Chriftopher*, I dare fay, will be more complaifant.

fant. No, no, interrupted the Clown, I am of *Colin's* fide, and 'tis but juft you fhould be paid in your own Coin———fince you have lived at the Caftle, you have been above looking at your old Acquaintance, and if you are little more civil now, 'tis only becaufe you ftand in need of us———as for *Colin*, I'm fure you don't value him of a Straw; and if I were as he, I would not have now you are fo much blown upon.

So much the better, reply'd I fiercely, and glad of a Pretence to quarrel, I am not fo much charm'd with his Perfon, but that I can very eafily refolve to fee him no more———fo farewel———it is now broad Day, and I can find my way to the Caftle without your Af-fiftance.

Colin was furprized at the Sharpnefs, with which I had anfwer'd, and as he loved me ftill, was forry *Chrif-topher* had fpoke to me in that manner, this he teftify'd by a Frown; then turning to me, ftay, *Jeanetta*, faid he, I will conduct you thither: No, no, purfued I, you fhan't refufe me any more Requefts.———I fhall know all that has happen'd without your telling me: In fpeaking this I offer'd to go; but they both laid hold of my Arms and ftopp'd me.—No, faid *Colin*, we fhan't quit you fo———you fhall go back to your Father and Mother.———I have their Promife, that if you were found, you fhould be my Wife, fo I have an Authority over you, and will make you return to the Village, whe-ther you like of it or not.

With thefe Words they in a manner forced me along, and I found it in vain to refift, therefore faid little, but my Tears which flowed from the two Sources of Grief and Spite, fufficiently made known the Vexation I was in. See, faid *Colin*, how afflicted fhe is———any one now that did not know the Caufe would pity her———all this is only becaufe fhe is like to lofe her dear Marquis. ———You fee they were not miftaken, that faid there was fomewhat more than ordinary between them——— her Behaviour is a plain Proof of it———one would think fhe fhould be overjoy'd to fee her Father and her Mother, and all her Neighbours again; but inftead of

that

that she does not care to hear them spoke of——Well, *Jeanetta*, for all that, you may one Day think it was happy for you to come among us again———what if we have no laced Coats, nor Feathers in our Hats, we may be as good as the fine Sparks you are so much taken with—befides, I can tell you after what has happen'd at the Castle, which is all laid to your Charge, your Godmother fays she will have no more to do with you.

This Intelligence, which he gave me without Thought, touch'd me to the quick———it brought a thousand things at once into my Mind.———I had a lively Sense of my Reputation, and to think of going Home under any Suspicion was insupportable to me———the Love I had for my Mother stagger'd my Resolution———one Moment, methought, I saw her lamenting my Absence, and all in Tears for the Uncertainty of my Fate, the next severe, and believing me guilty of whatever Mischiefs had happened on my Account.———I shall be reproach'd at Home, said I, to myself, and shall not dare go abroad for fear of being pointed at.———Besides, how know I, but that Brute the Chevalier *D'Elbieux* may lay wait for me, and get some Opportunity to effect his wicked Designs———if I were not secure when under his Mother's care, how can I hope to be defended by my poor Parents; what can they do against such a Man as he ?———O ! Heavens ! to what shall I be expos'd———these Reflections made me resolve to get by some Means or other to *Paris*, and go to Service, which was infinitely less shocking to me, than to be oblig'd to marry *Colin*; and then I thought, when I was far enough off, to write to my Mother an Account of every thing, and the Reasons I had for not returning to her.

As I was contriving these things, a Horseman appear'd on the Road at some Distance : As he rode at a great Rate, he was soon up with us, and cry'd, did you meet any where near this Place a young Maid.——— Ah ! what do I see !———continu'd he, in discovering me, 'tis she———'tis she———O ! Mademoiselle *Jeanetta*, how happy am I to have found you———

what

what a Satisfaction will it be to my Lord! He alighted in speaking these Words, and running toward me, presented me his Hand:———how great was my Joy, when I found it was *Dubois*; the Presence of my watchful Conductors could not hinder me from giving him Proofs of it; and this faithful Servant transported with seeing me, had taken my Hand, and was going to kiss it, when *Colin* interpos'd and push'd him away——— go, said he, and kiss their Hand you wrote to———you have no Business here—I know you well enough. Is this one of your Kindred, Mademoiselle, cry'd the Valet, surpriz'd at this Behaviour.———No, no, reply'd I, looking scornfully at *Colin*; what then would the Creature be at, resum'd *Dubois*, still holding my Hand. Creature! resum'd *Colin*, softly———softly, Friend——— your lac'd Hat does not make me afraid of you, and tho' we are Countrymen, we are no Cowards———you can be saucy, I find, said the Valet———saucy yourself, cry'd *Colin* in a Passion. With these Words he took *Christopher*'s Gun, and stepping back two or three Paces; go your way, continu'd he, or we shall serve you as we did the Wolf just now. *Dubois* wanted not Courage, and was not daunted with this Threat; but tripping briskly up to him, put the Muzzle of the Gun aside, and seiz'd him by the Collar; *Christopher* seeing his Companion over-power'd, quitted me to go to his Assistance. I took the Advantage of this Moment of Liberty, and flew from them as fast as my Strength would give me leave.

I pass'd through Thickets, over Hills, climb'd the Banks of Ditches, and explor'd the very wildest Parts of the Wood, without staying to consider whereabouts I might find the Road, yet I happen'd upon it before I was aware: Seeing a Woman driving two Asses before her, I ran to overtake her, which when I had done, she immediately ask'd what was the Matter, and the Occasion of my Flight: And I framed a Story, that having been at Service, my Master had attempted my Virtue, and I was compell'd to run away, having no Friends, nor no other way of preserving myself.

That

That's my good Maiden, answer'd she. be always careful of your Chastity, and Heaven will protect and bless you————I assure you if there be any thing in my power can serve you, I shall not refuse it————if you want a Service, I have a Daughter at *Paris* to whom I can recommend you, as she is in a good Place herself she may hear of one for you. I thanked her, and said, I should be glad to accept of her Kindness. On which she told me she was going to *Valvins* with some Cloaths for her Daughter; and that if I thought fit, I might go in the Waggon that carry'd them, and which. they should find at that Town.

The desire I had of escaping the Pursuit, that I knew would be made after me; the avoiding such Reflections as I had just now heard from *Colin*, and the Lout his Companion, join'd to the Fears of *D'Elbieux*; and the Pleasure of living in a Place, where I knew the Marquis for the most Part resided, soon determin'd me to take this Journey.

The good Woman assur'd me she would speak to the Waggoner to take care of me; and offer'd if I had not Money to defray my Expences, to lay it down for me, and let me pay it to her Daughter when I should arrive at *Paris*; I was much oblig'd to her for her Kindness, but told her I had sufficient for my Purpose————well! so much the better, said she, Money is no Burthen, and often prevents the Ruin of young Creatures, who like you are in Difficulties.

We had walk'd about two Miles talking in this manner, when my Conductress propos'd going to Breakfast, which, indeed, I was extremely glad to hear, being almost faint with Hunger: She pull'd a piece of Bacon and some Bread out of a little Wallet, and we seated ourselves under the Shade of some Willows, that grew by the side of a clear Rivulet, and the Asses, as is usual, readily stopp'd to graze. Never shall I forget how delicious this homely Repast seem'd to me, and to this Day whenever I have no Inclination for Food, and am over delicate, if I but think on that Bacon, my Appetite returns, and I eat with Satisfaction.

While

While we were eating, the good Woman looking earnestly upon me, had Tears in her Eyes, she sigh'd bitterly, and the Morsel rested in her Mouth.   Alas! said I, you seem troubled————what's the Matter ?———— you put me so much in mind of one, who once was dear to me, reply'd she, that I cannot behold you without Grief————she was about your Age, and had a great resemblance of you.————Ah! would to Heaven she had been less beautiful, for it was her unhappy Charms that brought her to her Grave ; yet lovely as was her Person, her Soul was yet more so.————But I'll relate to you her whole Story as we go along————it may be of Service to you ; for nothing prejudices the mind of a young Person in favour of Virtue, so much as Examples of it in those, from whose Situation we may draw a Parallel to our own.

After we had refresh'd ourselves, we continued our Journey ; and the good Woman, in pursuance of her Promise, began in this manner.

The History of MARIANA.

MEAN as I now appear, said she, the first Years of my Life were past among the great World. ————My Husband had a Place at Court, which entitled him to an Apartment there ;   and we lived in a manner, such as might render any one who had not an exorbitant Ambition, perfectly contented ; but on his Death, which too soon happen'd, myself with two Children, both Girls, were oblig'd to yield it to the Person that succeeded to the Employment.————I was made to hope a Pension from his Majesty's Bounty, for myself and little Ones ; but the Favourite, in whose power alone

K

it was to obtain this Grant for me, was my Enemy; because I would not be his Friend in a dishonourable way, and I never had the least Consideration from the Royal Favour. As I had not wherewith to support my Family, without entring into some Business; I bethought myself of dealing in Lemonades, and accordingly took a House, and settled in *Fountainbleau*, which tho' a small Place, yet by reason of the King's coming thither every Season, has a great Concourse of People in it.

Mariana, my eldest Daughter, was near twelve Years of Age when her Father died, so that she had the Opportunity of a much better Education, than I could have given her after that Misfortune.———I had the Satisfaction also to observe, that Nature had endued her with so great a Memory, and so strong a desire of Improvement, that she not not only retain'd all she had been taught; but by the help of a few Books, and a proper Application, she made a surprizing Progress in every thing she had begun to learn, when it was in our power to allow her Masters———in fine, she was look'd upon as a Prodigy, by all that were acquainted with her good Qualities; and as for her Person, think it not owing to the partial Fondness of a Mother, that I say few could vie with her in Point of Beauty.

Happy did I think myself in her till she attain'd the Age of Seventeen; when her once gay and chearful Temper gave Place to a heavy Melancholly———the beautiful Colour of her Cheeks and Lips vanish'd by Degrees, and was succeeded by a livid Paleness——— her Eyes grew languid, and her whole Form so alter'd, she was hardly to be known.

She was too dear to me, for me to behold so visible a Decay without the greatest Concern.———I could not but think she labour'd under some Discomposure of Mind, and pressed her to reveal the Cause, assuring her I would do every thing I could to remove it, be it of what Nature soever; but she still answer'd, that she knew it not herself.———I then had recourse to the Physicians, they allow'd her to be very ill; but confess'd they

they could not find out of what Diſtemper.————She grew, however, ſtill worſe and worſe, inſomuch that we all thought her, as, indeed, ſhe was, on the Verge of Death. She was ſenſible of her Condition, and one Day as I was ſitting weeping by her————my dear Mother, you have often deſired me with the utmoſt Sincerity and Tenderneſs, to let you know if any ſecret Grief has taken Poſſeſſion of my Heart ; and I, O! pardon it, as often, and with as much Falſhood and Ingratitude, deny'd I had————but I no longer dare impoſe upon you———— I feel that I am going very ſhortly to render Account of all my Actions before the Divine Tribunal, and I ſhould think it an Addition to my Guilt, not to con-feſs to you my Weakneſs.————Can there be a greater or more ſhameful one, than to fall in love firſt with a Man, and then inform him of it?————The Violence of my unhappy Paſſion, has thrown me into the Con-dition you ſee.————Bluſh not for me, my dear Mo-ther, continued ſhe, the Grave will ſoon expiate this in-voluntary Crime.

I was, indeed, very much alarm'd at this Acknow-ment, and the more ſo, as it was of all things leaſt ſuſpected by me, I concealed it, however, this not be-ing a time for Severity ; no, no, my deareſt Child, ſaid I, Heaven will, I hope, preſerve you, I ſhall be earneſt in Prayers for you.————Comfort yourſelf as much as poſſible for my Sake ; for, O! my Child, my dear Child, I cannot ſurvive your Loſs.

Your good Senſe and ſincere Piety, anſwer'd ſhe, will enable you to bear our Separation————but in Compaſſion to my Agonies, purſued ſhe, ſeeing me over-whelm'd in Tears, let me not ſee you weep————your Griefs pierce me to the very Soul.

The Mother of *Mariana* was here oblig'd to pauſe, the Repetition of ſo melancholy an Incident, renew'd in her ſome part of the Anguiſh ſhe felt at the time it hap-pen'd ; but after giving Vent to her Sighs, ſhe became more compoſ'd, and able to proſecute her Relation, which ſhe did in theſe Words.

I reſtrain'd my Tears, ſaid ſhe, as much as was in my power, that I might not add to her Diſorder.——— Dear Child! ſhe too wept, and for a time neither of us could offer any thing to conſole the other———at laſt, with a Preſence of Mind, which was wonderful, conſidering the Situation ſhe was in, both of Mind and Body; ſhe deſir'd me to be attentive, while ſhe gave me the Narrative of her unfortunate Adventure.

You may remember, my dear Mother, ſaid ſhe, that one Night finding yourſelf a little diſcompos'd you went early to Bed, leaving me alone in the Shop: To divert myſelf till the time of ſhutting up, I took the Hiſtory of *Hypolitus* ———fatal Hour!———dangerous Book, rend'ring the Heart capable of receiving the firſt ſoft Impreſſion that offers———the Paſſage I happen'd to pitch upon, affected me ſo much as to draw Tears into my Eyes———juſt at that Moment two young Gentlemen, one of whom was lovelier, even than the God of Love himſelf is painted, came into the Shop; they call'd for ſome *Lemonade* cool'd with Ice, and him I deſcrib'd, had ſo inimitable a Grace, both in the Tone of his Voice, and his polite Addreſs, that I was at once charm'd and pain'd. He perceiv'd I had been weeping, and the ſight of the Book, which ſtill was in my Hand, as well as my Bluſhes informing him of the Cauſe; how truly amiable you appear, ſaid he, when your enchanting Beauty is ſoftned by Tenderneſs———you weep then for Count *Douglas.*———How much to be envy'd is his Fate thus mourn'd.———Take heed you never render any Lover ſo unhappy by your Rigours———. think if you are ſo much touch'd with Woes, with which you have no Concern; how dreadful your Remorſe will be, if ever you hear your own Diſdain has been fatal to ſome faithful Heart.

He would have added ſomewhat more; but the Perſon who came in with him, interrupted his Diſcourſe, whether by Deſign, or that he had really Buſineſs I can't ſay; but he made an Excuſe for going elſewhere, and promis'd to call on him as came back.

I

I was now left alone with this too lovely Chevalier; I know not whether he had more the Art of Persuasion in his Words, than any of those who had hitherto addres'd me, or that my Heart melted with that fatal Story I had just been reading, was less capable of resisting the Assaults of Love; but it receiv'd the Impression, even before he declar'd his Passion; and that nothing might be wanting to compleat my Shame, I conceal'd not from him the Conquest he had made————never were Transports superior to his on this Occasion————he threw himself at my Feet————he kiss'd my Hands, and embrac'd me a thousand and a thousand Times.————I blush to this Moment to think with what Ease I permitted all this, nay, felt a Satisfaction all the time, which I could no more conceal than the Passion which occasion'd it ————'Tis true, indeed, all the Demonstrations he gave me of Tenderness, were only such as Innocence might suffer and Modesty approve————but cannot be excused, not only on the Account of his being so much a Stranger; but also, that his Love was unauthoriz'd by a Mother, who so well deserved to have had the sole Direction of my Heart and Actions.————O! Heaven! pursued the dear Creature to me, that you had not had so good an Opinion of my Conduct————that you had been more suspicious of me————then you would never have left me alone ———— you would have foreseen that one unlucky Moment, is enough to triumph over the feeble Reason of a young Maid like me. ————But Fate———— cruel Fate ordain'd it so, and set me down in its unerring Book, for Wretchedness and Shame.————

Notwithstanding the Delight I took in being with this Charmer of my Soul, and Bewitcher of all my Faculties; as I found it grew late, I was for taking leave and obliging him to retire; but he either was, or affected to be so much griev'd at that Request, that I could not refuse one quarter of an Hour more to his fervent Prayers.————He employ'd it in redoubling all the Tokens he had before given me of his Love, and render'd my believing Heart still more and more subjected to him————you love me, Monsieur, said I, and I could

not

not hinder myself from confessing, you are the only Man I ever wish'd should do so———shall I not have Cause hereafter to repent the Declaration I have made you?———According to all Appearance you are very much above me———what then can be the Event of this reciprocal Tenderness, or to what Purpose have you triumph'd over my Inclinations?———Oh! leave me ———I already condemn myself for what I have said ———Oh! why, reply'd he, with a dejected Air, do you think me capable of abusing so much Goodness? ———How unhappy am I, that you do not know me better.———No, my charming *Mariana*, I would suffer Death rather than deceive you———my Love for you shall be immortal as my Soul; and I will prefer you above all things the World calls great or powerful——— nor is my Condition so much superior to yours, as you, perhaps, imagine———I belong, indeed, to Monsieur the Count *Dc*———and have a fair Prospect of making my Fortune; whatever it be, I am ready to lay it at your Feet, and beg leave to share it with you.

These Words gave me new Life and Courage, I thought a Virgin had no Necessity to fly a Passion founded on Virtue, and that where Marriage was the End, the Means ought not to be disapprov'd.——— Alas! I did not consider how common a thing it is for Villains, to make this sacred Pretext the Dupe of their base Designs; and that it was a Rock on which Innocence was daily cast away.

We parted with Regret, but this first Interview giving an Assurance on my side of an eternal Constancy; I went to Bed full of pleasing Imaginations, and indulg'd a thousand vain Idea's, which till then were utter Strangers to my Soul.

Pardon me, Mother, said the dear Girl, that I carry'd on this Intrigue with so much Secrecy for near six Months: My perfidious Lover made me believe it was not yet time to reveal it to you, and begg'd he might have the Pleasure of doing it himself———the plausible Pretences he made from time to time, for this Delay, were such as might have deceiv'd a Person more wary

than

than myself.———I at least firmly depended on them for
Truth, and was zealous as himself in contriving Opportunities of seeing me, and keeping our Meetings from
your Knowledge.

All this while I waited with Patience the happy Moment, in which so tender a Passion was to receive your
Approbation; I depended wholly on his Honour, and
had so great a Confidence in him, that I look'd upon
it as one of the things impossible in Nature for him to
be false.

One Evening he came to me with a Countenance full
of Importance and Concern, my dear *Mariana*, said
he, I am oblig'd to leave you, and so well I love you, that
I am certain this Absence will be fatal, if you do not grant
me what I ask———the Respect I have for you, has laid
me under a Restraint this six Months, which no Tongue
can express; and should I leave you in this Situation,
you must never expect to see me more———yes, lovely Creature, either kill me, or secure my Happiness. I have already told you, answer'd I, that I love
you more than Life———what more remains for you to
ask? Ah? *Mariana!* cry'd he, if I lov'd you less, I
should have less Desires———but can I———can I———
is it in Man to bear eternal Agonies?———Can I forever
see you, and retain this cruel Distance?———much less
can I go from you, without receiving all the Satisfaction
in your power to grant, or my impatient Love to ask
———Love of yourself, not me, cry'd I, no longer at
a Loss for what he meant, indulging your own Wishes
without considering, that it must be at the Expence of all
that's dear to me in the World———my Honour, my Reputation, and my eternal Peace of Mind. Oh! Heaven! what say you, resum'd he, lifting up his Hands
and Eyes, is all you have named less dear to me than
to yourself?———do you know me, and yet use such Expressions?———Could you believe me capable of so
black a Crime, as attempting your Dishonour?———
Your Heart you say is mine, and all I aim at is to secure
the precious Prize by the most warrantable Means———
in fine, you must consent to a private Marriage with me,

before

before my Departure, or by all that's Sacred, the Difquiets I am in, will take me forever from you.

How weak does Love render us, I trembled at this Imprecation, and knew not how to refuse or grant what he defired———I figh'd———he prefs'd——— and at laft I yielded. The Reafons he urg'd for having it a Secret were of great Confequence.———His Ruin, he faid, was inevitable, if his Mafter difcover'd he intended to marry without a Fortune, he muft therefore make one of his own, before it was known he had a Wife; and that when he once fecur'd that Point, which he expected would be in a fhort time, he fhould acknowledge his Engagement with Pride and Pleafure.

You may remember, my dear Mother, that I afk'd your leave to vifit an Aunt about fix Miles off———that Journey was no more than a Pretence for my going out to be married.———Every thing, he faid, was ready for that Ceremony, and we took our leaves of each other, with the Defign on my fide, of being join'd for Life the next Morning.———But, Oh! Heavens! what a Change! this Moment I thought I was the happieft, the next found myfelf in reality the moft miferable.

Juft as my Lover was going out of the Shop, two Gentlemen exceedingly well drefs'd came in; he was no fooner pafs'd, than one faid to the other, was not that the Marquis *De*———? Yes, anfwer'd the other, but don't fpeak fo loud———he gave me a Wink and a Squeeze by the Hand, as I offer'd to falute him——— there is fome Myftery in it.—I have often feen him come in here.———I fancy he makes love to the beautiful *Mariana*. As I was in the little Clofet adjoining to the Shop, I heard them fay thefe Words, fo ftood clofe, imagining they would go on, as, indeed, they did to my Confufion.

I fhould eafily believe it, faid one of the Gentlemen, in anfwer to fomething had pafs'd; but *Mariana* is a Girl of Prudence, and I can't think fhe has yielded. How! cry'd the other, do you think it poffible for a Maid of her Condition to refufe any thing to a Man of his Quality———befides you know he has been always fuccessful in his Amours. I'll allow you to be right as to the Generality, said the first; but as to *Mariana*, I am convinced she is a modest Girl, and surprizingly superior to Temptation————a Friend of mine, and a Man of Consequence, offer'd her very valuable Presents, nay, would have made a Settlement on her for Life, but 'twas all to no Purpose. And what avails all this, resumed he, that knew so little of me; do you think a Girl like her would refuse to marry a Person of his Rank? You don't know, perhaps, that the Marquis scruples nothing for the Gratification of his Passion, and when he is what he calls violently in love, and can compass his Designs no other way, pretends an honourable Passion, and marries the admir'd Object under a borrow'd Name————and I believe I should not wrong him if I should say he had twenty Wives of this kind.

Guess, if it be possible, dear Mother, at my Surprize and Rage at hearing this, both were too violent to admit thought, and in the first Emotions I scream'd out, O! the Villain! we are overheard, said one of the Gentlemen, and by *Mariana* herself!————I am sorry for it, cry'd the other, we must prevail on her to hold her Tongue, on this they rush'd into the Closet, where they found me all in Tears.

They used their utmost Endeavours to comfort me; but I was asham'd to speak or look up, as if the Villany practis'd upon me had made me guilty too: They press'd me very much to tell them what was between me and the Marquis: and in Consideration of the Service they had done me, tho' undesignedly, as well as to clear myself in their Opinion, I related to them the whole Affair. They seem'd to believe, and pity me; but engag'd me never to let the Marquis know by what means, I attain'd the knowledge of his real Name, or the Intention he had of betraying me. They had no sooner left me, than I flung myself on the Bed without being able to pull off my Cloaths, in which Posture I remain'd all Night, and from the cruel Agitations I then suffer'd, I date the beginning of that inward Decay, which now deprives you of your Child.

All

All the Refolution, faid the afflicted Mother, that my dear Girl had affum'd, to me make this Narrative, here forfook her, and fhe was compell'd to vent fome Part of her Anguifh in Tears, before fhe was able to profecute it; but, drying her Eyes as foon as fhe could, fhe went on in this manner.

The Day following, refumed fhe, our Maid, who by Bribes he had made of his Party, brought me a Letter from him————in vain did Love plead in my Heart for this perfidious Wretch————in vain did the Idea of his Charms, his Wit, his Eloquence, rife in my Mind. ————I was determin'd never to fee him more, and to hate if poffible a Man, who under the facred Pretence of Love and Honour, had fo bafely impos'd on my Credulity, and gone fo great a way in the ruin of my Virtue. I fent the Letter back unopen'd, and charg'd the Servant never to engage in any Commiffions from him for the future; yet the audacious Creature prefum'd the next Day to bring me another, with a Meffage alfo from him, that he had fomewhat to acquaint me with of the utmoft Importance, and that he begg'd I would not condemn him without hearing his Defence. All fhe could urge on this Point either from him or herfelf, had not the defir'd Effect upon me, and I was fo provok'd at her offering to interfere, that I prevail'd with you on fome Pretence or other to turn her away, as you may remember.

Some few Days after this, I was cruelly alarm'd to find, when I awoke, the Deceiver kneeling by my Bedfide, and bathing one of my Hands with his deluding Tears ————I fnatch'd it from him; but with a Confufion, which gave him too much Reafon to believe, I had not yet overcome the Tendernefs I once had for him.

Well then, beautiful *Mariana*, you no longer love me, faid he, with a Look that pierced my very Soul, ————you refufe to fee me,————to hear me———— you banifh from you, all who would intercede for me. ————But in the Name of God what have I done to merit fuch cruel Treatment?————is it concealing my real Quality————I confefs I am the Marquis D————I

have,

have, indeed, deceiv'd you, but deceiv'd you on a Motive, which if you had known would have more endear'd me to you————is it a Crime to have a more refin'd and delicate Idea of Love, than my Sex ordinarily are capable of?————yet to this I owe my Misfortune————'tis this that has lost me all I value in the World————yet on whom lies the Blame, on *Mariana* or her Lover? Why did you not keep the solemn Promise you made me?————Why did you not meet me at the appointed Place?————There you would have known if it were to the Marquis *De*————or to the Secretary of the Count *De*————you were going to give your Hand.————Why, Oh! too cruel *Mariana!* did you disappoint me of the Satisfaction I propos'd in undeceiving you, by giving you a Husband more worthy of your Charms?————I address'd you under the Character of one, whom you might look on as your Equal, because if I had appear'd in my own, my jealous Heart might have suggested my Title and high Fortune had greater share in gaining you, than any thing you could find in my Person.————O! *Mariana!* my loving you too well, has made me criminal in your Esteem————but I have done————I owed so much to the Vindication of my own Honour,————you now know the bottom of my Heart, as to its Sentiments for you, and it remains for you to judge.

I am asham'd to confess, that while he spoke my Resolution stagger'd————my Heart was too much on his side————his Excuses were specious————I was sometimes ready to believe him, and to ask Pardon for having suspected him.————But Reason in the End overcome, it remonstrated to me that what I had heard from the Gentlemen could not be spoke with any Design, not only, as they were neither his Rivals nor Enemies; but also that their Discourse was between themselves, and not intended for my Ear, I assumed, therefore, Courage enough to desire he would leave me, protesting at the same time that all he could urge would be in vain; for I never more would consent to see him, or to think any otherwise of his Behaviour; but as he meant to deceive and abuse

abuse my Confidence. On this he committed a thousand
Extravagancies————offer'd to fall upon his Sword————
rav'd, wept, and omitted nothing that might testify the
most desperate dying Love————but I was still immoveable, and somebody luckily coming into the Room, he
retir'd, and deliver'd me for ever from the Alarms I
could not but feel, while he was present.

After he was gone————with how much Difficulty does
Virtue get the better of Inclination————I began to think
there was a Possibility of his being Innocent; and, if so,
said I to myself, what Punishment can be too great for my
rash and precipitate Proceeding————did Fortune design
me so vast a Blessing, as being the Marchioness *De*————
and have I wantonly thrown away her Favours!————but
these Suppositions soon gave way to more solid ones, and
I applauded myself for having so much restrain'd before
him, the Concern his Presence gave me,————I was, however, in a most unhappy Situation of Mind, till resolving if
possible to find out the Mystery, Chance and my own Endeavours brought me into the Acquaintance of a young
Maid, who had been one of the Examples of his successful Perfidy, and whose Story confirm'd me, that I had
plac'd my Affections on the basest of Mankind.————I
was asham'd then to reflect how far I had contributed to
deceive myself.————I hated the Character of my ungrateful Lover; but I could not love his Person less————
Time, however, might have worn out the Impression of
his Charms, had I been left to myself and heard no more
of him; but about eight Days since, I receiv'd a Blow
which I was quite unguarded against, and which has put
the finishing Stroke to my unhappy Life.

A Man of a good Aspect and well dress'd came to
me, and ask'd me if I were *Mariana*; after I had satisfied
him that I was, would to God, said he, any other than
myself had been employ'd on this Business.————I never
saw you before, Mademoiselle; but now I do, am so
much in your Interest, that I fear I shall be unable to
discharge my Commission in the manner it was order'd;
————but, continu'd he, as you must know it, forgive
me that I bring you the unwelcome News, that Mon-

sieur

fieur the Marquis *De*————is to be married to-morrow,
to Mademoifelle *De*————that Lady has been inform'd
of feveral Intrigues of her intended Spoufe, and among
the reft, that he has carry'd on a regular Correfpon-
dence with you, and fome have affirm'd that he is even
married to you in private; for which Reafon, though
every thing relating to the Ceremony is prepar'd, fhe
has made a folemn Vow never to become his Wife, till
the Affair between you is fully clear'd up: She will fend
a Perfon to you, to know your Anfwer, and on that entirely depends the Confummation, or breaking off the
Wedding.————It is in vain that my Lord Marquis
makes the moft folemn Affeverations, that he is a Stranger
to your Bed; fhe is inflexible, and affures him, that if
he has deceiv'd you, fhe will never fee him more. The
Marquis who adores her, and cannot live without her,
has fent me to you, to defire you will give fuch Replies
to the Queftions, afk'd you on this Occafion, as may
fecure his Happinefs; and withal commands me to tell
you, that if you act in any way, fo as to be an Obftacle to
his Happinefs, he will fend you to a Place, where you
may repent your Obftinacy at Leifure, and that————
go, go, Monfieur, go, interrupted I, exafperated beyond Meafure at this unworthy Menace; tell him who
has fent you with this honourable Meffage, that I defpife him too much, to give myfelf any Trouble concerning him, or his new Engagement; but I could
never have imagin'd, that after being guilty of fo many
Treacheries, of which I am better inform'd than he
thinks; he could have the Audacity to fend fuch a Meffage to a Perfon he has fo much folicited to be his
Wife; with thefe Words I turn'd from him, and he went
away aftonifh'd at my Spirit and Refolution.

But, vain Pride! unavailing outfide Appearance!
bitter Anguifh prey'd on my fecret Soul.————I was all
Horror, all Diftraction!————my Lover loft forever.
————Not only abandon'd by him; but facrificed to a
Rival. Nay, infulted by outragious Threats.————O!
this it is, dear Mother, that confumes my Vitals, and
                                                    has

has reduced me as you fee: What is all the World to me?———The Marquis is married;———all is done.

Her Tears put an End to this melancholly Narration. ———I endeavour'd to confole her, and omitted nothing to reftore her; but in vain, fhe ftill grew weaker, and about ten Days after expired———fhe died as fhe had liv'd, in fuch Sentiments of Piety, as afforded me great Comfort, and enabled me to fubmit to the Divine Will, but, alas! it coft me dear, and will do fo all my Life.

Here the difconfolate Mother ceas'd, and I was fo moved with this mournful Hiftory, that I wept bitterly: The liking fhe had taken to me, was very much encreas'd by feeing fuch Marks of my Affection, and fhe exprefs'd it in the moft grateful Manner. Reflections naturally arofe on the Inconftancy, the Perfidy, and Deceit of Mankind in Love Affairs, and I look'd on the Fate of *Mariana*, as a kind of Prefervative of my Innocence againft the Dangers I might expect to meet with in *Paris*.

At length we arriv'd at *Valvins*, where we found the Convenience before-mention'd; we bargain'd with the Perfon that drove it, for my Paffage and the Carriage of the Cloaths, *Mariana*'s Mother was fending to her furviving Daughter; and having taken leave of each other with mutual Demonftrations of Friendfhip, I fet forward on my Journey.

When I was alone in the Waggon, I abandon'd myfelf to the moft melancholly Reflections———Heavens! faid I, what am I doing———what will become of me ———what will People think?———what will my Mother fay?———that tender Mother who, perhaps, at this very Moment is half diftracted with her Fears for me———thefe Thoughts grew infupportable, and I cry'd to myfelf———no, no, I cannot, muft not be guilty of fuch a Breach of Duty———how know I, but it may break her Heart———I'll go no farther———I will return, better to endure all the Reproaches that can be laid upon me, than be the Death of fuch a Parent. ———Ah! had I never left her, I had not been involved in the Difficulties I now am.

In

In fine, I refolved to go back to the Village, and rather fubmit to any thing than be guilty of what I apprehended the Uncertainty of my Fate might be the Caufe of. I was juft going to call to the Waggoner to bid him ftop, that I might alight, when putting out my Head, I faw a Perfon well mounted, riding full Speed after us, and prefently after, to my Confufion, difcover'd it was no other than the Chevalier *D'Elbieux* : The Terrors that then feiz'd me are inexpreffible, fo I fhall only fay they were anfwerable to the Caufe———I trembled from Head to Foot————I knew not what to do in this Exigence————all I could think on, was to cover myfelf all over with a piece of coarfe Cloth, that was given me to preferve me from any Accident of the Weather ; and laid myfelf clofe down at the Bottom of the Waggon.————I remain'd thus above an Hour without daring to ftir, at laft Curiofity prevailing, I ventur'd to open one Corner of my Coverlet, and faw, Oh! Heaven, the Remembrance of what I then endur'd now makes me fhake, the Chevalier following the Waggon, and earneft in Difcourfe with him that had care of it.————What a Situation was I now in————how muft I now avoid the Danger that threatned me from his Brutality.————Good God! cry'd I to myfelf, what has brought him this Way !————who can have directed him————what may I not expect if he knows I am fo near him ?

The racking Myftery was foon unravelled ; for prefently after another Gentleman came galloping to the Chevalier, I have had no better luck than you, faid he, as he came toward us, I can hear nothing of her———— the Chevalier made no Anfwer, but put his Finger to his Mouth and pointed to the Waggon ; but when he came nearer, take heed, faid he, in a low Voice, we have her————if fhe now efcapes it muft be by a Miracle————tho' I fancy fhe fufpects fomething————fee how fhe has wrapp'd herfelf up————the Winding of the Road hindred me from hearing what farther pafs'd between them, and nothing is more amazing to me, than that the Fright I was in did not throw me into a Swoon ;

but

but the Almighty Difpofer of all Things enabled me to ftand againft this unexpected Blow, and infpired me with a Contrivance to preferve my Innocence.

In about half an Hour after I firft faw this formidable Enemy of my Virtue, the Waggon drove into a Forreft; the Remembrance of the Violence I had fo narrowly efcaped, in a Place much like this, from him who was now in Purfuit of me, for the fame wicked Purpofe, encreafed my Terrors; but the Road here being very bad, and the depth of the Rutts (occafioned by fome late heavy Rains) rendred it exceeding troublefome to ride, and compell'd the two Gentlemen to ftrike into a Path, between which and the great Road the Trees were extremely thick———fome of the Boughs luckily hanging over our Heads, I catch'd hold of one of them, and the Waggon driving from under me, I climb'd up into a large Tree, fully refolved to hide myfelf there till I could venture out with Safety, the Road being here ftrait I could fee a great Way from me.

I was foon convinced, that I had not taken this Precaution without fufficient Reafon, and fure it was Heaven alone that infpir'd me with the Thought, and prefented me with fuch an Opportunity———I could fee the Waggon when it had gone fome little diftance ftop———the Gentlemen quitted their Horfes, and having tied them to two Trees went towards it; one of them, but which I could not difcern jumped haftily into it, and having lifted up the Coverlet teftified a great Surprize at finding no Body under it———he then defcended, talked fome little Time with his Companion, after which they both remounted, look'd round, and then rode off taking different Roads.

I kept clofe all this while in my Poft, bleffing God for the Hope I now had of not falling into their Hands——— three Hours at leaft were elapfed without any thing appearing, yet did I not dare to remove; I was juft beginning to think my Danger over, when I faw the Wretches return, having met I fuppofe at fome appointed Place; it is to no Purpofe faid the Chevalier to fearch for her at fuch a Diftance———we did wrong———fhe can't be gone fo far, but muſt be hid ſomewhere this Way———it was here, or hereabouts we loſt her, do you place yourſelf yonder where the Roads croſs, and I'll ſtay upon this riſing Ground, from whence I can ſee a great Way round———How happy for me was this Information, I ſhould elſe have ventured down, and been a Prey to all a Virgin has to dread.

Night drew on apace, the Sun was already ſet, and I endured a great Deal both from my uneaſy Poſture, and my troubled Mind, my Strength as well as Patience was almoſt exhauſted, and I believe I ſhould have fallen from my Aſylum, had I not been happily relieved : A Chaiſe and ſix with a Lady and a little Girl in it, eſcorted by two Horſemen paſs'd by———the Moment I ſaw them, I thought it beſt to quit the Tree and beg their Protection, but in deſcending, I had the ill Fortune to have the upper Part of my Gown hook'd on one of the Branches, and my Foot ſlipping at the ſame Time, I hung dangling in the Air without being able to get quite down, or up again into the Body of the Tree. The fear of falling made me ſcream out, which brought the Lady's two Servants to my Aſſiſtance, they could not help laughing to find me in this Poſture, but having diſengaged me, and ſet my Feet on the Ground, good God, ſaid one of them, what Hazards do you run my pretty Maid———ſure you muſt love Birds dearly to venture paying ſo dear for taking their Neſts. I had no time to make any Anſwer, I ſaw the Chevalier *D'Elbieux* making towards me, and not above an hundred Yards diſtant———I ran, or rather flew to the Chariot crying out all the Way———for the Love of God, Madam, ſave me———as you tender your Happineſs here, or hereafter, protect a helpleſs Maid purſued by Raviſhers.——— My Cries occaſioned the Chariot to ſtop, and the Lady looking out, immediately beckon'd to me in Token ſhe gave a favourable Ear to my Requeſt ; and as ſhe afterwards told me, that tho' I was dreſt plain and like a Country-Girl, there was an undeſcribable Delicacy, a certain ſomething to which ſhe could not give a Name, that at firſt Sight intereſted her Heart in my Behalf ; ſhe bad me come into the Chariot,

and

and having ordered the Coachman to drive on, ask'd me the Occasion of my Fright: I made no Scruple of relating to her who I was, and all that had befallen me, concealing nothing but my Passion for the Marquis *de L——V——*, she listened to me with a great deal of Attention, and when I had done, why this is horrible, said she, and shews how dangerous Men are to those they pretend to love, where the Passion is not directed by Honour: Mothers therefore ought never to leave their Daughters to themselves, nor ought Daughters ever to take the least Step without the Advice of their Mothers; however, Child, continued she, you have nothing to fear from the Chevalier *d'Elbieux*——I don't think he will have the Insolence to insult you in my Presence, nor would the Servants who attend me suffer it if he did.—— I am well acquainted with your Godmother, and will write to her on this Occasion——I doubt not but she will lay her Commands upon him, to trouble you no farther. She had scarce ended these Words, when the Chevalier, who had stop'd a little on my being received into the Chariot, (I imagine to consider what he should do) rode up towards us, I perceived him coming, and cryed, Ah, Madam! he is coming——he is coming——the Lady then look'd out, and said to him as loud as she could, come hither Monsieur *d'Ellieux*, I am a particular Friend of your Mother's, and should be glad to give you some Advice——He had no sooner heard these Words, and seen who it was that spoke them, than cover'd with Confusion, he made a low Bow, and gallop'd back as fast as he was able.

Well, said she, I told you how it would be——you are safe and shall be so with me, 'till I have wrote to your Godmother, and her Answer shall determine in what Manner you must be disposed of.

I prais'd God for this happy End of an Adventure, which had threatned so much Evil, and bless'd my kind Protectress: She was a Lady extremely handsome, tho' at that Time past her fortieth Year; but her Goodness was hardly to be equall'd——I endeavoured by all the little Services I could do her on the Road, to testify my

Gratitude

Gratitude, and render myself acceptable to her; nor was my Labour thrown away; by the Time we reach'd *Paris*, I could perceive I had gain'd great Ground in her Affection.

The House we were set down at was very magnificent, both as to the Structure and Furniture; it was her own, and she was call'd (as I was soon after inform'd) Madam *De G*————, her Husband was a Man of Family, and Receiver of the Finances————the Number of their Servants spoke their Wealth; the Lady had three Women to herself, beside a Governess and Maid for her Daughter, who was about ten Years old, and was she who came with us in the Chariot

Her Husband kept not so many Servants to attend on his own Person, went plain in his Habit, and was very frugal in the Expences of his Household; but that was, as I found in a short Time, that he might have the more to dispose of in his private Pleasures.

Madam presented me to him, but he seem'd not much affected with what she said to him in my Favour, and indeed had a Kind of Indifference or Indolence, I know not which to call it, in his Behaviour to every body at Home; he only ask'd his Lady after an Absence of some Weeks, how she had enjoyed her Health in the Country, and turned into his Closet without staying for her Answer; as he pass'd by me, however, he gave me a Look, which young as I was, I could perceive had nothing in it of that Coldness he had affected in his Conversation.

He was about fifty or fifty-five Years of Age, he was a well made graceful Man, and had an engaging Aspect; I was soon told by some of the Family that he was of an amorous Constitution, but very private in his Intrigues, as indeed he well might, nothing being more ridiculous than for a Man to indulge those tender Follies after a certain Age, which in my Opinion ought not to exceed forty; he was at last sensible of the Errors he could not avoid falling into, and endeavour'd all he could, to pass upon the World as a Person who had entirely overcome them.

I made it my whole Study to ingratiate myself to the Lady, nor indeed was it difficult, her uncommon Sweetness nefs of Difpofition render'd every little Effort acceptable, and doubled every Service done her; fhe had a great Love for me and fhewed it in all her Behaviour to me—Her Daughter was taught Mufick, Painting, Dancing and Writing, and fhe was fo good to order I fhould make Ufe of that Opportunity for my Improvement———all the Mafters perceiving how much I was a Favourite, took the fame Care of me as they did of the young Lady herfelf; and to this I am indebted for great Part of the Accomplifhments, which at prefent I am efteem'd for; as my Voice was naturally good, and my Limbs turn'd for genteel Motion, I foon became a great Proficient in finging and dancing; nor was my Fancy lefs admired in my Painting, and I wrote well enough in a fhort Time to have my Hand equal thofe who inftructed me; and this latter Article pleas'd me above all others, becaufe I flatter'd myfelf I fhould one Day have an Occafion to ufe this Talent to one, I need not fay the Marquis, for whom, now my Fears were over, all my Refolutions to forget were over.

One Morning when I was practifing fome of my Leffons, in a little Room appropriated entirely for my Ufe, a Servant came to inform me his Lady would have me come to her in her Clofet; as I knew fhe had wrote to the Countefs *De N*———I made no Queftion but fhe had receiv'd an Anfwer, and made what hafte I could down; as foon as I came into the Room, *Jeanetta*, faid fhe, I have Letters here which concern you, and I fent for you to let you know the Contents.

She fpoke this with fo referved and grave an Air, that I apprehended there was little to my Advantage mention'd in them, and liften'd to her with an equal Share of Impatience and Fear.

This, purfued fhe, taking one in her Hand, is from your God-mother; fhe fpeaks of you with great Affection, but informs me of fome Particulars, which I think would be wholly improper to make you acquainted with—Your Heart I find is tender, and it might be dangerous to revive in you fome Sentiments, which have coft you much

Trouble,

Trouble, and if in the leaft indulg'd may involve you in more.

The Reader may judge whither this was not enough to excite in me the utmoft Curiofity, but I concealed it, determining within myfelf to try all poffible Methods to get that Letter into my Hands, that I might difcover what fhe feem'd to think of fuch ill Confequence for me to know.

This other, continued fhe, is from Madamoifelle her Daughter, who I find is not fo well affected to you——fhe thinks quite different from what he merits of the Chevalier, in Regard to his Behaviour to you——fhe advifes me to be cautious how I entertain any good Opinion of you, and to obferve all your Actions————fhe tells me you are a great Diffembler, very vain, and very malicious————that your Infinuations had like to have occafioned a great deal of Mifchief; that by your pretended Innocence you had inveigled the Affection of Monfieur the Marquis de *L——V*——that he had fought on your Account, and is much hurt————in fine, that you are the Reverfe of every Thing you would be thought, and have fo far forgot your mean Birth and Cottage Education, that you think you are on a Level with all who vouchfafe to give you any Encouragement ; and fays that fhe apprehends your Stay in my Houfe, will bring on fome ill Confequence or other, which may make me repent I ever fuffered you to come into it, fo wifhes me to difcard you immediately.————She alfo adds that the old Marquis de *L——V*——Father to him who is wounded, is highly incenfed againft you, and looks on you as the fole Caufe of the Danger his Son's Life is in, and vows the bittereft Revenge in Cafe he does not recover, which at prefent is very much doubted.

I labour'd all I could to refrain giving any Marks of the Vexation this Letter plung'd me in, and the ftill much greater Grief at hearing what had hapned to my dear Marquis ; but notwithftanding all I could do, my Tears forced a Paffage through my Eyes, and Madam *de G*————plainly faw the Anguifh of my Mind.

The

The Grief which you in vain attempt to conceal, said she, convinces me one Part of the Letter is true; as for the rest I regard it as the Effect of Prejudice————I see Madamoiselle *D'Elbieux* has an Averfion to you———— I know not wherefore, for indeed to me you appear of a fweet Difposition, and you muft be fo, unlefs you are the greateft Diffembler upon Earth.

I wept bitterly at thefe Words————fhe feemed moved at my Sorrows, and bid me compofe myfeif, telling me, fhe did not fend for me with an Intent to give me any Difquiet.————Behave yourfeif, faid fhe, as you have hitherto done, according to the Opinion I have of you, and I will take care of you.

I made a low Obedience in Token of my Gratitude, and was going out of the Room when fhe call'd me back————Stay, *Jeanetta*, faid fhe, I had like to have forgot one Thing, your Father and Mother would have you return to them; but in fpite of all Madamoifelle *D'Elbieux* has wrote, you fhall be at liberty to go or ftay————Ah, Madam! cryed I eagerly, as much as I refpect them I————well, well, replied my charming Benefactrefs interrupting me, I fee which Party you would wifh to take————you may have Reafons for not being fo willing to obey them in this Particular, as I doubt not but you would in other things———— be eafy therefore as I before told you, you fhall be your own Miftrefs, and are perfectly welcome to ftay where you are————I want not to lofe you.

I fell upon my Knees, and kiffed her Hands, quite overwhelm'd with this Excefs of Goodnefs, and having pour'd forth my Acknowledgements in as handfome a Manner as I could, retired from her Apartment; as I went out I was met by Monfieur *De G————*, and my Eyes being ftill wet with Tears, what is the Matter my pretty Maid, faid he taking me by the Hand, has any one affronted you?————I fhall be very angry with my Wife, for no one elfe dare ufe you in an unkind Manner————but do not grieve for any thing fhe does———— I'll take care you fhall not long be fo————I'll put Things in better Order————I have been thinking already

ready what to do for you. I am much obliged to you, Monsieur, answered I, your Lady being pleased to permit my being here, demands the utmost Gratitude from me, and I have a Soul, which will never let me forget her Bounties.

You do well to say so, answered he, but I see no such great Kindness to you————I perceive you have been in Tears, and I suppose you would not weep at receiving Favours————Some Time or other I will enquire farther into this Affair; but this is not a proper Place to hold any Discourse in————Farewel————with this he squeez'd my Hand, and went into his Lady's Chamber.

I was not so dull of Apprehension, as not to see he liked me better than he ought to have done, and was very much troubled at it, as being an Incident which very much endanger'd the Happiness of my present Situation; these Reflections however gave way to others of a different Kind, and which seem'd yet more interresting to me.

The Letter wrote by my Godmother to Madam *De G*———— ran very much in my Mind————I doubted not but it contain'd great Part of her Sentiments, concerning the Affection the Marquis had for me, and the very mention of that dear Name, was of itself sufficient to render me impatient to know in what manner; besides, I imagin'd I should thence be able to discover something more of that unhappy Adventure, in which he had been wounded, than Madam *De G*————was willing I should be acquainted with————I thought of nothing but how to get a sight of it, but could find no Stratagem, it being lock'd up in a Drawer, the Key of which Madam had always in her Pocket, it being a Place where she usually laid her Jewels and other Curiosities.

Chance, however was favourable to my Wishes; the *Sunday* following being somewhat later than ordinary before she was dreit, in her Hurry of going to Church she forgot the Key; as I had always a watchful Eye over that Place, since the Letters being laid there, I soon perceived the Opportunity was given me to read them, which I did with a great deal of Impatience.

The

The first I took in my Hand was that of Mademoiselle *D'Elbieux*, but that I pass'd slightly over and came to the Countess's : I found she spoke of me as Madame *De G*——had said, in very advantagious Terms, except where she mentioned the Marquis's Love for me, and there I could perceive a little Resentment : She acquainted Madam *De G*——that her Son had dangerously wounded him with a Pistol-Bullet——that the Coun-try talk'd variously on the Affair, but that she had come to the Truth by Means of an old Servant, whom she had entrusted with the Care of my Education——that tho' the Marquis was very cautious in his Behaviour, and refused to relate to any one the Grounds of the Quarrel between him and the Chevalier, yet the Disquiet he could not for-bear expressing at not knowing what was become of me, confirm'd the Truth of what the Servant had said——that she thought herself under an indispensible Obligation to acquaint his Father with the whole Business, that he might consider in Case his Son should recover, how to prevent any Consequences which might attend so violent and ill placed a Passion, which was the more to be fear'd, she said, as she believ'd me truly virtuous and my Lover a Man of Honour.

She concluded her Letter with advising Madam *de G*——to send me Home to my Parents, saying my Charms were dangerous and might in Time create much Mischief; but that if she resolved to keep me with her, at least never to let me see the Marquis, if he should re-cover and hear where I was.

I lamented with Floods of Tears the Condition of my beloved Lover, but I could not in my Heart condemn the Cautions given on my Account, nay I even resolved to make Use of them myself; what I had read reminding me of the Perplexities which must naturally attend such unequal Engagements, made me for a Moment wish I had never seen the Marquis——I say a Moment, for it lasted no longer——the Pleasure of loving and being beloved by such a Person, whatever Troubles it should involve me in, was preferable to an insipid Ease and a Life of Indifference.

2

After I had fully examined what I had so earneftly defired to know, I folded them carefully up in the manner I found them, and laid them in fame Place : I had but juft done, when Monfieur *De G*———came into the Apartment, and was very near furprizing me in the Fact.

O! are you here, my pretty *Jeanetta*, faid he, Well! I hope, you have had no farther Occafion for Tears fince I faw you laft. The Surprize of feeing him come in, had fent a Colour into my Face, which doubtlefs render'd me more amiable : That bold and forward Air, which a great many Women affect, being far lefs taking with the Men, than one that feems more timid and unaffur'd.

Monfieur *De G*———was juft then an Inftance of this Truth, at leaft in Appearance, by extolling the Modefty and Bafhfulnefs of my Air———but, faid he, you anfwer nothing to what I fay to you———is it becaufe you ftand in Awe of me, I affure you that is not one of the Sentiments I would wifh to infpire you with; neither is there any Occafion for it, I am more your Friend than you imagine———it is owing to me, that my Wife treats you with fo much Kindnefs———therefore if you are of fo grateful a Temper as you feem, you will think I deferve fome Regard from you ; I defire nothing more than that you will accept of my Friendfhip. I hope, Monfieur, anfwer'd I, that nothing in my Part has been wanting, to teftify the Senfe I have of all the Obligations conferr'd on me, fince the time I came into your Houfe, and as to your Friendfhip, 'tis fo great an Honour that———Well, well, cry'd he, you fhall be more happy than you think, at leaft it will be your own Fault if you are not ;———but take care, continued he, not to drop the leaft Hint of what I fay to you before my Wife———fhe is inclin'd to Jealoufy, and Peace muft be preferv'd in a Family.

I was at a Lofs how to reply to this Difcourfe, when fortunately Madam *De G*———was come from Mafs, and ran directly up to her Apartment, which her Hufband quitting, on hearing her on the Stairs ? What are

2

you

you doing here, *Jeanetta*, said she, to me?———Monsieur, I perceive, has just left you———what has he been saying to you?———let me know the Truth, continu'd she, throwing herself into an easy Chair, I shall not be angry whatever has pass'd———I know my Husband lives not without his Gallantries.——Therefore if you would preserve my Friendship, you must conceal nothing from me.

'Tis easy for me to satisfy your Ladyship, answer'd I, 'tis certain, Monsieur *De G*———has said very kind things to me; but I look'd upon them only as Words of Course.

Let me hear them, however, said she, and I shall be the better judge: On this I repeated Word for Word, the whole Discourse between us; after which, well, cry'd she, your Youth and Inexperience in the World, is an Excuse for your not answering him in a different manner, from what you did———But, remember, *Jeanetta*, that a Maid ought to nip in the Bud, all the Expectations Men may have of being able to dishonour her; for if they are once permitted to hope, they pretend afterwards a kind of Right, to take any Measures to compass their Designs.———So be wary for the future, and do nothing without first consulting me.

The Remonstrances of this good Lady were not unnecessary, for I was soon convinced she knew her Husband, but too well; and what befell me on his Account, not only prov'd it; but gave her an Opportunity of discovering an Excellence of Nature few Women can boast of.

Two Days after this, one of Madam *De G*———'s Women, for whom I had a particular Regard, as I found she was a great Favourite with her Lady, came into my Chamber before I was up———what in Bed still, you lazy thing, cry'd she, come you must rise and dress yourself immediately, I am going out and shall take you with me———with all my Heart, answer'd I, if you had given me Notice last Night, I would have been ready before this———well, 'tis Time enough, resumed she, however, make what haste you can.

This

This Woman could not be lefs than feventy Years old, forty of which fhe had pafs'd in the Family, where fhe was much refpected, efpecially by her Lady, whofe Mother fhe had waited on while fhe was in her Child-hood.———I had the greater Regard for her, becaufe I overheard her perfuade Madam *De G*———to keep me in the Houfe, when fhe feem'd inclin'd to fend me Home on the Countefs's Letter.

We went in a Hackney-Coach to *St. Honore*'s Street, where we ftopp'd at a Mercer's, fhe afk'd for flower'd Damafks, which being immediately brought, fhe would needs have my Fancy, and then bought the Piece I pitch'd upon.———Gowns then of light, gay Silks were fhewn us, fome befitting the Spring of the Year, and others the Autumn ; fhe ftill confulted me, and I fpoke my Mind, on which all I 'made Choice of were bought.

We then went to a Sempftrefs, the Purchafe we made there, was a dozen of fine laced Shifts, and a dozen plain ones, and fome other both Day and Night Linnen, fuitable to the reft.

After this we call'd at three or four other different Shops, and bought Headclothes, Tippets, Gloves, Stockings, Ribbons, Fans, made Flowers, and a thou-fand other Trumperies ; and at laft alighted at *St. Roche*'s *Bank*, where I was introduced into an Apartment, nei-ther large nor fmall, but very neat and commodious, and richly furnifh'd.

Madam *De G*———'s Woman had brought Table-Linnen with her, and a Footman who I knew belong'd to Monfieur came in, laid the Cloth, and every thing ready for Dinner, and then retir'd.

All this threw me into a prodigious Aftonifhment, I thought there was fome Whim it ; but could not com-prehend the Truth, the Character of the Perfon who was with me, preventing my having the leaft Sufpicion of any Defign upon me.

Prefently after fome body knock'd at the Door, the Footman brought up a Woman with Hoop-Petticoats : The old Directrefs chofe one of the handfomeft, and

gave

gave her the Price she demanded: After which, come, said she, to me, let us see how this will become you. I try'd it on, and thought it gave me a graceful Air, I look'd in the Glass, and confess, that I took a secret Pride in viewing myself with this Addition.

My Companion easily penetrated into my Thoughts ———you are not mistaken, *Jeanetta*, said she, in thinking yourself handsome———you really are very beautiful, and you must give me the Pleasure of dressing you according to my Fancy. I was ready enough to see how I should look in the Court-Fashion, and she accordingly curl'd, powder'd, patch'd me, and put on one of the fine Head-dresses we had been buying, only to try it as she said. I made some Difficulty in letting her put the Carmine upon my Cheeks——— what a Child you are, cry'd she, don't you see 'tis only for Diversion?———there remains nothing now, continu'd she; but to put some Ornaments on those pretty Ears, and I am luckily provided for that. As she spoke this, she drew out of her Purse, which seem'd well filled, a Pair of Brilliant Diamond Pendants?———How do you like these, cry'd she? O! magnificent! reply'd I, they even dazzle my Eyes———Well then, said she, we'll see if they become you as well as the rest.———I then look'd in the Glass, and was so astonish'd at the Change I found in myself, that I could not speak a Word.

While I was thus taken up with the Contemplation of my own dear self; and I must own overwhelm'd with Vanity———a Mantua-maker came in, and I was desired to pull off my Gown, that she might take measure of me———your Cloaths will be made to Admiration, Mademoiselle, cry'd this old *Jezebel*; Mademoiselle *Pagod* has the best Air in her Habits of any one of her Business in all *France*. The taking my Measure, and these Expressions open'd my Eyes.———Oh! Heavens! said I to myself, I am betray'd———how dull was I not to see it before——— to what can I have Recourse!

The surprizing Situation I was in prevented my speaking, while the Woman was examining my Shape, which

I perceiv'd fhe did with Looks that denoted more of Grief and Pity, than of that fawning Complaifance, moft of her Profeffion ufe to the Ladies who are their Cuftomers: This put me on trying a Stratagem which gave me fome Prorpect of Succefs, and if it faii'd could not render my Condition worfe than it was.

I made a Pretence to go out of the Room for a Minute, and on a Bit of Paper on which fomething had been wrapp'd, wrote with a Pencil, I luckily had in my Pocket, thefe Lines.

To Madam De G————.

POOR *Jeanetta* is left forever, if your Ladyfhip does not take pity of her Fate, and fnatch her from the Deftruction which threatens her————fhe has time to fay no more, than that a Moment's Delay may render all Affiftance too late.

I had nothing wherewith to feal this Billet, nor was it material, for as all my Hopes were on the Honefty of this Woman, this Proof of my defiring to preferve my Virtue, would render her the more induftrious in delivering it. As fhe was folding up the Silks intended for my Garments, I ftood clofe and pretending to help her, flipp'd the Note into her Hand, faying at the fame time, if you love Virtue, as I doubt not but you do, deliver this as directed with all poffible Expedition, and God I am fure will blefs you.

I fnatch'd the lucky Minute, for I had but juft given my Billet, when the Door open'd, and in came Monfieur *De G*————; tho' I had all the reafon in the World to expect him, after what had happen'd, yet I was Thunder-ftruck at his Prefence.————I became pale, ard had a trembling over all my Limbs. Ah! how beautiful are you now, faid he, without perceiving the Confternation I was in, I was not deceived when I thought that if once habited like our Ladies, you would furpafs them all ————with this he approach'd nearer, the Women being withdrawn on his Entrance, and look'd

at me on all Sides; but charming *Jeanetta*, continu'd
he, how do you approve what I have done?————are
you satisfied with your Condition?————do you not
think the Service of Monsieur *De G*————preferable to
that of his Wife?————but this is nothing in Comparison of what I will do for you————from the first Moment I beheld you, I resolv'd to make you easy————
but come, my lovely Maid, speak to me, you seem melancholly————is there ought else in my power that
you desire:————I think that beautiful Hand requires
an Ornament————a Ring————take this————'tis
yours. He concluded this Speech with plucking a fine
Diamond off his Finger, and presenting it to me: Oh!
what Shocks does a young Woman, who has any Share
of Modesty, endure in the Circumstances I then was.
I push'd away his Hand, and turning away, let me
alone, Monsieur, for Heaven's sake, cry'd I, take away
your Presents————I have not deserv'd such Favours,
nor expected them, much less an Adventure, such as I
am unwarily engag'd in.

What, said he, with a very serious Air, when I offer'd you my Friendship did you not accept it?————
No, Monsieur, reply'd I, not in this way?————I am
not accustom'd to the *Parisian* manner of Expression,
and we did not understand each other.————I have receiv'd many Marks of Friendship from Madam, nor did
I think you meant any other than such as were innocent.

Yet, nevertheless, resum'd he, you have laid yourself
under————Ah! Monsieur, interrupted I, bursting
into Tears, you have too much Honour to offer Violence
to a poor helpless Creature, betray'd merely by her Simplicity into your power. You know me not, said he,
or you would not suspect me capable of such a thing.
————No, *Jeanetta*, I love you too well to give you
any Disquiet, and shall ask nothing till you are less unwilling to grant————in the mean time dry up your
Tears, and be sole Mistress of yourself and me————
these Lodgings————all you see about you are yours————

the

the Servants shall be wholly at your Command, all that I desire, is leave to visit you sometimes.

This Discourse was so far from dispelling my Apprehensions, that it very much encreas'd them————how unhappy am I, said I, to have excited so ill an Opinion in you————Ah! rather let me die than accept of a way of living, to which I have so little Pretence.———— Great God! what Obligations must I lie under———— none at all, but what you shall approve, answer'd he,———— dispose of your Heart to whom and when you please: I give you my Word and Honour, which I assure you, I am incapable of violating, never to offer any thing disagreeable to you. Give me only, as I said before, the Liberty of seeing you sometimes, and supplying you with what you shall have Occasion for; that Pleasure shall be a sufficient Reward for all the Services I can do you———— when you have more Experience of my Humour, you will confess, I am far from thinking as some do; that wherever they confer any Favours, they have a right to tyrannize, and exact a servile Compliance to whatever they demand.————No, *Jeanetta*, I should not wish to gain you on such Terms————your Delicacy in this Affair raises my Esteem of you, and I again assure you my Behaviour never shall offend you————to convince you of this Truth, I will now take my leave, and not return till you think proper to invite me.

In speaking this, he made a low Bow, and went out of the Room without staying to hear what Answer I would make.

Till we attain a little Knowledge of the World, how apt are we to be influenc'd by Appearances: This Discourse of Monsieur *De G*————made a very great Impression on me, and I was sorry to have entertain'd an ill Opinion of him: I was not deceiv'd, however, the Conduct he afterwards observ'd in regard to me, prov'd that his Word and Honour were no less sacred to him, than he pretended.————I now almost repented that I had wrote to Madam *De G*————these Reflections I must own had a Mixture of Self-Interest.————I was before

fore a great Glaſs———I had the Opportunity of conſidering myſelf from Head to Foot———the Richneſs of my Dreſs, gave vaſt Advantages to my Perſon—the Red upon my Cheeks added, I thought, a greater Luſtre to my Eyes.———I could not avoid admiring every thing about me, and ſaid to myſelf———Well, who knows if the Marquis were to ſee me thus, to what a Height the liking he already has for me might riſe.———Then, added I, where can be the harm of accepting the Gifts of Monſieur *De G*———I am not engag'd to make any Returns.———He has given me his Promiſe not to exact any, and I believe I may rely upon his Honour.

I was taken up with theſe Meditations, when the old Chamber-maid came into the Room———ſhe was too wickedly cunning not to ſee into my Thoughts.—Well, my charming, *Jeanetta*, ſaid ſhe, Monſieur *De G*——— made but a ſhort Viſit———he ſeem'd melancholly, as he went out, you have ſaid ſomething unkind to him I fear. No, anſwer'd I, he has conferr'd too many Favours on me, not to demand the utmoſt Gratitude and Civilities from me.———Indeed, at his firſt Entrance, I thought he expected ſomething that was not fit for me to liſten to.———He! cry'd ſhe, with an inſinuating Air; alas! you do not know him ———the leaſt Good-nature will do any thing with him———and ſure he deſerves you ſhould be a little compliable———few Women in *Paris* would ſcruple to———

Very fine———very fine, indeed, cry'd Madam *De G*———who had been liſt'ning at the Door, and burſt that Moment into the Room, you preach moſt excellent Maxims to this Girl.———Go, Wretch, I am glad to find ſo timely what you are.———Heavens that I ſhould be the Dupe of ſuch a Hypocrite!—begone, get out of my Sight this Moment, and never more come into it— begone, and if you continue in *Paris* Four and Twenty Hours, depend upon it, I will ſend you to a Place where you would be glad to be turn'd out if you could. ———Oh! my God! continu'd this Lady throwing her-

ſelf

felf into a Chair, is it poffible I fhould ever employ fuch a Creature ?

The wicked Woman did not ftay to hear all this—— the firft Exclamation was fufficient to fend her away ; and as for me I ftood aghaft and trembling, as though I had been the Criminal myfelf.

Madam *De G*————remain'd in a profound Meditation for fome time ; but afterward recovering herfelf, and looking at me with a great deal of Sweetnefs, *Jeanetta*, faid fhe, your Difcretion and Virtue fhall endear you to me for ever.————I receiv'd your Note by a Perfon who feem'd, indeed, much to commiferate your Cafe, and gave me a Defcription of all I fee here.————Don't be alarm'd on the Account of Monfieur my Hufband, the very Virtue he in vain attempted to feduce, will create in him an Efteem far fuperior to what is call'd Love.————I know his Temper well, and dare affure you, he will after this, be always your Friend in the true meaning of the Word ;————but as for that unworthy Woman whom I fo long have cherifh'd, what does fhe not merit ?————no Punifhments can be too great for fuch Servants, who by an unworthy Compliance with their Mafter's Paffions, lead them into Vices they would elfe never put in practice.

In fpeaking this, fhe rofe from the Chair, and looking round, very pretty and well fancied Furniture, faid fhe ; but then cafting her Eyes on my Drefs, poor Girl, added fhe, how art thou trick'd up in all thefe Allurements fo fatal to Youth and Virtue. Thefe Words made me very much afham'd, I prefently fnatch'd up a Napkin and demolifh'd my Patches and Paint. Then tore off the Head-drefs, and threw it on the Ground—— let me embrace thee, my dear *Jeanetta*, faid this excellent Lady, I am charm'd with this virtuous Indignation.————Now thou, indeed, art lovely, truly lovely. But, added fhe, I muft not omit one thing, call up the Mafter or Miftrefs of the Houfe————'tis proper I fhould know who it belongs to, and on what Account the Lodgings were taken.

The

The Mistress came herself: I had not seen her before, but soon found she was one of those fawning half-bred Gentlewomen, who imagine it the heighth of Complaisance, to add to every Sentence,————may it please your Ladyship————I beg your Ladyship will do me the Honour to believe————I am so happy as to think with your Ladyship,————and such like Phrases; and I am apt to believe, if she were even to abuse any one it would be with————under Favour————with Submission————or I hope I do nothing out of Decorum. ————In fine, every thing, she said, was so larded with Interlocutions of this kind, that in spite of the Reasons Madam *De G*————had for being serious, I could perceive she sometimes had enough to do to refrain laughing.

This affected Piece of Formality inform'd us, that Monsieur *De G*————hired the Lodgings of her, and furnish'd them himself; that he told her they were for a Country Lady who was a married Woman; and on her Husband's squandring away great Part of his Estate in vicious Courses, was come to *Paris* to sue for a separate Maintenance. Adding, as she said, that he had Letters of Recommendation in my Behalf, from some of the best Families in *Bretagne*, to whom I was related.

A plausible Story I must own, reply'd Madam; but I can assure you there is not one Word of Truth in it; so would have you be more cautious for the future: A very little Consideration might have made you sensible, that if your Lodger was what he pretended, she might have had an Apartment in his own House, especially as he had a Wife capable of entertaining her. As you knew Monsieur *De G*————you must also know this————after this she lock'd every thing up, and taking me with her in the Chariot, went directly to her House.

Monsieur *De G*————was gone out, he was appriz'd of all that happen'd by the old Woman, and left Word at Home that he was gone into the Country————no doubt ashamed to see his Lady, as well he might after

so

so plain a Proof of his Infidelity; for tho' he had diverted himself with several Women, yet he had always been so extremely cautious, that she never before had the Means of proving what she had too much reason to suspect.

The next Day, however, she receiv'd a Letter from him, in which he entreated her Pardon for what had pass'd in the most tender and submissive Terms: Protesting never more to give way to the Dictates of a headstrong Passion, which generally brings on its own Punishment by one way or other————and as a Proof that he thought no more of me with any such View, desired she would send me, where he should never see me, nor hear any thing farther of me.

Madam *De G*————whose Kindness for me daily encreas'd, read me this Letter and her Answer to it: She told him that she was extremely sorry he should absent himself on so trifling an Occasion————that she knew no Man could be always master of his Inclinations; and if his were never plac'd on a less deserving Object it would be very well————that she herself had an entire Love for me, and could not think of sending me from her, being very well convinced of my Virtue, and concluded with repeated Assurances of Affection.

Did every Wife behave in this manner as often as the bright Sun of the *Hymenial* State is obscured by the dark Clouds of Jealousy, Divorces would be less frequent, and Women in greater Estimation; since it is certain that nothing shews Good-Sense, so much as over-looking those Frailties of Nature few Men are without.

It was now near a Year since I had heard any thing of the Marquis, and Time and Reason had a little abated that violent Ardor, mention'd in the first Part of these Memoirs. Indeed, all things contributed to render me forgetful of whatever could make me uneasy——Madam *De G*————treated me with such Affection, that there seem'd little Difference made between me and her own Daughter; and that young Lady, far from the Temper of Mademoiselle *D'Elbieux*, was never easy, but when I was with her; and Monsieur *De G*————had changed the

Love

Love he had for me into a parental Goodneſs; but what Marks ſoever he gave me of his Goodneſs, I was always on my Guard before him.

To add to this, I had ſeveral advantageous Matches offer'd me; but he of my Lovers who ſeem'd the moſt preſſing, was one Monſieur *Gripart*, Farmer-General of the Taxes: He was extremely rich, but of ſo diſagreeable a Form, that he ſeem'd a perfect Antidote to Love and Marriage; ſome regard, however, was to be paid to him, as he ſeem'd in earneſt, and Madam told me ſhe ſhould rejoice to ſee me ſo well diſpos'd of. I never durſt teſtify my Diſlike; but liv'd in hope that my mean Birth and want of Fortune, as he was the moſt avaritious Creature breathing, would keep him from coming directly to the Point; but I was ſadly miſtaken, tho' he had hitherto deny'd himſelf almoſt the Neceſſaries of Life, he could not deny himſelf the Gratification of his Paſſion for me; and informing Monſieur and Madam *De G*————of his Reſolutions, I was oblig'd to give them my Anſwer. But as he had a great ſhare in ſome of my Adventures, I think it will not be amiſs to preſent my Readers with his Picture; which, tho' it cannot be ſaid I flatter him, has nothing in it but what the Original may very well be known by.

He was of a middle Stature, and one half of his Body, like his Face, very different from the other, without being really crooked, he had the Reſemblance of it, to any one that met him; for when he ſtood as ſtrait as he could, one would think he was ſtooping to take up ſomething. His Phyſiognomy is yet more difficult to deſcribe: I never ſaw any thing in Man or Beaſt like it.——His Head was of an oval Form turn'd the wrong way:——His Eyes were as big as thoſe of an Ox, but had no Advantage as to Sight, their Lids ſeem'd to love each other ſo well, that they never parted without Tears.——His Mouth had ſomething of the Air of an Alcove, his Lips turning inward like a half-ſhut Door, which diſcovered here and there a dirty ragged Inhabitant——his Noſe look'd very proudly over the reſt of his Face; but on every Motion ſeem'd to give a gra-

cious

cious Nod, and when he laugh'd feem'd to be of one Piece with his upper Lip————his left Eyebrow was at such a Diſtance from the Eye to which it belong'd, that it took within its Circumference above half the Forehead, and the other ſo cloſe, that it could ſcarce be diſtinguiſh'd from the Eye itſelf: His Complection was neither black, brown, nor fair; but a Mixture of all three, a kind of motley Hue, and like the Rainbow varied, as you look'd earneſtly upon it. A great buſhy Perriwig ſerved as a proper Frame to ſo frightful a Picture; the reſt of his Dreſs, as well as his Hands, Legs and Feet were anſwerable; and altogether made the moſt droll Figure that Imagination can conceive.

This Creature, for it goes againſt me to call him Man, viſited me every Day; while I was ignorant of his Deſigns, the Looks and Behaviour which were of a Piece, ſerv'd as an Amuſement; and as it was a conſiderable time befoie he declar'd himſelf, I could not have believ'd he ever could have a thought of Love. Not that I would be thought to mean perſonal Deformity, as an Indication of a weak or ungenerous Mind; but neither his Character nor Principles, beſpoke his Soul at all more amiable than his Body.

I remember the firſt time he gave me to underſtand he thought me worthy his Addreſſes, he expreſs'd himſelf in this manner.

Do you know, Mademoiſelle *Jeanetta,* that for theſe eight Months, two Weeks, five Days and four Hours I have been in love with you————you laugh now; but I can aſſure you it is no Jeſt————a Deuce on't———— I would not if I could help it————there never was ſuch a thing in our Family before.————All the *Gripart's* from Father to Son, married without any Love in the Caſe————till now, I never look'd more at one Woman than at another————but you have wrought a Miracle————I could ſtare at you all Day.————

He embelliſh'd his Declaration with Flouriſhes appertaining to his Humour and Vocation, comparing me to a large Sum of Money, the employing of which was to be his Property, and told me as a great Proof of his

Paſſion, that he had given a Mau a whole Shilling for
having wiſh'd him good Luck that Morning————Ah,
ſaid he, he little thought the Buſineſs I was coming a-.
bout, and was ſo aſtoniſh'd at my Generoſity.

Well he might, anſwer'd I, that you ſhould beſtow ſo
conſiderable a Sum : yes indeed, reſumed he, with twelve
Pence much may be done ; why with ſuch a Sum I made
my Fortune, as I'll tell you ſome Day or other. He went
on with a great deal more to the ſame Purpoſe, which I
have now forgot, and I was every day wooed with a Politeneſs, which would have been entertaining enough to
me, had not thoſe to whom it became me to liſten, taken
Part in it ; a Waiting-Woman of Madam *De G*————
my Boſom Friend, told me ſhe had overheard ſome Diſcourſe concerning this Subject, that Monſieur *De G*————
was much in earneſt for this Match, and his Lady entirely
bent upon it ; I ſoon after heard it was concluded on, that
I ſhould be a Sacrifice to what they call being ſettled in
the World, and the Horrors ſuch an Apprehenſion fill'd
me with are unutterable.

I now began to run over in my Mind all that had
paſs'd between the Marquis and myſelf, call'd to Remembrance the Beginnings of that Paſſion once ſo dear to me,
and which never had been obliterated————Heavens !
cryed I, what can be become of him ?————Can he
forget his Vows————what can he think of himſelf, to
be ſo long without letting me hear from him————O !
how much did I confide in him————he muſt be falſe—
he muſt have forgotten me, and all he ſaid——my
fond Heart no longer can find Excuſes for his Abſence
and his Silence——Tears accompanyed theſe Reflections,
and as I was one Morning overwhelm'd with them,
Chriſtina came into my Room, and with a great deal of
Joy told me my Mother was in the Houſe, and juſt coming
up Stairs.

News ſo unexpected and withal ſo pleaſing ſurprized
me very much————and ſoon dryed up my Tears ; to
ſee a Mother to whom I had been ſo dear, after an Abſence of welve Months, was a Tranſport not to be expreſs'd :   ran to meet her, and having received her

Bleſſing

Blessing threw myself into her Arms————She held me to her, and in the tenderest Embraces testified a Joy, she had not Words to express; my Sister too was with her————I gave her also in her Turn the most sincere Marks of the Pleasure I felt in seeing her, and then conducted them to my Chamber: Our Discourse at first, through meer Eagerness of enquiring what had pass'd since we saw each other, was too confused to be intelligible; but by Degrees they became acquainted with my Adventures, and I learnt our Family Affairs; my Father they told me was in Health, and on his Way to Monsieur *De G*————'s, and that my Sister was married to *Colin*, which I was very glad to hear, because I knew the young Fellow was rich, and had withal a great deal of Honesty and Good-Nature.

The Steward of the House who had always been very civil to me, hearing my Mother and Sister were come, sent a handsome Breakfast to my Chamber————I exerted myself in entertaining them in a genteel Manner, and took a secret Pride in shewing how I was improved———— my Sister look'd at me with Astonishment, and cryed, observe Mother, this is not our *Jeanetta*, this is a fine Court-Lady————how she is drest————what fine Linnen! I had then on only a Bed-Gown, and Night-Dress on my Head, neither rich, nor gaudy, but being made after a different Manner from what was used in our Village, occasioned these Exclamations, which indeed gave me no small Satisfaction————Vanity is inseparable to all Degrees of People, and nothing sooths it more than to be admired, and wondered at by those of our own Country, especially when one has been absent some Time, and they see one again in a Fashion beyond their Expectations.————I was extremely alert about it in my Mind, and pleased myself with the Thoughts how much more I should surprize them, when they should see me what they call full dress'd.

But soon did these little Ideas vanish, my Mother as soon as she had done admiring every thing about me, asked me what I thought had brought her to *Paris*, and then again answer'd herself, by saying she was come to

see

see me married; these Words made me turn pale; she presently observed the Change, what, said she sternly, I hope you have not forgot the Education I gave you, so far as to have set your Heart upon any Man. No, my dear Mother, answered I, but the News you tell me has a little surprized me; but pray, continued I, to whom am I to be disposed?

'Tis strange you should be so near Marriage, as I am told you are, resumed she, yet be ignorant of the Person; the Lady into whose Hands you are so happily fallen, has wrote to the Countess very much in your Praise, but her last brings an Account, that she has now crown'd all the good Offices she has done you by providing a Husband, who would bring Wealth and Honour into our Family—— your Godmother sent for me on the Receipt of it, and ordered me to come to *Paris,* and be present at the Wedding, and this is all I am yet inform'd of.

While my Mother was yet speaking, a Footman came in to let her know Madam *De G*————desired to see her; on which she went immediately, leaving my Sister with me, whose Sentiments for me were now quite alter'd————the Envy and Jealousy that formerly occasion'd our little Quarrels, were now no more; and I had Good-Nature enough to forgive greater Injuries, than any I could possibly have received from her; the Joy she express'd at seeing me, banish'd from my Breast all Remembrance of her former Behaviour.

I would not however venture all at once to make her my Confidant, but having an irresistable Curiosity to know what had happened since I came away, I ask'd her in a Sort of careless Air, concerning the Family at the Castle; the Countess, replyed she, is much the same she was, and talks of coming very soon to *Paris* with her Daughter, who has been courted some Time, and they say will be married shortly to Monsieur *De F*————but as to the Chevalier *D'Elbieux,* no body knows what is become of him————he has appear'd very little, ever since that ugly Affair which has made so great a Noise, and is related a Thousand Ways————God knows how it was; but I am sure you did a very discreet thing not

to

to come near the Village afterward :————if you had
return'd as *Colin* perſwaded you, you would have been
pointed at————to this Hour you are in every one's
Mouth.

Dear Siſter, cryed I haſtily, let me know on what
Foundation they build their Cenſures, and then I can inform you how far I have deſerved them. You know,
anſwer'd ſhe, that in ſuch little Places as ours, every
little Trifle is made a thing of Conſequence————Every
Neighbour watches the Actions of the other, nothing
eſcapes without being talk'd on, and if they don't know
the real Motive, ſomething worſe is imputed.————
They ſay that the Marquis *De L————V————*held a ſecret Correſpondence with you and Madamoiſelle *Du Parc,*
and that it was agreed upon that he ſhould carry you
off; but that the Chevalier *D'Elbieux* being alſo in love
with you, by his Jealouſy diſcover'd the Deſign ; on
which they fought and the Marquis was dangerouſly
wounded ; they all lay the Blame of this Duel on you,
as having given Encouragement to both theſe Lords, and
this Belief paſſes the more current, becauſe Madamoiſelle
D'Elbieux declares ſhe never could ſupport your Coquet.
try with the Men.

My Mother, continued ſhe, endeavour'd with her u-
ſual Prudence to put a Stop to theſe Reports, by telling
every Body you were gone to ſtay ſome Time at a Relation's Houſe, and the Talk might have paſs'd off, if
Colin had not come home one Day beat almoſt to Death,
and in a terrible Fright————He ſaid that he narrowly
eſcaped with his Life, for offering to take you from the
Marquis's Valet de Chambre, and that you were grown
quite another Creature, with liſtning to the Flatteries of
fine Gentlemen ; in fine poor *Colin* was ſo incenſed with
the Uſage he had received from *Dubois,* and your Behaviour to him, that he was the firſt to ſpeak againſt
you, and told every body that he did not doubt but you
was conceal'd with the Marquis ſomewhere or other.

The ſame Day that *Colin* return'd Monſieur the Chevalier *D'Elbieux* arrived, and being inform'd of what
had happened made *Colin* be brought to him : they were
ſtrutt

shut up together some Time, and we saw him take Horse with Fury in his Eyes, swearing that he would revenge *Colin*'s Cause, and teach *Dubois* what it was to abuse any of his Tenants.

The Marquis, who then lay ill of his Wounds, sent every Day to the Village to know if you were return'd, but this was look'd upon more as a Feint for the better concealing you, than the real Truth that he was ignorant where you were, 'till the good Lady with whom you are placed, wrote an Account of it to Madam la Countess *De N*————, but one thing I must inform you of, which is, that since the Marquis has been recover'd and abroad, the Chevalier has never been seen————so People know not what to think as to that Article.

Madamoiselle his Sister continues to exclaim against you with all the Bitterness imaginable, and as she heard you were at Madam *De G*————'s, said she was very much concerned so good a Lady should be imposed upon by your seeming Modesty; and that she did not doubt but News would soon arrive of some fresh Mischief you had occasion'd; and that you strolled to *Paris* for no good, as she had reason to believe would be proved.

Bless me! cryed I, what can be the Meaning of the implacable Hatred she bears me? O! we are not ignorant, replyed my Sister, her Secrets can be divulg'd as well as those of meaner People————She is in love with the Marquis, he finds nothing in her worthy of making a suitable Return————she imputes his Indifference to your more prevailing Charms, and cannot but have an Aversion to what renders her Wishes ineffectual.

The Grounds of her Dislike to me are very mistaken ones, answer'd I, overjoy'd to bring her on this Topic, for since I quitted the Castle, I have never heard one Word of this Marquis you so much talk'd of, and have all the Reason to believe I am quite indifferent to him.

There is little sign of that, said my Sister, with a half Smile, when he so often sent to enquire what was became of you, tho' I readily believe that you may not have seen nor heard from him since; because when the Countess, out of Pity to my Mother's Concern for you,

let

let us know where you was, 'twas on Condition we
should conceal it from every body, left it should reach
the Marquis's Ear ; so that finding all the Enquiries he
could make unsuccessful, he gave them over, and has
never been seen in our Part of the Country since ; his
Father the old Marquis *De L———V———*would gladly
have had him return to Court, but he excused himself,
saying his Health would not permit ; and his Physicians
as they say, by his own Directions, declared it was absolutely necessary for his Re-establishment, that he should
go to some Place, I have forgot the Name of it, to
drink the Waters.

This Discourse awaken'd in me all the Tenderness I
ever had for the Marquis, and I felt an inward Grief,
which in Spite of me broke forth in Sighs—Ah, *Jeanetta*, cryed my Sister, you love this young Nobleman,
nor can I wonder at, or blame your Passion———it
must be own'd he has in him all that renders Man agreeable to our Sex ;———but remember the Disparity between you ; put the Case that his Designs upon you are
the most honourable that can be, yet still there are un-
surmountable Obstacles between you———'tis next to
an Impossibility you ever can be his Wife, and should
you give way to the Inclination he has inspired you with,
so far as to occasion the breaking off the Match now intended for you, and you should hereafter, fall into any
Troubles, who of your Friends would pity or assist you ?

I thank'd her for the Advice she gave me, which I acknowledged to be good, and promised to use my utmost
Efforts for putting it in Practice———Yes, said I, the
Marquis shall be forgot———I will obey the Dictates
of this severe Prudence———I will make a Sacrifice
of myself, and all that's dear to me———in speaking
these Words a Flood of ungovernable Tears burst from
my Eyes: hold, cryed my Sister, I cannot bear to see
you thus———I ought not to let you know I have a
Letter for you, but my Tenderness prevails in this Point
above my Reason———Here, said she, take it, Madamoiselle *Du Parc* gave it me the Night before our Departure———She loves you still, and I am much mistaken.

taken if she has not sent you News of what you love, for *Dubois* to my Knowledge, tho' it is kept a Secret, is often with her————they meet in a little Walk between the Castle and the Wood.

She held the Letter in her Hand till she had done speaking, and then giving it into mine, which trembled with Impatience, I hastily broke the Seal, and saw the inside was the Character of the Marquis————the Hurry of Spirits, the soft Confusion I was in, is not to be express'd on seeing from whence it came, but which was yet encreased when I read as follows :

To the loveliest, and dearest of her Sex:

WHERE are you————O my charming, my ever adorable *Jeanetta* ?————will this Testimony of a Love which knows no Bounds————a Constancy which can be equall'd by nothing but the transcendant Merit that occasion it, ever reach your Hand ?————O Heavens ! what have I not suffered in the Uncertainty of your Fate————a Thousand Deaths are infinitely short of the Tortures every Hour brings with it————where can you be conceal'd ?————has the Chevalier *D'El-bieux*————but I will not give Way to such Suggestions————no, the Divine Power will protect your Innocence————yet what can have happened ?————by what Means are all my Endeavours to find you rendered fruitless————I would search for you in the most distant Corners of the World, could I hope to find you there ; but something tells me you are near me————nay, I am sometimes flatter'd with the Hope that the happy Moment is at Hand, to restore you once more to my longing Eyes————O *Jeanetta*, ever charming, ever dear to my adoring Soul ! fain would I think the cruel Ignorance I am in of your Abode is not owing to yourself————and yet, wherever you are, or in whose Hands soever, you might, if you had thought me worthy of some little Contrivance, have found some Way to ease me of this racking Suspence————my Life as well as Patience is almost exhausted ; but my Love is still the

same

fame——in the Name of all that is dear to you in the World let me hear from you, if this diſtracted Epiſtle ever comes into your Hands ——I have ſometimes a Notion that Madamoiſelle *Du Pare* is in the Secret of your Reſidence, if ſhe be, ſhe is, alas! but too faithful to thoſe who have entruſted her with it——ſhe has however promiſed to ſend this to you, if ſhe can find a Poſſibility of doing ſo——How things between you are I know not, but know this, that nothing but the Aſſurance that I am not wholly forgotten by you, can ſave a Life long ſince devoted to you——deareſt *Jeanetta*—— but I will add no more——if I am not hated by you I have ſaid enough——if I am, leſs would be too much—— I will not however liſten to any thing my ill Genius in ſome deſpairing Moments tempts me to imagine—— but conclude with proteſting by all we have to hope above, or dread below, that whatever you are I never can be but

Your moſt faithful Lover, and Admirer,

Caſtle of *L——V——*
—— *April* the 7th.   *L——V——;*

Scarce had I read over this moving Letter, when my Siſter, who ſtood on the Staircaſe all the Time, ran to me, and told me ſome Body was coming up Stairs, I thruſt it haſtily into my Boſom, and had but juſt Time for doing it, when a Servant came to tell me I muſt come down to Madam *De G*——and my Mother——My Heart forboded the Buſineſs on which I was called, and I obeyed the Summons with inward Terrors, which I found it difficult to conceal.

As ſoon as I came into the Room, *Jeanetta*, ſaid Madam *De G*——to me, I rejoyce in having an Opportunity of recompencing your Virtue——what you refuſed for it are not forgotten by me, and I have ever ſince been contriving how to make your Fortune——you know very well that Monſieur *Gripart* has long endeavour'd to render himſelf acceptable to you, I hope you are enough
ſenſible

senfible of your own Intereft to confent readily to be his Wife, in which Confidence Monfieur *De G*——at my Requeft has fign'd a Contract in your Name ; and it is to be Witneffes of the Confummation, that I have fent for your Parents ————I own with you that your intended Hufband is not handfome ; but *Jeanetta* he is extremely rich, and will fettle on you twenty thoufand Crowns; to add to this he adores you, and there feems nothing wanting to compleat your Happinefs in fuch a Choice.

You anfwer me only in Blufhes, continued fhe, but I take your Silence as the Effect of Modefty : But that ought not to hinder her, rejoyn'd my Mother tartly, from throwing herfelf at your Ladyfhip's Feet, and thanking you for all your Bounties.

I was fenfible of this Repartee, and immediately did as fhe faid, and kifs'd Madam *De G*——'s Hand with a Gratitude unfeign'd ; rife, my dear *Jeanetta*, cryed that good Lady, tenderly embracing me;————I look upon you as my Child, and will provide every thing proper for your Wedding, which fhall be folemniz'd at my Country-Seat. As for *Mignonne* (for fo her Daughter was called) fhe loves you enough to give you the moft magnificent Prefents, but out of the little Treafure fhe is Miftrefs of, defires you'll accept of her Pearl-Necklace.

My Mother was fo much tranfported with thefe Teftimonies of the Affection I had gained, that fhe even wept for Joy, and was preparing to exprefs it in Words, when Word was brought of a great deal of Company being arrived ; on which we retired to my Chamber, and were followed by a great many of the Domeftics of Madam *De G*——, who having been told what had pafs'd, came to congratulate me on my good Fortune as they look'd upon it.

My Father came the next Day, and all things being now ready for the cruel Ceremony, it was fix'd for the *Tuefday* following————it was not in my power to oppofe the concurrent Will of all thofe, to whom by every Kind of Tye I was fo much bound————I had no Ob

jections

jections to make against it, but one that seemed of little
Validity, with Persons who having done with Love themselves, consider'd Wealth and Grandeur as the only Happiness in Life————*Gripart*'s Deformity was entirely
hid under the Advantages his Alliance brought with it;
and even my Mother, who had experienc'd the tender
Passion, and consulted no other Motive in the Disposal
of herself, was as inflexible as the rest, whenever I but
seemed to hint at the Disagreableness of him they were
about to give me for a Husband.

All Day was I persecuted with the odious Fondness of
Gripart, or in his Absence with the Discourses on my
approaching Happiness, so that I had only the Nights to
complain in, and give some Vent to those dreadful Considerations which agitated me with so much Vehemence,
that I have a thousand Times since wondered it did not
send me to the Grave. I was sometimes tempted to
write to the Marquis, and let him know the Situation I
was in————if he loves me but with half that Ardor
he pretends, said I to myself, he will find some Way or
other to break off this detestable Match; and if he
should not attempt to do it, such a Proof of his Perfidy
would make him almost as hateful to me as *Gripart*; and
I should have less Difficulty to give myself as they would
have me.————I determin'd one Moment to act in this
Manner: I took Pen and Paper, but before I could find
Words to express myself, Duty to those who gave me
being, and Gratitude to my Protectress interven'd, and
would not suffer me to obey the Dictates of my Inclination————in this State of Irresolution did I continue till
the Eve of that fatal Day which was to decide for me——
Gripart past some Hours with me, and brought me Jewels to the Value of twenty thousand Livres; but what
were all those glittering Toys————my Vanity was
not in the least flatter'd with them, and I now found my
Love for the Person of the Marquis setting aside his
Rank, was the reigning Passion of my Soul.

On the Morning following I was called up at four
o'Clock, drest and adorn'd, not according to my Birth,
but to the Condition of him to whom I was going to give

my

my Hand, and as I thought myself, a pompous Victim for a Sacrifice to Lucre. Never did any one receive greater Praises than were bestowed on me when thus equip'd— my Air, my Shape, my Face were extoll'd by every one, and tho' I could not hide my secret Emotions so far as not to force them to take Notice I look'd melancholly; yet they even thought that becoming, and said no other could be expected from a young Maid, so perfectly modest, on her Wedding-Day; but some among them knew how to judge better of the Cause, tho' they dissembled their Thoughts on that Head.

The invited Guests being come, I was conducted to the Altar, Mass was over, the Exhortation made——the Ceremony begun——*Gripart* had pronounced the fatal *I will*, and the Priest was turning to me for my Assent, when a female Voice, but extremely loud, was heard from the lower End of the Church, crying out——Stay—— Stay———

The Priest was surprized———all the Assembly turn'd their Eyes where the Voice proceeded, when presently a tall lusty Woman made her way through the Crowd and came up to the Altar———she desired to speak in private with the Priest, who conducted her into the Sacristy, followed by Madam *De G———*, my Mother, and Monsieur *Gripart*: I stayed in my Place, not able to imagine the Meaning of this Adventure.

The People seemed no less amazed, and crouded up to the Altar to stare upon me——Some cryed the Bride was very pretty and deserved her good Fortune———Others said 'twould be Pity any thing should happen to hinder it———and a Country Fellow bawled out———go, go, she'll get a Husband I'll warrant her if she loses this.

At length the Door of the Sacristy open'd, and a Man belonging to the Church came to call me, I followed him, and it was shut again immediately after my Entrance.

Your Wedding is deferr'd for this Day, *Jeanetta*, said Madam *De G———*a Person pretends a certain Promise made to her by Monsieur *Gripart* a long Time

I   ago

ago——it feems fhe lives in this Neighbourhood, and hearing he was about being married to you puts in her Claim——I think fhe has done it fomewhat of the lateft, and the thing might not have much Weight—— however, he fays that he will talk to her, and does not fear but to make all things eafy.

I am half diftracted, cryed Monfieur *Gripart* at this unlucky Turn——but there is no Man that has not been guilty of fome Follies in his Youth——I pro-teft no fuch Engagement ever came into my Memory, for doubtlefs if I ever made it, I never had any Inten-tion to fulfil it——but I flatter myfelf fhe will hear Reafon.

She defires nothing contrary to Reafon, fmartly re-plyed fhe, that had put a Stop to the Ceremony, fhe only infifts on your efpoufing her, or living always a fingle Life.

That would be fevere upon me, indeed, refumed Mon-fieur *Gripart*, but this is no Place to hold Difcourfe in, if you pleafe to ftep into my Coach, we'll hear what fhe has to fay, and if nothing lefs will content her. With thefe Words he prefented her his Hand, and after making a low Bow, went out of the Sacrifty.

We then all return'd to the Caftle, my Father and Mother were very much caft down, but I had Difficulty enough to conceal my Joy; I flatter'd myfelf that the Woman would be tenacious of her Right, and *Gripart* not able to compromife the Matter; but foon I found thefe foothing Hopes deceived me, he returned to the Caftle the next Morning with a Gaiety in his Counte-nance, which too truly informed me before he fpoke, that he had fucceeded in the Bufinefs he went about. Money does all things, and Mifer as he was, his odious Paffion for me had made him readily unload his Bags, and give the Woman a handfome Portion for her renoun-cing all Claim to him; a wife Exchange fhe made—— what would I not have given to have been in her Place——what not have hazarded for that dear Freedom fhe was paid for enjoying——? but it was now too late——a Day again was fixed for making
me

me for ever wretched, and I in vain repented that Nicety, which had hindred me from apprizing the Marquis of my Condition.

The Afternoon before the so much dreaded Day, we all took a Walk on a fine Terras at the lower End of Madam *De G*————'s Gardens, it over-look'd the Road, and was so high that it commanded a great Distance: ————The Company were talking of general things; but Monsieur *Gripart* kept always close to me, teizing me with the Pleasure he took in the Thoughts of his approaching Happiness.————To avoid answering him as little as I could, I lean'd over the Rail, and seem'd to amuse myself with the different Objects that presented themselves; when I perceiv'd at some Distance several Horses follow'd by a Pack of Hounds.————They pass'd leisurely by, this sight made me call to Mind the first meeting with the Marquis in the Forest of *Fountain-bleau*; I sigh'd, but felt a secret Pleasure in the Prospect, as tho' it foreboded me some good.

As I was contemplating on those past dear Moments, a single Person drest in green Velvet trimm'd with Gold, came gently along the Road, and cross'd into a little Meadow, at the very foot of the Terras————his Horse, taking the Advantage of the Reins lying loose upon his Neck, stopp'd frequently to graze.————His Rider had his Arms a-cross, his Head declin'd upon his Breast, and seem'd entirely bury'd in some Thought of great Importance.

People when they see any one in a Situation like their own, are apt to imagine it must be the same Cause that has produced the same Effect.————I presently thought so profound a Meditation, could proceed only from the Woes of disappointed Love, and felt a Pity for this graceful Stranger, which even brought Tears into my Eyes, and made me look very attentively on him;————but, good Heaven, when he came more near, I thought I knew him, and presently after fancied him to be the Marquis ————his Idea was too well graven in my Mind for me to be mistaken————and happening to lift up his Eyes just as he came to the Place where I was standing, Com-

plaisance

plaifance oblig'd him to pull off his Hat.————His Face was now fully difcover'd to me.————I was certain that I had not been deceiv'd, and in the fudden Tranfport gave a great Shriek, which prefently brought all the Company about me————the Marquis turning his Head at the Noife I made, had a full View of my Face, and between Aftonifhment and Joy being in a manner out of himfelf, as I had been, cry'd out, 'tis fhe !————by Heaven 'tis fhe, and clapping Spurs to his Horfe was out of Sight in a Moment.

The Change of my Countenance, together with my having fcream'd, made every one think I was taken fuddenly ill, and were too bufy about me to take Notice of the Marquis's Behaviour: My Father and Monfieur *Gripart* took me under each Arm, and led me into a Parlour where I was laid down on a Couch; but as it was only a fudden Emotion of Joy which had occafion'd my Diforder, no ill Confequences attended it, and I recover'd my former Looks.

Madam *De G*————having afk'd out of Curiofity the Marquis's Name of fome of his Retinue as he was paffing by, was not at a Lofs for the Motive of the Change had been in me; and fpeaking to my Father and Mother, who knew him again perfectly well, it was agreed among them that no Notice of it fhould be taken of it to me, and a ftrict Caution obferv'd never to mention any thing concerning him, in the Prefence of Monfieur *Gripart*, left it fhould fill him with any Notions in prejudice of me. I did not in the leaft doubt but this Adventure would occafion many Reflections among them, fo placed myfelf when I knew they were fhut up together, in an adjacent Clofet, where I overheard all their Difcourfe.

In the midft of it, I perceiv'd a Servant came to acquaint Madam *De G*————, that a Gentleman defired to fpeak with her; as I doubted not but it was either the Marquis himfelf, or fome one fent by him, a ftrange kind of thrilling ran through all my Veins.————I trembled between Hope and Fear, and was all Impatience for the Event.

My

My Suspense lasted not above a quarter of an Hour, Madam *De G*————who had entertain'd the Marquis (for it was he, indeed,) in her Closet, order'd I should be call'd.————I went with timid Steps, and had scarce Strength to push open the Door which I found half shut. Come hither, my dear *Jeanetta*, said she, and exert all the Influence you have over this Nobleman in the Behalf of your Fortune and Reputation.————He opposes your Marriage, and tells me he will have Recourse to every kind of Means to prevent your giving your Hand to Monsieur *Gripart*————you cannot be insensible of the Consequences, that must inevitably attend any such Attempt, and I hope may prevail on him to stifle a Passion, which never can be successful.

The Marquis who I found at the Feet of Madam *De G*————quitted her, and threw himself at mine as she done speaking, crying, Ah! *Jeanetta!* What have I done, that you should render me the most miserable of Mankind?

How powerful is a Lover in such a suppliant Posture————my Heart sympathiz'd in every Pang I saw him in, and forced the unwilling Tears into my Eyes; yet summoning all my Courage to my Aid, what is it you desire of me, my Lord, said I?————have I the power of disposing of myself.————I conjure you by all that is sacred to leave me, and not endeavour to subvert a Virtue too much shaken by your Presence.

Leave you, cry'd he, with great Emotion! Ah! unkind, and too forgetful *Jeanetta*, is it thus you receive a Man who adores you after so long an Absence?———— A Man who from the first Moment he beheld your Charms, became entirely devoted to them————but, continued he vehemently, your approaching good Fortune has dazzled your Eyes; and all that Love and Tenderness of which you have had so many Proofs must be sacrificed.————Yes, yes, ungrateful————I know I am to blame for ever presenting myself before you, after the Testimony I yesterday receiv'd of your Disregard———— but————

He was going on; but my Impatience would not suffer me to let him proceed————what Teſtimony my Lord, ſaid I, what have I done?————O! Heavens! reply'd he, is that a Queſtion to be aſk'd?————have I not wrote twenty Letters to you, tho' I know not whether they ever reach'd your Hand; and did you vouchſafe an Anſwer to any one, till laſt Night brought your final Determination?————Did you not tell me that you never lov'd, nor would have wrote but to let me know it.; that you deſir'd I would trouble you no farther, and that I never ſhould be made acquainted with the Place of your Abode, till you were free from my Importunities in the Arms of a Huſband————which you would the ſooner accept of, as if it would utterly deſtroy all the vain Hopes I might have conceiv'd.————

Ah, hold, my Lord, cry'd I, I deſerve not this Reproach————I never wrote to you————never wrote to me, interrupted he with a kind of a diſtracted Air! ————is *Jeanetta*, that *Jeanetta*, whoſe Innocence and Simplicity I ſo much ador'd, thus chang'd————can it be poſſible ſhe ſhould be capable of attempting a Deception of this kind? or am I not be credited without a Witneſs of the Truth of what I ſay?————but, here then, purſued he, let this ſpeak for me. With theſe Words he pull'd a Letter out of his Pocket, which I no ſooner caſt my Eyes upon, than I knew it to be the Hand of Mademoiſelle *D'Elbieux*. Madam *De G*———looking it over alſo at the ſame aſſur'd him of the Truth: Ah! Madam, cry'd he; you have reſtor'd me to Life, then turning to me, ah! *Jeanetta*, purſued he, if you have not really form'd that Reſolution this Letter contains, compleat what this Lady has ſo generouſly begun, and promiſe me never to eſpouſe this new Lover. Heavens! cry'd I, how can I avoid it?———am I the Miſtreſs of myſelf————can I, dare I contradict the abſolute Commands of thoſe who gave me Being?————Ought I to oppoſe the Will of this good Lady, to whoſe Bounties I am ſo much indebted?————God knows 'tis neither Intereſt nor Inclination

carries

carries me to the Altar————you will go then? cry'd
the Marquis, in a despairing Tone; you will then give
yourself for ever from me————do so, *Jeanetta*, fulfil
the Promise you have made my Rival.————Obey the
Dictates of this rigid Virtue; but be assur'd, to the Nup-
tial Rites a Sacrifice shall not be wanting; the Hour
that gives you to Monsieur *Gripart* shall also give me
Death.————Good Heaven forbid, rejoin'd I, bursting
into Tears; alas! I love you but too well for my Repose.————But how can I avoid this Marriage?————
What Reasons can I alledge for my Disobedience?
That you love me, answer'd the Marquis. Oh! my
Lord, said I, were that sufficient I would make the
Confession with Pleasure. 'Tis enough, my Charmer,
resumed he, pardon, Madam, my Transports, continu'd
he to Madam *De G*————on this Moment depends my
Fate————that Sweetness in your Countenance, tells
me my Love and my Despair have moved you to Compassion————I have already declar'd to you the Purity
of my Intentions————may I hope you believe me
sincere, and that you will fulfil the Promise you were
so good to make me?————Speak, Madam,————you
see this dear Creature does not deny her Kindness for me.
O! answer, continu'd he, pressing her Hands and bathing them with his Tears, yet do not, till you have well
weigh'd the Consequence of what you say————I perceive on you my Doom depends————*Jeanetta*, her
Parents, all will submit to your Decision.—O! Heavens,
you hesitate————you will not pronounce in my Favour
————you are resolv'd to see me die before your Eyes.

It must have been an obdurate Heart, indeed, that
had not been moved with these Words, and the Vehemence with which they were express'd; besides the high
Rank, and yet more elevated Accomplishments of the
graceful Petitioner, pleaded not a little with a Person of
Madam *Do G*————'s Humour————she was touch'd,
as she afterwards confess'd to me, to the very Soul, yet
not knowing how to comply with his Request, she reply'd to him in these Terms.

I am extremely perplex'd, my Lord, said she, were it in my power to make you happy in your Wishes, I were unpardonable to pause———but, alas! tho' I must own myself the the Person that first encourag'd Monsieur *Gripart*'s Addresses, yet I cannot see any way to render abortive, what I have taken some Pains to bring about———the Match is now so far advanced, that there seems scarce a Possibility of breaking it off, without incurring the Censure of all who hear of it—'tis true Monsieur *Gripart* is your Lordship's Inferior in every thing; but then he is our Friend, and a Person of some Consideration———what Colour can be put on our Refusal ?———on the other side *Jeanetta* is extremely dear to me———one Moment of Reflection brings a thousand different Ideas into my Mind at once.———I believe your Passion real, ———your Honour sacred,———your Word inviolable ———I doubt of nothing you have said ; but, Marquis, remember you have a Father, who will never be brought to accept of *Jeanetta* as a Daughter.———He has already sufficiently explain'd himself on that Head, and would never be brought to pardon any one, who had the least Hand in bringing about such a disproportionable Match———all therefore that I can do for you, my Lord, is to delay the intended Marriage with Monsieur *Gripart* for eight Days———if you can find any Means in that time to break it wholly off, without prejudice to *Jeanetta*'s Character, I am too much affected with the Condition I see you in not to rejoice in a Change for your Advantage. In concluding these Words she went out of the Room, and I was following her, but the Marquis stopp'd me.

Stay a Moment, cry'd he, with an Air in which the most piercing Sorrow was painted, or prepare to behold me die at your Feet ——O ! how can you abandon me in the Despair you see me in ?———Good God ! reply'd I, what can I do ?——What Answer would you have me make to the Reasons you heard just now alledg'd ?——— that you despise them all, said he, for the sake of a Man who may be able one Day to justify your Choice of
him.

him. How? continu'd I, would you have me entirely
lose myself with Persons to whom I am so much
oblig'd? No, answer'd he, they cannot condemn you
without being guilty of the utmost Injustice.———I am
ready to marry you myself———receive then my solemn Vows, I call Heaven to Witness I will have no
Wife but you———I never had any Design unworthy
of your Virtue.———I only waited a favourable Opportunity to convince you of it.———I have a Father,
who unknowing your Merit, is, indeed, inexorable, at
least he appears so at present; but if you consent to my
Happiness we may be married in private. ——— He
is old, and cannot live long———tho' far be it from
me to wish his Death———on the contrary I would
avoid giving him the least Disquiet; and it is for this
Reason that I would conceal our Nuptials———if you
love me, therefore, *Jeanetta*, you will.———If I
love you! interrupted I, yes, my Lord, I love you
more than Words can speak; but yet I never can consent to be yours in the manner you desire—nothing shall
ever make me vary from the Resolution I have form'd
———you are dearer to me, infinitely dearer to me than
my Life———and as a Proof of it I will disobey, since
it must be so, the Authors of my Being.———Yes,
continu'd I, with a Torrent of Tears, I will set all the
World against me———what can you ask more? O!
you suspect my Truth, cry'd the Marquis hastily, you
think me perfidious———a Villain that aims only to seduce your Virtue by the specious Pretence of Marriage
———you dare not trust my Vows———you———
no, pursued I, nothing can be more secure than I think
myself of your Honour.———I know the true Esteem you
have for me, and the generous Sentiments of your
Heart in my Favour; and I would render myself in
some Measure worthy of them, by surmounting the
common Weakness of my Sex———my Virtue is all I
have to boast; in the Name of God seek not to tarnish
the Brightness of it by such Proposals. The Moment I
had said this, I ran out of the Room with all the Speed

I

I could; and Madam *De G*———who had heard all
that had pafs'd, met me on the Staircafe, and taking
hold of my Arm, come into my Chamber, faid fhe, I
have fomething of Importance to communicate to you.
———She then fhut the Door to prevent any Interruption, and having made me fit down by her, fpoke to
me in this manner.

The End of the SECOND PART.

THE

THE
VIRTUOUS VILLAGER,
OR,
VIRGIN's VICTORY.

PART. III.

I NEVER shall forget the Proofs you have just now given me of your Prudence and Virtue, continu'd Madam *De G*———; but shall delay the Praises your Behaviour merits, till a more leisure time, and at present only conjure you, my dear Child, for as such I love and regard you, never to quit the Path you have so happily begun to tread, and which alone can conduct you to the End of your Troubles.

While my Ears were pleasingly entertain'd with hearing how nobly your Virtue triumph'd over your Love, my Eyes were turn'd towards the Park, where I was surpriz'd with the Appearance of several People, who I knew did not belong to us; they pass'd backwards and

forward several times, and coming nearer I found some among them had on the Livery of a Man, whose Name will make you tremble; I do so myself, while I tell you it was that of the Chevalier *D'Elbieux*————and soon after one of my Park-keepers accompanied by a Person, who I guess by his Air (for he was too distant for me to discover his Features) to be no other than that desperate Lover, join'd the others; and having talk'd together some time, as if concerting Measures, my Servant pointed to a Green-house which you know we have at the Entrance of the Wood, after which they separated.
————Ah! *Jeanetta!* some guilty Project is in Hand ————depend upon it, the Chevalier hurried by his brutal Passion, is come down hither to bear you hence by Force, if Stratagem should fail.

Madam, answer'd I, frighted almost to Death, your Conjectures are but too just, and reminds me of a thing, which filled me with a great many Apprehensions for the time it lasted, nor have I since been able to get it out of my Mind, tho' till your Discourse, I look'd on it only as the Effect of Imagination————Last Night, Madam, continued I, with a Voice faultring with Terror, I heard a a Noise at my Chamber-door, and wak'd *Isabella* your Ladyship's Woman who lay with me————she was in a sound Sleep, and I was oblig'd to speak very loud, on which I heard a Voice, not unknown to me, say, *let us retire*————the Fear I was in, made me throw myself into *Isabella*'s Arms and cling fast to her; but she laugh'd at me, and said it was only some of the Servants, who having, perhaps, been drinking, were going to Bed, and hearing me speak, were afraid of being discover'd and getting Anger for being up so late. Tho' what she said was probable enough, yet I could not be easy, the Sound of the Voice I had heard has never since been out of my Ears.————

It must be so cry'd Madam *De G*————interrupting me, there was certainly a Design of carrying you off last Night; but the great Company we had at Supper, and who staid late, render'd the Execution hazardous.————I am extremely troubled, nor know by what Methods to proceed
ceed

ceed————the Marquis is here ſtill, I ſuppoſe, and his
Retinue with our own, are more than ſufficient to prevent any Violence.————He is too much intereſted in
the Affair, and would not fail to give us his Aſſiſtance;
but then there alſo may be dreadful Inconveniencies in
letting him know it.

Yes, Madam, cry'd I, ſuch as I ſhudder but to think
on————remember what has already paſs'd between
theſe two Rivals, and the implacable Hatred they bear
each other.————Oh! Heaven! continu'd I, weeping,
what have I done, to draw ſuch Misfortunes upon me!
my Tears drew alſo ſome into the Eyes of this good
Lady; and that ſight reminding me of the trouble I
was likely to cauſe in her Family.————Dear Madam,
ſaid I, forgive what is not in my power to avoid, and
to prevent any farther Miſchiefs that may ariſe on my
Account, ſuffer me to quit your Houſe, while there remains
a Poſſibility of doing ſo.————Alas! cry'd ſhe, where
would you go?————or how get out of theſe Gates,
without falling into thoſe Ills, I would hazard every
thing to ſhield you from?————you may be ſure we are
obſerv'd————the Chevalier has doubtleſs Spies, who
inform him of all that paſſes.————However, I ſee no
other way, for tho' we are greatly reſpected here among
our Tenants, yet what could they do againſt the People
I ſaw in the Park, ſhould this deſperate Lover proceed
to Extremities, as there is too much Cauſe to fear he will.
—But, my dear Child, added ſhe, if you could even depart hence without the Knowledge of the Chevalier
D'Elbieux, the Marquis himſelf would be alſo an Impediment————then there is my Huſband, Monſieur
Gripart, your Parents, your Siſter, other Friends, all
have their Eyes on you. No matter, Madam, anſwer'd
I, were there but a Place where I could depend on being
receiv'd, I would run any riſque to arrive at it. The
Abbeſs of a Monaſtery not two Leagues off, ſaid ſhe, is
one of my Intimates.————I have done her Services,
and ſhe has Gratitude enough to acknowledge it.————
O! Madam, interrupted I, kiſſing her Hands, order
ſomebody to conduct me thither————every Moment

G 5

now is worth an Age————do you acquaint Monsieur
De G————with what has happen'd, while I go into
the Company and appear as unconcern'd as possible————
when you have contriv'd the Means for my Escape, be
so good as to give me a Hint, and I'll pretend the Head-
ake, or some other lit tle Disorder, and ask Permission to
retire to my Chamber, and while every one believes me
to be there, I can get on Horseback in some Disguise;
and meet the Person you appoint for my Guide at the
End of the Village.

Ah! *Jeanetta! Jeanetta!* said Madam *De G*————
embracing me, your Wit and Virtue charms me————
the Plot could not have better contriv'd, and I flatter
myself it will succeed————go, my dear Girl————
you shall ever be to me as my Child.————I will endeavour, Madam, answer'd I, to merit that precious
Title, by my following the Pattern you have set me,
and by obeying all your Precepts ;————but I shall lose
you, cry'd I, weeping.————No, *Jeanetta,* resum'd
she, I will always be a Mother to you————I will see you
often, and when Affairs are compos'd, bring you Home
to me again ;————but dry your Tears, and let us go
————no time is to be lost.

With these Words she embrac'd me in the most affectionate manner, and we were just going to leave the
Room, when on a sudden the Door was thrown open, and
in came the Marquis ; what, Madam, cry'd he, to Madam
De G————, you are going to take *Jeanetta* from
me ; but you shall first take my Life ?————What have
I done to merit so much Cruelty ?————He then threw
himself on his Knees between us, and taking each of
us by one Hand, protested both to the one and the other,
that whatever happen'd I should not be remov'd————
and that if we did not promise to forego the Resolution
he had heard us make, he would that Moment lay himself dead at our Feet.

These Words utter'd with so much Vehemence, the
Despair that appeared in his Countenance made me tremble ; but then the Apprehensions of the Chevalier *D'Elbieux,* who might in an Instant surprize us, and open
the

the moſt tragical Scene Imagination could conceive, gave me Courage and Reſolution, and enabled me to anſwer him in a Tone and Manner, very different from my Heart, or my uſual Manner of expreſſing myſelf.

My Lord, ſaid I, if it be true that you love me—— if I love you? ——Ungrateful Maid! —— interrupted this deſpairing Lover, is it now that you ſeek for Proofs to perſuade you of it?—— what I ſo long have ſuffered for you, might—— I deſire you will hear me out, cry'd I in a pretended Anger, and let me ſee how far I may depend on the Attachment you pretend, by complying with what I now requeſt; without which Teſtimony, expect not I will ever believe or liſten to your Vows. —— Call your Reaſon to your Aid, my Lord, Love, without it, is but a wandering Fire, and will lead you into Miſchiefs irretrievable.—— I know myſelf as yet unworthy of the Paſſion you have for me; and ſhould I ſubmit to the Conduct of ſo blind a Guide, ſooner or later, even you would make me repent my Weakneſs. As I doubt not your Sincerity or Honour, I am ſenſible of the Obligations I lie under to both; and will endeavour to merit the Condeſcenſions you make in my Favour, by ſuch Ways as you ſhall hereafter approve.—— It is no longer, my Lord, *Jeanetta*, an ignorant Country-Girl, that takes the liberty to hold this Argument with your Lordſhip, but a Maid, whoſe Sentiments are enlarged, and whoſe Mind is rendered capable of the moſt refined Ideas, by the excellent Example and Inſtructions of this Lady, and the generous Affection you are pleaſed to have for her. ——— Yes, my Lord, in ſpite of my mean Birth, my Love and Virtue ſhall enoble me: —— a Proof of the one, I give in ſacrificing to you a certain preſent Eſtabliſhment, for an uncertain one to come; and of the other, in refuſing both yours and my own Inclinations to be yours, but by ſuch Methods as ſhould call a Bluſh in neither of our Faces.——Beſides, my Lord, conſider, I beſeech you, that I am engaged to Monſieur *Gripart*, that I ſhould be married, that my Parents and all my Friends are waiting to be Witneſſes of the Ceremony. ——— Where, but in a Convent, can I be de-

fenced

fended from making good the Promifes made in my Name,
by thofe who alone have the Power of difpofing me ? —
Would you then oppofe a Refolution formed on purpofe
to fecure me to you, and compel me to perform an Engagement which will take me for ever from you.————
A Cloifter is the only Refuge I can take with Decency,
and by pretending that I have a Call to that Life, none
will take upon them to controul a divine Infpiration. —
This, my Lord, is all I have to fay, continued I with a
determined Air ; and if you agree not to fuch juft Reafons, and retire immediately from this Houfe, I have
nothing to do but to efpoufe Monfieur *Gripart*, and never
fee you more.

I was obliged to turn away my Face in uttering thefe
laft Words ; my Tears, in fpite of me, betrayed my
Heart, and would have fhewn him how great a Conftraint I put upon myfelf to treat him in the Manner I now
did, had the Surprize he was in to find me fo refolute, permitted him to obferve my Countenance.—He was altogether unable to reply, and only feizing one of my Hands,
with agonizing Grafps expreffed the inward Convulfions
he that Moment felt.—What then did not I endure amidft
the double Anguifh of his, and my own Griefs ! —— O
let all Maids, who would preferve their Firmnefs, beware how they behold a beloved Lover in fuch a Situation.———— Happy was it for me, that a Perfon fo much
refpected as Madame *De G*———— was prefent, elfe I cannot anfwer how far my Tendernefs might have tranfported
me.———— In fuch a Juncture, Flight is the fole Means
to conquer ; ———— I tore myfelf away, and fhut myfelf into an adjacent Room, leaving Madame *De G*————
to behave in what Manner fhe thought proper.

That good Lady was truly fenfible of the Marquis's
Defpair ———— fhe omitted nothing that fhe thought
might give him Confolation ———— fhe affured him, that
fhe would continually acquaint him with all that paffed
concerning me ; and, at laft, prevailed fo far as to fend
him away much lefs afflicted than he had been. I liften'd
all the time, and partook in all the Tranfports of Grief,

Love,

Love, Defpair and Hope, that he by turns expreffed, while Madame *De G*—— was difcourfing with him.

But when he was gone, and I had time to reflect on the Haughtinefs I had affumed towards him, and the Tendernefs and Submiffion with which he bore it, I melted into Tears ; and it feemed to me as if my very Soul diffolved.—— O Love, if thy Votaries are bleffed with Joys, exceeding all that the World without thee can beftow, the Pains they feel are not lefs exquifite.—— I might conceal the Weaknefs which then overpower'd my Refolution if I pleafed ; none can pretend to accufe me of what none but myfelf was Witnefs of, but as I begun thefe Memoirs meerly for the Service of my own Sex, I ought to hide nothing of the Truth, that they may be let into the Dangers to which a young Heart is expofed, and know at the fame time the Methods I was fo happy to put in practice for curbing the Impulfe of Inclination.——A fmooth and flattering Sea that hides beneath it Rocks and Quick-Sands, on which many are caft away, and which nothing can defend us from, if we once truft ourfelves upon it — the deluding Profpect muft be fhun'd——we muft turn our Backs upon it—we muft not even fuffer the Idea of it to dwell upon our Minds ; but take all Occafions of employing our Thoughts on different Objects.

As foon as Madame *De G*—— had got rid of the Marquis, fhe acquainted her Husband with all that had happened : he was aftonifhed, and troubled at the Temerity of the Chevalier *D'Elbieux*, and agreed with her, that the removing me from their Houfe was abfolutely neceffary. —— They confulted between them on a proper Perfon to entruft me with ; and I was conducted the fame Night to the Monaftery of Saint *N*——, where I was received by the Lady Abbefs and the Nuns, with great Kindnefs and Civility.

My Mind was too much taken up with this fudden Change of Situation for me to have any Appetite to eat, fo defired Permiffion to go to Bed, and was fhewn to a little neat Chamber, where I was no fooner alone than I abandoned myfelf to the different Paffions, which the Ad-

ventures

ventures of the Day had infpired; ——— at length however they gave way to Sleep, if that can be called fo which
prefents us even with more terrible Ideas than our wake-
ing Thoughts can do.——— Rapes, Murders, all that
is dreadful to Nature and to Senfe, were continually before my Eyes——— methought, I faw the Marquis and
Chevalier engaged with equal Fury ——— the former
was overpower'd ——— he fell ——— he died, and
with his laft Breath avowed his Tendernefs for me ———
I became a Prey to the Conqueror——— he dragg'd me
from a Tree where I had clung for Refuge——— I feem'd
to feel his favage Grafp, and awoke with Agonies unutterable!

The Sun was now above the Horizon, and lightned
my Cell. I caft a melancholly Look on the Objects that
furrounded me———a great wooden Crucifix, at the Foot
of which was a Death's-Head, was placed directly oppofite to my Bed——— on the right Side of the Room
was painted the tremendous Judgment-Seat, where all
the unnumber'd Millions that ever were, or are to be,
muft appear to receive their irrevocable Doom——— on
the left, a Picture of Hell, where all the Torments of
the Damned were decypher'd in fo lively a Manner,
that I was ftruck with Horror, and durft not venture to
look long upon it.———Alas, cry'd I, how miferable is
Humankind, to have by Nature a Propenfity to Actions,
which muft without an Infinity of Mercy bring them,
fooner or later, to fo fad a Place! ——— This Reflection
brought me on my Knees, and I prayed with the utmoft
Fervency to the Divine Being, that he would difpofe
my Heart to obey the Dictates of his holy Word, and
mortify all vain Defires in me.———After this, I got into
my Bed again, and my Door being foon after opened,
an old Nun came in, *Ave,* faid fhe in entering, how have
you paffed the Night? ——— I fear but indifferently,
that you are not yet rifen. Madam *De G*———'s in the
Parlour with our Superior, and asks to fee you.———Ah,
my God! cry'd I, with Tranfport, how long has fhe
been here? ——— How does fhe do? ——— What does
fhe fay? ——— I asked all thefe Queftions in a Breath,
but

but she answer'd to them only by saying, Put on your
Cloaths, and come down, you will know every thing
you desire when you see her ; —— but, continued she
very gravely, be sure not to quit your Chamber, till you
have paid to Heaven the first Duty of the Day——
some body shall come for you in a Quarter of Hour——
she left me with these Words, and I jump'd out of Bed,
saying my Prayers, and dressing myself at the same time,
through Eagerness to know what News Madam *De G*——
had brought me of the Marquis. —— So easily, alas !
does Devotion yield to Love —— I found it immediately in myself, but had the Assurance to argue in this
Manner.—— I love God with all my Soul, said I,
but it cannot sure be a Fault to give a little of my Affections to a Man who has no Designs upon me, but such as
are warrantable by the Laws of Heaven and Earth.——
These Reflections were combatted by others, which the
dreadful Pictures before me inspired, and I cannot say,
whether Heaven or Nature would have got the better ;
for a young and very beautiful Nun came to call me
down, and hindered me from thinking farther.——
Ah! said she, you have been weeping —— I dare
engage a Convent has no Charms for you —— but
you are not the only Person here to whom such a Life is
displeasing. I looked earnestly upon her while she was
speaking, and from that Moment conceived an Affection
for her, which afterwards arrived to all the Heights of
Friendship. We said no more however at that time to
each other, but went directly down Stairs.

The Moment I came into the Parlour, I ran, without
thinking of any thing else, and threw myself at the Feet
of Madam *De G*——. Good morrow, my dear
Jeanetta, said she, but you should have paid your first
Respects to your Reverend Superior.—— She is a good
Lady, and for my sake will take a particular Care of
you——you could no where have been so well placed
as with her. I turned myself then a little confounded to
the Abbess, and kissed her Hand. —— She embraced me in a very kind Manner, saying to me, do not
weep, for the Tears were then coming into my Eyes,

z   there

there is nothing so dreadful in a monastick Life —— Cuſtom will make it eaſy to you.   She is naturally pious, reply'd Madam *De G*———, but the very Air of theſe venerable Walls has ſomewhat in it alarming to a young Perſon at firſt ſight ; —— but there are certain Occaſions when ſuch a Retirement from the World is neceſſary; and ought therefore to be pleaſing ; theſe Words were accompany'd with a Look, which told me ſhe had ſomething extraordinary to acquaint me with, and made me very impatient at the Impertinence that delayed my hearing it.

The Abbeſs after a Fit of coughing, which laſted near a Quarter of an Hour, began to entertain her old Friend Madam *De G*———with all the little Animoſities that had happen'd in the Convent, ſince the Time they had laſt met; and it would have been Matter of Affliction to me, had I then had Time to conſider on what ſlender Occaſions, Perſons, who ought by their Profeſſion, to be of a more meek and humble Behaviour, take laſting Piques againſt each other, and diſturb the Peace of a Place conſecrated to Acts of Piety and Devotion ; but my Mind being employed on Things which ſeemed of greater Conſequence to myſelf, left me no Leiſure for Obſervation on the long Stories, which I was compell'd to hear.

At laſt this Converſation was happily interrupted by the coming in of one of the Siſterhood, who whiſpering ſomething to the Abbeſs oblig'd her to withdraw, tho' not till after making a great many needleſs Apologies to Madam *De G*———for being oblig'd to leave her.

Now, *Jeanetta*, ſaid Madame *De G*———as ſoon as we were alone, I'll take this Opportunity of informing you, of what you will ſtand in need of all the Aids of Religion, Prudence, and Courage to ſuſtain——— therefore guard well your Heart againſt the Aſſaults of Paſſion, before I begin the ſhort but tragical Recital.

I ſince have often wonder'd that ſo dreadful a Prelude, did not render me uncapable of liſtning to what was to enſue ; but from the Moment I came into the Parlour, I gueſs'd by the Looks of this good Lady, that ſhe had nothing

thing but ill News to tell me, so had anticipated her Commands, and indeed prepar'd myself for the worst.

After Madam *De G*————had made a little Pause, as recollecting what she had to say, you had not been gone many Minutes, pursued she, when Monsieur *Gripart* (who had it seems been walking in the Park,) came hastily into my Chamber, Madam, said he, how have I deserved this Usage ?————had not Chance been more my Friend than any I have in this House, I had been finely imposed upon————your *Jeanetta*, your virtuous Villager is a fine Creature I perceive————I overheard two Footmen talking to each other in your Park, which has let me into the whole Secret————she has a Lover, Madam, a Gallant, and I was to have been the Dupe of a Husband————but 'tis over now————the *Griparts* never were deceived yet, our Family is famous for Penetration————we are not to be drawn in———— we never were————and I will undertake to say we never will.

I cannot here forbear interrupting the Course of my Memoirs, by giving my Reader an Account of what soon after befel this self-sufficient Man ; for I think not right the Hero of my History, should be dropt without relating his Destiny. His Prediction in Relation to himself, proved equally fabulous with most other modern Predictions————He was some Years after *drawn in,* and married Madamoiselle *Fanchon De L*————all the World knew her————she had carryed on Intrigues in more Climates than one, and was indeed notorious ; yet she had the Address to behave so in his Presence, that he looked on her as a perfect Pattern of Modesty and Virtue, during his Courtship ; but they were no sooner married than she threw off the Mask————at first he raved, tore his Hair, and turned her out of Doors, but as she had been Mistress of Cunning enough to get a Settlement from him before the Ceremony, he was afterwards glad to take her again to avoid paying it, and the Conduct she continued to preserve, was such as convinced the World, there was a Possibility for the *Griparts* to be deceived.

But

But to return to the melancholly Account Madam *De G*————was giving to me; in spite of all I could say to Monsieur *Gripart*, pursued that Lady, either in Vindication of your Innocence, or mine of imposing upon him, he took Leave of me, and went into his Chaise with the utmost ill Humour. My Husband in the mean Time, was arming all the People we had for our Defence, in Case of an Attack, but these Precautions proved entirely useless; Chance disposed Things otherwise than we imagined, and indeed there was no foreseeing the Misfortune that happen'd.

When the Marquis *De L*————*V*————departed, he did it with so little Caution, in Spite of all I had said to him, that the Chevalier *D'Elbicux* was immediately inform'd of it, on which imagining that under the Pretence of marrying you to *Gripart*, you were in Reality to be given to the Marquis, he flew in Pursuit of him Sword in Hand————the Fright he put a poor Shepherd into, was perhaps the Cause that on his enquiring of him which Way his Rival went, he was directed to the Road Monsieur *Gripart* had taken instead of that of his Lordship. The Speed he made, soon brought him and his Attendants to the Heels of a Lackey, who was following the Chaise————He began the Tragedy by shooting this Fellow, and *Gripart* on the Report of the Pistol looking out of his Chaise, and supposing himself pursued by Robbers, jump'd out with all the Haste he could, and throwing himself on his Knees through Fear, begg'd they would spare his Life and take all he had about him————but the Chevalier without regarding what he said, rode furiously over him thinking to find the Marquis in the Chaise: As soon as he was got within Reach of it he discharged a Pistol, the Ball passing through the Leather shot the Postillion in the Shoulder; but he was strangely surprized when looking in, he found himself mistaken, and his Rival escaped————He turn'd back more desperate than ever, and the Road being narrow, gallop'd a second Time over the unfortunate *Gripart*; but he posted to his own Ruin————the Moment of Vengeance

Vengeance was at Hand, nor would Heaven any longer stand unconcern'd at his wicked Attempts.

The Marquis *De L———V———* had been pursuing his Journey toward his own Castle, when the Sound of the Pistols reaching his Ears, he turned hastily the Bridle of his Horse, and flew as directed by the Noise———O Heavens! cryed he, *Jeanetta* is on the Road———this may be some fresh Enterprize against her———Struck with this Idea, he enter'd full Speed the Road I just now mentioned, he knew the Chevalier too well to be mistaken in him; and seeing an empty Chaise, Men lying wounded on the Earth, others crying out for Help, all conspired to intimate to him a second Rape——— *D'Elbieux* had the same Opinion of the Marquis, and had sought him with too much Earnestness now to avoid him, they met with equal Rage, but the Chevalier's Impatience making him forget that both his Pistols were discharged, he attack'd his Rival with them unloaded in his Hands———Thou shalt not escape me now, cryed he, pulling the Trigger, I'll make thee know a second Time the Chevalier *D'Elbieux*——— the Marquis at the same Instant gave Fire, and lodged the whole Charge in the Body of his Antagonist——— he fell immediately from his Horse, and the Marquis alighting, and presenting the other Pistol to his Head——— you are this instant dead, said he, if you tell me not where you have convey'd *Jeanetta*: I have not seen her, replyed the late impetuous, but now dejected Chevalier; I own that I had form'd a Design of carrying her away this Night, but hearing you were at Madam *De G———'s,* and suspecting you intended to secure her to yourself for ever, I left the Place where I had laid conceal'd, and came in Pursuit of you———are you sincere, cryed the Marquis, fearing to be imposed upon?———I am, replyed his wounded Rival, you have vanquish'd me, and may take my Life———I value it not———Despair of being happier, and Remorse for what I have done, render it a Burthen to me——allow me but Time to recollect my Offences and implore Forgiveness———my

Eyes

Eyes are now open————I see my Faults, and pray you to forget————

He was able to speak no more, Loss of Blood threw him into a Swoon, and the Marquis, whose Sentiments are truly generous, was touch'd with the utmost Compassion for him ; he gave Charge to his Attendants to take Care of him, and to bring him to my House, where he hastened before to acquaint me with the History of what had happened——judge my dear, *Jeanetta*, the Grief and Confusion I was in at hearing such dreadful News.

Save yourself, my Lord, save yourself, cryed I, as soon as he had done speaking————this Accident is of the last Consequence, and I fear will involve us all in a Labyrinth, from which we shall have Difficulty enough to extricate ourselves————Madam, replyed he, there requires no more than the plain Truth to testify my Innocence————but I tremble for the adorable *Jeanetta*——should the Place of her Retreat be known at Court, she would doubtless be confined by a *Lettre de Cachet* all the Days of her Life. I am easy as to that, said I, the Precautions I have taken are such as cannot well fail ; there is but one Servant, and him I can depend upon, knows where she is————she passes in the Convent for a Neice of mine, who has a Desire of becoming a Nun, and I have prevail'd upon her Father and Mother, to say her Daughter has absented herself, and that they are wholly ignorant of what is become of her ; so that whatever Search is made, it is next to an Impossibility to find her. You give me a new Life, Madam, said the Marquis kissing my Hand ; go, my Lord, interrupted I, every Moment is precious————Perhaps they are already in Search of you————I will not have you stay to make me any Answer————As soon as you are secure from any Accident let me hear from you, and I will inform you of all that regards us.

The Marquis was but just gone when the Chevalier was brought in, the Motion had brought him to his Senses, but he was unable to speak————my Husband's Surgeon (who you know is constantly with us, on Account of the Danger he is in from an Apoplectic Disorder) searched search'd his Wounds, and finds them very dangerous, yet of such a Nature that there is a Possibility of his Recovery. The Lackey belonging to Monsieur *Gripart* was kill'd, and his Master is so full of Contusions, besides having two of his Ribs broke, that 'tis expected he will not be able to stir these six Months, and the Postillion is maim'd 'tis fear'd forever————in fine, my dear *Jeanetta*, my House is become an Hospital.————as we are very much beloved among our Tenants, we have desired it may be kept a Secret; and I have not heard it has been talk'd of this Morning; but I expect to have dismal News at my Return.————————I came hither thus early to apprize you, because if the Affair should reach the Convent, you may be upon your Guard, and behave so as not to be suspected as the Cause of these Misfortunes————be careful therefore I charge you to affect an unconcern at whatever is said————if you do not, you are lost for ever, and will involve all who love you in the same Perplexity————See, *Jeanetta*, see pursued she, the sad Effect of your unhappy Charms———— would to God you had been less beautiful, or that I had made use of the Advice given me by Madamoiselle *D'Elbieux* ————What an Infinity of Trouble I had then avoided.

These cutting Words, pronounced by a Mouth accustomed only to tender Expressions, struck me to the Heart————I was in such a Consternation that I became motionless, and without Power of Speech————my Tears as well as Words were obstructed in their Passage, and I should have fainted away, had not a Nun who came that Moment into the Room supported me. It was the same I mentioned before, whose Beauty and Sweetness of Behaviour had gain'd very much upon me at first Sight: She was now sent by the Abbess to make her Apology to Madam *De G*———— for not being able to return to her. This amiable young Woman was touch'd with the greatest Compassion to see me in that Condition————She took me in her Arms and gave me a thousand Caresses————Madam *De G*————who was moved at these Marks of Friendship from a Stranger, recommended

recomended me to her Care————do not forsake her,
said she, I perceive none can be more proper to console
her than yourself————her Father will have her placed
here in order to take the Vail, and her Repugnance to it
is the Cause of the Trouble you see her in————Ah,
my God! replied this charming Nun, why will a Parent
render a Child so miserable————for Heaven's sake,
Madam, take pity on her, and save her from so cruel a
Constraint. I cannot stay now to speak of this Affair,
replied Madam *De G*————assure her when she comes
to herself, that I shall always love her as my own Child,
and that she shall very shortly hear from me again; with
these Words she departed.

My Fainting had not hindred me from hearing all was
said. But my Protectress was no sooner gone, than I
found myself extremely ill, my Griefs finding no Vent
preyed upon my Vitals, and I felt as if I was struck with
the Hand of Death.

Take Courage, my lovely Sister, said the young *Saint
Agnes* (for that was the Name of this sweet-tempered De-
votee) I sincerely pity you————Endeavour to support
yourself————I will set you an Example, and when you
know the Woes I have undergone, and which are yet far
from being dissipated, your own will seem much easier to
be borne; with this she took me under the Arm and led
me to my Chamber, where having obliged me to lie
down, I was a long Time without being able to speak
one Word, or testify any other acknowledgment then
tenderly pressing her Hand. She sat down on the Bed-side,
and asked me how I found myself? Alas! cry'd I, half
drowned in the long stifled Tears, I find myself the most
wretched of all created Beings————a cruel Destiny
attends all my Actions————the most direful Events
succeed each other in a continual Round, as I were born
only to suffer————Sure never Creature was overwhelm'd with so many Miseries.

Ah, my dear *Jeannetta!* answered she, your Youth
and Inexperience of the World has not yet made you acquainted with the Calamities of it————Behold in me,
the most unfortunate of Woman————were your Afflictions

tions even greater than ever had a Name, they could not be compared to mine————you are at least at Liberty, I drag a double Chain————under this Vail I wear a Heart pierced with a thousands Darts————the deplorable Victim of an unaccountable Caprice————without Hope————without even a possibility of Relief I find myself doomed to bear continued Torments, which are the more unsupportable as I am obliged by Honour, Decency, and the Interest of my Relations, to stifle my too just Resentment————I have not hitherto had even the Comfort of one Friend, to whom I might safely vent the swelling Sorrows which ever and anon are ready to burst my Bosom————you are the only Person to whom I have utter'd any Part of my Complaints————Since therefore you are of the Number of the unhappy Ones, and seemed by Nature pityful and tender, let us blend our Sufferings————I will make you my Confidant, do me the Honour to let me be yours————we will mutually condole each other, and perhaps be able to find out some Ease in the melancholly Employment.————Shall it be so beautiful *Jeannetta?*

Yes, replied I ardently; how chearing is it in my present State to find such Compassion in a Place where I expected nothing but what is disagreeable? Your Aversion to a Cloyster, resumed *Saint Agnes,* is so conformable to mine, you merit for that alone to be trusted with the dearest Secrets of my unhappy Life————I will therefore make no Scruple to lay my whole Heart open to you———— we have still an Hour secure from interruption, and I am more than half persuaded my Story will be a considerable Alleviation to your Sufferings. Finding me prepared to *hear her,* she began in this Manner.

The *History* of SAINT AGNES *and* MELICOURT.

I Shall touch but flightly on my Birth, whatever Parti-
cularities there may be in it, faid this beautiful Nun,
and at prefent fhall only tell you I am of *Pont-a-Mouffon*
in the Dukedom of *Lorrain*, and the Daughter of a
Man of the firft Quality, who refided at fome diftance
from that City, but married my Mother thence on account
of the Charms of her Perfon ———— She was about twenty-
five Years of Age when fhe brought me into the World,
and for fome reafons which I fhall acquaint you with
hereafter, had concealed her being with Child, and lay in
as privately. as could be contrived————I was no
fooner born than committed to the care of a Gardener
and his Wife, who lived about fourteen or fifteen Miles off,
and paffed with every body as their Daughter————
the firft Years of my Life were employed in the meaneft
Occupations, and fuch as befitted the Profeffion of my fuppofed Parents————the ill Humour of my two Sifters,
as I then thought them, made my Life very unhappy;
and the ill Agreement between us made our Parents in
common Pity to me, fend me abroad to keep Sheep; the
cruel Treatment I had received at home from thofe Girls,
made this Vocation pleafing to me, and I thank'd Heaven
for the Change.

The Lord of the Village in which we lived was called
Monfieur *Melicourt*————He was Councellor in the Parliament of *M*————and came down to his Eftate always in the Time of the Vocation————He had a Son
who had not entirely finifh'd his Studies, but never fail'd
to accompany him when he came into the Country.

I
This

This young Gentleman was extremely lovely, well
ſhap'd, had the moſt inchanting Air, and was more reſerved and grave than is uſually found in Perſons of his
Sex and Age.   Inſtead of ſpending his Time in Hunting,
Gaming, Drinking, or any of thoſe Diverſions to which
moſt too much adict themſelves, he paſſed the greateſt
Part of it in Reading——his chief Recreation conſiſted
in walking either in the Fields or about the Village, after
the Sun had ſo far withdrawn his Beams as not to be of-
fenſive——few Evenings there were wherein I did not
meet him, and always with a Book in his Hand; he
never paſs'd by me without pulling off his Hat, but
ſeem'd inſtigated to that Civility only by the Complaiſance
of his Temper to any of our Sex, for I perceived he did
it to all he met without making any Diſtinction, or paying more Deference to me than others.

But, alas! it was not ſo to me, I was not then quite
fourteen, yet I could diſtinguiſh between Men, and when
I compared him with the reſt of his Sex he appeared to
me of a ſuperior Specie: I was, however, too young to
know from what Senſe theſe Idea's proceeded, neither
indeed did I examine into it——I bluſhed wherever I
ſaw him without being able, if I had been asked to ſay
for what Reaſon, and I caſt down my Eyes whenever we
met, yet nothing afforded me ſo much Pleaſure as to look
upon him——I have a thouſand Times wiſhed for an
Opportunity to gaze on him without his perceiving I did
ſo, and was never ſo much troubled as when any Chance
kept him at home, that I miſſed the pleaſure of beholding
him.

One Day when I had drove my Sheep towards a
Warren about half a Mile from *Treſe*, for that is the
Name of our Village, who ſhould I find ſleeping on the
Graſs at the Foot of a Tree but him, whoſe charming
Image was ever preſent to me——how happy did I
think my ſelf in having ſo far an occaſion of contemplating him without his ſeeing me——Emboldened by
that Security I drew nearer——I was alone——he
aſleep, and at laſt I ventured ſtep by ſtep till I was cloſe
to him——yet trembling leſt he ſhould awake and

surprize me, I rustled the Leaves of the Trees with a little Stick I had in my Hand, as an Experiment to try if his repose was sound, and finding it according to my Wishes, I stoop'd gently down the better to examine his Features, than which to me none ever appeared so charming————but I will give you the Picture as near as I can draw it————He is of what they call a sanguine Complection, very clear Skin, large sparkling Eyes, and tho' their Lids were then closed were not without their Beauties, the dark and shining Fringes which seemed to guard the precious Balls of Sight from any Offences by Dust or other Atoms wasted by the Wind, had a peculiar Grace, nor were his fine form'd Eyebrows less to be admired, his Forehead majestick, round and ample————his Nose admirably turned, and a Mouth round which every Grace inhabited————the Make of his Face neither long nor over short, and of an agreeable Plumpness————His Hair of a Chesnut brown hung in great Curls over his Shoulders————his Shape well proportioned, and his Limbs a fit Pattern for a Statuary to copy after for a perfect Model————think not, continued the lovely Nun, I speak as Passion guides these least prepossess'd in favour of *Melicourt* allow him such as I have described————a Book lay by him on the Grass, I had learned to read, and promoted by Curiosity to see what had been the Subject of his Meditations made me take it and put it in my Pocket————after this I thought of retiring, lest he should wake and discover what I had done, but indulging myself with one look more before I went, a Gnat that Moment happened to settle on his Cheek, I stooped again, too much interested not to stretch out my Hand to drive away this poisonous Insect, but the Confusion this Action threw me in made me execute my intent with so little caution as to wake him————he started as surprized, and spoke some Words which my Fright would not suffer me to understand————on my endeavouring to run away he catch'd hold of my Petticoat, and said with a Smile which added to his Charms, what have I done, my pretty Maid, that you should disturb my Slumber————indeed, Sir, answered I in a faultring Voice,

I beg

I beg your Pardon, I had no defign to hurt you, but being in Search of a ſtrayed Sheep, I happened as I paſs'd by to ſee a Gnat juſt going to ſting you; and in going to bruſh it off was ſo unlucky to awake you, while I was making aukwardly enough I believe this Apology, he looked on me with an Attention that very much flattered my Vanity————when I left off ſpeaking he would have thrown his Arms about my Neck to thank me as he ſaid for the good will I had ſhewn to him———— Covered with Bluſhes I avoided his Kindneſs and turn'd haſtily away, ſweet Creature, cryed he, miſconſtrue not my Gratitude, I will be more reſerved, if you do not ap-prove the Tranſports your Eyes have kindled in my Breaſt————you are the firſt I aſſure you that has ever been able to inſpire me with the Sentiments I now feel—good God! continued he, taking me by the Hand, how perfectly beautiful you are————I do not deceive you—I never ſaid ſo much to any of your Sex before, becauſe none but you ever appeared ſo in my Eyes.

I pretended not to underſtand what he meant, but young as I was, I comprehended very well that he would have me think he loved me, and that I ought not to liſten to any Diſcourſe of that kind; and notwithſtand-ing the Pleaſure it gave me to be near him, I retired with an unwilling haſte; Ah! dont leave me, cryed he, the Sun is not yet ſet————you will not be wanted— Cruel Creature! added he, when I was got ſome diſtance from him————better for me I had been ſtung by the Gnat————the Smart would then have ſoon been over, but the Wound I have received from you will never be healed.

By this Time I was come up to my Flock————*Me-licourt* followed me at ſome Diſtance, but when I ſaw him coming one Way I turned another, under the pre-tence of keeping my Sheep together————He ſoon per-ceived I was reſolved to give him no farther Opportunity of talking to me, and ſtood ſtill, but continued to look after me with an Air no leſs expreſſive of his Meaning than the beſt choſen Words could have been————without ſeeming to take any notice of him I went back to the

Village,

Village, but carried an Impreſſion in my Mind, which no Changes of Fortune has ever been able to erace——— O to what Misfortunes does the Heedleſſneſs of Youth tranſport us !

I will not tire you, my dear *Jeanetta*, purſued *Saint Agnes*, with the Ideas that ran through my Mind the Night after this firſt Converſation with the Man I had ſo long in ſecret admired———you may ſuppoſe they were of a mix'd Nature, divided between Hope and Fear, and both romantick enough in their Turns ; I will only tell you that *Melicourt*'s Diſquiet were not at all inferior to mine, as his Actions afterwards ſufficiently evinc'd——— I ſaw him the next Day, and every Day he declared his Paſſion for me in the tendereſt Terms, I was prepoſſeſſed in his Favour, and at length let him know the Influence he had gain'd———the Tranſports he expreſs'd on this Confeſſion, were ſuch as would loſe half their Energy in being repeated by any other Mouth, and notwithſtanding the vaſt Diſparity there then appeared to be between our Birth and Fortunes he gave me, the moſt ſolemn Vows never to be but mine———Ah what flattering Charms ———what gay Delights attend the Infancy of Love! ———how ſweet is mutual Affection before embittered by any adverſe Paſſions, or cruel Diſappointments !——— *Melicourt* and I indulged ourſelves for a Time in all the innocent Felicity that any Pair enjoyed, without once think- ing what was to enſue———the Vacation now expired, he was obliged to leave me, and this Separation firſt made us ſenſible that the Engagements we had entered into muſt infallibly entail on us a Train of Difficulties.——— nothing can be more mournful than our taking leave ; and tho' he endeavoured to conſole himſelf and me, with the Hopes of ſeeing each other again, yet I could eaſily ſee how deeply he was afflicted, and after he was gone, I did nothing for three whole Months but utter my Complaints to my poor Sheep, who were my only Con- fidents.

As I was going home one Evening more depreſt with the Anguiſh of my Mind, than with the Fatigues my Body had that Day undergone, I met running towards

z   me me one of the Daughters of those Persons who pass'd for my Parents————O *Minetta*, said she, for that was the Name they call'd me by, I have rare News for you—— what will you give me to tell you?————Somebody is come you'll be glad to see————as *Melicourt* was continually in my Head, I blush'd thinking she meant that Gentleman, and durst not ask her any Questions,———— you have little Curiosity, resumed she, but indeed you have seem'd very indifferent of late to every Thing——, now if my Mother would not be angry I would not tell you at all——but however you must come Home this Minute, there's a great fine Lady come to our House in her own Coach————She asked for my Mother, and went into our Chamber with her————I could not imagine what she wanted, so stood to listen————it seems you are not our Sister, and this Lady says you are her Daughter ————How, cry'd I astonish'd, you tell me strange Things indeed, and what I do not know how to believe————I fancy you only want to laugh at me————we were arguing in this rustick Manner, when the other Sister came quite out of Breath with running————why dont you come *Minetta* said she————you shall make such fine Folks wait for you indeed————pray go home, and leave me to watch the Sheep; my Mother charged me to do so.

I began to think there must be really something in all this, and went with her that came first; I was scarce got in when she I took for my Mother pull'd off my Handkerchief and shewed a Mark I have on my Neck to a very graceful Lady, whom I found sitting in the Room.

'Tis she I know, said she, not that I should have doubted it without this Testimony————her Face is sufficient————then turning to me in a very gracious Manner, will you come and live with me? pursued she, your Mother here has promised me you shall——I assure you that you shall be well taken care of; and as she has several Children and is not very rich it will be an Ease to her. Your Ladyship is mighty good, replied my supposed Mother, I'll answer for *Minetta* she will be proud to attend your Ladyship, she is a very good

Girl

Girl and tractable enough; but your Ladyſhip muſt excuſe her if ſhe behaves at firſt after a plain Manner, ſhe has not been accuſtomed to Gentry.

The Lady after this whiſper'd ſomething to her, and I was ordered to go and put on my beſt Gown; I obey'd, but was quite dejected in my Mind, as not able to reconcile what the Girl had told me with what I had juſt now heard from the Lady's own Mouth; to add to this the Uncertainty where I was going, and the Fears I ſhould not be able to acquaint my dear *Melicourt* where he might ſee me, made me put on my Clothes with a very ill Will. However I was at laſt ready, and re-entred the Chamber where they expected me, with down caſt Eyes————the little Concern which I ſtrove to conceal but could not, was conſtrued to my Advantage, the Lady taking it as the Effects of Tenderneſs and Duty to thoſe whom I imagin'd my Parents; and indeed I lov'd with very great Affection thoſe I was going to quit, and as I believe our Grief was mutual at Parting, it was a moving Sight.

When I was on the Road and alone in the Coach with this ſtrange Lady, what the Gardener's Daughter had ſaid again came into my Head, but it ſeemed all a Myſtery to me; if this were really my Mother, cry'd I to my-ſelf, what ſhould hinder her, now no Witneſſes are pre-ſent from embracing me, and acknowledging me as her Child?————I found ſhe was extremely penſive, and as ſhe did not ſpeak one Word to me, durſt not take the Liberty of opening my Lips to her————both of us obſerved a profound Silence for about ſix Miles of our Journey, and had perhaps continued in it longer, if a Gentleman on Horſeback had not rode up to the Coach ſide, and accoſted the Lady with a Familiarity, which ſhewed he muſt either be a Relation or a very intimate Friend————he looked very ſtedfaſtly on me, aſked ſe-veral Queſtions concerning me, and often ſaid I was very pretty.

At laſt we arrived at a magnificent Caſtle, where the Lady and Gentleman made me enter with them into an Apartment, which as I had never before ſeen any thing
like

like it dazzled my Eyes !————the Furniture was indeed
rich, gorgeous, and well fancied————I cou'd eafily
perceive they were expected to fup there, for the Table
was already covered, the Side-board fet out, and every
Thing prepared————I had my Supper brought me to
the Fire-fide, where the Lady had made me fit————
both fhe and the Gentleman had often their Eyes fixed
on me, and in fpite of my inward Difquiets, on the account of *Melicourt,* and my Confufion at fo fudden a
Change of Fortune, I felt a fecret fomething within me
which emboldned me to look on them in my Turn————
the Lady, cryed out feveral Times, this Girl wont appear aukward when fhe comes to be dreft————the
Gentleman feemed entirely of her Opinion————he
made me turn about————examined my Shape, my
Hands and Arms, and was for feeing the Mark upon my
Breaft ; but my Modefty would not fuffer that, till the
Lady told me I might permit this Perfon the Satisfaction
of his Curiofity, tho' I could not be too referved to all
others of that Sex.

He had no fooner beheld this Mark than he appeared
highly fatisfy'd, and embraced me with an extraordinary
Tendernefs, but I was in fuch a Confternation at all
thefe Things, that I could not eat ; they preffed me very
much however, and when they thought I had fupp'd, a
Chamber-maid, who they called Madamoifelle *Bretigny,*
was ordered to put me to Bed in a Chamber before prepared for me, and which was feparated from the Room
they were in only by a Wainfcot Partition and Glafs
Door.

This Woman undreft me from Head to Foot, and
while fhe was doing fo gave me a thoufand Carreffes,
then having put me to Bed, drew the Curtains round me
and retired, wifhing me a good Repofe.

The Occurrences of this Day were too particular and
furprizing to me, for me to have any Sleep in my Eyes
————there were fome Things in the Behaviour of
this Gentleman and Lady to me, that feemed to render
Probable what the Gardener's Daughter had faid to me,
and others again that utterly deftroyed it————My

Curiofity

Curiofity to be fatisfied in this Point was fo great, that I refolved to neglect no Opportunity of coming at the Truth: Accordingly I got foftly out of Bed and crept to the Glafs Door, and lifting up the Corner of a little Taffety Curtain that hung before it on the Infide, I could fee all over the Room, the Lady and Gentleman were ftill fitting at the Table, and Madamoifelle *Bretigny*, who I perceived was the Confident in all this Myftery, had taken my Place by the Fire-fide; they were earneft in Difcourfe, but fpoke fo low, that I could not under-ftand one Word they faid for a good While, and I was about to return to Bed hopelefs of fucceeding in my Attempt, when contrary to my Expectation the Lady raifed her Voice, and fpoke with great Emotion in this Manner.

What Hazard do we run, cryed fhe, what Prejudice can it be to either of our Reputations for People to be told the Truth——every Body knows you had the Misfortune to kill Monfieur the Count de *D*—— in a Duel, that you were banifh'd for it, and when it comes to be revealed, that inftead of being in the Ifland where it was given out you had retired, you lay con-cealed near your own Houfe, none can impute it to you as a Crime——the having concealed my Pregnancy, and the Birth of this Girl, will then be known to be only to favour your fuppofed Abfence——and fince that unhappy Affair is now at an End, let us no longer keep the poor Child in Ignorance of her Birth.

Blefs me, cryed my Father, for I could now no longer doubt if it was he, how much do you fuffer your Tender-nefs for your Child to overpower your Judgment, and ftifle all other Confiderations! ——Can you be fo forget-ful or blind to the Vexations fuch a Difcovery would bring upon us all——is not your eldeft Daughter, married to one of the moft felf-interefted Men on Earth ——what will he fay when you tell him this Adven-ture, and the Birth of *Minetta*?——Will he not look on it as a Fiction; and on her, as a fuppofitious Child, only brought in to rob him of his Expectations, and be a joint Heirefs with his Wife?——He'll certainly
profecute

profecute you, and not only fo; but the Court will be appriz'd of my Difobedience to the Royal Mandate——— you know very well that the Family of the Count *De D*———was prevail'd upon to ftop Proceedings againft me on Condition, that I departed the Kingdom; the contrary of which muft be prov'd, if you prove *Minetta* your Child and lawfully begotten, fo of Confequence I fhall be rendred liable to a frefh Indictment.———The repealing my Sentence of Banifhment, which has been fo difficult to procure, will be invalid when once it comes to be known, that I have not fulfill'd the Conditions impos'd on me, by the Order of the King.———Reflect therefore, my Dear, continu'd he, that in owning *Minetta* for your Daughter, you run the Rifque of your Hufband, and, perhaps, too without any Advantage to the Girl; for your Son-in-Law would without doubt oppofe all you can do in this Affair.———Thefe are my Reafons, added he, if you have any better to offer, let me know them, and I fhall be convinced.

Then, faid my Mother, this poor Child, who is your lawful Daughter, muft be depriv'd for ever of what is her Right, and pafs her whole Life in Ignorance of her Birth, and real Parents.

I acknowledge, reply'd my Father, that her Cafe is extremely hard; but as fhe knows it not will feel nothing of the Difquiet, which otherwife would naturally attend being cut off from what fhe was born to, and, indeed, feems to merit.———But Times, perhaps, may change, and fome Accident happen in her Favour, to render the Difcovery you defire both fafe for me, and prudent for yourfelf; but at prefent there is no Poffibility of reconciling all thefe things.

I am very much miftaken, interrupted Madamoifelle *Bretigny*, who having never been a Mother, knew not a Mother's Tendernefs, if there is not a way to folve thefe Difficulties, and make you all equally eafy———Mademoifelle *Minetta* is young———fhe knows not of how great a Defcent fhe is, or if fhe did, could make no Obection to this Propofal: It is, continu'd fhe, to put her immediately into a Convent, and when her time of Probation

bation is expir'd, make her take the Veil————after which you may if you pleafe acquaint her with her Birth, and give and receive thofe Proofs of Tendernefs which the near Relation between you demand:————Monfieur your Son-in-Law can then take no Offence, and the young Lady have no Caufe of Complaint.

This Advice of yours *Bretigny*, reply'd my Mother, feems founded equally on Reafon and Good-nature———— we muft confider on it————my Father, faid nothing; but teftified by his Looks that it was not difagreeable to him, they talk'd fome time longer on this Head; but having acquainted you with the material Part of their Difcourfe, 'twould be needlefs to trouble you with Repetitions.

Early the next Morning, Mademoifelle *Bretigny* came to call me up: She try'd upon me feveral Suits of Cloaths which had been my Sifter's, and dreffing me in that which fhe found fitted me beft, I found nothing wanting about me becoming a Girl of Condition.

As foon I was ready fhe conducted me into my Mother's Chamber, who being in Bed call'd me to fit down by her. *Minetta*, faid fhe, liften with Attention to what I am going to fay to you———— your Mother was formerly my Servant, I have always had a great regard for her, and promis'd to take care of one of her Daughter's; as your Countenance pleas'd me beft, I made Choice of you, and defign to put you into a Monaftery for Education————you are of an Age to be fenfible of the Gratitude you owe me, and I expect you will fhew it, by punctually obferving the Directions I fhall give you.————If they know you are born a Peafant, they would not fhew you that due Regard I would wifh you fhould be treated with; and if in Procefs of time, you fhould have an Inclination to devote yourfelf wholly to Heaven, and abandon the World, you would not be permitted to take Orders on Account of your mean Birth; therefore I am determined from this Moment to make you pafs for a Neice of mine juft come from *Provence:* I have order'd *Bretigny* to inftruct you farther on this Affair, and alfo to carry you to M——this Day, where every
thing

thing proper for a Perfon fo nearly allied to me, as I would have you believ'd to be, fhall be bought for you—— then you fhall return to me, and tarry till your Rufticity is entirely worn off, to the End you may not difgrace the Name you are to bear when you go to the Convent.

While my Mother was thus fpeaking, I look'd earneftly upon her——I felt within myfelf a Love for her, and a Propenfity to obey her, more than ever I had known for her who had brought me up, and whom till now, I imagin'd demanded all the Duty I could pay. ————How ftrong is Nature, and how weak is Policy when in Competition with it.—I burft out into Tears of Affection, my Mother with Difficulty reftrain'd hers from falling ; fhe gave me the moft ftrenuous Embraces ; I knew not as we were alone, but all might have been explain'd, had not *Bretigny*, who had left the Room to give fome neceffary Directions, re-enter'd it and found us in this tender Situation.————Ah ! Madam ! cry'd fhe, with a very expreffive Look, what are you doing————there wants here only the Prefence of my Lord. Take her away *Bretigny*, cry'd my Mother, wiping her Eyes, I can hold no longer————thefe Words made my Tears flow fafter ; but I began to prove myfelf a Daughter by my Obedience, and *Bretigny* led me down Stairs, where the Chariot being ready, we went directly into it.

All this Woman could fay, had not the power of getting one Word in anfwer from me, neither could I be prevail'd on, to eat when we were got into the Cabera, fo great were the Agitations of my Mind !————the fame Night we reach'd *M*————and the firft thing fhe did, was to fend for feveral Tradefmen to befpeak every thing for me, proper for my Condition, which they promis'd fhould be all got ready in two Days.

The next Day, having a great deal of Bufinefs in the City fhe went out, and fhut me into my Chamber, taking the Key with her. I fat down at the Window meditating on all the things which in fo fhort a Time had befallen me ; *Melicourt* was ftill uppermoft in my Thoughts, I call'd to remembrance all the tender Paffa-

ges

ges of our Love from the beginning of our Acquaintance to the time of his Departure; and was half loft in Thought, when all on a fudden I caft my Eyes on a young Gentleman going through the Street, on the other fide of the way————I imagin'd I knew his Air, and putting my Head out of the Cafement, found it was *Melicourt* himfelf————the Tranfport I was in at feeing him, made me clap my Hands together, and fend forth a Cry——on which he lifted up his Eyes, and in fpite of the Alteration was in me by the Change of Drefs, immediately knew me! O! Heaven! cry'd he, 'tis *Minetta*, he fpoke no more, but flew into the Houfe, and in an Inftant was at my Chamber-door. *Minetta*, *Minetta*, faid he, endeavouring to open the Door; will you not admit your ever faithful *Melicourt?*————What a Bleffing is it to find you here————have you taken this Journey to feek me————how happens it you are no longer a Shepherdefs?————Open the Door, if it be true you love me, diftract me not with this Delay——all this was faid in a manner at once, at leaft fo faft, that I had not time to make any Anfwer; but was all the while fumbling with the Lock on the Infide, as he was on the Outfide————at laft finding all my Efforts, as well as his were vain, I told him that I had a thoufand things to fay to him————a thoufand to reveal; but could not do it thus fhut in, becaufe we might be overheard by fpeaking through the Door.————But, he prefs'd to know wherefore I was thus made a Prifoner; but as I could not fatisfy his Curiofity, without entring into a Detail of the whole Affair, I advifed him to ftay in the Houfe, which as it was an Inn he might do without Sufpicion, and told him that when *Bretigny* return'd, I would find an Opportunity to get loofe and talk to him: On this he retir'd, and affur'd me that in fpite of his Studies to which he was ftill unhappily confin'd, he would not go out of the Houfe till he had entertain'd me with his Vows of Conftancy————we agreed upon a Signal, and he went down and order'd a Breakfaft below Stairs.

A

A Moment longer and Mademoiselle *Bretigny* had surpriz'd us in this Position: The Pleasure which the knowledge of seeing my Lover had inspir'd me with, spread itself over my Face, and made me look quite different, from what I was when she left me.——She easily perceiv'd the Alteration, and taking me in her Arms, cry'd, now I love to see you——you look a thousand times handsomer than you did Yesterday.—— There is a sweet Serenity in your Countenance, that makes me hope you are not dissatisfied with the Favours Madam *De*——heaps upon you. I answer'd to this Discourse in a Fashion that pleas'd her very well, and our Conversation afterwards was of the same Piece; for when the Heart is satisfied, it influences all the Faculties.

The chearful Temper I was in, contributed very much to my Designs, tho' I did not put it on with that View; for seeming perfectly contented, and sauntring about, as if I did not know what to do with myself, she had no longer any Guard upon me, and being charg'd with many Commissions, besides those relating to me, she went out again, without locking me up as she had done before.——She was no sooner gone, than I gave the appointed Signal to *Melicourt*, who immediately appear'd at the Bottom of the Staircase, I pointed with my Finger to a Room, the Door of which was open, he went into it, and I immediately ran down and join'd him.

I doubt, dear *Jeanetta*, continu'd the charming Nun, fixing her Eyes upon me, that I shall give you an ill Opinion of my Prudence in this Affair, and that the Steps I then took, will seem too inconsistent with that strict Reserve our Sex ought to observe; but my Youth and want of Education, I hope will in part excuse me. ——I thought there could be no harm in this Meeting; nor, indeed, was there as it happen'd, with one as little experienc'd in the Artifices of his Sex, as I in mine. ——As soon as he saw me, he threw himself at my Feet——neither of us were able to speak for some Moments,——Joy and Astonishment depriv'd us mutually

ly

ly of Words; but when we did it was in the moſt ſoft and endearing Terms————an Account of all that had happen'd to me,————my Birth, the ſecret Reaſons that induced my Parents to act as they did————nothing was forgot————I lov'd too well to conceal any thing from my dear Shepherd, for by that Title he affected to call himſelf, in Complaiſance to me, in our firſt Days of Courtſhip.

· The Change of your Fortune, my lovely *Minetta,* anſwer'd he, augments not the Eſteem I had for you, when I believ'd you no more than the Daughter of a poor Gardener;————but it rather mortifies me, in taking from me the Means of giving you the moſt ſubſtantial Proof in the power of Man to do, of my diſintereſted Affection—it was ſweet to me to think, I ſhould one Day make my Shepherdeſs's Fortune, and ſhew the charming Maid, I lov'd her for her own ſake alone—and can I, may I now depend that after the Knowledge of your Birth, you will continue to love your Shepherd? ————I aſſur'd him of my everlaſting Tenderneſs in the beſt manner I was able, and the Paſſion that dictated my Words is ſeldom without Eloquence.

I had not yet told him the Deſign my Parents had of ſecluding me for Life; but when at laſt the fatal Secret came out, never did Deſpair arrive at a higher Pitch—— he rav'd, tore his Hair, and curs'd his Deſtiny, which by not making him Maſter of himſelf, permitted him not the power of breaking all the Meaſures concerted on this Score.————And will you conſent to it, cry'd he? ————will you reſolve to be torn for ever from me? ————Are you willing to hazard nothing for a Man who adores you to Diſtraction; who cannot live without you, and who vows to be no more, when he no more can hope to be happy in your Society?

Alas! reply'd I, what can I do? young, unexperienced, friendleſs, oblig'd to a blind Obedience, and dependant even for the Bread I eat————my Tears and Griefs are all I can oppoſe, and what will thoſe avail? We were in this melancholly Converſation, when I heard Mademoiſelle *Bretigny*'s Voice; I had therefore only

time to prefs his Hand, and ran up Stairs. She faw I
had been weeping and began to chide, telling me I
fhould be left no more alone; but come, continu'd fhe,
let me hear how you can read, I'll give you a Book will
help to pafs the time agreeably, with thefe Words, fhe
put the *Lives of the Saints* into my Hand, and I opening it happen'd on that Part, where *St. Agnes* pour'd forth
her devout Soul, I read it aloud to her; but as where
the Heart is ftrongly affected one is apt to apply every
thing to our own Cafe——the very Ejaculations of that
Holy Maid, feem'd to me what I had reafon to fay on
my unhappy Love.——I hope, Heaven, will forgive
the Prophanation I was guilty of, I have feverely punifh'd
myfelf for it, fince I came within thefe Walls, and it
was only Ignorance and Prepoffeffion made me Criminal.

The good *Bretigny*, however, interpreted the Concern I
teftified while reading, merely to my Piety, and exprefs'd a great Satisfaction, in finding, as fhe faid, that
I had fo true a Notion of Spiritual Things——after
this fhe run into a long Exhortation, not to regard the
Pleafures, or rather the Follies of the World; and gave
fuch extravgant Praifes to a Monaftick Life, that I eafily perceiv'd, fhe had Inftructions to prepare me as
much as poffible to approve it.

When fhe had ended her Sermon we went to Supper,
and I waited for the Hour of going to Bed with Impatience, that I might recollect all that *Melicourt* had faid
to me: The more I thought on him, the more my Averfion for a Cloyfter encreas'd——I repin'd that things
happen'd fo averfe to all that could make me eafy—had
I never been taken from my fuppos'd Parents, faid I to
myfelf, I might one Day have been happy—*Melicourt* had
made me fo——or had not fuch crofs Accidents interven'd thofe who really gave me Being, would not
have made me wretched, by thrufting me as it were out
of the World, and burying me while I am yet alive.
——Strange that I fhould fuffer for Actions committed by my Father, before I had any Exiftence——yet
fuch is my deplorable and cruel Lot. The Sum of all this
Reafoning, was that I ardently wifh'd to be the Wife of
Melicourt;

Melicourt; and to be depriv'd for ever of that Hope, was what made a monaſtic Life ſo terrible to me. I freely confeſs my Frailty in this Particular, my dear *Jeanetta*, nor, indeed, ought a Perſon of our Profeſſion to diſguiſe any thing.

The next Day my Cloaths were brought, and I found myſelf ſo different from what I was, that I ſeem'd another Creature; I will not tell you but the Looking-Glaſs in ſome Meaſure alleviated the Griefs which had the Night before tormented me; Youth and Vanity made me take Pleaſure in contemplating an agreeable Object, ſuch as I then appear'd in my own Eyes; and the Variety of Habits, of Ribbons, of Artificial Flowers, of Feathers, and other gay Trifles, for which our Country is ſo famous for inventing gave me an Amuſement, which for a time render'd *Melicourt* and my own Circumſtances leſs remember'd. Nor till I came into the Chariot, and was leaving *M——*, did the not ſeeing him before my Departure, gave me thoſe Agonies which might have been expected from the Love I really had for him; but when I had turn'd my Back upon that City, and remember'd I had left him there, without knowing when, or whether ever I ſhould ſee him more, my Tenderneſs reſum'd its former Empire o'er my Mind; and I ſhould not have forborn teſtifying my Anxiety by ſome Extravagance or other, had I not found ſome Relief from that Pride, which the Knowledge I was not inferior to him now inſpir'd————were his Love for me equal to his Profeſſions, ſaid I to my ſelf, he might have contriv'd ſome Means of ſeeing me————if no Opportunity could have been found for ſpeaking to me, he might at leaſt have ſhewed himſelf to me in the Yard of the Cabera; he might eaſily have ſtood unheeded by all but me, and bid me Farewel with his Eyes at leaſt.————I now was piqued————I reſented as I thought became my Father's Daughter the Slight he put upon me————and condemn'd myſelf for having behav'd to him with ſo little Reſerve.

Theſe Reflections accompanied me for about three or four Miles of our Journey, and had, perhaps, continued
                                                                    longer,

longer, if Mademoiselle *Bretigny* had not rouz'd me from them, by making me take Notice of a Pilgrim, who walk'd by the fide of the Chaife.———Look, Mademoifelle *Minetta*, faid fhe to me, on that poor young Man———is it not pity to fee him travel thus bare-foot through this miry Way ?———His Face has fomewhat in it infinitely agreeable, and who knows but his Soul may be yet more worthy Regard———how fevere is Fortune———how unjuft———can there be a greater Proof of it than for a Perfon of his Age and graceful Appearance to undergo fuch Hardfhips; while others, who perhaps have not half his Merit, indulge in all the Exceffes of Eafe and Plenty. This Difcourfe made me turn my Eyes on him, that had occafion'd it; but how great was my Surprize, when her Words making me confider him attentively, I found it was no other than the faithful *Melicourt*, that Lover whom my Sufpicions even had wrong'd at the very time he was giving me fo painful a Proof of his Affection.

It was happy for me, that *Bretigny*, through an extraordinary liking fhe took to this young Man, had that Moment put her Head out of the Chariot to invite him to eafe his Feet by getting up behind it; fhe could not elfe have avoided feeing the Change of my Countenance: My Eyes met thofe of *Melicourt*, I blufh'd and caft them down; but my Heart rejoiced in fecret, and tho' I pitied his Fatigue, was highly delighted to behold with what Satisfaction in his Countenance he feem'd to bear it.

The Civility with which Mademoifelle *Bretigny* treated him, encourag'd him to enter into Converfation with her, he told her he was returning from a Pilgrimage, and that he was more than two hundred Leagues from Home———fhe made the Sign of the Crofs, and, faid he ought to take fome Repofe before he continu'd to profecute fo long a Journey. *Melicourt* perceiv'd he was very much in the good Graces of this Woman, and having learn'd from our Poftilion with whom he had been talking, that fhe rul'd every thing in the Family where I was, thought he could not any way fo well forward.

ward his Defigns, as by getting her into his Intereſt ————to heighten her good Opinion, therefore of him, he told her abundance of extraordinary Stories; ſome of which, perhaps, he had heard, and others that he invented to amuſe and pleaſe her————his Plot ſo far ſucceeded; for ſhe appear'd perfectly enchanted with him————he entertain'd her in this manner, till we came to the Place where we were to dine — ſhe made him ſit down at Table with us, telling me I muſt never behave with any Haughtineſs to the Poor, eſpecially, if they were Religious; and that we were oblig'd to do all we could to aſſiſt them at all times; but more particularly on the Road————ſhe need not have made half thoſe Apologies if ſhe had known all; but I agreed to what ſhe ſaid with a Chearfulneſs, which gave her a high Opinion of my Piety and Humility.

If ever you experienc'd the Force of Love, purſued the ſweet *Saint Agnes*, 'tis eaſy for you to imagine the Pleaſure, I felt in the Enjoyment of his Company who was ſo dear to me, and had given me ſuch undeniable Marks of his Conſtancy and Tenderneſs.————I will own to you that I was all Rapture————that every Care was lull'd to reſt, and I gave my whole Soul to Love and Joy————as for his Part, the moſt experienced Lover never behav'd with greater Caution and Addreſs————the Satisfaction he took in being ſo near me, he ſo well diſguis'd under a ſhew of Gratitude to Mademoiſelle *Bretigny*, for the Favours ſhe did him; that but for the Fears of being too particular, I believe ſhe would have incommoded herſelf, to have given him a Place with us in the Chariot.

While ſhe went down to defray the Expence of our eating, my lovely Pilgrim took the Opportunity to expreſs himſelf to me in the moſt paſſionate manner———— he threw himſelf at my Feet, he kiſs'd my Hands—— he vow'd eternal Conſtancy————loſt in the pleaſing Dream, I return'd his Tranſports; but the cruel Remembrance of the Fate to which I was decreed, made me at laſt interrupt this delightful Courſe.————Ah! *Melicourt*, what does all our mutual Tenderneſs avail,

ſaid

said I, we must part, and since it must be so, why should
we by any Proofs, how truly dear we are to each other,
render an eternal Separation more grievous to be borne ?
——it is not better we should now take the final Farewel ?
————How, *Minetta*, cryed he hastily, can you resolve
my Death ? Do you not know that my Life is attached
to the Joy of seeing you——Alas ! you know not what
it is to love like me, or you would neither be able to
give, nor take such Advice.

Troubled as I was to see him in this Situation, my
Reason came to my Assistance, dry up your Tears, said
I, endeavouring to restrain my own————'Tis but too
true, I love you, and with a Passion which never can be
out-done, but as we cannot hope,——since there remains
no Prospect of ever being united, what can this Love
produce but Misery and Despair ! Too ready are you,
resumed he, to plunge me into it————who knows what
unexpected Turns may arrive to render us more fortunate
——many Things are in the Seeds of Time, impossible
for us to forsee, and if we continue to Love and to see
each other, who knows but something may fall out to
make us happy, no less strange than the Circumstances,
which now make us miserable.

How easily are we flattered into a Belief of what we
ardently wish————I thought there was Reason in
what my Lover urged, and consented he should take all
Measures, consistent with Prudence, for our continuing a
Conversation with each other ; one of the most feasible
was his endeavouring to improve the good Opinion Madamoiselle *Bretigny* had of him ; we therefore agreed he
should seem entirely devoted to her, and as he was determined to remain near the Place to which we were going,
under the pretence of visiting her, we might frequently
meet without Suspicion.

The Return of this Woman put an End to our Discourse, and she having order'd the Postilion to make an
easy Seat, for the Pilgrim behind the Chariot, we all took
our Places, nor stopped any more till we came to a Castle
much finer than the other, to which I was first carried——
this, as I afterward heard, was the Place where my
Father

Father ufually dwelt, the other being one, where he had been only conceal'd during the Time of his Banifhment; my Mother received me with a great deal of Teudernefs, and according to her Commands, and the Inftructions Bretigny had given me, I pafs'd for her Neice, tho' with an Infinity of Conftraint; nothing I think being more difficult or uneafy than to pretend to be what one really is not.

No Age, no Degree, no Humour is exempt from the Power of Love !———Madamoifelle *Bretigny* was a Proof of it———She was not lefs than five and fifty Years old———She had faved Money in the Service of my Mother and Grand-mother——— and the Infidelity of feveral Lovers in her Youth, had made her for a long Time refolved never to think of Marriage; fhe could not however refift the Charms of *Melicourt*, all the Tendernefs of fifteen return'd———fhe figh'd———fhe languifh'd———fhe wifh'd nothing fo much as to infpire him with the fame Defires, and had ftill Vanity enough to flatter herfelf with the Hope of doing fo—— her Thoughts were wholly bent on making his Fortune—— Gratitude in a generous Mind fhe knew would be one great Step to compaffing her Point; and having had a long Converfation with him after fhe came out of the Chariot, and finding he was a Man qualified to look after the Affairs of a Family, fhe promifed to procure him the Stewardfhip of the Caftle; but as there was a Perfon in that Office, fhe told him he muft be content for a little Time to act under him, who by Reafon of his great Age and Infirmities could not hold it long———*Melicourt* propofed too much Satisfaction to himfelf, in being under the fame Roof with me, not to accept joyfully this Offer, and as I find 'tis eafy for Men to counterfeit Tendernefs, whenever they find it agreeable to their Defigns, he fo well acted the Part of a Lover, that fhe imagined herfelf perfectly happy, and refolved to make him fo by giving him her Perfon and Fortune.

Three Weeks paft over fince my coming to the Caftle, all which Time I was continually receiving Leffons for my Behaviour, when I fhould be fent to the Monaftery, which

which was intended as foon as my Father, who was then
at *Fountainbleau* fhould return———*Melicourt* had frequent Opportunities of talking to me, and we bewail'd
together the Fate which threatened us with an eternal
Separation; it was in one of thefe tender Converfations,
that he faid to me, dear *Minetta*, I adore you, I am
certain you have not the leaft Reafon to doubt it———
you tell me I am not indifferent to you, and I fhould be
ungrateful to fufpect your Truth———our Births are
equal, tho' yours is concealed, it is not the lefs certain,
and as for mine it is an Impoffibility to impofe on you——
No difparity obftructs our Union———'Tis Caprice alone,
that would make a Sacrifice of the moft tender Paffion
that ever was———therefore, my Angel, continued he,
preffing my Hands between his, reflect how unhappy
you muft be, when once the fatal Vow is paft, that renders it Sacriledge for you, even to think of me as a
Lover; and how impoffible it would be to avoid falling
into Griefs inexcufable, by the auftre Superior, when
you fhould hear your adoring *Melicourt* had been a Victim
to the Defpair you had occafioned———we have now in
all probability, but a fhort Time, that we can call our
own———Your Father will return, and then you will
be torn for ever from me, all our Wifhes, our Efforts
will then be vain———let us while it yet is in our
power, make fure of our Felicity———let us difappoint
the Views of thefe cruel Parents———and———

How is it poffible, cryed I, interrupting him haftily?
You would not fure harbour a Thought, that I would
give you any Proofs of the Affection I have for you, but
fuch as are confiftent with my Virtue? Far be it from
me, anfwered he, your Honour is mine, and infinitely
dearer to me than my Life; but if you would confent to
come into my Meafures; Fortune now puts it in our
power to avert the Malevolence of our Stars———Oh
let us not neglect it!———Madamoifelle *Bretigny* has for
fome Days paft been preffing me to marry her———
I have till now evaded it by one Pretence or other; but
this Morning it came into my Head, that by feeming to
confent, I fhould have the fure Means of being united
to you———

What

What mean you, said I eagerly, will your promising to be the Husband of *Bretigny*, forward your Espousal with *Minetta* ? either you talk in Riddles, or have some Design unworthy both of me, and of yourself.

I own it has the Appearance of a Mystery, replied he, but I have now no Time for Explanation———I hear somebody coming———I will give you a full Account the next Time we are alone———Adieu———if you love me with the Sincerity you profess, I still flatter myself we shall surmount all Obstacles.

It was my Mother who gave us this Interruption, and finding me alone, began to entertain me on the usual Topick, the Happiness of a Life secluded from the Cares of the World ; but tho' I found she endeavoured to refrain as much as possible all Tokens of a maternal Love, yet it would frequently burst out in spite of her.——— She told me, that my Father was expected that Evening, and that his Arrival would fix the Day of my Departure ———it was in vain, that I testified by Tears my Repugnance, she reminded me that I was not at my own Disposal, and that it was impossible to bring my Circumstances to what I wished, I ought to bring myself to a Conformity with my Circumstances.

At Night, indeed my Father returned from *Fountainbleau*, and when I was going to Bed, Madamoiselle *Bretigny* acquainted me that the ensuing Week, I was to be carried to the Convent : This News was terrible to me, tho' no more than I expected, and as drowning Men are ready to catch hold of every Twig, in hopes of saving themselves, so tho' I had built no great Expectation on what *Melicourt* seemed to have in his Head, yet I longed to know it with the utmost Impatience.

I had no Opportunity of talking to him the next Day, nor was the second more favourable ; but on the Third, meeting me in the Garden, he found means to slip a Note into my Hand, which as soon as I was alone, I opened hastily, and read in it these Lines.

Charmer

Charmer of my Soul,

IF you would preserve yourself and me, from the most terrible Misfortune, that can possibly befal two faithful Hearts, be at the Closet Window, that looks into the Garden this Night after all the Family are in Bed——— I have much to say————and much to hope, if you comply with this Request———without it I am lost for ever———

Yours while I have Life.

There was neither Direction, nor Name to this Billet, which I considered as a Mark of his Discretion, in Case by any Accident it should have fallen into other Hands, than my own. I doubted not but this Assignation was to acquaint me with what my Mother's approach hinder'd him before from telling me, and was as punctual as he could desire. When I opened my Window, I found him standing under it; but how great was my Disappointment, when he cryed I have only Time to say the Passion *Bretigny* has for me at once, both forwards and prevents my Designs———She is coming into the Garden, I had no Way to get rid of her, but she goes out in the Morning on Business, which I am sure she will not neglect———be therefore in the Jessamin Walk behind the Grove, as soon as you find she has left the House———good Night———may pleasing Dreams attend my Charmer.

With these Words he withdrew, and I shut the Window, and went to Bed, not a little vixed at this Delay———after a sleepless Night, one of my Mother's Women came to tell me, her Ladyship would speak with me, on which I went directly to her Apartment————She was sitting at her Toylet in a pensive Posture, leaning her Head upon her Hand, and before she spoke, her Eyes informed me, the Business she had to Impart. She call'd me to her, and having made me sit down on a little Stool, began in this Manner.

You know very well, *Minetta*, said she, who you are, and the abject Manner in which you must have spent your Days, had I not taken a Fancy to you, and commiserated your Condition————I dare answer, that when you kept Sheep, and were exposed to Wind and Rain, to scorching Heats, and freezing Colds, and all other Inclemencies of different Seasons, you have a thousand Times lamented your hard Lot, and wished to be any Thing, but what you were—'Tis I who have taken you from this Misery—received you into my House—cloathed you, and to make you respected, pretended you were even of my own Blood————I do not mention the Favours I have done you by way of Reproach, I believe you deserve I should do yet more for you, but I would have you love me, and be assured that whatever I shall command on your Account is intirely for your Good——in fine, *Minetta*, I am now going to crown all I have done for you, and compleat your Happiness, by fixing you in a Convent————I expect you will think yourself more obliged to this last Testimony of the Kindness I have for you than to all the others————believe me, *Minetta*, pursued she, after a Pause, the World is full of nothing but Disquiets————those who seem most fortunate, have many Things in secret to bewail——every Step we take, every Measure we concert, renders us liable to Disappointments————if you had more Experience, you would see the Truth of what I tell you, in a thousand Instances————Marriage above all Things with Persons of mean Birth and Fortune, entails a Train of Wretchedness, even tho' you were not to fall into bad Hands——a Cloyster is a secure Asylum from Woes of every Kind, and when you have once brought yourself to be satisfied with it, you will look down with Pity on the fleeting Pleasures, the vain Hopes, and the eternal Hurries of People who continue their Attachment to the World——if a Grate looks frightful at the first, Custom will make it agreeable————one cannot but in such a Retreat ever come to a true Knowledge of one self, and without that can be no perfect Happiness, either here or hereafter.

Some

Some indeed there are, who are compelled to take the Veil, and others, who out of a present Pique to the World, threw themselves suddenly into a Convent, still carrying about them the Restlessness they in vain go there to avoid——these indeed cannot live easy, because under an Engagement they repent, would fain break through, but never can——you, my dear *Minetta*, will have nothing to regret——the Innocence and Simplicity of your Youth and Inclinations leaves your Heart at liberty to entertain those pure Ideas which befit the sacred Order ——you will be able to taste all the Charms of it, I will often visit you to partake and envy your Happiness.

As she spoke these last Words, I could perceive the Tears came into her Eyes, but she turned her Head away to conceal her Disorder as much as possible—— Ah, Madam, cry'd I; quite transported at this Effect of her Tenderness, what has your unhappy Child done, that you should resolve to Sacrifice her? These Words escaped me in spite of myself——and she looked on me with so much Kindness, that I believe had I taken the Advantage of that favourable Minute, Nature would have got the better of the Law, she had imposed on herself, not to trust me with the Secret of my Birth——. I durst not however presume to go any farther, and only threw myself at her Feet, and while I kiss'd her Hands looked up in her Face with Eyes streaming with Tears.

In this Posture, I remained some Time, the Agitation of both our Minds, neither permitting her to raise me, nor me to remove; at length, rise, *Minetta*, said she, embracing me, you are indeed my Child——I have in a manner adopted you as such——and I love you with perhaps more Affection than the Person to whom you have all along paid the Duty of a Child——when you are a Nun you will know that I am a Mother to you.

The Name of Nun struck me to the Heart, and finding she persisted in the Resolution of making me one, stifled the late Emotions of filial Tenderness, and enabled me to act with Caution, and as the more I seemed averfe to enter into that State, the more Care would be taken to prevent any Meafures I might attempt to fhield myfelf from it, I teftified no farther repugnance, but behaved afterwards with fo much Serenity, that it was impoffible for her to fee what pafs'd in my Heart.

People coming in upon Bufinefs, I took that Oppertunity of retiring to my Chamber, and there poured out the Anguifh of my Mind, in Tears and Lamentations————I was in this forrowful Employment when I efpied *Melicourt* alone in the Garden————the Family I knew were at that Time taken up with houfehold Affairs, fo I dried my Eyes as well as I could, and went down to meet him. He no fooner faw me at a Diftance, than he made hafte towards me, with an Air of Gaiety in his Countenance, that I could not help refenting, as ill befitting the Condition of a Lover, juft going to lofe his Miftrefs forever.

I expreffed my Thoughts to him on this Head pretty tartly, and told him I fhould leave the World with lefs Regret, fince I found it would be no Affliction to him ————Ah! beautiful *Minetta*, cryed he, interrupting me, with the moft tender and paffionate Look; how little do you know me!————if I appear eafy, it is becaufe I flatter myfelf, that a very little Time will lay you under Engagemeuts widely different from thofe they Defign for you————Yes, my deareft, purfued he, the Time is near at Hand to join us in Bonds indiffoluble but by Death————*Bretigny* has fent to a Prieft, who is her near Relation, and lives about two Leagues hence, to come hither under the Pretence of vifiting her; this holy Man is to perform the Ceremony, as fhe imagines, between me and herfelf; but it is you, my Angel, muft fupply her Place————Gold will do any Thing———— I have been privately to fee him————I have gained him to my Party, and inftead of marrying me tomorrow to *Bretigny*, he will this Night make me the Hufband of *Minetta*.

As much as I loved *Melicourt*, and how terrible foever a Cloyfter appeared to me, this clandeftine Marriage was what I could not relifh: Young and inexperienced as I

was,

was, the ill Confequences of fuch a Union glared me
full in the Face————He faw into my Thoughts, and
began to reproach me for want of that Affection I pro-
feffed ; but I foon convinced him that it was rather
owing to excefs of what he Thought me deficient in, than
the contrary, that I did not immediately accept his Propofal————What can become of us, anfwered I, after
fuch a Marriage————will your Parents admit of me
for their Daughter, without any other Fortune, than the
Difficulties mine may involve them in ?————Will not
your difpofing yourfelf in this manner, ruin you with
them——fhall we not both be expofed to all the Miferies
of Poverty, if once it is known what we have done, and if
it be kept a Secret, what will it avail, I fhall then, notwithftanding my Engagements to you, be forced as now
into a Monaftery ?————So my dear *Melicourt*, continued I, I find nothing in this Stratagem in the leaft
flattering to our Hopes.

As my Arguments were unanfwerable, by Reafon he
had nothing to alledge, but what Paffion infpired, which
he did in fo moving a Manner, that I confefs to you,
my dear *Jeanetta*, I was wholly overcome, and yielded
to run all hazards with him. On this we parted, and I
withdrew to reflect on the Promife I had made.

At firft, I gave myfelf up wholly to Love, and the
Profpect of endearing Joys of mutual Affection ; but foon
thefe fweet Ideas vanifh'd, and I began to tremble at the
Wretchednefs, fo deftitute a Pair as we in all probability
muft be, fhould be reduced to————all the Woes of
Poverty, of Contempt, came ftrong upon my Mind——
but above all the Remembrance that I had often heard it
faid, that Men, tho' the moft paffionate Adorers before,
grow Cool, Peevifh, and Unkind, when once the Storms
of adverfe Fortune difturb the Serenity of Love————
the bare Imagination that *Melicourt* might one Day be
of this Number was fhocking, and gave a Damp to my
warmeft Wifhes in Favour of what he defired of me——
in fine, I refolved to talk to him once more on this Subject, and be either fully convinced that no Misfortunes
would be able to leffen the Refpect he now had for me,

or else to retract the Promise I had made⸺a Nunnery disagreeable as it was to me, being yet less so, than to be ill treated by the Man I loved.

With this View I went into the Garden, believing he might still be there; but not finding him, I repaired to Madamoiselle *Bretigny*'s Chamber, then to a Gallery where he frequently amused himself, either with looking on the Pictures, or with some Book or other, he being seldom without one in his Pocket⸺in fine I left no Place about the House where there was the least Probability of seeing him, unsearched; but all this without Success⸺ I was uneasy at missing him, tho' I knew not why, my Heart fluttered, and presaged too truly some ill Accident at hand⸺I wandered at length into a Meadow adjacent to the Road, which led towards the Village, and no sooner came in Sight of it, than I beheld the Man, I had so vainly sought for, my dear *Melicourt* defending himself against four Men, who endeavoured to force him into a Chaise⸺He struggled but in vain ⸺their Strength overpowered him⸺he saw me, and gave a great Cry⸺I shriek'd and spread my Hands to Heaven; but my Prayers like his Efforts were fruitless⸺the Chaise drove on, and in a Moment he was out of Sight⸺I continued my Lamentations till I had no longer Breath, and happy was it for me, that no Persons were within reach of the Clamour I made; at last ashamed of what I had done, and confounded with what I had seen, I returned to the Castle, where the first Person I met was *Bretigny*, they were going to Supper, and had been in Search of me: She had an Air of Gaiety in her Countenance, which immediately vanish'd, on my telling her what had happened⸺ My God! cryed she, in a Sort of a distracted Voice, what can be the Meaning of this? —Who has any Power over him?—What has he done?⸺O! I am ruined; I will tell you the Reason another Time⸺go and sit down to Table, while I run to the Village, to try if I can get any Information⸺No, continued she, you are in Tears, poor good-natured Creature, you shall rather go along with me, and I'll acquaint you with the Cause of my Concern, for this Pilgrim.   With

With thefe Words fhe took me under the Arm, and we both went as faft as we could towards the *Cabára,* before which the Scene had been acted. The People of the Houfe refpecting Madamoifelle *Bretigny,* as a Perfon who managed every thing in my Father's Family, readily anfwered to all the Queftions fhe afked.

About four Days fince, faid the Mafter of the Houfe, a Gentleman came to lodge here, he had three Men with him, who I thought at firft had been his Attendants, and indeed I looked upon him as an Officer come hither to raife Recruits————the firft things he enquired after was, who was the Lord of the Village; how they lived at the Caftle; what Family there was of you; and if any Strangers were with you at this Time;————you know, Madam, purfued he, it is my Bufinefs to oblige every body, fo I gave him as full an Account as I could. He fpared no Expence for himfelf nor thofe with him; but what furprized me very much was, that he eat with them, and inftead of going in and out as Gentlemen ufually do to fee about them, when they are in ftrange Places, he never ftirr'd out of his Chamber, nor did any belonging to him go out, but one at a Time; and when they returned, gave an Account of what they had been doing only in a Whifper; if myfelf or any of my People happened to be in the Room. In this manner they went on till juft now, without my troubling myfelf about it, as they paid me well for what they had.

About an Hour ago, purfued he, him whom I took for the Mafter, came into my Kitchen, which he had never done before, and faid aloud to one of his People, go to that young Man you told me of, and let him know that a Perfon here would be glad to fpeak one Word with him; on this he went out, and immediately came back with Monfieur *Brunet.*

Brunet, continued the lovely Nun, was the Name my dear *Melicourt* affumed, and was diftinguifhed by at the Caftle, but to go on————the poor young Man, faid the Hoft, little imagined what was prepared for him, while the Meffenger was going for him, the Gentleman call'd me to him, and afked if I had any Intimacy with the

Perfon

Person he had sent for? On which I answered, no Monsieur, I only know he has lately entered into the Service of the Lord of this Manor, and is very much esteemed and beloved by all the Family; I believe as much, replied he, but they must lose him————therefore let the Chaise and Horses be brought before the Door immediately; for we shall take him away. Alas, Monsieur, cryed I, I hope he has been guilty of no criminal Action?————none but what will be easily forgiven, answered he, but to prevent your being alarmed I will let you into the Secret————He is the only Son of Monsieur De————Counsellor of the Parliament of *M*————and on some Project or other has quitted his Father's House, without leave, or indeed knowledge either of him or any of his Friends————nor could all the search we have been able to make prove successful till Monsieur *De R*————Lord of *Bisse* saw him here by Accident, and wrote a Letter to his Father; whose Valet de Chambre, I am, and sent with full Authority to force him hence if he offers to oppose the Will of him who gave him Being.

He had scarce spoke these Words, when the young Man came in, he presently knew this Domestick, and turned pale as Death; the other perceiving it, said come, Monsieur, take Courage, no ill is intended to you, unless you think it such to return to a Father, and a Mother whom your strange absenting yourself has brought almost to the Gates of Death. I know not whether this was heard or not by the Person to whom it was addressed, for he made no Answer to it, but took him that spoke by the Collar, and throwing him down had infallibly made his Escape, if the others seeing what was done had not seized him————He struggled hard, and in spite of all they could do got through the outer Court, and into the Road; but the Valet being by this Time recovered, joined his Assistants, and at last forced him into the Chaise which was ready waiting.

Here the Host concluded his Narration, and poor *Bretigny* was so confounded at what she heard, that she left the House without speaking one Word————when

we

we were alone, she fell into a Flood of Tears, I accompanied her in all the Demonstrations she gave of a perfect Grief, on which she embraced me with great Affection, imagining my Tears were the Effect of Pity for her Misfortune. She gave me however a Caution not to shew any Concern before the Family, to the End that when this Adventure came to be known, they might not suspect it related any way to her.

Three Days after this cruel Accident, which I passed as you may easily believe in Agnoies scarce to be supported, my Mother brought me hither, where I was received with all imaginable Kindness, and nothing omitted that might engage me to take the Veil, when my Year of Probation should be expired : The melancholly Air I carried with me, and which they know not the Motive of, made them with Reason suppose I had no Inclination to a monastic Life, which was too contrary to their Interest, as they expected a Portion with me, for them not to make use of their utmost Efforts to change. Liberty being a Thing desired by every one, they suffered me to go into the Parlour, whenever I would, without any of the Sisterhood to accompany me, or listen to the Discourses I had with those who came to visit me————tho' I must do them the justice to say, I do not believe they would have thus left me to myself, had they in the least suspected I had any thoughts of Love or Man.

Madamoiselle *Bretigny* came two or three Times a Day to weep with me, and told me she intended to go to M————to inform herself what was become of her dear Pilgrim ; alas, she little thought how much I languished to hear News of him ; nor did I flatter myself with enjoying ever that Happiness, unless by her Means, but what we least expect is often nearest at Hand.

One Day as I was walking in the Garden alone and meditating on my unhappy Fate, the Sister who attended the Gate told me, there was a young Officer, who called himself my near Relation, waited for me in the Parlor ————I was surprised and pleased, I had no Kindred, who would acknowledge me as such, nor knew any Man,

who

who should enquire for me, except one commissioned by my Lover, I went therefore, or rather flew to the Parlor, where I was immediately saluted with a Voice too well known, and too dear to me to be forgotten.——It was *Melicourt* himself————O Heavens! cried I in a Transport, it is you then————it is you!————I had Power to say no more, but came close to the Grate, and put forth my Hand, he seized it with an eager Joy—— he kissed it————he wetted it with Tears of Rapture ————my Senses were too weak to bear the Effusion of the mingled Passions, which at that Instant crowded into my Heart————I fainted away————he threw himself upon his Knees————he called to me, ————he wept ————he said a thousand tender Things ; but I neither heard nor saw in what manner he behaved.

The amiable Nun was in this Part of her History, when she was interrupted by one of the Sisterhood, who told us they waited for us in the Refectory ; on which we arose and went down, after agreeing to pass the Afternoon together in my Cell.

I cannot give any Description of that modest and tranquil Air with which thirty Nuns set down at their Meal, I was too much taken up with my own Affairs, to regard any thing, but what related immediately to them, or if I was obliged to give an Account of that pious Lecture, which was made before we rose from Table, I should find myself very much at a loss————the most pleasing Sound I heard, was the Bell, that Madame the Superior rung, as a Signal to say Grace, after which we all retired to our respective Apartments, and *Saint Agnes* and myself being shut up in my Chamber, she resumed the History of her Misfortunes in these Words.

The End of the T H I R D P A R T.

T H E

THE
VIRTUOUS VILLAGER,
OR,
VIRGIN's VICTORY.

PART. IV.

A Continuation of the History of SAINT
AGNES *and* MELICOURT.

AS the little Faintneſs I had been ſeiz'd
with, was occaſion'd only by an Exceſs
of Joy at the unexpected Sight of my
Lover, I ſoon came to myſelf; and the
firſt Uſe I made of my recover'd Senſes,
was to aſk by what Means he had eſcap'd
out of his Father's Hands: Are you ſo little acquainted with my Tenderneſs, ſaid he, as to be one Moment in doubt, if I would not break through every
thing to ſee you.————No, my deareſt, *Minetta*, were

every

every Star in the Firmament, as oppofite as at prefent they feem favourable to my Intentions, not Fate itfelf fhould have the Power to fhake my Conftancy—my inviolable Attachment, and if you have the fame Sentiments as I—if? cry'd I, haftily interrupting him, is the Love I have for you now to be call'd in Queftion?————Are not the Griefs I have endur'd in your Abfence, and the vifible Alteration they have made in my Looks a fufficient Demonftration how dear you are to me ?

Melicourt feem'd as much tranfported at this Declaration, as tho' it had been the firft Confeffion of Love I had ever made him, and teftified his Gratitude in Terms the moft delicate and touching————I could have liften'd to him all Day; fo true is it that while a beloved Lover fpeaks his Paffion, one's very Soul hangs on his Lips; and nothing but the Impatience I was in to hear, by what Miracle I now enjoy'd his Prefence, could have made me interrupt fo delightful an Entertainment. ————I began by telling him the prefent Situation of my Affairs, and added, that as I was now in a Convent, there appear'd, but little Probability of ever my converfing with him, but as at this time behind a Grate.

Yes, yes, cry'd he, with the utmoft Vivacity, I fhall foon fet you free from this cruel Confinement, and by a way more warrantable and conformable to your own Delicacy, than that I propos'd before our Separation;——but, to prepare you for the Tidings I am fo fortunate to bring you; 'tis fit I make you an exact Detail of all that happen'd fince my being torn from you in the Fafhion you were Witnefs of.

You cannot doubt, adorable *Minetta*, continued he, of my Defpair when all the Efforts I could make, were ineffectual againft thofe who feiz'd upon me————fo violent was my Fury, that the Valet de Chamber, and all thofe who affifted him, trembled even at my very Looks, and repented their having undertaken that Office ————during the whole Journey, I did nothing but curfe, vow Revenge, and meditate Means for getting out of their Hands; but all in vain, their Strength and Vigilance difappointed every Scheme I laid: I then refolv'd to ftarve myfelf to Death, and refus'd taking the leaft Nourifhment of any kind whatfoever————in this Condition, I was brought to my Father, who being inform'd of my Behaviour, and how determin'd I was not to live, chang'd the Conduct he propos'd to obferve toward me, and inftead of Rigour treated me with the greateft Sweetnefs; but as I feem'd indolent and unaffected with his Goodnefs, and continu'd obftinate not to eat or drink, till I faw myfelf at liberty.————He then us'd all poffible Means to conftrain me to it; but Force or Perfuafions were alike fruitlefs; four Days pafs'd over without my fwallowing any thing, and on the fourth I was feiz'd with a violent Fever.

I could not hear thefe Marks of his Sincerity without interrupting the Courfe of his Narration, by letting him know how deeply I was affected with them; he told me that were he capable of fuffering infinitely more, he fhould glory in it, and would facrifice ten thoufand Lives for the Pleafure of being pitied by me————after many other fuch like Expreffions, which a perfect Love infpires, and thofe poffefs'd of that Paffion are never wanting in, he refum'd his Difcourfe.

When my Father, faid he, was convinc'd by the Condition he faw me in, that my Life was really in Danger, for he had till now believ'd, that they had privately given me fomewhat to eat, he began to be in the utmoft Perplexity.————Paternal Tendernefs reviv'd in him;————he took me by the Hand————he even condefcended to entreat I would not make the remainder of his Days miferable, by the lofs of a Son, whom he had always look'd on with the greateft Affection; promifing me at the fame time, that if I would confent to take things proper for the Recovery of my Health, he would leave me at liberty to go wherever I pleas'd: As I knew him a Man utterly incapable of Deceit, thefe Words loft nothing of their Weight; and I affur'd him in my turn of a perfect Obedience to his Will, in all things in my power; and as the firft Proof took a little Cordial prepar'd for me in his Prefence. The whole Houfe was overjoy'd at this Change in me;

my

my Mother who had been continually in Tears since my Arrival, threw herself by me on the Bed, and embraced me with Transports, which shew'd how dear I was to her; she confirm'd over and over the Promise made me by my Father, and added she would contribute all she could toward giving me all the Satisfaction I wish'd. I cannot but acknowledge, and, indeed, should have been unworthy of this Goodness had I acted otherwise, than I did; I was sensibly touch'd with these Tokens of Love from those who gave me Being.————They were, however, failing in their End————long fasting had spoiled the Temperament of my Blood————my Stomach was unable to perform its Faculty of Digestion————my Head was disorder'd————all my Frame out of its wonted Tone; and I grew so ill, that for two Days my Life was despair'd of.

Tho' in that time I was wholly insensible of the Grief my Danger occasion'd, I might easily judge of it, by the Excess of Joy which appear'd in every Face, on the first Appearance of my Re-establishment.————I mended, however, very slowly, and my Mother who never left my Chamber, and observ'd my every Motion, was divided between Hopes and Fears, till at the End of fifteen Days, the Physicians who attended me, pronounced there was not the least Symptons of a Relapse.

As soon as I found myself able to hold a long Conversation; the Complaisance and Tenderness with which my Mother treated me, gave me Courage to make her a full Confession of the Motives, which had at first induced me to quit my Studies————the Passion I had for you————the kind Return you were pleas'd to make me————the History of your Birth, and the unhappy Circumstance that threatned us with an eternal Separation. ———— In fine, I made a Recital of the whole Progress of our Loves and Disappointments ; adding that tho' no Distemper should seize me, or Grief should fail to kill me, my full Resolution was not to survive the Day, in which you should be compell'd to take the Veil. Pardon me, continu'd he, my forever

dear

dear *Minetta*, that without your Permission I reveal'd
the Secrets of your Heart and Extraction: I knew no
other way to gain a Mother, by whose Favour I hop'd
great things——the Event, my Angel, as you shall presently hear, has answer'd my Wishes!——She listen'd
to me with Astonishment, mix'd with Compassion, but
no Signs of Displeasure; and when I had done, told
me it was necessary my Father should be made acquainted
with an Affair, which in my Person was of so much
Consequence to him; but bid me be under no Apprehensions, for she would reveal it to him in such a manner, as
should prepossess him in behalf of my Desires. I durst
not oppose what she said, and she went that Moment to
my Father, who was yet more amaz'd at the Relation
she made him, than herself had been on hearing it from
me. He came running into my Chamber, and would
know all the Circumstances from my own Mouth——
I obey'd him as well as I could, and he seem'd perfectly satisfied.——He told me he would that Instant
examine into the Affair of your Birth; and if there
were sufficient Proofs of it, he would consent with Pleasure to our Union; and had the Goodness to add with
a Smile, that as by what I had suffer'd he guess'd my
Impatience, he would return with all possible Expedition.

Judge of the Joy I felt, charming *Minetta*, at this
Readiness, with which both my Parents agreed to my
Desires, and how much I thought myself indebted to a
Father, from whose Mouth, never any thing but Truth
proceeded.——I would have thrown myself at his
Feet to acknowledge, as I ought, the wondrous Consideration he had for me; but he would not permit me,
saying the best return I could make to his Affection,
was to endeavour as much as depended on myself a perfect Recovery of my former Health and Gaiety; with
these Words he went out of the Chamber, and there was
little room to doubt, if I would be obedient to his Commands; the earnest Desire I had to see you, and to acquaint you with these things, made me omit nothing
that might put me in a Condition to travel.

In

In the mean time, my dear Father, for I muſt call him ever ſo, Source of my firſt and ſecond Life, was more induſtrious to render me ſatisfied, than even his Words had made me hope————he ſearch'd the Records ———— he conſider'd the Proofs ———— he added to his own great Judgment in the Laws, that of conſulting others, the moſt eminent of their Profeſſion, all concurr'd that the Right was on your ſide, and that you ought to be publickly declar'd the Daughter of Monſieur *De*————; but while you remain'd under the power of your Parents, it would be in vain, and therefore not adviſeable for any one to undertake your Cauſe; ————you ought therefore to remove yourſelf to ſome Place where you might be at Liberty, to follow the Dictates of your Inclination; and that if you married, the Right you had, being transferr'd to your Huſband, he would be entitled to ſue for, what they might elſe deprive you of, by compelling you to relinquiſh the World. In fine, purſued he, nothing can be done while you continue in a Virgin State.

Theſe Words were an Oracle to me, I preſently comprehended the Senſe of them, and communicating my Sentiments on that Occaſion to my Preceptor, who I knew was perfectly acquainted with my Father's Views; he told me that my Conjectures had not deceiv'd me: ————That nothing in reality could be more agreeable to him, than an Alliance with the Daughter of Monſieur *De*————, and adviſ'd me to go immediately, and endeavour to prevail on you to become my Wife; and that accompliſh'd, to bring you to my Father's Houſe, where he ſaid he was very certain, you would be receiv'd with open Arms. To eſtabliſh me in the Opinion, that he alledg'd nothing that he would not maintain, he offer'd to accompany me to the Village, and wait there with the reſt of my Retinue, till I ſhould get an Opportunity of ſpeaking to you at the Caſtle. There needed not half of what he urg'd, to make me do what I ſo earneſtly long'd for————accordingly we ſet out together, and arriv'd at the Village; but how great was my Diſappointment, when I was told the Neice of Madam *De*————

De————was convey'd to a Convent————By the help
of a very artful Fellow I have with me; however, I
soon found where you were placed, and flew directly hither, to tell you that it now depends on you alone, to
make me the most happy, or the most wretched of
Mankind,

Give me then, continu'd he, the Proof of that Affection you have so often charm'd me with—if you truly love
me, you will not hesitate one Moment to put yourself
into my Hands, to give me your Vows, and to receive
mine, and then to permit me to conduct you to a Father,
capable and willing to instruct us, in what we ought to do
in our present Situation; and to a Mother more tender,
and already, by what I have told her of you, more
sensible of your Merit, than she who gave you Birth,
and yet abandons you to a Fate, the most disagreeable to
you.

Melicourt here left off speaking, and fix'd his Eyes
upon me with an undescribable Tenderness, expecting my
Reply; but I was too much perplex'd to make an immediate one————what a strange Medley of Ideas run
thro' a Virgin's Heart, when press'd to give an Answer
on the like Occasion!————He easily guess'd the Situation of my Mind, and laid before me the strongest
and most moving Reasons————he represented to me
with a great deal of Wit and Eloquence, the little Regard my Parents had for me————he made me sensible that they were going to sacrifice me to a sordid View
————in fine, that I was lost, if I did not assume a
speedy and vigorous Resolution.————That I should
shortly be oblig'd to take the Veil, and that my Profession would soon after ensue, and that once over,
there was no longer any Hopes.————To this he added
many things to convince me, how barbarously I was
treated for the sake of a Sister, who ought to be no dearer
than myself————this rous'd that Resentment in me,
which I believe all People have some share of more or less,
when they are causelesly ill us'd, which together with
my Love determin'd me; retire, my dear *Melicourt*,
said I, lest too long a Conversation should render us

I   suspected,

suspected, and by being so, disappoint all our Views:
————Be here again To-morrow at this time, I will
then give a final Answer, and tho' I am not yet quite resolv'd, I fancy it will be such a one as you will have no
Cause to be dissatisfied with: I spoke these Words with
a Smile, and he departed very well pleas'd, after kissing
my Hand in the most affectionate manner thro' the
Grate.

I went back to my Cell after he was gone, in a good
deal of inward Agitation————the Aversion I had to
become a Nun, made me rejoice in having a warrantable Means of avoiding that Life; but on the other
Hand there appear'd Difficulties which I knew not how
to surmount————notwithstanding the Meanness of my
Education, the Pride of Blood had high Dominion over
my Mind, and inspired me with the most elevated Notions; conscious of what I was, not only a Cloister, but
even Death itself, seem'd less terrible, than being guilty
of any Action unworthy of my Birth; and I could not
find Arguments to convince myself, that to quit a Convent
where I was placed by those, who at present had the sole
Power of disposing me; and follow a young Man, who,
perhaps, was blinded by his Passion, was not a Trans-
gression of the Rules of Honour and of Decency. But,
then the Love I had for *Melicourt*, the Proofs he had
given me of his Passion————the Vow he had made not
to survive the Hour of my being initiated, together with
the Dread I had of entring into a State, where I could
not be allow'd to look back, on the tender Moments of
mutual Affection; nor even to think on the dear Man,
without being guilty of Sacrilege, all this balanc'd against
the other, and I remain'd in the most cruel Uncertainty for a long time.

At last Love grew most prevailing, as I believe it will
always be, when Virtue and Merit in the Object renders it worthy of that Name; I thought myself excusa-
ble in disobeying the Will of those who gave me Being as
they disclaim'd me for their Daughter—the Advantages
propos'd to me by *Melicourt*, appear'd such as were not
to be slighted.————I had Parents, but they permitted

me

me not to call them fo; I was offer'd others who would gladly receive me as their Child.————I had now no Name nor Family; in accepting *Melicourt* for a Huf-band, I fhould have both, and not inferior to thofe which of Right belong'd to me, fo I entirely yielded to thefe laft Confiderations, and began to fet myfelf in ear-neft to contrive fome way to get out of the Con-vent.

Love, ingenious in Invention, foon infpired me with an expedient, which from the Moment it came into my Head, flatter'd me with Hopes of Succefs: The Portrefs was extremely affable and good-natur'd, fhe had taken a great liking to me; and we were as intimate as any two People could be, that did not place fo great a Con-fidence in each other as to reveal their Secrets. Her Em-ployment engaging her in many Affairs, I fometimes of-ficiated for her at the Gate.————The Keys was always hung up in the Parlour, and the Grate open'd into a Room belong'd to the outward Portrefs, fo as I knew all the ways about the Houfe, I took my Meafures ac-cordingly.

It is not to be doubted but *Melicourt* was punctual to his Appoinment, I told him the Contrivance I had form'd of ftealing the Keys, and getting out the firft Op-portunity I found the Portrefs abfent————he feem'd fearful I fhould be furpriz'd in the Execution; the Con-fequence of which would be, that I fhould either be ftrictly watch'd or remov'd to fome other Place; he, there-fore, judg'd it moft proper, I fhould attempt making my Efcape in the Night; but I convinced him of the Impoffibility of that, becaufe according to the Rule of the Houfe, the Portrefs always brought the Keys of the In-clofure into the Superior's Chamber————it was, there-fore, agreed between us, that he fhould be ready with a Chaife, and the beft Horfes that could be got, and wait at a little Diftance from the Gate of the Convent, the next Morning at the Hour of Matins————fo having fettled every thing he took his leave.

I was too full of what I was about to do, for any Sleep to enter my Eyes that Night; the Thing that appear'd so feasible in Theory, was difficult enough to put in Practice, nor could it ever have been done, had I been in the least suspected by any of the Convent: It had always been my Custom to rise late, and to please me they indulged me in it, so I was not expected at the Morning Devotions———I was now up however, but kept close in my Cell, 'till I heard the Mother Portress pass by—I knew her Step, and as soon as she was gone to the Choir, I ran into the Parlour, and found the Keys in their Place, I took them off the Hook, and open'd the Door of the Inclosure; 'tis well for me I had the Presence of Mind to shut it after me, for if I had not, I should infallibly have been stopped by an old Lay Sister, who hapned to be there, and calling out to know who was at the Door, rang the Bell to alarm the Convent on my not answering.

The Street-Door had a very difficult Lock, and I was so long endeavouring to get it open, that on the Sound of the Bell several Nuns ran to the Window, and seeing what I was about, cryed out for Assistance; happily for me no body was passing by at that Time, and *Melicourt* being on the Watch, and hearing a Fumbling at the Lock, used his utmost Efforts on the outside to force it open, but in vain, the Gate was impregnable, and all our Hopes had been frustrated, had I not that Instant bethought myself of making Use of the other Key I had in my Hand, in Order to turn that which was in the Lock ——— this effected it, and the Gate flew open———I threw myself into my Lover's Arms, and scream'd out for perfect Joy. The Nuns who saw all this from above, and were desperately enraged at my Flight, redoubled their Cries in such a Manner that we could hear them at a great Distance; we drove on with the utmost Expedition the whole Day, without once stopping to take any Refreshment, 'till we came to a *French* Village, where we were in no Danger of being taken; the Preceptor of whom *Melicourt* spoke, waited for us at this Place, and having prepared the Curate beforehand, it was given out that he intended to say Mass the next Morning by Break of Day, and under that Pretence

we

we were married in the Presence of four Peasants, who served as Witnesses, and sign'd a Marriage Certificate, ready drawn up for that Purpose———after this we set forward on our Journey with mutual Satisfaction; all my Scruples being now over, I was very well pleased to accompany a Husband whom I loved, and whom to obey, was reconciling my Duty with my Inclination.

The Valet de Chambre who was on Horseback, went before us to apprize the Parents of *Melicourt* of all that had happened, and on our Arrival, I was received with a Kindness which made me forget the Vexations I had past————I was treated by them both with the same Tenderness as a real Daughter, and with a Respect superior even to my Birth————all the House were industrious to oblige me, and I thought I should have been ungrateful to Heaven, if I had not been perpetually acknowledging the happy Change of my Fate.————But alas! how cruel a Reverse was soon my Lot————this short Tranquillity was succeeded by the most dreadful Tempest, which shipwreck'd all my Hopes for ever, and plunged me into an Abyss of eternal Misery.————My Husband's Father who was impatient to have me acknowledg'd for what I was, not only that the World might see his Son had not demean'd himself by my Alliance, but also on the Score of that great Estate to which I was Coheiress with my Sister, when my Birth should be confirm'd, set himself about drawing up a Remonstrance from the Instructions I had given him, and as there was a Necessity it should be corroborated by substantial Witnesses; he went to the Gardener and his Wife, with whom I had been brought up as their Daughter, and that he might the easier come at the Truth, pretended he came from Madam *De*————and gave them Money which he said was sent by that Lady, as a Recompence for the Care they had taken of me. He took two Persons with him of Reputation, who were present during all the Conversation he had with these People, and whose Testimonies could not be suspected.

My pretended Parents mistrusting nothing, and supposing the Father of *Melicourt* to be a Dependant of

Monsieur

Monfieur and Madam *De*————went not about to difguife any Thing of an Affair he feem'd as well acquainted
with as themfelves: When he had gain'd as perfect a
Satisfaction from them as he wifh'd he threw off the
Character of Steward to my Mother, which he had affumed to draw the Secret from them, and fhewed himfelf
what he truly was, Counfellor to the Parliament of
M————and Commiffioner of the Jufticiary Court, and
obliged them to fign what they had in Words acknowledged, that I was none of their Child, but the Daughter of Madam *De*————and when this Form was com-
plyed with, he returned Home very well pleafed with
the Succefs of his Journey.

The Gardener and his Wife finding by this, that they
had been impofed upon, and fearful that the Confeffion
they had made, fhould draw on them the Refentment
of my Parents, no fooner faw themfelves at Liberty, than
they went to the Caftle, and acquainted my Mother with
what had happen'd, as thinking if they had unwarily
done amifs, the beft Attonement they could make was an
immediate Confeffion, which might perhaps prevent any
ill Confequences arifing from their Inadvertency.

They were in the right fo far, for my Father who had
been immediately inform'd of my Flight from the Monaftery, and was in the utmoft Diftraction to know
where or with whom I had withdrawn myfelf, being
now Mafter of that important Secret took his Meafures
accordingly, to fatisfy his own Defigns, and compleat the
eternal Ruin of his unhappy Child. He went directly
to Court, and formed a Complaint againft both my Hufband, and felf, fo efficacious, that he obtain'd from the
King a full Grant of all he defired on this Occafion.

My Hufband's Father in the mean Time believing he
had done all things for the beft, fent me with my dear
Melicourt to an Eftate he had about fix Miles diftant from
the Town; where imagining we had now efcaped all the
Rocks that threaten'd our Love, and reached the happy
Port, we indulged ourfelves in all the Delights, that
could be expected in fuch a Situation.

He

He thinking, however, that it would be proper to lie quiet for a Time, and not divulge our Marriage 'till obliged to it, happen'd of the most dreadful Consequence that could be ; indeed my little Judgment represented such a Conduct as entirely wrong, tho' as he was a Man of the highest Reputation for understanding the Laws, I durst not offer any thing in Opposition to what he did ; but the Event convinc'd him, too fatally for *Melicourt*, and myself, that our worst Enemies could not have acted more cruelly.

One Night as we were sleeping in our Bed, we were disturb'd by several of the Servants running into our Chamber, who with Tears in their Eyes told us we were undone, that the Castle was full of Soldiers, and the Officer who commanded them said they came in the King's Name————they had scarce Time to warn us of the Danger, before two Exempts appear'd, and signified their Orders to us————my dear Husband would have defended himself and me, but what was his Strength when oppos'd to twenty Men————I sent forth the most piteous Cries————I knelt, I wept, but nothing mollifyed these Barbarians————they tore me from the Arms of *Melicourt*, where I had thrown myself in the Extremity of my Anguish, and where they conveyed him, or what they did with him I never could learn ; but me they brought directly hither, where the first Persons that presented themselves before me were my Father and Mother—the most violent Fury sparkled in the Eyes of the one, and those of the other were full of Tears : Wretch ! cryed he, you have done well to fly in the Faces of those who raised you from Beggary, and to have Resource to Calumny in Order to become a Libertine— Vile Creature ! nothing remains for you now but to take the Habit to-morrow, or resolve to perish : In speaking these Words he pluck'd a Dagger from his Side, and menacing me with it, regard what I say to you, resumed he, and chearfully comply with what I ordain for you, or be assured you shall find in me no longer a Protector but an Executioner :————He added no more, but having push'd me before him to the inner Gate of the Inclosure

closure, where the Abbess attended to receive me, whisper'd something in her Ear, and then went out with my Mother, who I perceived was once about to speak to me, but he made a Sign to her to forbear.

I will not trouble you with the Repetition of the Reproaches made me by the Superior, for having as she said brought the Convent into Disgrace, by flying from it with a young Man ; I will only tell you, that she greatly added to the Disquiets of my Mind, by treating me in the worst and most unkind Manner she possibly could——She was for ever filling my Ears with Remonstrances, that the best Way for me was to pay a blind Obedience to what Monsieur *De*————enjoyn'd, for he would otherwise have no Mercy on me————and that when I was once profess'd, she would take such Measures as should compel me to look with Detestation, and Remorse on my past Life————what could she have said more, had I abandoned myself to Shame and Wickedness, yet I was obliged to listen to it without daring to utter a Word in my own Justification————I passed that Night and the next Day in Horrors which you may more easily conceive than I describe, and on the ensuing one, took the Veil.

I could not forbear interrupting the lovely Nun in this Part of her Story ; but, dear *St. Agnes,* said I, why did you not loudly declare your Marriage, and oppose your first Vows to those they now imposed upon you.

Ah ! do you think I did not, answer'd she, but what avail'd it————they knew very well I was married and to whom————Religion has no Pity in Societies such as these, when Interest is concern'd————they told me my Nuptials were illegal, without Consent of my Friends——that the Rites so solemnized were no better than Folly and Madness————that I but stole myself away from those whose Property I was, and now they had recover'd me might dispose, of me as they pleased——these, my dear *Jeanetta,* were all the Answers I could obtain, and I had no Friend to espouse my Cause————my Husband, if alive, ignorant, as were all his Family to what Place I was

carried

carried————the whole Year of my Noviceſhip, I was never ſuffered to appear at the Grate; and that Time expired, my Father (tho' I ſcarce can call him by that tender Name) came here to put the finiſhing Stroke to my Calamities, and having made me be call'd to him, told me in a Tone, which I never think on without trembling, that if I did not make my Profeſſion the next Day, or the Day after, he would come again and take me away, having taken effectual Meaſures for revenging himſelf on my Diſobedience.

What ſhall I ſay, Madamoiſelle *Jeanetta*, I was compelled to ſacrifice myſelf, my Vows, my Hopes, my All————and I am now bound forever to the Service of the Altar————I am uſed, 'tis true, with ſomewhat more Lenity than I was; but what Reparation can be made me for what I have renounced————tho' I do all I can to conceal from the Nuns the inward Agitations I ſtill endure, ſtill I bear in remembrance my firſt Engagement————*Melicourt* in ſpite of my Endeavours appears ſleeping and waking before my Eyes————the Charms of his Perſon, and thoſe of his Mind, his Truth, his Tenderneſs are ever preſent————my Profeſſion condemns the Regret I feel, that I no more am his————I am miſerable for my whole Life, and in perpetual Doubt of my eternal Salvation————ſhocking State.————

The unhappy *Saint Agnes* wept bitterly in pronouncing theſe Words, then lifting up her Hands and Eyes, Spouſe of my Heart, cryed ſhe, ſtill muſt I call thee by that precious Name given thee before the Holy Altar! Ah! nothing can ever erace thy Image from my Soul.

She here ended her ſorrowful Narration, nor could ſhe have proceeded had any more remain'd to relate, her Agonies were too great at this Repetition of her Misfortunes to leave her the Power to ſpeak, and her Sighs came with ſuch Vehemence as tho' they would have burſt her Breaſt————I was pierced to the Heart at this Sight, and my own Circumſtances at that time rendered it more affecting————I uſed all my endeavours to conſole her, but indeed looked on her Condition as irremedible————I

was

was however too much convinced of the Sincerity of her Friendship, by the Confidence she placed in me, not to return it with the most zealous Affection, and as I thought it might, at least for a Time, render her forgetful of her Sorrows, I gave her a full Account of my own Adventures, and she expressed a great deal of Pity for the Disappointments I had met with ; but, said she, as soon as I had done, these Things may change, beautiful *Jeanetta :* Beside, you have still room to Hope———— but alas, that is not my Case————all in this World is lost to me, beyond a Possibility of Redemption———— and Death, that gives a Period to the Woes of others, will perhaps to me open a Door, yet more terrible ————thus divided, thus doubly engaged to Man first, and Heaven afterward, how can I reconcile such different Duties————how comply with either, as I ought————here ensued a second Flood of Tears, and indeed I found her Despair too justly grounded to be able to urge any thing to mitigate it, so could only bear her company in Tears————we continued in this melancholly Employment, till the Rules of the House obliged us to go down to the Refectory ; but this mutual Intimacy between us daily encreased, and we were from this time forward very little asunder. I must confess I found a great deal of Comfort in her Society ; but it lasted not long, Fortune was not yet weary of persecuting me, and deprived me of this Relief, in a manner I least expected.

Tho' I am very sensible one ought not to give way to those superstitious Ideas, which are apt to creep into the Minds, especially of young People ; yet I could not keep myself from being very much affected with a Dream I had at that Time, and which has proved an exact and faithful Presage of what has since happened to me.

We had a Pensioner in the House, call'd Madamoiselle *Renneville,* a young Lady of an uncommon Vivacity of Temper ; she was the youngest of seven Daughters, and according to the custom of great Families, was destined to a religious Life, to the end her Sisters might live in the World with greater Splendor ; but the Aversion she had to a Cloyster, had made her resolute not to enter herself as a Novice, so that all they could do was to keep her there as a Boarder————she was too gay to let any thing affect her Heart, and always flattering herself that some lucky turn or other would fall out to rid her of this Confinement, was one of the most entertaining Companions in the World; among the rest of the Whims with which she amused herself, and those with whom she contracted any intimacy, was that of having recourse to the little Arts for discovering the Secrets of Futurity————throwing the Grounds of Coffee, laying a Pack of Cards in a particular manner, and a hundred other such like fancies, took up all the time she could steal from those publick Acts of Devotion, to which she was obliged to conform. *Saint Agnes* and myself were very fond of her Society, as she diverted our melancholly Thoughts———she always was with us when we walked in the Garden, she pertook in all our Recreations, and without making her a Confidant, we treated her with the greatest Freedom; neither of us concealing from her our dislike of a monastick Life, we were continually forming Schemes of Escaping, tho' such wild and chimerical ones, as only served to make us laugh, and never were intended to be put in Practice.

But above all the Mysteries *De Renneville* imagined herself skilled in, was the Interpretation of Dreams: She pretended to be Mistress of great Secrets on that score, and would persuade us she could draw Conclusions from every Image, which the ever waking Fancy presents while the Body is asleep————tho' my self as well as *Saint Agnes* was above giving credit to any such Follies, yet we could not help being a little merry at the serious Air she put on, whenever she talk'd on these Affairs. Few Mornings past over without her relating to us some Dream of the preceeding Night, and then would needs know what ours had been, which she construed after some rules she had by Heart; this she took such pleasure in, that whenever we were weary of her Company, it was but to tell her we did not depend on any thing she said on this Subject, and this would so mortify her that she would run away directly, and go to others more believing.

One Evening as I was sitting with *Saint Agnes* in my Cell, she came running in with a satisfaction in her Eyes, as had we been less acquainted with her Humour, we should have imagined had denoted no less than, that she had heard News of being delivered from the Convent— Now, said she, embracing us, my dear *Saint Agnes*, my dear *Jeanetta*, you'll never think me impertinent again : I have got an infallible Secret to know what shall happen to every one of us—O how rejoiced I am—continued she, clapping her Hands, and jumping a Yard from the Floor ; we could not forbear laughing at the Transport she was in ; Nay, nay, 'tis no Jest, resumed she ; I'll engage when you know it, you'll be as much ravish'd with it as I am————look here————said she, taking a Book out of her Pocket——here it is, and in Print too ;——judge if one can doubt of the Truth. I opened the Book to please her, and found the Title was,————*A Treatise on Dreams, and their true Significations, with many curious Secrets, to excite the Mind to operate, while the Senses were at rest.* There were several Methods laid down to procure what the Title exprest, but I shall relate only one, which if we had not made use on, we should never have been free from the importunities of *De Renneville*.

It was to go to Bed two Nights without eating any Supper, and on the third Day refrain from Dinner, taking no other Nourishment in four and twenty Hours, than a Cake made of half a Pound of Flower, without the least Grain of Salt, or Butter, and worked up with the Grease of a black Hen, and rain Water.

The black Hen made a great impression on the Mind of this superstitious young Lady————that alone was sufficient to make her warrant the Efficacy of it— we both complied with her request, to make a trial at least, and it was not to be doubted but she would experience it herself————so we all three, at different times pretended Indisposition, to be excused appearing in the Refectory.

Saint

Saint Agnes was the firſt inititated, and when *De Renneville* impatient to hear the Proof of what ſhe ſeemed ſo certain of, called me to go with her into the Cell of that beautiful Nun——ſhe aſſured us that ſhe had had a very extraordinary Dream————I knew it——I knew it, ſaid Madamoiſelle *De Renneville*: O, the black Hen could not fail.

But her Triumph laſted not long, for *Saint Agnes* preſently added, that indeed it was true ſhe had dreamed ſomething, which had ſurprized her for the time it laſted; but that on her waking ſhe could not remember any one particular of it. I laughed heartily and *De Renneville* looked down, but at length recovered herſelf, and laid the blame on *Saint Agnes* for having drank twice after eating the Cake, whereas it was expreſsly forbid to take a ſecond Draught. I had no Curioſity however to make this trial; but I was ſo teized that I at laſt conſented, and took care to follow all the Directions to a tittle.

It was not common with me to dream, yet whether talking ſo much on it, or whether there was really any Efficacy in the Secret I cannot tell, but that Night I had a Dream, or rather Viſion ſo ſingular, and ſo intereſting, that I never mention it without thinking I have ſtill the Images before my Eyes, which then preſented themſelves to me————my Reaſon tel's me, it was meerly accidental, nevertheleſs it had an exact conformity with the Adventures which befel me ſince.

I thought I had left the Convent, and had wandered into a troubleſome Road, full of Thorns and Briars—— The difficulty I found to paſs it, made me caſt my Eyes about for ſome better Path, and ſoon perceived thro' the opening of a Hedge, one that ſeemed very plain and ſmooth————it was of a good diſtance from me; but my deſires of reaching it, made me direct my ſteps that Way, and ſtruggle through a thouſand Obſtacles————ſometimes my Feet were cut with the rough flinty Pebbles, which lay ſcattered up and down before me————ſometimes I had much ado to preſerve myſelf from falling into Sloughs and Quagmires————in ſome Places huge Trees,

which

which Hurricanes had torn up by the Roots ſtopped my advancing, in others Brambles and Nettles twined about my Legs, and entangled me ſo that I had ſcarce Power to extricate myſelf——Waſps, Hornets and other venemous Inſects came about me, like ſo many Swarms of Bees, and I never ſhould have got to the Path I ſo much wiſhed, had not a Stranger that Inſtant appeared on it, and pointed out a Paſſage which brought me eaſily to him ; I was no ſooner arrived, than he began to lead the way, beckoning to me to follow, and ever and anon turning back and ſmiling on me, but never ſpoke to me the whole Time. He was habited in Black, but had ſo pleaſing an Aſpect, that I apprehended no danger from him, and went after him as faſt as I could.

We travelled in this Manner for about half a League, and then came to a large Stream, which cut the Road in two, I ſaw there was no getting to the other ſide without croſſing this Water, which appeared very rough and rapid, ſo ſtood trembling on the Bank without knowing how to proceed, when my Guide, who was at ſome Diſtance before me, ſeemed to make nothing of this Difficulty ; but walked over the Surface of the Water, with the ſame eaſe he had done on dry Land, he encouraged me by his Geſtures to follow his Example; but the fear of being drowned prevented me——He laughed at my Timidity, and ſtill perſiſted in inviting me, and had convinced me, I might venture without Danger, when I heard a Voice in the Air, which ſaid to me—— *Jeanetta*——*Jeanetta*, *take care of yourſelf*——*if you paſs the Torrent, you will be devoured by a Monſter*—— I lifted up my Eyes at theſe Words, and ſaw above my Head, a great Machine, on which ſat a Woman of a majeſtick Form, and beauteous Countenance, her Throne appeared to me like the Stern of a Ship, adorned with ſeveral Streamers wavering in the Wind, on which were wrote in Capitals of Gold, theſe Words,

YOU CANNOT WITHOUT VIRTUE ARRIVE AT YOUR DESIRED PORT.

I gazed with Aſtoniſhment, but in a Moment all diſappeared.

I

I then cast my Eyes with a melancholly Air towards the Stream, where I still saw the Man I mentioned, redoubling his Entreaties that I would come over; but what I had seen and heard would not suffer me to be prevailed upon, and I turned hastily away, resolving to return tho' I knew not where——Curiosity making me look back, when I had gone a few Paces, I was strangely surprized to find the agreeable Stranger was turned into the most hideous Monster, that imagination can suggest——I was terrified beyond Description at the horrid Metamorphosis; but much more so when I saw him in full Speed pursuing me——Fear gave me incredible Swiftness——I thought I was in an Instant a vast Distance from him, and looking behind me once more——the dreadful Form was vanish'd; but instead of the clear and serene Sky I saw before, there appeared in the Place of the Stream, a thick black Mist, sending forth pestiferous Vapours to the very Heavens. ——Sudden Flashes of Lightning every Moment darted from the Clouds, followed by the most dreadful Bursts of Thunder——the Prospect was too shocking to be long endured, and I began to run again with all my Speed.

The Path seemed now to enlarge itself gradually, and at last brought me to a fine Meadow, covered with Grass, and enriched with a thousand various Flowers, the produce of Nature without the help of Art——a most magnificent Palace, terminated the delightful Prospect——Heaven be praised, said I to myself, I hope my Troubles now are at an end——this Palace must certainly be inhabited, and some one there will have Pity on me, and admit me——on this I advanced towards the Building, but was cruelly disappointed when I came near it, and was not able to find any Gate——I went round it, examined the Walls in every Part, but could perceive no Entrance—— During this employment, Night came on——the Sun was set——Darkness began to cover the whole Hemisphere——the remembrance of the furious Monster I had so lately seen came fresh into my Mind and alarmed

me

me dreadfully———I ſhall be devoured, cryed I, no power on Earth can ſave me.

As I was in this Perplexity, a Lamb whoſe Fleece I thought excelled in Whiteneſs the new fallen Snow, and was adorned with Flowers and Ribands, came and fawned upon me ; he appeared ſo ſweet and beautiful, that I could not forbear careſſing him ; with which he ſeemed delighted, and at laſt looking up in my Face, he opened his Mouth and amazed me, with uttering in a diſtinct human Voice the following Words ;

> *Follow me,* Jeanetta, *lovely* Jeanetta, *and I will lead you to a Palace where you will find all manner of Felicity.*

Alas, charming Lamb, replied I, how can that be when I have vainly ſought all round it for an Entrance ? I anſwered in this manner believing he had meant that glorious Structure before us ; but he took no notice of my Miſtake (as it afterwards proved) and only ſaid,

> *Follow me, and I will find you a Gate.*

I did as he bid me, but was a little troubled to find he, paſſed by the Palace I ſo much admired, and longed to be admitted into. A range of Buildings, which I had not obſerved before, was at a ſmall Diſtance from it ; but as irregular and ill formed as the other was beautiful——— the Walls indeed were high, but black and frightful——— the Entrance vaſtly wide, through which I ſaw Crowds of People hurrying in, but very few at leaſt while I was there, came out ; this a little ſtruck me, and I ſtopped to conſider what I was about———the Lamb did all he could to perſuade me to go forward, but I replied, that I had no Inclination to enter ; this not being the beautiful Palace I had ſeen before, and into which only I was ambitious of being admitted.

The ſeeming Lamb on this refuſal, appeared incenſed, and raiſing himſelf up on his hind Legs, cryed, *Since Softneſs fails to move thee, it is fit I ſhould ſhow myſelf to thee ſuch as I truly am* ; while he ſpoke theſe Words, his late lovely Fleece, changed into a harſh grizly Hair, ———his Eyes enlarged themſelves, and Fire ſeemed to iſſue from their Balls———every Limb took another

Form

Form, and I beheld with Terror unconceivable the same
Monster, who had before deceived me under a human
Shape————He flew directly on me, and I screamed till
my Voice echoed through the Air.

I was on the Point of being made his Victim, when
a Voice loud and shrill, but at the same time harmonious,
suspended his Fury : Methought it spoke these Words ;

*Hold, fatal Enemy of human Kind————*JEANEATTA
*has of her own Accord, refused to go within thy horrid
Gates————Thou, therefore hast no Right to tempt her
farther————Begone, O Vice! the Proofs she has given
are sufficient ; and from this Time forward my Palace shall
be her Asylum.*

This spoke, the same Divinity which I had seen in
the Air appeared before, the Monster fled, and she presented her Hand to conduct me, to the so much wished
for Palace—we entered by a steep and narrow Stair-Case,
which till she shewed me I had not discovered, and I soon
found myself in the midst of a spacious Temple, the
Throne of Virtue, was placed at the upper End, and she
who brought me there seated herself in it ; about her
thronged not a numerous, but noble Company, in whose
Faces Joy and Contentment were most beautifully deline-
ated. However I still methought wanted something more
to compleat my Happiness, I looked round me, tho' unknowing what I sought, when in an Instant a lovely
Personage, who they told me was Wisdom, took my
Hand and led me to the Altar, where I found the
the Marquis de L——— V—he embraced me with tenderness————our Hands were joined————my Heart
unable to contain the overflowing Transport, broke the
Bands of Sleep, and I started up, Crying, O ! why good
Heaven is all this Delusion.

This Vision indeed strangely affected my waking
Mind————it was then but Break of Day, and I
thought of nothing else till *Saint Agnes* and Madamoiselle
De Renneville came in and surprized me in the Contemplation ; I'll engage, said the latter, that you have had
a Dream, and have not forgot it as *Saint Agnes* did ; as I
thought her not a proper Person to be entrusted, and had

a mind to reserve that Confidence for my dear Nun, I made use of her Excuse, and said I remembred nothing of it. You are both of you Deceivers, replied she, I know the Secret is a good one, and you have experienced the Benefit of it, tho' you conceal it from me; but I'll try it myself next, and for your Punishment, will follow your Example, and be henceforward as reserved as your selves. She spoke this with an air of Spite, and went out of the Room, which neither of us were troubled at, especially myself, who was impatient to communicate to *Saint Agnes* how I had passed the Night.

She was very much surprized at hearing it, and told me, she could not but be of Opinion there was somewhat very significant in it; you will go through many Difficulties and great Temptations, my dear *Jeanetta*, said she, but Time and Virtue will at length make you happy——whereas for me no Hope remains——my Doom is fixed——unalterably fixed! I endeavoured to divert her from this Idea seeing her Eyes full of Tears; and as a little Amusement made her write down my Dream, and we afterwards found a good deal of Satisfaction in putting down on Paper the Adventures that had befallen us.

One Morning as we were talking on the Misery it was to be condemned to a Cloyster, without having the least Avocation to that sort of Life; Madamoiselle *De Renneville* came to tell us, there was a young Lady, who seemed to be a Person of Quality, just come into the House——She looks extremely melancholly, said the talkative Thing, I dare answer she is some new Victim, one may see it in the very Air of her Countenance. Both myself and *Saint Agnes*, were too much taken up with our own Troubles to give any regard to this piece of News, Alas! I little thought how nearly this concerned me, so as we did not seem in a Humour to hear her chat, she left us, and we resumed our Conversation: *Saint Agnes* seemed that Day more than ordinarily dejected, and cryed, she had no longer Courage to support her ill Fortune, on which I took an occasion to tell her, that since she found it an impossibility to reconcile herself to

the

the Profeſſion ſhe had been forced into, I thought it adviſeable to take ſome Methods for being freed from it;
and perſwaded her to draw up an account of the whole
Proceeding, ſince ſhe was taken from her Huſband,
that when a favourable Opportunity arrived, it might be
ſhewn to the Father of *Melicourt*, who no doubt would
exert all his Intereſt to eſpouſe her Cauſe———this
Counſel ſeemed to revive her; ſhe immediately ſet
about writing a Memorial of the whole Affair, and added
to it a Proteſtation againſt her Vows;———this proved
a fortunate Step, tho' I then was far from imagining that
I ſhould ever be employed in it, or that I was on the
Point of being ſeparated from this agreeable Companion.

Juſt as ſhe had made up her Packet, the Bell rung
to the Refectory, on which we made all the haſte we
could down Stairs, having been often chid by the Superior for coming late. I took my Place as uſual at the
Penſioners Table; the young Lady *De Renneville* had
told us of was there, ſhe roſe when I came in, and
ſaluted me in a very polite Manner; but, Oh Heavens!
how great was my Confuſion, when I found in this
Stranger a Perſon I had little reaſon to love———a
Perſon whoſe very Name I trembled at———and who
to ſee in this Place, preſaged me nothing but Troubles
———in fine Madamoiſelle *D' Elbieux.*

I grew pale at this Encounter———my Heart beat,
and an univerſal trembling ſeized me, in ſo much that
I fell back fainting in my Chair———as I was very
much beloved, both Nuns and Penſioners ran to my
Relief———Madamoiſelle *D' Elbieux* among the reſt;
but not before having obſerved my Face, and now
knowing me, ſtarted from the Place, crying out, great
God! 'tis *Jeanetta*———the inſinuating, the dangerous
Jeanetta!———Ah! what brought her here———how
dare ſhe ſhelter herſelf beneath this ſacred Roof———
having been the occaſion of ſuch Miſchiefs———
Wretch, 'tis for her my Brother breathes his laſt———
I recovered enough to hear ſome Part of theſe Exclama-
tions, the reſt *Saint Agnes* informed me of; the religious
Company, were too much aſtoniſhed to be able to aſk

any

any Questions concerning the meaning of what they heard, and she went on raving against me, saying, I was the most wicked Creature in the World, and that by my Artifices I had caused her Brother to be assassinated ————then as not enduring to look upon me, she flew out of the Room, and filled the whole Convent with her Clamours; but before I proceed, it will not be improper to make my Reader acquainted with the Occasion, which unluckily for me, brought her to this Convent.

A *Valet de Chambre* belonging to the Chevalier *D'Elbieux* having been witness of the Misfortune, that had happened to his Master, took Post, and immediately informed Madam his Mother, and that Lady alarmed beyond measure at the Danger he was in, was just setting out in her Chariot, with her Daughter to go to him, when before she got out of the Court-yard a Messenger arrived from *Paris*, sent express by her Husband the Count *De N*————, who was then in the Bastile, on account of a Duel with another Person of Quality; desiring her to repair immediately to him, in order to solicit his Discharge; this Person informed her also, that there was no Time to be lost, his Antagonist being a Man of great Interest. The Countess was perfectly overwhelmed with this second Disaster————She remained some time in a most distracting suspence, divided between her Duty to her Husband, and maternal Affection for her Son; had she followed the Dictates of her Inclination, they would doubtless have carried her to the Chevalier; but her Reputation, as being known not to be on the best terms with the Count, and which neglecting him on so pressing an Occasion would have confirmed, at length got the better, and she resolved to go to *Paris*. Madamoiselle *D'Elbieux* was of the same Opinion, but the Tenderness she had for her Brother made her represent to the Countess, that he ought not to be abandoned by all his Family, at a Time when his Life was in such eminent Danger, so obtained her Permission to go to Madam *De G*————'s. But as her Castle was a considerable way out of the Road to *Paris*

and

and she could not set her down there without loosing a whole Day; her Ladyship bethought herself of this Convent, near which she was obliged to pass, and having determined what to do, ordered to be drove directly hither, where having left her Daughter, she went on to *Paris*, and Madamoiselle *D'Elbieux* was to take a Post-Chaise from the Village, and so proceed to the Castle of Madam *De G*———

My ill Fate ordained it so, that when Madam the Countess arrived, there was not a Chaise in the whole Village to be hired for her Daughter, and the Superior to remedy that Difficulty, offered to send to Madam *De G*———'s for one to fetch her; this Proposal was accepted with Thanks by the two Ladies, and the Mother proceeded on her Journey, while her Daughter waited at our Convent for the coming of the Chaise.

It was the Custom for Strangers to dine in the Parlour, but unhappily for me, Madamoiselle *D'Elbieux* entreated she might eat in the Refectory, and that occasioned our meeting. Chance often produces such odd Events in the Affairs of Life, that when one makes any Reflection on them, they appear rather brought about by Policy and Contrivance; and it is frequently to this, that Persons who make a great Noise in the World, either for good or bad Conduct, owe the Establishment of their Characters———I have known a lucky Turn set up a Coward for a Hero, and a Fool for a Politician; on the other Hand, a truly brave Man become rank'd among Cowards, and the ablest Statesman consider'd as a Blunderer———So true it is that Success is every Thing, and without it, the best laid Schemes become the Sport of Coxcombs. But to return.

The outragious Behaviour of Madamoiselle *D'Elbieux*, drew after her a great Number both of Nuns and Pensioners to enquire into the Cause, and her Resentment, or I may justly say her Malice against me, made her omit nothing that she thought might lessen me in their Esteem; she gave them the History of my Birth, made the Passion I had for the Marquis *De L*——*V*———appear in the most ridiculous Light, accused me of having encouraged

he

her Brother's Defigns upon me, and the betraying him to his Rival——told them I was the moft artful Hypocrite that ever was, and that under a feeming Modefty, couched a Temper that rendered it dangerous to hold any Converfation with me. Let any one judge what influence fuch a Reprefentation of me muft have among Perfons fuch as it was made to — the Abbefs above all was particularly piqued at being impofed on by Madam *De G*————on my Account, and affured Madamoifelle *D'Elbieux*, that fince I was fuch a Creature, fhe would not fuffer me to remain long under that facred Roof.

As I was informed of all this by Madamoifelle *De Renneville*, who would let nothing efcape her that afforded matter of Talk, I pafs'd all that Day and Night in the moft cruel Agitations————the amiable *Saint Agnes* quitted me as feldom as fhe could, and ufed her utmoft efforts to mitigate my Troubles : Take Courage, my dear *Jeanetta*, faid fhe, you will one Day furmont all thefe Difficulties, and triumph over thofe whofe are caufelefsly your Enemies. I am Prophet enough to affure you, that every thing that now fo much diftreffes you, will hereafter afford you only Satisfaction to reflect upon as Evils paft, enhance a prefent Good————but continued fhe, you muft practice in the mean Time, both Policy and Patience, if you appear too much dejected the whole Convent will give credit to what the malicious Madamoifelle *D'Elbieux* has faid of you————indeed the Venom of her Tongue exceeds all Defcription, and I believe fhe is yet worfe than you who fuffer fo much by her can conceive————however, you have this Confolation, that you are very much beloved here, and every one is loth to harbour an ill Opinion of you.

Ah ! my dear Friend, anfwered I, the force of Calumny is great, and finds an eafy entrance into the Mind————but that I look not on as the greateft of my Misfortunes ; when this cruel Woman arrives at the Caftle of Madam *De G*————have I not caufe to fear her Tears and Remonftrances againft me will turn the Heart of my only Protectrefs againft me————the good Lady has indeed had trouble enough on my Account,

and

and will not the Reflection of the Mischiefs I have innocently occasioned, render her averse to espousing me any longer————I well remember that before these fatal Accidents, the Letter wrote to her by Madamoiselle *D'Elbieux* half balanced her against me, and had it not been for my Behaviour on the Account of the Offers made me by Monsieur her Husband, I knew not whither I had so long preserved myself in her Favour————but added I, there seems now no other Probability than that of being cast off for ever—the manner in which she quitted me at our last Interview—her Silence since, are all Presages of my being totally abandoned by her, and to compleat my Misfortunes, I shall doubtless be turned out of this Convent, a Place once hateful to me, but since honoured with your Friendship no less agreeable————besides where can I wander————where hope to be received————. who for the future will afford any Asylum to a Wretch whose ill Fate is infectious, and brings a train of Miseries to every Place she comes ?

As I was thus lamenting, and the sweet tempered *Saint Agnes* endeavouring to console me, a Messenger was sent to call me to the Abbess, and told me at the same Time, that a Chaise from the Castle being arrived, Madamoiselle *D'Elbieux* had that Instant left the Monastery. See here, cried I, the beginning of the new Misfortunes that attend me. I said no more, but *Saint Agnes* making a Sign that she waited my return in her Cell, I followed the Nun who had come for me.

I entered into the Chamber of Madam the Superior, with trembling Limbs, and an akeing Heart, she was encompassed by several of the oldest among the Sisterhood, who I heard as I passed along were speaking with great Vehemence; but were all silent as soon as I appeared. Come near, said the Abbess, Madamoiselle *Jeanetta*, I desire you will inform me, as there is no room to doubt but you can, the Motives which induced Madam *De G*————to impose on me, by making you pass for her Neice—had she thought fit to have made me a Confidant in this Affair, perhaps it had been better for you, especially as I have many Obligations to that

Lady,

Lady, and never blushed to acknowledge them————
the whole Convent here can testify I never went about to
conceal the least Part of the Favours I have received
from her————in all appearance you are very dear to
her, the adopting the Daughter of a poor Peasant is a
convincing Proof of it————don't be under any Confusion,
continued she, seeing the Colour come into my Face at
this reproach, you came too well recommended to apprehend any ill treatment from me, notwithstanding all
has been said to persuade me to a contrary Behaviour————
but don't think to deceive me any longer————I know
too much not to be made acquainted with the whole, and
that alone can entitle you to an Abode here————consider
therefore, whether it is best for you to make me your
Friend, or to provide for yourself elsewhere.

This Discourse coming from the Mouth of a Person
reverend for her Years, as well as Profession, made me
shed Tears ; while I was drying my Eyes, I had time
to reflect what Answer I should make, and concluded
not to comply with her Desires, or pretend to give any
Explanation of my Affairs, till I had heard from Madam
De G————, who I doubted not but after seeing Madamoiselle *D'Elbieux* would come to some Resolution about
me, and either send a Messenger, or write to me what
I had to depend upon————so I replied to the Abbess
that I knew Madamoiselle *D'Elbieux* too well to expect
any thing from her but ill Offices ; but as to the As-
persions she had loaded me with, Time would best declare
whither I merited them or not————I added that I had
nothing that I desired to keep secret either from her or
the whole Convent ; but as Madam *De G*—had been
pleased to introduce me, I thought it would be a Breach
of the Duty owing from me to that Lady, if I said any
thing farther than she had been pleased to reveal, without
receiving Permission from her ; and that, tho' I found
nothing in the Convent, but what was perfectly agreeable
to me, I was ready to quit it, if it should be absolutely
required I should do so.

The Abbess seemed a little surprized at the Resolution
with which I expressed myself, and after whispering to
one

one of the Nuns, made a Sign to me to retire, which I gladly did, making a profound Reverence, and went to meet *Saint Agnes* in her Cell, where she impatiently expected me.

I found her in Tears, and was obliged to comfort her in my turn ; the Apprehensions of losing me alarmed her cruelly, she had no other Person in whom she durst confide, and had received as well as myself many Advantages in the mutual Trust we reposed in each other, and which neither of us were capable of abusing ; and sure there are Pleasures in the society of a faithful Friend, a kind of second-self to whom one may safely communicate the secret Wishes of one's Heart, which not only give a double relish to good Fortune, but are an infinite Relief in the most sharp and poignant Disappointments —We past the remainder of that Day in the most tender Protestations of preserving an everlasting Regard to each other, nor parted till the Night was very far advanced.

Notwithstanding the perplexity of my Mind, I was very near falling asleep, when I heard the Door of my Cell open, and somebody come in————I could not help being frighted, not being able to imagine who should enter at such an Hour————are you awake, beautiful *Jeanetta*, said *Saint Agnes*, for it was she ? O Heaven ! is it you, cried I, then venturing to lift my Head above the Cloaths, I protest you set me into a Fit of Trembling. Whom but me, resumed she, smiling, or one like me could you expect in this Place, ————in any other indeed, a Lover might have been natural enough ; but our History will afford no such Adventures, especially as the Men are much less enterprising in these Times, than the former, if we give credit to Romances : In finishing these Words she set down a Candle she had brought with her, and placed herself on my Bed-side. She had on a Night Dress, which became her so perfectly well, that I could not forbear complementing her upon it. Alas, said she, how can you amuse yourself with taking notice of such Trifles ; but it is a proof that we Women, tho' taken up with the most serious Affairs, have always a spare Place

in

in our Minds, for every thing that relates to Beauty—ought I not rather to have expected you should have asked me what had induced me to disturb you at this late Hour? Take care, cried I, in the same tone, that I dont accuse you of as great an Impropriety——is it possible for any thing so dear to me as you are to give me any Disturbance; but you seem to have Letters in your Hand, continued I perceiving she had Papers, have you received any News? Alas! from who? said she, these are what we wrote together the other Day. I was no sooner in Bed than I reflected on what had passed yesterday and to-day, and as I judge it will not be long before you leave this Place, I thought it would be a necessary Precaution to commit this Memorial and Protestation to your care, while I had an Opportunity; for who knows but your Departure may be too precipitate, and we may be too much observed for me to do it at the Time of taking leave——I beg also, that as soon as your own Affairs are a little settled, you will get these Papers conveyed by a safe Hand, to the Father of *Melicourt*——you see I have some Self-interest, mingled with my Friendship; but I only enjoyn this in Case I am so unhappy as to loose you; and the Certainty that you will not neglect me in a Business on which my very Life depends, is all the Consolation I have in the Thoughts of being separated from you.

I shall be far from attending the Certainty of my Fate for the getting these Papers delivered, answered I, you may depend upon it, my dear *Saint Agnes*, that when I quit your Society, to prove the Sincerity of my Friendship to you, and the Regard I shall always bear to the precious remembrance of it, shall be the first of my Cares——I have too much experienced the Torments of Suspence myself, to leave you a Prey to them, when I shall be happy enough to have it in my power to rid you of them——it was indeed my Duty to have prevented your Desires on this Occasion, and entreated you would entrust me with so material a Negotiation—that I did not do so, my Perplexities can only excuse—but I will endeavour to atone for it by my future Diligence.

Saint

Saint Agnes testified her Gratitude for this assurance by a tender Embrace, after which we passed great Part of the Night, in consulting on proper Measures for the delivery of these Letters, and for conveying the Answers to her, I took down in Writing the Names of the Persons and Places; and when we had fixed on every Thing proper to be done, she retired to her own Cell, and left me to my Repose.

Two Days passed over without my hearing any News, and what I suffered in this Uncertainty, of what was to be done with me, was not much inferior to the knowing the worst that could be decreed—On the Third, however, about ten in the Morning I was relieved; Madam *De G*————wrote a Letter to the Superior; desiring her to put me into the Hands of the Bearer, without mentioning any Thing farther, than that she would see her in a short Time. I was with her when this Express arrived, at which she shook her Head in Token of being not well pleased, and cried out, this is mysterious indeed! Then ordered me to pack up my things, and went to her Closet to write an Answer to Madam *De G*————. *Saint Anges* who was present would have accompanied me; but she was ordered to keep her Place————they doubtless had some Suspicion, that she would take the Opportunity of my leaving the Convent, to charge me with some Commission; but as it happened, they took this Precaution a little too late————so true it is, that one ought not to defer any Thing till to-morrow, that one can do to-day.

I went to my Cell, with a great Confusion of Mind; but that did not hinder me from getting myself ready in a very little Time; and as soon as I was so, I went to Madam the Superior's Chamber, to take my leave of her, which she received with a great deal of Coldness; but it was not so with the Community as well as Pensioners, every one of them embraced me, and gave me all the Demonstrations of their good Will, that can be imagined, and much more than I expected: Even the gay *De Renneville* shed Tears, but poor *Saint Agnes* wept bitterly, as I kissed her, and squeezed her by the Hand.

Till

Till now I had not seen the Person who was sent for me; but was extremely pleased when I found it was *Christina*, the favourite Woman of Madam *De G——* of whom I spoke in the second Part of these Memoirs. Ah, my dear *Christina*, said I, as we went into the Chaise, what have you to tell me? Has my excellent Benefactress the same Pity for me, she has been accustomed to treat me with? I have many Things, said she, to acquaint you with; but shall defer the Recital, till we get out of the Village———then looking on me more earnestly than she had done before, Oh Heaven! added she, how you are altered! Nothing, answered I, ought to be less surprizing, I have not enjoyed one Moment's Peace since I came into this Convent, and Grief you know is no Friend to Beauty; but I have this to console me, that if a small Affliction serves to cast me down, a little Contentment is sufficient to re-establish me.

It would be but impertinent to say I was impatient for the News she brought me, the Reader will easily believe I was extremely so——as soon as I found we were in the open Country, I reminded *Christina* of her Promise; yes, beautiful *Jeanetta*, answered she, I have abundance to say; for I love you too well to conceal any Thing from you———I dare lay a Wager you'll not be able to guess who is the occasion of your being taken from the Convent. No, said I, sure the thing is not so much a Riddle———I could be removed only by the Goodness of Madam *De G——*or the Malice of Madamoiselle *D'Elbieux*.

No, answered she, it is the Chevalier *D'Elbieux*, at the Point of Death, he repents him of the Injuries he has done you———He begs with sincere Tears to see you, and knowing the Aversion his Sister has to you, has made her promise to receive you kindly———that young Lady on her arrival at our House, was so outrageous against you, that my Mistress without quarrelling with her, could not urge any thing in your behalf; but she is grown much more moderate since her Brother has declared his Intentions, and to please him has consented

ſented to a friendly behaviour toward you; ſhe even ſeems concerned to have ever been your Enemy; but alas! 'tis eaſy to perceive this Change is but affected, and that ſhe ſtill retains a ſecret Rancour in her Heart.

I know her, ſaid I, and ſhall never place any Confidence in her——but what more have you to tell me, continued I? ——What do they ſay of me?——in what manner am I to be diſpoſed?——Ah, *Jeanetta*, *Jeanetta*, replied ſhe, 'tis eaſy to ſee the lovely Marquis is not forgotten by you, and that under all theſe Queſtions, the deſire of hearing ſomewhat of him is principally couch'd; and tho' it is what I am poſitively forbid, I think the command too unjuſt to be obeyed, and will let you into the ſecret of every thing, depending on your Diſcretion never to let it be known I have tranſgreſſed my Orders.

The ſame Day, continued the obliging *Chriſtina*, that Madame *De G*——came back from viſiting you at the Monaſtery, ſhe received a Letter from the Marquis, who begged in the moſt paſſionate Terms to hear News of you; adding that he ſtill flattered himſelf a Time would come in which he might be allowed to make her a ſuitable and publick acknowledgement, for the Protection ſhe had been ſo good to grant you. The Valet de Chambre who brought this, had Orders from his Lord to ſee you, and I ſuppoſe to deliver you a Letter alſo, had but juſt Time to receive an Anſwer from Madam *De G*—— ſhe obliging him to return immediately, being under apprehenſions that the Marquis ſhould not be ſoon enough apprized, that his Adventure with the Chevalier *D'Elbieux*, made more Noiſe than he imagined, and that his Valet if he made any Stay would be arreſted.

My Lady's Fears were but too juſtly grounded, *Dubois* had not left the Caſtle two Hours before an Exempt arrived with *Letters de Cachet* to ſearch for, and ſeize the young Marquis *De L—— V*——the Chevalier *D'Elbieux*, you, my dear *Jeanetta*, and all concerned in that unhappy Affair. Not only the Caſtle, but the Village alſo ſuffered the ſtricteſt Scrutiny imaginable—— So confident was the Exempt of finding thoſe he ſought
for,

for, and so exact in the execution of his Orders, that he would have taken the Chevalier out of his Bed and carried him away; had not the Surgeons who attended him, declared that to remove him in that Condition would be murder. On this he was obliged to content himself with drawing up a Process, and having left him in the Custody of proper Officers, returned to give an Account how far he had proceeded. Monsieur *De G——* set out at the same Time, and having joined his Interest, with that of the Friends of the Parties concerned, the Affair was a little mitigated, and those troublesome Guests the Soldiers ordered to leave the Castle; but tho' the Marquis as well as the Chevalier is connived at by particular Favour, the former is forbid appearing in Publick till farther Orders, and as for your Part, lovely *Jeanetta*, you are entirely exempted from the Grace granted to your rival Lovers; the Court being informed, that you were the Cause of this Duel has commanded, that whenever, or wherever you shall be found, you shall forthwith be seized, and put in Prison. Ah! my God, cried I, then 'tis to deliver me up that I am sent for from the Monastry. No, no, answered she, I am very certain that while you are with my Lady you will be secure, but as to how she intends to place you afterwards I cannot pretend to say; but I suppose you will know it from her own Mouth.

All that I can tell you farther is, that the most implacable Enemy you have is the old Marquis *De L——V——*, it was his Resentment against you, that first occasioned your Name to be inserted in the *Letter de Catchet*, and on his hearing you had escaped the search, and suspecting my Lady had concealed you somewhere, he wrote a Letter to her, in which he severely reproached her, for having given you shelter in her Castle, which he said occasioned the Rencounter that endangered his Son's Life. In fine, he will be satisfied, with no less than your Confinement during Life———he offers to pay your Pension in a Monastry, or even a Dowry with you, if you will become a Nun———She was going on, but I was too much interested to forbear interrupting her to ask

what

what Madam *De G*———said to all this———I cannot resolve you so far, replied *Christina*, her Ladyship has not communicated her Thoughts to me on that Subject; but there is no probability she will abandon you—the charge she gave me to draw up the Glasses, and hide you as much as possible, from the Sight of any one as we pass through the Village, may convince you how solicitous she is that you should not be apprehended.

The Good-nature of this Woman made her add much more for my Consolation; but all she could urge was ineffectual: Fear and Grief had the Ascendant over all, and I gave myself up to Tears, and to Complainings—I regretted a thousand Times during this little Journey, that I had ever left the homely Cottage, where I first saw Light———Ah! my dear Father, Mother, Sister and Relations, cried I, how easy were my Days, when under your Protection———O! that I were with you again in the safe and peaceful Village, harrassed with no Cares, diverted with innocent and simple Pleasures, my Sleep unbroken, and my waking Thoughts entirely undisturbed; but alas, those happy Times are past, and never———never shall I see the like again.

In this melancholly Humour, did I continue till we reach'd the Village, where agreeable to her Lady's Orders, the good *Christina* set herself in my Lap, and took all imaginable care to conceal me; the Postilion, who had likewise his Instructions, did not set us down till we came into the inner Court of the Castle, whence I pass'd by a Pair of back Stairs into the Closet of Madam *De G*—. *Christina* ran immediately to let her know I was there, while I waited her approach with a palpitation of Heart, and a trembling that I cannot express.

I see you then once more, my poor *Jeanetta*, said that Lady as she came into the Room, indeed your Fate is very averse———I wish I had never seen you———I love you too well not to take part in your Sufferings, and tho' you are far from meriting these Misfortunes, yet you are not the less wretched———what to do for you, or with you I know not———*Christina* has doubtless told you what has happen'd, and how strenuously

Monsieur

Monfieur the Marquis *De L——V*—preffes to have you put into his Hands.——Monfieur *De G*——— is alfo of Opinion that I ought to comply with that Nobleman's Requeft, who has engaged his Word and Honour, that you fhall be treated with all imaginable Lenity and Indulgence————yet notwithftanding this, the Friendfhip I have for you, renders me fearful and irrefolute.

Ah, Madam, cried I, throwing myfelf at her Feet, have pity on the unfortunate *Jeanetta* ; if you forfake me, I fhall die with Grief and Defpair. Tho' I fhould even depend on the Promifes of Monfieur the Marquis, in fpite of the Reafons he has to be diffatisfied with me, have I not caufe to dread frefh Adventures, perhaps, more fatal than the paft will enfue————you know his Son, and may guefs what his Paffion for me will make him do————no fooner would he hear I was in his Father's Power, than he would hazard every Thing to fee me, and deliver me from my Confinement———— thofe who had the charge of guarding me would doubtlefs oppofe it, what might not then be the Confequence— what Mifchiefs, Murders————diftracting Thoughts— O fave me, Madam, from thefe new Difafters————turn me rather out to wander in the Woods————commit my future Fate to chance————let me go hence this Night— I'll hide myfelf among Rocks, and take my Lodging in a Cave, rather than by my unlucky Prefence, create Confufion among thofe whom I would die to pleafe.

Comfort yourfelf, replied that excellent Lady, perceiving I was in great Agitation, I will confider farther on your Affair, and when I have refolved fhall let you know————in the mean Time ftay here, while I go to the Chevalier's Chamber, and fee if he is in a Condition to receive you————for four and twenty Hours he has done nothing but call for you————his Sifter, as I fuppofe my Woman has informed you, has endeavoured all fhe could to divert him from the defire of feeing you, but this Contradiction had like to proved fatal ; it threw him into a Fit little different from Death itfelf, and Madamoifelle *D'Elbieux* grieved to the Soul for having been the Caufe, implored his Pardon, and affured

I

him

him she would henceforward be your Friend, and if you were brought hither give you the sincerest Welcome——the unhappy Chevalier testified how kindly he took this Promise by a thousand Embraces, then said, that if he could once speak to you, he would give content to every body. He sent immediately after this for a Notary, who they say has made his Will——the poor young Gentleman is very ill, the Physicians affirm he cannot recover without a Miracle, his Fever being continually upon him——Farewell, *Jeanetta*, added she, as she went out——you shall soon hear from me——be as easy as you can——Perhaps the supreme Director of our Actions will have Compassion on you.

Madam *De G——* was scarce out of the Closet, before Madamoiselle *D'Elbieux* appeared——she turned Pale at Sight of me, and I doubt not but I did the same ; she had however more Courage than I, and was the first that advanced, so great a Trembling seized me, that I was incapable of even meeting her, as the vast Disparity between our Births required I should have done—— Dearest *Jeanetta*, said that Lady, I flatter myself, from a perfect Confidence in your Goodness, that you will pardon all the Vexations I have occasioned you——the Fears I was always in of the Misfortune that has now happened, made me look upon you with an Eye of Enmity ; but the Entreaties of my Brother, and the Patience with which you have born my ill Treatment, have entirely extinguished all my Animosity——but my Brother's Condition allows no time for Ceremony—come with me to see him, perhaps your Presence will contribute to restore him to me——alas, I fear they conceal half his Danger from me.

This Behaviour of Madamoiselle *D'Elbieux* was extremely touching to me, a Person sincere in their own Nature is easily imposed upon, by the appearance of it in others. I could make no reply to what she said, but returned her Embrace, accompanied with Tears, and perceiving she waited for me, presented her my Hand, for her to lead me to the Chamber of the Chevalier—the moment we came within the Door——be of good Heart,

my

my dear Brother said she, here is *Jeanetta* come to visit you———*Jeanetta* whom I shall henceforth love with the greatest Tenderness———nay doat upon, if I find the Sight of her as efficatious as I hope it will be———a pale and death-like Hand, then put the Curtain back, and strait I heard a feeble Voice cry, where, where is she if I see her I shall die content. As the Room was darkned they brought Candles, and I advanced towards the Bed-fide tho' not without some terror, remembering the Disposition he had been of; but that immediately vanished, and a real Compassion succeeded when I found the State he now was in.

Since I fee you again, said he, I have nothing more to ask in relation to this World———forgive me, O! too beautiful *Jeanetta*, for the effects of an ungovernable Passion———the Misfortunes I have brought upon you, my Death will soon atone———O! may all knowing Heaven convince you of my sincere Contrition for my criminal Designs upon your Innocence———All I wish to live for, is to give you Proofs of it, and to shew the World that divine Grace has enlightned my Heart, to fee with abhorence the Blackness of my Attempts to feduce so perfect a Virtue.

In the room of these wild Desires, continued he, with which I was formerly possest, accept I befeech you, lovely Maid, the fincerest Friendship and the purest Wishes, and believe that whether I live or die, I am incapable of changing the Sentiments I now have for you— let the Marquis know when next you fee him, that I regret the Difquiets I have occasion'd him——— as for yours I will make some small reparation———

As he was speaking some twitching Anguish feized him, and he broke off for a Moment, then cried out, O *Jeanetta*, *Jeanetta*, pray Heaven to forgive my Crimes, ———your Innocence will obtain Mercy for me— then lifting up his Hands and Eyes, feemed to pray internally; after which he turned to his Valet de Chambre, and bid him give him what he had ordered him to feal. The Gentleman than delivered him a Packet, which he prefented to me, faying, accept this, as fome Part of

Compensation for the Troubles I have caused you————
It is a Contract for twenty thousand Francs left me by
an Uncle, so of no Prejudice to my Family————
Madamoiselle *D'Elbieux* is already apprized of it,
approves my Intention, and has promised to make some
Addition to it————is it not true, my dear Sister, you
have loved me too well Living, to oppose my Will after
my Death.

The poor Chevalier who drew Tears from all about
him, seemed to have a glimpse of Joy, when he beheld
his Sister give me a Kiss, as a Confirmation of what he
said—O, I am satisfied—I am satisfied, cried he, this is
what I most earnestly wished—I have no more to do but to
implore Mercy from the divine Being, for all the irregularities of my Life, in speaking these Words he pressed
my Hand, weak as he was ; then embraced his Sister,
and having returned Thanks to Madam *De G*————for
all her Favours, and made an obliging Sign to all present, his Confessor was called in, and we all retired.

We past eight Days in suspense for the Chevalier's
D'Elbieux's Life————sometimes flattered with Hopes,
at others there appeared not the least sign of his Recovery,
—his Symptoms were so various, that the Physicians
were divided in their Opinions all that Time, but on
the Ninth agreed, that if the Fever left him in twelve
Hours he would be out of Danger————that Night it
did so ; every Body rejoyced at the Change, nor was
I less affected with it than the rest : The Sincerity there
appeared of his being truly Penitent, made me regard
him now with as much good Will as I before had done
with Detestation.————Madamoiselle *D'Elbieux* now
treated me with the utmost Tenderness ; it was she
who came running into my Chamber, and brought me
the first News of her Brother's Amendment, declaring
at the same Time, that if he recovered, she would ever
acknowledge herself obliged to me alone, under Heaven,
for so great a Blessing. I returned these Civilities with
a real Affection————Alas ! I little suspected that all
she did was Artifice, and that she feigned to love me
only the easier to undo me, and to put in practice Designs

she

she was then forming against me of the most cruel Nature.

The Chevalier *D'Elbieux* at last obtained new Life and Health, and proved that he had in good earnest also recovered those Sentiments of Honour and Probity, which had too long been dead in him. He shewed himself entirely cured of his Passion for me; but seemed opprest with a heavy Melancholy, and as if he was meditating some important Design: This made me sometimes apprehensive that he had but affected a return of Virtue, and was contriving some new Enterprize against my Virtue————when we have been once deceived by a Person, we are apt on every little Accident to fear the like again; but in this I was happily mistaken, Cares of a different and more sublime Nature, were now the employment of his Thoughts————who would have expected it————O Providence! how wonderful are thy Decrees.

One Evening attended only by his Valet de Chamber, the Chevalier went out of the Castle, as we supposed to take the Air, after so long a Confinement; but not returning the whole Night all the Family, particularly his Sister, were very much alarmed————I had my own Reflection on this Absence; but as it soon proved, were injurious to him: About Eleven in the Morning Madam *De G*————sent for me into her Chamber, I found her in Tears with a Paper in her Hand, and was apprehensive of some Misfortune; what Madam, cried I, more ill News, will my ill Fate never suffer me to enjoy a Moment's Ease? Don't be alarmed, my dear *Jeanetta*, said this amiable Lady, 'tis nothing that concerns you, or if it does, no farther than to engage your Pity and your Wonder————but I will not keep you in Suspense, read this Letter, and judge if it has not a right to make an Impression on the Mind; who indeed could have forseen an Event like this! With these Words she put the Paper into my Hand, and to my great Surprize I found it contained as follows:

To

To the most perfect Patroness of Virtue Madam De G—

PArdon me, Madam, that I departed without taking my leave, and thanking you in form for all the Goodness with which you have been pleased to honour me, while I was so long and so troublesome a Guest with you, and for, yet to me a greater obligation, your Care and Protection of that beauteous Innocence, who, but for you, might have fallen a Prey to my base Designs upon her, and I had Opportunity to commit a Crime, the Blackness of which no Time, no Penitence, no Tears, not even those of my vital Blood could have eraced——that I am saved from so dreadful, so irreparable a Mischief, and that Virtue triumphs over Vice in the preservation of *Jeanetta*, is owing, Madam, to you——Words would but poorly represent the Sense I have of such an excellence of Nature ; besides, I am at present not enough composed to attempt it ; all that I can say is you never shall be forgotten in my Prayers——I have wrote to my Sister to acquit the mighty Debt, far as is in her Power——I flatter myself she will not fail.

Fatal Experience, Madam, having convinced me, that this Life is subjected to nothing but Passions and Disappointments, and fully sensible, that the Things which seem of most Importance to us here, and which we pursue with the greatest Vigour, are in the Sight of Heaven but meer Trifles, often of pernicious Consequence to our eternal Happiness ; and that it is certain I must one Day die, and also give an Account of all my Actions, the Terror of those I have, and might hereafter be guilty of, should I continue in the World, have determined me to quit it, and seek an Asylum from the Temptations of it, among the holy Brotherhood of *Capuchins*. I have long been deaf to the Calls of a celestial Voice within me, which bad me retire before it was too late——Heaven has at last corresponded with my good Genius, and enabled me to obey its Dictates, by shewing me the Gates of Death, and then snatching me from them in order that I might recollect my Offences,

L 2

and

and endeavour to atone for all I have been guilty of.
I doubt not, Madam, but you will applaud my Reſolution——I fly to divine Mercy, and avoid all occaſions that might endanger a Relapſe into my former
Courſes——I recommend to Madamoiſelle *D'Elbieux*,
the amiable and virtuous *Jeanetta*, and hope that ſtill
dear Maid will in the Siſter's good Offices bury in Oblivion the Memory of the Brother's Ill——I ſend her a
Diamond which I before forgot, when ſhe is the Marchioneſs *De L—— V——*, as I doubt not but ſhe
will, and ſincerely pray that ſhe may, it will become her
Finger——I have now done with theſe Toys for ever
——I once more beg the Continuance of your generous
Care over her till ſhe is ſettled in the World——ſhe
merits it all, and is the laſt Requeſt of him who is, with
the greateſt Reſpect and Gratitude,

Madam,

From the Convent   *Your moſt obliged and*
of Capuchius, *at*   *moſt devoted Servant,*
M——   D'ELBIEUX.

I accompanied Madam *De G——* in Tears at the
reading this Letter, and thoſe being a little abated we
fell into Diſcourſe concerning the Inſtability of all
Things in this World——the wonderful Revolutions in
it of States as well as private Perſons, and as nothing was
to be depended on, could not but allow the Chevalier
was happy in his Reſolution of quitting—Nothing certainly being to be envied more than a monaſtick Life,
when it is entered into by Choice, as nothing more
dreadful when the effect of Force.

As we were in this ſerious Entertainment, we were on
a ſudden interrupted by Madamoiſelle *D'Elbieux*——
She flew into the Room more like a Fury than a
Woman, and finding me there loaded me with Reproaches, as being the occaſion of her Brother's quitting
the World, and all the Misfortunes of her Family, and
vowed ſhe would be revenged on my unlucky Face, as ſhe
termed it. In ſpite of the regard Madam *De G——*
had for her Mother the Counteſs, ſhe could not help reprimanding

manding this Sally of Paffion, and defired fhe would call to mind the Chevalier's Intentions, whom fhe ought not to difturb in his Retreat by the news of her Behaviour, in an affair which appeared of fo much moment to his Peace, and then fhewed her the Letter we had juft been reading ; on which fhe feemed more foftned, and having paufed fome Time, as I had afterwards reafon to fuppofe, to reflect that an open Enmity would be lefs prejudicial to me, than a pretended Friendfhip, came to me and embraced me, afked my Pardon, and begg'd I would impute the blame of all fhe had faid to the firft Emotions of her Grief for the lofs of a Brother, whom fhe fo tenderly loved, and not to any difguft to me, the innocent occafion ; I received thefe Excufes, and replied to them with the refpect due to her Birth. Indeed I could not determine in my own Mind, whether they were fincere or not, I was loth to be guilty of Injuftice, yet fearful of Confiding ; but it was not long before the matter was decided, and I found by experience, that where our Sex once take an Averfion, we are hardly ever reconciled.

This Lady to comply with her Brother's Requeft, as well as her own Friendfhip, as fhe pretended, was very zealous in perfwading Madam *De G*————to keep me in her Houfe, till I could be otherwife difpofed of to my Inclination————that Lady not fufpecting her black Defigns, as Candor takes all the World to be like itfelf, placed an entire Confidence in what fhe faid, and was truly rejoyced at this feeming return of Good-nature.

Madamoifelle *D'Elbieux* left us two Days after, to rejoin Madam her Mother, who wrote to inform her of the Enlargement of the Count, and to rejoice with her on the Recovery of the Chevalier, of whofe Retirement they had not yet heard. She took her leave of me, with all the Marks of a tender Affection, and kiffed me as fhe went into her Chaife—this was the laft Time fhe ever did fo, and was in order to prevent me from any Apprehenfions of the Blow fhe was going to ftrike.

Three or four Days after her Departure Madam *De G*————received a Letter from her, in which her Refpects to me were not omitted, and fhe fo preffingly

reiterated

reiterated what she before had said concerning my remaining in the Castle, that I began to depend on her Kindness, and to banish from my Breast all remembrance of her former Proceedings.

Early the next Morning I received a Letter of infinitely more Consequence : *Dubois* was the Bearer of a thousand tender Vows, from my dear Marquis : That faithful Lover acquainted me, he was then in *Lorrain*, that he escaped being taken by the Exempt only by two Days, that he now had hopes of receiving Permission to return to *Paris*, but that his Father had wrote to him, advising him to take a Journey into *Germany*, in order to make him forget his late Adventures ; but did not make any mention of me, which he was a little surprized at, as knowing the Humour of the old Marquis ; and feared he had some Intentions against me, that he could not as yet comprehend : He entreated me to give him a full Account of my present Situation, and that I would not yield to Affliction, assuring me that he would labour incessantly not only for my Interest, but my Peace of Mind.

What a charming Truce did this give to my Disquiets, ————secure in the most perfect Affection and Esteem of the Man I loved, all other Difficulties seemed for a Time unworthy my Regard : 'Tis indeed natural for a Person accustomed to Vexations to lay hold of every little matter of Consolation, and to be more elevated in those Intervals of Satisfaction, than one whose Life is unchequer'd with Misfortunes————the Bitterness of the one, renders the other doubly Sweet, and Pleasure is truly Pleasure when it succeeds Pain. I wrote a long Detail of every Thing had happened to me since the Marquis's Departure, and was not inferior to him in Point of Tenderness————he desired I should treat him without reserve, nor was I under any Apprehensions he would think I wanted Nicety, in paying this Deference to a Man who had suffered so much for me, and in whose Affection I was so much honoured.

Dubois assured me he would have my Letter in two Days, and said he, even that Time will be to him an
Age.

Age———Amidft all thefe Amufements which would engage the Heart of any other Man, he languifhes to hear News of his adorable *Jeanetta*, and all the Endeavours made ufe of to pleafe, ferve rather to fatigue him..

A fecret Inquietude of which I was not Miftrefs made me queftion this Man; he had told me that the Town where the Marquis refided was full of very lovely and accomplifhed Women, and that his Lord was greatly admired by them; I cannot fay whether it was Jealoufy or fimple Curiofity, that made me defirous of knowing what kind of Beauties thefe *Lorrainers* were, fo made him fit down while I dreft my Head, and he gave me the following Account.

The Town where we are, faid he, is called *Pont-a-Mouffon*; the Situation is extremely delightful, and one finds enough there not to regret the Pleafures of *Paris,* a thing one cannot fay of hardly any other City in the World———the Nobility are extremely Polite, and the Citizens very Obliging———the Women as well bred and eafy in their Converfation, as thofe who frequent *Verfailles.* But among thofe who are moft eminently diftinquifh'd by the Charms of their Perfon and Behaviour, I will name to you Madam *De Gombervault*; fhe is certainly one of the faireft Creatures in the World, her Skin is of the moft dazling Whitenefs: She has very light brown Hair, fine blue Eyes, a Mouth formed to captivate, every Feature regular, then her Wit and the Sweetnefs of her Temper, adds a Luftre to her other Perfections. Monfieur her Hufband is Captain of the Guards to his Royal Highnefs, and knows how to do the Honours of his Houfe in a very elegant Manner. My Lord Marquis eats frequently there, when he can difengage himfelf from Madam the Baronefs *D'Atel*; This Lady is a brown Beauty, has dark hazel coloured Eyes, quick and penetrating as is her Judgment: She is a great Scholar, well read in Philofophy, and can entertain on ferious Subjects, with as much eafe as on thofe more befitting the greateft Part of her Sex: Monfieur *D'Atel* her Spoufe is Chamberlain to the Prince, and there is united in him the greateft Complaifance and perfeft

feft

fect Sincerity————He has also a fine Library ; and a Stranger cannot more agreeably pass his Time than at his House.

The third Family where my Lord is perfectly well received, is that of Monsieur the President *De Landre*: His Lady is extremely amiable, and tho' her Complection is not so clear as those of the others; the inimitable Shine of her black sparkling Eyes make up for that Deficiency, nor is she wanting in any Thing that composes a compleat Beauty————her manner of entertaining Strangers is such, that none can quit her House, without desiring to return, nor does Time ever seem tedious in her Company ; but as if conscious of an Inability of pleasing in her own Person, she is perpetually promoting some new Object of Diversion.

Monsieur the President of *Vitry le Francoise*, has also a very lovely Woman for his Wife ; it would be difficult to give any Idea of her Perfections without seeing her, because they are of a Nature which strike the Eye too much for Words to describe: There is an irresistible Something, which is nor confin'd to one Feature, nor all of them, but spreads itself through all her Air, in so much that she cannot speak, or look, or move, without discovering every Time, some new Grace; but if one may say she excels in any one Thing more than another, it is in Dancing, of which she is a great Lover, and a Week seldom passes without her giving a Ball at her House.

The Provost of the Town must not be forgot, continued he, his whole Family are extremely agreeable— His Wife, tho' past her Bloom, is not without her Allurements, and if Age has destroyed some Part of her Charms in her own Person, they are still to be found in those of her two Daughters, the Eldest of whom is not inferior to any in *Pont-a-Mousson* . She is married to an Exempt of the Guard to his Royal Highness, and called Monsieur *De Saint Val* ; he is a great Musician, has frequent Concerts at his House, and plays admirably well on the Base Viol himself; which my Lord Marquis delighting extremely in, he seldom fails of passing his Evenings there.

there. Monfieur is befides a very good Companion, and has no Fault, but being jealous of his Wife, which indeed is to be excufed in him, that Lady having a Perfon and Accomplifhments to infpire the moft paffionate Sentiments. The Town will needs give her to my Lord for the Object of his Adoration, on Account of his frequent Vifits————

Dubois was continuing his Narrative, but fomething to which I know not how to give a Name feized my Heart, I was cold and hot at the fame Time————every Pulfe felt the Effect of it, and I could not keep myfelf from interrupting him————Yes, cried I, it cannot be otherwife in Nature————the Marquis finds fomething in Madam *De Saint Val*, which very well confoles him for the Abfence and Uncertainty of the Fate of a Woman he has pretended to love in the moft honourable Terms————How Madam! replied *Dubois*, with a Smile, I hope you are not jealous ?————if you are, tho' my Lord could not but be tranfported at that Proof of your Affection for him, I fhould receive little Thanks for having given you, by my foolifh Recital, any Caufe of Pain————No, anfwered I, endeavouring to compofe myfelf, I am not jealous————it is a Paffion I ought not to indulge————I know myfelf too well to prefume to controll the Marquis————I could not utter thefe Words without Tears in my Eyes ; *Dubois* perceived the Agitation I was in, tho' I turned away in order to conceal it as well as poffible, and vexed that he had given any room for it, as he knew how much it would difpleafe the Marquis, he grew ferious, and endeavoured to eafe my Alarms, by protefting in the moft folemn Manner, that the Beauty and other Perfections of all thefe Ladies were far from making any Impreffions on the Marquis's Mind————that his Heart was wholly devoted to me, and that there never was a more tender or more paffionate Lover ; to prove this he gave me an exact Detail of the manner in which his Mafter paft his Time, the Complaints he uttered for being feparated from me, the Refolves he made in my Favour whenever he fhould fee me again, and in fine, the Pleafure he took in Talking

of

of me, than which according to my Opinion there cannot be a furer Proof of a most vehement Affection.

Little Jealousies in Love, when not founded on Reason, are easily eraced, and only serve to render us afterward more secure ; and if any Disquiet remained in me, it was only occasioned by my Shame for having wronged so perfect a Lover as the Marquis, by my unjust Suspicion. *Dubois* after this recounted to me many entertaining Adventures, that happened at *Pont-a-Mousson*, since the Time they had resided there———Some may perhaps, if I have room, find a Place in the Course of these Memoirs.

I was laughing at one of the most pleasant of them, when Madam *De G*———interrupted us by coming in and bringing a Letter in her Hand she had just wrote to the Marquis ; as *Dubois* only waited for this Dispatch, he took leave of us and immediately departed.

I felt an infinity of Satisfaction in having wrote to the Marquis, it was the first Letter he had received from me, wherein the Secrets of my Heart were clearly demonstrated to him ; nothing sure is a greater Relief, than to unbosom one's self with freedom to a Person we love and have an entire Confidence in, it is the very Soul of Friendship, and the Essence of all the Joys attending that noble Passion———Modesty, however, would have restrained me from speaking half that to him which I wrote ; I could never have declared that to him with my Tongue, which I ventured to reveal with my Pen ; but that even with so much Tenderness, that he has since told me the reading some Expressions in that Letter, gave him Extasies little inferior to those he should have felt at seeing me. I frankly own the Weakness of my Soul was Love ; if it can be called Weakness to indulge a Passion founded upon Virtue and Gratitude ; in other Things I wanted not Resolution ; and as I grew in Stature, so I encreased in Courage, to bear up against what Misfortunes threatned me ; but for this as well as for many other Qualifications, I own myself indebted to Madam *De G*———, who had a great deal of Wit and Spirit, joined with a perfect Knowledge of the World———the

sincere

sincere Attachment she found I had for her, so endeared
me to her, that she would pass whole Days with me——
these improving Conversations enlightned my Mind,
and enlarged my Ideas, so that without what they call
Living in the World, I had learned all the Ways of it,
from the variety of Histories she related to me. When
I was alone I recollected all had been said to me, and
had Comprehension enough to compare the different
Events, and to draw this Conclusion, that every Station
of our Lives are subject to Dependancies ; that we never
were without somewhat to hope, and somewhat to fear ;
and that Life passed away in a succession of good and
bad Accidents, therefore did not despair of one Day ac-
complishing my Desires, which I do not blush to confess,
were all centered in being united to the Marquis. I had
thus begun to settle my Thoughts, and to make myself
easy in the expectation of something to fall out to my Advantage ; when alas ! I was on the very brink of falling
into the worst Calamity I had to dread.

I will not pretend to say that People have a Prescience
of what is to happen to them ; as a Woman it does not
become me to argue on this Point, nor would my Sentiments be of any weight in the Decision————all I can
say is, that after having been some time in a greater
Tranquillity than I had for a long while enjoy'd, I was
all on a sudden seized with an uneasiness, which I know
not how to account for————after passing a very
agreeable Evening with Madam *De G*————I retired
to my Chamber in a kind of spleenatick Humour————
it was the first Time I had ever known any Disquiet, without being able to say for what Cause, and was
now so angry with myself for it, that I did every thing
in my power to remove it————I took up a Book,
but could give no Attention to what I read————I would
have pray'd, but my Thoughts were too much distracted
to know what I said————I went to Bed endeavouring
to compose myself to Sleep, but had no Power to close
my Eyes————I turned from one Side to the other,
but all in vain——I could not rest, tho' my Thoughts
were bent on no particular thing to keep me waking——

at laſt the crowing of the Cocks proclaim'd the approach of Day, yet ſtill I continued in the ſame Agitations————Some Hours before the Hemiſphere was enlightned by the Sun paſt over, and I was the ſame, that cheating Plant had no effect upon my Mind: I was about however to riſe, when I heard ſomebody knock at my Chamber Door————I ſtarted up in a Fright————I knew it was very early, and they never uſed to diſturb me————I had both lock'd and barr'd myſelf in ; for ſince the deſign the Chevalier *D'Elbieux* had form'd of carrying me away, I always was very careful to ſecure the Door————a ſecond Knock confirming me I had not been deceived in the firſt, I aſked in a fearful Voice who was there ? and what they wanted ?
————Madam *De G*————anſwered, and bad me open the Door: but ſpoke in ſuch a Tone, as chill'd my Blood————I found ſhe was not alone, and that ſhe ſeemed talking to a Man————her Commands were not to be diſputed notwithſtanding, and I ſtept out of Bed, and having thrown my Robe de Chamber over my Shoulders unfaſtened the Door, and hid myſelf again behind the Curtains. As I looked between them, I ſaw her enter and a Gentleman with her, who ſeemed by his Dreſs and Air to be of Faſhion————He ſoon withdrew my Shelter, and was opening his Mouth to ſpeak ; but after having fix'd his Eyes on me, he turned them to my Protectreſs ; indeed Madam, ſaid he, I did not think to have diſturbed ſo pretty a Lady as this————I no longer wonder at the apprehenſions Monſieur the marquis *De L*———— *V*———— is under————a Beauty ſuch as I now behold, joined to a little Intrigue, may carry his Son great lengths. While he ſpoke theſe Words, Madam *De G*————threw herſelf on my Bed, where I lay quite overwhelmed with Apprehenſions—Ah ! *Jeanetta*, cried ſhe, how unhappy am I to have known you ſince I muſt loſe you ſo ſoon————if my Fears had left me any remains of Reaſon, this Exclamation deſtroyed them all————great God, returned I burſting into Tears, what is it you ſay, Madam—no, I

will

will never leave you————they fhall kill me firft, with this I threw myfelf into her Arms.

.The Stranger doubtlefs touch'd with the Grief his coming had involv'd us in, approach'd with a great deal of Politenefs, I am much concerned at the trouble I give you, beautiful young Lady, faid he, and much more at the Order which obliges me to put you under an Arreft ————you will find, neverthelefs, fome Reafons to confole yourfelf in this unavoidable Misfortune———— Monfieur the Marquis *De L———— V————* on obtaining a *Letter de Cachet* to confine you in a Monaftry, might have employed thofe Perfons who are appointed for that Purpofe; but having intrufted me with his Defign and the Motives he had for it, I defired this Commiffion more out of Curiofity I do affure you, than any Averfion I had for you————and to this I may add another Reafon, which I will not conceal before this Lady, who I perceive is too much your Friend, not to be the Confidant of the moft fecret Paffages of your Life; I am, Madam, a near Kinfman of your Lover, and not-withftanding his Referve, and the Care he took to con-ceal every Thing relating to you, from all his Family, I knew the whole Affair between you————as foon as the unlucky Adventure between him and the Chevalier *D'Elbieux* made it publick, and I underftood the In-tentions of my Uncle the old Marquis; I pretended to think as he did, and applauded his Refentments, that I might be the better able, when Time fhould ferve, to mollify them————So that, Madamoifelle *Jeanetta,* continued he, the greateft caufe of Grief you have, is that for a Time you muft be feparated from this excellent Lady————I doubt not but much happier Days here-after will obliterate the Memory of the prefent———— Your Tears and Beauty have touched me to the Soul, and tho' my End in taking upon me this Office was to ferve you, yet the Means is too difagreeable, and per-haps dangerous to myfelf.

Monfieur *De Saint Fal,* for that was his Name, figh'd as he pronounced thefe Words, and turned his Eyes alter-nately from me to her, and her to me again, with fuch

an

an Air of Pity, as very much confirmed what he had said : Madam *De G*———took the advantage of his kind Concern, to endeavour to prevail on him to return without me, and pretend that I had made my Escape two Days before his Arrival. Would to God, Madam, replied he, that it were in my power to oblige you thus far———but there is no Possibility of doing it——— My Uncle, is but too well acquainted, that Madamoiselle *Jeanetta* is at your House, and moreover, that there was no Intention of her removing———he even knows that *Dubois*, my Cousin's Valet de Chamber was here with Letters from him, and carried Answers back to *Lorrain*———in fine, there is nothing hid from him ; a Person whom I must not Name, has a Spy in pay under your own Roof, who sends every Day Intelligence of what Passes, and, in case Madamoiselle had left the Castle, was to have followed her and given Notice——— You see Ladies I speak sincerely, added he, and I think it is not difficult for you to guess from what Quarter the Blow proceeds.

No, no, cried I impatiently, the Treachery is too plain———it can be no other, than the false Mada- moiselle *D'Elbieux*———the barbarous Creature, who caressed me while she contrived my Ruin. Madam *De G*———tho' greatly interrested in the Affair, was yet less so than myself, and had not the least Suspicion of her, but on my naming her, looked on Monsieur *De Saint Fal*, and was answered with a Glance, which left her no room to doubt the Mischievousness of that un- sincere Woman———She shook her [Head, in token of Detestation of such Actions, than taking me in her Arms, protested her Friendship should follow me where- ever I went———I cannot oppose the King's Orders, said she, nothing else should tear you from me———the Letter your Lover's Father writes to me, is filled with Apologies for the Force, he is compelled in Honour, and as he says, to prevent fatal Consequences, to use in my House ; and would make me believe 'tis in Respect to me he sends one of his own Blood instead of an Exempt. ———He tells me also, that for my sake you shall be

treated with the utmost Tenderness, tho' at the same
Time he lets me know he looks upon me as no Friend
to his Family, in having favoured, or at least not opposed your Correspondence with his Son——But for
my Part, I am little concerned at what the World may
reproach me for on this Score, conscious I have acted
according to the Principles of Honour and Probity——
All I desire is, my dear Child, that you would summon
all the Fortitude you are Mistress of to your Assistance—
we must all submit to Necessity———Continue to behave as you have always done with Virtue and Discretion, and I dare answer Heaven will protect you, and
render you in the End triumphant over all ill Accidents.

She then entreated Monsieur the Count *De Saint Fal,*
to retire while I got myself ready for my Departure; he
readily did so, and all the Time I was Dressing, this
admirable Lady animated me with a Thousand kind
Remonstrances; she called to my Mind the many
Dangers I already had escaped, and from thence as she
told me, built an assured Hope that I should never be
abandoned by Providence, and that by these uncommon
Trials, I must be destined to some very extraordinary
Event———She added, that it was in the well enduring
Misfortunes that the true Sublimity of the Soul was best
proved; and by such Occasions it was alone, that I could
manifest myself worthy the Sentiments the Marquis had
for me, and put all those to Confusion who pretended
a Dignity of Nature was confined to high Birth———So,
my dear *Jeanetta,* said she, always bear this in your
Mind, that the more you suffer, the more you will be
endeared to your noble Lover, and this will enable you
to go through every Thing without sinking.

This Counsel was so conformable to my own Opinion,
and so greatly strengthned the Resolution I was bringing
myself to, that I dried up my Tears, restrained my Sighs
by degrees, and by the time all Things were prepared for
my leaving the Castle, I had resumed so serene a
Countenance, that Monsieur *De Saint Fal,* on his being
called into the Chamber, was surprized and scarce knew
me

me again————I behaved to him with all the Complaisance his Quality demanded, and told him I was ready to obey the Orders he bore. Requesting him to acquaint the old Marquis *De L——— V———*, when he should write an Account of what he had done, that I had the highest Regard and Veneration for every Thing that came from him————not even excepting his Severities, and should attend his Decision of my Fate, with all the Patience and Submission he could expect from those most devoted to him.

The Kinsman of my Lover, made a thousand Compliments on my Spirit and Resolution, and when he was told I waited only his Pleasure for going, he gave the Word for his Retinue—I then embraced my amiable Protectress with the greatest Tenderness————She held me a long time in her Arms, and neither being able to refrain in this Adieu, which we knew not but might be our last, we mingled Tears, accompanied with the most vehement Sighs————She had presence enough of Mind however to slip a Purse into my Hand, just as we parted without the Count's perceiving it————all the Servants who waited for me in the Gallery to give me their good Wishes, seemed greatly concerned for me, they followed me till I got into the Chaise, weeping as they went, and after I was seated, and the Coachman was driving away, I could distinguish the Voice of poor *Christina* above the rest, uttering the loudest Lamentations.

The End of the F O U R T H P A R T.

T H E

THE

VIRTUOUS VILLAGER,

OR,

VIRGIN's VICTORY.

PART. V.

DURING the Time of our Journey which was prolong'd two Days above what was neceſſary for Reaſons I ſhall hereafter explain, the Count *de St. Fal*, treated me in every Reſpect as if I had been a Woman of the firſt Quality, ——the firſt Day indeed his Behaviour had been different : The malicious Ideas they had given him of me, made him conſider me as a ſimple Country Girl without Education, and eaſy to be brought to any Thing—— this Prejudice made him talk to me in a familiar Stile, which my Modeſty and perhaps ſome Sparks of Pride,

made

made me anſwer in ſuch Terms as aſtoniſh'd him———
however he continued for ſome time the ſame ſort of
Phraſes, and thinking to intimidate me, ſpoke in a
tone, which made me ſee he was ſenſible of the great
Difference between him and me ; and under the Pretence
of giving me Advice, in order that I might not be miſerable, he told me that I ought to abate a great deal of that
Haughtineſs, the Marquis's Affection he ſuppoſed had made
me affect ; proteſting more Mildneſs and Humility would
become me better ; but ſoftning at the ſame Time the
Aſperity of theſe Reflections, with many Praiſes on my
Beauty, and letting me underſtand I was perfectly agreeable to his Taſte. He added alſo, that I was too lovely
and too genteel to be debarr'd all my Life, from the
Pleaſures of the World, and ſhut up in a Convent———
that there was no hope of alleviating the old Marquis's
Reſentment againſt me, and if I once entered the Place
he had Orders to conduct me to, I muſt never expect to
come out, for that either by Perſuaſions or Menaces they
would oblige me to become a Nun; but that if I would be
complaiſant to him, in fine, if I would endeavour to
bring myſelf to love him, he would not only ſave
me from falling into the Hands of the Marquis;
but alſo take care of me in a handſome manner all my
Days.

I am not, I flatter myſelf, to be condemned for
treating ſuch Diſcourſe with the Diſdain it merited ; for
whatever diſparity there was in Point of Birth, between
me, and the Count, Virtue enobles its meaneſt Votaries ;
as Vice degrades the moſt High-born, when they become ſubjected to its Sway. I entered therefore into no
Argument with him ; but only told him with an Air,
which I could perceive a little diſconcerted him, that I
deſired he would forbear talking to me on any ſuch
Matters, but to execute the Commiſſion had been given;
for neither the Ills that were prepared for me, nor the
Means of eſcaping them, would be in the leaſt capable
of making me change the Plan I had laid down for all
my Actions, which was in all Events never to ſwerve
from the Paths of Honour and Decency.

He

He endeavoured to laugh me out of these romantick Notions, as he called them, and displayed a more fashionable System of Morality, which finding made no impression on me, would have been no less free in his Actions than he had been in Words ; but I had the Art, without being guilty of any breach of Politeness, to give him a Rebuff, and make him sensible how unworthy of a Man of Honour or good Breeding such Proceedings were ; I told him that it was highly inconsistent with these Rules, which Persons of Quality above all others ought strictly to preserve, to endeavour either to fright or seduce a young Creature, whom Chance alone had put into his Power, and who had no other Defence, than what her Tears afforded————by so much the more you are above me, said I, by so much the more ought I to expect Protection from you————in fine, Virtue inspired me with Words so touching and persuasive, that this young Nobleman dangerous as he was, and who when it grew Bed-time could scarce prevail on himself to quit my Chamber, retired with a kind of Shame, for having given me Cause to make him Remonstrances, the Solidity of which he could not but acknowledge—He entreated me to think no more of what he had said, and promised to atone for his want of Respect, by a quite contrary Conduct for the future. I received his Apologies in a proper Manner ; neither dwelling too much on what had past, nor seeming altogether satisfied with the Assurances he gave me, and indeed went to Bed cruelly agitated, as well with Resentment for what had happened, as the Fears of what might ensue.

It was not without a good deal of Timidity, that I saw him approach me the next Morning, but his Words, his Looks, and his whole Air was so much the Reverse of that he had put on the Day before, that I soon lost all Apprehensions on this score————He seemed now to study nothing but to oblige me————treated me with all imaginable Respect————told many entertaining Stories as he said to divert me in my Journey ; and omitted nothing, that he thought might convince me,

he

he meant to keep the Promises he had made me the Night before.

His Conversation was perfectly genteel and easy, and shewed he knew the World very well, and did not want Wit; my Answers to him, giving him an Opinion that I had some share of it myself, I could plainly discover by his Looks, on some of the Repartees I made him, that he was amazed to find such ready turns of Thought and aptness of Expression, from one he had considered hitherto only as a meer Country Girl——so strangely does the Pride of Birth in those descended of a noble Family prejudice the Mind, that they cannot without great Difficulties bring themselves to believe, it is possible for one of mean Extraction to wear off the Rusticity of their Original. But Monsieur *De Saint Fal* should have considered the uncommon Opportunities I had of Improvement, first under my God-mother the Countess *De N*——and afterwards in the Family of that excellent and polite Lady Madam *De G*——which indeed were sufficient to render a small natural Capacity accomplished.

The third Day my noble Exempt, if I may be allowed to give him that Title, as he had undertaken the Business of one, spoke much less to me; but seemed to consider me with very great Attention, and in doing so frequently sent forth deep Sighs; this gave me an infinite Disquiet, I feared with Reason he was becoming Amorous of me, and trembled lest I should find in him a second Chevalier *D'Elbieux*; the Apprehensions I was under on this Score made me sometimes turn pale, alone as I was, and entirely in his power——Sometimes I had thought of attempting to make my Escape out of his Hands——but where should I have gone—— where hoped to find Protection against Royal Power? ——besides, with Confusion I must own it, since my living in the manner I had done since I had quitted my Father's Cottage, I was grown too delicate to bear the Fatigues I could before have chearfully gone through; and this last Consideration helped to make the Difficulties

of

of my Flight more numerous and formidable than they really were.

The Agitations of my Mind shewed themselves in my Countenance, too plainly for the Count not to perceive I was disordered, and imagining I might not be well, asked me several Times if I chose to stop and go into some House for refreshment; but on my answering him in the Negative, I fear, said he, the Journey is too great a Fatigue for you————I am very much deceived, if you are not on the sudden very uneasy; I hope, beautiful *Jeanetta*, you do not remember any Cause I might give you of Displeasure at our first setting out;————I beg it as a favour you will command any thing in my power, and deal sincerely with a Person, whose utmost Ambition is to repair the Wrongs he has done you, by a mistaken Pre-possession, and which a more perfect Knowledge of your Merit has entirely banish'd.

This Discourse, the Uncertainty of my Fate, the new Convent to which I was going to be carried, the loss of Madam *De G*————'s Advice and Protection, and to speak truth, the Improbability of seeing my dear Marquis any more————all these Things I say coming at once into my Mind, melted me into Tears————all my Fortitude forsook me, and my Heart-Strings seemed to break————Ah! cried *Saint Fal*, this is too much————I cannot bear to see you thus————your Grief overwhelms my Soul————notwithstanding a thousand Reasons for the contrary, a secret Impulse attaches me to your Interest, and will not suffer me to execute the Commission which gave you to my Power————'tis the Apprehensions of a Convent I judge has given you this Disturbance; if so, be easy lovely Creature; for whatever shall be the Consequence, I cannot do any thing which draws Tears from the finest Eyes in the World—he paused a Moment or two after these Words; then, yes, Madamoiselle, pursued he, you shall be convinced of the influence your Charms have on all who behold you————blush not at the Confession I make, 'tis an excuse for the Passion my Cousin has for you, whose Happiness I envy,

and

and profefs myfelf his Rival————But let not the knowledge of my Sentiments alarm you ; for here I vow by all we Mortals have to hope or fear, I will never take any advantage from the opportunity Fortune has put into my Power, to diminifh the Inclinations you have for the Marquis, much lefs to make ufe of any violent Means in favour of the Paffion you have infpired me with.———— You figh, continued he, perceiving I did fo, you ftill fear me————put therefore my Honour and Sincerity to the Proof, and you will then be convinced, O too beautiful Maid, how far I am to be relied upon.

The Count here ftop'd expecting my reply ; but I was too much confufed to make any, and my Eyes fixed on the Ground, difcovered my Perplexity.

To what can I impute this Silence, faid he, muft I look on it as a Mark of your Diftruft ?————Can you be-lieve me capable of deceiving you after the folemn Af-feveration I have made, and which in fpite of the gay Life I have led, I could not be tempted to falfify———— but if you judge thus of me, I fhall indeed pay dear for the Infenfibility I have hitherto boafted of, and feverely repent the imprudent Curiofity which has thus expofed my Liberty————I might indeed, without feeing you, have been affured from the Marquis's Affection for you, who I know to be fo great a judge of what is truly valua-ble, that you were the moft worthy of your whole Sex to be adored————Yet, charming *Jeanetta*, whatever Injuftice you may be guilty of in your Sufpicions of me, or whatever Treatment I fhall receive from you, I will not regret my having undertaken this Commiffion, as it gives me an Opportunity of ferving you, which without it I could never have been Mafter of—yes, cried he with Vehemence, you fhall foon fee that Deeds and Words are the fame things with me. He had no fooner faid this, than he put his Head out of the Chaife, and ordered a Servant that rode by the fide of it, to direct to take the Road to *Verfailles*, inftead of that he was pur-fuing.————The Servant feemed very much furprized, and replied, that Monfieur the Marquis had commanded the contrary————and that————he was going on, but

I

his

his Master prevented him by saying in a fierce Tone, is it for you to reason on these Matters———do as you are bid, and leave the rest to me; the Fellow offered no more, but spoke to the Postilion, and we soon quitted the great Road.

I knew not what to think of this Counter-Order; but as I began to flatter myself, that the Count had really no Intentions to my Prejudice, I could not avoid feeling a secret Pleasure in finding myself going to a Place, which I knew would be the Residence of my Lover, when his Banishment should be repealed, as I doubted not but it soon would———I knew also that it was the Palace of the King, and that, recalling the dear Remembrance of my seeing his Majesty at *Fountain-bleau,* which Accident had first given me the knowledge of the Marquis, inspired me with a thousand pleasing Ideas———alas! how easily do those in love pass, from one extreme to the other!———my Eyes now resumed their accustom'd Vivacity, and the innate Satisfaction of my Mind spread itself through all my Features.

The Count perceived with joy this Change in me, and not imagining it proceeding from any other Source, than that of the Prospect of being delivered from a Cloyster, reiterated the promise he had made me; and added, that I should always be the Mistress of my Actions; and be convinced by Experience, that if he was not so happy as to please me, he would at least deserve that Honour by his Services and Integrity.

I was going to return with all the Gratitude it demanded an Answer to those fresh Assurances of his Goodness, when on entring a Village where we were to dine, we saw a Crowd of People gathered about a young Female Pilgrim, who was carrying, or rather dragging a Cross of a most prodigious Size———Good God! cried I, how I pity that poor young Creature———how is it possible to see her, and not commiserate the Rigour of her Fate! As I got out of the Chaise, I asked the Mistress of the House, who came to welcome us, if she could inform us, what Obligation this Pilgrim lay under to travel in such a manner. It is what I cannot learn, answered

answered she, all I hear is that several of the Neighbours have given her Alms, she distributes it among the Poor about her, which occasions these Acclamations, and at the same time proves that she is a Person of no mean Condition.————My Husband had the same Curiosity you have, continued she, and went to enquire ; but all the Account he brought was, that she said, she was doing a voluntary Penance, and fulfilling a Vow she had made ; and that if she had enjoined herself infinitely more than what she suffered, it would not be a sufficient Atonement for her Sins, and that before she left the Village, we should be made acquainted with her History.

My Curiosity was greatly encreased by what this Woman said, and I could not help expressing it to the Count *De Saint Fal*, as he led me into the House, where as soon as he had left me he retired.

I imagined he had been gone into the Stable as was his Custom, to see sufficient care was taken of his Horses ; for tho' he had several Servants with him, he took a pleasure in overlooking the manner in which those poor Creatures were provided for. Being alone, I fell into Contemplation on the oddness of my Fate, and in particular the Circumstances I was at present in————'twas impossible for me to see the end of this Adventure, and what would be the Consequence of that Passion, I now found the Count had for me————I longed for a Friend to whom I might communicate both my Hopes and my Apprehensions. If my dear *Saint Agnes* were with me, said I to myself, my Misfortunes would lose half their Weight ! How unfortunate is it in some Situations to be abandoned to one self !

The Remembrance of *Saint Agnes* at this juncture, made me reproach myself for being so slow in the Service she expected from me ; but from the time of my leaving the Monastery, I had been in such a continual hurry of Spirits, and been also so strictly observed, that I had not had an opportunity of performing my promise to her—I might indeed have left her Papers with *Christina* at my coming from the Castle ; but as it was of the utmost Con-

I

sequence to prevent their being lost, and the Affair ought to be pursued with Vigour, I was fearful of entrusting them in the hands of one who was not in a Station to act as it required. These were the Reasons which had hitherto delayed my doing any thing for this dear Friend ; but as we are never so sensible of the Afflictions of others, as when we labour under great ones of our own, these Reflections so lively set forth to my Mind, the Grief *Saint Agnes* was in for my Absence, and how tedious Expectation is, that I resolved to acquit myself of the Obligations I owed for the Confidence she had placed in me, and to lay hold of the first occasion that presented itself to send an express Messenger to her Lover, who should deliver her Letters to his own Hand, or in his Absence to his Father ; this was now easy for me to do, as I had Money that Madam *De G*——— had given me, and which I had never thought of since, till this Design of serving *Saint Agnes* reminded me of it——— I now took the Purse out of my Pocket, to see what my generous Benefactress had bestowed upon me, and found it contained five and twenty *Lewis d'Or*, but what transported me much more was, that in opening a little Box I found the Picture of Madam *De G*——— ; I kissed it, and all her Tenderness coming fresh into my Mind a flood of Tears ensued——I was moved to that Degree, that to this Moment while I am writing these Memoirs, I feel some part of what at that time passed in my Heart———Yes, ever admired Lady, cried I, never shall I forget your Goodness and the Friendship with which you have honoured me———'tis said in reproach to our Sex, that Women are seldom sincere and lasting Friends to each other, I hope it is not true in general, but if it is, I am an exception to this Rule, for were I to live beyond an Antidiluvian Age, the tender regard I have for Madam *De G*———would never be diminished.

Her dear Picture was still in my Hand, with my Eyes and Heart attentively fixed on it, when I was pleasingly disturbed by the Count *De Saint Fal*, leading the Pilgrim into the Room. I take the Liberty, Madam, said he, to introduce this amiable Person, whose Fate you so much pitied; I have engaged her to remain here while we stay, and to relate to us the Motives that induced her to lay so severe a Penance on herself.———I am indeed no Stranger to her Name, and have heard much talk of her Adventures in my Province; but as she tells me, they are related there in a manner very different from Truth, my Curiosity is not now inferior to yours.——— I can assure you of this, however, that she is not a Person of mean Condition, and that her Wit and Learning excels not only most of her own Sex; but also equals some of ours who pass for celebrated.

I had rose from my Seat to embrace the beautiful Stranger on her first entrance; but this Character given of her by the Count, who I had perceived was not of a humour to allow Women more than he thought their due, made me redouble my Complaisance, which she returned in a fashion which shewed me she had been educated among the polite World. The Cloath being laid, I entreated she should dine with us, to which she readily agreed, on Condition she should be at liberty to eat in the manner she chose; in the mean time desired permission to give some Orders in the Kitchen; and while she was gone I took the opportunity to thank Monsieur *De Saint Fal* for obliging me with the Sight of this fair Pilgrim———Stay, beautiful *Jeanetta*, till I have done you some, real Service before you make me any such Acknowledgments, what I have now done serves only to shew you, that to fulfil the least of your Desires shall always be to me a matter of the utmost Moment.

The Pilgrim's return prevented me from making any reply as I would have done to this Civility; and while the Count was speaking to her, I examined her whole Person more heedfully than I before had done———She was tall, and her Limbs of so delicate and fine proportioned a Turn, that I question had the best Artist been employed to make her Statue, if it would have come up to the Original———She had on a close Waistcoat of very fine Cotton, which shewed to great advantage the Beauty of her Shape; her Petticoat was the same, and

over

over all a coarse red Mantle, and decorated according to the Custom of Pilgrims with Shells; a Rush Hat, cock'd Boatways and lined with yellow Taffety, became her better than the gay Ornaments some Ladies wear to set off their Beauties.————Her Face was much tann'd, having been exposed to the Inclemency of the Weather, but her Hands shewed that nothing could be more white than her Skin naturally was————the Lustre of her large sparkling black Eyes, however, neither her Sorrows nor Fatigues seem'd to have impaired, which, together with an exact Symmetry of Features, rendered her extremely lovely, in spite of a melancholy and dejected Air, which we might plainly see was only occasioned by her Misfortunes.

While I thus attentively considered her, I could not forbear sighing————when one is opprest with any Afflictions, the Sight of them in others excites our Compassion on our own, and I naturally passed to a Commiseration of myself; and imagined that whatever Woes this agreeable Pilgrim had to complain of, they could not be more poynant than those I laboured under. But this did not render me less willing to give her all the Consolation in my Power; whenever she burst out, as she frequently did, into Exclamations against the Severity of her Fate, I took her in my Arms with the same Tenderness as if we had long been intimate, and these proofs of a growing Affection in me, seemed a little to mitigate her Sorrows.

Dinner being brought in interrupted a Conversation, which was much more serious than could be expected among Persons of our Age; and after we had placed ourselves at Table, Monsieur *De Saint Fal* and I saw to our great surprize some coarse Bread and a Glass Mug of Water set before the Pilgrim, which was all she would be prevailed upon to taste, tho' we thinking she imposed too rigorous a Law upon herself, did all in our power to oblige her to partake with us. She said that all the Mortifications she had sustained were infinitely too little for the Cause, as we should hereafter confess on hearing the particulars of her Story; but added, she, my

Vow

Vow of Abstinence expires this Day, and To-morrow
I shall conform to the rest of the World.   This silenced
our Request, and as soon as the Table was emptied, she
prevented us on the Subject we were so desirous of knowing, especially myself, by saying she would now make
us sensible of the Motives which had induced her to undertake this Pilgrimage ; but, said she, if your Journey
requires to be immediately pursued, I will not detain you
by a Repetition of those Circumstances which may be
omitted, and only give you a Narrative of the Facts,
which have rendered me the Wretch I am.

By no means, cried the Count, this Lady is entirely
her own Mistress, and I dare answer would be loth to
lose any part of a History the Sight of you has made her
take so great an interest in; what say you, Madam,
continued he, turning to me, does not your Inclination in
this point concur with mine? Besides, I think it would
be well if you remained here till To-morrow————I see
the Journey has been already too fatiguing to you, and
some repose here will enable you to prosecute it with more
vigour. I had all the Sense it merited of this Complaisance,
and bowed in token of my Acknowledgment.

The Pilgrim told us she was rejoiced at this Proposal,
as it gave her an Opportunity of a longer Conversation
with me, she not being to go herself till the Day following ; when her Penance being concluded, she had appointed a Chaise to meet her, in which she intended to
reach her Journey's end.   Then finding we were impatiently disposed to hear her, she began to satisfie our
Curiosity in these Words.

The *History and uncommon Misfortunes of the beautiful* LINDAMINE.

I AM said she, the only Child of one of the most eminent, and wealthy Physicians of *Montpellier*, nor is
it a boast in me to say, that no Man of his Profession exceeded him in Learning or Experience ; both which he
had so great Reputation for, that I have known Persons
come a hundred Leagues for his Advice : it seem'd indeed
as if Heaven gave a peculiar Blessing to his Endeavours, for
scarce one in fifty of those, to whom he administred, died
under his Hands.

As I was the sole Fruits of a Marriage, the Happiness
of which had never been interrupted with any of those
Jealousies, Repinings, or Discontents, that too often are
the Portion of that State, and fright others from entring
into it ; it is not to be doubted but my Parents were ex-
tremly tender of me, and took all imaginable Care to
have me educated in such a Manner, as would become the great Fortune, that was to devolve on me after
their Decease. Soon as I arrived at Years capable of
receiving Instruction, I was put under the Tuition of the
best Masters.———My Father, far from thinking that
Learning was immaterial to the rendring our Sex accomplished, had an Ambition to make me as knowing
as the most celebrated of the other ; so that besides
Musick, Dancing, and those other Qualifications, which
all Girls of any Condition are taught, and which you
may easily suppose my Mother would not suffer to be
omitted, he made me in the first Place be well acquainted
with History, not only of my own but foreign Countries :

From this I proceeded to Geography, and Philosophy, and thence to the study of Physick, in which Science he was himself my Master: Charmed with the Facility with which I surmounted all its Difficulties, he set no Limits to his Lectures: My Memory, like a fruitful Field, yielded a plentiful Harvest, of whatever was sown in it: I comprehended Anatomy, Botany, and Osteology, and, in fine, before I was seventeen, had made so great a Progress in the Mysteries of *Æsculapius*, that I composed a Treatise of Physick, in *Latin*, and dedicated it to my Father. The Reputation I gained by this Book reached very distant Countrys, and my Father had the Satisfaction, of receiving convincing Proofs of it, by the Compliments made him upon it by the learned World.

Fatal Knowledge! Ruinous Accomplishments! Which by rendring me known to others, made me ignorant of myself——I heard every body say I was a Prodigy of Wit and Learning, and I readily believed them.—— To heighten my Vanity, the little Beauty I was mistress of was also extoll'd, and as every one sees their own Features with flattering Eyes, either they, or my Glass, made me imagine, I merited all the Praises could be given me.————In fine, I thought myself such, as no Man was capable of deserving to possess; and this Idea made me reject with the utmost disdain, all Addresses which had Love or Marriage for their Aim. This Disposition in me, troubled my Father very much, for being far advanced in Years he ardently long'd to see me disposed of before his Death: But greater far would his Concern have been if he had perceived, what I cunningly kept from him, the Motive of that Aversion I declared for Marriage: Could he, I say, have imagined that Pride alone was the Scource of my refusing the many advantageous Offers, that were daily made him on my Account, he would, I am very certain, in spite of all his Tenderness, have taken as much Pains to mortify that Passion in me, as he had done to give me those Endowments which had excited it; but I so well disguised it under the Pretence of the Love I had for him, and my dear Mother, whom I told

him

him it would break my Heart to be a Day separated from, that he concluded, I was only insensible of any soft Desires, because I had not yet seen the Man, destined by Heaven to inspire me with them, so rested himself contented, in the Expectation of what he wished would one Day happen.

At last, the Report of my Learning and other Qualifications, inspired the Son of a Nobleman, some few Leagues distant from *Montpellier*, with a Curiosity to see this Wonder as I was called————He came under the Pretence of asking my Father's Opinion on some slight Ailment, and by that means, having an opportunity of seeing me, became extremely enamoured, and to so great a Degree, that before he had been three Days at our House, he threw himself at my Father's Feet, entreating he would give his Consent to authorize his Addresses to me————The Count *de St. Fal* knew him perfectly well, and you, Madam, cannot but have heard of him, it was the young Count *de B*————; besides the Advantages of Birth, he had one of the finest Persons in the World, and was also every way one of the most accomplished of his Sex. My Father was transported at the Honour, and not doubting but I should receive it, as I ought to have done, immediately made him the Concession he desired————what Woman but me would not gladly have accepted a Lover of his Rank ?———— One would think, my very Pride should have made me embrace the Offer of being placed among the Nobility; but, alas! mine was a kind of Haughtiness, which, I know not how to account for; a Haughtiness, which as it was not at all perceivable in my outward Deportment, had the greater Empire over my private Thoughts————I could not avoid doing Justice to the Merits of this new Admirer, but I still thought my own superior, and could not think of entring into a State, in which it was my Duty to submit.———— The Pleasure of being adored, and being free to receive all the Homage paid me, by those who flattered themselves with being able one Day to engage

my

my Heart, was what I could not resolve to part with; and I answered my Father, concerning the Count, as I had before to the others who had sollicited him on the same score.

This tender Parent appeared so much surprized at my Behaviour, that he scarce knew what to say; but the Count, whose Passion for me really carried him to great Extravagancies, exciting his Pity, as well as regard for his Quality, he at last told me, that if I had any Respect for his Commands, or any Awe of his Authority, I must think of this young Nobleman as a Person destined to make me happy——— My Mother was not less importunate with me——— all my Friends and Kindred endeavoured to prevail upon me, the Count himself was every Day dying at my Feet, yet I was still unmoved, and all their united Efforts served only to disquiet me, without making the least Abatement of that Obduracy I had all along maintain'd.

For some Months did this faithful Lover endure all that neglected Love afflicts; and found that instead of making any Impression on my Heart, all his Assiduities but encreased my Aversion, yet still did the Excess of his Respect prevent him from making any Complaints to my Parents, or once desiring they would make use of their Power over me, to oblige me to listen to his Vows, with a more favourable Ear; but this manner of proceeding, continued so long, and my being urged to it by all who wished well to our Family, my Father at last began to think his Conduct to me had been wrong, and that he ought not to have left me in this Respect, so much my own Mistress. Possest with this Opinion, he told me, one Day, that since he found I was so little capable of judging for myself, or had indeed so little Regard to his Advice, he now would shew me, that I was not at my own Disposal; in fine, that he would force me to be happy in my own despite, and that he would no longer wait my Choice, and that I must prepare to marry the Count in a few Days

This

This Command uttered in a Tone, which was quite a Stranger to my Ears, threw me into the utmost Consternation.————I was terrified at so unexpected a Proof of his Authority, but I was not shaken in my Resolution; and I had the Audacity to tell him, that if he went about to do any Violence to my Inclinations in this Article, I wou'd that Moment fly for Refuge to a Monastry, or even to Death itself; neither of which, cried I, is not half so dreadful to me, as the Thoughts of Marriage. This Protestation was succeeded with a flood of Tears; and as he perfectly doated upon me, his Fondness got the better of his Resolves, and he gave me his Promise, never more to persecute me on a Theme, to which I had testified so invincible a Repugnance.

He had but just left me, before the Count *de B*—— came into the Room: He perceived I had been weeping, and uttered certainly the most tender Things, that Love ever dictated on the like Occasion. But at that Time I was so far from being sensible of them, that looking on him that spoke them, as the Source of my Perplexities, the Indifference I had for him grew into a perfect Hate.————Pretend not to pity, said I, what you alone have caused————your unwished Acquaintance——your luckless Love, and your fruitless Importunities, have very near deprived me of the Tenderness of the best of Fathers, have subjected my Actions, and my Sentiments, to the Scrutiny of a thousand impertinent Intermedlers; and, if you desire to repair the Vexations you have given me, it must be by never seeing me more. With these Words I flung from him, and shut myself into my Closet, refusing to hear what Answer he would make, tho' he continued a long Time at the Door, beseeching I would hear him speak.

This was the last Time I saw him, but not the last of my Troubles, on his Account; for, as I afterwards was inform'd, his Despair carryed him into the *Polish* Wars, were he was unfortunately kill'd——— I heard the News, at a Time when I was grown

more

more susceptible of the Power of Love, and was extreamly grieved at the Fate I looked on myself as the sole Occasion of——Alas! I did not then imagine I was born for the Destruction of all to whom I was dear——

The beautiful Pilgrim, was here interrupted in her Story, by a Torrent of Tears, which in spite of her Endeavours to restrain them, burst from her Eyes; but her Griefs having had a Vent, and composing herself as well as she could, after a short Pause she resumed her Discourse in the following Manner.

In a few Days after the Count's Departure, said she, my Father received a Letter from a Physician at *Lisbon*, acquainting him, that a Book wrote by me had fallen into his Hands; that having read it with great Attention, and form'd a Judgment of my Capacity, by this learned Production, he could attribute such a Prodigy, to nothing so much as the great Skill of the Master, who had been my Instructor in this abstruse Science, so thought him a proper Person, to improve an only Son of his; and beseech'd he would accept of the Charge of him; assuring my Father at the same Time, that he should think nothing too great a Gratification, if he could obtain a Favour he had so much at Heart.

My Father, who secretly persisted in his inclination of seeing me married; tho' he would not break the Promise he had made, consented to receive this young Gentleman, as a Scholar, and a Boarder, hoping that under the pretence of leaving the Care of his Studies to me on account of his great Age and Infirmities, he might have the Opportunity of ingratiating himself, and by being continually in my Company, if his Person was at all agreeable, wean me by Degrees from the relish I had for a single Life.

With this View the *Lisbon* Physician had an Answer agreeable to his Wishes, the Offer was accepted, every thing agreed to, and the young Gentleman was to set out on his Journey with all possible Expedition.

'Tis true, that before my Father gave his Consent,

he

he took the Precaution of enquiring, by the Means of some Correspondents he had there, concerning the Character and Person of him who was to be sent: and finding both such as he desired, the one without Reproach, and the other extremely amiable, he hesitated not a Moment, before he did his Part, toward making the Experiment, how far I could be influenced in Favour of Mankind. In order to which, he said to my Mother in my Presence, that there was nothing he disliked in having this Gentleman, who was expected in eight Days, but that he was so ugly, and deformed, as to create almost a Loathing in all who saw him. He enlarged very much on the Topic, how disagreeable a Thing it was to live with one of such an unhappy Make, and added he would gladly have been excused, but that he was pressed to it by Persons, whom he knew not how to disoblige.

I little regarded this Discourse, it only served to give me an odious Idea of the Person I was to instruct; but as I had no Thoughts of him, as one who would ever pretend to make his Adresses to me, the thing was a matter of perfect Indifference.

At length he arrived, but great God, how was I astonished, when instead of the most contemptible Figure in the World, I saw my Father introduce to my Mother and myself, infinitely, the most graceful Person I had ever beheld————Tall, majestick, admirably proportioned, a Face in which every manly Charm was blended, a certain Softness which stole itself into the Heart irresistable as Lightning, and no less swift in Motion. My Father perceived with Pleasure, the Astonishment I could not help betraying, and applauded himself, for having found out the right Method of compassing his Designs.

The Stranger seem'd to consider me with Admiration, and paid me an infinite Respect; but I was too much accustomed to be treated in that Manner, for it to make any Impression on me, it was his Person that accomplished what so many had fruitlessly endeavoured; but as I soon found it pleased me but too well, I examined it with the ſevereſt Scrutiny, in hope to find ſome part which ſhould take off the Enchantment of the reſt, but to no Purpoſe; he ſeemed all Perfection, and I was ſo angry with myſelf with being captivated, and with him alſo for having got the better of my hitherto impregnable Inclinations, that I made a Pretence to leave the Room, and retired to my Chamber.

I was no ſooner there than I reflected on the Motives, which had led my Father to impoſe upon me, in relation to this Gueſt, and ſoon diſcovered what his Aim in doing ſo had been——I then aſked myſelf, that if this charming Stranger ſhould make his Addreſſes, whither I would liſten to them or not; no cried I, with great Emotion, I will never ſubmit to the Authority of any Man, beſides that of him to whom I owe my Being, and thoſe Accompliſhments that render me ſo generally adored——No, I will ſooner die than ſuffer it to be ſaid, I had the Weakneſs to reſign my Liberty for Love, ——Love, ſaid I again, what is Love, to what does it tend?——if I love to ſee him, to hear him ſpeak, this I can do without Marriage; and when it goes beyond thoſe Bounds, it's beneath the Dignity of a Woman of Senſe——the Fondneſs I behold in ſome Women of my Acquaintance to their Huſbands, may be called Conjugal Virtues, but to me they are Follies; and ſhews thoſe who practiſe them, to be indeed Creatures made only for the Pleaſure and Convenience of Man ——ill would it become me to be one of thoſe.——

Thus did I ſtruggle with my Paſſion on its firſt approaches; but ſoon I found I had to do with a formidable Enemy. I every Day read Lectures of Phyſick, by my Father's Order, to this young *Portugueſe* ; but in the midſt of theſe grave Leſſons ſofter Thoughts crowded in upon my Soul; and the Pain it gave me to conceal them, made me ſometimes ſo ill-humoured, that every one wondered to ſee ſo great a Change in me.

Bellizay, for ſo the Invader of my Peace was called, perceived the little Propenſity I had to Tenderneſs, and tho' I have ſince had dreadful Reaſons to be aſſured he loved me with an Extremity of Paſſion, never ſpoke the

leaſt

least Word that I could censure as a Declaration of it——
I was however too well acquainted with the Language of
the Eyes, not to be sensible what his Sentiments of me
were, and the Pain I knew it must give him to conceal
them was a Proof of his Respect, which was very
pleasing to me.

My Father on the other hand, never gave me the least
hint, that he wished it might be a Match ; so I had no
Persecutions but what I received from the Capriciousness
of my own Temper ; those however were too violent to
sustain without a very ill Effect on my once healthy
Constitution ; the continual Constraint I put upon myself,
that *Bellizay* might discover nothing of my Weakness,
and the secret Conflicts I endured, between my Pride and
Inclination, made so great a Revolution in all my Frame,
that I fell extremely ill, and was obliged to keep my
Bed.

Bellizay never left my Chamber, but at those Times
when it was improper for him to stay ; but regulating
his Behaviour to the Antipathy I seemed to have for the
tender Passion, he was so circumspect in all his Words,
that nothing he said could pass for a Declaration of
Love.

The Excess of it, however, appeared in all his Actions ;
and when my Distemper began to be looked upon as
dangerous, the Transports of Grief he fell into, were such
convincing Proofs of it to my Father, that he promised
him nothing should prevent my being his, in case I
could be brought to approve it ; which he told him he
did not greatly question, because he had observed I
looked upon him with less Austerity that I had hitherto
done on any of his Sex.

This Discourse between them was over-heard by a
Maid that waited on me, and foolishly enough by her
repeated to me——Another would indeed have rejoiced to find Duty and Inclination go hand in hand in
promoting a Settlement for Life ; but I, on the contrary,
was only fearful that the same Authority with which I
had been menaced on the Count *De B*————'s Account,
should now in good earnest exert itself in favour of

Bellizay; for sure no Woman had ever more Dread of being compelled to marry the Man she most abhorred, than I had to be the Wife of him, whom in spite of my-self, I loved more than Life.———I say, in spite of my-self, for I could have torn out my Heart, for being sen-sible of that Weakness, and still continued firm in my Resolution, never to be overcome by it; or to do any thing that should give him the least Hope I could be in-fluenced by his Assiduities, or even my Parents Com-mands in his Behalf.

The Disease under which I had some Days languished, proved at last to be the Small-Pox; and *Bellizay* hav-ing never had them, my Father fearful the Contagion should affect him, would not permit him to come into my Chamber; but with what Reluctance he obeyed this Command, the Loss of his Appetite, and extreme Me-lancholy demonstrated.

I, who knew nothing of this Injunction, and missed him from my Chamber, was sensibly affected with his Absence———I presently imagined the Indifference I had shewn to him, had determined him to offer to some other those Vows he despaired I would receive; or else that the Disease I laboured under had so much im-paired my Beauty, as had entirely destroyed the Passion he before had for me———I knew not what to think, but was most cruelly alarmed———the Apprehension of losing his Affection seemed as terrible as Death, tho' yet less terrible than his knowing what I suffered on his Account———at length my Fears were over, the talkative Wench I before mentioned informed me of all had passed; and that my Father, by the Change that ap-peared in *Bellizay*, growing fearful his over Caution might bring on what he endeavoured to prevent, gave him Liberty to visit me again———O! if you had but heard the Extasy he was in, said she, when my Master told him he might see you, I dare say you could not be ungrateful to such a Lover. Judge the Satisfacti-on this Account was to my Love and Vanity; but I maintained my usual Reserve, and chid the Maid for troubling me with such Trifles.

Bellizay

Bellizay being re-admitted, resumed his former Chearfulness, and I in Proportion grew much better, what contributed also; very much to my speedy Recovery, was, that a Glass being brought me, I found that fatal Enemy to Beauty, the Small-Pox, would leave little or no Impression on my Face,

My Father, who had been in continual Alarms, during the Course of my Illness, testified his Joy at my Recovery, by large Alms, and other Acts of Piety. But these Acknowledgements were no sooner over, than I grew indisposed again: A frequent Vomiting, a Disgust to all Kind of Food; and a Sort of an unusual Heat about the Regions of the Heart, rendered me so weak and languid, that I had scarce the Power, and less the Propensity to walk or use any Motion————as this Disorder was imputed to some defect in my Stomach, I took proper Remedies, but without Success for three whole Months————in the fourth, I grew somewhat better, the former Symptoms ceased, and my Appetite was restored; but Faintings were very often the Consequence of my Eating, and I was, besides, troubled with those strange and whimsical Fancies, which have the Name of Vapours.

For these also I obeyed the Prescriptions of the Learned; but whither the Medicines had any Effect upon me, or that Nature of itself was sufficient for my Relief, I know not, tho' since I am inclined to believe it was to the latter, that I got rid of these vexatious Ideas; my Health seemed in a fair way of being re-established, and all our Family were again transported at the Change that appeared in me.

But short was the continuance of their Joy, it soon gave place to a Grief, which was to have no more Cessation————I was seized with such inward Twitches, as sometimes made every one about me, as well as myself, apprehend that Moment was my last————again I was put under a Course of Physick; but the more I took, the faster my Pains came on, and Night nor Day for near six Weeks was I two Hours together free from them. This Disorder was the more shocking to me, as neither my own Skill, my Father's, nor any other of those Physicians he would needs consult about me, could distinguish from what Source it proceeded———I imagined that I felt something stir within me, and would frequently cry out, *now, now it moves,* and then scream out between Astonishment and Pain.

Complaining to my Father of these extraordinary Movements, the Feel of which I could compare to nothing but a living Creature within me, struggling as it seemed for room, made him at length conclude that I really had something within me bred by a Conflux of Humours. Examples, tho' not very common, are not wanting of such a *Phenomenon,* and he began to assure himself to his great Grief, that it certainly must be my Case. As it was so nice a Point, he would not rely on his own Judgment, but had a Consultation of no less than seven able Physicians, to which three Surgeons were added———I was examined concerning the Motions; and my Answers to their Questions, especially when I told them I felt it most violent when fasting, or beginning to eat, made them all agree, that my Father's Opinion was stronger than any thing could be objected against it ; and that as the Case was no less dangerous than extraordinary, an Incision was the only means to free me from what sooner or later if suffered to remain in me must be my Death.

My Father came with Tears in his Eyes, to acquaint me with the Result of their Consultation, and to prepare me for the Operation———I must confess that I was seized with the utmost Terror, as I knew very well the least Accident must be fatal ; I beg'd I might have that Night to consider whether I could resolve to undergo it or not ; this Request was easily granted me, and it must be supposed in such a Situation I could get but little Rest. It was near Morning before I felt any Inclination to Sleep, at last my Eyelids growing heavy, my Cares had certainly yielded to a short Cessation ; if in that Moment a Voice had not reached my Ears, saying distinctly these Words,

Lindamine !

*Lindamine! Lindamine! Lindamine! take Care you
consent not to the Operation, in a few Days you will
be cured.*

I was so terrified at this Voice that I fell immediately
into a cold Sweat, and called out with all my Strength,
to my Father who lay in the next Room; on which he
presently rose and ran into my Chamber to know what
had occasioned my Outcrie:————when I had related to
him, what had happened, he endeavoured to persuade
me it was no more than Imagination————he told me
that in the Anxiety I was in on Account of the Incision,
nothing could be less surprizing than that I should dream
in this Manner; nay, that even waking, when the Mind
is oppress'd with any extraordinary Care, said he, your
own Judgment in Anatomy may inform you, that the
subtile Vapours mounting to the Brain, cause so great a
Confusion in the several parts about the *Pineal* Gland,
that it conceives Objects vastly different from what they
are in reality, and works so strongly on the Senses, as
to make us think we both see and hear things that
have no Being, but in the disturb'd Imagination.

But these Observations, however well grounded, made
no Impression on me: I thought myself too well convinced of what had happened; and as our Sex whatever Progress we make in Learning, always retains some part of
its natural Frailty, I was extremely superstitious————I
dreaded Apparitions, and imagining the Caution given
me to come from something of that kind, both believed
and trembled at it. I thought also the Tone of the Voice
was what I had been accustomed to, tho' I could not then
recollect at what Time, so concluded that it proceeded
from some Friend of our Family just departed, and as
it was always my Opinion, that at the Moment of Dissolution the Soul at once takes in a great number of
Events, among others had the Power of admonishing
me of the great Danger, to which I was going to expose
myself.

My Father could not help smiling at all this; but because he would not have me suffer myself to be guided by
the common Prejudices of the World, labour'd to convince

vince me by Philofophical Arguments of the Unreafon-ablenefs of fuch an Opinion. I was however too obftinate to yield the Point, tho' I pretended to do fo, and alfo to find myfelf much better, perceiving that was the only way to avoid the cruel Operation.

Notwithftanding the Danger with which the Phyficians threatned me, in cafe I did not confent to what had been agreed on for me, I could not refolve to come to that Extremity, and had a fecret Dependance in what the Voice had faid———I was alfo fomewhat mended in reality, excepting thofe interior Motions which I now did not dare to complain of.

One Morning being awake fooner than ordinary, for of late I had been exceeding drouzy, my Maid told me *Bellizay* begg'd leave to fpeak to me: As I was in Bed Decency made me at firft refufe his Requeft, but he reiterating it, and declaring he would not ftay a Moment, I permitted him to enter, ordering the Maid not to leave the Room while he continued in it.

He had a Letter in his Hand, and all the Marks of Grief in his Face and Air———I ftarted at Sight of him, tho' I knew not for what Caufe, and he trembled as he approach'd the Bed-fide———I am this Moment, faid he, obliged to leave you, Madam, having juft now received Advice that my Father lies at the point of Death; my Grief———its very natural, cried I interrupting him, and fcarce able to diffemble my Concern at lofing him, and I fympathize in your Affliction. O would to Heaven, refumed he, not regarding the Maid's Prefence, it were truly fo, and that what you have faid I might depend upon as fomewhat more than Words of Courfe———how great a Confolation would it be to think you partook in the Difquiet this Abfence from you muft occafion me. We don't underftand each other, faid I, it was the Danger your Father is in I meant, which has not the leaft Affinity with what you feemed to think by your Reply. Ye , cried *Bellizay*, it is indeed too evident, you either do not, or will not underftand me——I ought to blufh, indeed, when I confefs that the Accident, which calls me away is not the thing that moft

alarms.

alarms me———Could you but see into my Heart you would———but I dare say no more———whence comes this cruel Aversion in you to Love ?———Ah ! lovely *Lindamine* to what has this Idea prompted me !———how happy shall I be, if you one Day forgive the Rashness of a Passion which durst not break out in the open Day. I had no need to have Recourse to Dissimulation to pretend this Language was unintelligible to me : I was indeed amazed at it, and equally at his looking me full in the Face, which he never before presumed to do. You talk in Riddles answered I, what have you done that shuns the open Day ?———but your Actions ought not to be any concern of mine, I should rather ask what Encouragment I ever gave you, to entertain me with so much Freedom on the Subject of Love ?———My Rights are of such a Nature, replied he blushing that———he was proceeding to utter something more, which perhaps had let me into the fatal Secret, I but too late became acquainted with, when my Father's coming into the Room, broke off our further Conversation, I cannot but say I was troubled at it, because, tho' I know not why, I imagined myself greatly interested in what he was going to speak, and flatter'd myself with coming at the Sense of what at present appeared mysterious to me.

My Father, who by the same Post had received the News, came to settle with *Bellizay* the Particulars of his Journey, which was resolved should be immediately———the very Talk of it almost over-power'd my Reason, and I had enough to do in the Moment of his taking leave, to prevent the Discovery of a Weakness, I had hitherto so well disguised, from the loved Object himself, as from all the World beside. When they were gone, I sent the Maid away, and being alone abandoned myself to Tears, and to the most poynant Despair.

When I was called to Dinner, I sat down, but could hardly constrain myself enough to swallow a Morsel, and being much pressed to it, by the Tenderness of both my Parents, and equally fearful of the Incision, if I made any Complaint, as of the true Reason of my want of

Appetite

Want of Appetite being difcover'd; I pretended I had been fo foolifh as to eat fome Sweetmeats, which had quite cloy'd my Stomach for fome time. This paft well enough over, and when the Cloth was taken away, I return'd to my Chamber, and again gave a loofe to all the Extravagancies of Grief. Telling the Maid I was going to my Studies, fhe offer'd not to interrupt me; but about Ten at Night I was feiz'd with fo violent a Cholick, that I was glad to ring my Bell for her. —————She was fcarce got into the Room, when I fell into fuch racking Agonies, that I doubted not but I was on the point of expiring—————terrified at the Condition fhe found me in, fhe ran and call'd my Father, who with my Mother immediately enter'd—————their Prefence put no ftop to my Shrieks and Groans; and my Father with all his Skill, being miftaken in my Ailment, and imagining I fhould be fuffocated by that Animal, the Phyficians had agreed with him, was within me, order'd me to be let Blood directly.—————I was fo, and found a fhort Relief; but the cruel Cholick again came upon me with fuch Violence, that every little Fibre in my whole Frame was affected by it, and I fell into moft terrible Convulfions—————as it was not fuppofed I could poffibly live till next Morning, while I was employ'd in making my Confeffion to my ghoftly Father, the Gentlemen of the Faculty were again fummon'd, and having confulted among themfelves, they all agreed, except one, who after feeling my Pulfe, went away fhrugging up his Shoulders, that in this Extremity the Operation muft be immediately attempted.

My Father was beginning to make ufe of Arguments, in order to engage my Confent to this horrible Expedient, when on a fudden I fhew'd there was, to his Confufion, no Occafion for any thing of that kind.————— Oh! continu'd the charming Pilgrim, cafting down her Eyes, how fhall I find Words to acknowledge my Shame. —————Nature itfelf, willing to releafe me of a common Load, made fuch violent Efforts, that the Houfe refounding with my Cries, I brought forth a little Creature of a Species, that was little expected from me. My

Mother on seeing it struck her Breast, and my Father, as he afterwards said, felt the Bolt of Death that Moment at his Heart; he spoke nothing, his Grief, indeed, was too great for Words, and he withdrew to his Closet, and shut himself up, that none might be Witnesses of his Agonies.

My Mother fearful that Reproaches might be fatal, in the dangerous Condition I then was in stifled her Rage, and constrain'd herself to behave to me with Tenderness. ———I suffer'd myself to be govern'd by her, not in the least suspecting I had any way offended her, and she gave me the Assistance of a Midwife; while all the Time I was thanking Heaven, for having without the Incision so much talk'd of, freed me from a Burthen of so many Months Continuance.

Had not the Child been still-born, I could not have deceiv'd myself in this Manner; but, conscious of my Innocence, even in Thought, as to Mankind, it would have been more strange, had I guess'd at what had happen'd to me, than that I had not the least Thought about it. Doubtless it was the Things I had taken, and Want of proper Assistance in that Moment which requires it, was the Death of that to which I unknowingly had given Being: And this was the second Murder I was guilty of.

Ten Days past over without the least Hint being given me of what happen'd, during all which Time I never saw my Father; I was perpetually enquiring for him, and also asking a Description of that Lump of Flesh from which I had been deliver'd; but could never get any direct Answer to either of these Questions, Sighs and Tears ordinarily ensued, and this was all the Satisfaction I could obtain.

I was extremely uneasy at this Behaviour; but it did not hinder me from recovering my Strength, sooner than could have been expected, considering what I had suffer'd; and finding myself out of any immediate Danger of Death, I could endure this Suspense no longer, and resolv'd to rise, and see what had prevented my Father's Visits to me, in such a Situation, when I stood

so much in need of his Advice and Consolation.——
The extreme Grief that appear'd in the Face of my
Mother, and the heavy downcast Looks of all the Servants, and the Answers they gave me seem'd so ambiguous, that impatient to be convinced, I got out of Bed,
protesting I would see my Father, and know from himself the Motive of his Absence. My Mother came into
my Room, as I was uttering these Words; return to your
Bed, cruel Creature, said she, forcing me to obey, and
add not to the Number of your Crimes by destroying
my Life, which must attend the Loss of yours——
be contented with having overwhelm'd me with the bitter Anguish of reflecting, I have brought a Child into
World, whose Behaviour has kill'd her Father, and entail'd an everlasting Infamy on his Name.

What is it you say, Madam! cry'd I, struck with the
utmost Horror, my Father kill'd!——— I the fatal
Cause!———Yes, wretched *Lindamine*, reply'd she,
that tender Parent could not survive your Shame.——
He paid the Debt of Nature sooner than would have been
demanded, but for your Offences.———He died of no
other Distemper than a broken Heart, three Days after
that fatal one, in which your Dishonour was discover'd.

———The Tears and Agonies which accompanied
these Words were so violent, as would have melted me
in Grief, had not the Distraction they occasion'd in me,
left no room for the softer Passions ——

Great God! cry'd I, what have I done!———of
what am I accused———is it not enough that I have
languish'd under the most terrible and most extraordinary
Ailment that ever was, that I am now but just reliev'd
from it, and still in the power of Death, that in this
Weakness I have lost my dear Father ; is not all this
sufficient, either to turn my Brain or sink me to the
Grave ? but I must also be reproach'd, as if guilty of
some horrid Crime———what can this mean?———
O! what has turn'd my once fond Mother's Heart against
me, and fill'd her with Suspicions of her unhappy
Daughter, ——— I dishonour'd ——— I guilty of Offences———of what Nature ?———

Daughter

Daughter, Daughter, cry'd my Mother, interrupting me, if you would hope to be forgiven either by Heaven or me, ceafe this vain Pretence of Innocence——— rather confefs your Crime, and the Means taken to feduce a Virtue, I flatter'd myfelf had been impregnable.——— Can you hope to hide an Infamy, I myfelf was an Eye-Witnefs of, and is alas too publick, in fpite of all my Care to conceal it———for, Heaven knows, I would have fcreen'd your Shame ; but, alas, the whole Town is too well inform'd of it.

Inform'd of what? faid I, paft all Patience at her Difcourfe———explain yourfelf I befeech you, Madam ; for God who fees my Integrity, will enable me to juftify myfelf from whatever Afperfions are caft upon me

Hold, *Lindamine!* refumed fhe, dare not to prophane the facred Name, left immediate Vengeance fhould fall upon you : On the contrary, you ought, while Breath is permitted you, inceffantly to blefs the Divine Mercy, in preferving a Life you fo wickedly expos'd, and while you murder'd your own Reputation, and brought Shame and Confufion on your Parents, was the Occafion alfo of your Child's dying unbaptized.———O ! continued fhe, what fhocking, what accumulated Guilt is yours——— yet ftill you perfift in feigning your felf innocent——— Harden'd Criminal as you are———had you timely confefs'd the firft of your Crimes, and repofed a confidence in me, the reft had been prevented——— you fhould have had the Affiftance your Condition required———and by that means your Reputation been preferved, your Father and your Child had not been fent untimely to their Graves, your Mother not loaded with this Weight of Anguifh, and yourfelf might have deferved Pardon.

The Aftonifhment I was in had hindered me from faying any thing all this Time, and my Mother imagining by my Silence, that her Difcourfe had made fome Impreffion on me, and that Grief and Shame now tied my Tongue, took me affectionately in her Arms, and kiffing me, be comforted, however, continued fhe,

m)

my ftill dear, tho' unhappy Child, for what is paft
there is no Remedy———let us now look to the future
———what you fhould firft do, is to afk Pardon from
Heaven for all your Faults, I will join with you in Acts
of Devotion and Piety, that you may find Mercy——
The Death of a Child and Father indeed can never
be fufficiently attoned for———Neverthelefs we muft not
Defpair.———Come, purfued fhe, the holy Evange-
lift affures us, that true Contrition is a Sacrifice never
offer'd in vain.

Here fhe paufed, but I was almoft fuffocated with
my Tears, diftilling falter than my Eyes could vent
them, fo finding me unable to reply, and fearing I
fhould expire in the Agony fhe faw me in: We'll
talk no more at prefent, faid fhe, on Themes too
fhocking for the Weaknefs of your Condition to fuftain———your Griefs may throw you into a Fever,
which would now infallibly deftroy you; and guilty as
you are, I could not furvive your Lofs———No, my Child
my poor ruined *Lindamine*, added this unfortunate
Mother, do not increafe my Miferies———you know
my Life is wrapt in yours———Dry up your Tears,
———I forgive all, and the cruel Injuries we have
received, fhall be in part repaired, by your efpoufing
the Man, who in fpite of all your good Underftanding,
has found Means to delude you———let me know who
he is———perhaps he abfconds on this Occafion—
let him appear, how mean foever he may be, we have
a fufficiency to make him happy———let him not refufe
you this Reparation, and it fhall be my Study to content him.

This Difcourfe and the preceding one, was ftill a
Myftery to me; and as foon as I recovered the Power
of Speech, I took the Liberty to tell my Mother fo,
on which fhe ftarted from my Bed-fide, fearing, as fhe
afterwards told me, that in her Rage fhe might do fomething, fhe would hereafter have repented; and made no
anfwer to me, but crying out, Obftinate, obftinate,
wicked, abandoned Wretch, flung out of the Room,
clapping

clapping the Door after her with a Force that ecchoed through the House.

I cryed to her to stay with all my Strength, and perceiving she was gone, threw myself a second Time out of Bed, in order to follow her; but the Maid forced me to lie down again, and told me I should be the Author of my own Death by these violent Emotions. Yet how can I avoid them, cried I, in the Name of God, *Fancton*, explain to me what is the Meaning of all this———I fear the Death of my Father, has had a fatal Influence on my Mother's Brain———She doubtless is disordered in her Senses.

She has but too much Reason, answered she, to know that what she says is real. What, cried I, that I have had a Child? Yes, Madam, resumed she, and it is very strange since we all know it, that you will not discover who it is that has abused you. O the monstrous Assurance! return'd I, giving her a Blow, my Mother must say as she please, but for you———you Creature, to presume in this Manner———to what am I reduced———

The Reply she made me was so provoking, and she in such coarse Terms asserted the truth of what my Mother had reproach'd me with, that I had no longer Patience, and catching up a Torch, which stood near, I threw it at her, with such unlucky Force, that happening on her Temple, she expired in a few Minutes.

Judge, continued this unfortunate Pilgrim, the Terror that seized my Soul at what I had been guilty of, I forgot all my Weakness, jump'd out of Bed, and thence ran screaming, naked as I was, to my Mother's Chamber, I found her on a Couch half drowned in Tears; she seem'd frighted to see me thus, and led me back, forcing herself to treat me with more Tenderness than she thought I merited———but now great was her Consternation, when on entring the Room, she saw the poor Wench on the Floor weltring in her own Blood. She called for help, a Surgeon was immediately brought but Life was flown before he came.

This Murder was made to pass as an Accident, occasioned by her running too hastily against the Corner of a great Cabinet that stood near, and as we were very much respected no enquiry was made further.

In the mean Time this sad Adventure, joined to what my Mother had said, had so great an Impression on me, that I fell very ill and was judged at the Point of Death ————the convincing Proofs I every Day received from all the Family, that I had really brought a Child into the World, tho' I knew myself perfectly innocent, gave me a gloomy Light into my fatal Destiny————I thought there was a possibility some base measures had been taken with me————and then again I found other Reasons to persuade me that it could not be so————the various Contradictions which perpetually presented themselves, whenever I seem'd determined to lean either Way, perplex'd me so, that nothing is more to be wondered at, than that I retain'd my Senses; but thank Heaven, my Brain remained untouch'd, and the Horrours I endured only preyed upon my Heart, but that with such Violence that I thought every Moment was my last.

My Mother, notwithstanding all she supposed me guilty of, and even my persisting in denying it, which she look'd on as even superior to all the rest, could not think of losing me without being inconsolable; she never left me Night nor Day, was continually on her Knees, and made a Vow that if it pleased Heaven to restore me, she would go a Pilgrimage to our Lady of *Luxemburgh*.

Her Prayers were heard, and I recovered doubtless for my greater Punishment; but alas! instead of being able to perform her Vow, she fell into so languishing a Condition that from the beginning threatned Death———— Wretch that I am, 'twas I that kill'd her too; for finding neither Menaces nor Persuasions could bring me to confess, what she so much desir'd to be inform'd of, together with the Sense she had of my publick Dishonour, as well as my supposed secret Guilt, her Grief for my present State, and Fears for my future one, it was that threw her into the Distemper of which she died.

Finding her Dissolution at Hand, and seeing me on my Knees, by her Bedside, with Tears imploring her Benediction, she conjured me once more as I would wish her

Soul's

Soul's eternal Peace, or had any Regard for my own,
now in her laſt Moment to diſcloſe the fatal Secret——
what could I ſay?———how reveal what I was in invincible Ignorance of myſelf?———all I could Reply
was, that if any ſuch thing as I was accuſed of had happened, it muſt be brought about by ſome extraordinary
Means, which I could no Way fathom———and concluded with the moſt ſolemn proteſtation of my Innocence.
But this being far from convincing her, ſhe turn'd herſelf
in the Bed, that ſhe might ſee me no more, nor could all
my Tears or Entreaties prevail on her, to look toward
me or give me her Bleſſing; the laſt Words ſhe uttered,
being that ſooner or later, I ſhould be ſeverely puniſh'd
for my Hypocriſy.

The loſs of ſuch a Mother, was of itſelf enough to
throw me into Deſpair, but the cruel Circumſtances with
which her Death was accompanied, entirely depriv'd me
of my Reaſon———I made frequent Attempts on my
Life, but ſome of my Relations, who, ſince this laſt
Accident never left me, had ſo conſtant an Eye over
me, that to their Vigilance I am indebted for my Preſervation from an untimely End———I continued a-
bove a Month in the reſolution of deſtroying myſelf, my
Frenzy prompting me to believe it was the only Reparation
I could make, for the Miſchiefs I had occaſioned; at length
through the Grace of God, and the frequent Exhortations
of a worthy and pious Eccleſiaſtic brought me by little
and little to myſelf———he prevail'd on me, after hearing
a Recital of all my Misfortunes, to have recourſe to Heaven alone : My Sincerity and Innocence appeared plain
to him, and he accepted my Confeſſion as of that of a
ſincere Penitent; I was indeed ſo, that Pride which had
brought on all my Woes being now quite mortified in me,
the Spirit of Devotion took its Place, and in that I received a Conſolation no Words are able to expreſs———
Ah! when oppreſt by Cares too weighty for frail human
Nature to ſupport, where can we find Relief but in the
Boſom of our Creator———there alone we can hope
to enjoy true Peace———there alone be ſafe from the
Deceits, and Cruelties of an ungrateful, and enſnaring and

a barbarous World————the good Priest doubted not
from the Circumstances of my Story, but that some unnatural Means had been put in practise on me, assured me
that in spite of the dreadful Consequences which had attended it, I might reasonably hope Mercy————He
reminded me, that Providence by the most unexpected
Means often accomplished its Decrees ; and that Heaven
out of Love to its Creatures, made them sometimes appear most wretched, in order to render them in reality
most happy, by bringing the whole Mind and Dependance to itself, and entirely wean'd from the Follies of
the World————He added I had Cause to think myself
of that Number, and that these uncommon Misfortunes
were inflicted on me only to make me eminently pious.

These Admonitions frequently repeated, were like
Balsam to my wounded Mind, and after passing nine Days
as the holy Father enjoin'd in Meditation, Fasting, and
Prayer, methought an Inspiration from above induced me
to make a Vow of what my Mother had fulfill'd, if not
cut off by Death, and after that, resolved to become a
Nun, whatever incident should happen to tempt me, to
a continuance in the World, and divide the large Fortune
now devolved on me between publick Charities, and those
of my Kindred, according as their several Wants demanded, without regarding Proximity of Blood.

When I had formed this Design, I communicated it to
my spiritual Director————he sincerely rejoiced to find
in me such pious Sentiments, inspired as he said by Grace,
the greatest Mark we can receive of the divine Favour;
but he disapproved of the Pilgrimage, because of the In-
conveniences and Dangers to which a young Woman,
such as I was, might be exposed to in so long a Journey,
and offer'd me a Dispensation from my Vow ; but I was
so strongly bent upon undertaking it, that he at last consented, and gave me the best Advice for regulating my
Conduct, and avoiding those Perils his Prudence foresaw
would attend the Performance.

Before I began my Pilgrimage, I set my Affairs in
Order, and disposed as I had before resolved of my Es-
    rving only to myself what was absolutely ne-
                                                cessary

cessary for that state of Life, I had resolved to enter into —————My Relations used their utmost Efforts to dissuade me from making over my Fortune, remonstrating to me, that if any Accident should oblige me to change my present Way of thinking, I must be oblig'd to depend on others for my Subsistence; but my Steadiness surmounted all their Arguments, and when they saw I had in Sincerity no farther Consideration for the things of this World, they left me at Liberty to follow my own Designs.

The Evening before my Departure, I had an Attack little inferior to my former ones—————I received at the same time two Letters from *Bellizay*—————the first inform'd me how much he suffer'd by being separated from me, and was fill'd with a thousand Protestations of a most violent and faithful Passion—————it brought me also an Account that his Father was dead, and had left him Master of an ample Fortune, and concluded with assuring me that Decorum alone had prevented him from coming, the Moment he found himself at Liberty, to offer at my Feet all he was possest of. In a Postscript, he entreated me to reflect seriously on what he proposed, and added that I ought not to think I was so much my own Mistress, as to dispose of myself to any other Man.

This sort of Courtship, from a Man who had never presumed to mention his Passion to me, but in those ambiguous Words he said at parting, seem'd very particular, and I knew not well what to make of such an extraordinary Proceeding, till breaking open the second Letter, which was dated two Days after the first, and wrote lest I should hesitate in coming to a Resolution, I found all the Horrours of my Fate explored—————. He there declared himself my Husband—————that he had enjoyed me as a Wife, and vainly endeavoured to palliate the Villany, he employed to compass his Designs, by the Excess of his Passion, and the Excess of my Haughtiness of Nature. He acquainted me, that in the dread of ever being able to conquer my Antipathy to Marriage, he had given me a sleeping Potion, which at first he had no other View in prescribing, than to Remedy my too great Watchfullness during my Illness;

but

but the Opportunity appearing fo favourable to his future lawful Defigns, he could not refift taking the Advantage of it, flattering himfelf, that in Cafe a Pledge of his Love fhould appear, Decency would engage me to confent to what he doubted all his Sollicitations would not bring to pafs.

Now was the fatal Myftery explain'd——now the Source of all thofe irremediable Ills, I had fuftain'd, was no longer hid in Clouds.——I knew the Wretch who had undone me, and that all I had been accufed of, excepting my Hypocrify, was but too true.——Religion, however, and reftraining Grace, prevented me from any Extravagance.——I refented as I ought the Injury done me, and in fpite of all the Tendernefs I had for him, refolv'd to fee him no more.——I went immediately to Prayers, befeeching God to accept of the Sacrifice I now made of my Inclination, for this unworthy Lover, and begg'd that as Pride had before determined me not to receive his Addreffes, fo now Devotion might enable me to avoid both them and him. I then renew'd my Vow of becoming a Reclufe, and I thank Heaven have never once repented of it ; and I truft the fame Divine Infpiration which gave me Grace to make it, will always continue with me, and fupport me againft every thing that has a Tendency to break it.

It is now a Year and a Day fince I quitted *Montpellier*, in the Equipage you fee me ; I have had the good Fortune to meet with no troublefome Adventure to delay my Pilgrimage, which being now expired, To-Morrow I bid an eternal Adieu to the World

Thus, added the forrowful Pilgrim, have I given you the full Account of my Misfortunes, no Particular of which can ever be obliterated from my Memory—— and as Pride and Self-Sufficiency was my Ruin, for my great Humiliation, I made a Law in myfelf, never to refufe the Recital of them, to fuch as defire it ; with this Condition annex'd, which I did not before mention to you, becaufe I am perfuaded of your Compliance, it is to do fome Act of Piety in my Behalf, that the fupreme Being may enable me to perfevere in the holy
Sen-

Sentiments he has inspired me with, and Fortitude to carry them into Execution.

Here did *Lindamine* conclude, and the Tears which she had with so much Difficulty restrain'd, now burst forth in such Abundance, that even the Count *De Saint Fal*, gay as he was, could scarce forbear sympathizing in her just Griefs ; for my Part, I felt an Anguish little short of what I had done in the most melancholy Turns I had experienced in my own Fortune. As soon as these Demonstrations of Grief were a little over, we thank'd her for the Pains she had given herself to oblige us, and I then ask'd her, if the Convent she had made Choice of, was far distant from the Place where we were: On which she told me she had not fix'd on any particular one ; that it was altogether indifferent to her where she retir'd, and that she purpos'd on her Steward's Arrival, to send him to enquire out some Convent, where she might not be known ; for as she intended to quit the World intirely, she would not go into one near where she had liv'd, and elsewhere she had no Objection.

On her saying this, a Thought came into my Head that might be serviceable to her, and at the same time give me an Opportunity of relating my present Circumstances, both to Madam *De G*————, and my dear *Saint Agnes*, who was never absent from my Mind. With this View I recommended in the strongest Terms I could to *Lindamine*, the Monastery I came from, and told her I would direct her to a Lady, who honour'd me with her Friendship, and who partly on that Score, and much more out of her singular Piety and Sweetness of Disposition, would take Pleasure to oblige her in this Affair ; which I assur'd her lay greatly in her Power, as the Abbess was much devoted to her, and would receive with open Arms, any one that came from her.

Lindamine seem'd charm'd with this Proposal, and made me a thousand Acknowledgments : I gave her the Character of *Saint Agnes*, and made her sensible of the Consolation, she would find in the Society of that charming Nun. As nothing is more pleasing than to talk of those we love, I could not help expatiating a great deal

on

on this Topick ; but the Count having never feen her, and confequently could have no fhare in this Difcourfe, interrupted me, by asking my Permiffion, to go before it was too late in the Evening, and try the Benefit of the Air for a violent Head-Ach, which he faid had afflicted him fince Dinner. I anfwer'd him only with a low Bow, and he immediately retired.

When he was gone, I prefs'd *Lindamine*, again to think of no other Convent than that I had mention'd; and fhe affur'd me, fhe would go the next Day to Madam *De G*————, and as foon as that Lady had done what I had made her hope, fhe would enter directly; after this we began again on the Subject of *Saint Agnes*, and I related the Particulars of her Story, to the End the fair Pilgrim might believe her Misfortunes, were fuch as would readily induce her to pity thofe of another.————Ah! cry'd that unhappy Lady, if your fair Friend had the fmalleft of my Crimes to reproach herfelf with, the Cruelty of her Fate would be dreadfully extenuated ; but, alas, no Woes are equal to the Horrors of a guilty Confcience.

Lindamine perceiving by the Hiftory I gave her of my Friend, that I was entrufted with her Papers, which I was at a Lofs how to deliver, told me with the moft obliging Air, that if I would venture them in her Hands, that fhe would undertake they fhould be given to the Perfons directed to ; by the Means of a trufty Servant, who was to come to her the next Day, and who fhe would fend Exprefs with them, and return with an Account to her, how far he had been able to execute his Commiffion. I found this Way fo eafy and fo fpeedy, that tranfported to think the Satisfaction *Saint Agnes*, would find in having an Affair, fhe fo much wifh'd accomplifh'd, that I threw myfelf at *Lindamine*'s Feet to teftify my Joy and Gratitude. This beautiful Woman charm'd with my Good-nature, entreated to know in her Turn, who I was ; and imagining by the Sighs I fometimes vented, and a certain Air of Melancholy, which I could not always difguife, that there was fomething peculiar in the Accidents that had befallen me,

Preſſed me very much to relate my Hiſtory, aſſuring me at the ſame time no-body could be more intereſted in it. On which I told her with a Smile, that it would be a very ill Return for her Civilities, to trouble her with a Detail of my Misfortunes; but ſhe renewing her Requeſt, I ſaid *Saint Agnes* ſhould receive Permiſſion from me to ſatisfy her Curioſity; and added, the agreeable Manner in which that beautiful Nun would relate it, would render the Circumſtances leſs tedious.———The Politeneſs of *Lindamine*, oblig'd her to ſeem content with this Promiſe, tho' I could eaſily perceive it ſerv'd only to encreaſe her Impatience.

After ſome mutual Demonſtrations of a laſting Friend-ſhip to each other, I ſet myſelf to writing. My Letter to Madam *De G*———, was taken up with recommend-ing the fair Pilgrim, teſtifying the high Senſe I had of all the Favours ſhe had heap'd upon me, and entreating ſhe would always remember poor *Jeanetta* in her Prayers. That to *Saint Agnes* was much longer, I there poured out my whole Soul, related all had happen'd to me, ſince I left the Convent, and after letting her know how happy I was in having an Opportunity to ſerve her; begg'd that if the Marquis ſhould come to the Convent, or ſend *Dubois*, as I imagin'd he would, ſhe would aſ-ſure that generous Lover, that in all Events, my Heart ſhould as long as Life remain'd be devoted to him alone.

It was near Eight o'Clock before I had finiſh'd my Diſpatches, and this important Buſineſs being over, I began to think of *Saint Fal*, and was ſurprized to hear he was nor yet return'd.———The perfect Reſpect he now treated me with, had eraced from my Mind all Re-membrance of his Behaviour the firſt Day he had me in his Power, and the Confidence he repoſed in me, in leaving me to myſelf in a Place, where I might have had an Opportunity of eſcaping from him, if I had at-tempted it, created in me a kind of an Eſteem, and render'd me uneaſy, leſt ſome ill Accident had happen'd, and prevented him from coming back.———At Nine, my Surprize encreas'd, and I went down into the Court-

Yard

Yard of the *Cabara* to enquire of the People concerning him————they told me he was gone, as they imagin'd, to kill some Game, and that probably he was watching to shoot a Hare————as I knew very well that Sportsmen had no Consideration of Hours, I believ'd that might be the Case, and return'd to *Lindamine* better satisfied; but was strangely surprized to find at her Feet a Man of a very graceful Appearance, who seem'd to urge something to her with great Vehemence, while she endeavoured to get free from his Importunities, and struggled as he held her two Hands close press'd between his.

I was going to retire without testifying any Desire of prying into the Mystery of this new Adventure; but *Lindamine* cry'd out, no, no, beautiful *Jeanetta*, come in, and by your Presence and Advice assist me in defending myself from the Assaults of this base Man————. this most unworthy Wretch who dares pretend to call himself my Lover.————Behold here *Bellizay*, continued she, the Brutal Ravisher————the Author of all my Crimes, of all my Miseries; yet after having render'd me so unhappy, would needs persuade the black Designs he put in Practice, are Proofs of a warrantable Affection.

Yes, charming *Lindamine*, cry'd *Bellizay*, interrupting her with a most violent Emotion, may Heaven this instant strike me with its severest Vengeance, if ever I had the least impure Intention towards you————from the first Moment I beheld you, all my Desires center'd in the glorious Ambition of being one Day yours, by such Means as you and your Parents should approve; ————but you reproach me, ah, too unjust, and cruel as you are, with being the Occasion of your Misfortunes; how easy it is for me to retort it, and appeal to your own Heart, if that Distaste you express'd for Marriage, did not in a manner enforce me to be guilty of what you call a Crime,————The Parity between our Births, our Fortunes, our Years; your Father's desire of seeing me his Son-in-Law, all this joined together, and opposed only by an unaccountable Caprice, rather than any Disgust to my Person or Character, tempted me to take the

only

only Means, as I then thought it, of making you mine.
———I pleaded guilty, O! adorable *Lindamine*;———
but as I cannot think you hate me.———I have a thousand Inftances, which you unknowing to yourfelf have
given me of the contrary, render us not both unhappy.
———You are my Wife———my dear Wife.———
Hold! barbarous Man, cry'd fhe, weeping, call me
not by that odious Name———nor think I will ever
forgive the bafe Methods you took to enfnare me into a
Confent to wear it.———O! Heaven, purfued fhe in
the bittereft Agony, that you can dare to think you have
a Right.———Yes, refumed he, eagerly, I have a
Right which nothing can deprive me of, and I will die
before I renounce the Title of your Hufband. Be you
the Judge, Madam, faid this unfortunate Lover, addreffing himfelf to me———I leave my Fate to your Decifion. I take you at your Word, reply'd *Lindamine*
haftily, I am too well fatisfy'd of her Sentiments of Honour and Religion, to doubt if fhe will defer paffing
Sentence in my Favour.

Bellizay finding his Fate depended on me, rofe from
the Pofture he was in, and began to ingratiate himfelf by
exaggerating his Paffion, his Tendernefs and Conftancy;
he endeavour'd to palliate his Temerity, and the fatal
Confequences of it, by many fpecious Arguments, and
then proceeded to alledge, that as what was done was
impoffible to be recall'd, Hymen ought now to repair
the Fault of his paft Conduct, and that if he even lov'd
the charming *Lindamine* lefs, Honour would oblige him
to infift on being her Hufband in the Face of the World,
as he was already fo in the Eyes of Heaven. After this
he proceeded to paint the Torments he had endured, in
being abfent from her, in the moft lively Colours; he
gave me an Account of the many advantageous Matches
he had refus'd for her fake, and that being much urged
on that Head by his Relations, he left *Lisbon* to avoid
their Importunities, and came to *Montpellier* in order to
facrifice all thefe Offers to her, who had his Heart; that
hearing on his Arrival fhe had quitted that Place; he
had for near a Year wander'd in a vain Search of her,

till

till returning to *Montpellier*, he heard by Accident she had sent for a Chaise, which he follow'd without being observed by him that drove it ; and was now come either to obtain her Pardon, or put an End to his Despair before her Eyes.

I gave *Bellizay* all the Time he desired, to embellish his Defence with every Argument, Love and Wit could furnish him with ; and finding he had done, I turn'd to *Lindamine*, and ask'd if she had any thing to add to what she had before inform'd me of. No, Madam, answer'd she, nor do I think there needs any Addition to Facts, such as have been the Consequence of his fatal Inclination.

This being sufficient to make me know she persisted in her Resolution, I address'd myself to *Bellizay*, and gave my Arbitration in these or the like Terms. Since you think fit, Sir, said I, to refer your Fate to my Opinion in this Case, I am extremely sorry to acquaint you it is widely different from yours.————You must also forgive me, when I say, nay, will take upon me to maintain you are not only unworthy of the Happiness you aim at ; but even of the Society of Persons of any Delicacy, as you have broke through all the Rules of Honour, Decency and Integrity, to which you so vainly pretend————is it possible that with that fine Understanding and Education you have (for it would be Injustice to deny you either the one or the other) you could so far forget the Duty owing to yourself ?————The Crimes of seducing, or even forcing a Woman's Virtue, great as they are, are yet more excuseable than what you have been guilty of ?————The first may be compared to a Man, who conscious of superior Strength and Skill, attacks one no way equal to him, and goes to Fight with an Assurance of Victory, yet still some lucky Chance may save the Weaker, at least he has an Opportunity of attempting his Defence ; but your Conduct resembles that of an Assassin, who stabs his Antagonist in the Back, or when he is asleep, at a time when he is wholly incapable of warding off the Blow, or even knowing from whom he receives it :————Indeed, Sir,

Sir, it muſt be confeſs'd, that a Procceding ſuch as yours, is truly an Aſſaſſination.————You pretend alſo, that Love ſuggeſted to you to commit this Outrage; no, Sir, true Love never inſpired its Votaries with Baſeneſs: That Paſſion which centers in a Self-Gratification, is far unworthy of the Name of Love.————A Lady from whom I received ſome Part of my Education, and who is with Reaſon, highly eſteem'd for Delicacy and Penetration, always taught me, that the way to diſtinguiſh a real Tenderneſs, was to ſeem not always on one's Guard before the Perſon who pretended to it, and according as he took or declined taking any Advantage of that ſuppoſed Weakneſs, one might judge of his Sincerity ————Beſides Love in itſelf is an unvoluntary Paſſion ; what Obligation does a Man confer on his Miſtreſs, when he adores her becauſe ſhe appears beautiful in his Eyes ? But if it is not in his power to render her happy, and he makes a Sacrifice of his Deſires, and yields his hopes to a Rival every way qualified to compleat her Wiſhes, he is then, indeed, a Lover, becauſe he prefers the good of the beloved Object to his own. It muſt be acknowledg'd, indeed, the preſent Age affords but few Inſtances of ſuch a diſintereſted Affection; but, nevertheleſs, I am well aſſur'd there are Perſons, whoſe Greatneſs of Soul would enable them in ſuch an Occaſion to teſtify it.

In fine, continued I, there can be no true Love that is not accompanied with the niceſt Regard to Honour, neither can its Conſequences ever be ſortunate; becauſe Paſſions founded on Self-Gratification, will excite other Paſſions, which will claſh with each other; but when Love has Virtue for its Guide, it prevents all the Miſchief that frequently, if not always ariſe from the Sallies of a diſorderly Inclination.————How little Experience ſoever I have, I believe, I have given you the Outlines of the Picture of what a Lover ought to be ; and to ſuch a one, I think Mademoiſelle *Lindamine* is juſtly entitled ; and which had ſhe found in you, that Averſion to Marriage, which ſeem'd ſo unconquerable, Time and a perfect Knowledge of your Worth, might

have

have fubdued, and you would both have been compleatly bleft; whereas now nothing can be more unhappy.——— Reflect on the dreadful Ills your Indifcretion has occa- fion'd ———How wretched even to an extreme, you have made the Woman, whofe Felicity fhould have been your fole Care.———In the firft Place, fhe is unknow- ingly the caufe of her poor Infant's Death———in the next, fhe lofes the moft tender and beft of Fathers.——— Then provoked by an impertinent Anfwer, fhe embrues her Hands in the Blood of a Perfon appointed to attend her.———Then fends to the Grave oppreft with Grief a moft affectionate Mother.———After this attempts to lay violent Hands on her own Life; all which Crimes though innocently committed, or attempted, demand Attonement, nor can fhe do lefs than devote the reft of her Days entirely to Acts of Piety.———Religion and Honour require this of her, and a Cloifter can alone compofe the Tumults of Remorfe.———Let this generous Effort be equall'd on your Side, and if you cannot gain fo noble a Victory over yourfelf, give at leaft this laft Proof of your Love, not to moleft her in the Execution of her Purpofes.

I had no fooner mention'd a Cloifter, than this dif- confolate Lover threw himfelf again at the Feet of *Linda- mine*, with all the Marks of the moft fincere Repentance— His Expreffions were fo touching, his Defpair fo lively, that the Paffion fhe had formerly been poffefs'd of for him, began to revive; fome Sparks of it, in fpite of all her Caution forced their way, and *Ballizay* no lefs dif- cerning than amorous, eafily perceived the Effect his Pre- fence and Difcourfe had on her Heart; and purfued the Advantage he had gain'd with fo much Wit and Elo- quence; that fhe no longer had any Arguments to offer, and only infifted on her Vow, which fhe told him, fhe neither could nor would attempt to break.

I muft confefs I pitied her Situation extremely, and trem- bled for her Refolution, which I found was on the Point of being fhaken————as I thought it impoffible for her to enjoy any true Happinefs in the World, after what had befallen her, efpecially with the Perfon, whofe un-

fortunate

fortunate and ill-govern'd Paſſion had been the Cauſe, I heartily wiſh'd he might not be able to prevail on her; but ſhe ſoon eas'd me of my Apprehenſions and Suſpence, by a Behaviour worthy the Imitation of all, who have any Reaſons to put in Practice that difficult Virtue of Self-Denial, in the things their Souls moſt love.

Bellizay having made a long Harangue to prove, that a Vow ſuch as hers was of little Conſequence, and that any Prieſt had power to grant a Diſpenſation, eſpecially, as there were ſuch powerful and previous Reaſons, for her laying herſelf under other Bonds than thoſe of the Church; the charming Pilgrim ſtarted from her Seat, and without making him any Anſwer, flung herſelf upon her Knees, and lifting up her Hands and Eyes to Heaven. Oh! Power ſupreme! ſaid ſhe, who haſt inſpired me with a Reſolution of quitting this falſe World and all its Cares, enable me I beſeech thee, to fulfil the Vow I have made, and which I now confirm, to ſacrifice my future Days to thee alone.

Bellizay at hearing this, could ſet no Limits to his Deſpair ————— and drawing his Sword, cry'd, thus then I ſacrifice to cruel *Lindamine*: It was as much as the united Force of both of us could do, to hinder the Effect of his Raſhneſs, and our Strength in endeavouring to force the Weapon from him, had not prevented it from paſſing through his Body; had not *Lindamine's* more prevailing Words obliged him to ſheath it: Hold, cruel Man, ſaid ſhe, too much Blood already have I to anſwer for————let me not have another Death to mourn.————

To mourn, reply'd he, Ah! could I hope you would lament my Fall, Life would be worth preſerving;———— but, vain Thought————have you not vowed my everlaſting Miſery————do you not fly to a Cloiſter to avoid me.————Well, go; but firſt behold the End of him who cannot live without you.

With theſe Words he made a ſecond Attempt, but *Lindamine* threw herſelf upon him, ſaying you ſhall not die.————Do not *Bellizay* terrify me in this manner ————my Blood runs cold through all my Veins.————

I tremble, and in the Consternation you have put me, am unable to know myself, what I would do to save you————allow me but this Night to recollect; Tomorrow you shall have my Answer————perhaps, it may be conformable to your Inclinations.

He was about to reply; but she conjured him to retire, and leave her to the Privilege of Thought; I join'd in her Request, and told him that he ought to be satisfied for the present, with what she had said; on which doubtless flattering himself, that the Sight of his Despair had wrought the Effect he wish'd, he was at last prevail'd on to leave the Room, though not till he had utter'd things might have shook the firmest Resolution.

As soon as he was gone, *Lindamine* having wip'd away some Tears, which in spite of her, trickled down her Cheeks, ought I not to blush, said she to me, after having betrayed so much Weakness; but dearest *Jeanetta*, let me not be prejudiced too hastily in your Esteem; for notwithstanding the Force of a Passion revived at the Presence of him, who first inspired it, and the Despair he has testified before me; still will I persist in my Resolution, and you shall see me put in Execution, with the utmost Courage, what I have vowed to perform.

She had scarce left off speaking, when the Steward she had mention'd came into the Room; she acquainted him with her Uneasiness on the Account of *Bellizay*; and he before knowing her Intention of going to a Monastery, we all agreed, that the best way to escape the Vigilance of this distracted Lover, which doubtless would not rest at so critical Juncture, was, that she and I should change Bed-Chambers; and early in the Morning she should set out in the Count's Chaise, which might carry her to some Place of Safety, and return time enough for our Departure. I made no question, but a Person of Monsieur *De Saint Fal*'s generous Disposition, would readily assist in so laudable an Enterprize, and therefore gave Orders to his Postilion to have the Chaise ready by Day-break.

In these Contrivances a considerable time was past, and the Clock struck Ten without any News of the Count's arriving: I was really very much concern'd at

it,

it, and could not help expressing to his *Valet de Chamber*, that I thought his Indifference did not very well become him; on which he took a Guide and Lights with him, and went out to seek his Master.

What made me the more troubled, lest any Misfortune should have happened, was, that I look'd on myself as partly the Occasion: Being convinced that the chief Motive which induced the Count to go out, was to leave me the Liberty of entertaining the lovely Pilgrim, to take off all Appearance of Constraint on my Actions.

I perceived, indeed, he was possess'd of a very great Passion for me; but then as he behav'd with so much Honour and Respect towards me; I thought neither my Virtue, nor my Affection for his Cousin the Marquis, laid me under any Obligation to resent the Sentiments I had inspired him with————all required on my Side being not to encourage, or approve any Declaration of that Sort. Inclinations cannot be controul'd, but Actions may, and when a Woman by her Merit has created a real Passion in a Man of Honour, and after his avowing himself her Admirer, she has assur'd him her Affections are elsewhere engag'd, I can see no Reason, why she should scruploufly avoid his Company, provided she allows him no Opportunities inconsistent with Decency. ————Affectation and Precisenefs are no Proofs of true Virtue: Experience convinces us, that the most abandon'd frequently screen their Vices under those Masks, and I would not advise any Woman, who is truly valuable to wear them, however, censorious the Ill-judging World may be on what they call a free Behaviour. According to this Maxim, I treated the Count *De Saint Fal*, in a manner becoming his Quality, and as a Person to whom I was obliged, yet at the same time gave him no room to flatter himself, my Gratitude to him would extend to the Prejudice of the Man I loved. But to return.

Lindamine, desirous of setting out before *Bellizay* could have any Thoughts she was awake, went to my Bed as we agreed; but not till we had taken a Farewel of each other, more conformable to that of a long

Friend-

Friendship, than of the Acquaintance of a few Hours; and so great an Esteem had we mutually conceived for each other, that this Separation cost both of us many Tears. I entreated she would let me hear often from her, as soon as I should be able to send her proper Directions, and she assured me she should comply with my Request so readily, as by the Trouble she should give me, might, perhaps, make me repent I had given her that Liberty. After this she went to her Repose, but I could not be prevail'd upon to think of taking any, till I heard some News what was become of the Count.

The End of the FIFTH PART.

THE

THE

VIRTUOUS VILLAGER,

OR,

VIRGIN's VICTORY.

PART. VI.

ELEVEN, Twelve, and One o'Clock
was paſt, yet no *Saint Fal* appear'd, and my Uneaſineſs encreas'd
to that Degreee, that not all the Entreaties of the Woman of the Houſe,
could prevail on me either to
eat any Supper, or go to Bed ; till a
Horſe ſtopping at the Door, one of the Servants call'd
out haſtily, that a Meſſenger from the Count was arriv'd.
————Immediately after, a Man booted and ſpur'd
came into my Chamber, of whom I haſtily enquired
for Monſieur *De Saint Fal:* And he reply'd that he had
left

left him about 20 Miles off having rid Post with him so far. This News astonished me indeed, and I could not help asking a thousand Questions in a Breath, concerning the meaning of this strange Proceeding and what could induce him to so sudden and unlook'd for a Departure, on which he delivered me a Letter, and told me that he doubted not but I should find in that a fuller Information than any he was able to give me : I added no more but having hastily broke the Seal, I was supriz'd at reading the following Lines ;

To the beautiful *Jeanetta.*

AS I have reason to apprehend from the Observations I have made of your Sweetness of your Disposition, that my Departure and Absence might occasion in you some Disquiet for the Cause, I should have been utterly unworthy of that Friendship I would merit by my Actions, if I had not sent an Express with all possible Speed to put an End to your suspence. As I went on a Business meerly to serve you, I had not made a Secret of my Journey ; but that I flattered myself to have accomplished it, and returned with the News of it before you could have had any suspicion on what purpose I had gone ————— the pleasing Surprize it would have given you, flattered the Delicacy of those Ideas, which the disinterested Affection I have for you, has inspired me with, and the Accident which deprived me of that Satisfaction, has been no small disappointment to me.

My Intention, O ! charming *Jeanetta,* was to have prepared a Place for you, where you might remain with Safety and Convenience, till all the Tempests of your Fate were over, and you settled in the World, as you justly deserve ; but when I arrived at *Saint G————,* a Town which seemed to be most likely to answer both these Ends, how was I amazed to find at the entrance my Cousin the young Marquis *de L————V————* whom I thought in *Lorrain :* He appeared no less astonished at the Sight of me ————— the Confusion of his Behaviour gave me some room to imagine he suspected what my Business here

here was———I will acquaint you To-morrow, with the Reasons that would not suffer me to deal with him in the sincere manner I have been accustomed; but I know you have too much Wit, and Penetration, not to guess part of them————Never Man, however, was more perplex'd than I was, during the whole Time I was in his Company, glad should I have been to have avoided such an Interview, and the many Questions he ask'd me———but the great Intimacy between us, as well as Nearness of Blood, would not permit I should excuse myself from supping with him. Our Conversation turn'd on Matters wholly indifferent to either of us, and tho' I could perceive he was a thousand Times on the Point of speaking of his adorable *Jeanetta*, yet he as often re-strain'd himself; which confirmed me more and more that he had some Mistrust of me, and as nothing can ren-der a Persons Company less agreeable, we had no sooner given over eating than we separated under different Pre-tences : My Cousin said he was obliged to ride Post back to *Pont a-Mousson*, for having come with a Design to go to Court, as imagining he might now appear, the Cheva-lier *D'Elbieux* being recovered of his Wounds, but that he had met some of his Friends on the Road, who let him know it was proper he should absent himself a little lon-ger. But alas I was not to be imposed upon on this Head, I am too sensible of the Power of your Charms, not to know 'twas you alone that drew him from his Retreat——He doubtless has been inform'd of his Father's Resolution concerning you, and that I have been employed as his Instrument in the Affair———what he now judges at seeing me without you I cannot determine, but am con-firm'd in my Conjecture as to the Motive of his quitting *Lorrain*, for having had him watch'd, when he took Leave of me to go as he said to *Pont a-Mousson*, the Emis-sary I sent is just come back, and assures me that the Marquis, instead of taking the great Road turn'd into a Bye-Path, where having rode backward and forward several Times, he at last return'd into the Town by an-other Gateway. If in his Turn he has sent any body after me, he will find I have not deceiv'd him, for I told

him

him I was going to *Verſailles*, where I indeed expect to be to-morrow; and if he imagines I act in Concert with my Uncle, as I doubt not but he does, my future Conduct will ſufficiently convince him to the contrary.

It is for you to determine which way you ſhall act; but if I may be permitted to adviſe, in the Ambition I ſhall ever have of ſerving you, I ſhould think it moſt proper for you to meet me to-morrow at *Verſailles*——— I will provide an Apartment for you, where you ſhall be received under a Name that will infallibly ſecure you from all Enquires———You will find a Man in the long Walk, who ſhall watch your coming, and conduct you where you are to alight. Let not the Place give you any alarm, the old Marquis *de L——V——* is in the Country, and as he is far from ſuſpecting how ill I obey his Orders will have no other Thought but you are where I ſhall pretend I have diſpoſed you———ſo that tho' at his Return he ſhould happen to ſee you, he will never imagine you the Miſtreſs of his Son———Oh Heaven! with how much Pain do I give you that Title; but you take Pleaſure in it, and I will not preſume to complain of you at leaſt, whatever I may do of my Fate———happen what will, in all Events you ſhall ever find in me a ſincere Friend, who will not only ſecretly, but openly alſo, ſtand between you and every thing that might occaſion you diſquiet———I beg you will let me know your Pleaſure by the Bearer, who knows where to find me, and has my Orders to return immediately with your Anſwer———I am with much more than Reſpect,

O lovely *Jeanetta*,
Your moſt humble, *&c.* ———

De Saint Fal.

In a Poſtcript I found theſe Words.

P. S. Conſider I beſeech you, adorable *Jeanetta,* that in the preſent Situation of your Affairs, it is of extreme

3

treme Consequence you should avoid being seen by my too amiable Cousin.

I read this Letter over several Times, before I was able to fix on any Resolution : the Pleasure it gave me to hear these new Proofs of the Marquis's Affection, was so exquisite, that for some Moments it took up my whole Soul, and I could think on nothing else———his Quality ———the Charms of his Person———the Tenderness of his Passion, but above all his Sincerity might well be ravishing to a young Heart, and I could not but rejoice when I reflected that the Warmth with which I thought of him, had the Excuse of Gratitude for what he had done, and suffered for me, as well as his Perseverance in combating with such almost insuperable Difficulties for my Sake.

I could not however disapprove the Conduct of the Count *de St. Fal* on this Occasion, tho' I plainly perceived Love and Jealousy had the greatest Share in it ; but the engaging and respectful Manner in which this new Lover behaved toward me, made me no Ways apprehensive of the Consequences of either. I was entring into a Train of Reflections, when the Messenger reminded me that my Answer would be impatiently waited for, on which I set myself to consider what it was I ought to do ———the Absence of the Count, and the entire Liberty at which he left me, gave me now an Opportunity of throwing myself into the Arms of my Family———or indeed into those of the Marquis, whom I could soon have advertised of my Escape, and appointed him to meet me, but *Vanity* soon banished all Thoughts of the *one,* and *Decency* of the *other*———a *Cottage* was insupportable to my *Pride,* and a *beloved Lover* dangerous to my *Virtue;* the complying with the Count *de St.Fal's* desires, seemed therefore the Medium between these two Extremes, so wrote instantly to him, acquainting him that I relied so much on his Honour, as to resolve to be entirely guided by him, and that I would take the Road to *Versailles* the next Day, where I hoped to find no Room to repent, by any Discontinuance of his Goodness to me, that I had depended on him.

I

I had no sooner sent away this Letter, than I wished I had it back again————Ah! my God! said I, to myself, what have I done, to what hazard will not the following the Advice of Monsieur *de Saint Fal* expose me! to chuse for my Residence a Place where the old Marquis *de L———V———* has so much Power!————a thousand Accidents may happen to discover me to this provoked Parent, and the Hatred he has already to me would be justly encreased by my Presumption————to come into his very Presence, could be looked upon as no less than an Insult, a kind of Disdain, a daring of his Resentment ————But supposing I should be able to avoid the Knowledge of the Father, can I expect to escape the Vigilance of the Son; what Name, or, what Disguise can hide me from a Lover's Eyes, and then, Heaven! what have I not to apprehend! what may not Jealousy, Despair, and Amazement prompt him to?

These Reflections dwelt on my Mind some Time, till others of a different Nature made them give Place——How am I certain, cried I, that the Count will always retain the same Moderation he at present treats me with; may not all his specious Pretences of a disinterested Friendship, be but so many Wiles to ensnare my Heart, and win me by degrees to Love, and when he finds he has but deceived himself, may he not then have recourse to other means————May not the same Principles with which the Chevalier *D'Elbieux* was actuated lie hid within him, which as his last resource he may put in practice? O, too unwary *Jeanetta!* into what Dangers art thou running————should any of the Misfortunes thou now so justly apprehendest fall upon thee, who would compassionate thee!————Ah! 'tis too true, continued I, all the Troubles I now labour under, I am myself the Cause of————had I less Vanity, or less Love, these continual Turmoils had been prevented, and I been secure in the peaceful Cottage where I first saw Light————a poor Country Maid indeed; but more truly beautiful arrayed in Innocence and Virtue, than in all the pompous Trifles the World is so much dazzled with.

These.

These Ideas struck me so strongly, that I resolved not to perform the Promise I had made *Saint Fal* ; but lay hold on the Opportunity he had given of escaping from his Power, and all the other Mischiefs that represented themselves to me————the Goodness of Madam *de G*———, and the tender Pity she had always express'd for me, made me imagine she would again take me into her Protection, when she should hear of the new Dangers to which my Virtue was exposed ; and if it was impossible for her to keep me in her own House, she would at least recommend me either to the Monastry where I had been before, or some other of equal Security.————I therefore determined to have Recourse once more to this truly generous Lady, and go in the Chaise with *Lindamine.*

Having thus settled what I would do, I got out of Bed, and went to the Chamber of the fair Pilgrim————She was surprized to see me at that Hour; but when I communicated to her my Intentions, and the Motives I had for forming this new Design, she entered immediately into it, and told me it was her Opinion I ought not to act otherwise, and having embraced me in a very affectionate Manner, and offered to divide the remaining Part of her Fortune with me, or at least to pay what should be required for my Admission into a religious House, if I were disposed to that Life————Alas ! she little knew that all my present Terrors were only occasioned by the Danger I was in of being compelled to it. I made my Acknowledgments to her however, for her obliging Offer, but could not help saying with a Smile, that I thought such a Change of too much Consequence to be entered into without having well considered on it————She praised my Sincerity, and added, with a deep Sigh, that in the Situation she was, little regard was to be paid to her Decision.

As it now grew near the Hour in which the Chaise was ordered, we set about preparing ourselves to go, and the frequent Sighs intermingled with Tears, which the sorrowful *Lindamine* could not restrain, made me see how difficult it was, even for a Woman humbled to the Degree she was, and even fortified with such a Spirit of Devotion, to think of parting forever from the Man she loves.

We were no sooner ready, than Word was brought that the Chaise was at the Door; *Lindamine*, had muffied herself up for fear of meeting *Bellizay*, and was following me; but that diligent Lover had observed all our Motions the whole Night, and having over-heard Part of our Discourse (as he afterwards confess'd) quitted not the Chamber-Door after seeing me go into it, and when we opened it to go out burst in upon us; Pardon my Despair, dearest *Lindamine*, cried he, opposing our Passage, Death is a far less formidable Evil, than your unjust Designs————but ah! cruel as you are, how could you think of withdrawing yourself from the legitimate Right I have over you?————Right! replied the fair Pilgrim, in an angry Tone, legitimate Right! ought you not to be covered with Shame and Confusion at the very Word————what do you expect to prevail, because you have taken it into your Head to imagine you should do so; but henceforward I will have no Regard, no Pity for your Despair whether real or pretended, but pursue my Duty and Inclination, neither of which however you may flatter yourself with vain Hopes will ever be of your side.

Be pleased to return to your Apartment, replied *Bellizay* in a calm but resolute Voice; for be assured you go not hence without me————I ask your Pardon, Madam, said he, to me, for preventing the Execution of your Advice; but you and the whole World shall see that in this, I am not to be deceived. With these Words he would have taken *Lindamine*'s Hand to lead her in, but she chose to return of her own accord, rather than be compelled; Heavens! cried she, in an extraordinary Agitation, to what am I reduced, when those who should treat me with the greatest Respect pretend to command and tyrannize over me————with these Words she threw herself into an easy Chair, and then again, what, resumed she, is it not enough, that you have rendered me the most miserable of all my Sex, that you have

drawn

drawn Mifchiefs on me, which never had a Name but in my Fate !————are you not content that I am wretched in this World, beyond all poffibility of Relief, without wifhing I fhould forfeit all my Hopes too in another, and perifh everlaftingly?

Bellizay, liftned to all fhe faid, with a fullen Attenton, and after a fhort Paufe, I will leave you to compofe yourfelf from this unneceffary, as well as fruitlefs Grief, faid he, but before I go, I would have you confider, that if Love has no influence over you, Honour at leaft ought not to be banifhed from your Breaft———— at leaft I would advife you in my turn, to reflect ferioufly and judge for yourfelf, and then I am certain you will engage in no rafh Enterprize————when you recover your ufual Serenity of Mind, and refolve to behave in a manner your Circumftances demand let me know it, and you fhall find me ready to comply in every thing with your Defires !

He made a low Bow as he ended thefe Words, and retired giving me a look as he went out of the Room, which fufficiently explain'd his Refentments to me, tho' I pretended to take no Notice of it, nor had during this Converfation between them uttered on Syllable.

Lindamine, being very warm in her Temper, fell into violent Exclamations on the Severity of her Fate ; the Indignation fhe expreffed at this ill Treatment of her Lover, fhewed to me plainly, that in fpite of all her Endeavours, her natural Haughtinefs was not utterly eraced. A Flood of Tears fucceeded, and quenched the Fire of Rage, and having a little recovered herfelf, fhe recommended her unhappy Cafe to the fupreme Difpofer of all Things, in terms fo moving and pathetick, as fhewed them the Dictates of a Heart, that overflowed with Penitence and Piety.

After thus pouring forth her Griefs, where fhe alone could hope Redrefs, fhe appeared fomething more eafy ; I contributed all in my little Power, to ftrengthen her Refolutions, and enable her to regain her Tranquility ; and indeed fhe confeffed that had it not been for my Prefence, and the Refolution I infpired her with, fhe could

not

not anfwer how fhe fhould have behaved in fuch a trying Circumftance.

When the Inclination of doing any thing is very ftrong, Invention generally comes in to its Affiftance; nor did it now fail *Lindamine*, for the means of efcaping from a Lover, whom with fo much Reafon fhe was determined to avoid: The Scheme fhe formed for this Purpofe was, that I fhould quit the Inn in the Chaife that waited for us, and ftop at a little diftance behind a Chapple, which fhe very well knew and directed me to; and that when I was gone, fhe would counterfeit to be overcome by the Paffion of *Bollizay*, in order to lull him into a Security, and fo get an opportunity of joyning me.

I could not but approve of thefe Meafures, as affording a greater probability of Succefs, than any I could think of; and to give the Thing an Air of Reality, I took my leave of her in a loud Voice, and fhe, as I was going down Stairs, ordered one of the Servants to tell *Bellizay*, fhe defired to fee him.

I was juft ftepping into the Chaife in order for the Execution of our Defign, when the Count *de Saint Fal's* Valet de Chamber came near, and afked what I intended, and to what Place I was going: As I was not prepared for this Queftion it very much alarmed me, and my Countenance betraying my Confufion; I am afraid Madam, added he, the Departure of the Pilgrim, is but a Pretence, in order for you to take the Advantage of my Mafter's Abfence for your Efcape————I cannot fay indeed that I have any Commands from him to lay a reftraint on your Actions; but I think myfelf obliged neverthelefs to reprefent that you ought not to leave this Place without his Knowledge; the Civilities he has treated you with, and which I knew not how he will be able to anfwer to his Uncle, demand at leaft thus much from you; and I affure you, I cannot confent you fhall make ufe of my Mafter's Chaife, unlefs I have a pofitive Order for it from himfelf.

The Poftilion who was going to drive away, on hearing this Difcourfe, got down and took out the Horfes: In the perplexity I then was in, I had a Thought of
making

making a Confidant of the Valet de Chamber, and endeavouring to gain him to my Party; but he had naturally fo little Complaifance, befides, having always fhewn a fort of a Prejudice againft me, that I durft not run the Rifque of it, and was obliged to go into the Inn again, blafhing with Difdain and Refentment.

I was then extremely at a lofs how to behave; if I returned to *Lindamine*'s Chamber, I was fearful of rendering her more fufpected by *Bellizay*, and confequently prevent any new Steps, fhe might take for her Efcape; and not to let her know I was difappointed in what I had defigned for her and myfelf, might occafion her going to the Place appointed; where miffing me, fhe would not know what to make of the Adventure, and poffibly wait there till her impatient Lover might be apprized of her Flight, and purfue the fame Road——— Nothing could be in a greater Dilemma, than I was on this Occafion———My own Affairs alfo perplexed me very much; let me think which way foever, I faw no poffibility but either remaining where I was, or going to *Verfailles* as the Count defired, and I had promifed; but the Apprehenfions I before mentioned, returned with greater Force than ever to deter me from that Journey; what Madam *de G*———had often faid to me, concerning the Danger of giving the leaft Encouragement to a Man who had declared himfelf my Lover, now came frefh into Mind, and what had actually happened to me, on Monfieur *de G*———'s Account, affured me but too well of the truth of thofe Maxims fhe had laid down for my Conduct in that Point; when I reflected on the fudden Tranfition of Monfieur *de Saint Fal*'s Behaviour to me, the Facility with which he difobeyed the Orders given him by his Uncle, and the Liberality, not to fay Profufenefs, with which he had entertained me, with his Offers of fupporting me, till I was otherwife difpofed of, how could I keep my felf from trembling for the return he might one Day expect for fo many Favours.

It is true, I ought to have confidered all thefe things fooner, and rather chofe to have been carry'd to a Convent, or wherever elfe the Refentment of the old Mar-

quis

quis should have ordain'd, than to lay myself under such dangerous Obligations to his Nephew : I know that many of my Sex will condemn my Conduct, and say I ran myself into Adventures of this kind, and then boasted of my Virtue in resisting Temptations, I might easily have avoided. I acknowledge myself to blame, and that my Vanity, my Aversion to being a Recluse, and the charming Hope that I should one Day be what I now am, made me expose my Virtue to very dangerous Trials, and that I have reason to bless the Divine Providence alone for my Defence in many of them.—— I would, however, entreat the Favour of those, who censure me with too much Severity, to remember of what Age I was, and ask themselves the Question, if, in that unexperienced time of Life, they never acted with Imprudence.

I was now fully convinced I had taken a wrong Step, and which way to retrieve it appear'd difficult : I was as much in the power of Monsieur *De Saint Fal*, if I continued in the Inn, as if I went to *Versailles* ; and as I had agreed to his Proposals of going there, had reason to fear if I now refused, I should so far irritate him, as to make him lose that Respect which had hitherto preserved me.

In this Agitation, I bethought me of consulting *Lindamine*, so left my Door half open, that I might hear when *Bellizay* had quitted her, as I might easily do, my Chamber being under that where she lay. It was not long before I heard his Voice, giving some Orders as he came down Stairs ; I then went directly to the fair Pilgrim, who seem'd very much surprized at my Return ; but on my giving her a brief Recital of the Cause ; it will be easy for us, said she, to surmount this Obstacle, my Chaise is not yet gone. Pray Heaven we may find no greater Difficulty in escaping the Vigilance of *Bellizay*, from whom I have now undergone the most dangerous Attack.——This guilty wretched Man cannot be brought to Reason ; I was therefore oblig'd once more to feign myself moved by his Despair, and, in fine, have promised to go with him.——

Heaven,

Heaven, who knows it was my only Method to preserve myself, I hope will pardon the innocent Deceit.——— He now confides in me, and the more so, as he imagines you are gone; you must therefore, continued she, avoid seeing him all Day, and give Orders to the People of the Inn to tell him so, if he should ask any Questions: though being prepossess'd as he is of your Departure, I scarce think he will be inquisitive on that score. I have already told him, that before I undertake so long a Journey, my Servant must go to provide some things for me at a neighbouring Town; so cannot pretend to set out till To-Morrow Morning. To countenance my Design, I shall also pass this whole Day with him, and as soon as it grows late, and he is retir'd to his Chamber, I am to get softly out of the Inn, and walk about a hundred Paces where my Chaise is to wait for me, and I hope will carry me to Madam *De G*———'s, long before he can have any Notion of my being gone ———if you, therefore, keep close till the appointed Time, continued she, I will give a gentle knock at your Door as I pass by, and you may follow me with all the Security imaginable.

I was transported with this Contrivance, and immediately after took my leave, fearing with Reason the Return of *Bellizay*, should break all the Measures we had taken. When I return'd to my Chamber, I pretended to be a little indisposed, to the End my keeping shut up, might occasion no Suspicion in the House: I then bethought myself, that the Confusion I betrayed when the Count *De Saint Fal's* Valet de Chamber opposed my Departure, might make him think I had some Design on Foot, his Master would not approve, and consequently give him an Opinion, that it was his Duty to give an Account of my Behaviour; and besides I consider'd, that Good-manners and Gratitude demanded I should acquaint that Nobleman with the Motives which compelled me, to take the Advantage of the Liberty he allow'd me in making my Escape.

In order this Valet should have no room to suspect any thing, I sent for him into my Chamber, and shew-

ing

ing him the Count's Letter to me, asked him if he knew the Hand, and he answering that he did very well, and that it was his Master's; I told him I could very well justify myself for not being that Day at *Versailles*: You are sensible, said I, with a malicious Air, that I was going; but you, for what Reason you best know, thought fit to put a Step to the Execution of my Designs, and the Count's Desires. I, Madam! cry'd he, quite confounded at what he heard; I should never forgive myself to have done it, if an Excess of Duty to him who gives me Bread, had not, as I thought, oblig'd me to it——if, added he, you had mention'd to me your Intentions, and my Lord's Request, you should have been before this Time at the appointed Place.

I did not imagine, reply'd I very haughtily, that I was to give you any Account for the Motives of my Actions;——besides, I was so much surprized at your Presumption, that I could not speak one Word, nor am I yet, indeed, perfectly recover'd.——I sent for you to inform you of this, having no Design to do you Prejudice; but you must believe it impossible for me to avoid acquainting the Count with the Reasons, that prevented my meeting him as I had promised, or if you please, you may do it for me, I leave it to your Choice; as well as my going To-Morrow early in the Morning to *Versailles*; for as in the Absence of Monsieur *De Saint Fal*, I find I am to be under your Direction, I shall not take upon me hereafter, to do any without having first consulted you.

I spoke all this with so much Reservedness, and the Reproaches I made him seemed so just, that the poor Man seem'd Thunderstruck; he knew, without Doubt, his Master's Disposition, and having been Witness of the great Respect with which he treated me, fear'd the Consequences of his Displeasure, in having given me any Occasion for Offence.

He begg'd my Pardon a thousand times over, acknowledg'd himself greatly to blame, and protested he would never dare to call any of my Actions in question more ——in short, his Submissions were so much beyond **all**

all Bounds, that I could scarce refrain from smiling at them; and put me in Mind, that as mean Persons when they imagine themselves vested with any Authority, always execute it with the greatest Insolence; so when they find themselves mistaken, descend from their Height, to the most groveling and most abject Humiliation. This Fellow to repair his Fault, would persuade me to set out that Moment, assured me every thing should be ready as quick as Thought, and I might yet be at *Versailles* by Dinner.

I was very well pleas'd at the Effect my Resentment had on him, and chang'd my Countenance to more Serenity; but told him my Indisposition would not permit me to leave my Chamber that Day, but order'd he should hold himself in Readiness to set out the next Morning.

But though I spoke this to him with Sweetness enough, he was still under most terrible Apprehensions, nor would quit my Room, till I had assur'd him of an entire Forgiveness of his Rudeness, as he called it———— on which, as well as to get rid of his Importunities, I not only promised to think no more of it, but also that I would say nothing of it to the Count; but lay the blame only on my own Illness and Incapacity of travelling. ————He was now as much transported at my Condescension, as he had been abash'd at my Resentment; and told me, that as we were not many Leagues from *Versailles*, he would go thither himself, to prevent his Master from being uneasy at my not coming: He added, that he would send no other on this Business as he might do; but that he was willing to give me a Proof of the entire Confidence he had in me, and that he was not commission'd to be a Spy over me.

To avoid all Suspicion, I would have persuaded him to send the Postilion; but he said, that, as that Servant had been but lately hired, he might possibly make some Mistake, which might be prejudical to the Secrecy his Master desired might be observed, in all things relating to me. I seem'd to acquiesce to his Reasons with some Reluctance; but was really extremely rejoiced

to be freed from this watchful *Argus*, who might possibly have been an Obstacle to my Defigns once more, in
fpite of all his Pretences ; ftill dreading his Prefence
almoft as much as *Lindamine* did that of *Bellizay*.

After he was gone, I applauded myfelf very much for
my Managment in this Affair : But how little Pains do
Evafions coft our Sex ! That Hufband, therefore, who
has not a Wife fincerely virtuous, will never by all
his Watchfulnefs be fecured from Impofition ; and but
vainly depends on his own Management and Penetration, fince frequently it happens, that Women of the
meaneft Capacities in other Things, have Artifice enough
to deceive the wifeft of Men.

I ftaid in my Chamber all Day, as I had agreed with
the fair Pilgrim, and as I fometimes liftned to hear if
Bellizay was with her, found that paffionate Lover gave
her but fmall Truce from his Importunities. I doubted
not her Refolution and Management of him, however,
and paft the whole time in Reflections, on the many
different Circumftances which had befallen me ; I could
not but imagine fuch extraordinary things, muft neceffarily produce a Fate no lefs extraordinary in its kind,
and recommended myfelf to Heaven for a happy Event.
I was in thefe Meditations, when about Eight o'Clock I
was rouz'd from them, by hearing fome Horfes ftop at
the Inn ; I ran to the Wnidow and look'd haftily out,
fearing fome new Obftaele was arrived to thwart my Defigns : I was fo accuftomed to ftrange Adventures, that
I could neither hear nor fee any thing I did not know
the Meaning of, but I prefently imagined it related fome
way or other to myfelf.———As the Count *De Saint
Fal's* Letter had inform'd me, that the Marquis was in the
Neighbourhood, I knew not but it might be he, whom
Chance had directed to the very Place I was ; I cannot
fay this Idea was difpleafing to me, my Heart overflowing that Inftant, with the grateful Remembrance of
what he had done and fuffered for me, would have tranfported me fo far as to have thrown myfelf into his Arms,
and given him the moft tender Welcome after fo long an
Abfence ; though on Reflection, I fhould doubtlefs have
repented

repented fhewing myfelf to him, as the Situation of my
Affairs then was. I was once of Opinion it was Monfieur *De Saint Fal*, who impatient at my not performing my Promife, was come back from *Verfailles,* to
conduct me thither himfelf.————But I was foon eafed
of my Perplexity, when looking out a fecond Time, I
difcern'd by the Light of two Flambeaux, carry'd by
Servants in rich Liveries, a tall graceful Perfon getting
out of a Coach ; he feem'd pretty far advanced in Years,
had a venerable and majeftick Afpect, and by his numerous Retinue feem'd a Man of very great Quality : As
he was coming into the Inn he caft his Eyes up, and a
Candle happening to ftand in my Window, gave him as
full a View of me as I had of him ; he ftood ftill a Moment
or two, and looked fo earneftly upon me, that I was
obliged to draw back————the manner in which he regarded me, I thought had fomething of Admiration in
it ; a fmall fhare of Beauty, indeed, is fufficient to infpire fuch Imaginations in moft Women, and I freely
confefs I had the Vanity to believe, that even in this
tranfient View, I had made a new Conqueft. But tho'
I was too great a Friend to Sincerity not to acknowledge
I had in me a great Share of my Sex's Weaknefs in
this Particular ; yet I would not have my Reader imagine, this fuppos'd Effect of my Charms, afforded me
any Ideas prejudicial to that Affection I fo juftly bore to
my dear Marquis.——Indeed, I gave myfelf not the trouble to think much concerning it ; but having fat down
in an eafy Chair, the little Repofe I had enjoy'd the
Night before, had made me drouzy, and I fell into a
fort of Slumber, which, however, was every Moment
interrupted by the continual Expectation I was in of
Lindamine coming to inform me as fhe was ready to depart.

But how was I furprized when on opening my Eyes at
a little Noife, I faw two Men ftanding before me, one
of whom I prefently knew to be the Perfon that came
out of the Coach————the Emotion I was in at fuch
unexpected Vifiters, was vifible enough in my Countenance, and, indeed, I was that Moment feized with
fomewhat I knew not how to account for ; but though I

am

am no Friend to giving Credit to Omens, I have since thought it was a certain foreboding of a very particular Event, which this Interview was indeed the first Occasion of.

I beg, Madam, said that graceful Gentleman I mentioned, and whom by the Magnificence of his Dress as well as his noble Air, I supposed to be the Master, you will be under no Apprehensions on my Score————I little Thought of giving any Disturbance to a Lady, who seems born to command universal Homage—— It was an Accident brought me into your Apartment, which I mistook for that allotted for me, being on the same Floor————I confess, indeed, that when I found my Error, I ought to have retired, but few Men can at all Times practise the Virtue of Self-Denial————the Sight of so many Charms, compell'd me with a sweet Violence, to indulge the Pleasure of gazing on them; and I hoped to have stole that Satisfaction without your perceiving the Theft————No Age, Madam, is secure from the Assaults of Beauty, and yours seems accompanied with a Sweetness, which I hope will induce you to forgive the Boldness of my Admiration.

It may easily be imagined, that both the Visit and Discourse of this unknown Person gave me a great deal of Surprize, but perhaps the Reader will think it strange when I confess, that neither the one or the other was disagreeable to me————on the contrary there was something extremely pleasing in both————all the Time he spoke I listened with the greatest Attention, and when he left off, answered the Compliments he made me, with all the Politeness I was Mistress of————I felt indeed a Respect for him, which would not suffer me to do otherwise, and I endeavoured all in my Power, to inspire him with as high an Opinion of my Wit, as he seem'd to have of my Beauty————tho' I knew neither his Name or Quality, I thought nothing could be a greater Glory for me, than to be thought agreeable by him, and the Desire of Pleasing gave me so much the Power of doing so, that he seem'd in Raptures at my Complaisance, and the Manner in which I received the fine Things he said faid to me. Good Heaven! is it poffible, cried he, that, every Charm, every Grace of Womankind, fhould be united in one Perfon! Happy! happy will be the Man who fhall poffefs this Treafure————*Forfan*, continued he, to the Perfon that was with him, and on whofe Shoulder he fupported himfelf, thou art older than my-felf, yet tell me, doft thou not feel an Admiration, a fomething more than Refpect for this beautiful young Lady————fay, did'ft thou ever fee any thing fo perfect ————fo lovely.

This Dependant was about making fome Reply, when I prevented him by faying————take care, *Monfieur*, interrupted I, that fuch Praifes given me by a Mouth like yours does not infpire me with a Vanity, which would very much diminifh the little Merit I am Miftrefs of, which confifts at prefent only in a Confcioufnefs of my own Unworthinefs, and a perfect Efteem for all Perfons of true Honour and Good-Senfe, be they of what Age or Degree foever.

How conformable in every thing, refumed the old Gentleman, lifting up his Hands and Eyes! and then went on extolling my Way of thinking to the Skies : He embellifh'd his Difcourfe with all the Graces of Wit and Eloquence, and had a Facility in the Turn of his Expreffions, which very much added to their Agreeable-nefs————in fine, there was fomewhat in his Conver-fation that perfectly enchanted me, and I believe never two Perfons at firft Sight, without being infpired with that Paffion which is call'd Love, ever took fo great a liking to each other. He eafily perceived I was pleafed with entertaining him, and tho' I am perhaps too ready in confeffing the Vanity of my Sex, and my own in par-ticular, yet I cannot Help obferving that the Men, and the wifeft of them too, are no lefs liable to this Weak-nefs————there is certainly fomething inherent to hu-man Nature, that will not fuffer us to be difpleafed at the Praifes given us by People we converfe with, and the more Deference we pay to their Judgment, the more are we exalted————Nay, I will go further, and venture to fay, that we look even on their liking us as a Proof

of.

of their Judgment; elfe wherefore fhould this Stranger, whofe Years, Experience, and fine Underftanding, ought to have render'd him more cautious, cry up to that high degree he did, the admirable Penetration of a Girl he had never feen before, and could not confequently be acquainted with the Capacity of, any otherwife than by the Civilities he found himfelf treated with by her.

The Charms of my Perfon with which at firft he feem'd fo much tranfported, were now no longer mentioned, or at leaft had but the fecond Share in his Admiration; and on my telling him, that a young Perfon could not but look on an Acquaintance with one of his Turn of Mind, as extremely fortunate; have you really determined then, Madam, cried he, to make me forget my Age, and every Confideration, that might deter me from falling a Victim to the Power of Love? Your Eyes were indeed fufficient to captivate a Heart, not fortified as mine for many Years has been, but when you attack it in this Manner with the Beauties of your Mind, how difficult, nay, how next to impoffible is it to refift.

I feem'd a little confufed at this Declaration, and caft down my Eyes, being wholly unprepared for an Anfwer; on which, let not what I have faid, continued he, I befeech you, Madam, give you any Uneafinefs, tho' I fhould even forget the Difparity between our Years and Merits, you have nothing to apprehend, from a Paffion mingled with fuch Refpect, and a certain Awe, which nothing lefs than fuch fuperior Merits as yours could have infpired me with—— I look, added he, on your charming Soul, as a Ray of the celeftial Effence, fhining thro' the fineft Features its divine Wifdom ever created, and think I worfhip Heaven, in adoring its moft perfect Work. By this Time I had a little recover'd myfelf, and anfwered him in a fafhion which excited new Compliments. Our Difcourfe afterwards turning on the different Perfections of the Mind, he afked me, if among my other Accomplifhments I had practifed Singing, and I making but fome few faint Excufes, he earneftly begg'd I would favour him fo far as to give him a Specimen of my Voice; I thought it would appear affected in me to refufe his Requeft, queſt, and indeed knowing my Voice was good, and that I had made a conſiderable Progreſs in Muſick, I was well enough ſatisfied to ſhew him, that Part of Education had not been denied me. And ſung an Air, the Words of which were the Marquis's, a ſufficient Reaſon for my remembring it.

S O N G.

CLOE *has a Shape, a Mien,*
Sparkling Wit, does graceful move :
Where ev'ry Charm but Virtue's ſeen,
Then it is a Crime to love.

Mark my CELIA, *Goddeſs fair !*
With not ſparkling Wit alone,
Virtue gilds her Beauty's Sphere,
Then are Love and Virtue one.

After a thouſand Compliments on my Performance; well, *Forſan,* ſaid the agreeable Stranger to his Dependant, how fortunate ſhould I have thought myſelf, if the Perſon you know of had made Choice of ſuch a Lady as this——— O, that ſome happy Star had directed him to theſe Eyes ———they could not but have captivated him, and ſuch a Loſs of Liberty had been glorious for him, and an infinite Satisfaction to me———Your Pardon, Madam, continued he turning to me, that I wiſh one more had been added to the Number of your Adorers: Him I ſpeak of was not unworthy of that Honour, 'till he ſullied the Luſtre of his Birth, and Accompliſhments, by a mean and degenerate Paſſion.

As I took theſe Words only meant to introduce new Praiſes, I only ſaid, that Love was blind, and incapable of Diſtinction. I know very well, Madam, anſwer'd he, that when the Heart is prepoſſeſt by Beauty, it is too apt to exalt the Merits of the beloved Object——— but an Infatuation, ſuch as the Gentleman's I ſpeak of is, is not to be parallel'd———I will make you the judge———few, if any of his Quality, which I aſſure
you

you is not of the lowest among the Nobility, could boast a better Education, or had made a greater Progress in all those Accomplishments befitting his Age, and Sex————He was indeed the Darling of the whole Court, as well as of an indulgent Father, nor had ever once been guilty of any Extravagance, to forfeit the Esteem of those he convers'd with, 'till all at once he became the very Reverse of all he had been————forgot his Birth, his Duty, his Honour, and every thing that ought to have been valuable, to pursue a country Girl, the Daughter of a poor Peasant, who has involved him in continual Broils, brought his Life more than once in Danger, and made him guilty of Actions, which have driven him from the Presence of his royal Master, rob'd him of his Father's Love, and the Respect of all who knew him.

All the Softness and Serenity which had before appear'd in the Face of this old Gentleman, was at the speaking these Words entirely banish'd————his Eyes shot Fire, and his Cheeks flush'd with a glowing red————he even trembled with Excess of Passion————for my Part I found so much Resemblance between this Story and my own, miserably mangled, and misrepresented as it was, that I could not forbear blushing, but how great was my Surprize, when I heard *Forsan* immediately say————Ah! my Lord Marquis, the near Concern your Lordship has in this Affair, transports you to forget, that Love can make Perfections where there is none in reality————I dare engage the young Lord finds all those Charms in the Object of his Affections, as you so justly allow this Lady to be possest of.

The Title of Marquis, join'd with the Description of his Person, which I had often heard, but above all the implacable Rage he express'd against the poor country Girl, left me no Room to doubt, if my ill Genius had not thrown me into the Company of my Lover's Father————I was confounded, but had no Time to make Reflections on this odd Adventure. The old Nobleman immediately rejoin'd, I tell thee, *Forsan*, it is impossible, tho' I allow the Force of Prejudice in some

Cases

Cases, it cannot be of any Effect in this——what, continued he, a little Wretch brought up in a Cottage, a Creature who can have no other Merit than her Youth, and perhaps a tolerable Face, can she, can such a one as she, behave in any Fashion, to create Esteem in any Man of Sense? I could forgive his toying away an idle Hour with the pretty Trifler, tho' even that debases him too much——but to entertain a serious Passion—— to avow it too——to fight for her, to suffer every thing——to do every thing for such a one, I say cannot be call'd Love but Madness.——But by this Time I believe she severely suffers for all the Troubles she has occasioned, tho' never can attone for the Disobedience of a Son to his Father——you, *Forsan*, were one of the first to represent these Things to me, and indeed it was you, who put me in the Head of the only Expedient, to rid the World of such an Incendiary, who without Wit or Education, has had Artifice enough to set whole Families in a Flame.

I et any one judge of the Condition I was in to hear myself thus cruelly reproach'd: the Terror of being surprized by the quick-sighted *Forsan*, would not suffer me to speak one Word in Defence of the poor injured Villager, and this join'd with the Restraint I was under, made me ready to sink. The Marquis being entered into the Topic, could not easily get out of it, and continued for a long Time, uttering the most opprobrious Language against his Son's Mistress, that Malice sure ever dictated; at last good Manners reminded him, that as I was not at all interested in his Affairs, he ought not to entertain me with them; and changing the Conversation, he ask'd how far I was from Home, which Way I went, and if I intended to prosecute my Journey next Day? I replied with a great deal of Indifference, that I was only going to accompany a Relation to a Monastry; he then enquir'd if the Monastry was near *Versailles*; because, added he, I would do myself the Honour to attend you thither; I thank'd his Lordship, and told him that it was not far off, and that we should not set out 'till ten or eleven o'Clock; by which Time, thought I

to

to myfelf, I hope to be far enough out of your power. This gave him an Opportunity of acquainting me, that he was returning from a Caftle he had in the Country, and was obliged to ftop at the Inn, becaufe his Servants not expecting him fo foon, had not met him with frefh Horfes; fo that, added he, the Time in which I have now fent Orders for them to come, will fuit exactly with yours, and I fhall think myfelf extremely happy to accompany you. I anfwer'd to what he faid in a very complaifant Manner, and perceiving that by the reft of his Difcourfe, I was not in any Danger of being difcovered, I refolved to take my own Part a little in the Perfon of the young Villager, if a fecond Opportunity fhould offer.

I cannot here omit remarking, that tho' I was often on the Point of being ruined one way or the other, yet Providence, that never failing Friend to Innocence, ftill interpofed for my Protection————What in this Circumftance could have fallen out fo fortunate for me, as the Valet de Chamber of the Count *de Snint Fal* being gone to his Mafter; and to compleat the Service he did me on this Occafion had taken with him, I fuppofe for the fake of Company, another old Servant whom the Count had left behind, fo that there remained none of his Retinue but the Poftilion; who being hired but for the Journey, knew neither my Name, nor that of the Gentleman he attended; and as for the People of the Houfe, I remembred very well that Monfieur *de Saint Fal* had been cautious of letting them know either his Name or Quality, fo I was perfectly fecure in cafe the Marquis, tempted by his Curiofity, fhould make any Enquiry, as indeed he afterwards did.

The Defire I had of bringing my own Subject on the Tapis again, made me take the Advantage of the Regard and Admiration he paid me, and withdrawing one of my Hands, which he had juft been kiffing, I fancy, my Lord Marquis, faid I, that you are not entirely free from Prejudice yourfelf: If your Son be as eafily influenced by our Sex as your Lordfhip, you ought not to be furprized at his falling in love, with a Perfon who perhaps may
be

be much more amiable than I am;. There is a vaſt
Difference, Madam, replied the old Marquis very
gravely between allowing a Lady. her Merits, and falling
in love ; much more being guilty of all manner of Irregularities for the ſake of that Paſſion. Alas ! my Lord, ſaid
I, the Engagements between your Sex and ſuch a Girl
as you deſcribe, cannot be of any great Conſequence——
and I am inclined to believe her Kindred have much
more to fear on her Account, than thoſe of his Lordſhip can poſſibly have ; becauſe the meaner ſhe is, the
more ought ſhe to prize her Virtue, as the only Treaſure
allotted her by Fate. Nay indeed, cried the old Marquis with a Smile, I ſcarce can think, that in ſpite of all
he has done he will be mad enough to make her his Wife,
————and yet, continued he, growing ſerious again,
I am told ſhe is ſo artful a Jilt, and has ſo many Contrivances, that I am not ſometimes without my Fears
for him. Then, my Lord, ſaid I with an Air of Gra-
vity, I muſt applaud the Reſolution you have taken to
ſeparate them for ever, and am inclinable to wiſh ſo well
to your Family, as to hope you have taken care to do it
effectually. I expect as ſoon as I come to *Verſailles,*
anſwered he, to hear News of her being ſecured in a
Monaſtry, where I have given ſuch Orders, that ſhe
ſhall have a reception proper for a Perſon, who has occaſioned ſuch Diſturbances——I think ſhe cannot with all
her Hypocriſy have deceived a young Nobleman, who
being my Nephew, I entruſted with the Commiſſion :
He is pretty well verſed in the Arts practiſed by Creatures of her Stamp, and will but laugh at all the Tricks
ſhe may have recourſe to.

I was ready to burſt at theſe laſt Words, and I have
ſince, on recollecting this Paſſage of my Life, wondered
how I was able to contain myſelf from uttering ſomething, that might have made him ſee how nearly I was
touched with what he ſaid——any one at the reading it
may gueſs how they would feel at hearing themſelves
thus torn to pieces————thus accuſed: of things they
in their Souls moſt deſpiſe and hate : The Apprehenſions
I had, however, that all the Admiration this Nobleman
seemed

feemed to have of me, would not have defended me
from the Effects of his Refentment, had he once come
to know who I was, obliged me to keep within thofe
Bounds, which were neceflary to prevent him from Difcovering me, and I only faid, Good God, how greatly
does your Lordfhip furprize me ! The little Converfation
I have had with you, would have given me a high Idea
of your Son's Capacity, but this Defcription of his
Miftrefs deftroys it all————is it poffible a young
Gentleman of any refined Notions himfelf, can be
really in love with a Creature fuch as you have painted?
————the Blindnefs of Paffion concerns no more than
the exterior Part of the beloved Object, it extends not
to the Mind, and let a Man be never fo much charmed
with a Face, if he has Senfe himfelf, he will notwithftanding his Affection, fee the Defects of it in her. I
am therefore apt to imagine that this Girl, tho' meanly
born, has fome good Qualities, befide her Beauty, to
fecure her Lover's Heart.

I allow the Juftice of your remark, Madam, anfwered
he, and were I not perfectly convinced of the vile Difpofition of this intriguing Creature, I fhould believe as
you do, that fo lafting a Paffion as fhe has infpired in my
unhappy Son, was kept alive by fome good Qualities;
but Experience, Madam, fatal Experience convinces me
of the contrary————What ! has fhe not by her Artifices deprived a very excellent Lady her Patronefs of
an only Son ! Has fhe not ruined mine ! Engaged him
in Quarrels ! Difconcerted all his Affairs, and fet him
at variance with his Father ! Can any Character be
more abominable ? Is fhe not equally to be feared and
hated ?

One of that turn of Mind, indeed, faid I, is a Difgrace
to her Sex ; but if this Difcourfe did not affect you too
much, I would beg leave to afk your Lordfhip one
Queftion ?

With all my Heart, replied he, tho' I cannot fpeak of
this Affair without Emotion, yet I take too much
Pleafure in hearing you, not to be ready to anfwer any
thing you fhall take a Satisfaction in being informed of.

It

It is my, Lord, said I, looking earneftly at him, whither you have ever feen this fame Miftrefs of your Son, I mean the Country Girl, the Villager you have been fpeaking of; for poffibly he may have others, a thing they fay pretty common with Perfons of his Age and Rank? No, beautiful Lady, anfwered he, I have never feen her; but thofe who knew her but too well, have given me a perfect Defcription of her; particularly a young Lady, Daughter to the Lord of the Village where fhe was born; and who by the Misfortunes the Wretch's Hypocrify and pretended Innocence has brought upon her Family, has Reafon to regret the charitable Protection her Mother gave her.

Ah, my Lord! cried I, how are you certain they do not impofe on you, and taking the Advantage of your Lordfhip's Refentment on Account of her mean Birth, load her with Crimes, of which perhaps fhe is entirely Innocent.

No, Madam, no, refumed he a little peevifhly, I tell you they are Facts, and notorious to the whole World; befides, the Perfon I fpeak of, can have no Reafons for deceiving me in this Point.

Pardon me, my Lord, faid I, you fay the Lady is young, and your Son doubtlefs a fine Gentleman, why may there not be Rivalfhip in the Cafe, and Jealoufy has a cruel Tongue?————Perhaps not able to endure the Preference fhould be given to one, fo much her inferior in Birth, this young Lady may have taken thefe Means to punifh both the Infenfibility of your Son, and the Vanity of her Rival, for pretending to a Heart, fhe was ambitious of fecuring to herfelf.

Such an Incident as this, cried the Marquis, would do well enough in a Romance; but indeed, Madam, there it nothing in it————this Vagabond Peafant merits all the ill that can be faid of her, and were all the World to join in your Opinion, and would endeavour to make me of the fame, it would be in vain; for I am convinced, and when I once am fo, am no lefs inflexible.

This

This was utter'd with a Malignity, which teſtified, indeed, the Rancour of his Heart; and made me tremble with the Fears of one Day feeling the Effects of it. I would now have changed the Converſation; but he was grown too full of the Subject, and went on railing at the Country Girl, and praiſing me by Turns, till unable to ſupport it; I cry'd out for Heaven's ſake, my Lord, be more juſt, you either allow too little or too much, and neither your Indignation or Friendſhip, ought to have any Weight with Perſons who are unprejudiced in your Favour.

Theſe raſh Words eſcaped me, without thinking what I ſaid, and I had no ſooner ſpoke them, than I would have given the World to have recalled them. The Marquis ſeem'd aſtoniſhed, he looked at *Forſan*, then again turning to me, eyed me from Head to Foot; yet all this, as I afterwards happily found, without the leaſt Suſpicion of who I was.

How unhappy am I, Madam, ſaid he, after a long Pauſe, to have any way offended you.————You ſeem to have taken ſomething amiſs from me, and if in the Heat of my Reſentment againſt that pernicious Creature, I have uttered any thing unbecoming, I ſincerely aſk your Pardon.————I take you to be a Lady deſerving more Reſpect than I am able to pay, thus perplexed as I am with the Behaviour of an only, and once moſt beloved Son; therefore, I beſeech you tell me, wherein I have done, or ſaid amiſs, that I may be careful to avoid the like Tranſgreſſion for the future.

Theſe Queſtions very much puzzled me, I would fain have evaded giving any direct Anſwer, and only ſaid that his Lordſhip ſtood in need of no Apology to me, for he had neither done, nor I reſented any thing as an Affront; but this would not content him, the Cloud that ſtill appear'd upon my Brow, as well as the Warmth with which I had let fall thoſe unguarded Expreſſions, convinced him I was ſecretly very much out of Humour, and the Replies he made to the aukard Pretences, I made for this Change in my Countenance, and manner

of

of speaking, made me see I had to deal with a Person, whose long Experience in the World would not suffer him to be easily deceived. In the Name of God, Madam, said he, endeavour not to conceal from me, the Fault I have unknowingly committed.————Something I see has touch'd you very nearly————be assured it would give me a sensible Affliction to have created any Disquiet in you.————Nay, I will say further, that I feel something within me, that interests me in your Behalf, such a kind of Tenderness, as had I a Daughter, or a Sister, might be expected from me.————Speak, therefore, lovely Creature, continued he, seeing me in Confusion ————let Matters be clear'd up between us, and though it is the first Time I have the Pleasure of being in your Company, let me not despair of re-enjoying that Satisfaction by any Displeasure on your side.

Here I again attempted to make him believe I had no meaning in what I had said; but all I urged on that Score had so little Appearance of Truth, that he easily saw through it.————Ah! cry'd he, you would in vain attempt to deceive me, and your going about to do it, convinces me that there is some Mystery in it.————I remember too, you express'd yourself with great Earnestness concerning my Son.————Perhaps, you know him————you may also know me————or————or ————you may be of the Acquaintance of Madam the Countess *De N*————, or more probably of Madam *De G*————; both of whom have been Protectors of that insinuating Jilt that has so betrayed my Son————if you know the last of these Ladies, she, perhaps, being herself impos'd upon by her Artifices, may have given you Ideas too favourable of her————you blush:———— Nay, then, by Heaven there is somewhat in it.———— Ah! *Forfar*, continued he, turning to his Attendant, I am persuaded there is an extraordinary Motive for the Trouble this young Lady discovers, while she endeavours to conceal it.————I must know it————perhaps, It may concern me more, than yet I am aware of, of, and I am determin'd not to leave this Place, till I can solve the Riddle.

I reprefented to myfelf the Danger I was in, of being on the Point of being difcover'd, by the only Perfon on Earth I had Reafon to be afraid of, that I was ready to fink when he afk'd me if I knew his Son——the mention he made of my Godmother and Madam *De G*————, gave an Addition to the Alarms I felt; but his laft Words terrified me to that Degree, that I fell into a Swoon.

I was afterwards inform'd by the People of the Houfe, that the Marquis took Abundance of Pains to bring me to myfelf, he call'd for Affiftance, and while the Women were employ'd about me, made a ftrict Enquiry who I was ; but, as I faid before, his Interrogatories were fruitlefs, No-body could inform him of any thing concerning me.

I foon recovered my Senfes, but as I found the Difcourfe was about me, I pretended to be ftill in a Fit, that I might not be afked any farther Queftions, which muft infallibly have involv'd me in new Perplexities.

The Landlord and Landlady of the Houfe, I found were in the Room, of whom I heard the Marquis impatiently enquire who I was, whence I came, who brought me thither, and the Name of the young Lady that was going to a Monaftry, and I had mention'd as a Relation; but their Anfwers feemed only to render the Difcovery he aim'd at more difficult.————They told him the Pilgrim could be no Relation of mine, for I had never feen her before that Day, and had exprefs'd a great Curiofity to know her Hiftory————that a young Officer, whofe Name they were intirely ignorant of, had conducted me thither ; but that he was gone, and I had a Difpute with one of the Servants he had left behind, the meaning of which they were ignorant of ; and that they being alfo departed, there remain'd only the Poftilion who was wholly unacquainted with any thing. Well, cry'd the Marquis, this is aftonifhing————what think you, *Forfan*, don't you think there

muft

muſt be ſomething very extraordinary in this young Lady's Circumſtances, that ſo many Precautions are taken
to prevent any Diſcovery————we will, however,
ceaſe Enquiries for this Night.————To-morrow, perhaps, ſhe will of herſelf be complaiſant enough to put
us out of this Suſpence.————If not————I have infallible Means of coming at the Truth.

He had no ſooner ſaid this, than recommending me to
the Care of the People of the Houſe, he went out of the
Chamber; but return'd again immediately, to order that
if I continu'd long ill, they ſhould inform him of it,
for he would ſend to *Verſailles* for a Phyſician to attend
me: He then redoubled his Charge to them to be diligent
about me, adding that he now recollected who I was,
and that I was a Perſon of Quality, whoſe Family he was
well acquainted with.

He was no ſooner gone than I began to live again,
that is to give a Vent to my Breath, which I had ſo long
reſtrain'd, that I was in good earneſt almoſt ſuffocated.
While the Landlady remain'd in my Chamber, and was
helping me to Bed, which I ſeign'd would be the beſt
Remedy for perfectly recovering my Diſorder; I began
to conſider what could be the Motive that had induced
the Marquis to ſay, I was a Woman of Quality, and
flatter'd myſelf, that I was ſo happy as to be miſtaken
by him for ſome other Perſon; but whether I was deceiv'd in my Conjectures or not, ſhall be made appear
in the Sequel of theſe Memoirs

As every thing I had to hope or fear in the World,
now depended on my Eſcape, I pretended an Inclination to Sleep, that I might be left alone; and as ſoon as
I was ſo, I got out of Bed, dreſt me, and crept ſoftly
up to *Lindamine*'s Chamber, having liſtened at the
Door, and found ſhe was alone. A little Knock I gave
made her immediately open it, and ſhe receiv'd me
with open Arms; ſhe told me ſhe had heard that Strangers had been with me, and was in moſt terrible Apprehenſions, leſt their Arrival ſhould hinder the Execution
of my Deſigns. No, beautiful *Lindamine*, anſwer'd I,

the Adventure of this Night has render'd my Departure
in the moſt ſecret Manner, abſolutely neceſſary, as you
will be convinced, when you ſhall be inform'd of the
Particulars of my Hiſtory from my dear *Saint Agnes*;
but how, cry'd I, have you diſpoſed of *Bellixay?* Will
he be no Obſtruction to our Deſigns ? Not in the leaſt,
ſaid ſhe, he is gone to his Apartment, perfectly ſatisfied
with the Aſſurance I have given him of Pardon, for what
is paſt, and a Reſolution to lead the Remainder of my Life
with him. And as for every thing elſe, added ſhe, I
have taken ſuch Meaſures, that I have not the leaſt
Reaſon to doubt the Succeſs.

She then acquainted me that every thing relating to our
Journey was fix'd, and the Scheme ſhe had laid down for
it, appeared to me ſo well contriv'd, that it was next
to an Impoſſibility we ſhould be diſappointed————
But how little, alas ! ought we to depend on human Prudence————*Lindamine*'s ill Stars indeed ſeemed to be
tired of perſecuting her, and now conducted her to a ſafe
Aſylum from all the Storms and Terrors of the World,
but I was only beginning to Experience the Malignity
of mine ; and, as my Dream foretold, was entring into
a Wild of Dangers————an immenſe Labyrinth of Tryals, in which my Virtue, and eternal Peace of Mind,
were often near being loſt.

The Shades of Night had now extended themſelves
over all our ſide of the Globe, and covered all things
with Obſcurity for ſome Hours————the Houſe was in
a profound Silence, not a Creature waking but *Lindamine*
and myſelf within, and the Hoſtler, who having ſeen the
Reckoning diſcharged, had orders to wait without the
Door the coming of *Lindamine*'s Steward, that his
knocking at ſo late an Hour might not alarm thoſe,
whoſe Intereſt in this Affair might render not very
ſound Sleepers.

Exactly at the Time prefix'd, that faithful Servant
came to acquaint us every thing was ready, and conducted us down Stairs in the Dark, to prevent any Accident which a Light might have occaſion'd. When

WO

we were got into the Chaise, now, my dear, cry'd *Lin-damine*, I hope we are got clear of all we had to appre-hend, and before Day-break shall be in a Place of Safety. Pray Heaven we may, said I, but I tremble without knowing why; it is only the Darkness of the Night that frights you, reply'd she, I see you are but a Novice in these dangerous Adventures!————What would you do, if you were alone in a Forest at this dreadful Hour, as many a Time I have been during my long Pilgrimage! I made no Answer to this, but thought in my Mind, I had but too much Experience, in what she imagin'd me a Novice.

Her Steward, who rode by the side of the Chaise, now began to acquaint us in what manner he had executed his Commission, which the hurry of our quitting the Inn, had not before given him time to do; and gave a pleasing Cessation to my Fears, by assuring me, that *Saint Agnes*'s Packet, of which his Mistress had given him so great a Charge, would be safely deliver'd into *Me-licourt*'s own Hands; for, Madam, said he, I very luckily recollected that a very near Relation of mine, has serv'd that young Gentleman's Father for more than Twen-ty Years, to whom I have sent them by a trusty Hand, under a Cover from myself, and shall doubtless have an immediate Answer. I then ask'd him with great Ear-nestness, by what Means it would come to Hand; on which he told me, he had order'd the Person who carried the Letters, to go at his Return to the Village in which the Monastry stood, where his Mistress had told him, she intended by my Advice to take Refuge; and to wait there in Case he should return before he arrived.

I was charm'd with the Diligence of this Man, and cry'd out in a kind of Transport, O! my dear *Saint Agnes* then will soon have an Account of her beloved—she will be in Raptures! And I, in being with her by that Time, shall partake of her Felicity. The fair *Lindamine*, thought she could never sufficiently extol the Sincerity of my Heart, and told me no-body ought to think them-selves altogether unhappy, who had a Friend like me.

After

After some mutual Compliments on this Occasion, our Discourse turned on the new Way of Living, we were going to enter into.

We had not proceeded in our Journey above Six Miles, before the Postilion was obliged to rest his Horses, after getting up a very steep Hill. The Steward in this Interval turn'd about, as attentive to something, on which I asked him the Reason; or I am much deceived, Madam, answer'd he, or I hear the trampling of Horses at some Distance: Neither *Lindamine* nor myself made any Answer to this Information; but putting our Heads out of the Chaise, found alas! what he had imagined was but too true.——I am undone, cry'd she, *Bellizay* has certainly discovered my Flight, and is come in Pursuit of me.——Ah! rather cry'd I, full of Apprehensions on the Marquis's Score, it is me, unhappy me they seek! The Terror I was in, now was a Proof, that let our Friendship or Compassion for another be ever so strong, it will still recede, when once dear Self comes in question.——Good God! what shall I do, resumed *Lindamine*, how now shall I get rid of this impatient, this obstinate Disturber of my Repose, and Resolution. Compose yourself, Madam, I beseech you, said the honest Steward; you know I have made a Campaign, am no Coward, and in your Defence am ready to shed the best Part of my Blood;——but I do not think there will be any Occasion for this.——*Bellizay* has no right to controll your Actions, and if he should persist to follow you, can only learn the Place of your Retreat—His Importunities when you are there, in my Opinion, is all you have to apprehend, and those the Holy Orders of the Place will soon find Means to ease you of;——but should he——dare he attempt now to force you back, as I said before, Madam, I have a good Pair of Pistols and a Sword, which shall all fail me with my Life, before you shall be compelled to any thing against your Inclinations. *Lindamine* then told him, she was most fearful, that his Duty and Readiness to serve her should be fatal to him; but though she said this, and possibly might have disquiet on that Head, yet I could easily see she still had some remains of that Affection, she formerly bore to *Bellizay*, and that her greatest Terror was the being exposed to fresh Temptations from that dangerous Lover———I pitied her from my Heart, as indeed she deserved; for it must be confessed a Woman is very unhappy, while her Virtue is combating with her Affection.

However, the Noise of the Horses increased, and in spite of that our Chaise made, it being now in Motion, we could perceive they gained Ground upon us every Moment; we also thought we could discern some glimmerings of Light behind us on the Road———My Alarms now redoubled, I remembered what the old Marquis had said at leaving my Chamber, that he had infallible means of coming at the Truth, and no longer doubted if it was himself, or some he had sent after me, in order for the Discovery he so much desired. As the Light drew nearer we found it proceeded from Torches, and *Lindamine*, putting out her Head, for I had Courage to examine no farther. Ah! cried she, I know not which of us is pursued, but here are three Men on full Gallop toward us.———How far off are they, said I, scarce able to speak———Not two Pistol Shot, replied the Steward———In the Name of God, cried I, quite besides myself, order the Postilion to stop that I may get out———I am certain that I am the Person whom these Men seek, and more than my Life depends on avoiding them———the Darkness of the Night may conceal me behind some of these Thickets. Both *Lindamine*, and her Steward would have disuaded me from alighting; but the Terror I was in of falling into the old Marquis's Hands, made me resolute to hazard every thing rather than that; so they were obliged to comply. Our Horses stop'd, and neither *Lindamine*, nor myself being able to get the Door open, the Steward was obliged to alight, which took up so much Time, that those I endeavoured to avoid had the Opportunity of coming up with us, and surrounding us just as I was stepping out. By the Light of the Torches, dying as I was with my Apprehensions, I discerned *Saint Fal,* putting me gently back into my Place———— His Face was as pale as Death, and when he endeavoured to speak, his Voice quite forsook him ; it seemed to me as if this inforced Silence was occasioned by want of Breath with hard Riding, but as he afterwards informed me, it proceeded from a surprize of Joy at having overtaken me. His Valet de Chambre, enraged at the Trick I had put upon him, well supplied his Master's Deficiency of Speech, and perhaps imagining that after what I had done, he intended to reproach me ; Really, Madam, said he, in an insulting Tone, you make a fine return to the Civilities my Lord has treated you with, and if I were in his Place————Be silent, cried the Count, having now recovered herself, what Complaisance I have shewn to this Lady is infinitely beneath what her Merit demands from all the World————I have no manner of Right to controll her Inclinations, or Actions, and if I oppose her Intentions at this Time, it is only because her own Interest requires she should act otherwise than at present perhaps she is sensible of. After saying this he drew nearer to the Chaise, and made a great many gallant Apologies, both for having given me any Alarm, and for interrupting my Journey. Concluding with saying he would give me such Reasons for what he did, that he was certain I should myself approve of his Conduct. I was so much surprized at his Behaviour, and the Respect he paid me, after the manner in which I had abused the Confidence he reposed in me, that I was wholly incapable of making any reply to what he said ; but tho' my Tongue was silent, my Thoughts were not inactive, and I present'y cast about for something to alledge in my Vindication ; the having been thrown into the Company of the old Marquis appeared to me a very plausible Pretence, and I did not fail afterwards to make the proper Use of it.

The Count then addressed himself to *Lindamine,* and instead of upbraiding her with having contributed to my Escape, said the most polite Things imaginable to her ; and on hearing we intended to take Refuge in a Mo:

nastry, praised our Prudence; and assured the fair Pilgrim, that to repair the Misfortune of being deprived of so agreeable a Companion as myself, he would frequently wait on her himself, and bring her News of me as soon as he had settled me in a convenient Place.

While he was entertaining us in this Manner, a Servant rode up to him, and told him, he saw the Chaise coming; on which Monsieur *de Saint Fal* informed me, that guessing by the Time he heard I had left the Inn, that he should overtake me; he had ordered the Groom to get it ready and send it after him. A Precaution he said, he was rejoyced to have taken, because by this means it prevented any Interruption of *Lindamine*'s Journey. I found by his Discourse that it was by the Hostler, who had opened the Door for us, that he was informed of our Departure, and the Road we intended to take, having overhead the Direction given by *Lindamine*'s Steward to the Postilion: which shewed me how little Dependance there is on the Secrecy of such Sort of People. I also found that his returning to the Inn was wholly owing to the Valet de Chamber's going to *Versailles*, suspecting by what that Fellow said, that the Pilgrim and I had formed some Contrivance together, which might deprive him of me. I was extremely impatient to know, if on his calling at the Inn, he had met with the old Marquis, but I restrained my Curiosity till we were alone, not caring to speak any thing of the latter Part of my History before *Lindamine*, till she should be acquainted with the former.

The Chaise joined us in a short Time, and after I had embraced the beautiful Pilgrim, received a most affectionate return from her, and assured her of continuing a Correspondence with her, the Count assisted me in removing from one Machine to the other, and when I was seated was most tenderly diligent in taking all possible Care to defend me from the Inclemency of the Night Air———he wraped his Cloak about me, and obliged me to cover my Feet; in fine, did every Thing that could be expected from the greatest good Manners and

Respect, and then commanded the Postilion to drive on.

I now began as well to excuse my Flight, as to know whether he had seen the old Marquis, to relate the Adventure which had befallen me ; but never was Surprize greater than that which this little Narrative threw him into————Good God, cried he, my Uncle at the same Inn with you————you in his Company, and treated by him in that manner !————Why, said I, did you hear nothing of his being there at your Arrival ! not a Syllable, answered he, nor is it to be wondered at, all the Family were in Bed, except the Person, who was in the Secret of your Departure ; which after he had informed me of, I was in too much Confusion, and had too much Impatience to follow you to ask him any Questions, so only changed Horses for the more Expedition, and gave him Orders to send my Chaise after me, the Moment he could get it ready————How fortunate for me was it, added he, that the Marquis knew nothing of my being there————the unexpected Sight of him would have involved me in little less Perplexity that yourself, unprepared as I was to give him any Account how I had disposed of you.

He then made me repeat all the Marquis had said to me Word for Word, as near as I could remember, and after I had finished, confessed that after such an Accident he could not be surprized, that I had formed a Resolution of taking Shelter in a Monastry during my own Pleasure, since the Necessity of my Affairs made it seem the only way to prevent my being secured in one for ever, by the cruel Will of another. And I am well paid, beautiful *Jeanetta*, added he, for all the Pains your Flight occasioned me, in being informed by your own Mouth, that it was not any Aversion you had taken to me, or to punish any Offence I had given you, that you quitted the Inn in that clandestine manner. I replied to this Compliment in the most obliging Phrases I was Mistress of, and told him that I should always prefer the Honour of his Friendship too much to do any thing which might justly forfeit it, and that I valued myself highly

on

on the Civilities I had received from him. Ah!
Heavens! cried he, what Savage is there of the Race of
Men, that could behave otherwise to a Woman so every
way adorable !————all that I beg you to believe, is,
that I am not only truly sensible of your Merits, but
that also they have inspired me with Sentiments, that
must always influence me to serve you, even against the
Interest of that Passion, Beauty like yours cannot fail
of kindling in the Soul————Never, therefore, most
lovely *Jeanetta*, be under any Apprehensions from me!
Look not on me as one, who would obstruct your secret
Inclinations————I give you my solemn Promise, nay,
will confirm it by any Oath, you yourself shall invent
most binding ; that, notwithstanding the fervent Affection I have for you, I will rather promote, than any
way be an Impediment to your Happiness, with the
Man you love————I am sensible I know you too
late—your Heart was pre-engaged, and to one, who,
if any Man can do so, deserves the Esteem you have
for him, therefore may you both be bless'd, and I doubt
not but time will render you so.————All I entreat is
that, you will never forbid me your Society. Be assured,
charming *Jeanetta*, that unruly Passions have no Dominion over me————my Heart allows itself no Desires,
but of seeing and admiring you————should it ever
exceed those Bounds, I have too much Delicacy, not to
check the inordinate Sallies, and if nothing less would
do it, would tear myself forever from your Presence—
you should have no need to banish me, I would hide myself in the Bosom of Virtue, and be a voluntary Exile,
rather than give you the least Disturbance.

Such strong Assurances of a disinterested Friendship,
had a right to touch my Soul, nor could my dear Marquis, to whom I have since confest what I felt on that
Occasion, b'ame me for being greatly affected with
them ; I told him that if what he now said was sincere,
as I had no Reason to doubt, I should consider him as
the most generous Man on Earth, and should make a
suitable Return, which was all that Friendship, exclusive of Love, could bestow ; he answered, it was all he
desired,

desired, and whenever he asked more, would not complain if I treated him with the utmost Disdain and Resentment.

From this we fell into Discourse on the old Marquis; I told the Count, that I much feared when once he came to find I had not been secured according to his Orders, that he would make such strict Enquiry after me, that it would be impossible for me to avoid his Search. Make yourself easy, dear Madam, on that score, replied he, as I have ordered Things, you will be much safer at *Versailles* than elsewhere. The Person with whom you are to lodge, supposes you to be a Widow of an Officer, and come to sollicit a Pension, and the Name I have invented for you is the Countess *de Roches*, so can give no true Information of you, should she be inclined to talk of your Affairs: No Place can be so proper as the Court to screen you from too curious Observers: Every one who comes there, is taken up with his own Concerns, and there are every Day so many Strangers, that without making it the Business of one's Life, one cannot possibly dive into that of all who frequent it ———Strangers pass there for what they please, and I have known some that have establish'd themselves under pretended Titles, and their Posterity have succeeded to them.——— As to your Sex in particular, all who behave well have a right to be esteemed, and are never molested, unless it be with the too great Devoirs of ours.

Well, my Lord, said I, so far I am satisfied, and what you have been so good to contrive for me, has indeed the Appearance of shielding me from the Danger, I so much dreaded of the Marquis *de L———V———*; but pray my Lord, as you have made me a Woman of Quality, by what means am I to support myself as such? ———You know I have no Income, that a capricious Turn of Fortune took me from an humble tho' innocent Condition, and has left me in one altogether uncertain, without any means of subsisting———Yet would I a thousand Times rather prefer being reduced to my original

ginal Meanneſs, than ſhine out in all the Pomp of Grandeur at the Expence of my Reputation.

I ſhould not have given you Time for theſe Reflections,
ſaid the generous Count interrupting me, but for the
Pleaſure I take in hearing you. Ah! beautiful *Jeanetta,*
how worthy of that heavenly Form is the Soul that dwells
in it ! How does your Way of thinking make one forget
the lowneſs of your Extraction ?————Birth ! What is,
Birth, when not ennobled by ſuch Qualities as yours ?——
What Advantage does it really give us, if we act not up to
it ? In my Opinion the Son of a Duke belyes his Original, when he behaves like a Peaſant ; and the Peaſant
who acts with Honour, which is no more than Honeſty,
is in Effect the great Man.————No, no, he that prides
himſelf only on his Deſcent, muſt be inſignificant indeed,
ſince he has Recourſe to what was done before he had Ex-
iſtence, and may juſtly be ſaid, to adorn himſelf with the
Aſhes of his Forefathers————if you, moſt charming
Jeanetta, were not born in high Life, your Virtue entitles
you to live in it, and depend upon it you will always do
ſo. But how, cried I ? you will ſhortly ſee, replied he ;
Alas, reſumed I, with ſome Emotion, but let the means
of my Support be kept ever ſo much a Secret from the
World, I ſtill ſhall know it myſelf————and to be oblig'd for a Maintenance————

Obliged, Madam, interrupted *Saint Fal,* not in the
leaſt, true Merit lays a Tax upon a worthy Mind, 'tis
the Law every Man of Honour ought to lay on himſelf,
to relieve Virtue in Diſtreſs————Vice is too often
maintain'd by the vicious, ought not Virtue to find the
ſame Encouragement from its Lovers ? .

By Arguments like theſe the Count attempted to remove
my Scruples, but all his 'Wit and Eloquence, both of
which he was Maſter of in a very high Degree, were not
ſufficient to convince me, that receiving Favours of the
ſort he mentioned, from a Perſon of a contrary Sex, was
not intirely inconſiſtent with Honour————I told him, that
not all the Neceſſities I was reduced to, could excuſe ſo
dangerous a Step ; but alas, I muſt here again confeſs my

Fault,

Fault, I said all this, but did not enough persist in it as I should have done : I ought to have desired he would execute the Commission given him by his Uncle, and confined me in a Monastery, rather than thus have exposed my Innocence; I know the Duty I owed to myself, yet did but half discharge it————I was determined to preserve my Virtue, yet suffer'd myself to fall into Temptations, which Providence alone enabled me to withstand ————How few are there that are so happy to escape, therefore let all my Sex beware how they too much depend on their own Strength, a trifling Circumstance sometimes compleats their Ruin————real Virtue is most secure in Diffidence and Humility, they are our surest Guard, and our constant Lesson should be to fear ourselves————this laudable Timidity is the surest Way to Victory, and makes us triumph over the most dangerous Assaults of Vice.

I had these Reflections when I arrived at *Versailles*; how soon were they swallowed up in Ideas of a different Nature!————it was then past nine a Clock, the Sun shone bright upon the Palace, and afforded me the most gorgeous Sight I ever had beheld———— my Transport at the Magnificence and Grandeur which now struck my Sight, was so great, that I forgot every Thing beside, even myself. *Saint Fal* fearing I was giving way to those Meditations, which seemed the Consequence of my preceding Discourse, asked me with an Air of Concern the Occasion of my Silence. We were then at the End of the grand Alley, and just going to turn off to the left————Ah! my Lord, cried I, do not disturb me in the Contemplation of this delightful Prospect. The Count now perceiving the Cause of my Resvery, ask'd my Pardon, and told me I could not give a greater Proof of the Exquisiteness of my Taste, then in admiring the Beauties of this Palace ; and then ordered the Postilion to stop, that I might have the better Opportunity of viewing it. I gazed with so much Attention, that as Monsieur *de Saint Fal* afterward told me, I seem'd to devour it with my Eyes————indeed my Admiration was so great, that I could no otherwise express it, then by the Eagerness with which I turn'd my

Head

Head from one Side to the other, endeavouring as it were to enlarge my Sight, to take in at once all the Magnificence of the several Parts, and asking a thousand Questions without giving him Time to answer one of them.

After I had a little recovered myself, from the first Transports of my Admiration, is it, said I, at this glorious Edifice I am to lodge ? He could not forbear smiling at my Simplicity, but restrain'd himself as much as possible, and told me that this was the King's Palace, and inhabited only by such whose Rank or Employments placed them near his Person, of whom he gave me a Catalogue, which lasted till we came to the *Orangerie* Street, where the Chaise stopping at a very large handsome House we were set down.

A Gentlewoman of about twenty, or five and twenty, who I soon found was the Mistress, having been appriz'd by the Count's Valet de Chambre of the Time in which she might expect us, attended our coming at the Door ; and received me in a most obliging manner, valuing herself very much, as I soon found, on her Court Breeding. Good Heaven! said she turning to the Count, after having saluted me, How extremely young must this Lady have been married——why she is still a perfect Child ; but it is no Wonder with such a Stock of Beauty ; 'twould have been impossible to have long escap'd the persecuting Sollicitations of your Sex——and she'll remain a Widow but a short Time I dare engage. I could not keep myself from blushing at this Discourse, and the obliging *St. Fal* perceiving my Confusion, put a stop to it by presenting me his Hand, and conducting me up a very large light Staircase to the Apartment had been taken for me.

The Sun at that Moment shone out extremely bright, and the Reflections of that glorious Planet on the Glasses and Gildings, with which the Rooms were ornamented, cast a prodigiou Lustre.

I have more than once confess'd, that my Heart was too liable to be taken with Splendor and Magnificence, and I now gave a Proof of it, in feeling an infinite Satisfaction in the Finery of every Thing I saw about me——

all

all the Reflections which I had made on the Road, had now no Place in my Remembrance—the great Sconces, the Pictures, and the other rich Furniture engroſſed my whole Attention, and my former Apprehenſions were no more. The Count eaſily perceived how much I was dazzled with the gay Objects before me, and felt an inward Pleaſure, which ſince he has made no Secret of, in finding his Stratagem ſucceeded : which was to ſtrike my Imagination at the firſt Entrance, and thereby render the Place he had provided for me, agreeable hereafter to me. He was certainly right in his Judgment : The firſt Sight commonly makes a laſting Impreſſion, eſpecially in things where the Senſes only are conſulted, for in thoſe where the Mind is call'd to Council, Time and Experience of their real Worth alone can render dear.

After I was put in Poſſeſſion of my Lodgings, and Madam *De Geneval*, for ſo the Miſtreſs of the Houſe was called, retired ; the Count *De Saint Fal*, entreated I would endeavour to amuſe myſelf during the Time of his Abſence ; for, ſaid he, I think it will be proper for me to wait on the old Marquis *De L———V———* this Morning, and if I do, cannot well avoid paſſing the whole Day with him.———My fiery Trial now comes on, continued he, I muſt invent the moſt plauſible Story I can, concerning your making your Eſcape from me ; for I cannot pretend to ſay I found you not at Madam *De G———*'s.

Take care, my Lord, for Heaven ſake, cry'd I, what you ſay to him on this critical Point, your Uncle ſeems to me to be a Perſon of the greateſt Penetration, and when you tell him that I made my Eſcape from you ; and when he remembers the Meeting he had with me at the Inn, the Precautions that were taken to conceal who I was, my Departure in the Night, and the Confuſion I was in, at his mentioning the Country Girl with ſo much Indignation ; will he not be apt to ſuſpect the very Perſon he hated, and order'd to be confined, was the ſame he entertain'd with ſo much Gallantry ? And ſhould he once take that in his Head, will he not
employ

employ Spies to find me out?————May not a thousand Accidents, now I am so very near him, throw me
once more in his Way, and then I am lost for ever.
The Civilities he treated me with, when known for what
I am, will augment the Detestation he before had for
me, and I must hope no Mercy.

I have already given you my Word and Honour for
your Protection, Madam, answer'd he, and will keep
it in so strict a Manner, as to lay down my Life, rather
than suffer any Insult should be offer'd to you.————I
hope what you apprehend, will be prevented by a
prudent Management on both our Sides; but if not,
depend upon it, that the Force of my Uncle's Displeasure will fall on me.————

My Lord, said I, that is too much to think on————
I cannot bear you should suffer on my Account, and——
Ah, Madam, cry'd he, impatiently, what I have to
suffer from my Uncle, is little in Comparison with the
Apprehensions of other much more affecting Ills.————
'Tis not the Rage of the Father, but the Amiableness of
Son, that sooner or later will deprive me of the Pleasure of obliging you;————but, continued he, this is
too tender a Point to be agreeable to either of us; all
I ought to entertain you with, is the Readiness with
which I shall ever fly to execute your least Commands;
and the perfect Interest I take in your Affairs, entirely
exclusive of my own.————Whatever I suffer, myself
alone shall know, nor will I ever presume to appear
before you, when I cannot do it with an Air composed
enough, not to create in you any Uneasiness.

With these Words, accompanied with a low Bow,
he went out of the Room, leaving me astonish'd at his
Generosity, and full of the most grateful Sentiments
for it. When he was gone, the Chambermaid, who had
been hired to attend me, came up————she appear'd to
me to be upwards of Fifty, and doubtless was no less,
for I easily perceiv'd no Care had been omitted to conceal the Effects of Age. She had an insinuating Air,
and affected an Infinity of good Breeding; but while she

was making Abundance of Encomiums on my Beauty, and other Perfections, always found an Opportunity to introduce her own good Qualities, by way of Parenthesis. Her Name was *Brochan*, Madam *De Geneval* gave a very high Character of her.————It seems she had lately quitted the Service of a Dutchess, and the Reason she gave for it, was, that my Lord Duke's Secretary being violently enamoured with her, she must have run a great Risque of losing her Innocence, had she continued there much longer. I could not help smiling within myself at this Account; her Age, and the disagreeable Formality of her Behaviour, as well as the Plainness of her Face, I thought might have been a sufficient Security for her, against all Dangers of that kind; but in some Days after, I found she had the Weakness to persuade herself, that she had as many Admirers as Beholders, and that it was utterly impossible for any Man to look on her with Indifference. To this Folly she had another added, if possible, more ridiculous than the other, that of imagining she was nobly born; and as she was sensible every body knew her to be a Cook's Daughter, asserted very gravely, that she had been chang'd at Nurse.

Madam *De Geneval* came up soon after this Waiting-Woman, and as I now happen to be in the Humour of drawing Pictures, cannot resist giving my Reader hers. She had a very good Face, was tall, and well made, and had she been less sensible of what she owed to Nature, had it in her Power to have been a very agreeable Companion; but Vanity and Affectation, render'd even her Wit, of which she had a good Share, sometimes tiresome to those she conversed with.————With all this, she was so passionately fond of hearing herself speak, that she would scarce afford room for any other Person to utter a Word; and of all the Topicks of Conversation was most pleas'd with that, which gave her an Opportunity of finding Fault with the Conduct of those, who were so unhappy as to come upon the Tapis; but as it was impossible for me at first Sight to discover this Foible in her Temper,

per, and she behaving to me in the most affectionate
Manner, I could not help making her very sincere Returns, accompanied with a little too much Confidence;
the Consequences of which shewed me, that a young
Person cannot be too circumspect in their Behaviour before new Acquaintance, and taught me by a dear
bought Experience, to enforce as much as I am able
this Precept to others.

After a little Chat of ordinary things, Madam *De
Geneval* and *Brochan* open'd a Chest of Drawers, see
here, my Lady, said the former, how much Care I
have taken of your Things; Monsieur the Count *De
Saint Fal*, gave me a strict Charge concerning your
Baggage, and as he gave me the Keys I open'd all your
Trunks, and laid your Cloaths, as you may perceive,
in as neat a manner, as if yourself had been present.
————As I took them out. I wrote an Account of
every Particular, which I beg you'll look over.————
I am certain you'll find all Right, for I would trust no-
body but myself. With these Words she gave me a Paper, which I soon found was an Inventory of Wearing-
Apparel, Bed and Table-Linnen fit for a Woman of my
supposed Quality; as I knew not yet what the Count
had provided for me, I excused myself from looking
over either that, or the things, fearing to betray my Ignorance; and said, that as I had come a great Journey,
and travell'd hard, I would lie down some Hours and refresh myself————they agreed it would be best for me,
and Madam *De Geneval* having wish'd me a good Repose, quitted the Chamber, and soon after Madamoiselle
Brochan, after laying my Pillows, and throwing a Coverlet upon me, did the same, entreating I wou'd ring the
Bell, the Moment I had any Commands for her.

Though I had not been in Bed all Night, I was now
in too great an Agitation of Mind to think of Sleep,
and as soon as I found myself alone, I looked with
Pleasure on the gay Objects, that presented themselves to
my Eyes; the Beauty of the Paintings, the fine carved
Work of the Cabinets, had a kind of Witchcraft in
them,

them, and I could not refift the Temptation of taking a
nearer View of the Things, I was now in a manner
Miftrefs of ; I got up and bolted the Door, that I might
not be furpriz'd in my Curiofity, and then made a full
Examination of the Furniture ; after which I went to the
Drawers, that I might fee in what Fafhion I was to be
dreft, and was quite tranfported to find there Habits excellently well-fancied, and full as rich as thofe I had
feen worn by the Countefs *De N*————, or Madam
De G————, and much gayer than thofe even of
Madamoifelle *D'Elbieux*.

I will not pretend to give a falfe Glofs to my way of
thinking at that Time, in order to render my Character
more perfect than it is in reality ; and though I know I
lay myfelf open to the Cenfures of thofe of my Sex,
who will not acknowledge they ever did amifs ; yet I
chufe rather to fuffer their Reflections, than that Truth
fhould fuffer by me.

To fpeak of things then as they were, had I examined my Heart, I fhould certainly have found it more
taken up in thofe firft Moments, with the brilliant Situation I was in, than with the Murmurs and Remonftrances of an interior Virtue.————There is a wide
Difference between arming one's felf againft Things at a
Diftance, and encountering them when prefent ;————
we but faintly reject what pleafes us and is in our power :
————Many People, indeed, defpife Riches in Theory ; but we find few Examples of the Practice.

My Virtue, however, was not fo far lull'd into a
Lethargy, as not to make fome Efforts towards reftraining me from thefe Allurements ; but then a fudden
Thought came into my Head, that I ought to be well
acquainted with what I was fuppofed to have purchafed.
————What, faid I, to myfelf, when *Brochan*, according to the Cuftom of Ladies Women, fhall afk me
which Robe, or which Head-Drefs I would pleafe to
wear ; would it not difcover that I was only a kind of
Tenant at Will to all this Pomp, if I could not readily
order fuch a thing, or fuch a thing to be brought
me ?

Prepoſſeſſed with this Belief, that the indulging my Curioſity was abſolutely neceſſary ; I open'd every little Drawer and Box, and though I had ſome little Checks at the beginning of this Employment, they ſoon were felt no more, on finding ſtill ſomething to attract new Admiration.

The End of the SIXTH PART, and the FIRST VOLUME.

New Books, sold by *Eliza Haywood*, Publisher, at the Sign of *Fame* in *Covent-Garden.*

I. THE BUSY-BODY ; or SUCCESSFUL SPY ; being the *entertaining History* of Monſ. BICAND, a Man infinitely Inquiſitive and Enterpriſing, even to Raſhneſs ; which unhappy Faculties nevertheleſs, inſtead of ruining, raiſed him from the *loweſt Obſcurity,* to a moſt *ſplendid Fortune* ; interſperſed with ſeveral *humourous Stories.* The whole containing great Variety of Adventures, equally *inſtructive* and *diverting.*

II. ANTI-PAMELA, or Feign'd Innocence detected, in a Series of SYRENA's Adventures : A Narrative which has really its Foundation in *Truth* and *Nature* ; and at the ſame time that it agreeably entertains, with a vaſt Variety of ſurpriſing *Incidents,* arms againſt the frequent *Miſchiefs* ariſing from a too ſudden Admiration. Publiſh'd as a neceſſary Caution to all young Gentlemen. The Second Edition.

> *Fatally fair they are, and in their Smiles*
> *The Graces, little Loves, and young Deſires inhabit ;*
> *But all that gaze upon them are undone ;*
> *For they are falſe, luxurious in their Appetites,*
> *And all the Heaven they hope for is Variety.*
> *One Lover to another ſtill ſucceeds ;*
> *Another, and another after that,*
> *And the laſt Fool is welcome as the former ;*
> *Till having lov'd his Hour out, he gives his Place,*
> *And mingles with the Herd that went before him.*
>
> ROWE's Fair Penitent.

THE
VIRTUOUS VILLAGER,
OR
VIRGIN'S VICTORY:
BEING

The MEMOIRS of a very GREAT LADY at the Court of *France*.

Written by HERSELF.

In which the Artifices of defigning Men are fully
detected and expofed; and the Calamities they
bring on credulous believing Woman are particularly related.

Tranflated from the Original, by the Author of
La Belle Affemblie.

VOL. II.

In vain are mufty Morals taught in Schools,
By rigid Teachers, and as rigid Rules,
Where Virtue with a frowning Afpect ftands,
And frights the Pupil from her rough Commands:
But charming Woman can true Converts make,
We love the Precept for the Teacher's fake;
Virtue in them appears fo bright fo gay,
We hear with Tranfport, and with Pride obey.

LONDON;

Printed for FRANCIS COGAN, at the *Middle Temple Gate.*

MDCCXLII

THE

VIRTUOUS VILLAGER,

OR,

VIRGIN's VICTORY.

VOL. II. PART. VII.

 NDULGING, as I said, this dangerous Curiofity, I paft from my Bed-Chamber into a Clofet, adorned with large Pannels of Looking-Glafs, the Hangings and Window-Curtains were Crimfon Damafk fring'd with Gold : Twelve Pictures all curious Landfcapes, on which feveral little Children feem'd diverting themfelves, with Sports fuitable to their Age, were placed between the Glaffes, and at the upper end was a fine carved Book-Cafe, containing a little Library of entertaining Books.

This magnificent Cabinet opened into a Wardrobe, in the midst of which stood my Toilette, covered with blue Taffety, embroidered with silver Stars, and covered with a fine **Lawn** laced round with *Bruffels*. It was furnish'd with every gay Trinket, that distinguishes Women of Fashion from the meaner Sort————such as Bracelets, Ear-rings, Necklaces, Ribbonds, Fans and Gloves. I could have contemplated much longer on these gay Objects, if the Fear of being interrupted before I had gone thro' all the Rooms, had not obliged me only to take a **tranfient** View.

A small Alcove next attracted my Admiration, on account of a fine Settee supported by kneeling *Cupids*, and others which seem'd in act of flying, bearing over it a Canopy of white Satin embossed with Flowers, so natural, one could not without Difficulty imagine them the Effect of Art. The Chairs were of the same curious Workmanship, and this as well as the Cabinet was adorned with Pictures and Glasses.

From this I went into a Dining-Room, where I found a large Buffet well filled with all Manner of Utensils all of Silver, and some gilt fit for a Table, on one side ; and opposite to it another, no less furnished with China of the most elegant Taste————the Hangings here were Tapestry, and the Floor covered with a fine Carpet————the Window Curtains green Damask laced with Gold, and made in the Festoon Manner————and in one Corner a Screen of such exquisite Painting, that well deserved the Admiration of a much better Judge than myself.

At last I returned to my Bed-Chamber, and passing by a large *India* Chest, the Key of which being in it, I lifted up the Top, and found it full of rich Silks, fine Hollands, Lawns, Cambricks, and Muslins, all in whole Pieces, to be made up into Garments, as I should think them fit for, and was proper for all the different Seasons of the Year. Nothing was here omitted that could possibly be thought on, even of the most triffling nature, and so well fancied, that it was not possible for a Woman, who had spent her whole Life in

nothing

nothing but the Study of Dress, to have made a better
or genteeler Choice.

My giving a Detail of these Things, may possibly be
looked upon as tedious, but I thought it neceffary in
Order to give the Reader a just Idea of my new Admirer
———nor indeed can I to this Day remember his Generosity, and obliging Attention, without the greatest
Gratitude ; to say therefore, that I was not highly affected with it, at that Time, would be injuring Sincerity, and tho' I could not then be convinced, as I since
have been, that he had no criminal Views in what he
did, yet I freely confess, his settling me in a Manner so
pleasing to my Inclinations, flatter'd my Vanity more
than it alarm'd my Virtue. O how dangerous a Situation, would this have been to a young Creature, with almost any other Man than the disinterested *St. Fal,* or
who had not the good Fortune, as I had, to inspire in all
those who liked me a certain Respect, which would not
suffer them to exceed the bounds of Honour.

The little Repose however I had taken the preceding
Nights, fatigued me to that Degree, that the Pleasure I
took in looking over all the fine things before me, gave
way to the Desire of resting my akeing Eyes, so threw my-
on the Bed, and soon fell into a profound Sleep : the
present Contentment of my Mind prevented any unpleasing Dreams, and only soft and agreeable Ideas possest
my ever-waking Fancy.

I awoke not till the Day was very far advanced, nor
perhaps had then done so, but for the Noise of Coaches
hurrying pass my Windows ; and then remembring I had
fastened the Doors, I got up and open'd that of my Bed-
Chamber———I had no sooner drawn the Bolt than
my Waiting-Woman entered : O my Stars ! Madam,
said she, with a fawning Smile, you are very timorous
to shut yourself up thus at Noon-Day———I have been
a hundred Times I believe at the Door, to know your
Ladyship's Commands, but the fear of disturbing you
made me forbear knocking. I answer'd her in a very
careless Manner ; indeed there was somewhat in her
Countenance that was quite disagreeable to me———there

are

are involuntary Antipathies in Nature, and from my Childhood I was too liable to these sort of Prepossessions; but as they sometimes prove unjust, since I have arrived at Years of Maturity, I have taken no small Pains to correct this Disposition in me; and could wish all my Sex would do the same; for it argues a great Weakness in the Understanding, and frequently occasions our making an ill Choice of Friends: many People there are who have very unpromising Aspects, yet have Souls infinitely more noble, than those of the most engaging Countenances. But I had not yet sufficiently grounded myself in this Maxim, and *Brochan*, for so this Woman was called, experienced it, for I neither could look upon her, nor speak to her with that Affability I did to others, and which, according to the high Opinion she had of herself, she expected from me.

While she was doing something about the Rooms, I placed myself at one of the Windows————it was now near Sun-set, the Evening extreamly pleasant, and abundance of People were taking the Air————I had not been accustomed to such sights, having hitherto been shut up in Castles, or Convents in country Villages, and the great Variety of Objects which now presented themselves, afforded me a most agreeable Amusement. I was prodigiously charmed with the Elegance, and Genteelness of the Women's Dresses; I examin'd them with the strictest Observation, and those which most suited my own Fancy, and that I had a Mind to imitate, drew my Eyes after them, as far as I was able to distinguish one Object from another. Ah! that such Trifles should have the Power to engross my Attention, at a Time, when the most material Matter that could befall me, ought to have left no Room for any thing but itself————But I was young, and a Woman.

All my Sex, if they would deal with the same Sincerity I do, must acknowledge that to be curious in the Examination of each other, is blended in our Nature, and one of our most strong Propensities—and this Desire is most commonly attended with a kind of Envy, arising from Self-love—'Tis very difficult for one beauti-

ful

ful Woman to do juſtice to another, and as greatly as I have laboured to overcome this Meanneſs in me, even to this Day I am apt to feel ſome of its Impreſſions.

While I was thus employ'd in making my Obſervations on all that paſſed by, I felt myſelf claſp'd in the Arms of ſome Body, who taking the Advantage of the Poſture I was ſtanding in, took me about the Waiſt, without my being able to know who held me————I bluſh'd with Shame and Indignation, and ſtruggling with all my Might, diſengaged myſelf, and turning about ſaw it was Madam *de Genneval*, laughing very heartily at the Confuſion ſhe had put me in.

It would be no eaſy matter to ſurprize your Ladyſhip, ſaid ſhe, you are ſo much on your Guard, and are beſide ſo very ſtrong, that little would be got with ſporting with you in this Manner. I aſked her Pardon with a Smile, for the rough Treatment I had given her, and ſhe told me ſhe would accept my Apology for this Time; but that ſhe would not promiſe me the ſame Indulgence for the future, nor indeed, added ſhe, will I be entirely reconciled now, but on Condition you give me the honour of your Company at Supper. She made this Invitation with too good a Grace for me to refuſe her, and having given her my Promiſe, we returned to the Window, where having placed ourſelves, we began to paſs our Cenſures on all that came within the reach of our Obſervation.

Madam *de Genneval* had a particular Talent for this dangerous and ill-natured Pleaſure————Dreſs, Figure, Countenance, nothing eſcaped her, the Women found little Favour from her ; and thoſe who were moſt handſome, incurred the moſt ſevere Strokes of her ſatirical Genius : To the Men indeed, ſhe was ſomewhat more merciful, but praiſed none but thoſe who were of Quality, or at leaſt of great Faſhion in the World.

We had ſpent a conſiderable Time in this Amuſement, when the Sound of Trumpets, Horns, and Kettle-Drums, at well as a great hurry in the Street, made me enquire into the Cauſe. It is the King returning from Hunting, replied Madam *de Genneval*, we ſhall ſee him pre ſently paſs juſt before us. A ſtrange Palpitation of my Heart ſeized me at theſe Words————they brought to my Mind the firſt Time I had ſeen his Majeſty, and the Conſequences of my Tranſports at that Interview———— the Admiration my dear Marquis had teſtified at firſt Sight of me————the Means he took to render himſelf acceptable to me afterwards————the little Chat of our Villagers on that Occaſion ; and in fine, the whole Series of my Adventures ruſhed at once into my Head, and threw me for ſome Moments into the moſt profound Reſvery————in which perhaps I ſhould much longer have been buried, in ſpite of the gay Impertinence of Madam *de Genneval*, who continued ſtill talking to me, if the King's near approach had not rouzed my Attention, and drawn it to the Contemplation of thoſe undeſcribe-able Graces, which ſhone about his Royal Perſon.

I was now arrived at an Age more capable of diſtin-guiſhing, and needed no Inſtructions to point out to me my illuſtrious Maſter————'tis impoſſible to expreſs the Satisfaction I took in ſeeing this dazzling Troop, every one of whom by his Air and Dreſs ſeeming no leſs than a King, nor could have been taken for leſs, but by the Homage they paid to him who really was ſo. And in-deed ſince I have lived at Court, and ſeen the Strangers who daily reſort thither to view the State and Magnifi-cience of it, I have had the Pleaſure to obſerve, that they ſeem little leſs tranſported with it than I was at that Time.

The Court paſſed juſt under our Window, and con-trary to what was uſual, as I afterwards was told, moved very ſlow ; I was ſo deeply taken up with what I ſaw, that I never conſidered I was in a plain Undreſs, and Madam *de Genneval*, ſet out with all the Embelliſhments of a Woman fond of attracting Admiration.

Good Heavens! cried, that Lady with a Self-ſufficient Air, what Creatures theſe Men are————one can't be at a Window, but they ſtare one out of Countenance———— I beg your Ladyſhip will obſerve, continued ſhe, how all their Eyes are turned upon us!————theſe Words, made me indeed take Notice, that tho' all the Windows

were

were full, ours seemed to draw the whole Attention——but she went on————it does not much surprize me, pursued she, for I am so well known, that it is always so whenever I appear————the King himself has done me the Honour to look on me with some Consideration————not, continued the vain Woman, with an affected Air of Modesty, that I attribute this to any extraordinary Merit in me; but because my Husband goes every Day to Court, and is very much respected there, his Wife tho' even less agreeable than myself, could not fail of being taken Notice of————See, cried she, his Majesty looks up at us, he certainly remembers my Face—for Heaven's sake let us retire————I can stand it no longer I protest————my Cheeks are all over in a glow. She spoke this in so childish and affected Tone, that I could scarce refrain laughing.

In that Instant a Nobleman in an exceeding rich Hunting Dress, made several of those who were about him turn their Eyes on me, crying out, did you ever see any thing so exquisitely handsome as that young Lady!————the Negligence of her Dishabille, serves to set off her natural Charms————on this, above Twenty of them check'd their Horses, to make a low Bow to me: The King, who had stop'd to speak to one of his Retinue, looked up a second Time, and took off his Hat; I blushed at this Honour prodigiously, and believing I ought not to stand as if I were insensible of it, made a very low Obedience. O Madam, cried, Madam *de Genneval*, what is your Ladyship doing, no-body ever salutes the King————we shall be taken for meer Country Gentlewomen. She spoke this so loud, that several of the Courtiers heard it, as I could perceive by their whispering and smiling one at another; but I was so confused at the reprimand, that I believe I should not have been able to speak for a considerable Time, if Madam *de Genneval* had not endeavoured to divert me from making any Reflections on it, by giving me the Names and History of all his Majesty's Retinue; but I had not forgot the Mortification she had inflicted on me, and I still think my Resentment justifiable.

Supper

Supper-time drawing near, she entreated me to go down Stairs, I would fain have changed my Head-dress, but she would not suffer me, telling me I was killingly handsome, as I was———— we shall see you ornamented enough, I doubt not, said she, but for once, let us enjoy you in your native Charms. This Compliment was answered by me in the politest Manner I could, nor did I forget to let her see I had a very good Opinion of her Beauty, which pleased her excessively ; a Weakness too common with us all, unless corrected by a more than ordinary share of good Sense.

She thought herself so much obliged to what I said, that she took me in her Arms, begging Pardon for the Freedom, and cried, O how different is the Behaviour of a true Woman of Quality, any body may see your Ladyship, has never conversed with any but those in high Life. I could not here help smiling to myself at the force of Pre-possession, as indeed it soon after proved ; for as long as she took me for the Countess *de Roches*, she was all Complaisance, all fawning Flattery ; but when, as she soon after, had reason to suspect I was not of that Quality, nothing could be more gross in her Reflections.

Pressed as I was to go down to Supper in my Night-dress, I believe I should not have consented, if Monsieur *de Genneval* had not come into the Room, and surprized us in the Debate : This Gentleman paid his Compliments to me in a graceful manner enough————he had some share of Wit, but like his Wife was a little too sensible of it himself, and a Person of any Penetration, might easily perceive it in him————as Super-intendant to the Duke *d*.————he imagined himself Company for any Body, and in that Notion was sometimes rather too pert and familiar with those he conversed with : Tho' this was easily pardoned in him on Account of the Diversion the Sallies of his Wit afforded. How much more easily do we imitate the worst Part of a Character than the best ; Madam *de Genneval* had all the satyrick Disposition of her Husband, without the least Grain of his Good nature ; whenever he made a biting Reflection

the

the Politeness would not suffer the Person to feel the
Sting ; but when Madam *de Genneval* said any severe
Thing, it was done in a manner which shewed she took
a Pleasure in it, and was therefore extremely diso-
bliging.

The Table was served in a very neat and elegant
Manner, and both Monsieur and Madam *de Genneval*
acquitted themselves exceeding well, in doing the Civilities of their House. We were five in Company, a
Relation of Madam *de Genneval*, made the third Woman ;
she was upwards of Fifty, but extremely gay, and told
a great many diverting Stories, which had made her
pass for a Person of good Sense, had she not unluckily at
last fallen upon the Topick of herself, and then began to
tire us with enumerating the Extravagancies that several
Noblemen her Admirers had been guilty of on her Account, a Fault I could wish my Sex to avoid, especially
after they are past a certain Age, and ought to endeavour
not to be looked upon as Triflers by their Acquaintance.

A Gentleman, who, I was told, had a Place in the
Houshold, was the very opposite of the Lady I have
just mentioned————he could not be more than thirty
Years of Age, yet had a sullen Gloom upon his Brow,
a Moroseness which tho' almost inherent to Fourscore,
is scarce even then excuseable ; but seems out of Nature
in Youth. This sour-looking Gentleman never
opened his Mouth, but to contradict what other People
said ; but notwithstanding this Difference of Characters,
I perceived they all agreed to make me talk, I suppose
excited by their Curiosity to learn some Account of my
Affairs ; but Monsieur the Count *de Saint Fal*, forseeing
there would be impertinent Inspections of this Kind,
had given me written Instructions in what manner to reply to any Questions should be asked me, so that they
were little the better informed of any thing they wanted to know.

The Desert was but just brought in, when a Footman
whispered Madam *de Genneval*, and she turning toward
me, told me, that a Nobleman enquired for me————
as I doubted not but it was the Count, I ordered he should

be

be conducted to my Apartment, and was just rising from
Table to go and receive him, but the Servant hearing me
mention his Name, assured me that it was not him, but
that he guess'd by the Livery it was the Duke *de*—The
Name of this Nobleman surprized me, as I had not the
least Acquaintance with him.   Madam *de Genneval* perceived it, and presently told me, that if I had any Reasons to avoid his Visit, she would go and acquaint him
I did not sup at Home.   On which, I answered, that I
could not conceive so utter a Stranger as his Grace, could
possibly have any Business with me, and I therefore
chose not to be seen.   She then got up, and desired I
would be easy, for I should not be importuned in her
House by any Person whatever ; with this she went out
of the Room, making several Signs to me, which I did
not comprehend the Meaning of, nor indeed gave myself much Trouble about.

   While she was gone, a thousand Thoughts ran through
my Head at once : The Dread I had of the old Marquis
de L——*V*——made me sometimes imagine it
might be him, and that the Servant had made a Mistake
in naming the Duke *de*——at others I fancied it might
be some Friend of his Son's, who having traced the
Count *de Saint Fal* was employed by that impatient Lover.
But I was soon eased of these Apprehensions, Madam *de
Genneval* returned laughing very heartily ;——I told
you, said she, that we were observed at the Window,
she then run on in a long Detail of all those who had
looked up at us, and concluded with assuring the Company, that our Charms made a great Noise at Court.——
Who doubts it, cried Monsieur *de Genneval* ironically,
every body envies my Happiness in being possest of so
fine a Woman.   You think to pass th s for a Jest, replied
she, half piqued at the Tone with which he spoke ;
but perhaps I could give you Proofs of it, would make
you more serious——I have just now received Encomiums, which my Modesty wont suffer me to repeat,
from the young Duke *de*——, tho' indeed I am not
much flatter'd by him, for I know what he said to me
was on the Countess's Account——my Account!
                                                      Madam,

Madam, cried I! How can that be, I am but juſt ar-rived from the moſt diſtant part of the Kingdom, and have no Acquaintance————that's no Argument, ſaid Monſieur *da Genneval*, interrupting me,————your Lady-ſhip need to be but once ſeen, to engage a thouſand Ad-mirers——I happened to be in the Street when the Court paſſed by, and found it a Difficulty to anſwer the many Queſtions that were aſked me concerning you————I had not then had the Honour of ſeeing your Ladyſhip, bnt now I do no longer wonder at their Curioſity.

Madam *de Genneval* who could never bear to hear an-other Woman extolled, and being alſo naturally jealous, did not reliſh this Compliment made me by her Huſband, and it was eaſy to perceive Envy in her Eyes. It muſt be allow'd, ſaid ſhe coldy, that the Counteſs is very hand-ſome in reality; but if ſhe were not ſo, a new Face is never without its Charms to you Men————don't you remember, continued ſhe, turning to the Company, the famous *Lyonneſe* that was here about two Years ago, that made ſo great a Noiſe in the World————ſhe was very fair, had regular Features, and an Air of Grandeur—— She no ſooner appeared in publick, but ſhe drew all the World after her————the charming *Lyonneſe*, the beau-tiful *Lyonneſe*, was the whole Subject of Converſation; but the Wonder ceaſed as ſhe grew more known, and in a ſhort Time grew as unregarded, as thoſe of the moſt moderate Perfections————So that Novelty is all that now a days attracts the Admiration of the Crowd.

I preſently diſcovered the little Malice of this Story, and the Application Madam *de Genneval* deſired ſhould be made of it; but I took not the leaſt Notice of it, nor could any of the Company diſcern that I was in the leaſt offended, tho' in truth I was much ſo, and from this Time reſolved to enter into no Intimacy with a Woman of her Character.

After ſhe had vented her Spleen in this Manner; Well but, ſaid her Huſband, on what pretence did the Duke make his Viſit? on which ſhe anſwered, that he only told her he had ſeen a very beautiful Lady at the Window, who ſeeming to be a Stranger, he came to offer his Ser-

vice

vice to her, in cafe fhe had any Affairs that ftood in need of his Intereft or Sollicitation. Madam *de Genneval* added, that fhe had inform'd him who I was, and that on hearing my Name, he faid he was very well acquainted with my Family ; and had a great Regard for feveral of my Relations, and would beg to be introduced to me at a proper Time, fince the prefent happened to prove otherwife.

I am apt to believe, continued fhe, by the Confufion his Grace was in, when I told him it was the Countefs *De Roches*, that he had taken your Ladyfhip for fome little Creature that came here to make her Fortune, as feveral have done, and that he need no more than fhew himfelf to meet with a favourable Reception.———— This Vanity of Mankind muft certainly proceed from the Opinion they have of our Weaknefs ; but, for my Part, whenever I am expofed to Attacks of that Natnre, I always make them repent ; for I turn all they fay into Ridicule, and amufe myfelf agreeably enough at their Expence.

This, methinks, is not a very commendable Method, faid her Hufband, for under the Pretence of Indifferency, the Lover has the Opportunity of being liften'd to, and I am fure fuch an Indulgence cannot be for the Reputation of a married Woman, however fecure her Virtue may be : Nor can I think that altogether fafe, an unguarded Moment may arrive, and when a Man has the Power of agreeably amufing the Woman he has a Defign upon, and he perceives it, he would be wanting to himfelf, if he did not proceed to greater Freedoms, in hopes of being forgiven them alfo.

It would indeed have been a matter of Aftonifhment to me, replied Madam *de Genneval*, if you had not fhewn the Prerogative of a Hufband in contradicting me, but I muft tell you, that if you imagine your Honour at ftake, by any Conduct of mine, it is not altogether fo prudent to take all Occafions of difobliging me.

Your Underftanding is rather to be blamed, faid the Gentleman of the Houfhold ; I think your Hufband gives you daily Proofs of the Confidence he repofes in you, by allowing

allowing you such unbounded Liberties——Liberties, indeed, that all the World condemns him for.

This stung Madam *de Genneval* to the quick, and she replied with a great deal of Warmth——a Continuation of your Silence, would much better have become you, Sir, than the part I see you have now begun to take in the Conversation; and I desire for the future you will oblige us with your Taciturnity.

As he was far from a polite Man, he answered with a good deal of Severity, and made very bitter Reflections on her Vanity, and the little Reason she had for it, at which she was provok'd beyond Measure; and finding all she could say, could not put a stop to the malicious Volubility he now shew'd he was Master of, upon Occasion, turned to her Husband, and upbraided him with want of Tenderness, and even common Decency, for hearing her so ill treated at her own Table, without resenting it ———as the Dispute between them threatned to grow very high, I thought it best to take the Opportunity of retiring, which I did without any Ceremony. Monsieur *de Genneval* was the only Person who saw me go out of the Room, and to shew it was not in the Power of a Family Quarrel, to render him neglectful of what was due to me, he rose instantly, and come after me to lead me to my Apartment: I told him that I was extremely concern'd at what had pass'd, and feared Madam *de Genneval* would not easily be brought into Humour; on which, alas! Madam, said he, your Ladyship is not yet acquainted with her Temper,————she is one of those who in one moment are angry and pleased————she is apt to take exceptions at every thing, but then the least word in Praise of her Wit and Beauty, brings her immediately to herself————'tis owing to a certain Levity of Nature, which has this good Effect, that nobody regards any thing she says, when in the Humour of giving Offence.

I could not however help blaming him, for suffering the Gentleman to provoke her, in the manner he had done; to this he replied, that if she was not a very weak Woman, she would not have seemed to resent any thing he said: My Friend, said he, is a worthy and honest

Man,

Man, but of fo fpleenatick a Difpofition, that his whole
Pleafure, if it may be called fo, is in giving Pain to
thofe, who have fo little Difcretion, as to to be affected
with what he fays————in fine, the Love of Contradiction, is his diftinguifhing Characteriftic, and when that
is known, who, that has any Regard for his other good
Qualities, would not fubmit to bear with it. I yielded
to what Monfieur *de Genneval* faid, as fuch a Peevifh-
nefs could be look'd upon only as a Difeafe, and therefore
rather to be pity'd than refented : tho at the fame Time,
it muft be confeis'd, a Perfon poffeft of it, is very unfit
for Society ; and it is ufually faid of Hypocondriacks, that
they *fay* a thoufand ill-natured Things, and never *do* one ;
yet I think if what they fay puts one out of Humour, it is
in Effect doing one an Injury————One meets however
with few of this Way of Behaviour in *France*, and thofe
who are of it, are fure to be fufficiently mortified one
way or other. An inftance of it in this very Gentleman,
was given me by Monfieur *de Genneval*, which for the
oddnefs of it, I believe may afford fome Diverfion to
the Reader.

As little as he feem'd inclined to Softnefs, Love had
found the means of gaining Dominion over his Heart :
Nothing could have been more enamoured than he had
been of a very beautiful young Lady ; and was fuccefsful
enough in his Addreffes, to gain not only her Affection,
but alfo the Confent of her Father. Every thing was on
the Point of being concluded, and a great Supper made
at the Houfe of the intended Bridegroom, to which the
Relations on both fides were invited, in order to fign the
Marriage-Writings—the Father, and Lover of the Lady,
having both of them a great deal of Wit and Learning, recited many curious Paffages, but the Spirit of
Contradiction, even at this joyful Time, gaining Poffeffion of the Lover's Mind, made him here utter things
not very obliging by way of Argument, to him who was
foon to be his Father in-Law————the old Gentleman
however fupported it for fome time with Moderation, and
imagined his own Memory might fail him, 'till at laft
falling on a Point of Divinity, which he happened to be

a

a perfect Mafter of, he would not in the leaft recede; the other growing ftill more warm, the more he was oppofed, the Difpute grew fo high, that it was not in the Power of any one prefent to make either of them abate in their Earneftnefs——the Father to convince the Company how far he was in the right, went home and fetched a Book, which proved he indeed was fo; but the young Gentleman having nothing elfe to fay, difclaimed both the Author and Edition————this Obftinacy fo provoked the Father of the Lady, that he flew out of the Houfe without taking any Leave, nor did the other attempt to detain him ——After this their Friends endeavoured to make up the Breach, and the old Gentleman at laft confented the Marriage fhould go on, with this Provifo, that he who defired to be his Son-in-law, fhould confefs he had been miftaken; but the Friend of *Genneval* could never be brought to it, and not all his Paffion for the Lady, nor all the Advantages of the Match, which it feems were confiderable, could prevail on him to acknowledge himfelf in an Error——So the intended Nuptials were entirely broke off, and the Lady foon after difpofed of to another, who perhaps might make her much more happy, by being of a lefs perverfe Difpofition.

I could not help making fome Reflections on this Capriciousnefs of Nature, and how miferable People, who had the Misfortune to give way to it, made themfelves and all about them; Monfieur *de Genneval* was perfectly of my Opinion, and added, that fuch a Temper could arife in reality, from nothing but an exorbitant Pride, and that a Perfon who had any fhare either of Underftanding, Religion, Philofophy, or even common Goodnature, would endeavour with all his Might to curb fuch difagreable Sallies on their firft Approach; becaufe, if in the leaft indulged, they prefently grow enormous, and fooner or later were the Occafion of the moft pernicious Events. After fome Difcourfe on this Head, in which he difcovered indeed a great Fund of Senfe and Good-nature, he took his leave, and I fhut myfelf into my Apartment, in order to go to Bed.

Brochan,

Brochan was undressing me, when I heard some-body knock at the Street-door; as it was very late, I was curious to know what important Affair, had occasioned a Visit to any of the Family; so went to the Window, and that I might not be seen, made my Servant take the Candles out of the Room. I discovered a Footman holding a Flambeau, by whose Light I saw a tall Man stand at the Door, which was just then opened by a Ser-vant belonging to Monsieur *de Genneval*, and heard him ask if a young Lady, who arrived but that Day from the Country, did not lodge there. The Answer giving him to understand he was not mistaken in the House, he de-sired to know if I was up and could be spoke with. The Servant who had been present at Supper, when Madam *de Genneval* gave an Account of the Duke's Visit, and heard me say I desired no Company, answered the Stranger, that the Lady he enquired for was not to be seen, especially by Night, and then shut the Door very roughly upon him.

I gave myself no trouble of reflecting on this Acci-dent, not imagining it was any other than the Duke or some Person sent from him, and as soon as *Brochan* had undrest me, went to Bed, and slept with a Tranquility, which I may be ashamed to confess in the Situation I then was.

In the Morning my Waiting-Woman acquainted me that several Trades-People were come to receive my Commands; I had not in this Juncture, Presence enough of Mind to conceal my Surprize, and asked her if she had sent for them. No, Madam, replied she, but they say they came by your Orders. On this I presently supposed the Count *de Saint Fol* had given such Di-rections, and bid *Brochan* shew them up. I found they were all Persons who were to make the rich Stuffs I before spoke of into Garments, so was taken measure of for Stays, Gowns, Hoops, and other requisites of Dress.

I believe the Reader will scarce imagine that I could be enough taken up with these Trifles, not to be impa-tient to see the Count, and hear in what manner the
old

old Marquis *de L*————*V*———— refented my pretended Flight; yet in reality this was the Cafe————
the Splendor of every thing about me, the Homage paid
me, the different Contrivances the Work-People offered
to me for rendring what I was to wear moft becoming
quite tranfported me, and I know not whether I did
not for fome Hours forget that I was *Jeanetta*, and
imagine myfelf in effect the Perfon I reprefented—Even the
Marquis whom I loved, and the Marquis whom I feared,
had fcarce any room amidft the hurry of my Thought—
all that was of Importance was fwallowed up in meer
Trifles ; things of Nothing. when compared to the
Obligations I lay under, and the Dangers to which I
was expofed————How fhall I excufe this Indolence,
this Inactivity of Reafon ; it is in vain to go about it ;
and I am perfwaded that it is in fuch parallel Circuftances
many of my Sex are led into Errors, which their Inclination would never tempt them to be Guilty of. But I
had the Bleffing never to be long forfaken by my
Guardian Angel, and I look on the many Trials I went
through, as a peculiar Inftance of the Goodnefs of Providence ; which enabling me to overcome them, makes
me clearly fee the Dangers to which Vanity expofes our
Sex, and alfo to give them fuitable Warnings how they
fall into the like, fince not one in a Thoufand might efcape as I did.

It was near Noon, when Monfieur *de Saint Fal* came
to vifit me, and as he was dreft extremely rich, and I
had never before feen him to that Advantage, appeared
to me one of the moft graceful and genteel Men I ever
beheld————I confidered him, with the utmoft Attention, and tho' my Affections were prejudiced in favour of another, could not be fo unjuft as to refufe him
that Place in my Admiration which he deferved.————
He now behaved to me with greater Diftance and Refpect than ever ; as indeed all Perfons of a delicate way
of Thinking, will always do to thofe on whom they
confer Obligations————*Brothan*, being in the Room
when he came, he pretended no other Bufinefs than to
enquire

enquire how I liked my Apartment, and if I had been
able to take any repose in a Place to which I had been
so great a Stranger ; which I having answered, he would
have gone away; but I would not permit he should
carry the Decorum so far, and insisted on his dining
with me, to which with much Entreaty he at last consented. As I knew all this was but a Feint, before my
Waiting-Woman, and that he could not but have Tidings
for me of the utmost Consequence, I made a pretence
for sending her down Stairs, and then asked with an Impatience which was not to be wondered at, what I had
to expect from the old Marquis, and if there was any
probability I could be safe from his Enquiries.

Notwithstanding, Madam, said he, I had strained all
the little Wit and Invention I am Master of, to find a
plausible Story, for my having been disappointed of the
Power of executing his Commission, I am not quite af-
sured it passed current with him————He flew into the
extremest Rage I ever saw him in, when I first mentioned
your Escape, and afterwards would needs be informed
of every Particular. I was not to seek for Answers to
all his Interrogations, and mentioned a certain Time and
Place, and many other Circumstances of your pretended
Flight, and the Pains I had taken to regain you, tho' in
vain————seemed as much concerned at the Misfortune as he was incensed, and said as many ill-natured
Things of you as my Heart would give me leave, in
order to deceive him. The first Emotions of his Passion
being abated, he began to question me more closely then
before, and under pretence of laying the Blame on my
Valet de Chambre, sent for him and examined him in
the most artful manner imaginable, but I knew his Fidelity, and as I had before given him his Lesson, had the
satisfaction to hear he answered according to it in every
particular. After he was dismiss'd, my Uncle appearing
more easy, would have me pass the Day with him, and
for several Hours talked to me of indifferent Things :
at last, all at once resuming the Subject, Nephew, said
he, I am not half so angry at the Disappointment of my
Revenge on this Girl, as I am amazed at her Cunning :
————with

————with the Precautions you tell me you took, one would imagine she owed her Escape to some supernatural Means————I begin now to have a Curiosity to see her, and provided she would promise never more to make use of her Arts to seduce my Son, could almost be tempted to forgive what is past on Account of her Wit. ————I still preserved my Caution, and dropt not the least Hint could make him suspect I was prejudiced in your favour————till, unluckily for our Designs, he said, in a seeming careless Manner, tho' doubtless, at least I fear so, it had but too much Artifice, is the Creature so handsome as they tell us ? or is it only to her Youth and Subtilty she attracts so many Hearts ? on which I could not command my Tongue from crying out, yes, my Lord, she is more beautiful than Art can paint, or Heart without seeing her conceive. He took no Notice however of this unwary Exclamation, but went coolly on in asking me concerning your Shape and Stature, and whether you had fair, or dark Hair, with many other Questions, which in that Moment, forgetting the Interview you had with him, I answered with all the Sincerity he could have wished, or I made use of, had I really desired he should no longer doubt if you were the Person he had seen at the Inn.

Pardon me, adorable *Jeanetta*, continued he, I dread to think, what my unwary Tongue may have exposed you to ; but to atone for my Fault, be assured, that I will lose my Life, rather than see you suffer any Part of what my Uncle's Resentment would doubtless tempt him to inflict upon you, should he ever, which Heaven forbid, come to a true Knowledge of this Affair.

I must confess I trembled from Head to Foot, during the whole Time he had been speaking ; but concealed my Disorder as much as possible from his Observation, and after having assured him, that while I was happy in so generous and disinterested a Friend as himself, I could be enabled to support every thing, I entreated him to favour me with the Result of this important Conversation.

When

When I left off speaking, resumed the Count, I
perceived the Marquis in a profound Meditation, after
which, or, I am much mistaken, cried he, or, there is
no room to wonder at my Son's Affection!

These Words, with the Pauses which preceeded and
followed them, reminded me of the Error I had committed, and to retrieve it as much as possible, offered to
go in search of you all over the Kingdom ; saying, tho'
the Girl is exceeding handsome, my Lord, she must
not be suffered to impose her little Artifices on a Person
of my Cousin's Rank in the World———she must be
found, and put in a Place, where her Charms will have
no Power of doing further Mischief,———and such
like Expressions, which I imagined might take off the
Suspicion I feared he began to entertain ; but instead of
accepting the Service I proffered ; no, no, Nephew, said
he, you have had but too much Trouble about her already,
———what will be, will be———Fate must have
its Course, and I think to give myself no further Concern
about the Matter.

After this, tho' I continued late with him, he never
once mentioned you, and either was, or affected to be
in a very good Humour ; but I shall be always on my
Guard, and it happens very fortunately, that to-morrow
he sets out for *Paris*, and when he is gone, we shall have
the Opportunity of contriving what Means will be most
likely to secure you from his search, in case what he has
said to me be not sincere.

Whatever Apprehensions I was in before, to hear
that he was so suddenly to depart, dissipated them all,
and I behaved so chearfully on this Occasion, that Monsieur *de Saint Fal* was perfectly charm'd.

To convince him the more that I laboured under no
Disquiet, I gave him a Detail of what had pass'd the
Evening before, and of the Visit made me at Supper-
time by the Duke *de* ———, at which he seemed a
little alarmed, especially when I told him that the same
Nobleman, as I supposed, had been to enquire for me,
or sent some other on that Errand afterwards at a very
unseasonable Hour. I perceived his Dissatisfaction,
however,

however, and as I thought in Gratitude and Honour I ought to do, endeavoured to diffipate his Vexation by giving him my folemn Promife to avoid all Vifits, and the Occafion of them, fo far as not even to divert myfelf at the Window for the future. On this Condefcention, as he termed it, he appeared perfectly tranfported, and confefs'd that there was nothing he fo much wifhed, but had not dare to afk, left I fhould look upon it as a reftraint upon my Liberty, which he was always ready to allow me in the moft extended manner I could expect; and if I went beyond thofe bounds, he fhould think himfelf happy in my preferving, yet he would never prefume to complain of it tho' he might regret it, and that he faid more alfo for my fake than his own.

After this his ufual Tranquility refettled itfelf in his Face and Behaviour, he entertained me with diverting Stories all Dinner-time, and when Cloath was taken away, told me, that as he was then obliged to leave me, he hoped to be happy enough to pafs the next Day entirely with me, and that then he would endeavour to fix my Affairs fo as to be pleafing to me.

Thefe Proofs of his Generofity reminding me of the Dependance I had on him for my Support, gave at once a cheek to my Pride, and a laudable alarm to my Virtue, alas! My Lord, faid I, what Opinion will you have of me!————I am in the utmoft Confufion at receiving Favours, which I have no poffibility of ever returning. Oh, Madam! cried he, interrupting me, 'tis greatly in your Power, infinitely to over-pay all I have done, or am able to do. Thefe Words were accompanied with a Look, which made me tremble for their Meaning, and fully refolved never to derogate from the Rules I had prefcribed myfelf————my Lord, replied I, very gravely, I have already told you, that not all the Grandeur in the World fhould tempt me from what I think my Duty————and I would much rather return to my native Meannefs, or even dare the Fiercenefs of the offended, the revengeful Marquis, than confent even in a Thought to what would render me unworthy either of Heaven's Protection, or the World's Efteem.

A

A few Tears, in fpite of me, fell from my Eyes, as I
fpoke thefe Words, at the Sight of which *Saint Fal*
feemed in the utmoft Agony ; Pardon me————Pardon
me, cried he, moft lovely, moft adorable of your
whole Sex, that I have fuffered you even for a Moment
to be under any uneafinefs on my Score—No, Madam,
I once for all, give you my Word and Honour, and
defire to be look'd on as the moft abandon'd of Mankind,
if ever any Behaviour of mine contradicts what before
now I have protefted to you————I love you indeed————
it would be Madnefs to deny it————you know it;
but what do I flatter myfelf with from that Paffion ;
nothing but the hope of ferving you, without any other
View than that you will allow me to do fo————to
accept with Chearfulnefs, and void of Fear, all the Services I have Power to render you, by much overpays
my doing them, and is all the Happinefs I afk.

On thefe Conditions, replied I, I accept the Honour
of your Friendfhip, fhall rejoice whenever I fee you, and
make no fcruple of repofing in you, the moft hidden
and deareft Secrets of my Soul. That, indeed, cried he,
would perfectly fatisfy me————the Effects of Love,
charming *Jeanetta*, are various, according to the Difpofition of the Perfon it influences ; and I believe you
will find them in me widely different from the greateft
Part of Mankind.————I was always of Opinion, that
to love for one's own Sake, was no Merit. to the Perfon
beloved, the Paffion centered in a Self-gratification, and
miffing it, deferves only a bare Pity ; but where one defires only to make happy the Object of one's Affections,
that I think may, without going too far, claim fome fhare
of the Friendfhip, if Love is incompatible with former
Engagements, of her one loves————This, Madam,
is the fole Aim of the Paffion you have infpired me with,
and to prove it is fo, I will labour as eagerly to promote
your Union with the Marquis my Coufin, as he can do
himfelf : And tho' in lofing you, I lofe all that's valuable
in Life, I fhall have the Confolation to reflect you are
convinced of my Difinterestednefs and Generofity.

The

The Delicacy of his Sentiments raised an Admiration in me, which as I was not able to find Words to express sufficiently, kept me from replying at all. On which misconstruing my Silence, can you doubt my Sincerity, resumed he, you make no Answer to what I say———I fear you think it an impossibility for me to keep within the Bounds I profess to observe———perhaps you think I have some Views———yes, I confess I have, pursued he, rising from his Seat, will you be convinced of what I have said, if I pour forth before you the most secret Motions of my Soul?

I now began again to be alarmed, but resolved to know how far he expected from me———well then, my Lord, said I, what are they? if you really are that pure and disinterested Friend, speak without reserve. ———What is it you have to hope?———You ought to know me, and consequently not to flatter yourself, that I shall even in a Wish depart from the Engagements I am under, and which are so precious to me. Ah, Madam! cried he, hear what I have to say, and do not, I conjure you, believe, that under the Veil of Honour and Sincerity any base Designs are concealed———I love and adore it is true, and to merit you, would sacrifice my Rank and Fortune; but would owe the Blessing of being yours, to your own Choice alone, not any Solicitations of mine———Perhaps, had not your Heart been pre-engaged, I might by my Services and Constancy have been thought worthy of your Favour; but as it is, I would not even attempt to estrange you from the first Object of your Vows———Yet, do I confess I have some Views, tho' distant one's———Nothing is impossible to Fate, and there may come a Time, in which to hope your Love would not be a Crime———the Events of Life are various, not that I wish the Marquis should alter the Sentiments he at present has of you, nor that Death should deprive you of him; but if either of these Misfortunes should arrive, might I not naturally hope you might remember with how much Zeal I love you, and in Time be brought to reward it, when you had the Power of doing so without a Crime.

Monsieur

Monfieur *De Saint Fal* pronounced thefe laft Words with fo great a Tendernefs, that it pierced me to the Soul.————You are not deceiv'd, my Lord, cry'd I, in the Opinion you have of my Gratitude, and had not my Heart been given before I faw you, to one, who you are fenfible deferves much more than I can pay, none but yourfelf could have have engag'd my Wifhes, ————be affur'd, therefore, that next to him, you are the firſt in my Efteem.

My Love is too reafonable, anfwer'd he, not to be content with this Acknowledgment.————I no more will call myfelf unhappy!————Yes, beautiful *Jeanetta,* I afk no farther Return for all my Sufferings, my Cares, my everlafting Services————with thefe Words he threw himfelf at my Feet, and kifs'd my Hand in a kind of Tranfport. At this Inſtant the Door was puſh'd half open, and I heard a Voice, the Sound of which ran through every Vein————I knew, and did not know it————it alarm'd me————I was tranfported and frighted at the fame time————the Words it fpoke were thefe ;

How have I been deceived!————Ungrateful and moſt perfidious Maid !

At the fame Inſtant I heard thefe cruel Words, I faw the Figure of a Man, who in uttering them, vaniſh'd from my Sight.————His fudden difappearing, together with the Shade of great Screen, which in Part darkened the Door, hindred me from being pofitive as to the Perfon ; though the Voice, as well as the Exclamation at feeing me with the Count at my Feet, left me no room to doubt, if it were not my dear adored Marquis.————I ſtarted up and ran to the Top of the Staircafe, the Count *De Saint Fal,* who doubtlefs thought as I did, was there as foon as I, and immediately jump'd down the whole Staircafe after him ; I found he overtook him, and heard high Words betⱳeen them, fain would I have gone to prevent any fatal Effect ; but Terror de‧ prived me of the Power, my Feet forfook me, and I muſt have fallen down had not a Settee been near me, on which I threw myfelf in an Agony not to be ex‑

3

prefs'd.

press'd. To heighten it the more, *Brochan* came running in, and told me the Nobleman who had just left me, and another whom she knew not, were gone out together, so equally incensed, that she doubted not but a Duel would ensue ; on which that Fear which had at first taken away my Strength, now restor'd it with added Vigour, I flew to the Window, and called out to them, as loud as I could, but they were gone too far to hear my Cries ; and I turned to *Brochan*, for Heaven's sake, said I, run after them————endeavour to bring them back————or I am undone, and shall lose all that's dear to me in the World ;————but instead of obeying my Commands, God forbid, reply'd she, looking on me in a sort of contemptuous manner, that young Women should be seen running through the Streets after such Gentlemen as they are————a fine Character I should have, indeed !————if I had thought I was hired to a Place where such kind of Adventures were like to happen, I would never have undertaken it.

The Confusion I was in at this Moment was such, as I think in no Accident of my Life I ever before experienced ————what to do to prevent the Mischief that threatned I knew not————were it possible for me to overtake them, said I to myself, my Presence would but encrease the Marquis's Rage————he thinks me false———— what Influence would my Tears or Prayers now have on him !————Sometimes a dawn of Hope shot itself through the Horrors of my Mind, that the Prudence and Moderation of *Saint Fal*, would prevent any Tragical Event ; but it lasted not a Moment, and I again reflected how deaf all kinds of Passions are, and that it was not probable, the Marquis in the first Emotions would listen to any thing could be said————he will doubtless attack his Cousin, the first convenient Place they come at———— the other must defend himself————and then !———— Oh, Heaven ! What then————perhaps, the Marquis ————the Count————or both may fall———— those two noble Youths ;————those who for Love, Friendship, all that's valuable in Man, are not to be equalled in the World————and is it for me, cry'd I,

in a kind of Diftraction, for worthlefs me, that Lives
fo precious muft be thrown away?

In this Anguifh, I continued walking backwards and
forwards in my Dining-Room, when Madam *De Geneval* to compleat my Misfortunes, came in to me, in a
manner very different from her former Politenefs, and
afked me in a very abrupt manner, the Meaning of
what fhe had juft now heard? Telling me withal,
that her Reputation was unblemifhed, and it would be
worfe than Death to her, to have any Accident that
might give room for Cenfure, to happen in her Houfe.
————Thefe Apartments, cry'd fhe, difdainfully,
were not defign'd for any Purpofes, but what are confiftent with Honour; and I take it very ill, that Monfieur the Count *De Saint Fal* fhould expofe me to any
thing, wherein my Name might be brought in Queftion.

I was fo confounded at a Behaviour I fo little expected, that joined with my other Troubles, it deftroy'd in me the power of Speech, and fhe taking Advantage of my Silence, and, perhaps, confirm'd by it
in an ill Opinion of me, continued her Reproaches with
fo much Malice, that what at firft prevented my Anfwer, now made me give her fuch ones, as a little a-
bated the Infolence of her Air.————I told her, I
thought her impertinent, and that I fhould acquaint the
Count, whom I expected back in a Moment, with the
Incivilities I had receiv'd in the Apartment he had
chofe for me, and where I expected to have been treated
with Refpect, and that till then, I defired fhe would retire and leave me to myfelf.

I utter'd this with fo much Spirit, that fhe could not
prefently reply, and her Hufband coming in that Moment, and hearing part of what I faid, afked me with
a great deal of Concern, if any of his Family had been
wanting in their Refpects to me.————I thank'd him
in a cool Manner for the Notice he took of it, and
perceiving his Wife was going to fpeak again, went to
my Clofet and fhut myfelf in, refolved to hear no more
of her ill-turn'd Remonftrances.

I **now** abandon'd myself to Tears and to Reflections.————I look'd on all these Troubles as a just Punishment for accepting the Count's Offers?————Why did I not go into a Monastery, cry'd I? That would have screen'd me from all these tempestuous Hurries, I am perpetually involved in; Love, Virtue, and Reason would then have all been satisfied, my Innocence secur'd, as well as my Reputation.————The old Marquis would have desisted his Persecutions, and the young one had leave to converse with me, when there no longer was any Danger of my becoming a Disgrace to his Family?————Why have I this foolish Aversion to a Cloyster?————Why does my Vanity tempt me to appear in the World? Alas! how dear do I pay for the Admiration I excite, and what Mischiefs do the few Charms I am Mistress of, create to all those who are so unhappy as to feel their Force!————

The whole Afternoon, and part of the Evening I past in this melancholly Situation, and no Account from *Saint Fal* arrived ————what could my Thoughts suggest, but the most horrid Ideas.————I doubted not but one or the other was no more; and as the fatal Misconstruction the Marquis had put on my Behaviour, I suppos'd would make him think himself under no Obligation to acquaint me with what had happened, I imagin'd him the Conqueror, and that the poor Count had been the Victim to his Jealousy; because I doubted not, but if he still survived, he would have found some way to ease me of the Tortures of Suspense. This Belief gaining Strength in me, made me naturally consider the Consequences of so terrible an Affair ————I doubted not but I should be seized as the Occasion, though a very innocent one, of what my Imagination suggested to me had fallen out, and in such a Case I knew, unfriended as I was, little Favour was to be expected, especially, as it was highly reasonable to suppose, my real Origin, and all the former Accidents of my Life, would then be brought upon the Carpet; and I should not only be hated, but despised as an Imposture.

How natural is Self Preservation!————We may talk of dying for those we love; but few there are who

C 2

see

fee the fatal Dart at Hand, would bare their Bofom to receive it.————Not all the Grief I felt for the lofs of two fuch worthy Lovers, could render me forgetful of my own Safety; and as Flight feemed the only Method of Prefervation, I refolved immediately upon it.———— In this Difpofition I began to confider whether I fhould go ;————but the Impoffibility of being conceal'd at any Place where I had ever been before, threw unfur- mountable Difficulties in my way.————There feem'd nothing fafe for me, but to quit *Verfailles* by Night, and travel difguifed and on Foot, till I got to fome Town or Village, where was a Waggon to carry me to *Paris*. There, faid I to myfelf, no body will know me, and I may either be admitted into fome Family as a Servant, or take a little Lodging and work at my Needle. Thus did my Fears influence me to a Determination, which ought to have been the Refult of my Virtue ; but why do I call what then pafs'd in my Mind a Determination ! Alas, it lafted not three Minutes, Plenty, Eafe, and the Flatteries with which I had of late been treated, had render'd me too delicate to do any fervile Office :———— I had forgot how to wait on myfelf, and was quite inca- pable of waiting on others, and had my Palate too much vitiated by being accuftomed to the *quelque chofe* of great Tables, to take up with the coarfe Fare I muft ex- pect to live upon, when to earn it by my Labour.———— In fine, I was grown the Woman of Quality, and could not bear the Thought of defcending ; and though the Apprehenfions I had of being made anfwerable for any Misfortune, which might have attended the meeting of the Count and Marquis, yet I could not put in Practice any Means of efcaping.

In thefe Anxities did I remain till near Ten at Night, at which time my Cook-Maid, who from the firft Mo- ment of her coming, took a great liking to me, and was befides very innocent and good-natur'd, came to feek me in my Clofet.————I hope my Reader will not think me impertinent, if I give a brief Recital of what pafs'd between us at this time, becaufe it happened after- wards to be of Confequence.

Blefs

Bleſs me! cry'd ſhe, do you great Ladies live upon
Air————your Supper has been ready theſe two Hours,
yet you have never rung the Bell, nor I ſuppoſe once
thought of eating————*Jeſu Maria!* continued ſhe,
looking more attentively on me, you are weeping!————
Mercy on us, when ſuch as you find any thing to trouble them————I am rarely fitted, indeed,————my
laſt Lady was always grumbling, and ſcolding, and throwing things about the Houſe like a mad Fool, and now I
have got one that cries like a Child :————Well————
every one has their own way ;————but among us poor
People there are no ſuch Fancies ?————Why what now
in the Name of Goodneſs have you to make you un-
eaſy ?————You want for nothing————have a fine
Lodging and well-furniſhed————rich Cloaths————
a great Income to be ſure, and for Youth and Beauty I
never ſaw any thing come up to you.————I wonder what
People would have ;————but cry your Ladyſhip's
Mercy, added ſhe, with a low Curteſy, I had forgot, I
warrant you are thinking of your Huſband ;————but
he is gone, and there's an End of him————don't
grieve yourſelf, dear Madam, for one cold one, there
are a thouſand warm ones to be had, we live in a
Country where, Heaven be praiſed, Huſbands are as
Plenty, as the Plagues of a Cook-Maid.

I could not forbear ſmiling in the midſt of my Troubles at the Simile, and the manner in which this poor
Creature endeavour'd to give me Conſolation, I bid her,
however, leave me, and told her I did not intend to
eat.————Then I'll faſt too, cry'd ſhe, it would not be
right at all in me, I'm ſure to indulge myſelf while my
good Lady is in Trouble. *Barbara*, for that was her
Name, left me with theſe Words, the Good-nature of
the poor Creature affected me very much, and I could not
help calling her Back, and bidding her go to her Supper, well then, ſaid ſhe, if you will be ſo good to eat a
little Soup; I'll ſwear to you by my Guardian Angel, to
devour as much as any four People ;————but, if you
continue in this Mood, I can out faſt our Curate, and he
is the greateſt Penitent in all the Country, and a very

good

good Man if he did not love Money too well; if it were not for that, he might have been made a Saint long ago ; but like the reſt of the World he loves himſelf, and, indeed, I think he is not much to blame.

I grew quite impatient with this Babble, and bid her leave me a ſecond Time.——Yes, Madam, reply'd ſhe, without ſtirring a Step, I ſee you are very angry, and you muſt be obeyed——how one may be deceived in People's Countenances !——I could have ſworn that you did not know how to frown; but I ſee now that you can ſcold as well as Mademoiſelle *D'Elbieux.* ——Mademoiſelle *D'Elbieux !* cry'd I, haſtily, why do you know Mademoiſelle *D'Elbieux ?*——Know her, anſwer'd my Maid, yes, indeed, I have reaſon to know her, I was her Servant once, and had ſuch a Life with her, as I ſhall not preſently forget ;——but, purſued ſhe, are you acquainted with her, Madam ?

I judg'd it would be very improper to own any Concern, I had on this Lady's Account, to this talkative, ſilly Creature, leſt her Folly might occaſion her to blab ſomewhat that might diſcover me to that cruel Enemy, ſo only anſwer'd that I knew her but by Name. So much the better, cry'd *Barbara,* for ſhe is a very ill-natur'd malicious Lady, as her Huſband, poor Gentleman, will find I'll warrant him. Is ſhe then married ? ſaid I. Yes, Heaven be praiſed, reſumed ſhe, ſhe is married, and our Village is rid of her. Pray, ſaid I, what is the Name of your Village.——Ah ! Madam ! reply'd ſhe, with Tears in her Eyes, it is called *D*———, and though it is the leaſt in the Foreſt of *Fountainbleau* ; yet I can tell your Ladyſhip it is a Paradice on Earth : I ſhall never be happy till I get into it again, I hope to end my Days there at laſt ; but we poor Folks muſt do ſomething to get our Bread ; and thanks to Providence, we are all honeſt Pains-taking People, all I ſhould ſay, but one of my Neices, who ran away with a Marquis, and they ſay has done a great deal of Miſchief with her pretty Face; but I have never ſeen her ſince ſhe was little, I was at Service a great way off, when

when she grew up, so have nothing to answer for what she does.

She had no sooner utter'd these Words than she went out of the Room, and saw not the Confusion I was in, which was, indeed, too great for me to have dissembled before her ;————by what she said, I was convinced that she was my Father's Sister, so odd a Circumstance, could not but give my Pride a considerable Alarm.———— Good God! said I to myself, how truly miserable is my Condition! I have lost all the good Will of my Friends, am despised by my nearest Kindred, who tho' never so poor, think me infinitely beneath them, as they imagine, I have forfeited that which alone can make a Woman valuable; and for what have I done all this? ————Why to be a gaudy nothing! A Toy trick'd and set up to be gazed at and admired for a-while, then cast down much more below even my mean Original, than I am now exalted above ;————what solid Good has accrued to me for quitting those who gave me Birth! ————Alas! the incessant Perplexities and Apprehensions, as well as my present eminent Danger, too plainly shews me Heaven is offended at my Vanity and Presumption, and punishes me in the Effects.————Had all-directing Providence thought I should have been a fine Lady, I had been born such ; and I am now convinced, all People should conform themselves to the Rank from which they sprang, had I done so I had been blest in Peace of Mind, and loved by all who knew me. These Reflections were followed by a Torrent of Tears, which continued till *Barbara*, my Aunt I should say, brought me a small Bason of Soup, which though I had small Inclination, she in a manner forced me to eat.

I behaved to her with more Affability than before, and she was more pleased at it, than if I had given her an *Agnus Dei*, yet she was very fond of Relicks, and had a great deal of Devotion, though not exercised in that precise manner of Mademoiselle *Brochan*, my ill-natured Chambermaid. I durst not, however, enter into any Conversation with her, on the Score of Mademoiselle *D'Elbieux*, nor ask any Questions concerning

my

my own Family, or what was said of that Niece she had
mentioned ; for fear I should not be able to restrain myself enough, to hinder her from taking Notice how
deeply I was interested in it, so suffer'd her to depart
without asking any farther Speech.

When I again found myself alone, I abandon'd myself to new Reflections————in these Moments I was
sick of the great World, and wish'd for nothing more
than to return to my primitive Meanness, with my poor
Parents ; and while these Suggestions lasted, was two or
three times about to call back my Aunt, confess myself
to her, and contrive the Means of going with her to our
Village ; but the Thoughts how I should be received
under the disadvantageous Opinion, I found they had of
me, deterr'd me from that Resolution.————I then
thought of retiring to a Monastery, and concealing myself, so as never to be heard on more ; but that was impracticable without a Recommendation, and how to get
one speedy enough for my Purpose, I could not tell.
————Then I thought of going to Madam *De G*————,
and, as I could not hope to be secure in her House, entreat she would provide some Place for me ; but I had
already been so troublesome to that good Lady, and had
created so much Confusion in that part of the Country,
that I durst not attempt it————my disturb'd Imagination presented a thousand Projects, which all vanish'd
almost as soon as formed, either through the Impossibility there appear'd of carrying them into Execution, or
my own Want of Inclination to go about them.

At last, though with an Infinity of Difficulty, and a
long Struggle, I resolved to go to *Paris*, and try my
Fortune in some mean way or other : Having fixed this
Determination, I wrote a Letter to the Marquis, wherein I justified myself in as handsome a manner as I could,
from what, according to Appearances, he had reason to
think me guilty of, and ending with telling him that he
should never see me more, since he could bring himself
to make any Judgment to my Prejudice, without examining into the Foundation.

I

I also wrote another to Monsieur the Count *de Saint Fal,* in which I thanked him for all the Proofs he had given me of a sincere and honourable Friendship ; but concluded, with assuring him I was resolved to hide myself forever from all the Tumults which threatned me, in persevering in a Life above me.

I put both these Letters into one Packet, and was just going to direct them, when it came into my Head again, that possibly neither of the Persons they were designed for, might be in a Condition to receive them, and this Imagination threw me once more into Agonies which almost deprived me of my Reason———I then thought I could not quit *Versailles* without knowing the Fate of those illustrious Rivals, and that it was my Duty to run any Hazards rather than be guilty of such an Act of Ungenerosity.

I was in an Easy-Chair, my Face all bathed in Tears, and my Head reclined upon my Hand, when my Aunt came hastily into the Room, bidding me dry my Eyes, for all I feared was happily over———— What ? cried I impatiently ; here, resumed she, pointing to the Marquis and Count, who that Moment entered together, here is a Proof, that I tell you no Lies———— Heaven be praised, continued she, there's no Mischief done, and the wicked ill-natured *Brocban* will be forced to ask Pardon.

While she spoke, the Marquis threw himself at my Feet ; he took hold of one of my Hands, kiss'd it with a Fervency, which is not to be exprest, and looking up on my Face, would fain have spoke, but was not able————small need he had of Words, however, his expressive Eyes sufficiently informed me of what passed in his Heart, and in them; I read unutterable Love ! unutterable Joy.

Monsieur *de Saint Fal* continued silent also, leaning on the Back of my Chair, which I had no Power to rise from, nor to pay any of those Respects, which either my Love or my Civility required from me ; but after he had attended the first Emotions of my Surprise ; I always told you, Madam, said he, that my chief Happi-

C 5

nefs would be in procuring yours, and I think this is now fome Proof of what I faid————I have brought you back the only Man in the World worthy of your Affection————he fuffered himfelf not to remain three Minutes in doubt of your Conduct, and I had not the leaft Difficulty to convince him of the Truth———— He is now afhamed to think he could be capable of fufpecting you, and you cannot in juftice refent, but rather pity the Effects of his Paffion————you would have known all this five Hours ago, if my Uncle the old Marquis had not met us, and I durft not fend any Meffenger to acquaint you of what had paffed, fearing his Curiofity might tempt him to have the Perfon followed.

Recover yourfelf, therefore, Madam, continued he, and enjoy without Difturbance the Happinefs of feeing a Lover no lefs worthy of you, than you of him. To thefe Words, he added, that he was obliged to return to his Uncle ; but that he would wait on me the next Day ; and then left the Room with a Bow, full of Refpect and Tendernefs.

I eafily faw he took his leave for no other Reafon, than to give the Marquis an Opportunity of Difcourfing me with the more Freedom : but my Heart was fo fluttered in paffing from the Extremity of Defpair to a contrary Emotion, which the unexpected Sight of a Lover fo dear to me, could not but excite ; that I was fcarce able to return the Civilities of that generous Friend.

The hurry of Spirits, or to fpeak more properly, the tranfport I was in to fee at my Feet, the dear adored Man, whom but a Moment before I had believed was mine no more, that I had not prefence enough of Mind, even to bid him quit fo uneafy a Pofture————at laft, overwhelm me not, my Lord, I befeech you, cried I, with this Excefs of Tendernefs ; for tho' mine for you may claim fome fhare of it, yet it ill becomes me to fee you thus. No, my dear, my forever adorable *Jeanetta*, replied he, I'll never rife till that charming Mouth has pronounced a full Pardon for the Crime I have been

guilty

guilty of————I confefs I have committed the worft of Outrages againft you in my Thoughts————I was bafe enough to believe you capable of Perfidioufnefs———— I imagined my Coufin in poffeffion of your Heart———— I gave myfelf up to all that Jealoufy could fuggeft—— but I acknowledge I have been to blame————Excefs of Paffion hurried me to Extremities, which nothing but the Moderation and Prudence of my Coufin, could have prevented from being fatal to one or both of us

O, what have I not fuffered in thefe Apprehenfions, faid I, fure the Terrors of my Soul can be equall'd by nothing, but the Joy of feeing you, and finding you convinced how little poffible it is, I can have one tender Thought for any of your Sex, but yourfelf. The Blufhes which accompanied thefe Words, feemed to the Marquis to be fome Remains of Refentment in me———— again, he begg'd me to forgive him, and would not be prevailed upon to rife, till I had vowed to think no more of what had pafs'd, as to what concerned that which he was pleafed to own, had been a fault in him; but at the fame Time, added, that I thought myfelf under an indifpenfable Neceffity of entreating his Forgivenefs in my turn; for having given room for Sufpicions. which muft have been unavoidable to any Heart truly affected with Love. Forget, therefore, I befeech you, my Lord, faid I, the Anxieties my Behaviour has occafioned you. I know I ought not to have oppofed your Father's Orders, but fubmitted to my Fate, and fuffered the Count to have conducted me to a Cloyfter, rather than have accepted any Proofs of his Friendfhip, which muft naturally expofe me to the Cenfure of the World, as well as your Lordfhip's Sufpicion of my Conduct———— to all this, purfued I, what Defence can I make, but that the very Inclination you have infpired, enforced me to Things which for a Time, made me feem unworthy of yours————Yes, my dear Marquis, a Cloyfter had for me uncommon Horrors, becaufe it would have feparated me for ever from you, and I chofe to run the rifque of loofing your Efteem by fome Indifcretions, rather than yield to the cruel Certainty of feeing you no more. C 6 The

The Marquis preſſed my Hands with an Extremity of Paſſion, at my ſaying theſe Words, and ſeating himſelf near me ; no, my charming *Jeanetta*, ſaid he, I have nothing to accuſe you of——Deſpair and Ruin had been my eternal Lot, had you acted in a different Manner——my Father would have ſhut you up for Life,——he had taken ſuch Meaſures, and his Orders would with ſuch Exactneſs have been obeyed, that if you had fallen into his Hands, I muſt infallibly have loſt you for ever——This I was informed of but ſince I left *Lorrain*, an old Servant of the Marquis's, ſeeing my very Life at Stake, betray'd it to me, on which I took Poſt immediately, and arrived at Madam *de* G——'s, but a few Hours after my Couſin in Quality of an Exempt had taken you thence——Judge to what an Extremity of Deſpair I was reduced, when I found you were gone——that good Lady was truly touched with my Condition, and it was from her I learned that it was *Saint Fal*, who had been entruſted with this Commiſſion ; but ſhe engaged my Word of Honour to keep the Secret inviolably : Had ſhe not taken that Precaution, I ſhould have extorted the Secret from him, where he had placed you, tho' I had loſt my Life——I met him in my return to *Verſailles*, as you have doubtleſs heard, but could not behave to him with the Candor I had been accuſtomed——the Spies I placed about him diſcovered his coming here, and alſo that a young Lady, an entire Stranger at *Verſailles*, lodged in this Houſe— I preſently imagined it could be no other than yourſelf, and call'd laſt Night to enquire for you—being convinced he had diſobeyed my Father's Orders ; what Motive could I impute it to but Love !——your remaining at *Verſailles*——the Change of your Name—— theſe Lodgings——all conſpired to turn my Brain— I thought I was betrayed——I reflected on the Merits of my Couſin——your Youth——the little Proſpect of your being ever united to me——your being ſubjected to the Power of him you were with, made the dreadful Chimera of your eternal Loſs ſeem real——I watched him myſelf this Morning, and ſaw him enter, and immediately

mediately

mediately after I afked for you———a Woman pretty
well advanced in Years, who I find waits on you, refufed
to carry in my Name to you, telling me fhe was certain you would fee no body but the Count *de Saint Fal,*
who had taken the Lodgings for you, and was now
alone with you, and fhe did not think proper to interrupt you———all this was delivered in a certain Tone,
which ferved to encreafe my Defpair; yet as in all
Misfortunes, Sufpenfe is the moft terrible to be borne,
I refolved if poffible to come at the Certainty, and
offered her ten *Lewis d'Ors* to difcover to me what fhe
knew———the Prefent was greedily accepted———fhe
told me with a Sneer, that you pafs'd for a young
Widow, was called the Countefs *de Roches,* and that
Monfieur the Count *de Saint Fal,* was continually with
you, fhe fuppofed to give you Confolation for the Lofs
of your Hufband. To this, fhe added many infiduous
Reflections, which I will not fhock you to repeat, and
of her own accord, proffered to conceal me in the Houfe
where I might fee you together.

Here I could not forbear interrupting the Marquis, by
defiring to know what a Servant could fay of a Miftrefs
with whom fhe had lived but two Days? to which he
anfwered, that he was at that Time too much confufed
to give any great Attention to the particular Words fhe
uttered; but that all fhe faid tended to let him fee fhe
took me for a Woman who was come to Court under a
feigned Pretence, and had in reality no other Bufinefs
than to make her Fortune if fhe could   Pardon me,
deareft *Jeanetta,* cried he, perceiving I was ready to
weep at the Recital of fuch cruel Afperfions———mean
Minds will always imagine every one like themfelves——
I am more to blame to liften to what fhe faid———but
every thing confpired to make you feem guilty—this
Woman's Difcourfe———*Saint Fal's* Vifit———my
finding him at your Feet———hearing his Expreffions
———your not feeming to refent what he faid———O,
who but, like me, muft have yielded to the Suggeftions
of Jealoufy and Defpair!———I do not fay I ought to
have been fo credulous, but I plead the little Poffibility

there

there was for me to have been otherwife at fuch feeming Teftimonies.

He ended thefe Words, with all the Marks of the moft tender Affection that ever was, and from this we talked no more of what was paft, and I fuffered myfelf to be pleafing'y enchanted, while his melodious Tongue flowed with all that Love and Wit infpired————the Clock ftriking One at laft rouz'd me from this delightful Lethargy, and I reminded him, that a Perfon of his Sex ftaying fo late in my Apartment, might give the malicious *Brochan* room for frefh Impertinencies. After fo long an Abfence it was fome difficulty to part, but we confoled ourfelves with the Thoughts of feeing each other again next Day, he kifs'd my Hand at parting, but looking tenderly on me, as tho' he paffionately longed for a farther Confirmation, that he was not in-different to me; I prefented my Cheek, but with fo many Blufhes, and unaffected Confufion, that he might eafily perceive it was the firft Favour of that kind I had ever granted to any Man, and the Tranfports he was in at receiving it, were fuch as affured me he was convinced it was intirely owing to the Sincerity of my Paffion.

The many Reflections which attended this Day's Adventures, would not fuffer me to enjoy much repofe that Night; but as the greateft Part of them were pleafing, were far from giving me any Fatigue————I grew more compofed however towards Morning, and fell into fo found a Sleep, that I awoke not till two o'Clock; nor perhaps had not then done fo, had not my good-natured Aunt *Barbara* been a little furprized to find I lay fo long, and called me feveral Times: She told me, that the Count *de Saint Fal* had been to wait on me in the Morning, and I could not but admire the Refpect he treated me with on this Occafion; for fhe faid fhe would have brought him into my Bedchamber, but he refufed it, anfwering that he would not for the World take the Liberty to difturb my Repofe; we have not a great many Examples of fuch Modefty————the Marquis, now my dear Hufband, has fince confefs'd to me he fhould not have behaved with fo much Mode-ration.   I

I took this Opportunity, however, of remonstrating to my Aunt, that Decency required she should suffer no Man to come into my Chamber when I was in Bed; and as she had made *Saint Fal* the offer meerly through Simplicity, and no bad Intention, what I said to her on this Subject, made her extremely careful for the future.

It was near Dinner-Time when the Marquis came in, if possible he appeared more amiable in my Eyes that Day than ever: His Dress was exceeding rich, and so well fancied that one would have imagined he made the ornamenting his Person his whole Study, tho' in truth no Man ever did, or does, consult it less; the Satisfaction in his Countenance arising from our last Night's Conversation, no doubt added to the Lustre of his Eyes, and gave his Features an additional Softness— the Tenderness with which we met may better be conceived by those of my Readers who have generous gentle Souls, than exprefs'd by any Words I am able to make use of; and for the harsh and unsusceptible Part of the World, it gives me little Concern, whither they approve or not of the soft Emotions with which the Breasts of those who are capable of a perfect Passion, are filled, when in the presence of the dear Object, equally loving and beloved.

He asked me, without doubting it, a thousand and a thousand Times, if I were perfectly reconciled to him, and I as often assured him that I was———How swift the Moments passed, the Clock had struck Four, yet I never thought of Eating, and I believe should have suffered the whole Day, to elapse in the same manner, if my Aunt, who could by no means approve of Fasting, had not reminded me of the Hour. The Marquis made an Apology for having been the occasion of this Delay; but I told him that the only way to atone for it, and punish himself, was to stay and content himself with Part of what was prepared for me———he was too much pleased with this Invitation not to comply with it, and *Barbara* was ordered to serve up Dinner immediately———we had no want of a third Person to fill up any Chasm in Conversation, we had enough to entertain each other with; and after the Cloath was taken away,

I let him into the Secret of the near Relation my Cookmaid had to me, at which odd turn he could not avoid being a little surprized, but commended my Prudence in concealing myself from her Knowledge for the present; I then gave him the Detail of all had befallen me since our separation————related to him the Histories of *Saint Agnes* and *Lindamine*, and dwelt so strongly on the Misfortunes of the former, and the cruel Restraint she was under, that he assured me in Consideration of the tender Friendship he found there was between us, he would employ all his Interest to procure a Dispensation from her Vows.

From this the Conversation turned on Monsieur *de Saint Fal*, and I had reason to see the Greatness of this amiable Lover's Passion, by the Pain it gave him, while I made a full and sincere Recital of all that young Nobleman's Behaviour, not omitting, as far as I could remember, the most minute Circumstance or Word that pass'd between us, from the Time of his taking me from Madame *de* G————'s to the preceding Day.

I had the satisfaction, however, to observe that it was not in the Power of all his Jealousy to prevent him from doing justice to the Count's Merits; he even went so far as to say, that his Honour was so much to be depended upon, that tho' he knew him to be his Rival, yet if the Necessity of our Affairs required it, he could not be uneasy if I were yet more in his Power than I already was. I told him with a Smile, that there was something owing to me also, and that he ought to rely no less on my own way of thinking, than on that of his Cousin. He answered, that he never had a Doubt of it, but in those hurrying Moments, which I had promised to forget; and added, that he flattered himself, that beside my Virtue, I had a softer Defence in favour of him, which would enable me to resist all Attacks made to his Prejudice. I made no reply to these Words, but gave him a Look, which sufficiently gave him to understand he had not been deceived in his Conjectures.

I then asked him, if he could with as little Difficulty give me an Account of his own Adventures and Behaviour since I saw him? Alas! reply'd he, what Account have I to give my adorable *Jeanetta*; but a long Series of Perplexities, Hopes, Fears, and all the natural Consequences of Absence, from the only Object of my Affections.

Take Care, my Lord, said I, with half a Smile, left you swerve from your usual Sincerity, when you tell me you were involved only in Cares for me————the fair *Lorrainers* I am apt to believe had a different Opinion of the Situation of your Heart, than what you now would seem to represent.

Ah, cry'd the Marquis with the same good Humour, *Dubois* I suppose, has been tiring you with the Adventures *Lorrain* abounds with, and has brought me in for a Share, perhaps, to find how far it would affect you.

A good Turn, indeed, my Lord, answer'd I; but that shall not prevent me, from insisting on a Detail of what happen'd to you, during your Stay in that Country.

You must then be obey'd, my dear *Jeanetta*, said he, though what I have to inform you of, is little worthy your Attention. On my first Arrival a profound Melancholy seized me, I seldom went abroad but to Divine Service; I grew pale, wan, my Strength and Appetite decreased by swift Degrees, and *Dubois* fearing I was falling into a Consumption, was continually importuning me to take the Air, and see Company; but finding me averse to his Proposal, and that I every Day grew worse, sent without my Knowledge for a Physician, who being come, my officious Valet told me, that in spite of the Resolution I had taken to hide myself from all the World, I could not hinder myself longer from seeing Company, and that a Gentleman who called himself *De Meurtrav*, was come to visit me; I was afraid he had been impudent enough to invite People in my Name, and began to chide him in so severe a Manner, that he was obliged to confess it was only a Physician, whom he thought it very proper I should consult.

As *Dubois* had done this, I was obliged to order Monsieur *De Mourtray* should be admitted, and was a little peevish at the Thoughts of being compell'd, as it were, to listen to the affected Jargon People of his Profession usually entertain their Patients with; especially, as I imagined I stood in no great Need of his Prescriptions; but how agreeably was I deceived, when instead of a formal Coxcomb, as I expected, I saw enter a Man perfectly gay, facetious, and well-bred.————After the first Civilities were over, and he had in an easy Manner ask'd me some few, and those not impertinent Questions, concerning the State of my Health, instead of Physick he proposed a Party of Pleasure;————told me I had no manner of Occasion to keep my Chamber————that whatever Ailment I laboured under was of the Mind not the Body; and it being a very fine Day, his first Prescription was, that I should favour him with my Company to a small House he had about a League and a half Distance:————To induce me to accept his Invitation, he said, I should meet with some agreeable People there; and added with a Smile, that fine Women and good Wine were the best Remedies in all Hypochondriac Cases.

I was so taken with his Good-humour and easy Manner of Address, that I obliged him to stay and dine with me, and, indeed, the diverting Passages he entertain'd me with, gave the Repast a double Relish to my long depraved Appetite.————In the Evening we went, as he had desired, to his Country-House, and found some very good Company of both Sexes; the Men were perfectly polite, and the Ladies far from aukward, as some People represent them; on the contrary, their Dress was well-fancied, and their Conversation as free from all manner of Stiffness and Affectation, as those at *Paris*.

It was this obliging Physician, which first reconciled me to appear in Publick, and give and receive Visits; but when I had begun to do so, my Acquaintance soon grew pretty extensive, especially after the Arrival of a young Gentleman, with whom I had been extremely intimate; and though a *Lorrainer* by Birth, he

finish'd

finish'd his Studies at the same Academy at *Paris* as I
did ; and there appear'd so great a Parity in our Sentiments, that during his Stay we had been very seldom
a-sunder.   Judge how much I was pleased to meet so
agreeable a Companion, the many Diversions in which
he would always make me a Sharer.   It was that chiefly enabled me to support so long an Absence from my
charming *Jeanetta* ; among the many Ladies he brought
me acquainted with, was Madam *De Charcé*, whose eldest Daughter he was passionately enamour'd with——
she is, indeed, a most amiable young Creature, and has
so great a Resemblance of you, that I never look'd upon her, but with Pleasure mix'd with Pain.————
Saint Alu asked whether I approved his Choice, and I
answer'd in Terms, which very much flatter'd the
Judgment of this young Lover.————In fine, his Addresses were encouraged, and a short time put him in Possession of his Wishes.————In about a Week after
their Marriage, the Bridegroom gave a magnificent
Ball at his own House, to which most of the Nobility
and chief Gentry were invited.————I need not tell you
I was not omitted, after having given you an Account
of the Intimacy between us————indeed, I heartily
congratulated his good Fortune, as I look'd upon her as
a Lady of very great Merit, and every way qualified to
preserve the Passion her Beauty had inspired ; and went
that Evening to his House with a Chearfulness, which
did not afford the least Presage of what was to follow ;
and that a Time set a-part for Jollity and good Humour, should be the last of our Friendship, and I much
fear of his Happiness, or that of his Lady.

Indeed, my dear *Jeanetta*, I never think on the Accidents of this unhappy Night without Trouble, and
could gladly be dispensed with, from ever mentioning it ;
but as 'tis probable you may hereafter hear it from others,
and, perhaps, related in a Manner very different from
the Truth, there is a kind of Necessity you should know
it, as it exactly happened.

This Affair, continued the Marquis, is of so delicate
a Nature, that I know not well how to relate it, nor,
indeed,

indeed, am well convinced from what Motive the Occasion of it arose.————I assure you my Condition is very hard : I am formally accused of having violated all the Laws of Honour, Hospitality and Friendship———— Appearances are against me————my Innocence is my sole Defence ; and Malice fails not to interpret every Thing to my Disadvantage ;————before I enter into this little History, I therefore conjure you beautiful *Jeanetta*, to recollect the former Part of my Behaviour, in order to assure yourself, that the latter could not justly incur your Displeasure.

These Preparations with which the Marquis usher'd in his Story, made me impatient to hear it ; and the Pains he took to persuade me to be of his Party, seem'd to promise something extraordinary. I was twenty Times about to tell him, that if I was to judge of the ensuing Matter, all he said would only give me Reason to think I ought to pass Sentence against him ; but as this would have delayed the Satisfaction of my Curiosity, I remain'd silent, that he might have the Opportunity of prosecuting his Discourse, which he did in these Terms.

The vast Concourse of People at this fatal Ball, said he, made the Room extremely hot, and being a little tired with Dancing, I quitted it in order to breathe a little of the fresh Air ; and also to contemplate on my adorable *Jeanetta*, who in the Eyes of my Imagination, far outshone all the Beauties of *Saint Alu*'s Circle. I walk'd some few Turns in a fine Walk of Jessamines behind the House, and being about to return to the Company, not doubting but by this Time I should be miss'd and enquir'd for ; I came into the House by a Back-Door, which was somewhat nearer than the great Gate ; in my Return I pass'd through a Room which had a Bed in it, with the Curtains close drawn, prepared, as I afterwards heard, for a Person who was intended to lie there that Night ; as it had not been used as a Lodging-Room, a great Fire, notwithstanding the Warmth of the Weather, was made to air it, which was all the Light was in it.————The Change of this Apartment,

ment, which I had before been well acquainted with under a different Form, made me stop a little to confider it, and that Inftant I heard the Curtains move a little, and a Groan from the Bed : I ftarted and liftned, then faid, who is there ? And prefently a Voice, which I knew to be that of Madam *De Saint Alu*, anfwer'd, 'tis I, my Lord, for Heaven's fake, come to my Afliftance, I am fainting away.

I ran haftily to her, but before I could afk, or fhe give me any Account of this fudden Indifpofition, the Door opened, and *Saint Alu* came in.—He ftarted back at feeing us.———Heaven ! cry'd he, I am betrayed ! ———Falfe Woman ! Perfidious Traitor ! This Reproach, and the Occafion of it, took from me the Prefence of Mind requifite to make an Anfwer, and my Silence, I fuppofe, confirming him in the Opinion of my Guilt, he went on railing in the moft bitter Terms that Jealoufy could fuggeft.———When I had enough recover'd my Surprize, as to fpeak, it was too late ; he was not to be appeafed, and had we not fortunately left our Swords in the Ball-Room, one or both had doubtlefs fallen a Victim to this Mifunderftanding.———I endeavour'd to perfuade him to be eafy that Night, and not expofe himfelf and me to the Company, who could not but hear us, offering at the fame to give him any Satisfaction, he fhould require the next Morning ;——— but he was deaf to Reafon, and it foon after happened as I expected ;———feveral Ladies and Gentlemen came in upon us, and were Witneffes of a Scene fufficient to give room for Cenfure———Madam *De Saint Alu* on her Knees, weeping bitterly———her Hufband ftorming, myfelf in the utmoft Confufion,———every one was officious in attempting to make up this Breach ; though it was eafy to be feen, moft of them had their Zeal excited by their Curiofity of knowing the Bottom of the Affair.———Thus was all the Diverfion of the Night broke off :———I retired very much perplex'd in Mind, and I heard afterward, that *Saint Alu* loaded me with the moft opprobious Names his Rage could dictate ; all was in Confufion———and all the Company
broke

broke up, and went to their respective Houses, to judge, and talk as they pleased on what had happened.

When this now unhappy Pair were left alone, the imaginary injured Husband, threated to kill his Wife if she did not confess the whole Truth of what had pass'd between us ;—she terrified beyond Measure at his Rage, and the dreadful Imprecations he had made, told him that it was only a foolish Piece of Superstition that had given him this Cause of Jealousy :———You know, said she, that my Lord Marquis amuses himself with Cabalistical Operations, and I permitted him to take off my Garters, for a certain Experiment of bringing me good Fortune.

This poor Lady thought herself very Politick in framing this Story, which, indeed, being a very foolish one, look'd the more natural ; it succeeded, however, so well on her side, as to pacify her Husband so far, as to make him consent to live with her still ;———he thought her innocent, though weak ; but me he never could forgive, as believing I must have some farther Design in my Head, or I would not have proposed untying a Lady's Garters.

For my Part, when I heard this Story, as I did the next Day from several People, who were acquainted both with him and me ; I knew not in what manner to reply to it, to say the Lady had utter'd a Falsity I thought would be unmanly ; but never could be able to find out why she made so frivolous a Pretence, instead of the real one.

From this Time I never saw *Saint Alu*, and because I would not give any Reason for his continued Suspicions of me, avoided every Place where his Lady visited ; notwithstanding I am inform'd they lead a very ill Life together, and that seldom a Day passes without her suffering from his Reproaches.

Here the Marquis gave over speaking, and I reply'd with a Seriousness, which I was not able to dissemble, I am not all surprized at the Jealousy of *Saint Alu* ; for how innocent soever you might be of any Intention to wrong him ; I cannot say, and think I may do so

without

without being too cenforious, that his Lady acted a very indifcreet Part.———Accidents like this, indeed, might poffibly happen———a Woman may be taken fuddenly ill ;———but then to throw herfelf on a Bed, and call for Affiftance from you, when doubtlefs her own Servants were in hearing———her faying no more of it afterwards, and the Pretext of having her Garters untied, had in it fomething not quite fo decent, as one fhould expect from a Woman of ftrict Virtue.

My Lover I found had little to offer in Vindication of the Lady's Conduct ; but made fo many tender Affeverations of the Integrity of his own, that I could not avoid giving Credit to what he faid. He confefs'd that he was far from blaming the Refentment of *Saint Alu* ; but on the contrary pity'd him fincerely, and feem'd with me to fear, this would not be the laft Subject of Complaint he would have againft his Wife.

After this we fell into Difcourfe of what was more material to us both———I hinted to him the Difquiets I labour'd under, on Account of the Obligations I had to the Count *De Saint Fal* ; and told him, that I thought it would be better for me to take Shelter in a Convent, notwithftanding the Averfion I had exprefs'd to it, than to be expofed to Temptations, which I was not certain I fhould be able always to refift.

The Marquis liftened to me with great Attention, and feem'd very penfive, while I continued to reprefent the Dangers my Virtue run ; and as a Proof of the Truth of what I faid, related to him the Vifit intended me by the Duke *De*———the Conftruction put upon it by Mademoifelle *De Geneval*, and her Behaviour, as well as that of *Brochan* to me the Day before. Befides, added I, fhould your Lordfhip's Father, by any unexpected Means happen to difcover me, I were loft forever ; he would infallibly put the *Letter de Cachet* in Force againft me, and I fhould be confined for Life, whereas by a voluntary Retirement, I avoid all thefe Dangers, and fhall be at Liberty to reflect on what has paft, and wait with Patience my future Fate.

Having

Having mentioned all that I thought neceffary on this Subject, I was filent expecting his Reply, which was to this Effect, that he was perfectly fenfible of the Truth of what I faid, and that he would confider ferioufly on the Affair, and hoped to find fome Expedient, which I fhould approve of to ward me from all the Dangers I apprehended without going to a Convent. Concluding with a moft folemn Proteltation, that he was too nearly concerned in every thing that regarded my Peace of Mind and Reputation, not to be ready to affilt me in any proper Meafures for the Prefervation of both.

We talked near two Hours I believe on this Affair, without being able to come to any determination ; but he affured me he would not reft, till he had found fome method to fatisfy all my Scruples ; after which he took his leave with every Mark of Affection, that could be given by the moft paffionate and faithful Lover, as indeed he was, a long Experience having now convinced me, that in all he faid to me his Tongue never fwerved from the Dictates of his Heart.

The Pleafure which the Ardency of his Affection afforded me, banifhed for a Time, all other Emotions from my Breaft—I grew elevated, and in fpite of all the Impediments that lay in my way to fuch a Station, I flattered myfelf with the enchanting Idea of being one Day the Marchionefs *de* L———*V*———. After fome agreeable Reflections on this Score, I bethought myfelf of the Letters I had written the Day before to the Marquis and Count *de Saint Fal*, and went to the Place where I laid them, intending to read them over, and fee what in thefe violent Emotions of Grief and Defpair, my poor tormented Heart had dictated ; I fearched not only where I thought they were, but alfo in every Place where I imagined a poffibility of finding them ; but could fee nothing of the Packet : I could not help being a little furprized and uneafy at the firft, but afterwards recollecting, that no body had been in the Room, but the Perfons to whom they were directed, I was convinced that one of them muft have committed the Robbery, and was not difpleafed at it.

I

I wish'd indeed that it might prove the Marquis who had been the Thief; becaufe in thofe Letters I had fo lively demonftrated the Love I had for him, the Terrors I was in for his Safety, and the Uneafinefs I was under at being compelled to receive Obligations from any other Perfon than himfelf, that I thought it might contribute greatly to induce him to provide for me without my feeming to defire it ; for as he had talk'd of making me his Wife, and had never by any Word or Action given me Caufe to apprehend he had any other Intentions, I could receive Favours from him without any of thofe Scruples, which muft naturally arife on the Effects of Generofity from Perfons lefs interefted for me. If on the contrary the Curiofity of *Saint Fal* had induced him to take them, he would only thereby have found, that I had Gratitude and Honour, without any tenderer Sentiments, than what were confiftent with the moft inviolable Affection for his amiable Coufin ; therefore which ever of them, or both, had feen what I wrote at a Time when it could not be fuppofed, I had the Power of difquifing my real Thoughts, or any further Intereft in doing fo, could not but enhance the regard that each were already poffeft of in my Favour.

I had not the Pleafure, however, of having my Curiofity fatisfied ; the next Morning I received a Letter from the Marquis containing, as follows :

To my Souls everlafting Comfort, the dear, the faithful, and moft adorable *Jeanetta.*

*I*NCESSANT *Difappointments are fure a Lover's Portion, I flattered myfelf with paffing this Day, and many fucceeding ones with my Charmer, uninterrupted by any Fears ; but I have now the Mortification to tell her, that the Commands of the Marquis* de L——V—— *oblige me to attend him to* Paris, *where I muft ftay at leaft the remainder of this Week*——*I obey with the lefs Reluctance, as I have fome Affairs to difpatch there, which the Accomplifhment of, will be agreeable to her who*

takes up all my Thoughts———be not therefore impatient
for my Return———be assured that in Absence you are
ever present to my Mind, and that even Sleep takes you not
a Moment from me———I have many Things to say, but
have not Time for any more than to conjure you to depend
entirely on the Love and Honour of him who never can be
but in all Events,

> *My dearest* JEANETTA,
> *Your most truly devoted and*
> *passionate Lover,*
>
> De L——V——.

It would be needless to go about making any Description of the Satisfaction this Letter gave me, I shall only
say it well attoned for this enforced Absence, and filled
me with so many delightful Contemplations, that to
indulge them, I resolved to shut myself up in my Apartment, till the dear Author of them should return. But
this was but the determination of an Hour, I could not
refuse seeing the Count *de Saint Fal*, I owed too much to
his Friendship and Generosity to deny him the only
Reward he proposed for all his Civilities, that of seeing
and conversing with me, so revoked the Orders I had
given.

Madam *de Genneval*, who was now brought into
Reason, by the Remonstrances of her Husband, would
scarce keep an Hour out of my Apartment, endeavouring
to make me forget her late Behaviour by an Excess of
Civility, which she sometimes thought to heighten by
the most fulsome Flattery———as she perceived my
Disposition inclined to Gaiety, she proposed my making one in a Party of Pleasure ; she told me one of Monsieur *de Genneval*'s Friends, belonging to the Board of
Works, had promised him a fine Barge, in which we
were to go up the River *Seine*. When she made this
Invitation the Count *de Saint Fal* was present, and offer'd
to accompany us, so that I was too earnestly pressed to
take the Air in this agreeable manner to refuse, even had
my

my Inclinations been averse, which with my usual Sincerity I confess were far from being so.

Nothing could be more delightful than this little Voyage, Monsieur *de Saint Fal* shewed us the *Menagery*, *Marly*, and *Meudon*, and I found so much to admire in these Palaces, that I grew extremely impatient to see *Versailles*, and indeed a Person of less Curiosity than myself might well have been desirous of viewing the inside of a Place, whose exterior Beauties had so much charmed me.

After this we went into the Park, where were a great Number of Nobility waiting to see the King, who that Day happened to come pretty late ; at length his Majesty appeared, and by his Presence gave a new Lustre to all the illustrious Assembly. Madam *de Genneval* made me turn my Eyes on a very graceful Person, who had his continually fixed on me, and who she told me was the very Duke who on the Day of my Arrival had desired leave to visit me. This gave me some Apprehensions ; I desired not his Acquaintance, and the Probability there was, that he would join Company with us to gain an Opportunity of speaking to me, made me propose going home much sooner than I should otherwise have done ; my Desires were too much a Law to those I was among not to be immediately complied with, and we quitted the Place.

I must own I was glad to find myself again in my own Apartment, without being accosted by a Person, whose Character and Quality might have brought me into Adventures, not to the Advantage of my Reputation, which together with the fresh Air, gave me so good an Appetite, that I sat down to a little Repast I had ordered to be prepared against our return, and entertain'd my Guests, which consisted of the Count, Monsieur, and Madam *de Genneval*, with as much Chearfulness, as tho' I had no Lover's Absence to lament, no incensed great Man in search of me, no Parents who gave me over for lost ; in fine, as if I had nothing at Heart but how to divert myself, and make my Moments agreeable. *Saint Fal* was perfectly transported to see me in so gay a

Humour,

Humour, and seemed very loth to depart ; but it growing late, and perceiving Monsieur *de Genneval* and his Wife were preparing to take their leaves, he did so too, not to injure Decorum, nor give any one the Liberty of Censure ; and indeed I must do him the justice to acknowledge, never Lover behaved with more Respect to a Mistress, as much above him in point of Rank and Fortune, as I was in reality his inferior in both.

The next Day the same good Humour remained with me, a perfect Indolence, or rather a Forgetfulness of all that ought to give me Pain possest me, and even Hopes and Fears subsided. How easily, Alas ! are we enchanted with a Life of Pleasure ! Madam *de Genneval* came into me to pay her Compliments, and my Tirewoman, whom I had ordered to attend me, cut my Hair, I all the time looking in the Glass——I fancied I looked extremely amiable, and being drest went into my great Room, which affording me a fuller Prospect of myself, I could not help thinking that such a Form as mine might very well become a Title, and that no body could blame the Marquis for being desirous to bestow upon me that which he was born to. I hope my Reader will pardon this Vanity in me, which I so freely confess, and which has cost me much pains to humble.

After Breakfast Madam *de Genneval* asked if I would accompany her to see the King at Mass ; and I readily accepted the Proposal, having as I said before a great desire to be a Witness of the interior Ornaments of a Structure so magnificent ; besides, as I believed the old Marquis *de L——V——* and his Son were both of them at *Paris*, I ran no great hazard of being seen by any body who knew me.

As she told me it was Time to go, I made no hesitation, but followed where she led ; we pass'd by the Apartments of the Comptroller of the Household, and through the little Galleries which lead to the Castle. I was surprized to find we met with very few People, and could not help expressing what I thought on this Occasion to Madam *de Genneval*——O, said she. we are not come yet to the Court, your Ladyship will

soon

foon find yourfelf amidft a number of Admirers; for all our young Nobility are fo of every new Face; this brought to my mind the Story fhe had told me of the beautiful *Lyonefe,* who at her firft coming to *Verfailles* had been fo much followed, and afterwards as much neglected; but I regarded not the little Envy of this Woman, nor had much time to reflect upon it, for we prefently arrived at the Prince's Gallery, and thence paft into the Apartments, where I found enough to banifh all other Confiderations from my Mind————the Magnificence of every thing I faw————the Height of the Building, the long and fpacious Vifta's which opened themfelves to my View which way foever I turned my Eyes, and vaft Concourfe of People, put me into fuch a Confternation, that had not Monfieur *de Genneval,* who luckily for me happened to be there, and offered me his Hand to conduct me the way I was to go, I fhould have ran I know not where.

Madam *De Genneval* perceived the Confufion I was in, and could not forbear laughing, had it not been for her Hufband, who reminded her fhe was not now at Home, I believe fhe would have rallied me loud enough to have been heard by the Courtiers, who indeed took fufficient Notice of us without; but I foon had an Opportunity of laughing at her in my turn, and if I had been as malicious as herfelf, did not want fufficient to mortify that Vanity which fhe fuffered fometimes to furmount her Good-nature.

I have already faid fhe pretended to be well known, and have a great deal of Intereft at Court, an Occafion now fhew'd how much fhe deceived others, and perhaps alfo herfelf in this Point, by faying it fo often. As we were walking, the Doors flew open, and the King appeared with the Cardinal going to Mafs————every Body followed, and we among the reft—Madam *De Genneval,* with an Air of Familiarity, and an Affurance of being admitted, fcratch'd at the Chappel-Door, which a Centinel immediately open'd half way, and faid there was no Room————She told him her Name, and infifted on a right of Entrance; but he clapt the Door upon her as a Person of no Consequence———She was ready to burst with Spite, and ventured to scratch again, but he cry'd I have already told you, Madam, you can't come in———pray do not be troublesome———with these Words he was going to shut the Door again, when I advanced ; and whatever was the meaning, I know not, but he stretch'd out his Hand, and at the same Time cryed to her, pray, Madam, make Room—on this I came nearer, and he let me in with a low Bow, and the poor mortified Woman, was obliged to say she belong'd to me, in order to get Admittance : But this was not the only Vexation she endured———there was but one Place left upon the Forms, which was given to me, and she was oblig'd to stand the whole Time———I offer'd her my Place, indeed, but she would not accept it, telling me that People used no Ceremony in the King's Presence.

During the Time of divine Service, I cast my Eyes about, and was charm'd to behold with what Piety the Nobility in general attended the Prayers———no Whispering———no ridiculous Civilities to each other——— each seem'd collected in himself, and wholly taken up with heavenly Ideas, but I have since found, that all this was but in imitation of their royal Master, who was no less distinguishable by the Fervency of his Devotion, than by that Air of Greatness, which is inseparable from him.

Mass being over, I was so taken up with admiring the many curious Objects, that presented themselves to me in this fine Chappel, that I believe I should have remain'd there 'till every body was gone out, if a Hand taking hold of mine, had not reminded me it was time to go out ———I thought it was Madam *De Gennevel*, and answered without turning about, when presently she gave me a Pull by the Sleeve, and said———Madam, I beg your Ladyship will reply to my Lord Marquis——— these Words made me indeed recover from my Resvery of Admiration, and I immediately saw it was the Father of my Lover, who was standing close to me——— never shall I forget the Confusion of this Moment——— to find the Person I had so much Cause to dread, and who

I

I believed at *Paris*, was still at *Versailles*, and so near me, gave a universal Trembling to my whole Frame, and I was once or twice ready to sink.

Fortune, Madam, said he, more favourable than you to my Wishes, has once more brought me to the Sight of a Lady, whose Charms are too deeply engraven in my Mind, not to be easily recollected; and tho' you were cruel enough, to disappoint the Endeavours, I would have made to render myself worthy of your Acquaintance, when I saw you before, it shall not now be in your power, to hinder me from doing you all the Services your Merit demands.

As much as I strove to conceal the Trouble I was in, the secret Emotions of my Soul could not escape his Penetration————what is the meaning of all this, Madam? cried he, is my Presence always to give you Pain?—— for Heaven's sake, inform me what private Reasons occasion my being so unfortunate. In speaking this he look'd me full in the Face, as tho' he expected a sincerer Answer from my Eyes than Tongue. I was so confounded that I knew not what I should have said, but Madam *De Genneval* whose talkative Humour was at this Time of Service to me, prevented my replying, by saying, O! her Ladyship can have no Reasons for avoiding such a Person as the Marquis *De L——V————*, any Woman would think it an Honour to be taken Notice of by so polite a Nobleman. I am infinitely obliged to you, Madam, answered he, and shall be yet more so, if you can prevail on this beautiful Creature to think as you do.

In this Instant a Person who seem'd to be of great Distinction, by the Respect every one paid him as he pass'd, came up, and whisper'd something to the Marquis, on which he left us with a low Bow, and accompanied the Courtier.

Every one may imagine how glad I was to be eas'd of his Presence, though I had no room to hope where I lived would now be a Secret to him; I presently cast about in my Mind for Means of escaping, and knew very well the Count would assist me in it, as soon as he should be told of this Adventure. I was strangely sur-

priz'd

priz'd alfo, when I reflected on the the young Marquis's
Letter; and as I found the Journey to *Paris* had been put
off, had a right to be alarm'd at his not having acquainted
me with the Motive, either by Vifit or Meffage.——I was
fo bury'd in thefe Contemplations, that inftead of turning towards Home, as I left the Chappel, I wander'd
back toward the Royal Apartments; and know not how
far my unwary Feet might have tranfgrefs'd, if Madam
De Genneval, who as I found afterward, had been all this
time talking to me, without my obferving her, had not
taken me by the Arm, and afk'd me if I intended to ftay
all Day at Court.   On this I perceived the Error, which
my hurry of Spirits had made me guilty of; and having
turn'd back was amazed to find, what a Progrefs I had
made through the Apartments.————I now follow'd
her with as much hafte as I could, and finding Chairs at
the Bottom of the Stairs, threw myfelf into one, and
directed where to be carry'd; as they were moving me
off, I heard a Voice cry out, run———run———and beg
her to ftay; Madam *De Genneval*, who heard it as well
as I, ftopp'd the Chair, and told me the fame Nobleman, who had accofted me with fo much Civility in the
Chappel, was coming down the great Stairs, and defired
to fpeak with me.————What will now become of
me!————all my Fears redoubled————I doubted
not but I was difcover'd, or at leaft ftrongly fufpected
for the Perfon I really was.——I had not power to fpeak,
even to invoke Heaven's Affiftance, in fo perilous a
Juncture.————In the midft of my Terrors, the old
Marquis came to the fide of the Chair; I muft not fuffer you, Madam, faid he, without taking Notice of
my Confufion, to make ufe of that Chair:————Mine
is here, and will better become you.   He ended thefe
Words with taking hold of my Hand in order to oblige
me to remove; I might have made fome Excufes, but
all my Prefence of Mind forfook me, and I made the
Exchange without being able to utter one Word.   And
he continued, you will now, Madam, go Home with
more Eafe, and after Dinner I will beg leave to vifit
you;————I reflect with Pleafure on the happy Mo-

ments I paſt, when I had the good Fortune to meet you on the Road, and have ever ſince languiſh'd for a Repetition of them————you were then pleas'd to expreſs no Diſlike to the Converſation of Perſons of my Age, and I hope you are ſtill in the ſame Mind.

Doubtleſs the manner in which I now behav'd, would have made him think I was very ill bred, had he not had ſecret Reaſons not to be aſtoniſh'd at it————with a great deal of Difficulty, however, and a faultring Voice, I at laſt forced myſelf to thank him for his Civilities, and to tell him that I ſhould think myſelf honour'd with his Viſit.

The Chair moved off as I had ſpoke ; but afterwards putting out my Head and looking back, I perceived he was talking with Madam *De Genneval*, and that they ſeem'd very earneſt in Diſcourſe; if any thing could have added to my former Shock this certainly would ; for I had all the Reaſon in the World to believe, from the Humour of this Woman, that ſhe would mention the Count *De Saint Fal*, as the Perſon who took the Lodgings for me ; and alſo the Encounter which had been between him and the young Marquis, which if he were not already convinced I was *Jeanetta*, would infallibly make him ſo; theſe dreadful Ideas accompanied me Home, and I would have given the World, to have found either the Count or Marquis there at my Return, but was told neither of them had been to aſk for me ; but in ſpite of this vexatious Accident, and the Cares which ſurrounded me, I found ſome Satisfaction in receiving a Letter from my dear unfortunate Friend *Saint Agnes*.————I broke it open with an Impatience anſwerable to the Love I had for her, and read theſe Lines.

To my faithfully beloved, and faithfully loving Friend, the beautiful *Jeanetta*.

Dear and amiable Companion,

I Never valued myself so much on any Thing, as the Choice I made of you to be the Partner of my bosom Secrets——

I thought from the first Moment I saw you, that you were of a Soul wholly composed of Generosity, but I have the happy Experience that what I felt for you was not a partial Liking, but the result of a true Discernment——

How unhappy should I have been had I found myself deceived! And how transported am I to be ascertained of the contrary——Yes, my dear Jeanetta, I am no less pleased with your Sincerity, than I am with the Effects of it——the lovely Lindamine gave me the Proofs of your continued Friendship, the very Day she arrived, and I have now those of the Constancy of my dear Husband——your kind Endeavours have had the wished Success——my Letters reached the Hand of Melicourt, and I have received an Answer from him, that he will be with me very shortly, to convince me that his Affection is unalterable——I should have wrote to inform you of this, the very Moment I knew it myself, but till I had the favour of yours, I was ignorant how to direct you——As soon as Melicourt arrives I shall tell him to whom, and by what means I had the Opportunity of acquainting him his faithful Wife was still in being, and that I am certain will readily induce him to wait on you at Versailles, and give you all the Particulars of what we have to hope or fear ; for, my dear Jeannetta, my Fate is yet in the Balance——How it will be determined Heaven only knows——but this one Thing I am certain of, that if I am condemned to end my Days in a Convent they will be but few——Sweeten therefore the bitter Moments of Anxiety by your endearing Letters, I beseech you——You, alas ! know but too well the Distractions of Suspense, not to pity mine, and afford me all the Consolation in your Power, while

this

this terrible Situation continues. Lindamine, *whom I have now made acquainted with your History, and who has the greatest Tenderness for you, defires the same Favour, ——her Treatment here is such as her Merit demands from all who know her, and every Body contributes all they can to dissipate her Melancholly, tho' after all I find she receives the most Consolation in her own Piety, and sure never Woman was possest of more—— Acts of Devotion——nay of Mortification, I mean what to others would be so, are to her a Pleasure——and she seems better satisfied with a Fast Day, than some of us are with a Festival——In fine, the whole Convent are in Raptures with her Virtue, a convincing Proof of which she has given in resisting a beloved Lover, such as* Bellizay. *By some means he found out her Retreat, and committed numberless Extravagancies with the hope of prevailing on her to return into the World.*

The Rashness of his ungoverned Passion found some Excuse among those of us who have not forgot to love, but the others were so much incensed, that had he not retired on the Remonstrances of a neighbouring Convent, whose Superior is some way allied to him, I know not what Complaints might not have been made against him in the Ecclesiastick Courts. His Despair was such as greatly affected the fair Cause of it; but by her admirable Sense and Resolution, she surmounted this severest Trial our Sex can undergo——Would I were capable of imitating her Example——but 'tis in vain to attempt it.
——Adieu, my dear, dear Jeanetta, *I expect to hear from you with an Impatience, which can be equalled by nothing but the Affection that occasions it, and which will never grow cooler, while there is vital Heat in the Bosom of her, who is,*

With the most perfect Sincerity and Zeal,

Sweet Jeanetta,
Your devoted Friend,

Saint Agnes.

P. S.

P. S. *If you would bind me yours more than I am already, omit not giving me an exact Account of every particular relating to your Affairs ; as, I trust in Heaven, Melicourt, will shortly do of mine to you   Once more farewell.*

I read this Letter over and over with a satisfaction which only a true Friendship is capable of inspiring——it was indeed so great, that while thus employed, I felt not my own Cares, and for a time forgot the Dangers I was in——my Apprehensions might perhaps have had a longer Truce, but for Madam *de Genneval*, who came in and revived them all.

How reserved you were, said she, not to own you had any Acquaintance with the Marquis *de L——V——* it seems he knows you very well. He may do so, answered I, dissembling my Confusion, but then his Lordship has the Advantage of me, for till you told me I was ignorant of his Name. How, resumed she, with an Air of Surprize, did he not meet you at a Village as you were prosecuting your Journey to *Versailles.* Yes, said I, perceiving he had acquainted her with this Particular ; but he might have told you that it was but by Accident, and that we saw each other but for a short time. Ah, Madam, resumed she, he said that to avoid his Inquiries you quitted the Inn before Day-break——so his Curiosity remaining unsatisfied, I suppose occasioned his asking me a great many Questions—— but really, Madam, pursued she, your Ladyship has been so very reserved to me, that I was able to give but an imperfect Account of any thing relating to you, and was obliged to content myself with assuring him, that he had no Reason to doubt of being informed of all he desired to know from yourself.

My Aunt *Barbara* was then serving up Dinner ; which broke off a Conversation wholly disagreeable to me, Madam *de Genneval* retired and I sat down to Table, tho' any one may believe with little inclination to eat— Never was Distraction of Mind greater than mine was at this Time————I am now at Liberty, said I to my-self, am attended, am Miſtreſs of my own Table ; but Heaven only knows in what manner I may be ſerved to-morrow, or where diſpoſed ;—perhaps inſulted, upbraided both for what I am, and what I am not guilty of, by the inexorable old Marquis, who now but counterfeits a Com-plaiſance to make the Indignities he deſigns to offer me more grievous————O, where is his Son ?————ſhall I never ſee him more————what can have hindred him from letting me know the Journey to *Paris* was put off, ————and where *Saint Fal* ; am I abandoned both by Friend and Lover, at a Time when more than ever I ſtand in need of their Advice and Aſſiſtance ?

These terrible Reflections kept me from knowing even that I was at Table ; but my poor *Barbara* with a great deal of Tenderneſs, and as much good Manners as ſhe was Miſtreſs of, reminded me, and begg'd I would at leaſt taſte of what ſhe had provided————to get rid of her Importunities I forced myſelf to ſwallow ſomething, and telling her I ſhould perhaps have a better Appetite at Night, ſhe took away the Cloath, and I withdrew to my Cloſet, and ſhut myſelf in, that I might give myſelf up to Tears and Complainings.

The End of the S E V E N T H *P A R T.*

T H E

THE

VIRTUOUS VILLAGER,

OR,

VIRGIN's VICTORY.

PART. VIII.

I BELIEVE there are none of my Readers, but will allow I had sufficient Cause for Apprehensions, yet after having given Vent to my Sorrows, I did not, however, give myself over for loft.————Happy are they whose Misfortunes happen in their Youth, when Nature is in perfect Vigour, it throws off all Ills as well of Mind as Body, without any other Assistance than its own; and if a small thing depresses for a Moment, a smaller yet elates.———— I am very certain that now, though I am not old, I could not feel the Weight of any one of the number-

less

less Vexations, which are the Subject of these Memoirs, without sinking under it.————But to return————

I began now to flatter myself, that my Fears had painted the Danger of the old Marquis's Acquaintance with me, in Colours stronger than the reality———— reflected that he could not be certain, I was that *Jeanetta* whom he so much hated; that at the worst he could but have entertain'd a bare Suspicion of it; and that the best Step I could take in so nice a Juncture, was to behave in a Manner which should take away all Probability, I was the Person he was in search of. While this dwelt in my Thoughts, I endeavour'd to assume a Serenity of Countenance, that I might receive him when he came with a Politeness and Chearfulness, that should appear wholly unconcern'd; I was just about settling myself to act this Part, when it came into my Head; that there was a Possibility his Son might come while he was with me, and that to see him there, would infallibly confirm his Suspicions. This Considerations brought back all the Anxieties I had so lately banish'd, and the Terrors of such a Meeting, put me upon contriving Means to prevent it————all that I could think on was to write immediately to the young Marquis, acquaint him with what had happened to me, and desire him, if he design'd to see me that Day, to retard his Visit till pretty late at Night.

After fixing on this, I was not long in putting it in Execution, my time would not permit me to write much, but what I said was to the Purpose; but having finish'd my Letter, a new Difficulty started up, which was how to get it deliver'd; *Barbara* I knew was faithful, but then I should run no less Hazard by her Simplicity than I should have done by the Treachery of another, so resolv'd to trust no-body to be the Messenger but myself.

I therefore order'd a Chair, but having never heard where] my dear Marquis lodg'd, I ask'd the Men, if they knew the Marquis *De L————V————*, who told me they did, and would carry me thither. I bid them stop at the Door, and sent in him that seemed the most

proper

proper of the two to deliver a Message, with my Letter, strictly charging him to give it into his own Hand ; but the Agitation I was in, made me forget the most important Precaution, nor had I time to reflect I had done amiss, before the Fellow return'd, and told me, that my Lord Marquis was at Table ; but one of his Men was gone in to acquaint him. As I had no Design of speaking to him in so publick a Place, where I saw Servants continually hurrying backward and forward, I bid the Chairman go in again, and send my Letter up, and then return and carry me Home.————He was just going to obey me when I saw *Dubois*, on which I snatch'd it out of his Hand, and call'd that Valet to me. Never was any Surprize equal to his, at the Sight of me.————He look'd stedfastly on me for some Moments without being able to speak, and I believe the great difference of my Dress, from that I wore when he last saw me, join'd to meeting me in a Place, where of all the World he could least have expected I should come, made him at first a little doubtful if it were me, or some one who resembled me that called to him.———— My speaking a second time, however, assured him of the Truth, and as I held the Letter to him, Ah, Madam ! cry'd he, what is the meaning of this ?————to what Dangers do you expose yourself————how happens it that you thus run an your Destruction ?———— My Master is at *Paris*, and if it be him you want, as without all Question it is, some Accident or other has deceiv'd you ;————the old Marquis lodges here, and all is discover'd if you appear. O Heaven ! said I, what is it I hear————you may be certain, indeed, that I never design'd my Letter for him. Fly then immediately, resumed he, for my old Master will be here this Minute————he has been told a handsome Lady waits for him, and he has too much Complaisance for all who are so, to make you stay long————I tremble for fear he should come before you are gone.————

On this I called out to be carry'd Home, but one of the Chairman, imagining I should stay, was out of the way ; the Terror I was in, made me order the other to open the Door, chufing rather to walk to my Lodging, than be catch'd in this Vifit by the Marquis; but the Fellow, rather than lofe his Fare, would needs run and fearch for his Partner, fo that his Obftinacy took from me the power of making my Efcape; *Dubois* being called away as foon as he done fpeaking to me.

In fine, my Lord Marquis accompanied by the Duke *De———*, the fame who had been to vifit me, and was refufed by Madam *De Geneval*, and feveral other Noblemen, came into the Hall, and my Chairmen being order'd to carry me in, I was compell'd to introduce myfelf to all this Company. The Marquis no fooner faw me, than with an Air of Satisfaction——— good God! Madam! cry'd he, why have you done me the Honour to prevent a Vifit I ought to have made before, and which nothing but the good Company you fee here could have retarded: As he fpoke thefe Words he took me out of the Chair, and I fuffered him to lead me up Stairs with a Confternation, which it is utterly impoffible to exprefs.

When I reflected on what the Marquis muft think, to find a Woman who had taken fo much Pains to fly from him on the Road, and who had betrayed fo vifible a Confufion at feeing him in the Morning, now come to feek him in his own Houfe, and teftify an Impatience at meeting him again, I was ready to fink every Step———without doubt, thought I, if he does not know me for *Jeanetta*, and by that Knowledge penetrate into the Caufe of my being here; he muft look upon me as a very bold and alfo ignorant Creature, and, indeed, in fpite of the Apprehenfions I was in on his Account, I had fuch a Refpect for him, that to fuffer in his Opinion was almoft as dreadful to me, as all that could have happened on my Difcovery.

As we pafs'd through a Gallery that led to the Marquis's Drawing-Room; *Dubois* placed himfelf in my way, and put his Finger on his Mouth as a Signal to me, that whatever Queftions I fhould be afk'd to confefs nothing: And I think this Valet's Caution infpired me both with Prudence and Affurance; for by the time we

were

were got into Room, I had recollected how to behave, and so well dissembled the secret Confusion I was in, that I believe it was not at all visible in my Countenance. As soon as we were seated, if I had known who you were, my Lord, said I, addressing myself to the Father of my Lover, I should not have omitted waiting on you the Moment I arrived at *Versailles*, with my grateful Acknowledgments, for the kind Concern you were pleased to express for my Illness, when Chance gave me the Honour of meeting your Lordship at the Village. O! Madam! reply'd he, when Beauty and Merit such as yours suffers, it becomes a general Concern, and I am very certain no Man in my Place, but must have been sensibly touch'd at your Indisposition ; all that I can say is, that none could be more so than myself, though in some, perhaps, it might arise from different Motives. I was then at a Loss to comprehend the meaning of these last Words, though afterwards I found the Ænigma solv'd in a manner, which at that Time was far from my Imagination.

All the Company added to the Compliments made me by the Marquis, and I was praised in a Fashion so flattering to my Vanity, that all the Trouble of Mind I was so lately in, vanish'd by Degrees, and I sat with all the Indolence and Unconcern of a Person who had nothing to think on, but how to make herself admired. ————In fine, I appear'd so gay, so chearful, and answer'd the polite things said to me, in so easy and unaffected a manner, as charm'd the whole Assembly. The Duke De————asked me if it were in his power to be any way serviceable to me at Court; on which I answer'd according to the Story *Saint Fal* had framed for me, that I did not doubt but I should have Occasion for Advocates in the Affair which brought me to *Versailles.* ————I told him, that my deceas'd Husband had spent a handsome Fortune in the Service of his Country ; and that I had some hope of being thought worthy of a Pension sufficient to support me in a Monastery, where I design'd to pass the Remainder of my Days. I had no sooner mention'd a Monastery, than the old Marquis

and

and all prefent exclaim'd againſt my taking ſuch a Refolution.——— Every cne offer'd me his Intereſt for the
Succeſs of my Suit ; but ſaid it ſhould be on Condition I
would baniſh all Thoughts of ſhutting myſelf up ; and
each ſeem'd to vie with the other, which ſhould ſay the
fineſt things to me on this Occaſion : Indeed, for a young
Perſon, born as I was, to be treated in this Faſhion, by
Perſons who next to the Princes of the Blood Royal,
were of the greateſt Quality in the Kingdom, was almoſt enough to make the Brain grow giddy. It was
happy for me, that none of them thought of aſking in
what Regiment my Huſband had been ; for had that
Queſtion been put to me, I ſhould have been extremely
at a Loſs what to have ſaid, the Count *De Saint Fal*,
not thinking of my ever being in ſuch a puzzling Cir-
cumſtance, having forgot to give me any Inſtructions on
that Article ; but this not happening, I came off very
well in a Converſation, which it was a thouſand to one
had not involv'd me in the greateſt Confuſion.

After about an Hour's ſtay, I roſe in order to take
my leave ; but the Marquis oblig'd me to ſit down a-
gain, telling me he could not reſolve to loſe me ſo ſoon,
and that he had ſomething to propoſe to me, which I
muſt not refuſe to grant him. There is a Play to-
night, Madam, ſaid he, which, perhaps, you have
not ſeen : It is called *Iphigenia*, and is a Piece much celebrated : As it pleaſes all the World, I doubt not but it
will be an agreeable Amuſement to you, ſo beg you will
favour us with your Company, as we all intend to go.
I endeavour'd to excuſe myſelf as being a Widow, in
which State I ſaid, I look'd upon it as a Breach of Decorum to appear at any publick Diverſion ; but this over
Nicety as they term'd it, only ſerved to make them
laugh, they told me that my Dreſs denoted the time allotted for Mourning was over, and beſides I was not
known, or if I were, we did not live in a Nation ſcru-
pulous about Trifles : Nay, ſaid a young Nobleman, as
you intend to ſollicite the Court for a Penſion it would
be highly proper you ſhould be ſeen, that it may be
known.

known how very much you merit all the Favour that can be shewn you.

Certainly, added the Duke *De*————,and I will take upon me to declare even before his Majesty, that a Widow diftinguifh'd by fo many Charms ought not to be refufed.————I will become your Sollicitor to-morrow, added he, and if I do not obtain in three Days Time a Grant of your Petition, I will be content to fuffer the greateft of all Punifhments, that of being banifh'd from your Sight forever.

This was fpoke with an Air fo paffionate and tender, as made all the Company immediately give him to me for a Lover, and many gay and witty things were faid on the Occafion; on which I quitted my Seat a fecond Time, and told them I muft beg leave to go Home; for it would be highly improper for me to be feen at the Theatre, without another in Company of my own Sex. I forefaw this Objection, cry'd the Marquis *De L*————*V*————haftily, and have therefore fent my Chair for the Lady you live with, I know her very well, and that fhe will be tranfported at the Honour of accompanying you————and thus, Madam, continued he, re-placing me with great Refpect, all the Difficulties you can poffibly raife are now removed.

How could I anfwer to fuch polite and preffing Entreaties, but with Affent, and that being granted, there remains yet one thing to be agreed on, cried the Marquis, and that is, who fhall ufher thefe Ladies to the Play———— I am too far advanc'd in Years to acquit myfelf of that Piece of Gallantry with any tolerable Addrefs, befides it is the Time of my waiting, and fhall be too near the King's Perfon to do it. All that were prefent then made an Offer of their Service, and faid they fhould think themfelves highly honour'd to be fo employ'd; but the Duke *De*————, on Account of his Quality, was the Perfon pitch'd upon by the Marquis *De L*————*V*———— ; who thank'd him for the Diftinction, and faid he would fend to the *Exempt* on Guard, to provide us Places. No, replied the Marquis, your Grace fhall be fpared that

Trouble

Trouble———I have here *Dubois*, the notable Agent of my Son's Amours, he shall go, as a Person very intelligent in the Service of the Ladies. These Words, and the ironical Tone they were pronounced with, put me into such a Confusion, as I then wonder'd the Speaker did not observe ; but alas ! he knew better then I did how to dissemble his Thoughts, and seem'd not to examine me in that Moment. And the other Noblemen doubtless attributed my Blushes to my Modesty, and indeed the Flatteries they bestowed upon me were sufficient to countenance that Opinion.

Dubois having been called for, came into the Room, with a certain Timidity in his Air, the Meaning of which I could very easily comprehend : He doubtless thought the Marquis had discovered me, and that he was summon'd in order to answer to what should be ask'd him, concerning the Intercourse between his Master and I, but the Cloud upon his Brow immediately vanish'd, when he found us all in Good-Humour———the Command given him however by the Marquis, of procuring convenient Places at the Theatre, seem'd to renew his Astonishment, and he appear'd so stupid, that he was oblig'd to repeat the Message twice over before he well understood——— to hear indeed that I was going to the Play, on the Invitation of the old Marquis, was indeed matter enough for his Surprise, and I could not help smiling to myself at the Perplexity he was in.

Madam *De Genneval* came in that Instant, and her so seasonable Arrival, turning the Eyes of the whole Company upon her, prevented any one from taking Notice either of *Dubois* or me.

By what I had seen of this Lady, and the Experience I had of her Volubility, I imagined she would now be a great relief to me, in this Conversation : I doubted not but she was able to answer the whole Company round, but how much are we deceiv'd by Appearances, I then first found what I have since a thousand Times observed, that those who seem to have most Wit among People of their own Rank , are most at a loss when they come before their Superiors———Never did any thing appear

more ridiculous than fhe did, by aiming at feeming particularly well bred ; it might perhaps afford fome Diverfion to my Readers, if I made a Defcription of the Pains
fhe took to be thought a fine Lady, but it is a Piece of
Ill-nature I cannot allow myfelf, tho' at the fame Time
I find a Temptation to do it.

The Marquis *De L——V——* mingled but little
in the Confervation the reft of the Company held with
her, but kept his Eyes fix'd on me, with an Attention
which renew'd my Fears, and made me imagine he was
forming fome Contrivance with Regard to me, I remembered what he faid at the Inn, while he believed I was
in a Swoon, *that he had infallible Means of difcovering
who I was,* and was almoft certain in my Mind, that
he had not deceiv'd himfelf with a vain Conjecture ; I
was the more confirm'd in this Apprehenfion, as he never
mentioned one Word to me concerning the Difcourfe we
then had together, and as I had often been told, he was
a Man not only of the greateft Penetration, but Refer-
vednefs alfo, it feem'd to me as if he had fecret Reafons,
for acting in the Manner he now did.

Thefe Confiderations made me a thoufand Times in
a Minute repent that I had confented to go to the Play,
————the Dangers I ran by it, reprefented themfelves
now to me in the moft glaring Colours————I knew
not but the young Marquis might even return that very
Day to *Verfailles,* might come to the Theatre, and if
fo, how impoffible would it be, I thought to myfelf, for
either of us to contain the fecret Emotions of our Souls,
from being fo far vifible in our Faces, as not to make a
Difcovery of the Truth, even tho' it yet remained a
Myftery : But the matter was now too far gone, and
it was impoffible to avoid whatever Deftiny attended.

Dubois being returned, with an Account that the *Exempt* would take care of our Places, the Duke prefented
me his Hand to lead me down Stairs, the Marquis walk'd
on the other Side of me, and Madam *De Genneval* followed, led by a young Count. You will make a great
many Conquefts, to-night, I am fure, Madam, faid the
Marquis ; but remember, that, tho' a thoufand fhould

fall Victims to your Eyes, you are already in Poffeffion
of a Heart, no lefs devoted to your Virtue, than your
Beauty, and that a conftant Perfeverance in Love and
Refpect can alone merit your Return.

I am infinitely oblig'd to your Lordfhip, anfwered I,
for fo kind a Caution, but am in little Danger of receiving any Impreffions of the fort you mean. A Time
will come, refumed he, or I am much deceived, when
you will find you have indeed Reafon to think I am your
Friend in this Advice; but as to Love, Merit, Conftancy,
they are Points on which I beg leave to have a little
Difcourfe with you after the Play is over. I have much
to fay to you on thefe Subjects, and do affure you, I have
fome Uneafineffes for you on more than one Account.

What could I think of this Difcourfe? it feem'd to
contain an Enigma, which the more I endeavour'd to penetrate, grew but the more obfcure————fain would I
have repiyed, but knew not in what Manner, nor durft
afk an Explanation, for fear of rendring myfelf fufpected.
————He faid many more things to me, equally ambiguous, but the Duke *De*————who took them all
as Gallantry, ftill taking up the Word as the other left
off, faved me the Neceffity of replying. When we
reach'd the Hall we found Chairs there ready to receive
us: I was put into that which feem'd the gayeft, and
which I afterward heard belong'd to the young Marquis,
and Madam *De Genneval*, into that of the old Marquis.
Soon after we had left the Houfe, *Dubois*, who had waited
in the Street for that Purpofe, came running up to the
fide of the Chair, and faid to me in a low Voice; for
Heaven's fake, Madam, how came you thus to throw
yourfelf into the Acquaintance of our crafty Lord————
you will ftand in need of all your Wit to pafs long
upon him, for what I perceive you pretend to be. I
then gave him a brief Account of the Accident which
had occafion'd it, on which he agreed, that after meeting
the old Marquis at Mafs, my Behaviour was natural
enough; and, added, that neither my Lover nor the
Count *De Saint Fal*, had any Opportunity of apprizing
me that the old Marquis did not go to *Paris*; becaufe,

faid

said he, he accompanied them about a Mile from *Ver-sailles*; then seem'd on a sudden to change his Resolution, and came back, leaving *Forsan* his own Valet with his Son, and obliging me to return with him, in Order he told me to perform the Office of that Valet ; and as for my own Part, my Lord having not acquainted me that you were at *Versailles*, it was not in my power to give you any Intelligence.

From hence we both concluded, that the pretended Journey and the Return of the old Marquis, together with his exchanging Servants with his Son, was all done with a View to make some Discovery concerning me ; and that *Forsan* being entirely devoted to his Master, it was wholly impossible, for either my Lover or *Saint Fal* to write to me, without Danger of being known to do so by that watchful Spy.

Dubois, however, gave me the comfortable News that he expected both his Master and *Saint Fal* that Evening, and I then hoped to be extricated from all the Perplexities I was now involved in ; yet as the Affair was of the utmost Consequence to me, I could not help being frighted, and said to *Dubois*, that in case his Lord should not come back, I would have him get me a Post-Chaise, that I might make my Escape from *Versailles*, the Moment the Play was done————No, Madam, replied he, be easy at least 'till to-morrow ; for I am positive the young Marquis will be here to-night————and you may then concert Measures————but in the mean Time be cautious what you say to my old Lord.

By this Time we were got to the Door of the Theatre, where the Duke *De*———— waited to receive me, and as soon as I was placed began to entertain me with Discourses, which at another Time, would have been greatly flattering to my Vanity : From me he went to Madam *De Genneval*, and paid his Compliments to her in a very respectful Manner ; he had formerly had some Acquaintance with her, and he took this Opportunity of renewing it, in hopes through her Means to have the more free Access to me, I suppose taking her to be much more in

my

my Favour than she really was, tho' Decency obliged me to behave to her with Complaisance.

While they were talking together, I had Time to consider the Place I was in, and the illustrious Company it contained, for in spite of all the Terrors I was in, I could not help being very much taken with Shew and Grandeur; I look'd at the Ladies, examined their Faces, their Dress and Shape, and was not a little mortified, to find that tho' my Glass, as well as the Opinion of all that had seen me, had inform'd me my Beauty could not well be excelled, yet there was an Ease, an undescribable somewhat, in the Air of these Court Ladies, that gave them Charms infinitely more striking than Complection, or Regularity of Features————indeed my Vanity wanted this Humiliation, and as I knew it a Fault in me, was not sorry, when I came to confider, for its Correction.

The Presence of the King, who came that instant in, broke of these Reflections, and the Play beginning at the same Time, took up all my Attention. As I had never seen any Representation of this Kind, it had the more Effect upon me: The Distress of *Iphigenia* melted me into Tears, and where the Lover complain'd, the Idea of the Marquis came into my Mind, and I thought there was a kind of Parallel between the Thoughts of the fictitious Hero of the Drama, and him who was the Sovereign of my Heart. The Duke could not help smiling to see how much I was affected, and after telling me he was pleased to find I had a Soul susceptible of Tenderness; How happy, said he, would be the Fate of a Lover, who could draw such precious Tears! these Words made me a little ashamed of the Softness I had shewn, tho' I ought not to have been so; for I think those who are not touch'd at a well wrought Fable, will not greatly compassionate real Woes.————I endeavoured however to throw off my Concern, and answered with as gay an Air as I could possibly assume; whenever, said I your Grace becomes enamoured, in my Opinion, you will deserve little Pity, who are so insensible yourself of the Misfortunes of the lovely *Iphigenia*. Oh Madam! replyed he, how little do you know my Heart, if I seem now indif-

ferent to the Diftrefs the Stage prefents us with, it is only
becaufe the tender Paffions of my Soul are only devoted to
you, and were *Iphigenia* a thoufand times more unhappy,
and more lovely than the Poet would make us think, fhe
could claim no fhare in a Heart, entirely filled with your
Idea, and has no room for any thing in which you have
not a Share.

This Declaration was made with fo much Serioufnefs,
that I thought a modeft Silence would better become me,
than any Anfwer I could make, fo pretended to be too
much attentive to the Play, to regard any thing elfe ;
this pafs'd for a little Time, but the Duke who was in
good earneft very much charm'd with me, refumed his
Difcourfe with fo much Fervor, that I could not without
being very unpolite, and unlike the Character I had affumed, refufe making fome return to his Gallantries.

In Conformity therefore to my Part, I put on as chearful an Air as I could, and replied to what he faid in a
genteel kind of Raillery, as tho' I gave no great Credit
to his Affeverations, yet was not difpleas'd with them.
As I was acting this Piece of Coquettry, I happened to
turn my Head, and faw a Man leaning over the fide of
the Box as diligently obferving me : My Eyes met his
direct'y, and I faw it was my Lover the young Marquis
De L———V———; fo great was my Surprize that
inftant, that nothing is more to be wondered at than that
I did not fcream out———perhaps he fear'd fome fuch
Effect of his fudden Appearance, and immediately turned
away ; but tho' I reftrained myfelf from doing any thing
which might have occafioned a Difturbance, yet I could
not refrain from changing Colour, and indeed grew extremely ill———methought a Bolt of Ice fhot through
my Heart, too true a Prefage, alas ! of the Vexations
this fatal Interview occafioned———I grew extremely
fick, and was obliged to lean my Head upon my Hand :
The Duke De———prefently perceived the Alteration
in me, and fhew'd a great deal of Concern———I told
him I was unable to fit, as indeed I was, and that if I
were not carried into the frefh Air I fhould certainly fwoon,
at which he feem'd in fome Perplexity ; it was not cuf-

tomary for any Perfon, to go out while the King ftayed,
yet the Refpect he had for me made him refolve to wave
that Ceremony, and he whifpered the *Exempt* who open'd
the Door, and his Grace led me to a Chair, begging my
Pardon that he could not attend me Home, becaufe as he
faid, the fame Excufe which might be well received on
my Account, could not be made for him ; but that the
Moment his Majefty left the Houfe, he would fly to enquire after my Health.

I was very glad of the Neceffity he was under of ftaying behind me, and long'd to be at home, that I might
indulge the many Reflections that this Adventure occafioned.

Indeed nothing could be more alarming than my prefent Situation, I knew myfelf innocent, but Appearances
were againft me, even more and ftronger than when the
Marquis fuprized his Coufin at my Feet————he now
inftead of being fhut up in my Apartment, as he might
juftly have expected in his Abfence, fees me at the Play,
in Company with a young Nobleman, who had the Character of the moft amourous Man at Court; he hears him
addreffing me in the fofteft Terms, and perceives me
liftening to him, with the Indolence of a Perfon whofe
Heart was unengaged, and at Liberty to receive any
Offers made to her————He fees that the Moment I difcover him I am out of Countenance, afhamed of my Behaviour, am obliged to quit the Place with all the Marks
of confcious Guilt upon me————what could he think of
me, but that I was falfe, a Coquet, ungrateful to his Love,
and therefore unworthy of it.————my tender Heart was
ready to burft at the Idea, that he had Caufe to remain
one Moment in this Opinion of me.   Affoon as I got into my Chamber, I therefore took Pen and Paper, and
wrote a Letter to him, in which I gave him a faithful
Account of all that happen'd fince I faw him, expatiating
pretty largely on the Accident that carried me to his Father's, and the Neceffity I was under of complying with
his Requeft, of going to the Play ; and then acquainted
him with all my Apprehenfions from the old Marquis,
as well as thofe I might juftly have from the Duke *De*—,

who

who no sooner had conceiv'd a Passion for me, than took the Liberty to declare it, and entreated he would think of some means of removing me from *Versailles*, where I already was taken but too much Notice of.

I felt myself something easier having wrote this Letter, in which I so freely and sincerely laid open all that had pass'd in my Mind ; but then remembring that the Duke had told me he would make me a Visit after the Play, I rang the Bell for my Aunt *Barbara*, and charged her on her Peril to admit no Person whatever that Night, but say that I was gone to Bed.

Depending that I might send my Letter by *Dubois* next Morning, who I doubted not but would be with me early, I sat down to Supper, with a better Appetite than I had done at Dinner, and after the Cloath was taken away, was even easy enough to take a little Book of Novels out of my Closet, and began to read one of those whose Titles promised the most Amusement ; but I had scarce got through two Pages, befo e my poor silly Aunt, came to tell me that a Nobleman esired to speak with me, on which I flew into a greater Passion than I remember ever to have been sensible of before in my whole Life, in so much that I push'd her out of the Room, without so much as asking any Description of the Person, or hearing what farther she had to say, and then bolted my Door, resolved that no one, even she herself, should see me that Night ————How thoughtless was I at this Juncture———— how weak————might I not have expected my dear Marquis, surprized at what he saw, might not come to reproach my Conduct, or at least to be inform'd of the Motives had occasioned it? but alas ! my Head being taken up with the Fears of his Father on one Side, and the unwelcome Importunities of the Duke on the other, had no place for what was no less probable than either. It was not long however absent from me, and I called again for *Barbara* in a more mild Manner than that in which I had dismiss'd her, and the Account she gave me of the Dress, Shape, and Stature of the Person who had enquired, left me no Room to doubt, if I had not denied

Access

Access to him, whom of all the World I had the most Reason to desire the Sight of.

I was troubled indeed at what I had done, but could I have foreseen the cruel Consequences that attended it, I should have set no Bounds to my Despair; but, little imagining any such thing, I consoled myself with the Belief, that my Lover so far from resenting my Behaviour in this Point, as he could not take it meant to himself, would applaud my Reserve in giving Orders to be denied at such late Hours——But how unjust are all Mankind, when Jealousy enflames the Mind; the cruel Thoughts he then entertained of me, even now when all the Tempests are blown over, make me shudder to remember.

I pass'd the Night, however, in much more Tranquility, than I did a long Series of succeeding ones; but rose more early than I was accustomed, in hope of seeing either *Dubois* or his dear Master; I was every Moment in Expectation of them, but it grew towards Noon before any body came to ask for me, at which Time word was brought a Gentleman desired to know if I saw any Company that Day; I asked no Questions but gave immediate Orders for his Admittance, I was so confident it was *Dubois*, that I had my Letter in my Hand ready to deliver to him, and was sadly deceived when I found it was no other than the Duke's Valet, with a Message, from him, to know how I rested after my Indisposition, and if I was enough recovered to permit a Visit from him in the Afternoon, I was so vexed at the Disappointment, that I answered with little Politeness I believe, that I was obliged to be abroad the whole Day: after I had given him his Dispatch, I abandoned myself to a thousand perplexing Thoughts on the Marquis's neglect, and every Minute brought with it some fresh Idea to torment me. I was walking about my Chamber, in a Motion of Body as disorder'd as that of my Mind, when *Barbara* came in, and told me a Gentleman in a travelling Habit wanted to speak with me————tho' I could not conceive who this new Visiter was, I bad her shew him up, resolving to be denyed no more without knowing to whom.

A

A very graceful Gentleman immediately appear'd, and most agreeably surprized me with telling me his Name was *Melicourt*, and at the same time presented me with a Letter from *Saint Agnes*. In spite of all the Trouble I was in, to hear any Thing from that dear Friend, especially to have the News of her brought by a Person, in whose Favour her Story had so highly prepossest me, gave me an infinite Satisfaction————I received him with the Civilities of an Acquaintance, and having made him sit down, told him I hoped he would excuse the Impatience I had to read what his lovely Wife had favoured me with, and while I spoke, hastily broke the Seal, and found it contain'd as follows:

To her, whom I shall ever rank among the dearest of my Friends, the sincere, and most beautiful JEANETTA.

I WRITE to you now with a Tranquility of Mind, which I should have despaired of ever enjoying, but through your kind Offices; and imagine not that my Words exceed the Dictates of my Heart, when I assure you that the remembrance of this Circumstance, will always greatly add to the Felicity I flatter myself with soon enjoying in a Reunion with my dear and most deserving Husband—it is he, charming Jeanetta, who will have the Honour to deliver this to you; and by him you will be informed of all the Steps that have been taken to separate us eternally, and render me the most unfortunate of Women. Heaven, and you have render'd the worst Part of their Endeavours fruitless, and will I hope equally disappoint the rest. An additional Interest to that which is already made, would put an End to all our Fears, and give me the Opportunity I so ardently long for of embracing you, and renewing our tender Friendship: I doubt not therefore, but you will engage the Marquis De L————V———— to join our Friends in pressing my discharge from the Monastery.

Our mutual Friend, the virtuous Lindamine, *sends you her best Wishes, and charges me to tell you that you are ne-*

ver

ver forgotten in her Prayers———her Piety must sure be heard, and I doubt not but you will be no less happy in the Completion of all you desire, than I hope soon to be. I leave it to my dear Melicourt *to acquaint you with the Particulars and am, with the most perfect Affection, and Tenderness, the lovely* Jeanetta's

ever faithfull Friend, and obliged Servant

Saint Agnes.

P. S. *As I was sealing this up, I heard a strange Up-roar in the Convent, and was presently inform'd that it was occasioned by Madamoiselle* De Renneville *having made her Escape———I cannot yet learn the Circumstances, but imagine they will not long remain a Secret, and I shall have the Pleasure of diverting you with them by Word of Mouth. Once more, dear* Jeanetta, *Adieu.*

I was transported to find the Affairs of this much loved Friend were so near being concluded, and turning to her Husband, begged he would perform the Promise *Saint Agnes* had made for him, by informing me in what Man-ner they had proceeded. Alas, Madam, replyed he with a Sigh, that dear Creature would never more have heard of her *Melicourt*, and I should have been the most guilty and most wretched of Mankind, but for the Papers you were so good to forward———'tis to you———to you alone I owe the Happiness of finding a dear, a most beloved and virtuous Wife, whom till then I thought lost for ever— 'tis to you I am indebted for my Innocence.———'tis you I am to thank for not being involved in Crimes, which whenever I had known to be such must have turn'd my Brain———But I leave you to judge the Immensity of the Obligation you have conferr'd upon me, by faith-fully relating what has happened since the cruel Day, when the Artifice and Barbarity of Monsieur De——found Means to separate me, from all that ever was, or ever can be dear.

A

A Continuation of the History of MELI-COURT, *and the beautiful* ST. AGNES.

YOU know, Madam, continued this tender Husband, how I was torn from the Arms of your fair Friend————had my Strength been equal to my Fury, in that dreadful Moment a thousand Lives had been the Victims of it; all that I could I did, but Numbers overpowered me, and I was compelled to yield to the fatal Necessity of seeing her carried away before my Eyes————me, having secured, they treated with a great deal of Respect, notwithstanding the trouble I had given them in seizing me————I suppose they had their Orders for doing so, but I was wholly regardless of their Civilities, and tho' the Officer who commanded the Party appeared to be a Man of great Humanity, and to share in my Sufferings, I vouchsafed not to answer any thing he said to me—my Grief was mute, and preyed the deeper on my Heart as I would not give it vent.

After a Journey of four Days I arrived at *V*————where I was conducted to the Town-Goal, and not permitted the Use of Pen or Paper, so that I could acquaint none of my Friends with the Place where I was confined. The Governor came to visit me the next Day, behaved to me with much Civility, seemed affected with my Misfortune, and told me that it was in my own power to procure my Discharge, which alone depended on my complying with one thing required of me. I than desired to know what it was; to agree, answered he, to the means that will be used for setting aside your Marriage, and to deal ingenuously with you, continued he, you have no other way to regain your Freedom; I therefore would advise you to it, and flatter myself, that when you shall consider seriously on the Affair, you will

believe

believe I perſuade you to no more than I would put in
practice myſelf on the ſame Occaſion – I know what it is
to love, and the Anxiety you muſt feel in being for ever
ſeparated from the Object of your Affections ; but when
you reflect on the unſurmountable Obſtacles between you,
and the Ruin that muſt attend your Refuſal of what is expected from, Love will give way to Reaſon.

As I offered not to interrupt him during this Diſcourſe,
he imagined it had ſome Weight with me, and that my
Silence after he had given over ſpeaking, was a token of
my Approbation, and this Opinion I ſuppoſe it was
that encouraged him to reſume the Theme. Think,
ſaid he, of the terrible Effects of being obſtinate in a
Caſe where you have ſo powerful an Adverſary as
Monſieur de————to deal with————a long and ex-
penſive Suit between your Families, which muſt be
ruinous to yours, as having leſs powerful Friends, and a
ſmaller Eſtate————your own Confinement during all
that Time, and at laſt, when a Decree is paſt againſt you,
as it doubtleſs will, deprived of all you wiſh for as totally
as tho' you now reſign'd it willingly————make uſe
therefore of your Prudence, and ſubmit to Neceſſity.

I could now contain myſelf no longer, but burſt out
into Exclamations ſuch as made him ſee, that my ſuffering him to proceed ſo far, was not owing to any
adherence to what he ſaid ; and as ſoon as the firſt Emotions of my Rage was over, I deſired he would never
entertain me more with any ſuch Propoſals ; for I would
chuſe to ſuffer eternal Impriſonment, rather than conſent to break my preſent Bonds by diſſolving thoſe I had
ſo joyfully put on.

My Reſolution aſtoniſhed him, and from that Time
forward, whenever he came to viſit me, as he frequently
did, forbore any diſcourſe on that Head, any farther
than artfully introducing ſome Stories of parallel Caſes,
which he perhaps imagined would have a better Effect
than either barefaced Perſuaſions or Menaces. I under-
ſtood him perfectly well, tho' I thought it beſt not to
ſeem to do ſo, and eaſily perceived he was a Friend of
my dear Wife's inhuman Father, which made me en-

deavour

deavour to behave before him in a Manner that should make him think my Confinement was less grievous to me than in reality it was. I never asked him any Questions even concerning the Prosecution against me, nor how my Father defended the Cause; so that finding my Reserve, and that there was nothing to be hoped from me, he by Degrees refrained coming to see me, and I was entirely freed from his Importunities.

As easy as I had appeared before the Governor, I was notwithstanding forever contriving means for my Escape; but, alas, I was too well provided against for any of the Attempts I made to prove successful. How impossible, Madam, would it be for me to describe to you the Torments I endured at finding there was no hope of getting from this detested Prison, and wholly ignorant what was become of my dear *Minetta*, for I then knew not she had assumed the Name of *Saint Agnes*, or how the Affairs of my Family stood; you can only form an Idea of what Words would but imperfectly represent; some Months did I languish in this terrible Situation, till at last it came into my Head to make the Turnkey my Friend, so far as to procure me Pen and Paper, and to send a Letter to my Father: I had the more Hope of him as he appeared to have a compassionate Soul———I had often heard him lament the Severity of his Fate in throwing him into an Office for Bread, which obliged to the continual Sight of Misfortunes he was no way able to redress; and the Confidence he reposed in me, by making these Complaints, gave me room to flatter myself I might gain him to my Party—— I therefore began with making him little Presents, telling him I liked his Countenance, was sorry he was not in some Employment to which he had less repugnance, and promised that I would procure one for him if ever I obtained my Liberty; the Fellow was quite transported at the Kindness I had shewn him, and when I had brought him to a Pitch, as I thought, proper for my purpose, I communicated to him my Request; but instead of complying, he seemed thunderstruck at the Proposal, and represented the Punishments inflicted on

those

thofe who betrayed their Truft in the manner I would
have him do, and repeated many fhocking Examples of
Wretches, who had fuffered on that fcore, in fuch
lively Colours, that I began to fear my Hopes in him
had deceived me, fo preffed him no farther at that
Time. But as this was my laft recourfe, I refolved not
entirely to give over the Purfuit, and talking fomewhat
of it every Day, till by degrees he feemed lefs averfe,
at laft, on the Promife of a great Reward, he fur-
nifhed me with Materials for Writing, and undertook
to be himfelf the Bearer of my Letters, fearing as he faid
to truft any other Perfon with a Secret fo dangerous to
him.

You may eafily believe, Madam, continued Monfieur
Melicourt, how glad I was of having gained this Point,
which in effect was gaining all ; for I did not doubt when
my Father fhould know where I was, he would have
Intereft enough to procure my Liberty on proper Bail for
my Appearance ; and when I was once out of Prifon, refolved to be fo indefatigable in the Search of my dear
Minetta, that I could not fail of finding her. I wrote a
long Letter to my Father, with one enclofed to my
Wife, in Cafe he fhould be happy enough to have difcovered to what Place they had conveyed her, and having recommended Speed and Diligence to the Turnkey,
he fet out with my Packet, begging me to be eafy till his
Return ; but that happened much fooner than I expected,
in two Hours he came again into my Chamber, which
made me conclude fome ill Accident had happened, and
threw me into frefh Exclamations on the Severity of my
Deftiny.

He opened his Mouth two or three Times to fpeak,
but the Defpair I was in would not fuffer me to liften,
till at laft, Monfieur, bawl'd he out, your Impatience
prevents your being told what cannot but be agreeable to
you. On that I ceafed, and bad him tell me the Occafion of his coming back ; he then proceeded to inform
me, that in his Way he luckily had met his Brother,
whom he had not feen in fome Years, coming to vifit
him, and that on relating to him the Bufinefs he was

going on, the other offered to take the Office on himself, which, said he, will save me from all Danger
in Case the Affair should ever be discovered, and your
Letters go equally as safe; for added he, I will engage
my Life for the Fidelity of my Brother. This Story
seemed feasible enough, and I made no Difficulty of
believing it.

The delightful Expectation of receiving some agreeable
News from my Father, gave some truce to my Disquiets,
and I waited with a tollerable share of Patience for the
Event; but eighteen Days being passed over without
hearing any thing, the Time now began to be tedious;
and five more elapsing, insupportable————I knew not
what Conjecture to form on this Delay, unless it were
occasioned by sending the enclosed to my dear *Minetta*,
who might probably be conveyed to a great Distance;
but then I reflected again, that the Tenderness my Father had for me, would not permit him to let me remain
so long in suspense; he would have inform'd me immediately of every thing he could, and not waited for
more.

I was one Night in the utmost Impatience, I may say
indeed Despair, alone in my Prison, and tho' it was dead
of Night, not yet in Bed, when an unusual Noise at that
late Hour, made me imagine somewhat extraordinary
had happened; but I continued not long in my Surprize,
my Door opened, and the Turnkey came in, with a
satisfaction in his Countenance, that seemed the Omen of
good News. Here, Monsieur, said he, presenting me
a Packet of Letters, I hope these will give some abatement to your Disquiets————My Brother is but this
Moment returned, and I tremble lest any Suspicion
should arise on my admitting him at this unseasonable
Hour————I must feign a Pretence for it————Adieu,
my staying in your Chamber may be dangerous; but I
could not forbear coming to bring you these joyful
Tidings. With these Words he was going out, but I detained him so long as to make him accept of a small
Diamond I had on my Finger in Token of my Gratitude,

with

with which he went away highly contented, tho' I dare
say much less so than myself at that Moment.

But, alas! of how short a Duration was this Interval
of Comfort, and how long a Series of Misery and Despair
succeeded————I opened my Packet in great haste,
where the first Letter I found was from my Father, tho'
the Character so altered, occasioned by a Hurt it inform'd me he had got in his Hand, that I should not have
Thought it his, but by the Tenderness of the Contents;
within it I found another, which imagining was from
my Wife, I kissed it a thousand Times with eager
Transports before I was able in this hurry of Spirits to
read either that or my Father's, but when I had a little
recovered myself, it will not seem strange to you, Madam,
that Passion prevailed above Duty. I chose to see what
my dear *Minetta* said to me, it being the first Letter I
had ever received from her before I read that of my
Father. But, good God! what was it I felt, when I
found, instead of the Softness of an endearing, a most
affectionate Wife, these shocking Lines:

To Monsieur M E L I C O U R T,

*A F T E R the Folly we have both been guilty of, I
could have wished never to have heard any mention of
you; but as you still seem to bear an Affection for me, I
could not be so ungrateful as to refuse an Answer to your
Letter; I am sincerely sorry for what you have suffered on
my Account, but if you continue in your Troubles, it is your
own Obstinacy, you are to blame, not me; if my Advice
has any Weight with you, they will soon be at an End by
your submitting to what is required of you————I am no
longer an Obstacle, I thought myself obliged to comply with
the Will of my Parents, and now release you from all
Engagements between us————I own I had some Difficulty
in bringing myself to do this, but am now convinced that
our first Duty is Obedience, and that all Promises, all
Oaths are invalid, when made without the Consent of
those to whom we owe our being,————I flatter myself
you have Resolution and good Sense sufficient to enable you
to follow my Example; or if not so, at least too much Re-*

2   *gard*

gard for me not to disturb my present Tranquility by any future Letters or Messages, much less to make any Attempt to see me——there being no Person on Earth, whom, for many Reasons, I would so much wish to avoid.

The Agonies this cruel Letter threw me in, would certainly have made me lay violent Hands on my own Life, had not some Sparks of Pride that Moment rose to my Assistance, and made me think it beneath the Dignity of my Reason to fall for so perfidious, so ungrateful a Creature——What, cried I, throwing the Letter away with the utmost Disdain, did Love and Constancy like mine deserve so base a Return!——I'll follow your Advice, forgetful, thankless, unfaithful Woman! I'll never think on thee but with Scorn and Detestation— in this manner did I rail for at least two Hours without being able to examine what Account my Father had given me of so unlooked for a Change. At last I gained Composure of Mind sufficient to read his Letter, and found he began with exhorting me to be patient, and having confess'd to me in a very free manner, that his Interest being far inferior to that of the Father of my unworthy Wife, he had been forced to drop the Suit; but had an Assurance of my being set at Liberty the Moment I yielded to the Dissolution of my Marriage, that being, he said, the sole Impediment to hinder her, I once thought mine, from giving her Hand to a Person her Parents had made choice of. He added, that, she had refused their Importunities but a few Days, and to obtain her Pardon, had consented to marry the Moment my Release from her former Vows should arrive, till which he said I must remain in Prison, it not being in his Power to free me.——

He enforced the Arguments he made use of, to bring me to a Resolution so conformable to Reason, and what I owed myself, with the most strenuous Commands that Words could form; and after many Pauses and Struggles with a Passion, which was far from being extinguish'd by this ill Treatment; I at last determined not to languish out my Life in a miserable Goal, for the sake of
one

one who after the moſt ſacred Vows, and all the mutual Endearments of Conjugal Affection, could ſo eaſily conſent never to ſee me more, and give herſelf into the Arms of another.

Two whole Days, however, paſs'd over without my being able to put in Practice what I had reſolv'd; I ſtill loved the dear Ingrate with the ſame Paſſion, as when I thought her true, and happy in my Affection.————— Her Charms were too deeply engraven in my Heart for even her Infidelity to erace; but when I reflected on her Beauty, and the Pleaſures I had enjoy'd in her Society, her Falſhood, her Levity, her Hypocriſy, render'd her ſo unworthy that I even hated myſelf, becauſe I could not hate her as I ought.————Never was ſuch a Chaos as my Brain, ſuch a Medley of perplex'd Ideas, were, indeed, enough to drive to Diſtraction; yet I at laſt aſſumed the Man, exerted my Reaſon, and in ſpite of all I felt within appear'd ſedate; I ſign'd the Renunciation ſo much deſired of me, and gave my ſolemn Promiſe, nay, aſſured them in Terms more ſtrong than they exacted from me, that I would never attempt to ſee the dangerous *Minetta* more.————O! Madam, purſued *Melicourt*, how heavenly good is your fair Friend to pardon what the Dictates of my jealous Rage then ſaid of her.————I curſt her————even from the Bottom of my Soul I curſt her Perfidy, though at the ſame time I ſecretly adored her Beauty.————My Behaviour, however, making them believe I had now a real Abhorrence of her, forwarded my Liberty, and I was diſcharged from diſmal the Priſon, where I had near a Year been confined.

You may ſuppoſe, Madam, that as ſoon as I had the power I went directly Home, where the Surprize of ſeeing me alive and at liberty, had like to have been fatal to both my Parents; my Mother fell into a Swoon, and my Father, though of a ſtronger Conſtitution, was alſo very near being in the ſame Condition.————Exceſs of Joy entirely over-powered their Spirits, and when they had recover'd their Voices, could ſay nothing for a great while; but————is it poſſible!————By what
Miracle

Miracle do we fee you again.————Is it really our
Son, or an Illufion.————And fuch like Exclamations,
which were to me unintelligible, as I had fo lately wrote
to them the whole Circumftance of my Situation, and
had receiv'd an Anfwer from them, containing the Conditions of my Freedom; I thought there was fomewhat
unnatural in the Aftonifhment they both expreffed, and
began to fear fome Diforder in the Mind had feized
them ; but the firft Tranfports of unruly Joy being a
little over, and I beginning to mention the Letters, how
confounded was I in my Turn, to hear they had never
wrote to me, nor knew where I had been fecreted from
the time I was forced away, to the happy Moment of
my Return. On this I fhew'd the Letters I had receiv'd
by the Hands of the Turnkey, and my Father affuring me, that fign'd with his Name was a Forgery, I
began to hope that from my Wife was the fame alfo ;
but, alas, that pleafing Idea lafted not long, both my
Parents confirmed the Story of her Falfhood, having
heard it from all Hands, and, indeed, fo induftrioufly
had Monfieur De———— caufed the Report of her intended Marriage to be fpread, that it was a thing not
doubted of, by any who were any way acquainted either
with her or me. From thence it was natural to infer,
that the Letter was really wrote by her ; though the
other was a Contrivance the more to haften me to give
up my Claim. The Imagination that fhe was concerned
in this Stratagem render'd her more unworthy than ever
in my Eyes, and I laboured inceffantly not only to forget all that had endear'd her to me, but even to hate
her. As this was a Difpofition which could alone reftore me to my former Peace of Mind, my Mother endeavour'd all in her power to divert me, continual Balls
and Entertainments were given at our Houfe to all the
neighbouring Gentry ; and as nothing is fo effectual to
eftrange the Heart from an Object it has been accuftomed to, as a Variety of new ones, fhe took care to
have always fome agreeable young Lady or other with
us. Among this Number there was one, no lefs admired
for her Beauty, than for her Wit and good Humour,

her

her Name is Mademoiselle *De Marcy*, and her Family and Fortune, perfectly conformable to our own.

I muſt confeſs there was ſomething in this young Lady which extremely pleaſed me, I was never ſo happy as when in her Company, and whenever I quitted it felt a Regret, mix'd with an Impatience to ſee her again; yet could not all this be called Love; it was rather Friendſhip founded on the Knowledge of her good Qualities, an Eſteem, an Admiration of the Mind, in which the Body had no ſhare, nor did I ever once think of the difference of Sexes in all the Converſations I had with her.

My Behaviour, however, made every one give me to her for a Lover, my Parents were infinitely pleaſed to find me as they believ'd, engaged in a Paſſion ſo agreeable as to Circumſtances, and thinking they acted extremely prudently, propoſed a Match between us to the Friends of the young Lady, who readily accepted it, after having found ſhe had no Averſion to it; and every thing was in a manner concluded on, without my knowing any ſuch thing was in Agitation.

I was all the time endeavouring to forget my dear *Minetta*, but in vain————ſleeping and waking her Image was ever before my Eyes, and I was but juſt awaked from a Dream of her, which gave me ſome Diſquiet, when my Mother came into my Chamber with a more than ordinary Satisfaction in her Countenance.

Now, my dear Son, ſaid ſhe, I flatter myſelf the Remainder of your Days will attone for the Anxieties of the paſt; Mademoiſelle *De Marcy* thinks you not unworthy of her, her Kindred agree to your Happineſs, and all things are ſo diſpoſed, that the Contract between you may be ſign'd this very Evening. The Surprize I was in at ſo unexpected a Salutation, and the little Satisfaction I expreſs'd, very much alarm'd this tender Parent, what, cry'd ſhe, are you not in love with Mademoiſelle *De Marcy*? Has our Endeavours to make you happy proved the Reverſe? Do you not think her deſerving of you? Yes, Madam, reply'd I, that Lady's Merits may juſtly entitle her to a more exalted Fortune than
ſhe

she could share with me ;————but, alas, I never entain'd one Thought that way, I am incapable of making her happy, and in spite of all her Charms, I should languish even in her Arms for the dear absent, though ungrateful Object of my first Vows.

My Mother, though by Nature one of the most sweet temper'd of her Sex, could not hear me speak these Words without flying into an Extremity of Rage; my Father when he was told of my Refusal was not less provoked; all our Kindred highly blamed me, my Acquaintance wonder'd, and, in fine, all the World blamed my Stupidity as they term'd it, and Meanness of Spirit to retain enough of my former Affection, for one who had proved herself so unworthy of it, as to make me slight a young Lady every way qualified to make me happy, and who had preferr'd me to a great Number who sigh'd in vain for her.

Indeed, Madam, though I would not adhere to the Remonstrances made me on this Head, I secretly allow'd the Justice of them, and extremely condemn'd myself for having given Occasion for them: When once we are brought to believe that Reason demands our Assent to any particular Action, though Inclination may oppose, a Person with any share of Resolution may overcome it, and prevail with himself to do as seems most just. This join'd with the Importunities of my Friends, and, indeed, the Menaces of my Father, who told me, I had already brought him to trouble enough, and that he would risque no more, but determin'd to disown me as a Son if I did not comply, at last engaged me to consent.

The Day before that prefix'd for my Marriage with Mademoiselle *De Marcy*, the Letters you were so good to forward came to Hand, which gave a most fortunate Reverse to this Affair.————My Parents were too just, and, indeed, too much attached to my dear Wife now proved innocent, not to rejoice at the timely Discovery; the Family of Mademoiselle *De Marcy* had no Occasion for Resentment: And the young Lady herself had the Generosity to congratulate me on the seasonable Disco-

very,

very, which had it arrived but two Days later muſt have
involv'd us all in Miſery. Every Body join'd with me ſn
deteſting the Cruelty of Monſieur and Madam *De———*
in barbarouſly attempting to ſacrifice their Daughter to a vile Intereſt : We conſulted the Laws a ſecond time in favour of this charming Woman, and
my Father having well weigh'd what he was to do, entered the Proteſtation *Minetta* had made againſt her
Vows, and revived the Suit which had ſo long lain dor-
mant againſt Monſieur *De———*, in order to oblige
him to acknowledge her as his Child. It had only been
through the Power of a favourite Miniſter, that he had
got the better of my Father before; but that Perſon
was now in Diſgrace, and we hoped, that when the
Cauſe come to be try'd before impartial Judges, he
muſt either own himſelf her Father, or ſuffer the Penalty
of the Law, of aſſuming a right over her, and forcing
her into a Convent, while he confined me in unwarrantable Bonds.

Our Opinion did not deceive us, Monſieur was now
obliged to appear himſelf before the Court of Judicature,
and was caſt.———The Proofs were as clear as the
Day : My dear *Minetta* is decreed Co-heireſs with her
Siſter, and her Father forbid ſeeing her till further Permiſſion : The whole verbal Proceſs is ſent to *Rome*, and
there is no doubt but a Diſpenſation will ſoon arrive,
and we ſhall be re-united with all the Forms neceſſary for
the Occaſion.

As in all Probability the *Nuncio* will have Orders to
decide it, the Marquis *De L———V———*'s Intereſt
to that Prelate, to whom we have not the Honour to be
known, would be of great Service toward haſtening the
Affair to a Concluſion; and this Favour, Madam, the
long ſuffering *Minetta* begs you will endeavour to procure for her.

Thus did Monſieur *Melicourt* finiſh his Story, and having thanked him for the Trouble he had given himſelf
in acquainting me with theſe Particulars, told him I rejoiced
to have it in my power to do any thing that might haſten
his

his Felicity; that I doubted not of the Marquis's Readiness to comply with my Friends, as well out of his love of Virtue, as his Attachment to me; that I had now wrote to him, and would break open my Letter on purpose to infert a Poftfcript on the Bufinefs he mentioned. I had no fooner faid this but I broke the Seal, and recommended my dear Friend's Bufinefs in Terms the moft ftrenuous, my Tendernefs for her could fuggeft.

After this, we enter'd into a Conversation on the many Difficulties which are frequently the Attendants on Love, though of the moft perfect and honourable kind; no body had more Experience than myfelf of this, and therefore could fpeak feelingly upon it; indeed, I had at this time a fufficient fhare of Anxiety, to render me more than ordinarily eloquent on the Occafion. *Dubois*, whom I fo impatiently expected many Hours before, was not yet come, and I could not imagine now to account for this Neglect; it was now paft Noon, and my Uneafinefs grew fo vifible, that Monfieur *Melicourt* could not but take Notice of it. On his afking me the Caufe, I made no Scruple of revealing it, with the Danger I was in from the old Marquis, if his Son were not acquainted with the Accidents that had happen'd fince I faw him. The Hufband of *Saint Agnes* feemed concerned I had not given him a Commiffion to deliver it, telling me it was a Thing of too much Confequence for me to have delayed, through the Complaifance of liftening to his Story, and begg'd I would that inftant permit him to go with it, and bring me an Anfwer back. This Offer was too obliging to be refufed, I gave him his Inftructions and he departed.

As it was fo fmall a Diftance, I expected him foon again, but two, three, and four o'Clock paffed over, yet he was not return'd: This Delay gave me fome alarm ————a thoufand ftrange Ideas came into my Head, concerning the Occafion of it; and, to add to my Terrors, Madam *De Genneval* enter'd my Chamber, and told me the Marquis *De L————V————* was come to vifit me————he would not be delayed, faid fhe, 'till I could apprize you of the Honour, but told me he was certain
you

you had too much Good-Nature not to difpence with Ceremony. As fhe fpoke he followed her in, and took from
me, by his Prefence, the Opportunity of replying to what
fhe faid, as otherwife I fhould have done, and perhaps
not in a manner very obliging to her, in the Humour I
then was. How difficult is it, when the Heart is oppreft
with Cares to affume a Serenity of Countenance ? yet it is
a Piece of Diffimulation, in fome meafure neceffary for
People that live in the World ; but I was too little practifed in this Art, to elude the Penetration of a Man fuch
as the Marquis : He prefently perceived the Conftraint I
put upon myfelf, and afk'd if he was come at an improper
Time. No, my Lord, anfwered I a little faultring in my
Speech, and if I appear not altogether fo fatisfied with
this Honour, as I ought to be, I beg your Lordfhip to
impute it to a little Diforder, occafioned by want of Sleep
laft Night. This Excufe, which was all I could think on
at that Time, gave him an Opportunity of faying many
gay and gallant things, on the Occafion of my Watchfulnefs————among other Things he told me, that nothing
but Love could have the Power of breaking the reft of a
Lady of my Years and Circumftances, and while he fpoke
this, looked at me with Eyes, which methought faid
JEANETTA, *you in vain endeavour to hide yourfelf*————
I know you————*and can read your inmoft Soul.* Tho'
this was only my own Imagination, yet it frighted me
little lefs than the reality would have done.

'Tis a received Maxim, that the moft filly Girl has
Wit enough to manage a Love Intrigue, but I was an
Exception to this Rule; as I was every Moment expecting
Melicourt, either with a Letter, or fome Meffage of very
great Importance, nay knew not but even the young
Marquis might have come with him, I ought in Prudence
to have made fome Pretence to ftep out of the Room, and
given orders to *Barbara*, to let whoever came to vifit me
know who was above ; but tho' I thought of this, I had
not Courage to put it in Execution, I fear'd the leaft Action would make me fufpected more than I already was,
and fo run a Hazard of being much more fo, of being
fully

fully difcovered, as I muft have been, if my Lover, or even *Dubois* had come at that juncture. ·

Whenever the old Marquis look'd upon me, I had not the Power to meet his Eyes, but caft mine down with a Confufion that fometimes made him fmile, and willing I fuppofe to increafe it, he drew his Chair nearer me, and began to beftow the moft lavifh Encomiums on my Beauty : the Name of Father to the Man I loved, gave him fuch an Afcendant over me, that tho' I could not have liftened to feveral of his Expreffions, from any other without Contradiction, Fear and Regard would not fuffer me to give him any Interruption. But when Madam *De Genneval*, to make her Court to him I fuppofe, as well as to fhew her Wit and Sprightlinefs, went to pluck back my Handkerchief, to fhew as fhe faid the Whitenefs of my Neck, I drew it clofe again, and gave her fo fevere a Look, as fhew'd them both I was not of a Humour to bear fuch Freedoms, nor would be jefted with too far. The Air I put on, on this Occafion, made the Marquis affume a different Turn of Behaviour, and I could perceive that from that Moment he ever after treated me with more Refpect, and Madam *De Genneval* with lefs. Which I think is a plain Demonftration, how much 'tis in our Sex's Power, to give an Awe, even to thofe whofe Fortune and Character makes them apt to imagine every Thing becomes them.

The old Nobleman, however, left not off my Praifes, but then a certain Serioufnefs accompanied them, which, tho' I could not avoid feeling fome Confufion at the extravagant Compliments on my Beauty, took of all Motives for Refentment. He was ftill on that Topic, when *Meficourt* thinking I was alone, and impatient for his return, came haftily into the Room, with a Letter in his Hand, I turn'd pale as Death at the fight of him, and had fcarce Power to rife from my Seat to receive him. The Marquis could not but obferve this change in my Countenance, as he had his Eyes never off me, but taking no Notice of it to me, got up and return'd the Civilities paid him by the Hufband of *Saint Agnes*,

who

who judging him by many diftinguifhing Marks to be a Perfon of Quality, made his Reverence in the moft profound Manner.

When we had all replaced ourfelves, the Marquis and *Melicourt* entered into a Converfation, which tho' indifferent, gave this young Gentleman opportunity of fhewing he wanted neither Wit nor Education; and by Degrees, as People are apt to fpeak of what they have moft at Heart, artfully enough introduced his own and Miftrefs's Story, with a View no doubt of interefting the Marquis in his Favour; who feeming defirous of doing every Thing to oblige me, afked me if I fhould find any Satisfaction to fee the Affairs of that beautiful Nun accommodated' I was too zealous for my Friend, not to affure his Lordfhip there were very few Things I fo earneftly wifhed. Well then, Madam, anfwered he, I give you my Word and Honour, that I will employ all the Credit I have with the *Nuncio*, which I flatter myfelf is of fome Weight, to engage him to a fpeedy determination in her Favour. Be pleafed, added he, turning to *Melicourt* to fend me an exact Memorial of the Proceedings, and I will not only be your Advocate myfelf, but oblige my Friends to join with me in doing you all the good Offices in our Power.

I thanked the Marquis for this Condefcention, with a Warmth which manifefted how zealoufly I efpoufed the Caufe of my Friend; and this Proof of my Sincerity drew on me frefh Compliments; but not all the fine Things faid of me by Perfons, who fo well knew how to judge, could make me eafy; my Love had much the Prehemicence over my Vanity great as it was, and I impatiently longed to be alone with *Melicourt*, that I might know what my dear Marquis faid to my Letter. But my fufpence was not yet to ceafe, and to add to my Perplexities, a new Adventure happened which was very near betraying at once all I had fo carefully concealed.

My poor unthinking Aunt, who by accident was in the next Room, when fome Body knocked very loud at the Street-Door, looked out of the Window to fee who it was, and then came running into the Chamber where we

were,

were, crying, Madam, Madam, here is the fine young Gentleman that dined with you one Day, come to visit you. The Blood immediately forsook my Heart, and flew into my Face, at these Words, I knew it must be either my Lover, or *Saint Fal* she meant ; and which ever it were, if seen by the old Marquis, must betray my Secret————in this Confusion, I got up and ran out of the Room without being able to make any Excuse to the Company————I heard the Door open, and knew the Person was let in————I flew to the Stairs, and met *Saint Fal* half way————fly, cried I, out of Breath with the haste I had made, the old Marquis is here———— unlucky Accident, returned he, I have things to tell you of the utmost Importance————endeavour to get rid of my Uncle as soon as you can, and I will return when I think he is gone————what News of the Marquis, said I ? Mad, answered he, but this is not a Time nor Place to tell you————in speaking these Words he made towards the Street-Door, and at that Instant some Body knocked————Perhaps he is here, cried I, more dead than alive at the manner in which he had spoke ; but if it be, let him instantly depart. You need be under no such Apprehensions, replied the Count, it cannot be him, I wish to Heaven it were————we would find some way to conceal him from his Father. What is it you mean ? My Lord, resumed I trembling, what has happened ? *Saint Fal* was going to make some Answer but the knocking redoubled, and I bethought me of making him run into the Kitchen, till the Person should be let in ; and returned to the Company, having ordered *Barbara* to see who it was that knocked———— the Consternation I was in at the few Words the Count had said to me on his Cousin's Account, joined to the Fears of being discovered, rendered me so wild and disordered that I could scarce make any Apology for having left my Visiters so abruptly.

The Marquis, who suffered not the least Look or Motion of mine to escape his Notice, asked me in a low Voice, if any thing had happened to me in which he could be of no Service, assuring me, at the same Time,

that

that I might command any thing in his power. I was
about to reply, tho' I believe it would have been with
Diftraction enough, when I was prevented by the entrance of the Duke *de*————I was glad of this Interruption in one Senfe, and vex'd at it in another: being
unprepared to make a fuitable Return to what the Father
of my Lover had offered, this Excufe for my Silence was
opportune; but then any addition to the Company I had
before, threatning to delay my talking with *Melicourt*,
and alfo to prevent my fpeaking a fecond Time to *Saint
Fal*, who had promifed me to come again, was the moft
unfortunate Incident that could be.

When every Body had paid thofe Civilities to the
Duke, which his Quality demanded, the Converfation
was renewed with a great deal of good Senfe and Spirit—
every Body but myfelf feemed to exert their Wit and
Eloquence; but I believe my Reader will eafily imagine
the Situation of my Mind at that Time would not permit
me to make ufe of my little Talents that way.

They were rallying the Marquis on the Admiration he
had fome time before teftified for the Lady of a certain
Count, who came to follicite an Affair at Court, when
we heard *Barbara* give a great Scream, and prefently after faw that poor Creature come running in a moft terrible
Fright, crying, Thieves! Thieves! ————where,
cried J, all the Company joined with me in the demand,
and the three Gentlemen immediately had their Hands
on their Swords. In the Kitchen, anfwered fhe, I was
going in and found the Door held faft againft me, and
on attempting to pufh it open, out rufhed a Man, the
Paffage was dark, and I could not diftinguifh what fort
of Perfon he was, but I am afraid he has left fome of
his Companions, for never a Rogue of 'em all would
have the Impudence to come alone to rob a Houfe at
Noon Day. I doubted not but it was *Saint Fal* fhe
meant, and was glad to find he had got off undifcovered;
but was obliged to feign myfelf under Apprehenfions, and
Barbara begging that the Kitchen might be fearched,
faying that till it were, fhe durft not venture down
Stairs, every body ran down in compliance with her

Fears————————not the least Corner escaped their Scrutiny, but no Man was to be found ; in looking earnestly about, however the Duke took up a Glove fring'd with Gold, which *Saint Fal* in his hurry had let fall ; upon my Honour, cried the Marquis, with a Smile, this Thief is certainly a Man of Fashion, I imagine he came with an intent to steal something more valuable than any thing in the Kitchen————————I wish he had not some Designs on *Barbara*. Ah! cried the Duke, who knows but she might have other Reasons than those she pretended for crying out. The Tone in which these Words were spoke, and the Laughter that ensued, made my good Aunt, who was but a droll Figure at the best, look exceeding silly ; and the grave Answers she made, and the Asseverations that she knew him not, and that he could be no other than a common Thief, heighten'd the Mirth, and I believe it would have continued a much longer Time, had not the Hour for the Marquis's Attendance at Court approach'd, and he was oblig'd to take leave, tho' as he said with Regret. The Duke I perceived had an Intention to stay behind him, but as I had not the same Awe of him as I had of the other, I had Resolution enough to let his Grace know, I was obliged to write some Dispatches about Affairs of Moment to me, for which that Gentleman, pointing to *Melicourt*, waited, and had done so a considerable Time, his Grace was too polite to oppose my Desires, and took his leave at the same Time the Marquis did ; Madam *de Genneval* also retired, and I was at last at Liberty to entertain *Melicourt* on a Subject I was so impatient to hear : But, good Heaven ! how little did I expect or deserve what I was going to receive, I tremble to this Day, and my Blood runs cold through all my Veins, when I reflect on the dreadful Tryal to which my Fortitude was put.

After having asked Monsieur *Melicourt* if he had seen the Marquis, and what was the Effect of his Embassy, he gave me a Letter ; there, Madam, said he, is an Answer to what you wrote, I fear it will not be very pleasing to you, and am extremely grieved to be so unfortunate

fortunate in the firſt Buſineſs I have the honour to be
employed on by you.

I rather ſnatch'd than took the Paper he preſented to
me, in the Agony his Words involved me, and haſtily
opening it, found in it theſe diſtracting, theſe ſoul-
rending Lines.

To Madamoiſelle JEANETTA.

The very Addreſs, ſo different from the Stile of a fond
Lover to the Object of his Affections, was near making
me faint away, but I ſummond all my Reſolution to my
Aſſiſtance, and with much ado, read on as follows:

*I Am ſurprized, Madam, that a Lady ſo much admired,
and ſo much taken up with the Gallantries of the Age,
ſhould find Leiſure to make any excuſes for her Behaviour
to a Perſon who has it not in his Power to make thoſe
publick Acknowledgments of his Paſſion, which I find are
ſo agreeable to her*———*Miſtake me not, Madam, I pretend not to complain of the Conduct you have been pleaſed to
obſerve, ſince your Arrival at* Verſailles———*I have
too much Regard for your Happineſs to diſapprove of thoſe
Civilities, which ſeem due to the Quality and Merit of the
Duke De*———*if he ſhould happen to have the ſame
Intentions for you as I had. I ſhall never upbraid you
with having put the firſt Hand towards raiſing your Fortune*———*the delicacy of my Sentiments will prevent me
from ever giving you Diſquiet*———*your Inclinations ſhall
not be diſputed by me, and as you receive his Grace's Viſits,
permit him to attend you to the Play, liſten to the ſoft
Things he entertains you with, it would be unpardonable
in me to offer any Interruption to an Intercourſe ſo ſatiſ-
factory to you.*———*You are certainly independant, and
I have no right to demand any Account of your Actions*———
*I wiſh you more Happineſs than I can now ever hope to
enjoy myſelf, and ſhall take care never to diſturb your new
Engagments by Viſits no leſs unprofitable to myſelf, than
diſagreeable to you*———*Farewell, therefore*———*Forever.*

L———V———.
P. S.

P. S. I beg you will give yourself no trouble to answer this, for be assured nothing of yours will evermore come to my Hand.

Let any Woman who has ever known what 'tis to love sincerely the most perfect Object in the World now put herself in my Place, for none but such a one can judge of what I felt————my Despair was so great, my Grief so poignant, that I could neither vent it in Tears nor in Complaining————motionless as a Statue did I stand some time————*Melicourt* endeavoured, to console me as I afterward was told ; but I heard not any thing he said————all my Senses were overwhelm'd, insomuch that I saw not the Count *de Saint Fal*, who entered while I was in this State of Insensibility. The fatal Letter had dropt from my Hand, and lay near me on the Floor, and on his casting his Eyes on that and on me, he no longer was at a loss for the meaning of the Condition he found me in. His tender Soul was touched with the utmost Compassion for my Distress, and taking me by the Hand, dear Madam, cried he, mitigate your Sorrows, and pardon the Author of them ; all his Fault is occasioned by an Excess of Passion————No, no, my Lord, replied I, just then recovering the use of Speech, he loves me not————he never loved me as he ought ; for if he had, he could not have treated me in this cruel Manner————if there is any Sincerity in Man, cried I wildly ; if all your Professions of Friendship, be not as false, as wavering, as his are of Love, assist me to fly from this detested Place————never more will I be seen of the World, never more endure the Sight of barbarous unfaithful Man !————Ah ! My dear *Saint Agnes*, why did I not follow the prudent *Lindamine*, and past my Days with her in the peaceful Cloyster ! the Society of two such Friends would have enabled me to bear up against the Treachery of a designing Lover, who wanted but a Pretence to abandon me, and no doubt triumphs in that which my Necessity, not Inclination enforced me to give him.————But, continued I, what need have I of any help to go where only Peace of Mind

Mind is to be found―――I'll difcover inftantly who I am, to the Father of my ungrateful Lover ; his Hate will do all I could hope for from Affection―――he will fend me where I no more fhall hear the Name of him who has undone my Quiet.

Thus did I exclaim till I had no longer Breath, without fuffering either *Melicourt* or the Count to fpeak one Word ; but the former having taken his leave, being obliged to go where his own Affairs required his Prefence, the other made known the Generofity of his Soul, in a manner few Men, if any befide himfelf, could put in Practice ; inftead of taking any Advantage of my Rage againft the Marquis, for the Intereft of his own Paffion, he employed all his Wit and Eloquence in favour of his Rival : he told me, that difobliging as this proof was of his Love, there could not be a greater than the Jealoufy he expreft.―――He then endeavoured to lay before me what Appearances there were, that I merited fome little Refentment, and begg'd I would not give way to a Defpair, which he was certain would be more afflicting to his Coufin, than any thing I was capable of doing.

I fuffered him to proceed without any interruption ; but the Fury with which I was at firft poffeft fubfiding by degrees, an adequate fhare of Grief took its Place, and burfting into a Flood of Tears, Ah, my Lord! cried I, I am but too fenfible of the Truth of what you fay―your amiable Coufin did certainly once love me―――that he does fo no more is owing to myfelf―――my Imprudence and Ill-management has forfeited the Pretenfions I had to his Heart―――I have been fo unhappy as to difpleafe him, perhaps too, to give him fome Uneafinefs―――O, tell him, my Lord, that I confefs the Faults I have been guilty of, tho' led into them only by an Excefs of Tendernefs for him―――tell him, that I will punifh myfelf for them by forfaking the World, which has nothing in it for me without his Love.

But I will not trouble the Reader with all the incoherent things I uttered in this terrible Situation ; it fhall fuffice to fay, that all Monfieur *Saint Fal* could do, was ineffectual to bring me to any tollerable Compofure of

Mind, and he was obliged to leave me, it growing late, with an infinite Concern.

The next Day he came again, but found me in the same Distraction, *Melicourt* also employed all his leisure Hours, in endeavouring to assuage my Griefs; but every Attempt to that Purpose was in vain. Those two were the only Persons I would see, and tho' the old Marquis most earnestly begg'd to speak with me, I made *Barbara* put him off sometimes on one Pretence, and sometimes on another. As for the Duke *de*——he had been five times at my Lodging without being admitted, in one of which, since he could not see me, he left for me a handsome Sum of Money, which the Bounty of the King had bestowed on me, through his Hands, in consideration of the Services my supposed Husband had been said to have done. But this Favour caused me afterwards much Trouble, as will be seen hereafter in the Course of these Memoirs. Common Gratitude obliged me to suffer his Grace to be admitted once after this, I thanked him for the Recommendations he had given me to the King, but received him in so cool a Manner, that it was easy for him to perceive his Visits were not at all agreeable, and testified a Concern at it, which convinced me, he was entirely serious when he told me he loved me.

At length I was also obliged to see the old Marquis, but the Constraint I put on myself to assume a Chearfulness which was far distant to my Heart, was such a Pain that I could scarce support it, and besides, counterfeited so ill the Part I endeavoured to act, that a Person of infinitely less Penetration than his I had to deal with, might have perceived it. The Views he had at that time in his Head, however, made him take not the least Notice of any Alteration in me, and he always behaved to me with the greatest Good-humour and Complaisance.

For eight Days never Creature suffered more than I did, during all which time I heard nothing of my Lover, ————from the second Day after I had received that cruel Letter neither the Count nor *Melicourt* seemed willing to mention his Name, and tho' I seldom spoke of any else, I could observe that they evaded all the

Questions

Queftious I afked, by putting others to me foreign to the Purpofe; this ftrangely perplex'd me, and growing quite impatient to be kept thus in the dark, in a thing which fo nearly concered me, I at laft got out of them, that the Marquis had left *Verfailles*, and was gone to join his Regiment in *Germany* where the War was broke out. What an Addition was this to what I felt before !———— Can Words exprefs what 'twas i fuffered————No, 'twas unutterable————inconceivable————the very Remembrance, even now bleft as I am in the utmoft of my Wifhes, ftrikes me with Horror————I am able to proceed no farther ; but thofe who take Intereft enough in my Story to wifh for the Event muft have Patience till I recover myfelf, and continue a generous Pity for me————they fhall foon fee, that the Happinefs I now enjoy has been brought about by all the Trials of Fortitude and Patience that Woman could fuftain.

The End of the E I G H T H P A R T.

THE

THE
VIRTUOUS VILLAGER,
OR,
VIRGIN's VICTORY.

PART. IX.

 F T ER this laſt mentioned dreadful Shock, I ſhut myſelf up from all the World, not excepting the Count *De Saint Fal* or the obliging Huſband of my dear *Saint Agnes* : Nothing but the beſt Conſtitution that ever was, could have enabled me to ſuſtain the Weight of Anguiſh, which I then labour'd under—I endeavoured to bring myſelf to ſome Reſolution where to go ; for *Verſailles* and all the Gaieties of it, were now deteſtable to me : I had very often thoughts of diſcovering myſelf to my Aunt *Barbara*, and return with her to the Village. As all the Misfortunes I had undergone, and even the Errors I had been guilty of, aroſe from the violent Affection I had for the Marquis, not excepting even that for which I was forſaken, it ſeem'd as if Providence did not
approve

approve my Tenderneſs, and I ought in Obedience to the divine Will, to lay this voluntary Puniſhment on myſelf, to return to my native Meanneſs, and ſubmit to all the additional Ills, which the Inſults, I muſt expect to receive for my Behaviour, ſince I left it, muſt inflict upon me.

————I reflected on the Penance *Lindamine* laid on herſelf, in being obliged to relate her unhappy Story wherever ſhe came, and thought my Vanity deſerved no leſs a Humiliation ; but alas ! how little do we know ourſelves, that very Vanity which I wiſh'd to mortify, had ſtill too much dominion over me, to permit me to continue long in this Reſolution ; after a long Struggle, therefore, a Monaſtry was the only Refuge I could conſent to take.

I then wrote to *Saint Fal*, deſiring he would come to me immediately, and as ſoon as I ſaw him, conjured him to comply with what I deſired : Can you doubt if I will do ſo, anſwered he ? no, my Lord, ſaid I, your Honour and Sincerity are too well known to me, and I ſhall not heſitate to entreat you will crown the Work you have begun, 'tis all I ſhall ever aſk of you. As I ſpoke this, the Tears trickled down my Cheeks, and riſing Sighs obſtructed the Paſſage of my Words : Permit me, cried the Count, to ſpare you the Trouble of mentioning your Commands————I know what 'tis you expect from me————you would have me overtake the Marquis, convince him of the Injuſtice of his Suſpicions, and bring him to your Feet a Penitent : I will this inſtant go about it, and if Deſpair has not rendered him deaf to Reaſon, you ſhall be ſatisfied. No, my Lord, replied I, my paſt Conduct, as to that Nobleman, has made you put a wrong Conſtruction on the preſent————ſo far from purſuing him with my unhappy Love, I wiſh not to ſee him more——His Eyes are now opened————a tranſient Paſſion in my Favour had blinded him, but he now ſees the vaſt Diſparity between us, is aſhamed of the Weakneſs he has been guilty of, and attones for it by abandoning me————I blame him not for remembring the Dignity of his Birth, I only think, he might have quitted me without cruelly accuſing me ;————but I will talk

no

no farther on that Subject————the happy Moments, in which I indulged too flattering Ideas, must now be buried in eternal Oblivion————the Follies into which a headstrong Passion hurried me, be punished,————my Aim now, my only Aim, is to pass my whole Life in a Convent, and there in the lowest Station, humble the Pride your Cousin's Addresses kindled in me————I flatter myself, that Heaven in Pity of my Youth and Innocence will enable me in Time to get the better of a Tenderness. which not all his Severities has yet extinguished————my constant Prayers shall be to free my Heart from an Image too deep'y engraven on it, and my Tears incessantly poured at the Feet of the holy Altar, will perhaps prevail, and restore to me that Peace which at present is a Stranger.

I uttered this in Accents so moving, and accompanied what I said with a Flood of Tears, that *Saint Fal* could not forbear sympathizing with me, yet was far from a-greeing to my desire of excluding myself from the World for ever: he represented to me the Danger I should incur of being miserable, where I expected Ease ; by suffering the worst of. Torments, that of a too late and fruitless Remorse : Despair, he told me, would infallibly be the Consequence of such rash Vows, which would no sooner be made, than I should wish to break. He insinuated artfully, that I was not of a Disposition for a Cloyster, and that tho' I was at present out of Humour with the World, Time, or perhaps said he, the Repentance of my Cousin, might work a Change in my Sentiments.

Here I interrupted him, and with an Air which was not without some Mixture of Disdain in it, no, Count, said I, tho' I love the Marquis with the utmost Tenderness, and I fear in spite of my Efforts shall always do so, yet if he should return to his first Vows, on no Confidation whatever will I ever be prevailed upon to see a Man more, who has once abandoned me————this is my fix'd Resolution, and the whole World shall never shake it.

Monsieur *de Saint Fal* seemed to think very seriously on what I had said for sometime without speaking, and
when

when he did, argued but faintly against it : He owned the
Marquis deserved I should resent his hasty Determination
————that I ought not to have been condemned without
hearing at least what I had to say in my Defence ; but
still insisted on the Manner of my doing it. And after
repeating the same Arguments he had before made use of,
against my being a Nun, charming *Jeanetta*, said he,
your Heart is made for Love————you have too lively
an Imagination to live in a state of Indifference————you
will always love, and what is in Nature cannot be era-
dicated————would to Heaven that whenever the Object
changes, it may be in Favour of one, who would make it
the Business of his Life to merit you, and who could never be capable of suspecting you. He was going on,
perhaps to speak even more plain, when *Barbara* imagining, because I had sent for *Saint Fal*, I would see Company as usual, brought the Duke *De*————into the
Room. I was a little vex'd, being not in a Humour to
speak to any, but those who knew the Cause, however
I received him with the Civility his Rank, and my late
Obligations to him demanded. But I could not so far banish the Cloud from my Brow, as to hinder him from perceiving it, and after we were seated, as I was told Madam,
said he, you admitted few Visits for some Days past, I
would have chose rather to deprive myself of what I look
on as my greatest Happiness, then have broke in on your
Privacies, had not an odd Affair happened which I thought
proper to make you acquainted with————perhaps, continued he, your Ladyship knows of it already, and that
has occasioned the Uneasiness I see you under, but, Madam, I would not have you disquiet yourself too far, depend
upon it, you have Friends who will give you convincing
Proofs of their Respect for you.

I was prodigiously surprized at this Discourse, as I
could not imagine what new Accident had happened, in
which I should want the Interest of any Friends of his Acquaintance ; but as I thought whatever it were, it would
serve as a plausible Pretence for the Perplexity he found
me in, I pretended not to be wholly ignorant of what

he

he came about, but begg'd him to repeat it, having had, as I said, but an imperfect Account.

Nay, Madam, answered he, it ought not to alarm you————those kind of Impostures are frequent here, and I do not question but all will be set right in a Day or two————'tis true, the Affair might occasion a good deal of Trouble to some Ladies, but with you, Madam, whose Beauty and Accomplishments have interested all the Court in your Favour, it is quite otherwise; and if there were no other Persons than the Marquis *De L*————*V*———— and myself, and the Count here, to espouse your Cause, I dare answer we should be sufficient to maintain it, against all such impudent Pretenders.

Judge kind Reader, how greatly this Prelude heightned my Curiosity, Monsieur *De Saint Fal*, guessing at my Impatience, and feeling no small Share of it himself, desired the Duke not to keep me in Suspence, but relate what he knew of this Adventure.

I think myself obliged to do so, replied he, because perhaps it may have reach'd this Lady's Ear, in a manner very different from Truth. About four Hours ago, Madam, a Woman of much the same Age with your Ladyship, tho' not a thousandth Part so lovely, sent in your Name, to beg a Moment's Audience of me ; I was at that Time very full of Company, but not imagining it could be any other than yourself, I quitted them immediately, and went into another Room to receive you ; but I was strangely surpriz'd to find instead of you, a Person I had never seen before————as I did not offer to disguise it, your Grace, said she, is not the only one, who expresses an Astonishment at seeing me, I have heard the whole Court is prejudiced in Favour of a Woman, who has taken my Name upon her, and pretending that the *Count de Roches* was killed in the Service, has received a handsome Present from the King: my Husband, continued she, Heaven be praised, is still living, tho' in an ill state of Health, and unable to sollicit for himself, has sent me to *Versailles* to implore some Portion of his Majesty's Bounty, nor should doubt the Success of my Petition, had not this Imposture prevented me.

That

That Word, Madam, continued he, obliged me to hinder her proceeding any further, I told her that nothing but the Confideration of her Sex, prevented me from treating very ill, a Perfon who fhould take upon herfelf the Name of a Lady, whom I was well acquainted with, and had the greateft Refpect for ; fo advifed her to make no farther mention of fo impertinent an Affair ; and added, that if I heard any more of it, I fhould be lefs fcrupulous in what Manner I refented it.

To this fhe replied, that it was very unjuft to prefer the counterfeit to the real Perfon ; but that fhe faw how matters went, and would complain to the War Office ; for as to the Favours received from the King in her Name, fhe did not fo much regard that lofs, as the giving out that her Hufband was dead, by which Report his Commiffion might be difpofed of to another, and his Family ruined—fhe faid much more to the fame purpofe, but I was not of a Difpofition to hear her, and fhe went muttering away————fince this, I have been told, fhe has actually prefented a Petition to the Council of War, and offer'd to produce a Certificate from the Colonel of the Regiment, in which fhe affirms her Hufband is a Captain.

The Secretary has juft now fent me a Detail of this Affair, and feems inclinable to believe the Clamour fhe makes has fome Foundation ; I am therefore, now come, Madam, continued he, to know in what manner you would have me act ; for I believe we fhall be obliged to prove at the Office, that no Fraud has been put in practice, and that tho' there fhould happen to be another of the fame Name, yet that you are the Widow of one Count *De Roches*, who died in the Service, and the Perfon whofe Name was inferted in the Memorial I prefented in your Behalf ; and if you will take my Advice, you will immediately put the thing paft Difpute, by giving an account of the Place and Particulars of your Hufband's Death, that a proper Enquiry may be made, and your Ladyfhip acknowledged for what you are.

The Count, who all the Time the Duke was fpeaking feemed in a deep Study, no lefs perplexed than myfelf, as he had innocently been the Caufe of this new Trouble

to me, anſwered with a Gaiety, which very much ſurpriz'd me, that the Woman who called herſelf the Counteſs *De Roches*, could only be a Cheat ; for ſaid he this
Lady can bring ſufficient Proofs, in two Hour's Time,
who ſhe is.———But, purſued he, turning to me, I remember you told me that urgent Buſineſs obliged you to
go out, tho' your Politeneſs would not permit you to ſay
ſo before his Grace———you may therefore, I ſuppoſe,
defer giving the Proof expected from you 'till to-morrow ?
———O by all means, replied the Duke, any time
within theſe three Days will ſuffice ; and I am extremely
concerned, if my Viſit has detain'd the Lady a Moment,
from proſecuting her Intentions. I ſaw that the Count
had ſaid this for no other Reaſon than to get rid of the
Duke, that we might conſult together on what was to be
done, and ſaid, that indeed the Affair which called me
abroad, was ſuch as could not be well diſpenſed with,
and hoped his Grace would pardon a Rudeneſs, which
Neceſſity enforced. He ſaid a thouſand polite Things in
Anſwer to this, and took his Leave : *Saint Fal* went out
with him to avoid Suſpicion, but gave me to underſtand
by a Sign, that he would ſoon be with me again.

After I was alone, if one can be ſaid ſo to be with a
thouſand tormenting Ideas, I grew more reſolute than
ever to quit *Verſailles*, this laſt Adventure had indeed
rendered my Departure abſolutely neceſſary, and the
Count returning immediately, I expreſſed ſuch an Impatience to be gone, that he had nothing to oppoſe againſt
it. This generous Friend was perfectly overwhelm'd
with Grief, for having given me this new Diſturbance,
by making me paſs for the Counteſs *De Roches*, but as
he knew not there was any ſuch Perſon in being, it was
impoſſible for him to foreſee the ill Conſequences attending
what he had done ; but I told him it availed nothing to
reflect on the paſt, Time was too precious to be loſt in
Diſcourſes of this Nature, and I muſt now think of ſe-
curing myſelf, from any ſuch Vexations for the future ;
I therefore reiterated my Requeſt, of being conducted to
a Monaſtery, whence, I ſaid, nothing ſhould prevail upon
me to go out, for the whole remainder of my Life.

Monſieur

Monfieur *De Saint Fal* perceiving I was fo bent upon
it, and that all he had faid to diffuade me, ferved only to
make me find more Arguments for what I had determined, very artfully defifted any Attempt to alter my
Opinion, but told me, that 'till things were prepared
for my being received into a Convent, it was proper I
fhould retire fomewhere. This I agreed to, and the next
Morning was fix'd for my parting from *Verfailles* ; and
in order to deceive Madam *De Genneval*, whom we had
all the Reafon in the World to diftruft, *Saint Fal* acquainted her, that being ftraitned for Room, I had taken a
Houfe, which I intended to furnifh, expecting very foon
an Increafe of my Family————She who fufpected nothing of the Truth, made anfwer that fhe was forry to
lofe me, but fuppofed I was going to be married, and as
foon as I thought proper to declare it, would not fail
coming to congratulate me. The Count anfwer'd her
only with a Smile, and that inquifitive Woman imagining the Thing was as fhe faid, enquired no more about
it.

Early the next Morning, as we had concerted, all my
Furniture was taken down ; but inftead of being removed to the Place intimated to Madam *De Genneval*, it
was conveyed by one of the Count's Servants to *Paris*,
on Carriages hired for that Purpofe.

Juft before my Departure, I fent for Monfieur *Melicourt*
and acquainted him with my Journey, and the Motives of my undertaking it ; promifing to write to him,
as foon as I was fix'd, that he might fend me an Account
of his Affairs from Time to Time. He teftified the utmoft Senfe of my Regard for him, and faid he hoped to
be at *Paris*, in a fhort Time, and would then infallibly
wait upon me

When we defire moft Secrecy, Fortune for the moft
Part throws fomething in the Way to endanger a Difcovery————*Saint Fal* fet out before me on Horfeback,
and was to wait for me at a fmall Village near *Verfailles*,
I went with *Barbara* in a Poft-Chaife, which he had
provided for me, and was bleffing Heaven, for having
made my Efcape without any crofs Accident interveening,
when

when turning towards the great Alley, I met a Coach and Six, in which I saw the old Marquis *De L—V—*, he pass'd close by me, and tho' I was pretty much muffled up, I could discern he knew me, by the Earnestness of his Looks and a Smile; what he discovered in my Countenance I know not, but I believe there was Confusion and Fear easy to be read in it, but we presently lost Sight of him : My Chaise went at a great rate, and pursued the Road to *Paris*, and his Coach drove on to *Versailles*. As he did not stop, nor as I could perceive sent any Body after me, I flattered myself, that the Surprize I had been in, was all the Consequence of this Rencounter.

Tho' I had but a short Way to go before I met the Count, yet did many Reflections run through my Mind in that Time,————the Unkindness of my dear Marquis was still the most predominant—He no longer loves me, cried I to myself, he abandons me to be the Sport of Fortune, and interests himself no more in what ever shall befall me————Ah ! that I could behave with the same Indifference to him————that I could free my Heart from his too enchanting Image,————I am told I am formed for soft Desires—that Love has the greatest Share in my Composition, why then cannot I reward the Services of the most generous Man on Earth—the complaisant, the tender, the faithful *Saint Fal*————he never would have used me thus————I then began to think how happy I might be, if I could once bring myself to love the Count ————and, as in these Moments I wish'd to do so, I took Pains to recollect all he had done for me, his Disinterestedness, his Politeness, his noble Behaviour, and when I made a Comparison between the Marquis and him, with regard to me, the one seemed an ungrateful, the other a constant Lover ; and tho' I was far from being able to change the Object of my Passion, yet I look'd on it as a Proof of the greatest Weakness in me. These Meditations remained with me, 'till I arrived at the Place appointed, and *Saint Fal* waited for me with a livery Coach, into which I went with him, and set *Barbara* on a Horse, sending back the Chaise, in order to prevent the Place I was going to, from being suspected.

No

No Difficulties attended our Journey, we arrived at *Paris* in good Time, and *Saint Fal* conducted me to a neat handsome Apartment, consisting of four Rooms and a Kitchen. I thanked him in the most obliging Manner, for the Care he had taken of every Thing, and thinking myself happy in such a Friend, appeared infinitely more chearful than could be expected from a Person in the Situation I then was in, and the Despair I had so lately testified : He was charmed with the Change he found in me, and as he has since acknowledged, nothing but the Apprehensions that betraying any Transports might have rendered me more determined of retiring to a Cloyster, hindered him from throwing himself at my Feet, and expressing his Satisfaction in the most tender and passionate Terms——what a Proof of Delicacy did he give in putting this Restraint upon himself—— how few Men there are that are capable of acting in that manner, and how much ought a Woman that contracts a Friendship with such a one to value him !

We supp'd together, and the next Day he came again to visit me, I would needs keep him to dine, and after the Cloth was taken away, he desired I would examine my little Library, to which he told me he had made some Addition. I complied with his Request, and found several entertaining Books, which I had never seen before ; among them were the celebrated Novels of Madam *de Gomez*, the Title of one pleasing me extremely, I singled it out with a Design of amusing myself with it, after he was gone, and this gave him an Opportunity of entring into a Discourse of those little Treatises.

There is nothing, said he, that gives a better turn to the Mind, than reading such Histories, wrote in this manner, for whether there be any thing of reality in them or not, Virtue is always inculcated——a Nobleness of Soul is always represented in the most lively Colour, and it's contrary rendered so disagreeable, that whoever finds in themselves the least likeness of such a Picture, will, if not hardned in Vice, endeavour to put another mode upon their way of Thinking. Besides, there are many who would fly a grave Remonstrance, are insensibly led

by

by the gay turn generally found in Writings of this Nature to imitate the good Examples contained in them——— no Instruction makes so great an Impression on the Mind, as that which is conveyed through the Canal of Pleasure———there is a Love of Liberty so inherent to Mankind, that any Thing that carries with it the air of Compulsion is sure to be avoided ; but it is my Opinion, that the roughest Nature in the World may be soothed into Good-manners, and be capable of doing every Thing that can be wished, when the Change shall seem to come from itself alone.

He said many more things to the same Purpose, and concluded with an Apology for having been so tedious ; for, said he, I fear I am so unfortunate as not to enter upon those Subjects of Conversation that are most agreeable to you. I assured him that he could speak of very few Things, that would not be rendered so by his manner of expressing. He returned this Complement with a low Bow, and then said, charming *Jeanetta*, how truly amiable is your Mind, that can lay such a Restraint on yourself to oblige your Friends. I have now enjoyed the Pleasure of your Society for almost two Days, yet you have never once mentioned the Marquis ; in speaking these Words, he looked me full in the Face, as tho' he would read my inmost Thoughts, whatever Gloss I might put upon them by my Words.

I felt my Heart flutter, and an unusual Warmth o're-spread my Cheeks at that Instant ; but calling all my Courage to my Aid, why my Lord, cried I, would you remind me of a Man I am desirous of forgetting ?——— why would you recall any Reflections of what has been, since it is now so no more ?———the Struggle is hard ; but still I flatter myself Reason will get the better of an ill-treated Softness———no, continued I, with an Air of Haughtiness, great as he is by Blood, his Instability, his Inconstancy sets him below my Notice———perhaps even now he offers to another those Vows, that Heart he a thousand Times has sworn should never be but mine.

Oh !

Oh! what a Medley is a Lover's Mind! what contra-dictory Ideas rise in the same Instant thwarting each other ; while I spoke, Indignation and Tenderness had an equal share in my divided Heart———at once I hated and loved. The Count was too quick-sighted not to discover this Truth, and with a Sigh which seemed to rend his Breast, Ah, *Jeanetta! Jeanetta,* cried he! this Anger of yours informs me but too well of what I longed, yet feared to know———the Marquis still is, and will be ever dear to you, and *Saint Fal* forever wretched—but I revere and adore the Mouth that pronounces my Doom, and before eight Days are past, will give you a convincing Proof, that my Passion for you is greater even than yours for my too agreeable Cousin, and that is go-ing to the greatest height it can arrive at.

The Surprize I was in at these Words, whose Meaning I could not comprehend, and yet seemed to imply some great Design, shewed itself in my eager Reply. What Proofs, cried I, and in so short a Time ?———what relation can any Proof of your Affection have to that of the Marquis ?

Alas! resumed he, how impossible is it for you, Madam, to conceal how precious he is to you!———you would not have been thus impatient for unriddling this Mystery, had my Words regarded only myself ; but, for your Punishment, added he, with a forced Smile, I will not ease you of this Suspence, till I have your Promise not to think of going to a Monastry till my return.

Return! said I, more amazed, whether are you going ? Ah, my Lord, you will not forsake me sure, till you have seen me settled according to my wish ? How obliging, replied he, would be that fear in other Circumstance———Ah! Count, interrupted I, can you make a doubt of the Friendship I have for you, which I owe to you, and which you are so truly worthy of——take not a Pleasure therefore in giving me these Alarms———what Riddle is this, that is not to be solved, but on Condition ?———I conjure you add not to my Dis-quiets that of Uncertainty———believe I cannot rest

while

while I think there is any thing relating to you that requires Concealment.

Ah! Madam, cried he, lifting up his Eyes, how greatly am I indebted to your Friendſhip——would to Heaven the leaſt ſhare of this kind Concern proceeded from a ſofter Motive; but I muſt be content, nor ſuffer you to continue longer in Suſpenſe——know then, moſt adorable·of your Sex, purſued he, that my Duty calls me to the Army, where I ought to have been ſooner, if I could have prevailed on myſelf to have left you ſurrounded with the Perplexities you were in at *Verſailles*; but as you are now without all Queſtion, ſafe from my Uncle's Enquiries, I go with more Tranquility———I ſhall ſee the Marquis the Moment I reach the Regiment, and in eight Days time you ſhall have an Account of his Behaviour, and Sentiments concerning you———. whatever they may be at preſent, I ſhall ſoon convince him how deſerving you are of his Affection, and probably my Letter to you will be accompanied with one from him no leſs ſatisfactory, than the laſt you received from him was the contrary.

O Love, how powerful art thou! the Count had no ſooner given me hopes of being ſtill dear to the Marquis, and that I again ſhould ſee him, the fond, the engaging Adorer he had been, than my Soul imbibed the rapturous Idea, and felt immeaſurable Delight——I now no longer regretted the Departure of Monſieur *de Saint Fal*, on the contrary I wiſhed him gone—— my Thoughts out-ſtrip'd the Wind; he had not left off ſpeaking a Moment before my Imagination preſented him talking to my Lover, atteſting my Innocence, all Things cleared up, the dear Man at my Feet, entreating Pardon for his unjuſt Suſpicions, a Reconciliation, mutual Tranſports, and ten Thouſand Day-Dreams, which none but thoſe who love with an equal ſhare of Warmth and Delicacy can be capable of concealing.

Monſieur *de Saint Fal* pretending not to obſerve what paſſed in my Heart, tho' as he afterwards told me it was eaſy enough to be read in my Countenance, entertained me on indifferent Things, for which I was not a little diſobliged;

difobliged: I had forbad him to fpeak of the Marquis to me, but I now did not thank him for obeying my Commands: The flattering Idea of being again beloved by him, fo took up all my Thoughts, that I wifhed to fpeak of no other Topick.

At laft this noble fpirited Friend took his leave, and while doing fo, I could perceive fome Tears trickle down his Cheeks, in fpite of his Endeavours to reftrain them, and juft as he left the Room, beautiful *Jeanetta*, faid he, make yourfelf as eafy as poffible,——be affured you fhall foon hear of me, and of him likewife whom you moft wifh to be informed of: Thefe Words reminding me that he faw through all the Efforts I made for difquifing my Affection for the Marquis, made me call him back, and engage the moft folemn Promife from him not to inter- fere too far in my behalf—the Thought of making any advances on my Part, was equal almoft to the lofs of him, and in fpite of all my Tendernefs, I difdained to owe his return to any other motive than his Love. I made him alfo give me his Word and Honour to write me a full Account of all that paffed between him and his Coufin with regard to me, without fuppreffing the leaft Circumftance on any Confideration whatever ; and in return for this, affured him I would not make any alteration in my way of Life, much lefs think of a Monaftery till he returned.

The firft Day after the Departure of this incomparable Friend I was very much dejected : Solitude feemed frightful to me, and indeed it muft be confeffed, that a young Perfon fuch as I was, without any Acquaintance, any Diverfion, muft be at a great lofs how to pafs her Time——my only Comfort was in the expectation of hearing foon from the Camp; the charming hope that *Saint Fal* had infpired me with of the Marquis's ftill loving me, gave me fometimes fuch Spirits, that whoever had feen me would not have fufpected I had any thing to trouble me ; but then at others I had different Senti- ments, and could not perfuade myfelf I fhould ever fee him more——I was one Moment all Extafy of Joy——the next all Sorrow and Defpair—— hoping, doubting, perplexed, I would walk whole

Hours

Hours together, backwards and forwards, looked through the Windows, without having any Object in view—— went from one Room to another, without knowing why, and fatigued myself more than if I had been employed in some laborious Work: when the Mind is greatly oppressed it always obliges the Body to feel some share.

At last I betook myself to Reading, and the Relief I found in it is inexpressible. *La Belle Assemblée* was a Book that infinitely pleased me: the vast Variety of Adventures it contains, the many fine, and always just Quotations from History, both amused and instructed me, while the excellent Lessons of Virtue and Morality every where inculcated, served to strengthen me in those Principles, I had always made it my Resolution to continue in. Next to this, I was most delighted with the Works of Messieurs *De Crebillon* and *De Marivaux*; had it not been an Indecorum, for a young Woman, to seek the Acquaintance of Men, I should have endeavoured to have obtain'd theirs; and very much envyed the Happiness of those who enjoyed the Couversation of such agreeable Persons. Nor do I think myself to blame in this particular, 'tis ungrateful, methinks, not to allow some Portion of our Favour to those whose Writings please us; and, also, a very high Injustice to suffer ourselves to admire the Books, and at the same Time despise the Authors, 'tho' this is too common a Practice: And since I have come to more knowledge of the World, I have often observed Volumes in the Libraries of the great, most richly bound and gilt, while those who have laid out their Brains in the composing them, have been cloath'd in Rags; but then it must be confess'd, that it is only among a certain Number, who have taken it into their Heads to discourage every thing, that has more Wit than themselves. For my own Part, I shall always acknowledge, that if I have any thing amiable in Conversation, I owe that Advantage to Reading; and I would recommend to all those of my Sex, who would wish to create a lasting Admiration, to pass a great Part of their Time in a Closet of well chosen Books.

3

Time

Time, in this Employment, glided away with much less Anxiety than it had done before, and I began to find no want of any other Society, 'till one Morning as I was getting out of Bed, my Ears were agreeably surpriz'd with one of the moſt melodious Voices I had ever heard. I could eaſily diſtinguiſh it proceeded from a Perſon of my own Sex, and was in the Apartment over me: from that Moment I wiſh'd to be acquainted with her, and *Barbara* informing me, that it was a young Lady who lodged in that Floor, I ſent my Compliments to her with an Invitation to come down; ſhe very readily complied with my Requeſt, and in the Afternoon made me a Viſit.

Her Appearance was no leſs agreeable than her Voice had been, ſhe was three or four and twenty, had a fine Face and Shape, and ſomewhat in her Air that made me think her a Woman of Condition, which her Diſcourſe afterward confirmed, ſhe making mention of ſeveral Perſons of Quality, who were related to her.

She had beſides her other Perfections an infinity of Wit, and even in this firſt Viſit ſo agreeably entertain'd me, that I was quite impatient for a ſecond. She ſeem'd to have taken no leſs a Fancy to me, and we became in a ſhort Time as intimate, as if we had known each other from our Infancy.

We dined together almoſt every Day, but generally paſs'd the Afternoon in our reſpective Apartments, I expreſs'd ſo much my Deſire of living a retired Life, that ſhe, who ſaw a great deal of Company, did not judge it proper to break in upon my Manner, any more than I to be a Witneſs of who came to her———in fine, we had our Reaſons for being ſeparate at thoſe Hours, tho' mine were vaſtly different from hers, as it afterwards proved.

Indeed, I was ſo charmed with her Converſation, that could I have enjoyed it alone, I could have been glad never to have been ſeparated from her; but an Adventure ſoon after happened, which ſhewed me, ſhe had a way of living, which I little ſuſpected, and alſo convinced me how dangerous a thing it is, to enter into an Intimacy with a Perſon of one's own Sex, without being previouſly acquainted

quainted with their Morals and Characters. What hazards do young Creatures, with any tolerable Share of Beauty run, when left to themselves! How little are they able to forsee the Snares laid for them, too often by their own Sex! Without a great deal of Prudence, and that too supported by Advice, Virtue may be surprized into Ruin, even when it thinks itself most safe————Happy is it for me, I did not buy this Experience too dear ; for which I think myself not all indebted to my own Discretion, but, as I have often said, to the Interposition of an all-ruling Providence, which ever snatch'd me from the Precipice of Infamy and Destruction, when I was the nearest falling into it.

One Evening, I was reflecting with great Anxiety, that I had not yet heard from the Camp: Monsieur the Count *De Saint Fal*, having ever been the most punctual Man in the World, and as he had assured me that he would write immediately on his Arrival, nothing could be more strange, than that three whole Weeks were elapsed without my receiving any Letter. My Imagination therefore was on the Rack, to assign some Motive for this Omission, when Madamoiselle *Junia*, for so my new Acquaintance was called, came into my Chamber, and ask'd me if I would not do her the Favour to sup with her. I have been unusually dull all this Day said she, I know nothing but yourself that can dissipate a Melancholy for which I can ascribe no Cause————come then, my Dear, and help to chace away this Fit of the Spleen. The Humour I was in that Moment, so much resembled what she described, that I presently accepted her Invitation, and went with her into her Apartment.

The Entertainment she gave me was very elegant, and render'd much more so by her enlivening Conversation, as dull as she pretended to have been, her sparkling Wit adding a thousand Graces to all the little Stories she told for my Amusement infinitely charm'd me————in the height of her Gaiety, however, she let fall some Words which I could not sincerely approve, and sometimes made me look very grave, but she rallied me upon

my

my over great Nicety, as she termed it, mimicking the Countenance I put on, whenever she said any thing that I thought seemed too free, and by that Means obliged me to quit it for a Smile. Are we not alone, said she, and may we not, as we are of the same Sex, indulge a little Liberty in Conversation, by way of Compensation, for the severe Restraint we are obliged to put on ourselves before the Men.

This Woman was certainly the most artful Creature that ever was, as will appear by the Stratagem she had contrived to bring about, what by any other Means she imagined impracticable. As short as our Acquaintance was, she might easily be convinced I was virtuous —— I had no Men that visited me, I liv'd without doing any thing for my Support, so that all she could think was, that I was a young Widow in good Circumstances, and so much concern'd for the loss of my Husband, that I avoided all Company. I had been one Day at Church with her, where an Acquaintance of hers seeing me, became very much enamour'd with me; and, as it afterwards proved, engaged her to introduce him to my Company. But this was no easy thing for her to do, though in Order to effect it, she had for several Days press'd me to make one at *Quadrille* in her Apartment; but I plainly told her, I was resolved to make no new Acquaintance, and excepting herself, would see no Company; on which she gave over her Importunities; but not her Design upon me, the Baseness of which will presently appear, and the narrow Escape I had, I hope will be a Warning to my Sex, how they enter too precipitately into any Intimacy with Strangers.

In order to chear my Spirits, as she said, this insinuating Creature was continually filling my Glass with a small Muscadine Wine, the Flavour of which, notwithstanding my natural Temperance, pleas'd me so much, that I drank more than was customary with me. By Degrees I grew exceeding chearful, and at last went so far as a Song, which till then I had never done in her Company. Mademoiselle *Junia* was so delighted with the Sweetness of my Voice, or pretended to be so, that

I was eafily prevail'd upon to fing again ; and when I had done, well, faid fhe, you are certainly in the right to fhut yourfelf up from the Men, for if they once were acquainted with you, you would have no Truce from their Sollicitations

I was not indebted to her for this Compliment, but return'd it with equal Politenefs, and I am fure with much more Sincerity. After which, looking on me with a great deal of Sweetnefs, you little know how frolickfome I am, faid fhe; but as much as you praife me, and imagine yourfelf acquainted with my Shape and Air, I would venture any Wager you will not believe, prefently, that I am the real *Junia* your Friend. I offer'd to ftake on that Head ; no, no, returned fhe, I am certain of your lofing, and don't defire to win your Money. I'll tell you, therefore, before-hand, how I will difguife myfelf: I love prodigioufly to act the Part of a Man, my Woman can tell you how naturally I do it, and have a rich Suit for that Purpofe, whenever I have a Mind to be innocently merry.————I'll go and drefs myfelf, continued fhe, and you fhall hear how I can make Love. I burft out into a Fit of Laughter at the Oddity of this Whim ; but told her, that I was pofitive that whatever Difguife fhe put on, fhe would be always agreeable.

Juft as I was fpeaking, fomebody knock'd at the Door? Ah! my good God, cry'd fhe, who is this now, that comes to interrupt us? Go————continued fhe to her Chambermaid, fee who it is, I am not at home to any body but my dear *Saint Clare*————fhe will join with us in the Frolick ; but as for any other, make fome Excufe.

This Order made me eafy, for befides that I was not drefs'd, I had laid it down as a Rule, that I would fee no Company. The Lady whom *Junia* had mentioned enter'd immediately, and was fo agreeable, that I was not at all concern'd fhe had been admitted. Having been inform'd of the little Comedy her Friend was going to act ; I am glad of it, faid fhe, for though I have feen you do it a hundred Times, I believe, yet I fhould

never

never be weary: You cannot imagine, Madam, conti-
hued she, addressing herself to me, how very diverting
she is————you would swear she was a real Man.
About six Months ago, she 'was thus disguised in the
Country————made Love to a very pretty Woman,
who, knowing nothing of the Deception, was charm'd
with her in good earnest ; the unravelling the Mystery
was whimsical enough, for though she had resolv'd never
to marry, the Addresses of *Junia* gave her an Inclination
in Favour of the Sex; and in a Fortnight after, she became the Wife of one who for Years had pursued her in
vain.   This Story made me laugh, and begin to be impatient for the Proof how good a Mimick she was————
she did not make me wait long, for going into another
Room with her Maid, in order to dress as she said, left
Saint Clare to entertain me in the mean Time.

In less time than I expected out came a Gentleman
richly habited, he threw himself at my Feet, and behaved with all the Tenderness of the most respectful
Lover.————Mademoiselle *Saint Clare* laugh'd immoderately, and every Moment cry'd to me, does she not do
it excellently ; beyond Imagination, answer'd I ; but why
does she wear a Vizard ? If we had laid any Wager on
my not knowing her in this Habit, if that had not been
out of the Question, I should have taken the Liberty to
have drawn Stakes.   O ! said the other, she wears that
Mask, which is very handsome, to make the thing look
more natural ; we Women you know have always a
certain Modesty in our Faces, which does not agree with a
Masculine Habit.   This passed very well with me, and
I suffer'd my Gallant to press my Hands, and caress me
in a very amorous Manner ; on which growing more
bold, he put his Arm about my Waist, and I to revenge
myself attempted to pluck off his Mask, then seeming
offended at my Coyness he carried his Devoirs to *Saint
Clare*, then turned to me again ; while I suspecting no
manner of Deceit, suffer'd myself to be very much diverted with this Metamorphosis, for I believe near an
Hour ; but, good God! how was I thunderstruck,
when I heard the supposed *Junia* say to *Saint Clare*, I

am

am quite tired of this dumb Shew, for Heaven's sake contrive some way to put an End to it————she is a lovely Creature.

How ought I to bless Providence, who that Instant, frighted as I was, inspired me with a Presence of Mind to avoid the Snare laid for me. I found now the Trick put upon me, and that all had been a Pretence to introduce a Man, who could have no other than a dishonourable Intention, and this also manifesting what Company I was in, terribly alarm'd me : However, I shewed not the least Uneasiness, but under the Pretence of giving some Orders, which I had just then thought of, to *Barbara*, I went down Stairs, and being got into my Apartment, made all the Doors to be fast locked and bolted.

As I did not return, *Junia* came down, and knock'd at the Door; but my Aunt *Barbara*, to whom I had told the Story, refused to open it, saying I was not well and was going to Bed. The other insisted on speaking to me, as did Mademoiselle *Saint Clare* who also came down; but all their Entreaties were ineffectual, and they were obliged to go back.

Though I was very positive in my Mind, that it was really a Man whom *Junia* had substituted in her Place, yet I was resolved to be more assured that I did not wrong her by a false Conjecture; I sat up till I heard *Saint Clare* come down, and looking through the Keyhole, could perceive she was led by the very Person whom they would have imposed upon me for *Junia*: Though they spoke very low, I being very attentive, heard enough to convince me, my Ruin had been agreed upon, and to have been compleated that Night. I shudder'd while I reflected on the intended monstrous Piece of Villany, and resolved henceforward to be very circumspect, and always upon my Guard.

Junia, who no doubt expected to have been a considerable Gainer had her Plot succeeded, could not but be very much mortified at the Disappointment; she had the Assurance, as what will not Women of her Character attempt, to come the next Morning to make me a Visit, but *Barbara* would not admit her : She com-

plain'd

plain'd of this Ufage, and faid, fhe thought I had been a Woman of more Senfe, than to quarrel with her for a harmlefs Frolick ; all which I taking no Notice of, fhe wrote to me, but I fent her Letter back unopen'd ; and fhe, finding my Refentment was not to be appeas'd ; and, I fuppofe, fearing I might fpeak of this Adventure, fo as to have her manner of Life call'd in queftion, removed in three Days after from her Lodging, and I for fome time neither faw nor heard any thing of her.

I had now fufficient Matter to employ my Thoughts, I receiv'd two Letters, the one from the Camp, and the other from *Verfailles* ; as I could not imagine who fhould write to me from thence, having left no Acquaintance behind me, that I could fuppofe knew I was at *Paris,* my Curiofity prevail'd, even above my Love for the Marquis ; and though I paffionately long'd to hear fome News of him, yet the firft I open'd was that from *Verfailles,* where to my inexpreffible Aftonifhment I fourd thefe Lines.

The Marquis De L———V——— *to* Jeanetta de B———.

*I*N *vain you fly me———in vain flatter yourfelf with deceiving my Penetration———whatever Qnality you affume, or wherever you conceal yourfelf, I fhall always know where you are, and in what manner you pafs your Time.———I can eafily comprehend how much this will alarm you, and the Apprehenfions which muft naturally rife in you, at fo unexpeeted an Event ; but they ought to vanifh, when I give you my Word and Honour, that fo far from doing you a Prejudice, the Knowledge I have of you, fhall turn wholly to your Advantage.——— Believe me, beautiful Maid, I am more your Friend, than ever I was your Enemy, and inftead of punifhing you am refolved to fix your lafting Happinefs.——— Doubt not of what I fay,———a Man of my Age, and Charaeter in the World is above Deceit, and on no Confideration can be tempted to break a Promife once*

made.

made.————*Be you on your Part as sincere————*
an open Confidence in me will make me more your Friend,
than you can possibly imagine.————Above all things,
therefore, beware how you enter into any Measures that
the Fear of me may suggest. To morrow I *shall be at*
Paris, *where I expect you will not endeavour to avoid*
my Visit ; and as I am acquainted with your Virtue, it
will be your own Fault if you don't receive convincing
Proofs of the Value I set upon it.————One Trial more
is all you will be put to————I am much mistaken, if,
like Gold, you will not shine brighter by the Test, and
then, charming Jeanetta, *you will have Reason to bless the*
Channel which brought you to meet me at the Inn.

Your Godfather and Friend,

L————V————.

If my Reader does not here help me out with the
Force of Imagination, it will be impossible for any Description I am able to give, to form a true Idea of what
I felt after reading this Letter.————Heavens ! cry'd
I, have pity on me and assist me !————What can
have occasion'd so strange an Alteration ?————What
can be the old Marquis's Designs ?————How can he fix
my Happiness ?————What Trial is it he will make
me undergo ?————Ah, said I again, it is too plain
———— his Son has given me up ———— renounced
me, and to put a sure End to any future Claim I might
make, has barbarously sacrificed me to his Father's Re-
sentments————it must be so, continued I, this incensed Parent satisfied with this, lays aside his Hatred
and Revenge, and either through Generosity or Policy,
will settle me in such a manner, as to prevent any future Intercourse between me and my ungrateful Lover,
in case he should relent, and be willing to perform his
Vows.————This is what he calls fixing my Happiness,
and my well enduring it, is the Trial he mentions————
well then————let it be so————I no longer will attempt to fly from an unavoidable Destiny.————I will
submit with Fortitude and Patience to my Doom, and if
it

It be a Cloifter, will pafs the remainder of my Days in Warnings to my Sex, to beware of the faithlefs Vows of barbarous, inconftant Man!

These Exclamations were fucceeded by a Torrent of Tears, which gufh'd in fuch Abundance from my Eyes, that for fome time I had not Power to read my other Letter.——Nor, indeed, was my Impatience for the Contents, in any Proportion equal to what it had been; I expected to find in it nothing but Confirmations of the young Marquis's Ingratitude and Cruelty; however, I at laft ventured to open it, and received a frefh Subject for Tears and Complainings.

To the moft adorable *Jeanetta.*

I Should not till now have delay'd Writing, had I not hoped Day after Day to have received the News of fomething material to have acquainted you with; but none being yet arrived, the Apprehenfions of fufpecting me capable of neglecting what you fo earneftly recommended to me, has made me at laft take up my Pen, though I have nothing to fay, but what will be rather difagreeable than pleafing. However, to comply with my Promife of concealing nothing from you; in the firft Place, I was fo unhappy as not to meet the Marquis at my Arrival at the Camp, he being gone on a Expedition, on which at his own Requeft he was fent.———As he is not returned, all his Friends are in great Anxiety for his Safety, and they alfo inform me that he came hither overwhelm'd with a deep Melancholy, which he vainly endeavour'd to conceal; and it is fuppofed that it is owing to a Defire of diverting this inward Grief that he procured this Command.———I was not at a lofs to guefs the Caufe of his Affliction; you cannot but be fenfible, too lovely Jeanetta, of the great Share you have in it.———I beg, however, that you will not give way to Sorrow, 'tis poffible before this comes to your Hand, we may receive fome News of this dear Relation, and you may be affured of having it conveyed to you by a Courier, whom I will difpatch the Inftant.

It

It is suppofed the Campaign will be fhort, and that after a Battle, which is every Day expected, and much defired, we fhall be fent into Quarters. This Notion is very delightful to me, fince I fhall then have an Opportunity of being near you; for tho' in the prefent Circumftances, I trouble you with nothing relating to myfelf, be affured I can know no Happinefs equal to that of feeing you, nor any Merit above that of deferving by all manner of laudable Acts, your Friendfhip and Efteem. Thefe will ever be the Sentiments of him, who is,

With an unalterable Zeal,

Moft charming JEANETTA,

Your faithfully devoted,

SAINT FAL.

One is never fenfible onefelf how great our Tendernefs for a beloved Object is, till we are in Danger of lofing it————my Notion of War was certainly very imperfect, yet no fooner did I know the Marquis's Life was in Queftion, than my Imagination reprefented it with all its Horrors————O, Heaven! cried I, half drowned in Tears, why am I overwhelm'd with fo many Afflictions at once!————how fhall I be enabled to endure fuch a variety of Anguifh————O, grant my Lover to be fafe——protect him, blefs him, whatever fhall become of me——tho' he forfakes me——refolves no more to fee me, his Welfare fhall ever be the Wifh of my adoring Soul.

It would be too tedious to relate the thoufandth Part of what my Grief made me utter on this Occafion, I fear I have already made too much mention of my Tears; but the Time will come when I have nothing but Joys to entertain my Reader with, and this Truth demonftrated, that the Happinefs which Virtue obtains for us, can never be too dearly purchafed.

Although, I had fufficient Notice of the old Marquis's Vifit, to prepare myfelf for it, I found myfelf terribly confounded as the Time drew near; and when

he

he came, received him with, a Timidity which indeed was
fufficient to have excited his Pity, if he had not already,
as it afterwards proved, been already fo greatly pre-
poffeffed in my Favour, as to imagine, that let me do
what I would every thing became me.

As I was now affured he knew the vaft Difparity between us, is it poffible, my Lord, faid I, receiving him
with great Humility, and prefenting him a Chair, that
your Lordfhip can condefcend to fee me after the Difcovery you have made————to what am I indebted
for an Honour I am fo utterly unworthy of————and
in what manner fhall a poor Country-Maid, and one
who has been fo unhappy to incur your Difpleafure, be
able to look you in the Face ? Let us talk no more of
that, beautiful *Jeanetta*, replied he, making me fit down
————I have no longer the Caufes of Complaint I had
formerly againft you————I was mifled by the idle
Stories which I now find had no Foundation in them,
and your Virtue, of which I have received convincing
Proofs, has excited in me a due regard for the fair Pof-
feffor of it————a mean Birth is meerly cafual, and none
ought to be upbraided with it, but when Vice renders it
truly fo————a fine way of Thinking, and good Actions,
raifes the Peafant above the Prince, when Royalty degrades itfelf by a low Behaviour————you, *Jeanetta*,
are very fenfible of this Truth, and have regulated your
Conduct, fo as to wipe off all Remembrance whence·you
fprung————This, however, is not the Affair that
brought me hither, what I have to fay to you is of a
different Nature ; but before I explain myfelf any farther, I expect you will inform me with that Sincerity,
which is always the Attendant of Innocence and Honour,
upon what terms you are with my Son ; I have very
great Reafons for afking you this Queftion, and if you
give me a full and perfect Account, it will lay an Obligation on me more to your Advantage than you can
yet conceive.

From the Moment I received the Marquis's Letter,
and knew he intended to vifit me, I expected to fuffer
an infinite Shock from the Converfation I was to have

with

with him, so was the less alarmed at what he said to me, tho' on the most tender Point he could have hit upon.

It would be in vain, my Lord, answered I after a Moment's Pause, to deny that your Son has been dear to me; the amiable Qualities he is possest of, might have rendered him so to the noblest Maid, how then could a Girl like me resist the charming Condescension he made me in an Offer of his Heart?———Was it possible to refuse the Acceptance of a Treasure such as his Affection, and could I, ought I to return his Vows with indifference?

———Pardon me, my Lord, continued I, you have commanded me to give you a perfect Account, and I will disguise no Part of the Truth———I did love the Marquis, I might make use of the Word *Esteem* instead of *Love*, but I will not impose upon you ; I did love your Son with the utmost Sincerity, and had not his late Behaviour forbid it, I should still preserve the same Regard ;———I dare not say I do not still, even in spite of all the Reasons I have to the contrary, I do not pretend to know myself so well, as to be assured I either have, or ever can throw off a Tenderness, I once thought my Gratitude as well as Inclination obliged me to confess. This, my Lord, is all I can say, and Heaven and your own great Experience in the World, I hope, will make you see I have not dissembled with you.

The Tone with which I spoke these Words, and the Blushes that accompanied them, I believe pleaded very much in my Favour, however it were, the old Marquis appeared charmed with the manner in which I had expressed myself. This free Confession, said he, enhances the Esteem I before had for you———continue to treat me with the same Sincerity, and you may depend upon it, I shall never abuse the Confidence you repose in me ———I have but one thing more to be resolved in——— tell me, my pretty Creature, continued he, looking full in my Eyes, as if he would penetrate into the inmost Recesses of my Soul, tell me I say, what your Designs are, and own from whom you receive, wherewith to supply the Expences of your Living ? While my Son and Nephew were here, I could easily account for it ; but

but suppose you should never hear more from either of them, how will you be able to support yourself in the manner you have began ?———Look upon me, *Jeanetta*, as your Friend, and dissipate all Anxiety on my Account; I once more give you my solemn Promise, you have nothing to fear, and much to hope from the Sentiments you have now inspired me with, and did I not truly interest myself in your behalf, I would not enquire into these Particulars.

After most humbly thanking him for the Goodness he was pleased to express for me, alas ! my Lord, said I, with a Sigh, I here must acknowledge the Imprudence of my Conduct; my Reason has often reproached me with it ; and it was with great Difficulty Monsieur the Count *de Saint Fal* prevailed on me to accept of the Tokens of the most disinterested Friendship that ever was——— some Time ago, I was determined to pass my Days in a Convent, and more than once press'd him to assist my Intentions ; but his Persuasions have detained me hitherto. You always talk of my Nephew, interrupted the Marquis, whom you do not love, yet never mention my Son in the Provision made for you. Yet its more reasonable to attribute your little Revenue to him than the Count *de Saint Fal.*

My Lord, answered I, Heaven prosper me as I speak with Sincerity, I will not absolutely say the Marquis has had no share in what has been done for me ; but this I affirm, that whatever I have received hitherto has been from your Nephew's Hands, as so much lent to me, and to be repaid by me, if ever Fortune should put it in my Power———a Train of Events continually alarming me made me accept his Generosity, and prevented my coming to any Determination how to dispose of myself.

Say no more, beautiful *Jeanetta*, replied the Marquis, I pretend not to call your Conduct in Question, I am convinced, more than you can be sensible of, that it has been without Reproach ; and assure you I am so far from desiring you should be shut up in a Monastery, that I would be the first to oppose it———excuse therefore the Questions I have put to you, an exact Examination into

your

your Affairs, was highly neceffary for me, in order to perfect the great Defigns I have for your Advantage—you have anfwered me in the manner I wifhed, and expected from the Idea I had conceived of your Honour and Veracity————I was infpired with an Efteem for you the firft Moment I beheld you, nor is it at all leffen'd fince the Difcovery who you were————Unknowing you, I hated you; but knowing you, am become an Admirer of your Virtue————rank me therefore among the Number of your Friends, or rather believe me the Chief of them————you will find me fo in the End——wait therefore with Patience the refult————I leave you at prefent, but in two Days you fhall hear from me, and as I come often to *Paris*, and fometimes pafs whole Weeks here, will be a conftant Vifiter.

With thefe Words he rofe from his Chair, and having pafs'd fome Compliments on my Shape and Air, and told me that he intended to invite me to Dinner fome Day to have the Pleafure of hearing me fing again, he took his leave, and left me in an Aftonifhment impoffible to be expreffed.

What indeed could I think of this Adventure! to find a Man who had expreffed himfelf with fo much Bitternefs againft me, and feemed impatient for my Ruin, changed at once into my Friend, anxious for my Good, and fatisfied with every Thing I did, an Alteration I fay, fo fudden, fo undreamt of might well appear a Myftery—was I not the fame *Jeanetta* for whofe fake his Son has twice endangered his Life, and who has coft him fo much Trouble, what had I done to merit, that the Deteftation he fo lately had for me, fhould be converted into fo great a liking?————I was fometimes tempted to imagine the little Beauty I was Miftrefs of had made him entertain Sentiments for me, which would have been no lefs a Misfortune than his Indignation had been; but then, when I reflected on the Praifes he had beftowed upon my Virtue and good Conduct, I could not think he had any aim to deftroy what he feemed fo much to value me for.

This

This laſt Conſideration gave me ſome Peace, and I was reſolved to wait the Event of thoſe great things he had made me hope, and ſhould it even prove that he had any diſhonourable Intentions toward me, to truſt in Heaven's Protection which had never yet abandoned me.

My Thoughts being a little more ſettled, I ſat down to anſwer Monſieur *De Saint Fal*'s Letter, but before I began, hearing ſome Voices on the Stairs, the Sound of which very much ſurprized me, I roſe haſtily, and looking through the Key-hole, immediately ſaw my Father and Mother embracing my Aunt————had I followed the firſt Dictates of my natural Affection, I ſhould have ran and thrown myſelf into their Arms, but the remembrance how improper ſuch a Diſcovery would be at this Time, checked that Impulſe, and I drew back and threw myſelf on a Settee, to conſider within myſelf what was beſt for me to do.

Neither my Love nor Duty would have ſuffered me to let them depart without ſeeing them, and as Time had made a very great Alteration in me, not only as to my Stature, but my Features alſo, which joined to the vaſt Difference in my Dreſs and Behaviour, made me pretty poſitive they would not know me, and in this Aſſurance rang my Bell for *Barbara*. She came in looking a little perplexed, and I aſking her the Occaſion of it, ſhe told me that ſhe hoped I would not be offended, for that having wrote to her Brother and Siſter the Happineſs ſhe enjoyed in my Service, they were now come to viſit her, ſome Buſineſs having brought them to *Paris*. No, no, anſwered I, ſo far from being offended, that I am glad you like your Place, and will make your Relations welcome : pray tell them they muſt dine with me. O, Madam ! cried ſhe, your Ladyſhip is too good———— ſuch an Honour is not for ſuch poor People as they are. I will have it ſo, returned I, therefore let me have their Company while you are getting Dinner ready————I aſſure you I long to ſee them. My poor Aunt went out of the Room quite tranſported at the Favour I ſhewed to her, and obeyed my Commands.

My

My Heart was in a violent, tho' not unpleasing Agitation, at the Sight of those who gave me Being; but I suffered a great deal from the Homage they paid me, and did all I could to put an end to it.

At last, by telling them I was an enemy to all kind of Ceremony, and that if they meant to oblige me it must be by treating me in a familiar Manner, I prevailed with them to sit down————the prejudice of my supposed Superiority made them however very fearful of speaking, and I should never have got out of them what I wanted to be informed of, if I had not luckily put them on talking of the Village where they lived; I told them I had past through it some time ago in a visit I made at the Castle, where I had stayed several Months: My Mother on hearing this appeared like a Person who was endeavouring to call something to Mind, and looking earnestly on me, said, that ever since she came into the Room, she imagined she had seen me somewhere, but could not recollect; but on my mentioning the Castle, she no longer doubted but that it had been with Madam the Countess *de N*————my Father said the same thing, and added, that things had been strangly changed since the Count's Death. I then asked him what was become of the Countess, to which he replied, that she lived with her Daughter Madamoiselle *de Elbieux*, now Madam *de Estival*. O Heaven! cried I, is she married, and as ill-humoured as ever? Yes, Madam, said he, I find your Ladyship knows her————sure never was a worse Woman in the World————she has quarrelled twice with her Husband, and enough to do there was to make it up again between them; but the third Time she carried Things to such a height, that he was obliged to part from her; but unfortunately for him he had put so much in her Power, that this Separation has left him in very ill Circumstances, but he chose rather to suffer any thing than live with her. To this, my Father added, that she lived not above three Miles from *Paris*, where she always passed the Winter Season, and that every body, even her own Servants, held her in Detestation.

The

The many Misfortunes this Woman's Cruelty had brought on me, made me curious to know the Particulars of her Hiftory, and I cannot boaft of fo forgiving a Nature, as not to be pleas'd with hearing thofe who injure me without a Caufe, have in their turn alfo fomething to complain of————I am fenfible of this Fault, and lay it as a Penance on myfelf, to confefs it in this publick Manner.

I had no fooner teftified my Defire of hearing in what Manner Madam *D'Eftival* had behaved, and the Circumftances that attended her Marriage, than my Father readily obliged me with the Detail, which tho' given in his ruftic Way, was perfectly intelligible to me ; but I fhall prefent my Reader with it in my own Words.

The Hiftory of Madamoifelle D'ELBIEUX, and Monfieur D'ESTIVAL.

AS long as Monfieur the Count *de N*————lived, Madamoifelle *D'Elbieux* his Daughter kept herfelf within tolerable Bounds, fearing his Severity, as having experienced it, on the firft Difcovery fhe made of her perverfe Inclinations. But he was no fooner laid in Earth, then fhe gave a loofe to all that the Badnefs of her Heart fuggefted————Her Quality, her Youth, the Reputation of her Wit, but above all the vaft Fortune fhe was then in Poffeffion off, attracted a great Number of Admirers. She had Vanity enough to pride herfelf in the Crowd who daily made their Court, but her greateft Pleafure was in creating Quarrels among them : No lefs than ten Duels were fought on her Account. She received all the Addreffes made to her with fo much feeming Sweetnefs, that every one imagined himfelf the happy Man ; but fhe no fooner found fhe had engaged the Heart, than fhe began to change the Encouragement fhe had given into

Difdain,

Difdain, and acted with fo much Infolence and Tyranny, that at length fhe faw herfelf abandoned by all but one. This unfortunate Gentleman, who truly loved her, and had befides great Intereft in the Match, ftill perfevered, and fhe continued to treat him with a fhew of Affection, much longer than fhe had done any of his Rivals.

This Gentleman had an Eftate within twelve Miles of the Caftle, belonging to the Countefs *De N*———, and this near Neighbourhood gave him an Opportunity of vifiting there very often——He was tall, handfome, well made, and had an Air of Grandeur, which was very engaging————Madamoifelle *D'Elbieux* was highly pleafed with having a Lover, for whom fhe knew feveral of her Acquaintance figh'd in vain: But I cannot think a Soul like hers capable of being influenced by that tender Paffion ; fhe might perhaps *Like*, but not *Love*, and the Event has fhewn I am not deceived. She left no Arts untryed to fecure him, but as foon as he was fo, refign'd herfelf entirely to Caprice and Ill-humour ; always reftlefs and mifchevious, fhe took a Pride in perplexing and rendring him uneafy, and found the means of doing it, in as ample a Manner, as her Propenfity to it made her wifh.

The Countefs her Mother, as I obferved in the beginning of thefe Memoirs, was naturally gay, and tho' pretty much advanced in Years, was very well pleafed to be told fhe was handfome : Monfieur *D'Eftival*, for fo her Daughter's Lover was called, eafily perceived this Foible in her, and did not fail to humour it, as he thought her Intereft would be very effential towards haftening the Match, which for many Reafons he was ambitious of, and which as the young Lady now behaved, he began to be in doubt of.

The Countefs was highly delighted with the fine things he faid to her, and the more fo, as he was now the only Perfon who entertained her in that Manner. Madamoifelle *D'Elbieux*, who was no Stranger to her Mother's amorous Inclinations, took a wicked Pleafure in heightning them in Favour of Monfieur *D'Eftival*, by continu-

aily

ally telling her of the Encomiums he made on her Wit and Beauty————He makes his Addresses indeed to me, cried the artful Creature, but I can see very well that if he durst to lift his Hopes to your Ladyship, he would much rather have me for a Daughter, than a Wife.

The Countess's Vanity, flattering her into a Belief that it might really be as her Daughter said, and approving of Monsieur *D'Epival's* Person, from that Moment began to treat him with an extraordinary Respect, mixed with some Share of Tenderness; while on the other Hand Madamoiselle *D'Elbieux* grew also still more kind to him, and pretending that her Mother's Consent was absolutely necessary for their Marriage, told him that the only Way to gain it was to feign a Passion for her. You are very certain, said she, of not being taken at your Word, even tho' you should carry it so far as to offer Marriage, but tho' part all soft Desires, she has still a Stock of Pride, that will not suffer her to have any Friendship for a Man, who she thinks prefers any Woman, even her own Daughter, to herself. This I assure you has been the true Reason of my continuing 'till now unmarried————I have been obliged to reject all the Offers have been made me, because not one of those who have done me the honour to address me, have found out my Mother's Foible, which if I betray to you, you ought to look upon it as a Proof of my peculiar Regard, since I have never done it to any before.

D'Epival believing all she said on this score, was so transported at this Testimony of her Condescension in his Favour, that he threw himself at her Feet, acknowledging the Honour she did him, with the most sincere Affection: and in Obedience to her Commands, redoubled his Assiduities to the Countess, in such a Manner, that every body imagined him her Lover. She, who was easily deceived on that Article, now plumed herself in the belief her Charms had lost nothing of their former Force, since they had captivated the Heart of a young Gentleman, who came at first to her House, with a view of addressing her Daughter, and could not be ungrateful for the Deference he paid her.

To

To like the Love, is a great Step towards liking the Lover, her Heart grew compassionate to the Pains she supposed herself to have created in his, and at last she confess'd to him, that he was not indifferent to her. Mademoiselle *D'Elbieux* by her Mother's Pensiveness guess'd what Sentiments she was possest of, and pleas'd herself with the Perplexity in which she should now involve both her Mother and Lover. Never had she any real Satisfaction but in giving disquiet to others, and as she did not want Wit was seldom at a loss for Opportunities, to indulge this wicked Impulse of a perverse and vitiated Disposition.

She now began to receive Monsieur *D'Estival* with Coldness, and on his complaining in a tender Manner of this change in her Behaviour, with Scorn, and Insolence. As he little imagined the Occasion, having done nothing but what her own Commands obliged him to, Jealousy took Possession of his Heart, and made him recollect that of late his Mistress had treated with Civility a certain Gentleman, who lived also in the Neighbourhood, called Monsieur *Destourneaux*, a vain, gay, fluttering Coxcomb, vers'd in little else than the Art of Defamation, and in that excell'd sufficiently, to make his Company acceptable sometimes to a Woman of Mademoiselle *D'Elbieux*'s Humour.

Such as he was, however, the Reception he met with at the Castle, gave Monsieur *D'Estival* an infinity of Pain ; he observed every Motion of his supposed Rival, and the Passion he was now inflamed with, having this peculiar Quality of representing every thing its own Way, the more Pains he took to be assured made him the less so, and as he truly loved the Lady, exclusive of her Fortune, he suffered all that can be imagined in such a Circumstance. Mademoiselle *D'Elbieux* presently discovered his Disquiet, and the Motive ; she gloried in it, and to encrease her Triumph over this unhappy and too constant Lover, carried her Complaisance to *Destourneaux* even to a seeming Fondness.

The Countess *De N———* was in a quite different Situation ; she had given Encouragement to the pretended Addresses of Monsieur *D'Estival*, but finding them cease on a fudden, and her fuppofed Lover grown extremely melancholy, fhe took an Opportunity when they were alone together, to afk the meaning of fo ftrange an Alteration in his Behaviour ; on which, Madam, faid he, I fhould little deferve to have the Paffion I profefs be believed fincere, if I could without the utmoft Anxiety behold the favourable Reception of a Rival. O Heavens! cried the Countefs, what is it you mean ? whom do you fee entertained here that can give you any Uneafinefs. Ah, Madam ! replied he, too well your Ladyfhip is acquainted with the Caufes of my Defpair————why will you therefore cruelly compel me to mention a Name fo hateful to me————But, O good Heaven, continued he in the utmoft Agony, in what does *Deflourneaux* merit the Encouragment he is bieft with.

Deflourneaux, faid fhe interrupting him haftily, is it poffible the Vifits of that Trifler can give you Pain ? but to convince you of your Error, I will fend to forbid him ever coming here any more————and be affured, that to render you eafy and contented, would do the fame by thofe infinitely more worthy of my Efteem.

Monfieur *D'Eftival* thought himfelf fo much obliged by this Promife, that he threw himfelf at the Countefs's Feet, and kifs'd her Hands, with an Eagernefs which might well be taken for the Effects of Love, as indeed it was, tho' not for the Object in prefence. Madamoifelle *D'Elbieux* came that Moment into the Room, and furprized her Lover in that Pofture, and imagining fhe was herfelf the Dupe of her own Plot, and that by counterfeiting an Affection for her Mother, he had work'd himfelf up into a real Paffion for her, was ftung to the very Soul, and fhe flew out of the Room, muttering fomething which was not very pleafing to the Countefs, who rofe haftily from her Seat, in Order to follow her, and give her fome Tokens of her Refentment————Monfieur *D'Eftival* perceiving the Fury fhe was in, kept her from going out of the Room, and in endeavouring as he thought to appeafe her, let fall fome Words, which let her into the Secret of his Behaviour, and that fhe had been but the Property of his Defigns on her Daughter. This Difco-

very

very put her into a very great Confusion, and she sat down again without being able to speak. *D'Estival* asked very respectfully if he had been so unhappy as to have done any thing to offend her. No, Monsieur, answered she, but I have something in my Bosom which I cannot be easy 'till I disburden myself of——tell me, therefore, continued she, if you have dealt sincerly with me, and if you have not, let me no longer be a Stranger to the Motive which engag'd you to deceive me——in fine, am I to depend on the Professions you have so often made me of Love, or am I not.

What a Perplexity was now this poor Gentleman in, he had been made to believe that nothing would engage the Countess to favour his Addresses to her Daughter, but imagining he gave the Preference to herself; to confess the Truth therefore, he thought would ruin all he had so long been endeavouring to bring about, and how to persevere in his pretended Passion he knew not, for fear, as there was but too much Probability, she should take him at his Word : Madam, answered he after a pretty long Pause, I can see no cause for your Ladyship's harbouring any doubt of my Sincerity. The Countess De N— ought to know herself too well, to doubt if any Charms can come in Competition with those she is Mistress of.

Well, replied she, I am willing to believe your Passion represents me such as you say ; and confess to you in my turn, that I look upon no Man in the World so worthy as Monsieur *D'Estival* ; but yet we ought not to enter into Engagements, which we should hereafter have Reason to repent——we are both of us past five and twenty, and should well weigh the Consequences of things of this Nature——to be plain with you, Monsieur, I have a very great Affection for my Daughter, and will never consent to marry to her Prejudice ; so as I would make her happy, and you also, I offer you your Choice, either to take me with only my bare Dowry, or her with the vast Estate, which by the Death of her Father, and the Retirement of her Brother, is now devolved on her ; for I have always promised her, and will not break my Word, that whenever I marry, she shall be immediately put in

possession

poſſeſſion of all the Wealth I am poſſeſt of——if your Paſſion ſtill continues, to give me the Preference even under theſe Diſadvantages, you have nothing to do, but publiſh the *Banns* of Matrimony ; if the Riches of my Daughter outbalances your regard for me, then prepare for your Nuptials with her : I leave you to reflect on what I have ſaid, and expect your deciſive Anſwer to-morrow about this Time.

With theſe Words ſhe went out of the Room, leaving Monſieur *D'Eſtival* in a Conſternation that is not eaſy to be expreſs'd ; he was ſo poſſeſt with what Mademoiſelle had told him, concerning her Mother's Caprice, that he was ſometimes ready to believe ſhe offered herſelf to him in this Manner only to try him, and that if he feigned to fix his Choice on her, with the Diſadvantages ſhe mentioned, that ſhe would then give her Daughter to him, contenting herſelf with the Vanity of having it to ſay ſhe had refuſ'd him. The Affair however ſeem'd ſo nice, and ſo much depended on the Anſwer he was to give, that it involved him in a moſt terrible Dilemma, and he went out of the Caſtle, ruminating on the Adventure, and full of diſturb'd Emotions.

Madamoiſelle *D'Elbieux* hapened to be at her Chamber Window, and ſaw his Coach drive through the Court-Yard ; as he had not uſed to quit the Caſtle without taking leave of her, ſhe imagined it the Conſequence of what ſhe had ſeen, and grew more confirm'd than before, that her Mother had ſupplanted her in his Affection——'till now ſhe knew not that ſhe loved him, but no ſooner did ſhe imagine he was devoted to her Mother, than ſhe thought herſelf the moſt unhappy Creature in the World, in the loſs of her Lover, who now appeared ſo amiable in her Eyes. Hurry'd with all the Impatience of Love, Jealouſy, Deſpair and Revenge, ſhe reſolved to omit nothing that might gratify each of thoſe outragious Paſſions, tho ſhe ſhould trample under Foot all the Rules of Duty, and of Decency.

Even her darling Pride was now no more remembered——*D'Eſtival* muſt be regain'd, and her Mother mortified, whatever ſhould be the Event ; ſhe then ſat herſelf down

3 and

and wrote a little Billet to him, in which she told him, that intending to go very early the next Morning before the Countess was stirring, to visit a Relation at a Monastery about a League distant, she desired he would meet her in the Road, having something to impart to him, that it was absolutely necessary he should know, and which she added, she believed would not be disagreeable to him to hear.

This she entrusted to the Care of a Farmer's Son who was frequently about the Castle, charging him to be secret, and bring her an immediate Answer ; to engage his Fidelity she gave him a handsome Reward, and promised him yet more at his Return. The young Fellow, for all his Simplicity, was sensible of the Consequence of what he was about to do, and dreading the Countess's Displeasure if it should ever be discovered, that he had a Hand in carrying on such an Affair without her Knowledge, thought it was best to go upon sure Grounds, and resolved to shew her the Letter.

Accordingly he did so, assuring her Ladyship, that though her Daughter should resent it never so much, he would hazard every thing rather than disoblige her.

The Countess highly prais'd his Honesty, gave him a handsome Gratuity, and promised that Mademoiselle *D'Elbieux* should never have any Reason to suspect he had betrayed her Secret. On opening the Letter, she was amazed at the Appointment she found it contain'd, and in order to penetrate into the Motive of it, she determin'd to write another, and send it instead of her Daughter's. She made use of the same Words, only changed the Time and Place, appointing an Ally in her own Park, which had a Door that opened into the Garden, and the Hour 12 at Night, instead of early in the Morning.

When this was ready she sent it by the young Peasant, and order'd him to bring to her whatever Answer Monsieur *D'Estival* should send ; after he was gone, she began to consider in what manner she should behave, in an Affair in which she had a double Concern.————She doubted not but it was owing to the Posture, in which

her

her Daughter had found *D'Eſtival*, that ſhe wrote to deſire this private Conference; but then if he ſhould comply with her Aſſignation, as ſhe ſometimes feared he would, in what Faſhion to reſent it ſeem'd to her very difficult to reſolve. But as no Judgment could be form'd till his Anſwer arriv'd, ſhe was oblig'd to wait the Event.

The Peaſant in the mean Time was highly delighted with his own Conduct, not doubting but he ſhould alſo be paid by the Lover for his Trouble, and went merrily on his Errand; but in the way happening to meet with an Acquaintance, went into a Cabaret, where drinking too plentifully he fell aſleep, and awoke not till it was dark. He reproached himſelf not a little for this Negligence, but thought to make up his loſs of Time by his haſte, and invent ſome Excuſe to the Ladies for having ſtaid ſo long.

The Hurry he was now in, occaſion'd him to miſtake his way, and happened to take that Road, which led to the Houſe of Monſieur *Deſlourneaux*, having never been either there or at Monſieur *D'Eſtival's*, he was only guided by the Directions he had received; and ſeeing before him a great Court-Yard, which had a row of Elms leading up to it, he imagined himſelf right, and went directly to the Gate, and enquired of the Servant who open'd it, if his Maſter was at Home, and being anſwer'd in the affirmative, ſent the Letter into him deſiring a ſpeedy Anſwer.

The Counteſs, in the hurry of Spirits ſhe had been in, forgot to put a Superſcription, which gave it very much the Air of a Myſtery to this Gentleman.———The Contents, however, ſeem'd yet more ſo: To be wrote to in that familiar Stile, and deſired to meet a young Lady of Mademoiſelle's Quality and Character, was an Honour he could little expect; and had he not been vain enough to think every thing was due to his Merit, he would from the beginning have imagined there was ſome Miſtake in the Affair.

But, as I ſaid before, Self-Sufficiency kept him from once thinking on any ſuch thing, and he order'd the
Meſſenger

Meffenger to acquaint the Lady who fent him, that he thank'd her for the Honour fhe did him, and that he would not fail the Time and Place appointed.

It was very late before he return'd, and both the Countefs and her Daughter fuffer'd not a little from their Impatience; the former to prevent her feeing the Fellow before her, had order'd Mademoifelle *Du Parc* her Woman, to watch for him at the Poftern, and this old Waiting-Woman was too diligent, not to conduct him into her Lady's Clofet, without Mademoifelle *D'Elbieux* feeing him.

The Countefs no fooner was told that *D'Eftival* would obey the Summons, than fhe wrote a little Note in his Name to her Daughter, entreating fhe would give him a Meeting that Night, having confider'd that the Morning would render her more liable to be obferved, and then named the Park-Gate. This fhe order'd the Fellow to give to her Daughter, as from the Gentleman to whom he had been fent.

'Tis eafily perceived that the Countefs laid this Plot, in order to be near the Place of Meeting, that by the Converfation they fhould have together, fhe might difcover the real Sentiments of Monfieur *D'Eftival*, fo went thither fomewhat before the Hour prefixed, and ftood concealed behind a great Tree, in cafe the Moon fhould happen to fhine out, and thereby endanger a Difcovery.

Mademoifelle *D'Elbieux* on the other Hand was extremely punctual, and came accompanied by her Maid, who was in the Secret: They fat down on a Bank near the Gate, and cough'd by way of Signal to *D'Eftival*, if it fhould happen that he were already near the Place: They waited not long before a Ruftling among the Trees made them not doubt, but the expected Perfon was approaching; on which the Confidante of Mademoifelle *D'Elbieux* ftepp'd forward, and faid, Monfieur, fpeak low, in Cafe any Wanderers fhould happen to be in the Park. The fuppofed *D'Eftival* anfwer'd that he would be wary, and prefenting her his Hand, fhe led him to her Miftrefs.

The

The Obfcurity of the Night happened to be fuch, as to render it impoffible for any Objects to be difcern'd, fo they were both oblig'd to content themfelves with faying a thoufand endearing things, without being able to converfe with thofe true Intelligencers of the Heart, the Eyes. *Deflourneaux* told her how happy he thought himfelf in this Opportunity of entertaining her, and fwore he adored her beyond all things upon Earth: on which fhe interrupted him, by faying, hold, Monfieur, I will not liften to one Word you tell me on this Score, till you inform me truly on what Terms you are with my Mother.;——'tis to be convinced of that from your own Mouth, I appointed this private Meeting, and will never fee you more, if you comply not with what I defire.————Therefore, tell me, if you have any real Paffion for her, I fhall be far from being any Bar to your Defigns.

Nothing could be more amazing than this Difcourfe was, to the Perfon to whom it was made.——Heavens! Madam, cry'd he, I a Paffion for the Countefs———— can you imagine me ftupid enough to doat upon Antiquity————can fhe have any other Merit in my Eyes, than being the Mother of the fineft Creature in the World?————No, no, Madam, her Charms have long fince been faded, and if fhe imagines her Paint, falfe Curls, and affected Airs have any Influence over me, fhe but deceives herfelf————one only Woman I love, and that is your beautiful Self.

Had he been Mafter of all the Eloquence of the greateft Orator that ever was, he could not fo well have pleafed Mademoifelle *D'Elbieux*, as he did in thefe ill-natured Reflections on her Mother : Malice was a Regale peculiarly adapted to her Tafte, and fo far from interrupting him, that fhe let him go on with many other, and more grofs Epithets if poffible, on her who had given her Birth. At laft, well, but, faid fhe, all this is not fufficient to fatisfy me ; for I am credibly inform'd you are under fecret Engagements.

Thefe

These Words ſtruck a Damp on the Gaiety of *Deſiourneaux*; when ſhe had mentioned the Counteſs, he was not at all alarmed at her Suſpicions becauſe they had no Foundation, and he knew very well how to clear himſelf; but this Gentleman had been weak enough to give his Hand to a Woman of mean Birth, and worſe Fame, which having immediately repented of, he was obliged to allow her a conſiderable Share of his little Fortune, in order to prevail with her to keep it a Secret.————— Imagining, therefore, by what Mademoiſelle *D'Elbieux* laſt ſaid, that ſhe had made a Diſcovery of his Marriage, he was extremely at a Loſs what to ſay.

The Lady taking his Silence as an Effect of his Guilt.————I find, ſaid ſhe, that what I accuſe you of is but too juſt, and you are now ſeeking ſome plauſible Excuſe for it;————but all you can ſay will be in vain, I'll never ſee you more. She was turning away, when *Deſiourneaux* took hold of her Hand, and gently drew her back ————Pardon me, my Angel, cry'd he, that I heſitated one Moment to lay open all my Soul to you. ————I feared to mention what, ſince you are ſo good to bleſs me with your Favour, I look on as my great Unhappineſs and Shame;————but I will now own to you, that I am, indeed, under a ſecret Engagement. ————I was unwarily drawn in, and am——————married ————Married! ſaid Mademoiſelle *D'Elbieux*. Yes, Madam, replied he; but as the Ceremony was not according to the Forms which ought to be obſerved on ſuch Occaſions, I can eaſily be reliev'd from it.

Wretch! reſumed ſhe, haſtily interrupting him, haſt Thou the Inſolence to hope I will ever regard thee after ſuch an Action.————No, no, proclaim your Nuptials ————be the Jeſt of all who know you, and the Object of my eternal Hate.

With theſe Words ſhe burſt haſtily from him, and flew toward the Gate, with too much Precipitation for him to have overtaken her, had the Surprize he was in permitted him to attempt it. He now curſed himſelf for his frank Confeſſion, and quitted the Park with as
much

much Mortification, as he had entered it with Pleasure.

The Countess could not but be heartily dejected, she had
heard the Man she loved speak of her in the most contemptible Terms, and her own Daughter seemed delighted
with his Bitterness against her; but all the Indignation
she conceived at this unworthy Treatment, was short of
her Astonishment at his pretending to be married to
her; and she returned to the Castle full of Perplexity
and Perturbation.

Thus was every one deceived by the Darkness of the
Night, and the Exchange of the Letters. The Countess never once thought it could be any other than *D'Estival*, whom she had heard with her Daughter.————
Deslourneaux went away, not doubting but he was the
Person for whom the Appointment was intended————
and Mademoiselle *D'Elbieux*, assured that her Mother
was married to *D'Estival*, though he now repented of
it.————All these Mistakes could not but produce very
odd Circumstances; but I must beg my Reader's Patience for a while: Dinner being brought in as my Father
was in this Part of the Story, interrupted him from prosecuting it, and after that other Accidents intervened,
which prevented my being told the Sequel till a long
time afterward.

While we were at Table, I long'd prodigiously to
hear what they would say of my Self, and would fain
have mentioned that Niece, of whom I had hear *Barbara* talk, but knew not how to do it without appearing too much interested; especially, as I saw both my
Father and my Mother, look very much and earnestly
on me, as often as they could do it without being rude.
But *Barbara* eas'd me of this Inquietude, by asking
them, as she was setting on the Desert, whether they
had been able to hear yet what was become of me.
Alas! no, Sister, said my Mother with a deep Sigh————.
we are entirely ignorant where she is at present————
some time ago we were told she was in a Monastery; but
that on Mademoiselle *D'Elbieux* happening to come

there,

there, she was taken suddenly away, and I can't find
any body that has ever seen her since.

Perceiving the Discourse was like to end here, I revived it, by asking how it was possible a Daughter
should neglect acquainting her Parents with the Place of
her Abode.————Sure, added I, you must have used
her very unkindly, or she could not be guilty of so
much Disobedience. No, Madam, cry'd my Father,
far from it————on the contrary, she was used with too
much Fondness, and that has been her Ruin ————
She was always suffer'd to have her own Will, and to
that we owe all the Vexation she has brought upon us
————where she is, or how she spends her Time no-
body knows; but she'll one Day answer for all the
Tears she has cost her poor Mother————for my
Part I am come to a Resolution never to trouble myself
any more about her; but e'en abandon her to her unhappy Fate.

Good Husband, don't talk so, reply'd my Mother,
wiping away the Tears, that in spite of her trickled
down her Cheeks, I hope she will see the Error of her
Ways one Day:————Besides, we don't know the
Truth of Things————she may not be so wicked as
People say.————I am sure her Inclinations were virtuous, and if she does not write to us, it may be because
she is in some Place where she is not permitted, or has
no Conveniency————we ought to condemn no-body
without hearing them, much less our own Child. You
are much in the right, Sister, said my poor good-natured
Aunt, the Girl may make a good Woman yet, for all
the Stories told of her.————One does not know what
may have happened, and should always judge the best.

I like you, said I, for taking your Niece's Part, there
is no judging by Appearances, and if it should one Day
be proved that she is wrong'd, it would inflict a lasting
Remorse on those, who have censured her Actions, without knowing the Motive of them.

Your Ladyship is excellently good, cry'd my Mother,
to have so favourable an Opinion of my poor *Jeanetta:* I

do

do affure you, Madam, fhe would not have fpoke in the manner thofe do, who accufe her, if they had been guilty of worfe things than can be laid to her Charge. My dear Mother melted into Tears as fhe utter'd thefe Words, and my Eyes that Inftant meeting hers, Nature exerted itfelf, and excited a Sympathy in my Heart, which, unable to reftrain fhewing fome Tokens of, I made a Pretence of going into my Clofet, and ftaid there till I had recover'd my felf.

I could hear my Father chide her, for giving fuch a loofe to her Tendernefs before a Lady of my Quality, and fhe excus'd herfelf by faying, fhe fancied there was fuch a Refemblance between me and her poor *Jeavetta*, that it was impoffible for her to forbear. My Father own'd he was of the fame Opinion, and if he durft would have mention'd it before.

After this they began to afk my Aunt who I was, and in what manner I lived: fhe told them that I was of very high Birth to be fure, for at Court where fhe had been with me, nothing but People of Quality, all my Relations fhe believ'd, came to vifit me; and as to my Behaviour I was a perfect Nun, and fo good humour'd and fo generous, that fhe did not think my equal was to be found in the whole World. My Parents congratulated her good Fortune; and then began to inform her, how very far from being happy they were, being fcarce able to fubfift, feveral of their Sheep having been devour'd by the Wolves, and two Cows, which were their main Support, ftolen from them. This pierced me to the Heart, and made me prefently fet about contriving how I might relieve their Neceffities, without difcovering myfelf, or giving any room for Sufpicion.

After having confider'd on the Matter fome little time, I return'd to them, and took an Occafion of telling them I was very fond of the Country, and as foon as I had finifh'd fome little Affairs, intended to pafs a few Weeks in fome pleafant retired Part. Ah, Madam, cry'd *Barbara*, your Ladyfhip cannot find a fweeter

Place

Place in all *France*, than the Village of *D——* in *Fountainbleau*—— there is not a better Air, nor a finer Prospect any where.—— Your Ladyship eats nothing here ; but if you would once go there, I'd venture my Life you'd have a good Appetite.

Well, said I, 'tis very likely I may make tryal of it : I am ordered to drink Milk for the Recovery of my Health, and if your Brother and Sister will be so good to comply with what I desire, I will think on no other Place but their Village ——— Be so good, cry'd my Aunt, quite transported ! Ah, Madam, i'll answer for them, you need only let them know your Commands ———— Both my Parents seconded what she said, and added, they should think themselves highly honour'd to serve me.

I am much oblig'd to you, answer'd I ; in the first Place, I will lodge at your House ; but I must desire you will buy me two young Cows that the Milk may be better. I will also give you Money to furnish a Chamber for me, and as I am fond of Country Amusements, you must purchase a little Flock of Sheep. It was pleasant enough to observe the Countenances my Father, Mother, and Aunt put on when they heard me speak in this manner ;———— but I gave them not time to reply, for plucking my Purse out of my Pocket, I counted out seventy-five *Lewis D'Ors* upon the Table : And when they had seen the Sum, I gathered it up together, and wrapp'd it in a Piece of Paper, then put it into my Mother's Hand ; I depend on you, said I, good Mademoiselle *B*——— to get the Cows, the Sheep, and the Chamber against I come. The Confusion I was in was so great, at being obliged to receive all the Acknowledgments their Gratitude poured out ; my Father, and Aunt especially, being ready to fall down and kiss my Feet, that to put an End to it, I pretended to have Affairs of the utmost Moment to dispatch, and taking my leave of them, retired to my Closet ; where I indulged that Satisfaction, which always attends con-

ferring

ferring Benefits, and being happy enough to give Happiness to others; and though I had done no more than what my Duty bound me to do, yet did the Consciousness of having acquitted myself of that Duty, give me an Infinity of Pleasure.

The End of the NINTH PART.

H 4 THE

THE

VIRTUOUS VILLAGER,

OR,

VIRGIN's VICTORY.

PART. X.

FTER my Parents were gone, and I
had recovered myself from the Emotions
their Presence gave me, I wrote an Answer to Monsieur the Count *de Saint Fal*'s
Letter. I thought proper to acquaint
him with the Epistle I had received from
the old Marquis *de L———V———*, his Discovery of
me, and the Visit he had made me ; with all that passed
in that Conversation ; concealing no Part of the Truth,
and entreating he would use me with the same Sincerity,
and also continue to favour me with his Advice, how to
behave in so critical a Circumstance.

When I had sent this Letter away, I divided my
Time between Acts of Devotion for the safety of my
dear

dear Marquis, and in reading Books of Philofophy and Morality to infpire me with Fortitude, to fuftain whatever Ills might ftill be ordained for me.   As the Time in which I expected the Father of my Lover drew near, I began to be no lefs impatient to fee him than I had been fearful before————the great Defigns he faid he had form'd for me, elevated me to Hopes I had little reafon to expect would ever be fulfilled, and tho' I endeavoured to check Ideas, which then feemed fo vain, yet would they ftill return, and in fpite of myfelf I was compelled fometimes to look on myfelf then, as what I now in reality am.

It was the third Day from that in which I had feen him, and I begun to doubt if he would keep his Promife, when about fix in the Evening, I heard him on the Stairs, enquiring after my Health of *Barbara*, in a very polite Manner ; when he entered my Apartment, it was with the fame Complaifance, as to a Dutchefs, tho' bended with the Freedom and Sweetnefs of a long Acquaintance and intimate Friend————this is true good Breeding, for one cannot call a Man a fine Gentleman, if a due Refpect, is not accompanied with a certain Eafe, which lays no Reftraint on the Perfon to whom it is paid.

One of the firft things he faid to me was this,———— charming *Jeanetta*, you have never been out of my Thoughts fince I was here ; and among other things, it has been fome matter of Aftonifhment to me, that you do not feem tired with this folitary Life————Women at your Age are ufually fond of Company and Diverfions, whereas you partake of none, and live in the World, as tho' you were out of it————I queftion if the Life of a Reclufe, which you fo much dreaded, is not to be prefered to yours.

Conftraint, my Lord, anfwered I, renders thofe things irkfome which in themfelves are not fo———— as I am now at Liberty, I prefer Solitude, but condemned to it, fhould think it dreadful————but, continued I, I find ways to divert all my time, and between Reading, Working, and Mufick, 'have feldom any vacant Hours.

You

You are never to be sufficiently praised for being thus every Thing to yourself, replied the Marquis, nor is it at all to be wondered at, that you inspire such lasting Affection in those who truly know you.

He looked at me as he spoke these Words, with an infinity of Tenderness, and perceiving I did not immediately reply, you know not, continued he, the whole Force of your Charms, nor the Conquest they have gained over a Heart, which very lately imagined itself incapable of being influenced in the manner it now is.

————There is a Person in the World *Jeanetta*, who tho' far advanced in Years has a very great Affection for you————he is a Man of Quality, and has Honour and good Sense————he has entrusted me with the Secret, and I have promised to be his Advocate————what say you, lovely *Jeanetta*, will the greatest Complaisance and Tenderness (both which I will undertake to answer for) make up for want of Youth ? ————I must own, that considering your fine way of Thinking, I cannot suppose he would run any Risque in declaring himself immediately, but I could not persuade him to discover to you his Name, till he was assured his Passion would not be rejected.

Any one may guess the Surprize I was in at hearing the Father of my Lover talk to me in this Manner ; and thence infer how difficult it was for me to reply————as I was wholly unprepared for any such Attack I thought it best to evade it by treating what he said, as a peice of Raillery: I therefore affected to be very gay, tho' in reality I was very much the contrary ; the Lover he mentioned had so great a resemblance of himself, that I secretly trembled, for the Consequence of what my unlucky Beauty might occasion ; his Love appearing, with Reason, no less a Misfortune to me, than his Hate had been.

The Marquis perceived the little Artifice I now put in Practice, you have a great deal of Wit, said he, it must be confessed————I see you would turn a Proposal you don't relish into a Jest; yet nevertheless I assure you nothing is more serious————I will however say no
more

more of it at present———perhaps, hereafter a more favourable Time may offer———a Lover of Sixty must have Patience.

After this, the Conversation turned on a different Subject; the old Marquis told me he had been solliciting in my behalf at Court, that he had reminded the King of what his Majesty had done for me before, and represented my Merit, and the Gratitude I expressed for that Bounty in so strong a Light, that he did not doubt but a good Effect would come of it. The King, said he, being told I am your Godfather, and that I espouse your Interest, will I believe allow you a Pension, and I flatter myself, such a one, as will support you without being obliged either to my Son or Nephew.

This Service was indeed very acceptable to me, and without reflecting as I might have naturally done, whether this was not a generous Artifice in the Marquis, to confer this Favour on me, without letting me know how far I was obliged, I thanked him with the utmost Humility and Sincerity, for interesting himself so far in my Behalf. The Affair is not yet concluded, said he, the better to conceal from me what Part he had in it; but I don't doubt but to wish you Joy of it the next Time I see you.———I shall be extremely glad not to be disappointed in my Hope, for I solemnly protest I have nothing more at Heart, than to see you perfectly easy.

I returned this Compliment as became me, and whatever passed in my Bosom, behaved with a Chearfulness which was very engaging to my Guest; he asked Permission to stay to Supper with me, and as it was a Favour I did not dare to refuse, granted it, as tho' satisfied with the Honour he did me———he said many fine Things to me, on my acquitting myself so well in the little Forms observed at Table between Persons of Distinction, and often cried out in a kind of Transport; good God! who would believe this admirable Creature was born in a Cottage.

When it grew towards Eleven a Clock, he took his leave, saying, he never would exact any thing from me

that

that trespassed on Decency; that tho' he could never think the Hours tedious in my Company, yet for my sake he judged it Time to retire, which he did with the greatest Complaisance, and a Promise of seeing me the next Day.

He failed not in his Word, and during eight Days, that he stayed at *Paris*, was never absent in an Afternoon. No Respect could exceed that with which he treated me; but every Time he came, dropt one Expression or another, which made me fear the few Charms I was Mistress of had made but too much Impression on his Heart.

The Day of his Departure he told me he was obliged to leave me, and as it would be impossible for him to return in less than a Fortnight, protested he never undertook any Journey with more regret. I tear myself from you, said he, and in this short Time, that I have been accustomed to your Company, am convinced I can't be happy without being eternally with you———if you at present, continued he, comprehend not the meaning of these Words, and many other others I have said, hereafter they will be sufficiently explained.

Alas! thought I, they are but too easily accounted for———I dissembled however my Disquiet till he was gone, and then fell into most terrible Agitations, to think of the Event of so unexpected an Accident——— Now, said I, all my ill Fortune is compleated———were the Marquis to return repentant of the rash Judgment jealous Rage has made him pass upon me, will he presume to Rival his Father?——and will the Father recede to the Son———will he, who would not consent to his Union with me, when he not loved me, ever be prevailed upon to yield that he should marry the Woman he unhappily has a Passion for himself?—

These Reflections, which after what had passed between me and the old Marquis were highly reasonable, joined to the Uncertainty I was in for the Fate of his Son, made my Breast a perfect Chaos of Confusion———I slept little that Night, and rose next Morning, not much more composed, when as I was looking for something in a

Drawer

Drawer in my Toylet, I difcovered a little Packet, which not having feen before, I haftily opened, and fonnd it contained a Purfe, fuch as Counters are ordinarily put into, but by the Weight I judged it to be Gold; nor was I deceived in my Conjecture——there were in it Two thoufand Livres; and a Letter as follows:

To the charming JEANETTA,

THE King has granted you Two Thoufand Livres, by my Hands; and has fettled on you one Thoufand more, to be conftantly paid you by the Year.———For fo good an Oeconomift as I know you are, this little Revenue I flatter myfelf will fuffice———I chofe this way of delivering you the Money, becaufe I would avoid any Acknowledgments your Excefs of Complaifance and Gratitude might have drawn from you———and defire that when I next have the Pleafure of feeing you, you will mention nothing of it———You are under no manner of Obligation to me, as your God-father, it is my Duty to efpoufe your Intereft, and I but fpoke, and my Requeft was granted.———if hereafter I fhall be fortunate enough to do any thing that may deferve your Friendfhip, I fhall not in that fo eafily give up my Pretenfions———Be affured there is nothing I more ardently defire, nor will go greater lengths to obtain———I have well weigh'd your Merits, and it is to them, much more than to your Beauty, admirable as it is, that you are indebted for all can be done for you by him, who is,

With the moft perfect Honour

and tendereft Affection,

The lovely JEANETTA'*s*

Admirer and Friend,

De L——V——.

So great an Act of Generofity, and the Manner of doing it, both furprized and charmed me, for I had then a firm Belief, which has been fince confirmed, that it was from the fincere Friendfhip of this truly valuable Nobleman,

man, not the Bounty of the King that I received this
Favour; which indeed came very seasonably; my little
Stock of Money being very near exhausted by the Assis-
tance I had given my Parents, I must without this Re-
lief have soon been driven to very great Straits. Afflicted as
I was on many Accounts, this gave me great Consolation——
People may say what they will, but Money is a vast
Alleviater of Misfortunes.————I from my Heart ad-
mired and acknowledged the Goodness of Providence——
Divine Service approaching I went to Church, and
joined in it with a greater Fervency than I had ever done
before, even at the Time when I was in that dreadful
Pit mentioned in the Beginning of these Memoirs, and in
Expectation of being every Moment devoured by a Beast
of Prey. The Poor were amply remembered by me,
and I gave Money to the *Sacristan* to have Prayers
offered up for the Preservation of the Marquis and the
Count, from all the Dangers to which they were exposed.
I was taught from my Youth to have a Confidence in
such Acts of Piety, and have experienced in many Instances that they are never thrown away, and tho' those
who have little Charity themselves, are apt to say what
is given that way, is in Danger of being misapplied, I
look on this only as the excuse of a narrow Soul, since it is
the good Intention that renders the Gift acceptable to Heaven————the Guilt of the Perversion lies alone on the
Person's Head, who is entrusted with the Distribution,
but the Merit in the *Donor* is the same, and never misses
its Reward.   And this I may venture to affirm, that if I
have not always received an immediate Relief from the
Misfortunes I laboured under, yet my Prayers have been
efficacious in obtaining a Fortitude and Resignation to
support them without those Murmurs and Repinings,
which are the certain Tokens of an abject Mind.

Great indeed were the Trials I sustained, and such as
nothing but a due Consideration from what Hand they
came, could have given me a share of Patience requisite
to preserve me from Despair.   That very Morning at
my return from Church I found a Person whom I
had ordered to bring me the *Gazette,* waiting for me,
————I

————I looked earneſtly for that Article relating to the Affairs in *Germany*————and found a Paſſage which too plainly confirmed what the Count *de Saint Fal* had wrote to me concerning the Marquis————the Words were theſe :

' A Detachment, commanded by a young Nobleman,
' is entirely cut off, having been ſurrounded by the
' Enemy, and the Commander with ſeveral other
' Officers of Diſtinction left for dead in the Field.'

Ah, Heavens! cried I out, the Marquis is no more! wretched————wretched *Jeanetta*————this was all I had Power to ſpeak ; overwhelm'd with Grief, my Senſes quite forſook me, and I fell motionleſs into a Chair : I remained it ſeems two Hours in this Condition ; during which my Cloaths were plucked off, and I was put into Bed, without my being in the leaſt ſenſible of any thing done about me, or ſhewing any ſigns of Life.

When I came to myſelf, I found my Bed encompaſſed with Perſons I had never ſeen before, and *Barbara* on her Knees weeping bitterly, and wringing her Hands, having given me over for dead; a Prieſt whom ſhe had ſent for in her Fright, aſked me how I did; alas! anſwered I, more ſick in Mind than Body : Have Courage then Madam, reſumed he, and caſt your Cares on God, who in his good Time will relieve you. As he ſpoke theſe Words, the Company withdrew, and I caſting my Eyes more heedfully upon him than I had done before, remembered I had ſeen him officiate at the Chapel where I uſually went to Prayers, and had taken a particular Notice of him on Account of the extraordinary Devotion, he ſeemed inſpired with above the reſt of his Brethren : —I look'd on him in this Juncture as one ſent from Heaven for my Conſolation, and made no Scruple of acquainting him, that the Condition he found me in, had been occaſioned by hearing of the Death of a Perſon who was very dear to me, and whom I had looked upon as a Man that was to have been one Day my Huſband.

The good Eccleſiaſtick conformed himſelf to my Weakneſs, the better to enforce his Doctrine, and ſhielded me from that Deſpair, he perceived was ready to lay hold on me, by making me fenfible how little Regard was to be given to Publick News-Papers, the Accounts of which he affured me were very uncertain; and then exhorted me to fubmit to the DivineWill, which it was my Duty to do in all Events, and which knew what was beft for me, and would order every thing for my Good, if I endeavoured fincerely to refign every Thing entirely to its Difpofal; he added, that a too great Attachment to any created Being, brought on nothing but Mifery and Vexation, and that it was a Crime to indulge Grief at the Expence of my Health.

His Admonitions failed not of their Effect, I promifed him I would ufe my Efforts to do my Duty, on which he took his Leave, affuring me he would conftantly re-member me in his Prayers.

Immediately after he was gone, a huge tall Man with a monftrous black Wig, came to my Bedfide and offered to take me by the Hand: His Afpect and Man-ner of approaching me, put me into fuch a Terror, that I fcreamed out and fnatched my Hand away————I had no Thoughts of a Phyfician being fent for, and my Head being a little out of Order through the Weaknefs which my late Fainting had left me in, made me not prefently comprehend what bufinefs he could have with me; but he foon folved the Riddle, when addreffing himfelf to an old Lady who ftood by; thefe Symptoms, Madam, faid he, denote a manifeft Delirium,————fhe muft be let Blood this Minute————Run, purfued he, to *Barbara*, and fetch Monfieur *Lancelot* the Surgeon, that he may perform the Operation, while this little Interval of Senfe continues. I was fo much amazed at being looked upon as 'mad, that I could not make any Anfwer to convince him and the reft of the Company, that I was not fo. How kind is Providence, faid the Lady, to whom he had fpoke, if Monfieur *de Pourpre*, had not happened to be at Home when I fent, what might not this pretty young Creature have fuffered! During this Lady's Exclamation I recovered my Voice, and looking on this frightful Doctor with Contempt, I ftand in no need, faid I, neither of a Surgeon, nor your-felf;

felf; fo defire you'll leave my Chamber————A————
Ha————cried he, the Fit is coming again————I
wifh Monfieur *Lancelot* were here————fhe muft have
ten Ounces at leaft taken from each Arm; and twice
that Number from under the right Ear ;————then turning to me, have a good Heart, Madam, faid he, I'll
engage we'll fet you up again, tho' it muft be owned you
are far gone————very far gone indeed.————See, continued he, to the old Lady, who I perceived had a great
Confidence in him, what a Wildnefs there is in her
Eyes————Ah, I am never deceived, if I once look
in the Eyes of a Patient————our Phyficians, generally fpeaking, are very ignorant, they cannot read
Difeafes by the Face, and therefore envy me for my
fuperior Skill————they talk of obliging me to leave
Paris ; but they fhall repent it if they offer to moleft
me in my Practice. I have a whole Volume ready for
the Prefs, which I'll have printed in *Holland*, and put
them all to Confufion.

The old Lady feemed to approve prodigioufly of
what he faid, and then afked him, what Remedies he
intended to prefcribe for my Cure. None Madam,
anfwered he, but what are perfectly fimple————the
Gentlemen of the Faculty will fometimes keep a Patient
under their Hands, three or four Years; but my Medicines never fail doing the Bufinefs in nine Days at
fartheft————I'll have her bled twice a Day for three
Days fucceffively————the too great Height of her
Spirits, muft be brought down by three Days Fafting,
and the Heat of her Liver cooled by Bathing————
fo that for the laft three Days, I'll have her fet up to the
Chin in cold Water, for at leaft fix Hours together ; and
if this, with the help of fome few Lenitives and Eme-
ticks, does not remove all her Complaints at the End of
nine Days, I'll be content to forfeit all the Reputation I
have acquired, and be looked upon as ignorant as thofe
really are, who pretend to call me fo.

The murderous Defign which I found this Emperick
had formed againft me, frighted me to that Degree,
that I cried out : *Barbara*, who was now returned from
going

going to the Surgeon's, came to me, and asked me tenderly what was the matter——O, said I, send that Man away, pointing to Doctor *Pourpre*, the very Sight of him will throw me into Fits. Is Monsieur *Lancelot* coming, cried he, without regarding what I said?——O, here he is, continued he, perceiving him enter: Come, Monsieur, here is your Patient——be speedy in performing the Operation. The Surgeon, without making any reply, presently plucked out his Lancet, and called for warm Water and a Fillet! while these Things were preparing, the terrible Doctor repeated to him the Number of Ounces of Blood he was to take from each Arm, and I making a sign to *Barbara* to draw my Curtains close about me, threw a Gown over my Shoulders, and escaped from the Bed's-Feet into another Room, where I bolted myself in, resolving not to open the Door till the Doctor and Surgeon had left the House.

I could hear the Uproar they made, when they found I was gone——See! cried *Pourpre*, can there be a more evident Proof of Madness, than to fly from Remedies, and such necessary ones as I always prescribe?——you, Madam, continued he, who sent for me, and know my Skill, can be a Witness that this young Lady is mad——you see how she uses me——for my Part, I think in Charity we ought to force open the Door, and bind her till the Operation is perform'd——it will be a meritorious Action to cure her against her Will; and if ever she comes to her Senses, she will thank us for the Violence we are now compelled to offer.

As no body opposed this Advice, and I heard them draw near the Door, I doubted not but they would do as he ordered, so was forced to cry out, and protest if they attempted such an Outrage, I would call for help from the Window, and have them all prosecuted.

The Surgeon, who was a Man of more Reason, and doubtless had not the best Opinion of Monsieur *Pourpre*'s Advice, begged me to moderate my Passion, and assured me he knew too well what he ought to do offer to bleed me without my Consent. I am ready to believe you Monsieur, answered I, but that Doctor has certainly
some

some Intentions of destroying me, and he will oblige you to do it. No, Madam, returned he, I give you my solemn Promise, that I will be the first to oppose it, unless commanded by yourself.———I beg, therefore, pursued he, that you will open the Door, that I may have the Honour of knowing by what Accident this Mistake has happened, and you will find I shall obey no other Orders than your own.

The Lady whom I mentioned was truly good natured, and moved with my Tears, made the same Protestations that I should not be molested, and *Barbara*, frightned lest I should catch Cold, as she knew I was half naked, cried to me, that they should kill her before they should offer to touch me———all this together emboldned me at last to open the Door, the Surgeon and the Lady came in, and the Doctor was pressing in after them ; but on my saying he should not enter, they shut the Door against him. Recover yourself, Madam, I beseech you, said Monsieur *Lancelet*, and favour me so far, as to inform me, what has occasioned the Trouble we have given you. On this I relate! to him all that had passed, and this with so much Calmness, that he shrugged up his Shoulders, saying, it was not the first piece of Folly that *Pourpre* had been guilty of, and that for his Part he was amazed he had been suffered to practise ; but added, that he did not want Skill, if he were less self-sufficient and precipitate.

The old Lady, who it seems had been so good to come to my Assistance, when *Barbara* cried out on my fainting away ; told me, that imagining my Case was desperate, she had sent for the Doctor, in whom till now she had placed great Confidence, and also for the Clergyman : I gave her my hearty Thanks for both, as she meant well ; but told her I should always think myself under an Obligation, for bringing me acquainted with that pious Ecclesiastick from whose excellent Remonstrances I had received great Benefit ; but as for the other I desired to see him no more, for I looked upon him to be more mad than he imagined me to be.

This

This whimsical Adventure ended with my ordering a Gratification to the Surgeon and Emprick, who went away well enough satisfied, but created in me such an Aversion to all Physicians and Prescriptions, that I could never since, even on the most pressing Occasions, be persuaded to have recourse to them————'tis true, I am sensible that this is Prejudice, and that all are not Doctor *Pourpre's*, but yet it is what I cannot get over, and so strongly is it rooted in me, that I believe I shall carry it to my Grave.

As soon as I was free from the Company of these Gentlemen, the good old Lady, to whose mistaken Zeal I was indebted for their Presence, told me, she should be very glad of my Acqaintance, that she had conceived a great liking to me for seeing me so constantly at Church, where she went twice every Day, and had observed I offered up my Devotions with greater Fervour than could be expected from a Person of my Years. I answered her in the politest Manner I cou'd, but evaded the Offer she made me, as not suiting with my Humour to see any Company, even tho' they were of my own Sex. Indeed, I had suffered so much by my too readily entring into a Familiarity with Madamoiselle *Junia*, that I had fixed my Resolution to avoid all possible Dangers of that kind, and nothing could persuade me to break it.

After she had taken her leave, I again took up the Paper, which had occasioned all this Bustle, and whether it was owing to what the Clergyman had said to me, or that in the hurry of my first reading it my Apprehensions had magnified the Danger, I know not, but methought it did not now seem so positive as before, and left room for Hope——the Marquis's Name was not inserted, and there might be many Detachments commanded by Men of Quality, and possibly it might be some other who had fallen the Victim of War, not him for whom I was so nearly concerned; this soothing Reflection, joined to the Fatigue I had undergone, made me fall into a sound Sleep the Moment I went to Bed.

I

I would fain have perſwaded my poor loving Aunt to have gone to her Bed, but all I could ſay would not prevail on her, ſhe inſiſted on watching by me, and happy was it for me ſhe did ſo, I had otherwiſe died through Fear, if not been murdered, as the Accident I am going to relate will ſhew.

The Confuſion and Trouble I had been in that Day, left Impreſſions on my Imagination, which was doubtleſs the Occaſion of a very frightful Dream———— Methought a Ghoſt, loaded with Chains appeared before me, looking on me with a very mournful Aſpect ————I endeavoured to avoid ſeeing him, but could not, and I beheld in his Arms a Corpſe covered with Blood and Wounds, which I immediately knew to be the young Marquis *De L————V————* ; behind this ghaſtly Phantome, many others equally diſmal ſeemed to ſtalk, with ſolemn and dejected Pace————among them was the Father of my Lover, who led a Woman in Stature, Shape and Features perfectly reſembling myſelf————ſhe ſeem'd to move as if by Compulſion, and had ſomething in her Air, more melancholy and forlorn than the reſt———— The old Marquis knelt down with her at the Feet of the dreadful Phantome I firſt mentioned ; on which the Corpſe of my Lover ſeem'd to revive, his Eyes opened, and the Blood no longer iſſued from his Wounds————By degrees he came to himſelf, and quitting their Arms which had held him, he took his Father's Hand, and that of the Woman who was in every thing my other ſelf, and joined them: I was, methought, in ſtrange Emotions at this Sight, but looking again was ſurpriſed to find the Bridegroom changed into the young Marquis, and the old one entirely diſappeared————caſting my Eyes a ſecond Time on the Spectre, I perceived he now had in his Arms another Corpſe embrued in Blood, as the former had been— this I preſently knew to be the Count *de Saint Fal,* his Countenance appeared ſo mournful and pity-moving, that I was running to give him ſome Conſolation in the exceſſive Sorrow with which he appeared to be overwhelmed,

whelmed, when on a sudden I was waked by my Curtains being drawn back————I started as People generally do when rouzed too haltily from their Sleep, and discovered by the Light of a small Taper, which was burning on the Table, a Man arm'd with a Ponyard, which he presented to my Breast, saying at the same Time, you are a dead Woman, if you offer to cry out, or make the least Noise————your Purse, or your Life this Instant must be mine.

O Heaven! to whom I owe my Preservation in this dreadful remembrance of thy Goodness to me, keep for ever in my Mind an humble and grateful Remembrance of thy Goodness to me! My Aunt *Barbara*, who as I said before, would needs remain in my Chamber, imagined she heard something breath in a Closet just behind the Chair in which she sat:————she liftned for some Time, and hearing the same Sound again began to suspect the Truth—She then cast about in her Mind how to avert the impending Danger,————to call out, or do any Thing that might give the concealed Person room to believe he was discovered, she thought would be certain Death, both to herself and me, so hit upon a method, which considering her Simplicity in most other Things, was very much to be wondered at. Instead of seeming afraid of any Thing, she pretended to yawn, and threw herself from one side of the Chair to the other as if sleepy and tired with her Position, and soon after got up and came to my Bed-side and looked at me, and then cried, ay, she's fast———— I knew no business I have to sit here————I'll e'en go to my own Bed in the Kitchen————so having pulled the Door softly, as if fearful of waking me, ran down Stairs, and called up a Merchant that lived at the next House, and she knew had several Men belonging to him————they made such expedition that they were all in my Chamber, just as I was preparing to rise and give my Money to the Villain. The Wretch let fall his Ponyard at this unexpected Interruption, and fell at my Feet begging for Mercy————the Merchant and his People presently secured him, and I a little recovered

from

from my Fright, then I knew him to be the Man who brought me the *Gazette*———he confeſſed his Intention of robbing me, had been owing to my Imprudence in opening a Drawer before him, where lay a great Quantity of Gold, when I went to pay him for the Paper ; ————that Sight, he ſaid, had tempted him to this Wickedneſs, having always till then behaved himſelf honeſtly : But, Madam, continued he, Opportunity and extreme Neceſſity ſtifled all other Conſiderations.

Your fainting away, ſaid he, and the Buſtle it occaſioned in the Family, gave me the Opportunity while every body was buſy about you, of hiding myſelf in that Cloſet, where I waited in hope your Maid would either fall a-ſleep or go out of the Room ; the latter happening, though not as I expected it, I proceeded to the Accompliſhment of my intended Deſign, which was, indeed, to murder you in Caſe you made any Reſiſtance.

Barbara then relating by what a Stratagem ſhe had rendered the Deſigns of this wicked Creature fruſtrate, made me admire the Divine Providence, who when he is pleaſed can inſpire the moſt fearful with Courage, and the moſt ſimple with Cunning.————Never was its power more manifeſt than in the Inſtrument made Choice of, for my Preſervation in ſo eminent a Danger.

It was doubtleſs the ſame Power who inſpired me with a Reſolution of ſaving the Life af the Wretch, who had attempted mine———a Moment later had prevented the Effects of my Pity, for one of the Merchant's Men, inſtead of accompanying his Fellows, had ran to alarm the Watch, as imagining, perhaps, there might be Occaſion for more Aſſiſtance ; but this I was ignorant of, and had prevailed with my Neighbours to let him make his Eſcape ; I was, indeed, ſo much moved with his Neceſſities, which he deſcribed with Tears, and the moſt bitter Remorſe, for having urged him to ſo deteſtable a Crime, that I gave him Two *Lewis D'Ors*, for the Relief of Ten Children, he to'd me he had upon his Hands ; requiring of him to live honeſtly for the future, and promiſing him farther Aſſiſtance from time to time, in Caſe he would ſend his Wife or one of his Children for it, andnever let me ſee him more.   G!

O! how heavenly a Satisfaction do they deny themselves, who, having the power to relieve, are insensible of the Miseries of their Fellow-Creatures! the Pleasure that arises from Acts of Mercy and Benevolence, is certainly the most perfect we can enjoy on Earth; and in my Opinion, he who wants a Soul to *give*, is much poorer than he who by Necessity is compell'd to *ask!* But neither Precept or Example is of Force, where an innate Compassion fails to excite,————Every one will act of himself, and the World must be as it will; for my Part I was so overjoy'd that the poor Fellow, vile as he was, had made his Escape, and had something to comfort his distress'd Family, that it more than compensated for the Terror he had put me in.

He was but just gone when the Watch came in, and search'd the House; but finding no-body, return'd laughing among themselves, I do not doubt, at my groundless Apprehensions.————As for the Merchant, I made him a Present of a Gold Snuff-Box, and gratified his Men for the Disturbance I had given them.

When all was over I embraced my dear Aunt *Barbara*, to whom under Heaven I owed my Life; and assured her, I would not leave the World without giving her ample Proofs of the Sense I had of the Obligations I had to her————fain would I on this Occasion have declared to her who I was, but I restrain'd that Testimony of my Gratitude, her Indiscretion might have occasion'd Consequences of such Moment, that I was oblig'd much against my Inclination to be silent on that Head.—I made what Amends I could, however, by treating her with all the Tenderness of a near Relation, though I own'd myself not as such; and she had all the Reason in the World to be satisfied with my Behaviour to her.

When all this Hurry was over I went again to Bed; but had not power to close my Eyes till Day began to break; but then slept so sound, that I knew not when I should have awoke, had not *Barbara* come into my Room, and told me that a Gentleman in a long Black Gown, with two Attendants with him, was come to speak with

me

me on Bufinefs of Importance. As I could not imagine
what any Gentleman that profefs'd the Law, as I fuppofed
this was, could have to fay to me, I afk'd her
feveral Queftions concerning what they faid, and in what
manner they enquired for me: And fhe told me that
he who feem'd to be the Mafter, afk'd her, if Madam
De Roches was at Home, (for by that Name I foolifhly
enough ftill continued to be call'd) and on her anfwering
that I was afleep, he told her I muft be waked, for he
muft fpeak with me, on a Bufinefs wherein Life was
concern'd.

What fhe faid affording me no Satisfaction, I got up
with as much Expedition as I could, and went into my
Drawing-Room to receive this extraordinary Vifit.———
I found it was a Commiffary, who having made a civil
Apology for giving me this Difturbance, addrefs'd himfelf
to me in the following Terms.

Laft Night, Madam, faid he, the Watch brought a
Man before me, who they found running through the
Street, as if he was making his Efcape from fome, that
he expected were purfuing him; on which they feiz'd
him on Sufpicion, but it being late I ordered he fhould
be fecured till this Morning, when being brought to
me again, he appear'd fo confufed, and gave fuch incoherent
Anfwers to the Queftions I put to him, that I
fent him back to Prifon, till he fhould give a better
Account of where he had been, and what had occafion'd
that Terror, which made the Watch take Notice of
him. A Letter directed to you, Madam, and entrufted
to the Turnkey to deliver to you, was intercepted and
broke open. He begs your Mercy, and fays his Life is
in your Hands. I examined him upon this, and he
pretends that having brought you the Gazette, he ftaid
to Supper with your Servants, and that was the Occafion
of his being out fo late. This agrees fo ill with
the Contents of his Letter to you, that I am come to
know what it is that he would have ftifled, and what he
means by faying his Life is in your Hands.——Pleafe,
therefore, to permit me to take down your Information,
and you may afterwards act as you think proper———

though I beg a perfect Account, becaufe Witneffes will be called, and any Deviation from Truth, might be of ill Confequence : As I heard your Quality demanded this Deference, I came to wait on you myfelf, inftead of fending an inferior Officer.

Thefe Tidings made me more and more admire Divine Juftice, which purfues Wickednefs even to its inmoft Receffes ; but was forry at the fame Time that my Compaffion was like to prove unavailing. I was very much at a lofs how to reply, as the Wretch's Life depended on my Words, and I naturally abhorr'd all kind of Lying or Prevarication ; at laft, it is true, faid I, that being juft going to Bed, I found the Fellow you mean in my Chamber, at which I was fo frighted that I fcreamed out and rais'd the Houfe ; but on Enquiry I heard that after Supper he fell afleep in the Kitchen, and that when he waked in endeavouring to get out, miftook his Way and came into my Room, and that being frighted himfelf at my taking him for a Thief, he ran away to prevent being feiz'd as fuch.

The Commiffary appear'd fatisfied with this, and went away ; but I prepar'd the Landlord of the Houfe and his Servants, that they might agree in the fame Story, in Cafe farther Enquiry fhould be made, as, indeed, there was ; but nothing appearing againft him, he got his Difcharge in two Days, as his Wife informed me, who came and returned me Thanks upon her Knees, protefting that fhe and all her Family would in that Pofture, never fail once a Day to invoke the Bleffing of Heaven on every thing I undertook.

Thefe two laft Accidens, though but Trifles in themfelves, joyn'd to the other Difquiets I laboured under, had an ill Effect on my Conftitution————I grew pale, fell away, my Appetite as well as my Sleep forfook me, and in a Week's time I was alter'd to that Degree, as hardly to be known.————Poor dear *Barbara* did all fhe could to divert me, and, indeed, with her odd Phrafes would fometimes make me fmile ; but, alas ! this was a Winter's Sun, which was prefently obfcured by the gloomy Clouds of Grief————my ominous

Dream,

Dream, the Uncertainty of my dear Marquis's Fate, the Impatience of hearing more of him from *Saint Fal*, was ever prefent to Mind, and I believe no one, who did not directly yield to Defpair, ever fuffer'd more than I did at that time.

I was fitting one Day at my Window in a very penfive and heavy Turn of Mind, when I heard a Coach and Six ftop at the Door, on looking out I faw it was the old Marquis's.————I ftarted, though I knew not why, but foon found fufficient Caufe to be alarm'd, when entring my Chamber, I perceived on his Countenance fo great a Melancholy, as in a Man of his Temper, could not proceed but from fome very extraordinary Occafion. It terrified me the more alfo, that I found he laboured very much to conceal it from me: and fpoke not any thing which could give me any light into the Affair that troubled him, I took the Liberty of queftioning him in my Turn; your Lordfhip, faid I, has been pleafed to honour me with the Title of your Friend, and I confefs myfelf too proud of it, not to do every thing in my power to merit it, and would alfo not be denied the Privileges of fo facred a Name.————There is a Cloud upon your Lordfhip's Brow, the meaning of which I cannot comprehend; if any unwary Act or Word of mine has given rife to it, I befeech your Lordfhip to acquaint me with the Nature of my Offence, that I may entreat your Pardon, and attone for it by my future Conduct————if I am no way acceffary, give me leave to fhare in your Concern.————

I was going on when he interrupted me, by crying out in a kind of inward Agony————Oh, *Jeanetta!* ————*Jeanetta!* how cruelly do you make me feel my Tendernefs for my Son.

He had fcarce utter'd thefe Words, than a cold Trembling feiz'd me from Head to Foot.————I was now affured my Dream was fatally accomplifhed, and the dear Man for whom my Vows and Sighs were offer'd was no more————in that inftant of Horror all Difguife was forgot, my Soul unguarded yielded to the dreadful Blow.————I fhriek'd, and the Tears burft ie Tor-

rents

rents from my Eyes————to speak I was unable; but heard from the old Marquis that his Son was dangerously, it was fear'd mortally wounded in the Head, in giving the most signal Proofs of his Bravery; and that the Count *De Saint Fal* was taken Prisoner in the Battle, which happened two Days after.

The Marquis, whether it were that he thought it ill became his Character, to offer any thing of Consolation to me in this Circumstance, or that the sight of my Grief made his own more sensible, I cannot pretend to say, but he staid with me but a little time; though I heard him as he went out, bid *Barbara* be careful of me, and promised her to come again the next Day.

He did so, but found me in a Condition little capable of receiving him————the melancholy News he had brought me, threw me into a Fit of Sickness.————I was than in Bed, which I stirr'd not out of for a considerable Time. This excellent Nobleman made his own Physicians attend me; but on the fourth Day they gave me over, unless Nature, they said, by a prodigious Effort, could throw off the bilious Matter from about my Heart, which was on the Point of suffocating me. They were not wanting in their Endeavours; but my Stomach was too weak to retain any of the Remedies they prescrib'd, long enough to operate on the Cause which still remain'd behind, and left no hope of my Recovery.

The old Marquis, who came at least ten times in a a Day to my Bedside, no sooner heard this, than he bethought himself of a Medicine, which though never given but in desperate Cases, he had seen some good Effects of————this he made me take, and sat by me during the Operation.————His kind Endeavours had their wish'd Success————the Emetick Dose staid with me for near half an Hour, during which time I suffered Tortures equal to the Rack; but at last was happily relieved, not only from those poignant Pains, but also from that obstinate Bile, which had render'd so violent a Remedy absolutely necessary. Nor was this all he did for my Recovery; after I had slept a little, and seemed more composed, a Courier came into my Chamber,

booted

booted as from the Camp, and deliver'd a Packet to the
Marquis, which he haſtily open'd, and having ſeemed to
read to himſelf ; I expect, *Jeanetta*, ſaid he, aſſuming
a pleaſant Countenance, that you will congratulate me
on the good News I have juſt received———my Son
is on the mending Hand, the Account we had of his
Danger proved a Miſtake, and he had only a ſlight
Wound in the Shoulder.

This Intelligence, which I then little ſuſpected was no
more than a Stratagem contrived to rectify the Diſorders of my Mind, was of ſuch Efficacy, that in a few
Days after I began to look once more like one, who
might be rank'd among the number of the Living.

Being now judged to be paſt all Danger of a Relapſe,
I made my Acknowledgments to Heaven, and to the
Marquis for the uncommon Tenderneſs he had ſhewn
to me———he ſeemed tranſported at the good Succeſs
of his Scheme, and continued to feed me ſtill with the
flattering Hopes of his Son's Recovery, and that he
would ſoon be on the Road to *Paris.*———Nay, went
ſo far as to forge Letters in his Name, which he read
to me, that I might be perfectly eaſy on that Article ;
and did all this, without ſeeming to penetrate how great
an Intereſt I took in it ; but as though his own Satisfaction would not ſuffer him to keep it a Secret.

This pleaſing Deluſion continued, till I was ſo well as
to be able to walk about my Rooms, and the Father of
my Lover having then Buſineſs, which call'd him to
Verſailles, took his *leave* of me ; but not without leaving a Servant at *Paris,* who was to carry him an Account of my Health every Day till his Return.

I gathered Strength very faſt, ſtill delighting myſelf
that the Marquis would be ſoon at *Paris,* and imagining
that when he ſhould come to hear the Truth of my Behaviour, he would not think me unworthy the Tender-
derneſs, he once had honoured me with. Never did it
once enter into my Head, that his Father had
deceived me, till I received by the Poſt a Letter
from the Count *De Saint Fal* ; I broke the Seal with a
pleaſing Impatience, expecting a Confirmation of what I

I 3 moſt

moſt wiſh'd on Earth ; but how great was my Diſappointment, when I read in it theſe Lines.

To the moſt beautiful *Jeanetta.*

IN Compliance with the ſolemn Promiſe you exaſted from me at my Departure, I now give you a little Hiſtory inſtead of a Letter, in which you will find much to lament, and much to rejoice at———let not, therefore, the firſt Part overwhelm you ſo far, as to render you incapable of proceeding to that which will afford you Conſolation ; if I hear it does, you muſt expeſt I ſhall not hereafter treat you with the ſame Sincerity.

My laſt acquainted you, lovely Jeanetta, *that my Couſin had obtain'd the Command of a Detachment, and that I apprehended from the Account I heard of him on my Arrival at the Camp, that his Melancholy might hurry him too far.——My Fears, alas! were but too well grounded. —Courage, doubly invigorated by Deſpair, put him upon attacking a Convoy, eſcorted by more than treble his Number ; and beſide that fell into an Ambuſcade, and without what is in our Days eſteem'd a Miracle, a faithful Servant, muſt have inevitably periſh'd———it was to* Dubois *his Valet de Chamber that he owed his Life.———He ſaw him fall, and tranſported by his Zeal and Affeſtion flew amidſt the thickeſt of the Enemies, and caught his bleeding Lord upon his Back, and bore him, in all Appearance dead, to the Camp : This Behaviour of his ſeem'd ſo new, that it aſtoniſh'd both Parties, and for a while occaſioned a Ceſſation of Deſtruſtion ——— all admired, and none attempted to render fruitleſs an Aſtion which appeared ſo brave.*

The Marquis had all this Time no ſigns of Life, but on the Surgeons ſearching his Wounds they were found not mortal, and that his greateſt Danger was his loſs of Blood. ——But make yourſelf eaſy, charming Jeanetta, *he is too much beloved here, for our Fears for him not to magnify every unpromiſing Symptom.*

Two

'Two Days after this melancholy one, the Armies fought a pitch'd Battle; we were the Victors, but I was made a Prisoner, and still continue so; the loss of my Liberty, is an inexpressible Misfortune to me, as it deprives me of the Pleasure of seeing you so soon as I expected, and of doing you what little Services are in my Power.

I send you here enclosed a Letter, which the Marquis had begun to write to me before the Action, and finished after he was wounded; it will serve to convince you, he is not so ungrateful as you imagin'd, nor in so much Danger as you, perhaps, apprehend.———I sincerely wish, whatever becomes of me, his Love and Life may one Day make you perfectly blest.———As what I say on this Account, has no less Sincerity in it than the rest, I know you are too just and generous to refuse me the Continuance of your Friendship, and in that charming Hope, I am enabled to endure all the Tryals a Lover can be put to.

If you think any thing I have done worthy of a Return, it must be in giving me as speedy Intelligence as you can, that you are well.———I should also be glad to hear if my Uncle continues his Visits to you———what you wrote concerning his discovering who you were, fills me with Amazement; but his Behaviour to you yet more, though I know him to be the most artful Man on Earth.—I cannot conceive, however, what Motives should induced him to dissemble with you.—Perhaps, your Beauty and your Virtue may have made him a Convert, as they did me; though I would not wish them to have altogether the same Effect on him, because I fear he would not be so resigning. — In all the Letters he has wrote to me, he has never once mention'd you; I follow his Example, for what I have done in that Affair will not bear clearing up to him, at least as yet.

I am well treated by my Conquerors, and till an Exchange of Prisoners is made, that I am happy enough to receive your dear Commands in Person, should think myself overpaid by a Line, for all I either have, or can do, or suffer. All I am, or ever can be, being entirely devoted to the charming Jeanetta; but I will delay no longer the Satisfaction you may find in reading the en-

closed,

clofed, which to give you, affords no fmall Share of to him, who is

With a Sincerity and Tendernefs,

great as the Charms which infpired them,

Moft adorable Jeanetta,

From *Mimkcim.*   *Your faithfully devoted*

De Saint Fal.

Though from the Moment I perceiv'd there was a Letter from the Marquis, I had, indeed, an inexpreffible Impatience to fee what it contain'd ; yet I would not be guilty of fo much Ingratitude to this generous Friend, as not to go through his Letter firft.———— 'Tis true there were no Witneffes of what I did on this Score ; but I had a Judge in my own Breaft, which would never fuffer me to do that thing in private, which if known would ftand in need of an Excufe. But now, having fatisfied the Demands of Friendfhip ; Love might be without a Blufh obeyed, and I examined my dear Marquis's Letter to *Saint Fal.* The Contents were as follows.

To Monfieur the Count *De Saint Fal.*

I Left Paris, *my dear Coufin, quite frantic with Rage, and I am now running into an Engagement, where my Defpair more than my Honour calls me————the Occafion of thefe Emotions is a Secret to all the World, but fhall not be fo to you ———— Jeanetta has deceived my good Opinion of her————She is falfe——— Unconftant————you will not perhaps believe this, but imagine fuch a Surmife only the Effect of a too ardent Paffion, which it is certain always borders on Jealoufy————yet what I tell you is fact————She no longer loves me, but gives the Preference to the Duke De————; his fuperior Quality, and perhaps fuperior* Merit,

Merit, *has fwayed her Heart in his Favour, and I am no more remembered by her———this made me quit all that was dear to me———this drove me to the Army———this pufhes me on to feek an honourable Death, rather than preferve a miferable Life ———I fay a miferable Life, for what is capable of affording me any Satisfaction, when fhe, in whom I had treafured all my Hopes, has fo ungratefully betrayed me.——— In vain have I ftrove to tear her Image from my Breaft———though fhe is no longer worthy, yet fhe is lovely ftill———the World has no longer any Charms for me, now fhe is loft.———Fatal Paffion, that leaves no hope of Relief but in the Arms of Death.*

My Scouts inform me, that a Party of the Enemy is but two Leagues diftant——— I fly to feek them ——— Farewel, dear Saint Fal, *remember me, and be affured, that though it is fomething unnatural to love one's Rival, yet you have been always dear to me.*

If the new Lover of my fair fallen Angel fhould deceive her, I beg you will be her Comforter.———We both know her Circumftances, do not therefore forfake her.———

I would not give way to thofe Emotions, which reading this cruel Accufation raifed in me, but pafs'd haftily on to the other Part, which I found was in a different Hand.

My dear Friend,

I Have been defeated, oppreft by Numbers, was laid for dead, but am now revived and happy———this laft Word may feem a Paradox, after what I have faid above; but I will explain it by telling you, that fince my Misfortune, I have received a Letter from a Gentleman, call'd Melicourt, *which affures me, I am ftill bleft in the pure Affections of my dear* Jeanetta: *If it be true, as he informs me, I can fubmit to every other kind of Ill. ———I am obliged to the Pen of* Dubois *to tell you*

this.

*this.————— I would entrust no other, and am unable to
make use of one myself,————write to me soon, I beseech
you, and let me know your Sentiments, on what so much
concerns my eternal Peace; for if what that unknown
Friend affirms he has been Witness of be real, I shall
content myself with the loss of an Eye, which is in some
Danger, so I have the other left, to behold the dear
Object of my Passion, and admire her Charms.———————
Assist me, I conjure you by all our Friendship, in making
my Peace with her, unless you think my late Behaviour
has render'd me unworthy of it————if so I should have,
indeed, no more do with Life; but I hope better both
from her and you.————I am sensible this is putting your
Friendship to the severest Tryal;————but I know to whom
I speak, and that's enough.*

Yours,

With the utmost Sincerity,

L———V———.

What Tears of mingled Grief and Tenderness did not
this Letter cost me! again and again did I read over
these Marks of his Affection————what would I not
have given that Instant to have been present with him?
————Ah! cryed I, why will not Decency permit me
to take a Post-Chaise and fly to the Camp. and convince him that I think none but his dear Self worthy
of my Love, and capable of making me happy?

After a long time spent in the most endearing Reflections, I began to think on *Melicourt's* Behaviour————
his taking the Trouble of writing in the Justification of
my Innocence, without my desiring that Favour of him,
or even without his mentioning to me that he would do
so, was an Action appeared so truly generous and so
noble, that it deserved my utmost Acknowledgments.
————I concluded, that a Person who could confer a Benefit for the sole Pleasure of doing it, had a Soul who
would think nothing too great a Trouble that Friendship demanded, and made me resolve to entreat him to
take

take a Journey to the Camp, in order to perfect the good Work he had begun, and assure my dear Marquis, that I was not unworthy of the Affection with which he honoured me.

Having determin'd on this Project, I wrote immediately to *Melicourt*, and sent my Letter by an express Messenger; I did not in the least doubt but on the Reception, he would come to *Paris*, having had such a Proof of his Inclination to serve me. Especially, as I had heard his own Affairs would not be decided in six Weeks; the *Nuncio* having been obliged to write again to *Rome* concerning some new Difficulties started by the Parents of *Saint Agnes*, and, therefore, he would have Time much more than sufficient to go where I required.

This worthy Husband of my dear *Saint Agnes* no sooner came to *Paris*, than I made him sensible how kind I took what he had done for me; and then acquainted him with the News I had received from the Army; I expatiated so much on the Concern I was in, to have a full Account of the Marquis's Condition, that he perceiving what I aim'd at, was so far from raising any Objections, prevented my making the Request I was preparing for, by offering to go; saying at the same time that I could not confer a greater Obligation on him, than to give him this Opportunity of becoming acquainted with a Nobleman, for whom he had so great Respect, as the Marquis *De L——V——*.

How greatly does the manner of conferring a Favour, add to the Value of it——they have no generous Souls who wait to be asked, before they grant what they know is wanted.— I was charmed with the Good-nature and Politeness of *Melicourt*, and immediately wrote a Letter, and gave him Directions how to manage the Affair.

We supp'd together, and during the little Repast, all our Discourse was on his intended Journey.——I chiefly insisted on his not delivering my Letter to the Marquis, till there was no Danger that the Surprize of hearing from me would affect his Health; and that he would

without

without concealing or disguising any thing, send me Word in what Condition he found my Lover, and in what manner he received my Letter.———Every thing being thus concluded on, he sent his Servant to order Post-Horses to be ready for his setting out next Morning by Break of Day.

All this being settled, and *Melicourt* on the Road, made me much easier than I had been for some time, and though I had still enough to trouble me on the old Marquis's Account, the excessive Tenderness and Concern he shewed for me in my late Indisposition, but too much confirming the Conjectures I before had of his being enamour'd with me ; yet did the charming Thoughts of being reconciled to his Son engross all my Attention. ———I had no leisure for any other Hopes or Fears ; when one is truly in love every thing centers there, and whatever one says, or does, or thinks, is dictated by that alone.

I cannot present the Reader with the Letter I sent by *Melicourt*, the Marquis by some Accident has lost it, and I remember only that it contain'd all the endearing Expressions a Soul overflowing with Love and Tenderness could suggest, without any Expostulations on the Injustice of his Suspicions———the Condition he was in took off all Resentment, and I laboured only to make him perfectly content.

Two Days after the Departure of *Melicourt*, it being the Festival of our Blessed Lady, and finding myself well enough to go abroad, I went to Church to return Thanks for my Recovery, and offer up Prayers for that of the Marquis. It was to Matins I went, but hearing there would be a Sermon in the Afternoon, I order'd Dinner more early than was my Custom, and returned in the Afternoon not to lose a Discourse, which I was told, there was great Expectations of being extremely elegant.

The Character I had heard was just : A Capuchin preached with so much Energy, Learning and Eloquence, that the whole Congregation seemed affected with it—there was nothing in his Discourse that had a Tincture of the

Pedant, and what he faid had more the Air of a Gentleman, recommending Morality to the World, than the fuperftitious Cant of fome of our illiterate Priefts.

The great Admiration I had of his preaching, made me look very much upon him, and the more I did fo, the more I fancied I had feen him before, tho' in what Place, or on what Occafion I could not prefently recollect. I know not how he came to caft his Eyes towards me, but he had fcarce looked upon me, when his Speech began to faulter, he turned pale, and tho' he feemed ftriving to repel fome inward Emotions which at that Inftant feized him, his Endeavours were in vain, and he fainted away.

Every Body was furprized and frighted, and many inquifitive Whifpers flew about the Church : one who fat by me, gave a fmelling Bottle to a Perfon that was affifting the Capcuhin, and feeming to know him, was afked by another who he was; to which he anfwered, that he was the only Son of a Nobleman, who having an extraordinary Vocation had quitted a great Title and Eftate to pafs his Days in a Convent, and then told the Name of his Family. I was very near falling into the fame Condition with the fubject of this Difcourfe, when I heard it was no other than the Chevalier *D'Elbieux,* ———Heaven, however, was pleafed to give me Strength to fuftain fo great a Surprize; but fearing it might yet have an Effect upon me, I took the Opportunity, while all were bufy about him to go out of the Church without being obferved.

When I came home I could not help reflecting on the Oddnefs of my Deftiny, which would not fuffer fcarce a Day to pafs over my Head without bringing on fome extraordinary Incident or other ; but this was not all, more and greater Matter of Speculation befel me before I flept.

In the Evening, *Forfan,* the old Marquis's Gentleman, made me a Vifit, and as he has fome fhare in the Accident of my Life, I believe it will not be improper to give a flight Sketch of his Character.

He

He had been always bred in high Life, without the Means of supporting himself according to his Birth, so was obliged to be a Dependant on others; to gain the Confidence of whom he seemed ever complying to the Humour of those he had a Design upon.———In a Word he was an artful, insinuating Man, and had so much the Appearance of Sincerity, that wherever he attempted to please he surely did so. As penetrating as was the old Marquis *De L———V———*, and certainly no Man was more, he suffered himself to be deceived in the Temper of this Servant; he made him his Confidante in most Things, not excepting the Tenderness he had for me, and the other to please him, was perpetually flattering him with an Assurance of obtaining me; but the end of these Memoirs will shew whither in this he fathomed the Bottom of his Lord's Intentions.

He imagined me of so mild and easy a Temper that he should be able to bring me to any Thing, so willingly undertook the Commission of waiting on me, and fathoming my Thoughts concerning the Passion his Lord had for me, which he supposed was arrived at that Height, that he would spare nothing for the Gratification of it.

He began with praising my Beauty to a degree of Fulsomeness, than proceeded to tell me the Effect it had on a Nobleman of the first Rank in the Kingdom, and added, that I ought not to refuse the Addresses of a Person such as the old Marquis *de L———V———*.

I doubt not but he would have had the Insolence even to propose Terms for my Compliance; had I not answered his first Attacks in a manner which shew'd I did not approve of any such Discourses, and on his discloseing his Errand, bid him quit my Apartment, and presume to come into it no more, unless it were to ask my Pardon for the Affront he had put upon me.

Any Man but himself would have desisted from a Prosecution which promised so little Success; but imagining the Continuance of his Lord's Favour depended upon his Skill in this Business, he had the Boldness to come again the next Day, and provoked me so far by his

Solicitations

Solicitations that I loft all Patience, and told him with
an Air, which nothing but the Occafion could excufe the
Pride of, that if he ever dared to approach me any
more with fuch fawcy Offers, I would find fome way
to make him repent it.

In this Inftance now did I find the Misfortune of the
Meannefs of my Birth————this vile Negotiator, fo
far from being daunted at what I faid, told me with
a fcornful Smile that I forgot myfelf————and that
fure I did not learn thefe Airs of Quality in the Village
of *D*————; to thefe Taunts he added Menaces, that
he fhould find means to difappoint all the chime-
real Ideas I had formed————that he would enquire
into my Behaviour, which he did not doubt but would
give the lye to all my Affectation of Virtue, and that
he would not fail to reprefent me in my proper Colours.
Having thus vented the Rancour of his Soul, he left me
to meditate on what he had faid.

I cannot fay but I was weak enough to be ftung with
thefe Reflections, and fhed fome few Tears; but they
foon paffed of, and my Innocence made me perfectly
eafy. I forfaw indeed that his Endeavours would not be
wanting to ruin me in the good Opinion of his Lord,
therefore without being ill-natured, I thought I might
do my beft to circumvent him in any Plot he
might be capable of forming againft me, by refenting
in a proper Manner, the firft Time I faw the old Marquis, the Ufage he had given me.

I was too much confufed to be able to do thing this
Day, but the firft Employment, after my Devotions,
that I took in Hand the next Day, was to write an
Account to Monfieur *de Saint Fal* of the Treatment I
had received from *Forfan*; I acquainted him alfo with
my Defign of getting him removed, in cafe the old
Marquis did not fuffer himfeif to be prejudiced againft
me, by his vile Offices. But I did not once mention
the young Marquis, having wrote fo fully to himfeif by
Monfieur *Meliccurt* all I had to fay.

I had juft concluded, when the old Marquis came *into*
my Room; the Surprize of feeing him at a Time when I fo
little

little expected him, put me into such a hurry of Spirits, that I could scarce rise from my Seat to receive him. You are writing to my Son, I perceive, *Jeanetta*, said he, snatching at the Letter, which I was hastily conveying into a Drawer. I find, continued he, by your Endeavours to hide it from me, you have no Inclination to make me your Confident in what passes between you.

I could easily convince your Lordship to the contrary, answered I, by shewing you to whom, and on what Occasion I have been writing ; but to what Purpose would it be for me to undeceive you in one Point, when it's probable your Gentleman may have insinuated things against me, in which, tho' equally innocent, I could not so easily clear myself.————as I perceived the Marquis appeared a little surprized at these Words, I took the Liberty to continue ; the manner, said I, in which you have been pleased to treat me by Monsieur *Forsan*, shews you have little Inclination to entertain favourable Thoughts of me.

Don't let us confound one thing with another, replied the Marquis, who for all his Subtilty was a little out of Countenance, I commanded *Forsan* indeed to wait on you with an Offer of my Heart————this was the Extent of his Orders, and if he has gone farther shall resent it————I have it's certain received some Intelligence, no way to your Advantage ; but my Intentions were to discourse you in a friendly Manner on that Head, and gave him no Commission to mention it to you———— but all this is foreign to the Letter you hide from me ; if you satisfy me in that Point, it will lay me under an Obligation to do as much in my turn————few Women are without Admirers, and Charms, such as yours, cannot fail of attracting a great Number————so that all the hazard you run in shewing me your Letter is, entrusting me with the Secret who is the happy Man : but I assure you, and will bind myself by an Oath never to divulge it ; and to make you readier to grant what I request in this Particular, will own to you, that I had much rather it were any other Man, than my Son, whom I would cease to acknowledge as such, if I found he had disobeyed my Commands.　　　　This

This is too cruel my Lord, cried I, burſting into a
a Torrent of Tears, and what I could never have expeſted,
nor deſerve————But you ſhall be convinced I am
not of the Diſpoſition you would ſeem to intimate.————
Mean as I am, I know what Honour, Virtue and
Decency demand from me, and have never even in
Thought deviated from their ſtricteſt Precepts————nor
by the Aſſiſtance of Heaven ever will————Here, my
Lord, continued I, preſenting him with my Letter, this
may convince you of the Intrigues I carry on———— I
know my Complaiſance involves your Nephew————
but he will pardon me, my Character, which is infinitely
dearer to me than my Life, is at ſtake————if to be
ſenſible of Inſults and outrageous Behaviour be a Crime,
I confeſs myſelf guilty.   With theſe Words I went
into my Cloſet and gave a looſe to my Grief

I know not whither the Impatience the Marquis was
in, to ſatisfy his Curioſity, gave him leave to take any
Notice of what I ſaid; for he had no ſooner laid hold
on the Letter, than he began to read it, and I ſuppoſe
with ſo much Attention that he well weigh'd every
Word, for he was a great while in this Employment.

This Girl's Conduct is reaſonable enough, ſaid he to
himſelf, not reflecting he was overheard————ſhe may
be aſperſed, and I impoſed on, but if I find I am ſo————
then he ſtopp'd, and read again, after which————
ſhe did not expect my coming, ſaid he, and it's plain
had no Deſign I ſhould ſee this Letter————there ſeems
to be no Guile on her Part————but I muſt, and will
fathom the bottom of this Affair.

All theſe Soliloquies I plainly heard, and have ſince
found that People in Years are very apt to talk in this
Manner to themſelves; I conceived great hopes however
from what he ſaid, and from that Moment began to
flatter myſelf with the Belief I ſhould have no Difficulty
in clearing up whatever was alledged againſt me.

The Marquis having finiſhed his Examination of the
Letter, came into my Cloſet and found me overwhelmed
in Tears————there is your Epiſtle, beautiful *Jeanetta*,
ſaid he, returning it to me————I aſk pardon for
having

having exacted such a Compliance for me————but I had my Reasons————Time will convince you they were not for your Prejudice————dry up your Tears I conjure you, if the Suspicions I have been made to conceive of you are without Foundation, I will not leave your Apartment till you have ample Satisfaction for the injury————I acknowledge to you, *Jeanetta*, that you are very dear to me, and it was my Affection which gave me so sensible a Concern for what I have heard in relation to your Conduct————I am informed that you have a secret Lover, who possesses all the Favours in your Power to bestow————that all the Pretences you make to Virtue, are but Disguises for your Passion————that in spite of your Fondness for this unknown Person, your aim is to make your Fortune by Marriage, and that my Son is the Man you hope to ensnare for that Purpose. That your Affectation of Virtue is only a Bait laid for him, and that you imagine the Passion he is possest of for you, will bring about your Aim at his Return, if Heaven shall preserve his Life.————Now, lovely *Jeanetta*, continued he, in all these idle Stories, supposing them to be such, there are yet some Truth———— I know my Son adores you————I know also you make him a very tender Return, at least appear to do so; his Misfortune of being wounded, and the Condition the News of it reduced you to make me apt to think you are sincere in your Professions to him————and yet what I have been told perplexes me————you best can unravel the Affair, and tell me whether I am imposed upon or not.

I must confess that while the Marquis was talking to me in this Manner, I forgot my Birth, and the vast Disparity between us, and full of the Pride of conscious Innocence, was eager to reply before he had half concluded what he had to say.

My Lord, replied I, looking on him with Eyes which I believe informed him of my Thoughts before my Tongue could utter them, I am more surprized than angry at such base Calumnies thrown upon me————I thank all gracious Providence, who has given me a

Mind

Mind difdainful of all bafe Actions, and that my Conduct baffles all Occafions of this Sort————were I really guilty of giving way to any loofe Attacks, my Anfwer would be very fhort; I fhould tell your Lordfhip in three Words, that I was not accountable to you for my Actions, becaufe then I fhould have Friends who would defend me from any Profecution of yours; but as I am, unfriended only by my own Innocence, and the Charms it has had for my moft honourable Protector your Nephew, I am bound to clear myfelf to your Lordfhip, from whofe hitherto good Opinion I have received fuch Favours.

As to the laft Particular your Lordfhip mentioned, and in which you doubtlefs have moft right to be concerned, I fet too great a value on Truth to deny I have been beloved by your Son, and that he is dear, and will ever be fo to me : This you may think a Crime, I am fure it is a Misfortune, and the Source of all I have fuffered ————without that unhappy Paffion my Life had glided on in filent and peaceful Obfcurity————but yet, my Lord, I was ever far from expecting the Honour you mention as my due————I am not fo partial to the few Merits I am Miftrefs of, nor can fo far forget my native Meannefs————tho' at the fame Time, permit me to affure you no other Pretenfions could ever have made an Impreffion on me.

I faid no more, expecting the Marquis would have replied, but as he did not, and feemed very penfive, and as it were wavering in his Thoughts————you ftill fufpect my Veracity, my Lord, refumed I, or are perhaps offended at the Truth I have been bold enough to utter; but I know how to clear myfelf from all the foul Afperfions thrown upon me, and at the fame Time to eafe you of all the Apprehenfions you have on the Score of my Tendernefs for your Son————before to-morrow Night, I will take a Step which fhall force you to acknowledge, I deferved more of your Compaffion than Contempt or Anger, and gave your Lordfhip no juft occafion to treat me in fo cruel a manner by Monfieur *Forfan.*

The

The Marquis at these Words seemed rouzed from the Resvery he had been in, and drawing his Chair near mine, took hold of my Hand, and looking on me with more Tenderness than he had done before, let us, beautiful *Jeanetta*, said he, be reconciled:————I have more than you imagine pleads for you in my Heart————you are restored to my Esteem and Friendship ; and I am persuaded you neither are, nor will be undeserving of it.

No, my Lord, resumed I, with a Resolution which I knew not if it might not be thought too presuming for one of my Rank to one of his, but as I have already said, Virtue is allowed some Pride, your Friendship is as fickle and uncertain as your Prejudice : I have a right to think so from your easy Credulity against my Innocence, and after the Treatment I have received already, what may I not expect————there is no Refuge for wounded Fame, but a Convent————there will I seclude myself from the base World, and never more be in the Power of such a Wretch as *Forsan* to traduce me.

It must not be, cried the old Marquis, interrupting me, ————I'll never permit such a Resolution to take Place ; I have Reasons to oppose it, which you cannot yet conceive. I desire not, my Lord, returned I with the same Tone I had spoke before, to dive into your Lordship's Secrets, but I know my own, and that I am so far the Mistress of myself, as that nothing shall prevail upon me to alter my Determination, except on one Condition.

What Condition, cried the Marquis impatiently ? it is my Lord, answered I, that you will oblige the Author of these Calumnies to reveal before my Face the Motives which induced him to load me with them, and if I have any secret Enemies to disclose and give them up ; for it must be that either he has been told these Stories, or invented them himself, and I desire to be convinced as well as cleared.

The Marquis seemed perfectly alarmed at my Thoughts of Retiring, and immediately complied with my Request : he sent a Servant to order Monsieur

Forfan to come to him, and in the mean Time omitted nothing that might affure me I fhould never more have Reafon to be diffatisfied with his Behaviour, provided I would not entertain any Defign of concealing myfelf from him.

Forfan obeyed the Summons, and the Marquis gave me the Satisfaction of reprimanding him for the injurious Treatment he had given me; during which the ill-natured Man gave me Looks full of Envy, and when his Lord had done fpeaking, whifpered fomewhat in his Ear, I fuppofe by way of Excufe; but whatever it was, the Marquis took no Notice of it, and infifted on his naming the Authors of thofe Reports he had brought of my Behaviour————*Forfan* turned pale at this Command, and fain would have evaded it, faying it would be cruel to betray Perfons, who out of Friendfhip to him had given him the Intelligence? At which the Marquis appeared highly incenfed, and looking on him with Eyes, that fparkled with Indignation, thefe Reafons are deteftable, cried he, an Accufation not fupported by Proofs, argues the Accufer the greateft Criminal ; and I begin to believe you had fome very unwarrantable Views in prejudicing me againft this young Lady. *Forfan* with many Imprecations declared what he had faid was not occafioned by any ill Will to me, and only repeated by him in Duty to his Lord, that he might not be deceived by falfe Appearances.

Let me then know from whom you had thefe Informations, faid the Marquis fiercely————have you lefs Refpect for me than for thofe you feem afraid to name ?

Forfan, terrified at thefe Words, and finding Evafions, would no longer be of any Service to him, confefied at laft ; that what he had heard was from a Lady of his Acquaintance, called Madamoifelle *Junia*, who had lately lodged in the fame Houfe with me, and was Miftrefs of my Secrets.

When I heard the Name of *Junia*, I no longer was furprized at the malicious Calumnies thrown upon me———— Women of her Character never forget an Affront ; and as fhe could not in reality bring me to be like herfelf,

3   tool;

took at least a Pleasure in making me be thought so. I gave the Marquis an exact Account of all that passed between us, and had given rise to the Malice she discovered on my Account, and then begged of him, that she might be sent for, that we might confront each other, being determined to have my Innocence made fully appear.

The Marquis seemed to think this Request entirely needless, and assured me he was perfectly satisfied, but all the little Passion I had in me being now worked up to the highest Pitch it could be, I insisted so vehemently on it, that *Forsan* was ordered to go and conduct her to my Apartment. He seemed ready enough to do as he was commanded, and was going out of the Room, doubtless to prepare her for the Business she was called upon to answer, when the Marquis called him back. No, said he, you shall not quit my Presence till we have heard what this Woman has to say: I will have one of my Pages carry a Message as from me to her.

The Page accordingly was sent to her Lodgings *Forsan* being obliged to give Directions where she lived, and as it was but in the next Street she immediately came, and with as much Assurance as tho' she never had been guilty of any thing against me.

I was about to open my Mouth to complain of her Ill-nature, when the Marquis put me back, and desired leave to discuss this matter himself——I beg, Mademoiselle, said he, that you will do me the Favour to relate to me what passed between you and *Forsan*, with Relation to this Lady———I do assure you that no ill use shall be made of it ; therefore must insist you will act with Sincerity.

Junia had been formerly acquainted with the Marquis, and knew very well that he was not a Man to be trifled with, so freely confessed, that hearing Monsieur *Forsan* came frequently to visit me, she had imagined he was my Admirer, and had rallied him on that Subject, telling him that she was very certain he would have no Success, for I had a Lover of a much superior Rank. The Marquis then asked who that Lover was that she

meant.

meant. Yourself, my Lord, anfwer'd fhe, in a gay
Manner——I know your Lordfhip has no Averfion
to pretty Women, and that you both wrote to, and vifited this Lady was no Secret ; fo I from thence concluded you were the happy Man.

The Blufhes with which my Face was cover'd at this
Difcourfe, fpoke at once my Anger and Confufion ; but
I forbore giving any Interruption to it, in Refpeft to the
Marquis, and *Junia* went on.

For my Part, faid fhe, I little thought this Converfation would be called over again, nor had fo ill an
Opinion of Monfieur *Forfan*, as to fufpeft he would
talk of fuch idle Matters ; he afked me feveral Queftions, indeed, concerning this Lady's Behaviour, in
none of which I could inform him ; therefore, if he
pretends to receive any Intelligence from me, any more
than the few unmeaning Words I have confefs'd to your
Lordfhip, he is a Villain, and muft have fome Defigns
to which I am utterly a Stranger.

Having fpoke this, fhe made a low Curtefy to the
Marquis, and another to me, and quitted the Room ;
as for *Forfan*, I believe, he would have given all he had
got by the Favour of the Marquis, to have been that
Moment an hundred Miles off———he look'd fo
downcaft and mortified, that in fpite of the Injury he
would have done me, I could not forbear pitying him. The
old Marquis feem'd to meafure him with his Eyes from
Head to Foot for fome Minutes without fpeaking ; but
it was eafy to perceive, he was incenfed againft him to
a very great Degree.

At laft, *Forfan*, faid he, you have fhewn yourfelf utterly unworthy, not only of my Protection, but alfo of
all civil Society, and ought to be banifh'd both———
you have abufed the Confidence of your Lord and Pa-
tron———you have endeavoured to blacken the Character of an innocent Lady———you are detected in all
this———fhamefully detected ; and cannot fure add to
your other Crimes, the Prefumption of flattering yourfelf, that I fhall ever fuffer you to appear before me any
more——begone——

This

This laſt Word was pronounced with ſo ſtern an Accent, that the poor Gentleman retired in the moſt fearful and ſubmiſſive Manner. If I ſhould ſay I was not highly pleaſed with the Victory, I had gained over his Malice, I ſhould be guilty of an Untruth———it is natural to rejoyce at ſurmounting Injuries, and of all others, thoſe on our Reputation are moſt ſenſibly felt ; yet now my Innocence was clear'd, I was ſorry for the Diſgrace of the Calumniator, and interceeded very ſincerely with the Marquis for his Pardon. No, *Jeanetta,* ſaid the Marquis, I may be deceived once, but will never be ſo a ſecond time by the ſame Perſon.

When the Emotions which this Affair had occaſion'd were a little over, the Marquis deſired me in the moſt obliging Manner, to forget the Diſquiets he had occaſion'd me, and as he had Buſineſs of the utmoſt Importance, which call'd him from me at that time, begg'd I would allow him the Favour of dining with me the next Day———he added, that he would one Day make me ample Compenſation for every thing, and ſaid ſo many complaiſant and reſpectful things, that I was highly ſatisfied with his Behaviour.———Alas! I little thought of the Troubles in which he afterwards involved me.

The next Morning at Six, *Barbara* waked me to tell me that a Man about Thirty, very poorly dreſt, blind, and led by a Boy of about ſeven Years of Age deſired to ſpeak with me———good God, ſaid I, why did you diſturb me, I know no ſuch Perſon in the World as you deſcribe ? But, ſince it is ſo, go and ſee what he would have.

Barbara went away and returned immediately in a kind of Extaſy ; well, Madam, ſaid ſhe, the blind Man was in the right to make me wake you———he tells me, he brings you the beſt News you ever heard in your Life.———News that will dry up the Tears you ſo long have been ſhedding———I was ſo rejoyced to hear him ſay this, that if it had not been for Shame, I would have taken him about the Neck and kiſſed him.

I

I could not forbear laughing at my Aunt's manner of testifying the Pleasure she took in every thing that promised Satisfaction to me; well then, said I, since he is the Messenger of good Tidings shew him up to me, I had no sooner utter'd the Word than she flew down Stairs, and immediately the blind Man and his Boy appear'd.

Go on, Child, said he, as soon as he enter'd the Room, lead me to the dear Creature, that I may throw myself into her Arms————that I may tell her how much I have suffered since I saw her————Where is she ?————Why does she not meet me————perhaps, Excess of Joy at my unhoped Return, has thrown her into a Swoon————else why does she not speak ————is she not here————does she not see us ?

Yes, indeed, Pappa, said the Boy, she sees us, but looks at us as if she did not know us. Hold your Tongue, replied the blind Man, her Silence is the Effect of her Surprize and Joy; but guide me to her ————'tis I alone that can recover her, she had always a gentle Heart, and 'tis no Wonder that my sudden Appearance, after being so long supposed dead, has overwhelm'd her.

The Figure of this blind Man, his swinging his Arms about, as if feeling for something, and the Discourse he had to his Boy, I thought so whimsical, that I could not help bursting into a Fit of Laughter. At which he seem'd very much offended, how is this, cryed he, does she receive me with Contempt ? Sure Child thou hast mistaken the House————pray somebody inform me, if these are not the Lodgings of Mademoiselle *De Roches,* who passes for the Widow of an Officer ! Yes, certainly, said my Aunt, and here is my Lady herself. Why then this unseasonable Mirth, resumed he ?————Has she forgot me, or does she not think me worthy of being acknowledg'd for her Husband, because I have had the Misfortune of losing my Eye-sight since I saw her ? ————I could never have believed a Wife for whom I have done so much, would ever have been so ungrateful ;————but 'tis no Matter, I'll endeavour to love her as little for the future.————I'll see the End of it,

however————in the mean time I shall make no Ceremony————wherever my Wife is there is my Home,
and here I shall take up my Quarters.

In speaking these Words he groped out a Chair and
sat down; the Boy crying all the while to me————
Mamma!——Mamma————pray speak to my Father
————you know how passionate he is, and you had
better keep him in Humour.

I thought there was something so extraordinary in this
Mistake, for I could think it no other, of finding myself claim'd as a Wife and a Mother, and my imaginary Husband taking a formal Possession of my House,
that I could not forbear continuing my Laughter to an
immoderate Degree.————*Barbara*, whom I had told
I knew nothing either of the Man or his Boy, was as
much diverted as myself, which so provoked him, that
he called us both a thousand Names, attempted to strike
us with his Cane, and stamped with his Feet like a Man
distracted————indeed, at last I began to think he was
really so, and was angry with myself for having turned
into a Jest, what rather deserved my Commiseration.
To be rid, however, of the Impertinence, I bid
Barbara take him by the Arm and lead him out;
but the poor Creature suffered for going about to
obey me: On her offering to molest him, he gave her
such a Blow as was very near throwing her down; vile
Woman, said he to me, are you not ashamed to give
this Reception to a Husband, who took you from an
infamous Course of Life, and loved you more than he
ought to have done; but I suppose you have taken up
your old way of living, and prefer that to Honesty
————don't think, nevertheless, that you shall escape
being made an Example of, you shall find I have
Friends that will take my Part.

The Seriousness with which these Words were spoke,
made me grow a little uneasy, and beginning to think
he was not mad, thought it best to answer him in a
proper Manner: I am very sorry, Monsieur, said I,
for the Ill-Manners I unwarily treated you with: I assure
you it was wholly owing to my not being able to com-
prehend

prehend your Difcourfe————your Miftake of claiming me for a Wife, I now perceive to be owing to the Agreement between our Names; for I do affure you I am a perfect Stranger to you.————O! perfidious Woman, cryed the blind Man, did I not take you from the moft wretched Condition in the World, and make you my Wife?————Have I not had feveral Children by you, of which this is the Eldeft, and the only one living————go, ungrateful Creature, I would have no more to do with you, I would abandon you to your ill Fate, if it was not for the Pleafure of Revenge.

Keep you Temper, Monfieur, replied I, a little more haughtily, otherwife you'll oblige me to expofe you, by fending for Affiftance to force you from my Lodgings. Was ever fuch Impudence, interrupted he, do you think I'll bear this?————no, follow if you will your wretched way of Life————I won't ftir a Step to hinder you; but affure yourfelf I fhall ftay here, and all the World fhall not drive me out.————Go, Child, added he, to the Boy, bid my Man bring up the Luggage, and then he fhall order fomewhat for us to eat, for this vile Woman, I fuppofe, will prepare nothing for us.

I was fo aftonifh'd and and perplex'd with all this, that I knew not what to fay————*Barbara*, no lefs confounded, cryed, what muft we do, Madam? And, indeed, had any one come in, and feen me ftand as I did like one ftupified, they would have imagin'd the Man had really fpoke the Truth.

His Commands were obey'd, and feveral Trunks and Boxes brought into my Dining-Room————a *Switzer* Servant, whofe Whifkers made me tremble, prefented my pretended Hufband with a Night-Gown and Cap, and having undrefs'd his Mafter, and received his Orders in a Whifper, laid the Cloth, but not finding the Key in the Buffet broke it open and took out what he wanted, behaving in every thing, as if he had been really at Home.

The Confternation I was in, took from me the power of Speech, and I went into my Clofet to meditate what was beft to be done; *Barbara*, who followed me no lefs

terrified

terrified than myself, advised me to call in the Neighbours and demand their Assistance; but alas! the unhappy Circumstances I was in, of having pass'd for a Person I was not, deterr'd me; I knew very well that to prove myself not the Wife of the blind Man, I must prove also who I really was, and this was a Step I dare not take without the Consent of the Marquis; and as I expected him that Day, I thought the most prudent thing I could do, was to wait with Patience till he came; which, indeed, was sooner than I expected: for as I was talking with my Aunt, I heard his Coach stop at the Door; I sent my Aunt to acquaint him with what had happened to me, and to beg he would come into my Closet, for I dreaded to pass through the Room, where the blind Man and his formidable *Swiss* were eating, as I must have done, had I gone to receive him in my Dining-Room.

He was much surprized at the Relation she made him, but could not help laughing at the Perplexity he found me in. I must own, said he, the Adventure has somewhat in it very particular; but certainly the poor Man must be mad; for no one in his Senses could be guilty of such an Extravagance; but, continued he, we will go and try if we can recover him.

With these Words he went into my Chamber, where my pretended Husband was smoaking his Pipe: And after telling who he was, desired he would inform him on what Pretence he took Possession of a Lady's Lodgings, whose Quality was not to be insulted by any one. To which the blind Man answer'd, that he knew too well the Respect due to the Marquis *De L——V——* to offer to contend with him; but at the same time begg'd leave to assure him that I was his Wife; and had been married to him many Years, however my Artifices might impose upon his Lordship to the contrary.

It was now my greatest Blessing, that the Marquis in Reality knew who I was, for had he not, the Assurance with which this Imposture spoke, and the Circumstances he brought to prove, as he supposed, what he averr'd, would

would have made this old Nobleman, penetrating as he was, ſtagger in his Belief; for my own Part had I been a Stranger, and heard any thing related in the manner the blind Man did this Story, I ſhould have given it on his Side; ſo careful ought we to be how we judge by Appearances.———

The Marquis now found I did not exaggerate the Impudence and Obſtinacy of this Invader of my Lodgings, and having liſtened to him with a great deal of ſeeming Patience, he ſtood for ſome Moment's conſidering on what he heard; at laſt, well, Monſieur, ſaid he, the Arguments you have brought to convince me this Lady is your Wife, are ſuch as muſt be left to time to confute ———if ſhe be really ſuch, you doubtleſs can bring ſome Evidences beſide yonr own Aſſeveration to prove it; and if ſo the Law muſt determine in your Favour; till then be pleaſed to accept of an Apartment in my Houſe, for I think you cannot inſiſt on living here, as ſhe diſclaims you for a Huſband.

The ſeeming Softneſs which the Marquis treated him with, render'd him more audacious, and imagining doubtleſs that there were ſome ſecret Reaſons for his not openly eſpouſing my Cauſe; declared boldly that no Man, be he ever of ſuch Rank, ſhould prevail on him to quit his Home, for ſuch that was which belong'd to me———on this, the Marquis appear'd more ſubmiſſive ſtill, and to ſound him farther, even condeſcended to entreat he would accept his Offer, which the cther perceiving, cry'd, no, no, my Lord, my Wife is young and handſome, and your Viſits here may occaſion ſome Diſcourſes not conſiſtent with my Honour; though I have had the Misfortune to looſe my Sight, I am an Officer, my Lord, and have had the Glory to receive many Wounds in the Service of my King and Country.———I am not, therefore, to be perſuaded to any thing that will occaſion a Blemiſh on my Character———I ſolemnly proteſt that Woman is my Wife, though for ſome ſecret Reaſons ſhe thinks fit to diſown me, and her Child too; and I will maintain Poſſeſſion here, in ſpite of all that would oppoſe me.

I

I perceived on the Marquis's Face a kind of malicious Smile at the blind Man's Assurance, and turning to me said in a low Voice, I now perceive this is not a Mistake as you apprehended; but conceals under it a Design which we shall soon discover————then stepping to the Door gave some Orders to one of his Servants, which I did not hear. On his Return he bid me be easy, for he would engage all would soon be over.

He had some farther Discourse with my would-be Husband; but the more he affected to sooth the Wretch, the more insolent he grew; and nothing gave me a greater Insight into the Subtlety of this Nobleman, than the Patience with which he endured his gross Behaviour.

Half an Hour had not pass'd over before the Servant return'd with a Commissary, to whom the Marquis related the whole Affair, adding, that he would be bound to make it appear that the blind Man had no Pretensions to me, for that he was my Godfather, and knew every Step of my Life, from my Birth, till that very Hour.

The Confusion of my unwelcome Guests at hearing the Marquis make this Declaration was such, as is not to be exprest; both the dreadful *Swiss* and his Master, would now have been gladly out of a Place they so lately pretended a right to, if they could any way have made their Escape; but the Officers who attended the Commissary immediately secured them; and only waited the Word of Command to carry them to Prison. Now, said the Marquis, we shall make you, Monsieur *De Roches* as you call yourself, prove by what right you bear that Name, and when and where you were married to this Lady.

The Fellow trembled, and perceiving they were going to lay hold on him, fell on his Knees and begg'd Mercy of the Marquis, protesting that it was with no intent to rob, much more to murder me, that he came to my Lodgings; but was put upon it by one who said it was only a Frolick to punish and give a little Confusion to me.

Who

Who is that Perfon, faid the Marquis, if ycu are fin-cere in your Confeffion, 'tis poffible this Lady may have the Goodnefs to forgive you. The pretended blind Man now open'd his Eyes, and own'd that he was a De-pendant on Monfieur *De Beauhaye*, and that it was to oblige him and Mademoifelle *Junia*, he had undertaken this Bufinefs———adding, that they had given him In-ftructions how to behave, in Cafe I fhould have any Friend to take my Part, and that the Plot was wholly theirs, though he was employed in the Execution of it.

I was more amazed to hear fuch Bafenefs in one of my own Sex, if poffible, than I had been at the Infolence of this Inftrument of her Malice; but when he men-tioned a Gentleman, as concern'd with her in this vile Stratagem, it ftruck into my Head, that it was the fame who had been difappointed in his Defigns upon me; and concluded that out of Revenge he had joined with *Junia* to give me this Difquiet.———I communicated my Thoughts to the old Marquis, who agreed with me that nothing could be more probable; and on our queftioning the Criminal concerning the Complexion, Shape and Stature of his Mafter, his Defcription agreed fo exactly with the Perfon I had feen come down Stairs, the Night I had fo narrow an Efcape, that I was confirmed in what I before believed.

Having obliged him to difcover as much as he knew of the Affair, the Marquis told him, in Confideration of his free Confeffion, and as what he had done was not out of any Malice in himfelf, but in Obedience to a Per-fon he depended on, he would not infift on his fuffering thofe Penalties the Law would have inflicted; fo bid him and his Confedeates be gone with all their Luggage, and take care how they meddled in fuch Matters for the fu-ture. The Word was fcarce out of the Marquis's Mouth, than they took up the things, and bleffing both him and I, made the beft of their Way out of the Houfe. The Marquis after this, made a handfome Pre-fent to the Commiffary for his Trouble, and thus con-cluded an Adventure foolifh enough in itfelf, yet might

have

have been of very ill Confequence, but for fo powerful
and penetrating a Friend.

When we were alone, the Marquis was very pleafant
on what happened, and told me I ought to think myfelf very happy, that I was not condemned to pafs my
Life with fuch a Hufband as this amiable blind Man ; he
would have continued his Raillery on this Subject much
longer, as it feem'd very much to divert him, but that
he was obliged to leave me; and that I was fo luckily indebted to his Vifit that Morning, was owing to his not
being able to give his Company at Dinner, having
Bufinefs, he faid, which would detain him till Six or
Seven in the Evening.

After this Storm of my unequal Fate was over, an Hour
of Sun-fhine broke upon me ; the old Marquis had not
left me three Minutes, before I received a Letter from
Melicourt, with one enclofed in it from my Lover :
I looked upon it as highly fortunate, that the Poft did
not arrive while his Father was with me, to whom I
could not well have avoided fhewing the Contents of
both, and how improper that would have been, the
Reader may judge. That from Monfieur *Melicourt* was
in thefe Terms.

To the moft beautiful and admirable *Jeanetta.*

Madam,

*I Should be far unworthy the Honour of your Friendfhip,
or the Truft you were pleas'd to repofe in me, if I delayed one Moment the Satisfaction I dare anfwer you will
receive from the enclofed————for that Reafon I fhall
defer giving you any Account of my Journey, till I have the
Honour to fee you————this Night having done all the little
Service required of me I fet out for* Paris, *where I fhall
be proud to receive any other Commands, you fhall think
me capable of executing ————I hope your Health is by*
this

this Time fully recovered, if it is not, flatter myself the happy Tidings I send you will have that good Effect.——

    I am,

      With the greatest Respect

        and Admiration of your Virtues,

          Mademoiselle,

            Your most humble and

              most devoted Servant,

                MELICOURT.

It was well this Letter from *Melicourt* prepared me for what I was to find, in that of my dear Marquis's: Excess of Joy being often more dangerous than Excess of Grief, the Transports I felt, however, were scarce to be sustain'd when I read these dear, and never to be forgotten Lines.

To my Soul's only Joy, the lovely, the adorable and faithful *Jeanetta*.

I Live *my Angel, and receive a double Pleasure in Life, since it is by you I live*———*your Letter was an infallible Balsam to my Wounds*———*Death that conquers all Things, withholds his Dart at your Command, and spares me to make what Compensation is in my Power for all the Sufferings I have occasioned you*———*O! how shall I express my Gratitude for your Forgiveness, for the Continuance of your Affection, after having proved myself so unworthy of it by my foul Suspicions!*———*Words* cannot *do it*———*Actions* must———*be assured of this? O thou most charming, most excellent of all your Sex; that the whole Employment of my future Days, shall be to make you happy.*———*I wait with the utmost Impatience the Recovery of my Wounds, that I may make*

you

you mine forever, and declare to my Father and the *whole
World, that I cannot live without you.*——*I rejoice
to hear by Monsieur* Melicourt, *of the favourable Disposition he is in towara you*——*pray Heaven encrease it
to a just Proportion with your Merits.*——*Adieu, my
Charmer, my Weakness will not permit me to explain to
you the thousandth Part of what my Heart dictates.
Monsieur* Melicourt, *who has been Witness of my Transports on your Account, I am certain will be so generous as
to make you in Part sensible of them; but if you love,
as I will no longer doubt if you do, that Love will inform
you better in my meaning than any Description whatever
*——*once more farewel*——*think of me as your own,
for it is inconsistent either with my Power or Inclination,
ever to be but*

My ever adored JEANETTA'S

Most faithful and most tenderly devoted,

L——V——.

P. S. *Be under no Uneasiness for my Wounds, the Surgeon this Moment assures me he finds so great an Amendment,
that I may expect a perfect Cure in a few Days.*———
See the Efficacy of your endearing Letter.———

From the Camp.

Where now was the Remembrance of my past Misfortunes !——Where the Apprehensions of any future
Ills ! All were swallowed up in the ravishing Idea of my
Lover's Constancy, his Recovery, and the Hope of seeing him in a short time——my Head run now on
our mutual Felicity at meeting, and the Means he would
employ that we might part no more.——I was all Extasy, all Delight, and it seem'd as if Heaven had decreed
I should receive this Letter to give me Strength of Spirits to support me in the most terrible Trial, I had yet
ever under undergone, and which was immediately coming on.

After

After having put my Letters carefully up, I sat mu-
sing on the dear Contents, and was in that Posture at
the old Marquis's Return: The Satisfaction at my Heart
made me receive him with an unusual Gaiety ————
he seemed pleased to find me in that Humour, which, I
suppose, he imputed to having been eas'd of the blind Man,
and the Discovery of the Baseness of those who had
employed him: We had some little Conversation on that
Head; but the Marquis seem'd less disposed to Raillery
than he had been in the Morning, and ever and anon
was very pensive, a Frame of Mind not usual with him.
I took the Liberty of asking if I had any way offended
him, as I had some Reason to fear from his Reserve;
no, *Jeanetta*, answer'd he, I am, indeed, thoughtful
on your Score; but the Sentiments I have for you, are
far from those of Resentment.————I have been calling a Council in my Heart about you, and after some
Struggles all is determined in your Favour————I
have more than once told you I had great Designs in
Agitation for you————they are now compleated, and
it is in your power to become one of the happiest Women in *France*;————but Secrecy, Prudence, and Sincerity are necessary in order to it.————I see you are
impatient for my Meaning, and I will not keep you
long in suspence————if you'll allow me the Pleasure
of supping with you, when that is over we may discourse at leisure.

His postponing what he had to say, made me imagine he intended to prepare me by Degrees for something, that he knew would very much surprize me. I
cannot but say I had some Anxiety, lest it should be a
Repetition of those Offers he had commission'd *Forsan*
to make me; but then the high Encomiums he had since
given my Virtue, made me think he would not pretend
to destroy, what he seem'd to account so worthy his
Praise.————Sometimes I was tempted to flatter myself, that he would no longer oppose my being united to
his Son.————Various were my Conjectures, but none
of them were right, as a little time convinced me.

During

During Supper we talk'd only of indifferent things, but when that was over, he defired that I would give Orders, that whoever came we might not be interrupted, which I having done, he drew his Chair near mine, and addrefs'd me in the following manner.

The time is now come, lovely *Jeanetta*, faid he, that I fhall difclofe to you the great Defign I have fo often told you I had for you. Your Virtue, of which I had a high Idea from the firft Acquaintance with you, is now fo well confirmed, that I will no longer delay letting you know I am determined to reward it by raifing you to a Rank and Fortune, which you could not but for that have any Reafon to expect: not that I make any Reflections on the Meannefs of your Birth————Souls have one common Parent, all are alike derived from the great Source of Wifdom and Virtue, who indeed endues fome with a much larger Share of his own Divine Effence than others———— thofe whofe Reafon triumphs over Vice, I therefore look upon as the Favourites of Heaven, and as fuch infinitely more to be refpected than the Favourites of Kings, or even Kings themfelves, when they act beneath the Dignity of their Royal Function.

You, my dear *Jeanetta*, are one of thofe happy few, whom Providence has bleffed with thefe celeftial Emanations in a peculiar Manner————in you I find thofe Perfections of Mind, which I fo highly reverence, and I now difcover to you, that I cannot behold them united to fo many perfonal Charms and engaging Ways of Behaviour, without defiring to be allied to them———— I know very well, that Cuftom and the common Practice of the World is againft me, and that among the Nobility, mean Alliances are never pardon'd———— were my Intentions, but even fufpected before accomplifhed, I muft expect Remonftrances on Remonftrances, and even what I refolve, perhaps may be difappointed by the Interpofition of fuperior Authority————on this Account therefore every thing muft be done with the moft perfect Caution and Privacy, and I doubt not

your

your Difcretion in acting according to the Rules I fhall prefcribe.

I believe after what I have faid, you are no longer a Stranger to my Meaning————there remains yet but one Thing to inform you,————you know I have an only Son, who pays me back in Duty all the Paternal Affection I have treated him with————I deferred declaring myfelf to you till I had firft confulted him——— he feems to confider this Mark of the Deference I pay him with the greateft Gratitude————but fee what he writes to me, in anfwer to a Letter I fent him on that Score.

In fpeaking thefe Words, he took a Letter out of his Pocket, and gave it me to read, which I did with very great Emotions the Contents were as follows ;

To my Noble and ever honoured Father, the Marquis *De L——V——*.

My Lord,

THE Marks I have juft now received of your conde-fcending Tendernefs to me, are fuch as demands much more than a Son can pay, fince all I can do in Return, is no more than what I am bound in Duty to do, were you lefs good. Believe, however, I befeech your Lordfhip, that I think myfelf much more indebted to you, for your think-ing me worthy of this Honour, than for the Life you gave, and alfo, that had you Thought fit to have acted otherwife, I fhould ftill have had the fame regard for the Lady in whofe Favour you are determined; being, with a fincere and profound Duty and Submiffion,

My Lord,

Your Lordfhip's

moft Obedient Son and
humble Servant,

L——V——.

Whether

Whether it were that one is naturally apt to believe what pleases us, or whether I had really Reason from the Discourse of the old Marquis, and the Letter of the young one to imagine I was going to be as happy as my utmost Wishes could suggest, I will not pretend to say, but its certain I doubted not but the next thing this Nobleman spoke, would be the fiat of my Bliss. I returned the Letter, and trembling between Hope and Fear, there was no need my Lord, said I, of this Proof to convince me of your Son's Duty and Affection.

But it may serve, replied he, to shew you the regard I have for him, in consulting him in an Affair, in which I was entirely my own Master.———However, as you seem methinks not yet able to comprehend my meaning ———know, charming *Jeanetta*, that notwithstanding the Reasons which opposed my Inclinations, I have resolved to make you the Marchioness *de L—— V——.*

Who would not have thought these last Words contained a Decree in which all my Hopes were centered ; overwhelm'd with the most grateful Sense, and as it were out of myself between Astonishment and Joy, I threw myself at his Feet, testifying by that Posture, what in the instant Transport I had no Words to Express.

How happy am I, my dear *Jeanetta*, said the Marquis tenderly raising me from the Ground, that what I am resolved to do for you, is received with so much Satisfaction———I must confess I hesitated for a long Time before I could bring myself to declare my Intentions———I feared your Passion for my Son, might have taken too deep a Foundation in your Heart, and should have been shocked to have found myself refused— But I see my good Opinion of your Prudence has not deceived me, and do assure you that the manner in which you accept my offer has done what I thought impossible, augmented the Love I before had for you; and in Gratitude for this Softness depend upon it, my charming

Jeanetta,

Jeanetta, I shall always behave to you in such a manner, that you shall confess my Complaisance makes full Attonement for the Disparity of my Years.

I am amazed that it was possible for me thus to remember what the Marquis said on this Occasion, so confounded, so stupified as I was at this unexpected Stroke of Fate, this somewhat so infinitely worse for all my Hopes, than I had ever conceived could happen————— the utmost that my Fears had ever suggested from his uncommon Complaisance was, that he would one Day make some Proposals of being his Mistress, and then that Virtue which he had allowed in me, and so much praised, would have enabled me to have evaded any such Offers without offending him; but to find he condescended to make me his Wife, left me without any excuse for a Refusal, excepting such a one as could not be agreeable to him———— it was plain that he must be passionately in love with me, to resolve on a Match so every way unequal, and it was therefore natural to believe he would go to any Extremities rather than be disappointed————the least of His that could befall me was the being separated from his Son, whether I seemed to approve, or absolutly refused the Honour he intended————never was a young Creature in so terrible a Dilemma, nor knew less what to answer to Addresses at once so advantageous and distruction————to heighten this Perplexity, the Letter I had just been reading from the young Marquis came fresh into my Mind, I now found that his Father had wrote to him concerning his own Marriage, and not, as I had imagined, a Consent for him to enter into that State; I doubted not therefore but my Refusal would now irritate him no less against my Lover than myself, and that Suggestion made me resolve to conceal my Aversion to his Proposals, and gain Time, which in Effect is gaining a great deal, as Chance frequently presents occasions of Relief which we could never have dreamt of.

How is it possible my Lord, said I, for me to reply to you————you see the Confusion I am in, nor can you wonder at it—good Heaven, shall the Daughter

cf

of a poor Peafant, with no other Recommendations nor Merit but her Virtue, and a tolerable Face, marry a Nobleman of your Lordfhip's Rank and Character in the World !

All this Time I had been filent, and while I was fpeaking this, I perceived he looked at me with enquiring Eyes, and taking me up with fome Impatience, I have already told you, faid he, that in my Judgment, Virtue much more than fupplies all Deficiencies whatever ; and without you difapprove my Offers, you have only to comply to prove the Sincerity of them.

I then pretended that the great regard I had for him made me fearful of his debafing himfelf in my Favour, but he fo well knew how to anfwer all the little Evafions I was capable of making, that at laft I had no more to fay, but to appear fatisfied with my Lot.

Having thus feemingly agreed, he told me that he had many Reafons to keep the Affair a Secret for fome Time, and began of himfelf to ftart fome Difficulties on that Score————if it fhould be done at *Paris*, faid he, the numerous Retinue which always attend me hither would infallibly difcover it; and if at any of my Caftles, People in the Country are ordinarily more inquifitive into the Actions of their Superiors than thofe in great Cities.

The Dilemma which he now appeared to be in, infpired me with a fudden Thought; fuppofe, anfwered I, your Lordfhip fhould defer raifing me to the Honour you vouch-fafe, till the King goes fome Journey, as his Majefty frequently does : your Rank and Employment oblige you to be near his Perfon, and while fo, your Retinue muft be with you————cannot you then, pretending fome fudding Bufinefs calls you to *Paris*, come with one Servant on whofe Secrecy you can depend ; while I in the mean Time prepare every Thing ready for the Ceremony : which accomplifhed, you may return wherever the Court is————as for my Part I fhall remain in the fame way of Life as before, till the Time arrives that you fhall think proper our Marriage fhall be
owned ;

owned ; and this, my Lord, I look on as the fureſt means for preſerving it a Secret.

The Marquis told me he was infinitely pleaſed with my Contrivance, and would leave the Managment of every Thing wholly to me. The remaining Part of the Evening was paſt in regulating our future Wedding— more gay, nor more magnificent Proſpects were never laid out———we talked of nothing but Rejoycings, Balls, Equipage and Grandeur, when I ſhould be a⸮knowledged for the Marchioneſs *De L*———*V*——— I came readily into every Thing he ſaid, and feigned a Pleaſure in the Pomp I was to enjoy ; but alas! what did not my poor Heart endure in this diſtracting Neceſſity of Diſſimulation ! and what had not have given to have it over, that I might be alone to give a looſe to my Sighs, and conſider what Meaſures would be moſt proper to take in ſo critical a Juncture.

At laſt the long wiſhed Moment arrived, the Marquis finding it grew late took his leave, and I ſhut myſelf up in my Cloſet———I had now not leiſure for Complaints or Reflections, ſome immediate Reſolution muſt be taken to avoid the Storm, which was already gathered, and was ready to burſt upon my Head. The old Marquis appeared too paſſionate a Lover to wait long———I could not depend on his adhering to the delay I had invented———he might poſſibly change his Mind the ne t Day, carry me to one of his Caſtles, and hazard a Diſcovery for the Gratification of a Paſſion, which muſt indeed be great to oblige him to marry a Woman, whom he had looked upon as ſo unworthy of his Son.

As I had talked of going ſome Time to our Village, and had given my Parents Money to furniſh an Apartment for me, I thought that Place the ſecureſt Aſylum I could find———as I had paſſed unknown by my own Parents, I might reaſonably hope not to be ſuſpected by others, and it greatly rejoyced me to think I had never mentioned the leaſt Word to the old Marquis that I had ſeen them ; for I could not make a doubt, but that when

my

my Flight was difcovered he would leave no means untried to find out the Place of my Retreat, and that if ever I fhould fall again into his Power, I muft expect all that Revenge could inflict upon me————from Love to Hatred was a Change I could not but be affured of from a Man of his Humour, when exafperated by Difappointment and Defpair from a Perfon of my Station.

Having thus determined once more to revifit my native Village, I confidered what was to be done before I left *Paris*; what feemed moft material was to inform the young Marquis of his Father's Defign of marrying me, the Meafures I took to avoid him, and the Place to which I withdrew————this Letter took up the beft Part of the Night, and I was fo greatly fatigued at the finifhing it, that I was obliged to go to Bed; my Imagination however was too much difturbed to fuffer me to Sleep long; in every little Slumber I fell into, I fancied I heard a Noife, and that the old Marquis was coming to take me away and conclude the cruel Marriage———— the firft Thing I did next Morning, was to write to *Saint Fal*; for I muft have been ftrangely ungrateful to have omitted making him the Confidante of the furprizing Adventure which had befallen me.

Juft as *Barbara* returned from carrying thefe two Epiftles to the Poft-Houfe, I received a Packet, and a Bafket from the old Marquis, the one was filled with the ftrongeft Affurances of his everlafting Tendernefs, and a Prefent of five hundred *Lewes d'Ors*, the other contained a rich Toylet and its Furniture all of gilt Plate, curioufly engraved; but I gave myfelf not the Time to examine either with much Attention———— every Moment now was precious, and I fet about packing up my Things with all the Expedition I could.

I forbore acquainting *Barbara* with my Defign, being apprehenfive her over Joy at it, might render it impoffible for her to keep the Secret————People are as often betrayed by the Simplicity and Babbling of their Servants, as by their Treachery————but to return, in two Days I had got every Thing ready for my Journey,

————as

———as it was impoſſible for me to take all with me, without hazarding a Diſcovery by the Quantity of Luggage, I intended that *Melicourt* at his return ſhould take Charge of them and ſend them to me as I wanted them, in different Parcels, to avoid any Notice being taken.

———I was going to write a Letter and Directions to him, for that Purpoſe when happily he arrived——— I was tranſported when I heard his Voice, and running to the Stair-caſe to meet him ; you are come very ſeaſonably, Monſieur, ſaid I, a few Hours hence I had been gone.

The Earneſtneſs with which I ſpoke theſe Words ſurprized him, and made him impatient for the Motive ; but I was no leſs eager to hear what Account he had to give me, and obliged him to yield to my Importunities. ———I bad him conſider, how dear the Perſon from whom he came was to me, and then aſk himſelf if any Thing ought to poſtpone the News of him.

Indeed, Madam, replied Monſieur *Melicourt*, the Marquis deſerves all the Tenderneſs you can pay, and he on the other Side is indebted to you for his Life——— his Life was deſpaired of at my arrival ; but your endearing Letter diſſipated that deep Melancholy, which, joyned to the exceſſive loſs of Blood, muſt ſoon have brought him to the Grave———I am utterly unable to expreſs his Tranſports ; weak as he was, he would needs read over the Lines you ſent him I believe an hundred Times in a Day———Monſieur *Melicourt*, ſaid he to me, the precious Treaſure you have brought me, has given me more than Life———the Angel!———the Charming Creature, did he cry out in his Extaſies, what Tenderneſs! ——how does her lovely Soul ſhine out in every Line !— what Excellence of Nature! ſo kindly to forgive my unjuſt Suſpicions !———but her Generoſity ſhall never be forgot———acquaint her with this, and that as ſoon as I am recovered, nothing ſhall be omitted for the accompliſhment of our mutual Felicity.

In fine, Madam, continued *Melicourt*, the little Time I ſtayed with him, was wholly taken up in Demonſtrations

tions of his Affection for you————he could talk of
nothing but you, and would have sent *Dubois* to you, to
give you a more perfect Account of his Heart, than he
was able to write ; but that I told him it was needless,
as I intended to return immediately; on which he
entrusted me with his Commands, in which I think
myself much honoured, and would be glad they had
been of a more difficult Nature, that I might the more
have proved my sincere Attachment to so worthy a
Nobleman.

After this I acquainted him with what had happened,
and what I was obliged to do ; he approved highly of
my Conduct, and added, that when the yonng Marquis should come to know the Sacrifice I had made,
there was nothing to fear but that Excess of Gratitude
would overwhelm him.

I then shewed him the Presents I had received from
my old Lover, and told him my Resolution of returning
it ; by no means, replied, *Melicourt*, I can put you in a
way of making a better use of it : As to the Toylet indeed
I think it adviseable not to keep it ; but as to the five
hundred *Lewis D'Ors*, they are wanted where I believe
you will think them well bestowed————the young
Marquis has commissioned me to take up about that
Sum for him at *Paris*, the Expences of the Campaign
having exhausted his ready Money, and the Remittances
from his Father are much more tedious than he expected ; so that you never can have an Opportunity of
obliging him with greater Delicacy.

I embraced this Opportunity of serving my Lover
with an infinite Satisfaction, and immediately put the
five hundred *Lewis D'Ors* into *Melicourt*'s Hands in
order to get remitted to him ; but still continuing in the
Opinion, that it was best for me to return the old Marquis all that he had presented me with on the Account of
being his future Bride, I gave Orders to have some Part
of my Moveables sold in order to raise that Sum for
Melicourt to deliver to him after I was gone————as
to the Toylet, and all the Furniture belonging to it, I
left

left it neatly packed up, and after confulting with *Melicourt*, wrote to the Marquis in the following Manner,

To the Marquis *De L——V——.*

MY LORD,

*T*HE exceſſive Favours your Lordſhip has heaped upon me, would render me the moſt ungrateful of my Sex, if I retired without acquainting you with the Reaſons, which compelled me to take this Step————know then, my Lord, that ſo high a Dignity as you were pleaſed to honour me with the Offer of, demands my utmoſt Acknowledgments and Gratitude, that I am not capable of accepting it, impute to a Conſciouſneſs of my Unworthineſs————None, my Lord, can Merit to be your Wife, but who has it in her Power to make an adequate Return to that abundant Love, which engaged you to make her ſo————Alas! all I have to give is the extremeſt Honour, and Reſpect————the Deficiency is therefore ſo great, that I chuſe to retire to expiate my Misfortunes; believe, however, my Lord, that wherever I go, or wherever I am, the utmoſt Gratitude to you will ever dwell with me———— Pardon, therefore, my Conduct on this Occaſion, ſince to have acted otherwiſe, would have been unſuitable to the Sincerity, on which I value myſelf, and which you have ſeemed to approve in her, who is with the moſt perfect Gratitude and Submiſſion,

Your Lordſhip's

moſt humble and

moſt obliged Servant,

JEANETTA DE B——.

P. S. *I received the magnificent Preſent you were pleaſed to ſend me; I durſt not return it for fear of diſobliging you, nor did I think proper to take it with me—— the Perſon in whoſe Care I have left my Affairs will* ſend

send it to you, when ever you give Orders, as also the five hundred Lewis D'Ors, *all which are in the Lodgings where your Lordship vouchsafed to favour me with your Visits———I repeat my Protestations of an eternal Gratitude, and entreat you will believe no Day shall pass without my most ardent Prayers for your precious Life.*

This Letter being finished, I delivered it to *Melicourt,* that he might send it to the Marquis two or three Days after my Departure ; and it was agreed between us, that he should continue in my Lodgings, till after the Time it could be supposed the Letters I had sent to the young Marquis and Monsieur *Saint Fal* were come to Hand, in case any Answers to them should arrive, which he was to enclose, under a Cover to me directed to Madamoiselle *De Mainville,* for I was resolved never to be known by that of the Countess *De Roches* any more. Every Thing being thus fixed, he provided me a Post-Chaise, and I set out with *Barbara* the next Morning at four a Clock, to the great Amazement of that dear good-natured Creature, who did not as yet know one Syllable of the Meaning of this precipitate Departure, nor where I was going to carry her.

The End of the T E N T H P A R T.

T H E

THE

VIRTUOUS VILLAGER,

OR,

VIRGIN's VICTORY.

PART. XI.

EHOLD me now once more a
Wanderer, my Head and Heart full
of the various Changes of Fortune I
had undergone, and wholly incapable
of forming any Judgment what would
be the Event of so many perplexing
Adventures. All my past Life occurring
at once to my Imagination made me extremely pensive and
sometimes in Tears, which my poor Aunt observing, shall
I never see you out of these Afflictions, said she? bless me!
how you People of Quality torment yourselves for Trifles,
if you were poor, indeed, or did not know where to go, I
should pity you; but, Heaven be thank'd, that is not

your

your Case————you have enough of every thing, and a good Character into the Bargain ; you are not obliged to go away for Debt as a great many are, and some very honest Folks too ; but you have left good Effects behind you, which you may have whenever you please, and wherever you go all the World loves you and pays you Respect————for my Part, I can't see what occasion you can have to be melancholy.

It is a Habit I have contracted, answer'd I, but I flatter myself that when I have been a little while in the Country, the Air will make me more chearful. Do you design to live in the Country then, said *Barbara* overjoy'd ; Heaven be praised that I shall once more see the Fields again, and hear the Larks and the Nightingales————O! what a a Blessing!————I hate the rattling of Coaches, and all the hurly burly of *Paris*, where one is every Moment in danger of being thrown down.————And pray, my dear Lady, continued she, where are we going; to your own Village, answer'd I, you know I have given Money to have an Apartment prepared for me at your Brother's ; I would have told you of it before, but as I did not chuse any body should be acquainted with the Place of my Retreat, I was afraid your over Joy would have betrayed the Secret.

Indeed, my good Lady you were in the right, cried she, I should never have contain'd myself that's certain. ————O! the dear sweet Place————why your Ladyship will be admired like a little Queen there———— they'll all croud to see you, and the Curate I warrant will come to pay his Compliments————he's no Clown I'll assure you, and keeps the best Company ; in my time they were never without him at the Castle.

Barbara was so transported at the Happiness she was going to enjoy, that she could talk of nothing else the whole Journey.————I did not send a Messenger before to apprize them of my Arrival, because my Father had wrote some Days before to acquaint my Aunt, that all my Commands had been punctually fulfilled, and that every thing was ready for me, so that I knew the Indolence, indeed I may say Laziness, which long Ease

I   and

and Plenty had given me a Habit of, was in no Danger of being interrupted.

No Accident intervening, at length we arrived at the Village, where the sight of our Steeple gave me an odd kind of Emotion, between Pain and Pleasure; but sure no Creature was ever in greater Raptures than my poor Aunt—look there, Madam, said she, there is the Church ————and where you see those Turrets is the Castle, it is all surrounded with fine Trees, we shall pass by the Gates; and you'll see the pretty Place, where the young Men and Maids dance on Sundays and Holidays. Still as we pass'd she explain'd all the Particulars, and that with such an innocent Satisfaction, as is unknown to those who live in the great World.

Just on our Entrance into the Village, an old Woman was spinning before her Door, my Aunt no sooner observed her, than she made the Postilion stop, and calling out to her made herself be known, and asked a thousand Questions all in a Breath————this good Country-Woman, after recollecting who it was that spoke to her, told her next Neighbour who was folding some Sheep, she ran with the News who was coming to a third, and so on till we had half the Village about the Chaise.———— I bad the Postilion drive on to *John De B*————'s, upon which several little Girls who were playing about, offer'd their Service to shew the way, and ran skipping before the Horses, and brought me in a sort of Triumph to the House.

My Father and Mother, who by this were inform'd of my Approach, came with a great deal of Joy to help me out of the Chaise: My Agitation was so great, that I did not hear half the obliging Welcomes they gave me.————As I was stepping into the House, my Mother made a Motion which frighted me, apprehending I was discover'd: I heard afterwards she was on the Point of throwing her Arms about my Neck, so great an Impression did my Face make on her; but she check'd herself, and conducted me with the Respect due to my imagin'd Quality, to my little Apartment, which consisted only of a small Dining-Room and Bed-Chamber ——— the Furniture they had provided for me was plain, but new and convenient, and with what *Melicourt* was to fend after me, would make my Situation comfortable enough.

My Father feemed tranfpoited with the Honour of having me for a Lodger, and fhewed me from one of the Windows a very neat Garden, the Walks of which he had laid out, and made a Parterre of Flowers on Purpofe for me. I thanked him for the Care he expreft for my Satisfaction, and affured him I thought myfelf very happy in being with him; nor did my Tongue in this Particular belye my Heart.———Not Abfence, nor all the various Changes I had paft through, had ever alienated my Affection from thofe dear Authors of my Being, and whatever Mortification my Vanity received from the Meannefs of the Place, I had ftill a fecret Satisfaction in feeing, hearing, and having it in my Power to relieve them.

After a fmall Repaft I went to Bed, to recover, as I faid, the little Fatigue of my Journey; but in reality to have the better Opportunity of meditating on a Plan for my Conduct, while I continued there. I refolved that whoever fhould feem defirous of being acquainted with me, to lay it down as a Rule to fee no Company; but to pafs my time either in Working, Reading, or Walking in the Garden: I alfo determined to avoid all the Expence I could in my Table, and to eat in a more plain manner, than for a long Time I had been accuftomed; to the End, that whenever the Time that I fhould be difcovered fhould arrive, I might not be accufed of having acted the fine Lady in my Father's Houfe; but I found it highly neceffary I fhould dine alone, left too great a Familiarity might give ground for Sufpicion, and add to the Impreffion which my Features, notwithftanding the Alteration in me, had made on both my Parents, which I could eafily perceive by their looking fo earneftly upon me, whenever I turned my Head away, and did not feem to obferve them.

But

But there was one Difficulty in preferving the Secret, which till this Moment never occurred to my Mind. ———The young Marquis on his Return from the Campaigne would doubtlefs be impatient to fee me; he had been at our Village, and had then been too much talked of and obferved, on the Account of the Prefent he brought me from the King, not to be known if he fhould come again; and as fome Part of my Adventures on his Score were no Secret, his Vifits to Madam *De Maixville*, joined with the Refemblance between her and the Daughter of *John De B*———, might give too much room for Belief, that they were one and the fame Perfon————this I knew not how to avoid, and as often as it came into my Head very much perplex'd me. I pafs'd the Night, however, better than I had Reafon to expect: In the Morning my Mother coming into my Chamber out of Good-manners to know how I had flept; told me the Gentleman at the Caftle had fent to enquire who I was, and whether I defign'd to make any ftay in the Village; to which Queftions, fhe faid, fhe had forbore giving any pofitive Anfwer, till fhe had received my Commands in what manner fhe fhould do it.

I praifed her Difcretion in Terms, which made her fee I was highly fatisfied, and then told her that I had fome private Reafons, befides a natural Propenfity to Solitude, which made it inconvenient for me to fee Company, fo defired that fhe would on no Account give any Encouragement of that Sort. She affured me that my Defires fhould be complied with; after which I made her fit down on the Bedfide, and remembring that my Father had began to entertain me with the Hiftory of Mademoifelle *D'Elbieux*; I entreated fhe would fatisfy my Curiofity with the remaining Part, which fhe readily did in thefe or the like Words.

The

The Sequel of the History of Mademoiselle D'ELBIEUX.

I Think, Madam, said my Mother, that my Husband left off where that odd Mistake of Monsieur *Desflour-neaux,* for Monsieur *D'Estival,* occasioned various Conjectures both in the Countess and her Daughter; in the mean time that Gentleman little suspecting what had happened, was considering within himself what Answer he should make to the Mother of his Mistress, and having resolved, came early the next Morning to the Castle ———a little later he would not have had Admittance, and must have return'd without being able to comprehend the meaning of his being refused. The Countess imagining she had reason to be higly incensed at his Behaviour, had determined to have him forbid the House; but not expecting him till Dinner, as she thought he had been up so late, had deferr'd giving any Orders concerning him, till she rose herself.

Having for a long time been accustomed to use no Ceremony there, he ran directly up to the Countess's Chamber, and 'tis easy to guess the Consternation she must be in, to see him at her Bedside, accosting her with an easy Air, which is always the Companion of Innocence. She was scarce able to command her Resentment enough to forbear breaking immediately into Reproaches; but either her good Sense, or the Uncertainty in what Terms she should upbraid him, kept her silent, and she only turn'd on the other Side as he approach'd, though that was done with a Disdain, which he could not but have taken Notice of, if he had had the least Suspicion of the Cause. But far from thinking on any

such

such thing, and also taken up with what he was come about, he enquired in his usual free manner how she had rested, and the meaning of her lying so long in Bed. His speaking in this Fashion had so much the Appearance of Dissimulation, prepossess'd as the Countess was of his Falshood, that it but provoked her the more : She nevertheless contain'd herself to hear how far he would carry his supposed Artifice. The Villain, said she to herself, after endeavouring to deceive both Mother and Daughter, now discover'd and discarded by the one, imagines he may still impose on the other————but why should I be troubled at his Perfidiousness ?—What is it to me that the Wretch is married ?——to seem angry would be too great a Proof of my Weakness, and give him an Opportunity to triumph over me.————No, I'll rather seem ignorant of his Baseness, and turn his Behaviour into Ridicule, that will better become my Character than a serious Resentment.

This last Reflection got the better of her former ones, and she turned towards him as just waking, saying she had not slept well in the Night, and that she could not have pardon'd any other than himself for giving her Disturbance. But, added she, I am so impatient to hear the Result of your Determination on our last Conversation, that if you will go into the next Room while I rise, we will talk together as long you please.

No, Madam, replied Monsieur *D'Estival*, I will not believe you heartily forgive my having broke in on your Repose, if you banish me from so delightful a Situation, as I now enjoy in contemplating your Beauties, in the Posture you are at present.——Permit me, therefore, to sit down by you, and I shall declare myself with that Sincerity you exacted from me.

The Countess was too sensible of Flattery, not to be pleased with this Compliment, even though she believed it far from being dictated by the Heart————at another time she would have been charm'd with it ; but the Proofs she thought she had of his Falshood, prevented her from giving any Answer to it, and she only bid him

declare

declare in as brief a manner as poſſible, what Reſolution he had taken.

I owe too much, Madam, ſaid he, to the Civilities your Ladyſhip has honoured me with, to deal inſincerely in a Matter, in which you are nearly intereſted, and in which it would ill become me to uſe diſguiſe, when preſs'd ſeriouſly to declare my Sentiments.——I will, therefore, no longer make a Myſtery of the Paſſion your lovely Daughter Mademoiſelle *D'Elbieux* has inſpired me with, and though I have all the Regard and Admiration poſſible for your Charms, yet it is to her my Soul is devoted————this, Madam, continued he, is ſaying enough, and I think I need not make any Apology, when I aſſure you that I am ready to marry her whenever you judge our Union proper, and ſhall with Tranſport receive her from your Hand, as a precious Pledge of your Eſteem and Friendſhip.

The Counteſs was ready to burſt at theſe Words—— the Anſwer was, indeed, conciſe and plain ; but diſſembling as well as ſhe was able the Indignation ſhe conceived at it ; ſo, ſaid ſhe, with an Air of Irony and Contempt ; you are willing to ſacrifice all the Paſſion you have for me, and marry my Daughter merely to oblige me.————I am prodigiouſly obliged to you, without Doubt ; but, Monſieur, I cannot return the Favour by forgetting I am a Mother, and conſenting to my Daughter's Ruin ; for to be plain with you, I hear you are already married, and muſt be fully convinced in ſo material a Point, before any thing can be concluded on concerning Mademoiſelle *D'Elbieux*. —— It will, therefore, be much more to your Honour to confeſs what ſecret Engagements you are under, than to ſubmit to an Enquiry, which I cannot otherwiſe avoid making.

Monſieur *D'Eſtival* was too much ſurprized at this Diſcourſe, to be able preſently to make any Anſwer : He look'd earneſtly in the Counteſs's Face, in order to diſcover if ſhe were really ſerious, or talk'd in this manner only to perplex him, by way of Puniſhment for preferring her Daughter to herſelf.

Aſſured

Affured as fhe was of his Guilt in this particular, fhe took his Silence as a token of it, come, Monfieur *D'Eftival*, refumed fhe, you are not the only Perfon who has been drawn into Engagements they have afterwards repented; but fince it is fo, the beft thing you can do is to acknowledge your Wife.————Pray, bring her to the Caftle, you may depend upon it, I fhall be glad to cultivate a Friendfhip with her for your fake.

D'Eftival loft all Patience at thefe Words, if, faid he, your Ladyfhip means this as a Jeft, I muft beg leave to tell you, it is carried fomewhat too far, and is but an ill Return for that Sincerity, I juft now behaved to you with————if you really are in earneft, continued he with fome Warmth, common Juftice without my requefting it, will certainly oblige you to difcover the Authors of fo bafe an Information, that I may punifh them as their Calumny deferves.

Mouftrous Deceit and Infolence! cry'd the Countefs, if my Daughter had offended me, yet more than fhe has, I could forgive her for the fole Merit of having difcarded with the juft Scorn fhe has done, a Man capable of fuch mean Actions, and then as meanly denying them.

For Heaven's fake, Madam, explain yourfelf, cry'd Monfieur *D'Eftival* impatiently interrupting her, my Honour is too much concern'd in the Treatment you give me, for me not to be refolute in having the Occafion of it cleared up————what Wife, what Marriage is it you reproach me with ?————What reafon have you to imagine your Daughter has difcarded me with Scorn ?————I do affure your Ladyfhip there is not one Word of Truth in all this, and if you perfift in talking in this manner for ever, I fhall ftill be in the dark for your Defign in it.

The more he protefted his Innocence, the more the prepoffefs'd Countefs's Rage encreas'd: Is it poffible, faid fhe, that you can carry the Deception to this Height ?————dare you deny that you are married ? Yes, Madam, reply'd he, and on that Truth will ftake my eternal Salvation. This is unfufferable, cry'd fhe,

know

know then, Monſieur *D'Eſtival*, that I was Witneſs of the Converſation you had laſt Night with my Daughter in the Park———will you deny ſhe wrote to you,——— that you agreed to meet her there———that both you and ſhe mentioned my Name, in a manner no way becoming either of your Characters———that ſhe accuſed you of a previous Engagement——— that you at laſt confeſs'd you were married ; but that ſome of the Forms being wanting you could get off it———that you offered to do ſo, and Mademoiſelle *D'Elbieux*, on this Diſcovery of your double Perfidy, treated you with the Scorn you merit, flew from you, and forbid you ever ſeeing her more ?

Nay, then, cry'd *D'Eſtival*, lifting up his Eyes to Heaven, I am either run mad, or you dreamt all this. He then re-capitulated the various Points of her Accuſation, and at the End of each, proteſted his Innocence and Ignorance.

Mademoiſelle *D'Elbieux* came into the Room as he was ſpeaking, ſhe knew not of his being there ; but making no Doubt but that he was the Perſon ſhe had met with in the Park the Night before, was not ſurprized to find him in her Mother's Chamber———aſſured as ſhe was of their Marriage, ſhe fancied he had enter'd privately, and had lain there all Night.—— She was the more confirm'd in this Conjecture, as ſhe found by the loudneſs of his Voice, as well as by the Diſſatisfaction in both their Countenances, that they had been quarrelling as married People too often do ; and being vex'd to meet a Man, who after the Diſcovery ſhe imagin'd ſhe had made, ſhe deteſted, was about to retire, when the Counteſs perceiving her commanded her to ſtay, ſaying her Preſence was neceſſary to clear up an Affair, which, added ſhe, with a diſdainful Smile, is worthy of your Confirmation and Teſtimony.

Monſieur *D'Eſtival* who was half diſtracted at what had been laid to his Charge, took hold of her Hand, and having drawn her nearer, repeated the Articles alledg'd againſt him by her Mother, and appealed to

her

her for the Decision, at the same conjuring her not to be sway'd by any thing but Justice.

Mademoiselle *D'Elbieux* was extremely surprised to find her Mother was so well acquainted with her Proceedings; but notwithstanding her Resentment to *D'Estival*, she was very well pleased that he denied the Meeting, and thought it was her Business, to second what he said, which she did with so much Assurance; saying, that she knew nothing of all he had mentioned, and that it was contrary to Common Sense, that the Countess enraged to the last Degree at hearing herself contradicted in a thing which she imagined was true; and, indeed, was so on one side, that she gave her a Blow on the Face; then turning to Monsieur *D'Estival* bad him leave the Castle, and never come near her more.

Yes, Madam, cryed he, rising from his Seat, you shall be obeyed——you never shall see me more; but remember, and I repeat it before this young Lady, that I never left my own House last Night, as several People in the Village, besides my own Servants can witness ——that I had not the Honour of seeing your Daughter either by Appointment or otherwise—that I never told her I was married——and to conclude, that all you have said is a mere Chimera——this is the Truth ——so farewel, and I engage my Word of Honour never to expose myself again to such injurious Treatment, as you have been pleased to give me.

With these Words he went hastily out of the Room, leaving the Countess no less astonished then enraged, at his impudent persisting in the Denial of a thing, she believed her own Eyes and Ears had witnessed to the Truth of; but recovering herself from the Thoughts of him, she vented her Fury on her Daughter, who still continued in the Room, and after loading her with Reproaches; there, perfidious Girl, said she, throwing the Letter she had intercepted at her Feet, assume the Front too if you dare to deny this too——you see I know you——your wicked Heart betrays itself in every Action —— Go, most ungrateful, most unworthy of what I have done for you. And I should act with Prudence after this Discovery of the Vileness of your Nature, to secure you in a Place that would take from you the Means of behaving to me so undutifully hereafter.

Insolent as Madamoiselle *D'Elbieux* was, she was a little awed at this Menance; and pretending the most perfect Contrition sued for her Pardon in such Terms that she at last obtained it, from a Mother who very much loved her, in spite of the Coquetry and Vanity of her own Humour.

Having thus made her Peace, she no longer remembered the Occasion she had given of Offence, and valuing the Countess no otherwise than for the Power the Law had given her over her, she bent now her whole Study how to be thoroughly convinced of the Truth of this ambiguous Affair————had there been the least room to doubt she would have concluded *D'Estival*, was not the Person she met in the Park, but the improbability there was, that any one should take his Name upon him, would not suffer such a Thing to enter into her Head————what most confounded her, was, to see the Letter she had wrote to him in her Mother's Hands————she could not think he had sacrificed it to her by the Behaviour of them both, much less now believe they were married, as the supposed *D'Estival* had confessed to her the Night before————the whole Business was indeed too puzzling for a Woman of a much better Capacity than Madamoiselle *D'Elbieux* to comprehend, and as she could not fathom it herself, she resolved to try once more her Power over her Lover to unriddle it if possible.

Monsieur *Deflourneaux* in the mean Time reproached himself, that he had not made better use of the Opportunity that young Lady had afforded him, and also that he had been so imprudent to suffer the Secret of his private Marriage to be sifted by her. Had I taken the Advantage, said he to himself, which the Night and her kind Advances in proposing a Meeting, gave me, I might easily have become Master of her Person and Fortune————the Girl to whom I have unadvisedly tied myself, would for a small Portion been content to have renounced all Claims to me, and every Difficulty,

under

under which I at present Labour, would have been removed.

To retrieve therefore what he imagined nothing but his own ill Conduct had deprived him of, he resolved to visit Madamoiselle *D'Elbieux*, and pretend that all he had confest to her the Night before, was only a Stratagem to discover how far he might have gained on her Affection, so having convinced his Wife that it would be for her own Interest to deny their Marriage in case any Enquiry should be made, he set himself forth with all the advantages Dress could bestow, and went to the Castle.

The Countess *De N———*, and her Daughter, both in a very ill Humour, were just set down to Table, when Word was brought that Monsieur *Deslourneaux* was come to wait upon them, and neither of them supposing they had any Reason to be offended with him, Orders were given for his Admittance.

Madamoiselle *D'Elbieux* was in too sullen a Disposition to receive him with any Part of that Gaiety she was accustomed to do, on the Account of his satirical Vein of Conversation; but the Countess on the contrary seemed extremely glad of his Company, she knew that Monsieur *D'Estival* had an Aversion to him, and in the Humour she now was, that was a sufficient Motive for her treating him with the greatest Complaisance: As he was naturally vain he grew very much elated with the Reception given him by the Mother, and as for the Daughter's Coldness it did not at all surprize him, because he looked upon it as the Effect of their last Conversation, which he should soon set right again——He was impatient for an Opportunity of entertaining her to that End, nor was it long before the Countess obliged him with one, she perceived her Daughter did not like his Company, and to mortify her, made some Pretence to retire as soon as Dinner was over and left them together.

Deslourneaux on this lost not a Moment, but began to address Madamoiselle *D'Elbieux*, with all the rhetorick he was capable of, which she receiving with Disdain, I see, Madam, said he, that the Severity you treat

me

me with, is oweing to the Folly I was guilty of laſt Night, in pretending to you I was married ; but I beg you will be aſſured I meant it no otherwiſe than as a Jeſt, and had you ſtayed but a Moment longer I ſhould have convinced you of it. Theſe Words made her ſtart, but not being yet well able to comprehend the Myſtery, what do you mean, cried ſhe haſtily ? what Concern is it of mine, whether you are married, or not ? How, Madam, replied he, with an Air of Aſſurance, you ſeemed to be of another way of Thinking when I had the Honour of your Company laſt Night.————My Company, interrupted ſhe, laſt Night, where for Heaven's Sake————you are certainly run Mad, or think to divert me with croſs Queſtions ; but I am not in a Humour at preſent to laugh at your Wit, ſo would have you reſerve it for others, that may think it more agreeable.

As bold as Monſieur *Defleurneaux* was, theſe Words quite confounded him, but recovering himſelf in a Moment, and pulling the Letter out of his Pocket, which had been brought him, inſtead of that the Counteſs had intercepted, I have heard, ſaid he, of ſome Ladies who have denied a verbal Aſſignation, but thought none would have done it, where their own Hand could be produced as an Evidence againſt them.

On this ſhe caſt her Eyes on the Letter, and to her great Aſtoniſhment found in it the ſame Words ſhe had written to *D'Eſtival* excepting the Time and Place of meeting altered ; this made her examine it with more Attention, and ſhe then found it was her Mother who had put this Trick upon her. She was yet however far from getting any Light into the Bottom of this Adventure——ſhe could eaſily imagine that the Counteſs had contrived this Interview on purpoſe to perplex her, but then ſhe could not account for having accuſed Monſieur *D'Eſtival*, with having been in the Park, and of ſaying thoſe Things which ſhe now found had been ſpoke by *Defleurneaux*. All the Satiſfaction he could give her in this Point was, that ſuch a Letter had been brought to him by a young Country-Man, and that he complied with the Summons, and then repeated to her all the
Particulars

Particulars of their Conversation———she was now well assured that he did not deceive her; but was so enraged at finding herself thus outwitted and exposed, that she could not help venting her Fury, on him who had been no way guilty of her Vexation.

The Countess heard all this from an adjacent Room, and the whole Affair, being now no longer a Riddle to her, and *D'Estival* quite cleared of what she had accused him, thought the Mistake so whimsical, that she returned to *Deflourneaux*, and her Daughter laughing prodigiously. He imagined by her Mirth, that she had laid this Contrivance on Purpose to turn him into Ridicule, and began to convince the Countess how much he thought himself affronted by telling her this should be the last Visit he would make her; but this Lady, who was naturally complaisant, and besides, fearing if he should divulge this Adventure, it might occasion some Discourse to the prejudice of her Daughter's Expectation, endeavoured to pacify him, and told him that he was no otherwise concerned in the Affair, than by a Mistake, which had been owing meerly to chance———She confess'd also that she had made use of a little Stratagem, in order to punish some Errors in the Conduct of Madamoiselle *D'Elbieux*, and said enough to let this young Lady into the Mystery of every Thing, which perfectly restored *D'Estival* to her good Opinion, and as he was the most constant of all that had pretended to her, and she in her Heart was most inclined also to favour him, from that Moment she began to take a Resolution of rewarding what he had suffered for her sake.

An Opportunity soon presented itself———the Countess being sensible of the Injustice of her Behaviour to Monsieur *D'Estival*, thought herself obliged to acknowledge her Error, and invite him to the Castle again. ———As he truly loved Madamoiselle *D'Elbieux*, he had quitted it with infinite Reluctance, and was equally transported at returning to it again without appearing of too mean and abject a Disposition———accordingly he came the next Day, and this short Absence served only to make him appear more amiable in the Eyes of
his

his Miſtreſs than he had ever done before this little Interruption of his Viſits.

He renewed his Addreſſes with greater Fervency than ever, and was ſo fortunate, if the obtaining ſuch a Wife can be called ſo, as to engage from her a promiſe of marrying him———the Counteſs convinced of the neceſſity there was of her being diſpoſed of, ſince ſhe had given ſuch a Proof of her Diſpoſition to intriguing as her late Sally, made no Difficulty of conſenting to the Match, on which the Nuptials were celebrated with all convenient Speed, and for the firſt few Days, nothing could be more happy than the new married Pair.   The Behaviour of Madamoiſelle *D'Elbieux*; now Madam *D'Eſtival* was ſo changed for the better, that the whole Family were aſtoniſhed and bleſſed the Occaſion; but their Joy was ſhort lived, her Humour was ſtill the ſame and ſoon exerted itſelf, with greater Vehemence if poſſible than ever.

This Harmony had not laſted above fourteen or fifteen Days, when one Morning as ſhe was riſing ſhe bad her Woman to give Orders that the Coach and Six, with all the Equipage, ſhould be got ready. Monſieur *D'Eſtival* aſked her with a great deal of Complaiſance, if ſhe intended to dine abroad ?————Yes, anſwered ſhe, in a cool and unconcerned Air, and ſup too——— I am going to *Paris*: to *Paris!* cried he amazed—— Ay, reſumed ſhe, I am tired of the Country, where one ſees nothing new, and can ſupport it no longer—— pardon me, my Dear, ſaid he, I cannot think you are in earneſt————I am ſure you have too much good Senſe to take ſuch a Journey with ſo much Precipitation, and without conſulting your Mother, and hearing her Opinion I hope, anſwered ſhe in the moſt haughty Tone ſhe could aſſume, I have too much good Senſe not ſo look upon myſelf as an Infant, or to aſk any one's Advice in what I have an Inclination to do—— it would be very extraordinary indeed if I ſhould marry to be a Dependant on the Humour of any body. What I ſaid, anſwered he, was not intended to give you room to imagine I ſhould wiſh you were ſo—you certainly are and ever ſhall be the Miſtreſs of your own Actions,

1   ———but

———but there are Difficulties in this Step, which perhaps you have not confidered———you know we have no Houfe at *Paris*, nor fince our Marriage have yet had an Opportunity to order one to be prepared for us, and I know not were you can lodge in a manner befitting you ———Pleafant enough, cried fhe, with a Laugh, which had more in it of Ill-nature and Contempt than Mirth ; as if I could be at a lofs for a Habitation to my Mind in fuch a Place as *Paris*——— do not imagine, I befeech you, that all the wife Things you can utter fhall be any hindrance to my Journey— No, no, I fhall fet out immediately, and no body fhall prevent me———I have contrived how to manage at my Arrival, and don't ftand in need of any Directions.

But, faid the Hufband, beginning now to be ftung a little at this Treatment ; do you think it becomes a Perfon of your Birth, to leave your Relations in fo abrupt a manner? I give myfelf no Paint about that, replied fhe, fo all your Arguments are anfwered.

Monfieur *D'Eftival* was going to make fome Anfwer, and, perhaps fuch a cne as would have fhewn he was not of a Temper to countenance fuch Extravagancies, when a Lady, who happened to be a Vifiter at that Time at the Caftle, came to wifh Madame *D'Eftival* a good Morning, came in and prevented any farther Difcourfe on that Subject.

At firft, they talked only on indifferent Affairs, when all on a fudden, without the leaft Preparation or Connection with what had been faid before, pray, Madam, cried the Wife of *D'Eftival* what is your Opinion of a Hufband who glories in playing the Tyrant over his Wife, and takes a Pleafure in contradicting her in every thing ? The Lady was extremely furprized at this Queftion, as well as at the abrupt manner it was uttered in, and guefling there was already fome little Pique between them, anfwered, that fhe did not think any Man was fo unreafonable. I will foon convince you then of your Miftake, refumed Madam *D'Eftival*, pointing to her Hufband with an Air full of Derifion, that worthy Perfon is of the Number———I have an In-

clination

clination to go to *Paris*, have indeed some Business there, and I asked his permission for the Journey ; nay, even begged it in the most tender and obliging Terms, yet he is so cruel to refuse me, pretends he has a Right to keep me Prisoner here, and will not suffer me to stir a Step without he is the first that proposes it———is not this playing the Tyrant ?——— I little expected such Treatment from a Man that pretended to adore me, and whose superior I am in Birth and Fortune———I am so provoked, that I know not to what Lengths his Barbarity may transport me.

The Astonishment Monsieur *D'Estival* was in to hear himself thus falsly accused before his own Face may more easily be conceived than expressed———I know not, Madam, what you mean, said he to his Wife, with a Voice interrupted by Passion, but this I know very well, that no other Answer is due to you than such a one as I do not chuse to give any Woman, much less my Wife———I leave you therefore to repent so vile a Piece of Forgery, and reflect what Attonement you ought to make me for it.

With these Words he flung out of the Chamber, and went directly to the Countess's Apartment——— the Disorder he was in was too perceivable for her not to take Notice of it, and on her enquiring the Occasion, he readily related the whole Affair to her; it would have been ridiculous for her to have attempted any Justification of her Daughter's Behaviour, but as there was nothing in it, she did not forsee from a perfect Knowledge of her capricious Humour, she neither was nor affected to be surprized, and told him that she was extremely sorry for what had happened, and assured him she would take proper Measures to prevent any Provocations of the like Nature for the future. Monsieur *D'Estival* thanked her, and was glad she undertook to bring so untameable a Creature to Reason, rather than himself, who he now to his great Misfortune, found had but little Influence. To avoid being even within hearing of the Clamour, which he doubted not would ensue, he took Horse, and went to dine at a Friend's House about three Miles distant, hoping at his return to find all things quiet, and

3   his

his Wife in a better Humour, and poffibly concerned for having given him this Proof what fhe could be on Occafion.

But alas! he was yet far from being acquainted with all the Extravagancies his Wife was capable of————— the Countefs her Mother, received no other Anfwers, than difdainful ones for her Advice————the other told her fhe was no longer under her Direction, and would act in every thing as fhe herfelf thought proper————— it was in vain that this ill-treated Parent remonftrated to her that to go without her Hufband's Confent, or even without his Company, as they were fo lately married, would render her liable to Cenfure————and that to difoblige a Man of his Character, was both wicked and weak; her Reply ftill was, that fhe would be under no Subjection, and that fhe faw no Reafon for the pretended Superiority of Men, who, tho' the moft fawning abject Creatures in the World before Marriage, no fconer became Hufbands, than they fancied themfelves Mafters, and ufurped an Authority which neither became them nor was their due————that if other Women fubmitted to fo foolifh a Cuftom, fhe would not————and added, that if a Journey to *Paris* was even difagreeable to her, fhe would take it, becaufe he had oppofed it, and that fhe was determined to proceed in this manner with him all her Life.

The Countefs provoked not only at her Obftinacy, but the little Regard fhe paid to herfelf, faid fome Things that ftung her to the Quick; the other returned the Sarcafms, and Words grew very high between them, ————an old Servant, who had attended Madam *D'Eftival* from her Infancy, for only entreating fhe would remember it was her Mother that fpoke, was immediately turned 'out of Doors————the other Servants finding a Perfon whofe long and faithful Services demanded fome Love and Refpect, was difcharged, knew they muft expect the fame Fate, if they fhould offer to delay the Commands of their imperious Miftrefs, fo went about preparing for the Journey with fuch Alacrity, that in an Hour every Thing was ready.

Madam

Madam *D'Eſtival* being informed of it threw herſelf into the Coach, and tho' her Mother condeſcended
ſo far as to follow her to the Door, and even entreat
her to conſider what ſhe was about, yet ſhe was deaf to
every Thing, and ordered the Coachman to drive away.
————The Counteſs was exceſſively provoked, the
young Lady before mentioned as a Viſiter quite amaz'd,
and the whole Family in the utmoſt Conſternation at
her Obſtinacy, all imagining, with good Reaſon, that
this was not the laſt Trial to which ſhe would put the
Patience of her Huſband.

Her Mother thinking ſhe ought in Juſtice to acquaint
Monſieur *D'Eſtival* with what had paſſed, diſpatched
one of her Servants with a Letter to him immediately :
He remounted his Horſe on the Reception, alarmed beyond Meaſure, to hear his Wife had puſhed her In-
diſcretion ſo far as to go not only without his Conſent, but
even without ſeeing him before her Departure, after the
Diſpute they had with each other—this ſeemed ſo unkind
and ſo contemptuous withal, that if he could not bring
himſelf preſently to hate her, it was becauſe he had
loved her with a more than ordinary Paſſion

The Counteſs allowed his Reſentment to be juſt, and
offered to make no Apology for her offending Daughter,
but on the contrary commiſerated his Misfortune, and
perſuaded him to take Poſt and follow her, endeavour
to overtake her at Night, and if he could not prevail
upon her to hear Reaſon, to exert the Power of a Huſband and bring her back by Force.

This Advice was too conformable to his own Opinion,
for him not to follow it————He immediately ſent for
Poſt-Horſes, and came up with her in a little more
than four Hours : She was juſt entring a Village, when
ſhe perceived him; but far from being daunted at his
Preſence, or any way wavering in her Reſolution, ſhe
contrived to get rid of him, by one of the moſt wicked
and ſhameleſs Stratagems that ever was invented.

When he came to the Coach-ſide, and ſpoke to her,
ſhe pretended not to know him, and threatened that if
                                                    he

he did not leave her and go about his Busineſs, ſhe would declare he came to offer ſome Violence to her; all the Time he was ſpeaking, ſhe ſtill called out to the Coachman to drive faſter, but being under a neceſſity of ſtopping in the Village, having tired the Horſes ſo much, that they could not have gone much further without baiting, the Huſband thought it beſt to ſay no more to her till ſhe alighted, and as ſoon as he ſaw ſhe was in the Houſe, came up to the Door; but on his advancing to enter was met by two or three Men, who with great Clubs ſeemed to guard the Paſſage, and aſked him what he wanted————I am come, ſaid he, to dine with my Wife, what Impertinence is here?——continued he diſmounting, ſome of you take care of my Horſe.

The Man who kept the Cabaret, and was the Perſon who aſked this ridiculous Queſtion, had juſt received his Inſtructions from Madam *D'Eſtival*, who told him ſhe had been purſued by a mad Man, who was in love with her, and ſo outrageous, that he fancied himſelf married to her, he is juſt behind me, added ſhe, and I charge you to hinder him from coming into the Houſe, for if he does, there muſt inevitably ſome Miſchief happen.

As ſhe came in a Coach and Six, with ſuitable Equipage, and Monſieur *D'Eſtival* on a Poſt-Horſe and no Attendants, what ſhe ſaid was readily believed, and the Maſter of the Cabaret preſently called all his People about him, and oppoſed the injured Huſband's entrance, in the manner already mentioned. Finding he had quitted his Horſe, and was making his way into the Houſe, they told him there was no Room for People in his Condition————that they were ſorry for him; but he muſt not think to diſturb a Lady of Quality, who did them the Honour to call there, and bad him endeavour to compoſe himſelf and go quietly away.

It is impoſſible to ſay, whether the Aſtoniſhment or Rage of Monſieur *D'Eſtival* was greateſt to hear himſelf thus treated, the latter, however, made him draw his Sword, and attempt to force a Paſſage; but their Clubs ſoon rendered that Weapon ineffectual; it was

preſently

presently broke, and he received several Blows in the Skirmish, the Master of the House and his People calling out for help all the Time, and saying they would manage him for coming there to play his mad Pranks. The whole Village was gathered about them in an Instant, and had it not been for the interposition of the Parish Priest, who came running among the rest, to know the occasion of this Uproar, the unfortunate *D'Estival* might have been almost murdered. It was in vain for him to protest he was really so unhappy as to be the Husband of that wicked Woman, who was all this Time at the Window laughing, and highly diverted to see the Reception he met, not a Creature there but immagined him to be really distracted, and by the Advice of the Priest, and some of the Heads of the Village they laid hold of him, and in spite of all he could urge carried him to the Prison, in order to secure him from doing any Mischief, till they should hear who his Friends were, that they might be sent to, to take care of him———some of the Clowns diverting themselves at his Extravagancy as they thought it, and others pitying him as they went along.

In the mean Time, those who attended Madam *D'Estival* were shocked at this Behaviour, and one of them in particular, took the Liberty to tell her, he was amazed to see she should put such a Trick on so worthy a Gentleman, and her Husband; on which she turned him away immediately, and told him, that if he dared to mention this Adventure, or offer to contradict what she had said, she would find a way to make him repent his Sawcyness.

But this Menace did not intimidate the Fellow, he went and expostulated with the Priest, and several others of those who had been Instrumental in carrying Monsieur *D'Estival* to Prison: He assured them, that he was really the Husband of that Lady who had seen him used so unmercifully, and so far from being mad, that he was one of the most sober and worthy Gentlemen in the World; but they were all prejudiced in Favour of the Lady, as indeed believing it impossible a Woman of

her

her Figure could be guilty of fo abominable an Action.

The honeft Servant provoked at their Obftinacy, and refolved to ferve his Mafter if poffible, rode immediately back to the Caftle, and acquainted the Countefs *De N——* with the whole Proceeding, who afflicted beyond meafure at fo horrible a Conduct in her Daughter, fet out the next Morning by break of Day, in order to procure the fuppofed mad Man his Liberty.

The Prieft, the Inn-keeper, and indeed the whole Village were terribly alarmed, when they found by the Countefs, who was known to fome of them, the indifcretion their Credulity had made them guilty of: They entreated Pardon in the moft fubmiffive Terms of Monfieur *D'Eflival,* who not caring the Adventure fhould make too much Noife in the World forgave them, but tho' he thanked the Countefs for the Trouble fhe had given herfelf, told her that he would never fee her Daughter more, or if poffible even hear her mentioned—— fhe had nothing to offer by way of appeafing his Refentment, on the contrary fhe owned it was but too juft, and agreed to caft her off as a Daughter, as he did as a Wife.

But what Prodigies cannot Love effect——how eafily are Injuries, tho' of the moft bitter Nature forgiven where the Heart takes the Offender's Part !—— it's indeed punifhing ourfelves too much, to be angry with thofe who are very dear to us, and human Nature feeks but its own Eafe in this Particular. The good Senfe of Monfieur *D'Eflival* indeed would not fuffer him to think fhe merited any Part of the Tendernefs he had for her, and for a Time, whoever mentioned a Reconciliation were fure to receive fuch Anfwers as made them foon give over their Mediation.

In the mean Time Madam *D'Eflival* enjoyed all the Pleafures of having gained her Point; but at Length growing weary of *Paris,* and beginning to reflect, that a Woman of Condition makes but an odd Figure in being feparated from her Hufband, fhe vouchfafed to make fome Overtures to him, which he at firft rejected
with

with a Difdain, worthy of the Wrongs he had received
————the more Difficulty fhe found, the more eager
fhe was; and in fpite of the Haughtinefs of her Tem-
eer, defcended to Submiffions, which he could never
have expected from her; thefe Condefcenfions making
him hope, fhe was entirely changed and truly penitent,
he again received her with a Promife, never to reproach
her with what, fhe faid, nothing but Youth and Inexperience had made her guilty of; and which fhe fwore
to attone for by her future Conduct————to preferve her in
this Temper, he treated her, if poffible, with more Tendernefs than before this Breach, and, in fine, feem'd to
make it the whole Study of his Life to oblige her; but
the Return he received at laft for all this Indulgence,
ought to render her the Object of Deteftation to her
whole Sex, fince it may poffibly deter other Hufbands,
from behaving with Mildnefs to their Wives, for fear
they fhould be encouraged by it, to act as fhe did.

About Three Months after this Reconciliation, Madam *D'Eftival* proved with Child: The Countefs *De
N*————inftead of rejoicing, as moft Women do, in
the hope of being a Grandmother, was very much
troubled, not doubting, after the Experience fhe had of
her Daughter's Humour, but that fhe would make her
Pregnancy an Excufe for a thoufand capricious Fancies,
that would be tormenting not only to her Hufband, but
to ever body elfe that came near her; but poor Monfieur *D'Eftival*, whofe Love had caft a Mift before his
Eyes, except when fome very flagrant ill Humour a
little diffipated it, was under no fuch Apprehenfions; his
Tendernefs redoubled, and he was all Tranfport at the
News; the Pleafure of being the Father of a legitimate
Offspring, moft certainly exceeds all others; but, alas!
full dearly did he pay for it————all that the Countefs's Imagination had fuggefted to her, was more than
accomplifh'd, and Madam *D'Eftival* immediately
gave into fuch Extravagancies, as one would think no
Woman that was not totally deprived of Reafon, could
have been guilty of.

To

To say nothing of her Longings, which were for almost every thing to which she could give a Name, whether possible to be procured or not; she affected to take Disgusts sometimes to one Acquaintance, sometimes to another, which must accordingly be forbid the House; till Monsieur *D'Estival* in time, was obliged to banish all his Friends———one Day all the Servants in general were discharged, and others taken in their Places, the next they were turned out again, and the former restored ———the Furniture of the Rooms were also continually changed, nothing but pulling down and putting up——— selling one thing and buying another, which was no sooner fixed, than it became as offensive to her Eyes as that she had exchanged for it———in fine, always restless and impatient herself, she tired every one about her; yet no one durst presume to contradict her or complain. ———Monsieur *D'Estival* was ready to comply with every fantastick Whim that came into her Head, and as he set the Example, all that belong'd to them were obliged to follow it.

It would be endless to recite the many Ways she invented to create Disquiet, to whoever was so unhappy as to be in the way of it; but I cannot omit giving one Instance of her Behaviour, which, indeed, may serve as a Specimen of the rest.

Monsieur *D'Estival* had been from his Youth acquainted with a *Capuchin*, a Man, who being descended of one of the best Families in *Provence*, had renounced with the Gaieties of the World a very handsome Estate; and who for his great Learning, as well as exemplary Life, was highly esteemed by all who had the Pleasure of knowing him: To add to his other excellent Qualifications, he was a Man of singular Good-nature, and had nothing of that Austerity, which instead of making Religion amiable, gives it a disagreeable Air, rather forbidding than inviting to its Embraces.

This Reverend Father, Monsieur *D'Estival* was so unfortunate as to bring with him Home one Day to Dinner, many Friends happened to be there at the same time, and every one was charm'd with the elegant Discourfes he entertain'd them with. The mifchievous Madam *D'Eſtival*, perceiving the high Refpect paid to him, thought of nothing but how to turn the good Humour and Pleafantry of this Company into Vexation. At laſt, as no one had more wicked Wit, ſhe bethought herſelf of the Means; the *Capuchin* had a very long and venerable Beard, and ſhe imagin'd, he was not a little fond of it, by his frequently ſtroaking it while he harangu'd the Company; ſo as he was in the midſt of a long Story, he had been requeſted to relate, ſhe interrupted him, by pulling him by the Sleeve, and faying, Father *Raphael*, how much longer do you defign to wear that Beard————the Abruptneſs of ſuch a Queſtion a little difconcerted the good Man; but without feeming much moved, my Life, Madam, anſwer'd he, is in the Hands of the Almighty, who alone knows when he ſhall be pleaſed to refume it.————I talk not of your Life; but of your Beard refumed ſhe peeviſhly; I want to know if you are not tired with wearing it fuch a length of Time, and would not be glad ſome Friend would rid you of it? No, Madam, faid he, little fuſpecting her Defign in afking that Queſtion, I hope to preſerve it as long as I live.————I am very certain I ſhall never conſent to part with it, and I fcarce think any one will have the ill Manners, not to fay Impiety, to attempt to deprive me of it by Force.

Why not, cry'd Madam *D'Eſtival?* would you be lefs the venerable Man you are, without that odious Beard?————I am furprized a Man of the good Senfe you are taken for, ſhould fet your Heart on Trifles.

Monſieur *D'Eſtival*, the Counteſs, and all who knew the Temper of this Woman, trembled for the Confequence of her concerning herſelf about the Beard; but, Father *Raphael*, who little fuſpected what was in her Head, turning to ſome of the Company, was beginning to refume the Difcourfe her impertinent Queſtion had oblig'd him to break off; when Madam *D'Eſtival* cryed out, well, I wifh I had never feen that Beard.————I am with Child, and it may be fatal to me, if I have not the handling of that Beard.

Impof-

Impossible was it for the gravest Person at the Table, to forbear laughing immoderately at these Words; but the poor *Capuchin* was both confounded and ashamed; however, his good Breeding got the better, and making a very low Bow, Madam, said he, as much as I have hitherto priz'd my Beard, I should be now grieved to have ever worn it, if to the Prejudice of a Lady for whom I have the utmost Esteem; but as your Ladyship's Desires tend only to the handling it, I see no Necessity for its being cut off to yield you that Satisfaction, since you are at liberty to treat it as you please, exclusive of the Razor. That's all I ask, cry'd she, and immediately rose from her Seat, and stood before the *Capuchin*, who presented his Chin to her with all Humility. Every body wondering all the Time what would be the Effect of so whimsical a Fancy.

The Scene was certainly very diverting; you are exceeding good, dear Father, cry'd Madam *D'Estival*, I have long'd these two Hours for a pluck at that reverend Beard, and your Complaisance gives me a new Life; these Words were accompanied with a Look so maliciously arch, which together with the modest Air the *Capuchin* put on, as she approach'd, set the whole Company into a loud Laugh;————but when she seized the Beard with such an Eagerness, as if she did not design to let go her Grasp easily, they were not able to contain themselves————she tugg'd at it with a Force, which was not a little painful to the good Father, and render'd him little able to endure the Mirth, he found her Behaviour excited; for the Love of God, Madam, said he, be more merciful, if you oblige me to gape in this manner, I shall have all the Owls about me fly into my Mouth.

This Piece of Wit made those that laugh'd ashamed, that they had seemed diverted with the Humour of Madam *D'Estival*, but it had not the least Effect on her; for having now the Command of the favourite Beard, she held it fast with one Hand, and with the other began to pull the Hairs up by the Roots, and that with so much Expedition, that Father *Raphael* not doubting but she would demolish his whole Beard in the same manner, started from his Seat, and endeavouring to disengage himself, threw the Lady on the Floor; Monsieur *D'Estival*, the Countess, and, indeed, all in the Room, ran to help her up, and enquired if she was hurt; no, answered she, but I shall certainly expire, if I have not the whole Beard torn up by the Roots. Had any one been disposed to gratified her Humour in this Point, it would have been impossible; for the *Capuchin*, resenting the Treatment he had received, no sooner had his Chin at Liberty, than he very prudently made all the haste he could out of the Room, with a full Resolution never to come again into a Place, where he might be in danger of seeing Madam *D'Estival*.

That Lady no sooner perceived he had made his Escape, than she called to her Husband to run after him, and either bring him back, or tear his Beard off; but all Monsieur *D'Estival*'s Complaisance to her, could not influence him so far; on which she fell into violent Exclamations, told him she was certain he desired nothing so much as to see her dead; and that he chose rather to oblige a *Capuchin*, than his Wife to whom he had such great Obligations. Monsieur *D'Estival* remonstrated to her the Injustice of her Request, begg'd her to consider, that as the Father was resolved not to part with his Beard; how unreasonable it would be to force him to it; and that besides it might be of very ill Consequence, to offer a Violence of that Nature to a Person of his Order, and who was so greatly respected by the Church. The Countess said much the same things, and all the Company joined with them, to beg her to think no more of this unlucky Beard; but nothing was effectual to appease her; she vowed she would sooner destroy herself and the Child she was pregnant with, than be disappointed in a thing she had so much set her Heart upon; and that if she could not have the Beard, the least Attonement her Husband could make her, was to revenge her on the brutal *Capuchin*, who had not only denied the gratifying an Inclination so natural to Women with Child; but had also, without any

Re-

Respect due to her Birth, Sex or Condition, opposed his Strength against her Weakness, and thrown her on the Ground.

Thus what at first seem'd only a Matter of Ridicule, had like to have to have turned out of the most serious Consequence to Monsieur *D'Estival* ; for being prevail'd upon by his Wife, to prosecute Father *Raphael*, for an Assault, he was near being cast with the Loss of all he was worth in the World.———The *Capuchins* all over *France*, took the part of their Brother, and the Ecclesiastical Court gave it entirely on their Side ; so that had not the Friends of *D'Estival* made a very powerful Interest, he would have repented as long as he lived, the engaging in an Affair, which was only pardon'd in Consideration of his Wife being frantick, and who it was alledged, had represented to him the Hurts she pretended to have received, in a manner different from the Truth.

Soon after this was concluded, Madam *D'Estival* brought a Son into the World, who was born without a Beard, though some, to humour her, had seemed to apprehend the contrary ———Her Husband rejoiced extremely at this Blessing from Heaven, flattering himself that he was now at the End of all his Troubles, and that his Wife now made a Mother, would come to a more just way of thinking, and give him no farther Occasion to curse the Ceremony that united them ; but he was sadly mistaken, a very short time convinced him, that there was no End of his Misery with a Woman of her Temper.

One of the first Places she appear'd in after her going abroad was at the Celebration of a Wedding, a young Lady one of her most intimate Friends was married to a Count ; and the Thoughts of being obliged to give Place to the Bride, who was before her inferior, made this restless Woman quite beside herself, and nothing now would serve her, but being made a Marchioness, that she might still preserve her Precedence.

What a new and unforseen Affliction was this to Monsieur *D'Estival*, he endeavoured to convince her, that

the

she ought not to indulge so inconvenient an Ambition, told her that his Estate was too small to support the Dignity of such a Title; and that as he had never been in the Army, he should be look'd upon as mad to solli-cite such an Honour. On this she flew into an Extre-mity of Rage, reproach'd him with having demean'd herself by marrying him, and said, that as she brought him a large Estate, she would have Part of it sold to buy a Marquisate————it was in vain that the Coun-tess her Mother, and all the Relations on both Sides, used their utmost Efforts to get this Whim out of her Head;————nothing would pacify her, she raved, throwed things about the House, broke all that came near her, and, in fine, behaved like a Creature quite deprived of Reason: but, Monsieur *D'Estival*, still continuing inflexible, she had recourse to Artifice, fell into pretended Fits, feign'd herself sick, did all that wilful, wicked Woman could, but all to no Effect; which she at length perceiving, she resolved to be re-venged, and to that Purpose stifled her Resentment, seemed to grow easy in her Mind, and to have entirely forgot all that had passed: In the mean time was form-ing a Stratagem, which had not Fortune assisted her Husband in the Disappointment of, must have been his Destruction.

Happening to be walking one Morning in a fine Meadow adjacent to the Castle, he met one of his Te-nants crossing hastily into the Road; on Monsieur *D'Estival*'s bidding him Good-morrow with his ac-custom'd Affability, the Fellow look'd earnestly at him, and seem'd troubled————what's the Matter, said *D'Es-tival*, has any Misfortune befallen you? The other knowing, as the whole Country did, the Disposition of Madam *D'Estival*, could not forbear replying; I know not whether what has happened to me just now, is for my good or ill, or what Consequence my acquainting you with it may occasion;————but I cannot forbear letting you know, I am sent by your Lady to put a Letter into the Post, with a strict Charge not to tell any body of it; it being she says of such Moment, that she

I durst

durſt not truſt the Care of it to any Servant ſhe has.
———Now, continued the Peaſant, methinks, you being her Huſband ſhould not be a Stranger to the Contents, and if you think fit I ſhould carry it, I will make
the beſt of my way, otherwiſe I think it is but honeſt
to put it into your Hands.

Monſieur *D'Eſtival*, as he had reaſon, doubted not
but there was ſome Myſtery contain'd in it, which it
would be highly proper for him to unravel.———So
took the Letter, bidding the Man return to the Lady,
and tell her he had punctually obeyed her Commands,
and at the ſame time gave him a *Lewis D'Or* in recompence of his Fidelity ; exacting alſo from him, that
he ſhould never divulge, either that he had been entruſted with ſuch a Letter by her, or in what manner he
had diſpoſed of it ; all this the Fellow aſſured him of performing, and, indeed, was as good as his Word, Monſieur *D'Eſtival* being as much beloved, as his Wiſe was
the contrary.

This perplex'd Huſband was no ſooner alone, than he
began to examine the Letter ; the very Superſcription of
which had reaſon to alarm him, it being addreſſed to
the firſt Miniſter of State; but infinitely more was he
ſo, when after breaking the Seal, he found the Contents
as follows.

The LETTER.

My Lord,

*N*OTHING *could apologize for the Preſumption of*
encroaching on Moments ſo precious as yours ; but the
juſt Concern of a faithful Wife, for the Honour and Safe-
ty of a moſt beloved Huſband.———*I have received*
certain Intelligence that Monſieur D'Eſtival, *that Huſ-*
band who is ſo truly dear to me, has accepted of an Offer
made to him, to engage in a Foreign Service, and is now
on the Point of leaving the Kingdom.———*I know not on*
what Motives he has been prevail'd upon, to ſwerve from

the

the Duty he owes his King and Country, and the Affection he once pretended to a Wife, who has made his Fortune ; yet so, my Lord, it is, and he will very soon quit all that ought to be dear to him for ever, if you do not interpose your Authority, to prevent a Misfortune I cannot hope to survive.———I know it can be done by no other way than by securing his Person for a Time ; but, in that, perhaps, he may recover those Sentiments of Loyalty and Love, which I once thought were incapable of being interrupted by any Temptation whatever.———How terrible is it to me become his Accuser, yet would it be yet more cruel to keep Silence in such an Affair ; besides, rend'ring myself in some Measure a Partaker in his Guilt.———Pity, therefore, I most humbly beseech your Lordship, and pardon the incoherent Dictates, of a distracted and almost broken Heart.

> *I am,*
>
> > *My Lord,*
> >
> > > *With the greatest Respect,*
> > >
> > > > *Your Lordship's*
> > > >
> > > > > *Most humble and*
> > > > >
> > > > > > *most obedient Servant*

A. D'Estival.

As much as Madam *D'Estival* had done to convince her Husband of the Mischievousness of her Disposition, he could never have believed without this Testimony under her own Hand, that it would have carried her to such enormous Lengths ————He perceived now that her Design was to get him confined, and that while he was so, having the Management of the Estate in her own Hands, she would try all Methods of satisfying her Ambition.————All the Remains of Love, which had hitherto pleaded so successfully in her Behalf, this last vile Action dissipated, and he came to a Resolution of

making

making himself easy once for all, which could be done no other way than by an eternal Separation.

For this Purpose he imitated her Example, concealed his Resentment, dissembled an Affection he no longer felt, and pretending the sudden Death of a Relation called him to *Paris*, took Post the next Day, and went to *Versailles*, where being admitted to the Minister, he laid open his Grievance, and to prevent the Effect of any future Letter she might send, produced that which he had intercepted.————The Statesman, skill'd as he was in Stratagem, was amazed to find so much Artifice in a Female Breast; and after being perfectly convinced of the Innocence of Monsieur *D'Estival*, granted him his Protection.

The next Step took by this unhappy Husband, was to apply to Parliament for a Separation, which he easily obtain'd on shewing the Letter, and proving it to be his Wife's Hand.

Madam *D'Estival* in the mean time was not idle, and though it was not in her power to prevent him from carrying his Point in this particular, she was no less successful in another: As he, infatuated by his Love, had acknowledg'd in the Marriage-Articles, a larger Dower than he in reality received, in Order, as it was pretended by the Countess, to give the Match a greater Air in the Family; she sued in her Turn for a Separation of Estates real and personal; alledging that her Husband was a Gamester and a Prodigal, and would squander away what belong'd to her and her Son.————All the Relations of her Father's side, thought themselves obliged to support this Cause, and as they were very powerful, their Interest carried it; and Monsieur *D'Estival*, was oblig'd to refund all he had receiv'd at Marriage, and to sell his own Estate, to make up the pretended Deficiency———— a sad Warning to all Men, how they depend so much on the Love of a Woman above them, as not to secure something to themselves in Case the Tide should turn.

Monsieur *D'Estival*, however, did not appear greatly dejected, the Wrongs he had sustain'd procured him much Favour from the distinguishing and truly wor-

thy

thy Minister, that he has since given him a handsome Employment; on the Salary of which he lives, and with with more real Comfort, than he did in his late Grandeur, with a Woman of such a vile Humour, as was that of his Wife.

Thus did my Mother conclude her History ; and I cannot say, on reflecting how much I had suffer'd from the Cruelty and Malice of that Lady, that I was sorry she had proved to all the World, what I but too well knew she was.

After this we fell into Conversation of several who lived in the Neighbourhood, and as my Mother naturally loved talking, she entertained me with many things, which I knew as well as herself, having happen'd before I left her ; but this she was ignorant of, and thought she did me a Pleasure ; by Accident having mention'd the *Financier*, who was the present Lord of the Village, I entreated she would give me his History ; which she did, beginning with his Intentions of marrying one of her Daughters, and the Occasion of breaking off the Match ; but that Part my Readers are already acquainted with, so I shall omit all my Mother said of it, and come to where she mentioned his purchasing the Lordship of the Village, and his Behaviour since his living at the Castle ; which she did with a Bitterness, which was not usual with her ; but I soon learned the Occasion of it in these Words.

A

A *Merry Adventure of Monfieur* GRI-PART, COLIN, *and his Wife.*

I Never had but three Children, faid my Mother, two Daughters, and a Son who died young————the Eldeft of my Girls it was whom I have inform'd your Ladyfhip, was very near being the Bride of Monfieur *Gripart* ; the youngeft, who though not altogether fo beautiful as her Sifter is accounted very amiable ; fhe married one *Colin* a Farmer, but a young Man of tollerable good Senfe, and very honeft————they love each other, and I have the Satisfaction to fee they live together with more Harmony and true Comfort, than is frequently the Portion of the Great. For fome Months after their Marriage they remain'd with us, and it was during that time, that Monfieur *Gripart* became Proprietor of the Caftle.————He had not been long in the Neighbourhood before he became ridiculous by his Amours, which were fometimes with his own Servants, and, indeed, he behaved with fo much Indecency to all the young Women that came in his way, that his Prefence was avoided with Deteftation.————All who were truly modeft, or defired to be thought fo, fled whenever he appear'd, and fhunn'd him like Infection.

He was, indeed, very complaifant to our Family, though the Inducement he had to it, was far from being guefs'd at by us.————He fent for my Hufband, and having heard he once had the Care of the Caftle-Gardens, told him, that if he would undertake the fame Bufinefs again, he would allow him the fame Wages had been formerly paid by the Countefs *De N*————. The Propofal was too advantageous not to be accepted with

M 5 Joy ;

Joy; but my Husband declined living their altogether on the Account of his Family; but went at Five o'Clock every Morning, and returned at Eight at Night.

As soon as Monsieur Gripart had thus secured *John B*——, who he knew very well was not to be imposed upon in any thing, where the Virtue or Reputation of those belonging to him were concern'd; he came very often to our House under various Pretences, sometimes desiring to rest himself, being, he would say, fatigued with walking; at others, call to know if we could recommend a Servant to him for such or such a Place—— at first he spoke indifferently to me, and to my Daughter; but after coming a few times he took more upon him, and began to be more free with her, than was becoming to a married Woman, and at last told her in plain Terms that he was in love with her;——as she is, Heaven be praised, very virtuous, she rejected this Declaration with the Disdain it merited, and solemnly protested, if he ever offer'd to talk to her any more on that Subject, she would complain to her Husband and the Curate.

Gripart was too much a Coward, to be willing to cope with so lusty and resolute a Fellow as *Colin*, and too covetous to be willing to come under the Rebuke of the Church, which seldom pardons without making the Delinquent pay pretty dear for his Offence; so promised he would be more discreet for the future, and begg'd she would not betray him; she consented to be silent on that Condition, though less for his sake than for her Husband's Peace, who she knew to be a little inclined to Jealousy;——but, the *Financier*, was either too much enamoured, or too foolish to keep his Word; and as he durst not speak to her any more, he contrived a Scheme by which he hoped to compass his Design, without exposing himself to any Danger.

He knew that *Colin* went every Week to a small Town about four Leagues distance to sell his Corn, and and that he never came back the same Night; but was often oblig'd to stay two or three Days away, and on this Absence he founded his Project.

Towards

Towards the Evening of one Day, that my Son-in-Law was gone on his accuftom'd Bufinefs ; *Gripart* fent a Peafant, whom by Bribes he made his Creature, to my Daughter.———I remember we were juft going to Supper, when the Fellow came in a vaft Hurry, and told her fhe muft go with him immediately, that *Colin* had fallen from his Horfe, and being let Blood was obliged to ftay at a Farm-Houfe in the Road, fo defired fhe would make all the hafte fhe could to him ; in order to go on with the Waggon early the next Morning, to fell the Corn for him. My poor Girl, not in the leaft fufpecting the Truth of what was told her, got up behind the Meffenger, and trufted entirely to him to conduct her.

It was two Hours after Dark when fhe arrived at the Place, where fhe expected to have found her Hufband ; but where in reality the bafe *Gripart* was waiting for her, now imagining himfelf fure of his Prey ; having, indeed, laid fuch a Scheme for her Ruin, as nothing cou'd have prevented from taking Effect, but the Interpofition of the all merciful and ever watchful Providence.

This Farm-Houfe, as the vile Tool of his Defigns call'd it, was no other than a little obfcure Inn, where the meaner fort of Travellers ufed fometimes to bait : *Gripart*, to avoid being expofed, in Cafe any Difappointment fhould happen, difguifed himfelf like a plain Countryman, and had invented a Story plaufible enough, to make the People of the Houfe of his Party : He to'd them, that being married to a young Woman for whom he had a very great Affection, he had of late heard fome Stories, which made him fearful her Conduct was not fuch as it ought to be ; but that not being willing to condemn her on a bare Report; he was refolved to make tryal of her, and to that End had pretended to go a Journey, that fhe might think herfelf at Liberty to act as fhe pleafed ; and that he had now fent for her to come there, in the Name of the Perfon with whom it was fufpected fhe had too great an Intimacy.———So, faid the wicked *Gripart*, if fhe comes it will be a convincing Proof of her Infidelity, and if fhe refufes I'

fhall

fhall know to give the lye to thofe who have fpoke ill of her.

The Mafter and Miftrefs of the Houfe approved very much of his Proceeding, and on his telling them that, perhaps, his Wife on finding fhe was difcovered, would cry out; they affured him, that neither themfelves nor any of their Family fhould interfere between them, if he had a mind to correct her, it was none of their Bufinefs— and that they fhould not be againft his bringing her back to her Duty.————Thus was every Obftacle, that could be forfeen, removed from hindring the Perpetration of his black Attempt.

Colin in the mean time happening to meet fome Officers, who were employed in furnifhing Provifions for the Army, and on the Watch for the Corn-Waggons, expecting to buy fomewhat cheaper than in the Market fold all his Wheat to them, and after drinking together, was on his return Home, overjoyed that he had difpatch'd his Bufinefs fo foon. And defign'd only to bait a little by the way, and then travel all Night, that he might reach the Village by the next Morning.

The Inn where he ftopp'd for Refrefhment, was the very fame where Monfieur *Gripart* waited for my Daughter, and on his Arrival, found his Horfes were too much tired, the Waggon being that Day more than ordinarily heavy loaded, to go any further; fo on the Waggoner's Perfuafions, he confented to yield to Neceffity, and to lie there all Night.

He was fitting drinking with his Man by the Firefide, when my Daughter came in: He was furprized to fee her, but fhe, who expected him there, ran directly to him, and throwing her Arms about his Neck, ask'd him how he found himfelf, and faid he was in the wrong, not to be Bed after fuch an Accident.

What Accident, cry'd he, what do you mean?———— your Words are as myfterious to me, as the fight of you at this time of Night, and fo far from Home? Good God! faid fhe, did you not fall from your Horfe?———— are you not bruifed very much, and oblig'd to be let Blood?————did you not fend *John Bibart* the Vine-

Dreffer

Dreffer to bid me come to you in all hafte ?——Prithee, continued fhe, turning to the Man that brought her, who thought was juft behind ther, what did you mean by telling me fuch an untruth ? But fhe might have fpared herfelf the trouble of afking this Queftion——the Fellow on his entrance, feeing *Colin*, thought he fhould make but a bad Figure in this Bufinefs if he were examined, fo ran out of the Houfe as faft as he could.

Colin confidered a little on it, and was convinced in his Mind, that this Contrivance to get his Wife abroad could not be made for nothing, and was refolved to fathom the Bottom of it if poffible ; in order to which he bid her fit down, while he went to watch what would enfue at the Gate——no body here knows us, faid he, nor has heard what paft between us at your coming in, fo when I am gone, you may afk if there is no Company, or if they don't expect fome body here, and by that means it's poffible we may find out fomething. My Daughter no lefs anxious than himfelf, promifed to do her Part, and as foon as he was gone out of the Room, called for the Woman of the Houfe, and enquired of her according to her Hufband's Directions, but was anfwered by her, that having been abroad herfelf fhe could not fay any thing to the Matter ; but if fhe pleafed fhe would fee. On this my Daughter obferved fhe went up Stairs, and foon after came down again, which as foon as fhe was, fhe whifpered in her Ear, and bid her go up the Party was above——very well, cried my Daughter, and immediately tripped up Stairs, where fhe was met by the wicked *Gripart*, who catch'd her in his Arms, crying now my pretty Peafant I will be revenged on you, for all your Coynefs——fhe fhrieked out, but as he had prepared the People, her Cries would have little availed, had not *Colin*, who fuffered nothing of what pafied to efcape him, flew to her Relief, followed by his Man both armed with Cudgels, which they did not fail to exercife with all their Might, on the Arms, Back, Legs, and every Part of the intended Ravifher, who fell upon his Knees, begging for Mercy, but

but in vain ; *Colin* would not be prevailed upon to desist till he was no less weary with giving Blows, than the Criminal was sore with receiving them———— then leaning to rest himself on his Cudgel, after loading *Gripart* with all the opprobrious Names he could invent, he bethought himself of yet a farther Revenge, which was to bind him Hand and Foot, and in that Posture carry him before the Curate, to be punished as the ecclesiastick Court should determine————this was much more terrible to *Gripart* than all he had suffered :—— he begged *Colin* not to carry Things so far as that, and offered a handsome Sum of Money, to be let depart quietly away ; but *Colin*, who took a Pleasure in tormenting him, would not seem to know him, tho' he did so from the Moment he came up, and cried, you do well to think to impose upon me————where should such a Clown as you have the Gold you talk of ?————in fine, he made such a Jest of him, and at the same Time, appeared so positive in complaining to the Curate, that *Gripart* was at last obliged to acknowledge who he was, beg *Colin*'s Pardon in his own Name, and entreat him to accept of his Proposal, which with some seeming Difficulty he was at last prevailed on to take, and with that Money soon after brought a Farm, on which they now live in a comfortable manner.

Since this Adventure, Monsieur *Gripart* has behaved with more Decency to Women in general, and I dare Answer is sufficiently cured of his Passion for my Daughter, who he now treats wherever he sees her with a great deal of Respect, as also her Husband, not daring to do any thing to disoblige them for fear they should expose him.

My Mother concluded her little Narrative, with telling me it was on the Account of his Curiosity concerning me, that she had given me this Account of his Disposition, in order that I might be upon my Guard.

I thanked her for her kind Caution, tho' she was far from imagining how little need there was of it, being resolved to avoid as much as possible, a Man whom I

knew

knew but too well, and who, even tho' he should not remember me for what I was, might take it into his Head to be troublesome to me in the Person I assumed.

The next Day I received my Goods, which Monsieur *Melicourt* had sent me, and with them a Letter, which cautioned me to be extremely careful how I saw any Strangers. He told me that the old Marquis was outrageous at my Flight————that he had dispatched Persons all over the Kingdom to learn News of me, and to encourage their Diligence had offered a large Sum of Money, as the Reward of him who should be successful enough to find me————*Melicourt* exprest his Apprehensions of my being discovered, and the Effects of the old Marquis's Resentment to me, if ever I should fall into his Hands, after having thus disappointed his Expectations————He informed me also, that supposing his Son was privy to my Departure, he intended to write to him, in order to compel him to discover the Place of my Retreat, or by his refusing Compliance with that Command, to banish him for ever from his Presence. How terrible this Intelligence was to me, any one who loves, and has such Reason to fear for the beloved Object, may easily imagine————*Melicourt*, however, assured me, that the Marquis, in spite of his Indignation, exprest a Concern, that I had not taken the Toylet with me, and said he was very unhappy in being so little known to me————that he would by no means suffer the Effects I had left behind me to be sold, in order to make up the Money he had bestowed upon me————and added, that since he knew not where to send them to me at present, he would order them to be secured for me till I should be heard of.

In fine, all that *Melicourt* wrote, convinced me that the old Marquis's Quarrel to me, was only occasioned by my Departure, and that his Passion for me was not in the least abated————this, tho' it defended me from all Apprehensions of being cruelly treated by him, if he should find me out, gave me others of a more

dreadful

dreadful Nature, on the Score of being loved too much.

The little Furniture which came down, occafioned much Difcourfe in the Village, it confifted of Plate, inlaid Cabinets, and fome other Toys in an elegant Tafte, and which had an Air of Grandeur————my Father and Mother could not fufficiently exprefs their Admiration, and my Aunt, who took a great Pride in the Honour, as fhe thought it, of belonging to me, told the Neighbours that this was nothing to what I had at *Paris*. I was fometimes very much diverted with her repeating to me what the People faid of me; but there was things fhe informed me of, which made me fee I ought to be extremely circumfpect, if I intended to avoid giving Sufpicion who I was.

She told me that her Sifter, meaning my Mother, could never look upon me without the Palpitation of the Heart; that the more fhe faw me, the more fhe thought me like that Daughter of whom I had heard them fpeak, and of whom they could not hear the leaft News, but that I never refembled her fo much as when I was in an Undrefs; and on my Father's faying he thought indeed there was a diftant Likenefs, but far from what fhe fancied, fhe had told him, that fhe would convince him by bringing him up on fome Pretence into my Chamber before I was out of Bed.

This Hint was very ufeful to me, and to bring them off from any Notions of the Truth, from this Time I dreffed every Morning as I ufed to do at *Verfailles*, and *Paris*; and tho' I had never made ufe of any Art before, I now put fome Red upon my Cheeks, to take off the natural Palenefs, or rather too great Delicacy of my Complection. I wore it Day and Night, fo that it paffed for the good Effects of the Country Air rendering me more robuft and healthy, and took away great Part of that Refemblance I fo much dreaded, fhould firft or laft difcover me.

There was one thing that gave me a great deal of Pain how to behave in: I had been in the Village now twelve Days, and had never once been at Church; the Excuse of bad Health would no longer pass current, when I looked so rosy, and besides, it was a Duty which I thought I ought not on any Motive to dispense with————Heaven, said I, to myself, can conceal me from the most inquisitive Eyes, when Piety obliges me to be seen, and tho' I were to hide me under the Earth, could also betray me————to that to the same Providence which has hitherto vouchsafed to protect me, will I still trust, fearing nothing so much as rendering myself unworthy of it.

This Reflection determined me to go the next *Sunday* to Church, but as I did not doubt that my Intentions would be a Secret, and consequently a great Number of People would be there to see me, I dressed myself in one of the richest Gowns I had, that I might appear as little like my real self as possible————I also put on a Hood very forward to conceal a good Part of my Face, and went along with my Head declined as looking on the Ground, so that it was very difficult to get a full View of my Face.

What I had imagined was true ; the Church was crowded not only with Parishioners, but also with a vast many Strangers, I went up to the Women's Benches, which were immediately cleared by those who were there before me ; but I obliged them to resume their Places, and I could hear them whisper to one another, that I was as affable as fair————so infinitely were they charmed with what seemed so great a Condescension in me.

But I was not suffered to remain long in the Place I had made choice of————a Verger came to me in the Name of the Lord of the Village to invite me to his Chapel, I answered him that I liked my Situation very well, and tho' I thanked him for his Civility, desired to stay where I was. The Messenger left me at these Words, but Monsieur *Gripart* then came himself, and told me he could not bear to see a Lady of my Appearance so incommodiously placed, and protested, that if I

perstited

perfifted in refufing his Requeft, he would kneel down by me on the Pavement.

His coming to me in this manner, drew more than ever the Eyes of the whole Affembly upon me, and to put an end to it, I thought it beft to comply; fo prefenting my Hand, permitted him to lead me to his Chapel, where I heard Mafs without making any Anfwer to the Compliments, with which he endeavoured to interrupt my Devotion.

He was over and above follicitous in acquitting himfelf politely, and as his Quality was but of a fhort Date as well as my own, I could not help fmiling to myfelf at the Ceremonies that paffed between us—— when Mafs was over he made me an Offer of his Coach to carry me Home ; but as my Lodging was not above an hundred Paces from the Church, I told him I chofe to walk, and indeed it would have been ridiculous to have done otherwife, even if I had had a Coach of my own————at leaft, faid he, I beg your Ladyfhip will do me the honour to fee the Caftle, I can affure you the Gardens are pleafant and well defigned, *John B*————where you lodge was the Contriver of them ; befides, Madam, continued he, our Country-Maids dance in the Avenues, and may afford you fome Diverfion. I thanked him for his obliging Invitation, but begged to be excufed, faying that it was my Determination to go no where except to Church ; but I fhould not fo eafily have got rid of his Importunities, if the Curate had not joined Company with us, as we were talking ; I could eafily perceive there was fome Mifunderftanding between them, for Monfieur *Gripart* immediately took his leave and went into his Coach, and I afterwards heared that good Prieft had very feverely reprimanded him on Account of his loofe Behaviour, which made him afterwards not very eafy in his Company.

He addreffed himfelf to me with a great deal of Refpect, and told me he had taken great Notice of my Behaviour during Divine Service, that I was a Pattern,

which

which he should rejoice to find his whole Congregation
endeavour to imitate, and that as the Manners of
People of Condition, had for the most Part an Influence
over the meaner Sort, he hoped mine would lose nothing
of their Force. I answered this Compliment with the
Humility due to his Function, and had no sooner done
so than my Father and Mother came up to us, and
after saying some handsome Things on the honour
they had of having me for a Lodger, he desired they
would use all the Interest they had with me, to prevail
on me to dine with him that Day————He told me,
that he had a Neice who was dying with impatience to
see a Lady , whose Praises she had heard from the Mouth
of every body in the Village————my Father and
Mother seconded his Request, and I was so beset on all
sides, that notwithstanding my Resolution, I was
obliged to comply.————The Curate appeared infinitely
satisfied and thought he had Reason to be more so, as I
had refused the same Favour to the Lord of the Village,
and when we came to his House, the Neice he mentioned, who was a very agreeable young Woman,
received me with the greatest Complaisance and
Respect.

The Curate, who little imagined I was that *Jeanetta,*
whom the Marquis *De L————V————* had sent *Dubois*
to enquire after, as mentioned in the beginning of these
Memoirs, had a very great Curiosity to know who I was,
and hearing I was called Madam *De Mainville,* said to
me at we were at Table, I once knew a Gentleman
named Monsieur *De Mainville* who belonged to the Sea,
perhaps, Madam, he might be a Relation to you.

I easily perceived he introduced this Discourse in order
to discover by my Answer somewhat concerning me, so
was entirely on my Guard, and beseeched he would not
oblige me to enter into Conversation, which would remind me of the loss of a beloved Husband.

This Reply of mine agreeing exactly with the Account my Aunt had given, that I was always lamenting
for the Death of my Husband, obliged him out of good
Manners.

Manners to talk of other Things ; but I, who wanted very much to be at home, for fear of any Accident happening to betray me, appeared so much dejected, and counterfeited so deep a Melancholy, that he was extremely troubled at having occasioned, as he imagined, so great a change in me.

I was just about to take my leave when *Colin* and his Wife came in ; as I had never seen my Sister since my coming, and was easily persuaded to sit a Moment longer, that I might have the pleasure of being in her Company, but indulging this natural Affection occasioned me some Alarms, and convinced me that the Passion of Love is stronger than the Tenderness of Consanguinity. ————*Colin*, who had felt that Passion for me, had my Features more deeply imprinted in his Memory than in that of either my Father, Mother, or Sister.———— He looked upon me with Astonishment, and cried out, I am sure I have seen that Face before ! ————That may possibly be true, replied I, with an Air of Reserve and Dignity which awed him, and I believe made him repent his Abruptness, for he hung down his Head and spoke no more. I could not help however being terribly confused, which the Company taking as Resentment for his ill Manners, my Father, Mother, and Sister thought they could never make sufficient Apologies for him————the Curate and his Neice also asked Pardon for him, and I was obliged to protest I thought of it no more, before they could be easy.

All this took up so much Time, that the Bell-rung for Vespers, on which I came away, the good Priest and his Neice would fain have engaged me to return after Prayers were over, and pass the Evening, but I excused myself, pretending I had Letters to write, and could not possibly do myself that pleasure.

His Neice came the next Day to pay her Compliments, I received her with all imaginable Affability, but was very reserved, so she stayed but a short Time. Soon after I invited her, and her Uncle to dine with me, and having paid that Debt, evaded any farther

meetings

meetings————all my Behaviour made it evident I did not care for Company, and at length I was not importuned on that score.

If the fear of Discovery had not given me just Reason to avoid Company, the trouble I was in, would have made me desirous of Solitude————a Month was now past over since I left *Paris*, and I had received no Letter from the Marquis, and the various Apprehensions that perplexed me on this score, rendered me as unfit for Society as unwilling to come into it———— I was all in Tears one Morning, when my Mother came into my Chamber, to tell me a Man on Horseback asked to speak with me, but would not alight till he knew if I were at home and alone————a sudden Trembling, with a Pain mix'd with Pleasure, seized me at hearing what she said————I fancied he came from the young Marquis, and at the same Time dreaded lest he were sent by the Father of that dear Man—— Suspence however was not to be borne————it was proper I should know the Message, be it from either the one or other, so desired he should be admitted, and then retired to a Closet I had next the Garden, that I might hear what he had to say to me, without danger of having any other Witness of it.

As the Person entered, a spring of Joy came over my Heart, in hopes it was *Dubois*, from whom I knew I might be certain of hearing a full Account of every thing, but when I saw it was not he, but a Man with a large Plaister on his Forehead, I turned away my Eyes, and received a Letter which he delivered to me, without taking any farther Notice, than to give him a Crown, and bid him go and refresh himself at the next Cabaret, adding, that I would send for him when I had wrote, in case the Letter he brought required any Answer.

I then looked on the Superscription, and found it was in the Character of my dear Marquis————I then, impatient for the Contents, broke it hastily open, and to my inexpressible Amazement, saw there was no more
wrote

wrote on the Paper than one Line : The Words of which were thefe ;

Deareſt *Jeanetta,*

The Courier will tell you all the Soul of your Adorer.

L———V———.

O Heavens! cried I, what can this mean ?———where is this Courier ?———why did he go, if he had any thing to ſay to me!

I was juſt turning to ring for *Barbara,* to call him back. unable as I was to comprehend this Myſtery, when I ſaw him on his Knees before me——what do I ſee! then ſcreamed I out in a Tranſport of Joy, and throwing myſelf on the Neck of this charming Courier, for it was no other than the Marquis himſelf, who thus diſguiſed, had been his own Meſſenger———is it you my Lord ?———is it you ?———I could ſay no more ———ſo dear and ſo unexpected a Sight overwhelmed me, and I was near ſwooning with Exceſs of Joy.

The Marquis was troubled that he had thus ſurprized me, and aſked my Pardon a thouſand and a thouſand Times ; but alas! what Occaſion was there for doing ſo———the Tranſport well over paid the little Alarm I felt at its firſt too violent Emotion ; I obliged him to ſit down, and made in my turn an endearing Apology for not having known him. Indeed I could not forbear ſmiling at the Reception I gave him, eſpecially when he mentioned the grave Air with which I put the Crown into his Hand, and bid him go to a Cabaret, till I ſent Orders to him ; we were very merry ſome time on this, after which I began to think he might in good earneſt ſtand in need of ſome Refreſhment, ſo called to *Barbara,* to lay the Cloth.

He was indeed ſo much weakened by his Wounds, that the Journey had fatigued him more than it would have done at an other Time, and he readily accepted of my Offer ; while Breakfaſt was getting ready, we began

to

to confider in what manner we fhonld behave, fo as to give no occafion to any Difcourfe to the prejudice of my Reputation; and after various Projects it was agreed upon between us, that he fhould pafs for my Brother. He told me all the Servants he had with him he had hired but that Day, and had not acquainted them either with his Name or Quality, fo that knowing him only for an Officer juft arrived from the Army, it was not in their power to make any Difcovery, in cafe they fhould be queftioned concerning him. I applauded his Prudence in this, alfo for wearing that large Patch on his Forehead, which altered him fo much, that there was no Danger of his being known by Perfons who had never feen him but once, when he came to bring me the Favour conferred on me by the King.

My Suppofition that the Patch was only worn for a Difguife, kept me from afking any Queftions concerning it, till at length remembering one of the Wounds he had received was on his Head; I afked if it were entirely healed. No, anfwered he, my Surgeon, at my leaving the Camp gave me Medicines, with which my Servant dreffes it every Day, but affured me that all the Danger that arofe from it was over, and that in eight Days there would be nothing but the Scar remaining. O Heaven! cried I, frighted at what he faid, why would you venture to ride Poft before you were perfectly recovered? fhould any ill Confequence attend this Journey, what would become of the unfortunate *Jeanctta*, who has been the innocent Occafion of it?

The Marquis took this Exclamation fo kindly, that he catched both my Hands between his, and preffed them to his Mouth, with fuch an Eagernefs as if he meant to devour them with his Kiffes, make yourfelf eafy, my charming *Jeanetta*, faid the dear Man, and the foft Concern you exprefs for my Safety, will compleat my Cure much fooner than could be expected———— Be affured, had I been deprived much longer of your Society, I muft have funk under the burthen of my Grief and Impatience—*Dubois*, who plainly faw that my

Abfence

Abfence from you was the chief Obſtacle to my Cure, propoſed my taking this Journey————Neither did I ride Poſt as you imagined, but came in my Chaiſe, which is very eaſy, and with my own Horſes, till I came within two Miles of the Village, and then came hither on one of thoſe belonging to my Men.————Yes, my deareſt *Jeanetta*, continued he, I am convinced how abſolutely neceſſary your Preſence is to my Recovery by the Effect, the very Thought I was drawing nearer you have had upon my Wounds————every Day I felt ſtill more and more the Benefit, and if you permit me to remain in a Place where I may enjoy the Pleaſure of your Converſation, I am very certain you will ſhortly ſee a wonderful Experiment, how far the Contentment of the Mind, ſerves to render the Body in perfect eaſe——Conſent therefore, my Angel, added he, that I may continue for a few Days at leaſt in this Village ; what I have ſuffered ſince our parting, demands this Recompence, and I flatter myſelf you will not refuſe it.

How could I indeed refuſe ſo ſmall a Requeſt, to ſo great a Paſſion! and at the ſame Time, what was ſo pleaſing to my own Inclinations————had I been leſs acquainted with the Honour of him who aſked it, I ſhould not have ſo readily agreed, however my ſecret Wiſhes might have pleaded in his Behalf; but I had experienced his Moderation in a thouſand Inſtances, and it muſt have been owing either to Injuſtice or Affectation had I ſeemed to ſuſpect it now, ſo that without making any Difficulty or Heſitation, you are determined to pretend yourſelf my Brother, anſwered I, and under that Name may ſtay here as long as you ſhall find it not inconvenient————for my Part I have ſo perfect a Confidence, both in your Love and Virtue, that I joyfully agree to accept of the precious Moments you are ſo good to devote to me, and am perſuaded I never ſhall have any Reaſon to repent it.

O, there is not the leaſt room for doubt on this Occaſion, cried he, kiſſing my Hand a ſecond Time
————I

————I never can be capable of forgetting what is due to you————the Letter I wrote to you to thank you for the Money you sent, ought to convince you how sensible I am of the Delicacy of your Sentiments and Behaviour————that Moment had I been able I had flown hither to testify my Gratitude at your Feet, and not have trusted to vain Letters, which speak the Mind but by halves, to assure you how entirely I was devoted to you.

Hold my Lord, cried I, interrupting him, no Acknowledgements to one who is so infinitely your Debtor, but satisfye me, if you please, concerning a Letter which you say you wrote, and I have never received.

How! said the Marquis, with a great deal of Emotion, did not Monsieur *Melicourt* send a Packet to you, with a Picture, which I enclosed under a Cover to him, in order that the Place of your Abode might not be known, and sent by a Servant of my own, who went Post on purpose to deliver it to that Gentleman's Hand?

That Servant then, replied I, has betrayed his Trust, for I know *Melicourt* is too exact not to have forwarded it, with all imaginable Expedition. What you tell me, cried the Marquis, both surprizes, and alarms me———— there is a Mystery in this Affair, which I cannot comprehend————I remember indeed, that I thought it strange that *Melicourt* sent back my Servant, without writing one single Word to me, and I expressed as much to the Fellow, but he readily told me, that the Gentleman was just going a Journey, and was in haste; but said he would write to me by the Post at his return. Since which I have impatiently expected to hear from him, and indeed through him from you; but no Letter arriving, the Disappointment served to hasten my Journey.————There is something so extraordinary in this Business, continued he, after a Pause, that neglecting one Moment to unriddle it, may be of very ill Consequence————the Servant whom I entrusted with this Letter belongs to me still, and has now the Charge of conducting my Baggage; I'll send one of those I have here directly to the Camp to bring him to me, that I may force him to confess what he has done with my Letter.

I, who was no less alarmed than the Marquis, as indeed our concern in this Affair was equal, approved of his Design, and hastened the execution of it. He went away directly, but soon returned, and told me he did not doubt, but that the Person he had sent would make an extraordinary Dispatch, in hope of ingratiating himself; on this I could not help asking if his Favourite *Dubois*, had any way offended him, that he came not with him. Not in the least, answered he, but as he has been in the Village, has talked to the Girls, and has a very remarkable Face, I was fearful he might be better remembred than was consistent with the Secrecy which our present Circumstances require, so I left him with the Count *De Saint Fal*, who in his Confinement stands in need of so faithful a Servant.

The Name of Monsieur *De Saint Fal* made me blush, when I reflected how ungrateful I was to defer till now enquiring after so generous and noble a Friend———— I acknowledged my Sentiments on this Occasion very frankly, to him who wholly taking up my Thoughts left no room for any Thing but himself; and he replied in a manner, both becoming the Lover and the Friend, and added, that he would shortly be at Liberty, an exchange of Prisoners being agreed on.

We dined together that Day, and to oblige me I perceived he eat more heartily than could be expected from his Weakness————I forbore talking of any thing that I thought might give him Disquiet, and always took care to interrupt him whenever he mentioned the old Marquis, and artfully turned the Conversation on some other Topick; he smiled upon me from time to time, as I would not suffer him to speak, and his Looks methought tho' pale and languid, had somewhat Heavenly in them; and certainly nothing can have a greater Resemblance of it on Earth, than where a tender Passion is accompanied by a perfect Innocence.

He was too dear to me for me not to consider every that thing was necessary for the Re-establishment of his

Health————

we had no fooner dined then I infifted on his going to lie down, and endeavour to take fome repofe, protefting that I would not permit him to return till Supper-time.
——————He earneftly entreated I would fuffer him to ftay one Hour longer, but I was not to be prevailed on, and told him I would fend my Maid to his Inn to be fatisfied, if he complied with what I required:——————Thefe little Regards charmed him to the Soul, and he declared at going out of my Chamber, that never till now had he known there were fuch Joys in Life.

When I was left alone, I indulged myfelf in the moft agreeable Reflections, had it not been for the Letter, which muft be either loft or intercepted, my Happinefs might have been envied, but as I had already experienced fo many ill Effects of Chance, it was natural for me to apprehend this Accident portended me no good——————this Notion no fooner gained Ground, than it diffipated by degrees that Harmony which before feemed eftablifhed in my Mind——————the impetuous love the old Marquis had for me, prefented a thoufand Dangers to my view, and fhewed me, that I was ftill at a greater Diftance from my wifhed for Point, and with which I was fo ready to flatter myfeif.

As I was buried in Meditation on all thefe Things, I heard a Coach and feveral Horfes ftop at the Door—————I prefently imagined that the old Marquis had difcovered where I was, that he was come to furprize his Son and me together, and feparate us eternally——————I fell into a fit of Trembling, and I know not how far the frightful Idea I was then poffeffed of, might have tranfported me, if *Barbara* had not come haftily in to acquaint me, that a very beautiful young Lady, and as fine as a Queen, was come to vifit me. I had not Time to think, who this unexpected Gueft fhould be, before *Saint Agnes* appeared——————I flew to her, and fhe by her affectionate Embraces, teftified I was no lefs dear to her, than when we were together in the Convent.

How happy am I, my dear *Saint Agnes*, faid I, to fee you at Liberty, and that this Change in your Fortune has made no alteration in your Sentiments towards me.

I fhould make an ill Ufe, anfwered that charming Woman, of the favours Heaven has beftowed upon me, if I could be ungrateful to her, who put the firft Hand to my obtaining them. After the firft Tranfports were over, and we were feated, I defired fhe would inform me by what means fhe had furmounted all the Obftacles, which feemed to be thrown by adverfe Fortune, between her and Happinefs ; to which fhe immediately yielded.

Sequel of the Hiftory of SAINT AGNES.

INDEED, my lovely Friend, faid fhe, it is but a fmall Time fince I defpaired of ever being in the Situation I now am——in fpite of all the Intereft the Friends of *Melicourt* could make, our Affair went flowly on, and when through the Remonftrances of my Lord Marquis *De L——-V——*, the *Nuncio* feemed inclined to favour us, fome unlooked for Accident requiring his return to *Rome*, all was at a ftand till a new one fhould be fent in his Place————this gave my Father time to employ all his Friends to influence the *Cardinal*, who was to fucceed the other as *Nuncio* here, on his fide ; and this fucceeded fo well, that having been prejudiced by the Accounts fent to him, my Hufband found him on his arrival no lefs our Enemy than my Father. ————I was all this Time kept in Ignorance of what was done, permitted to fee none but who were fent by my Parents, and even when there was moft probability of the Decifion being made in favour of me, told by the Superior and thofe Nuns, who were gained by my Father, that I ought not to flatter my felf with ever living in the World again, and all I fhould gain by having ftirred in the Affair, was, that when all was concluded I fhould be obliged to undergo a fevere Difcipline for my
little

little regard for these holy Orders, I had once taken upon me.

No Letters from *Melicourt* were now suffered to come to my Hand, and for some Weeks I looked on myself as utterly abandoned both by Heaven and Earth————— I was but very rarely permitted to come near the Grate, and if I did it was in Company with one who they knew would have a watchful Eye over me; it was in one of those Times, however, that a Woman was there offering Oranges to sell, my Companion bought some, but I who am no great admirer of that Sort of Fruit, could not a long Time be prevailed on to be a Customer; at length moved by the poor Creature's Intreaties, who said she had a number of Children, and no way to maintain them, but the Profits of this little Merchandize, I at length drew near the Basket, and being about to make Choice, the supposed Fruiterer, under pretence of giving me one she could recommend, pulled one from the bottom of the Basket, and put it into my Hand, with so significant a Squeeze, that I presently found their was somewhat very extraordinary in this Adventure: I concealed my Surprize, however, put the Orange into my Pocket, paid the Woman, who immediately went away, and I then retired to my Cell, in order to discover if there was any thing supernatural in my Orange or not.

On looking upon it a second Time, I easily perceived it had been cut, and the Rind cemented again, so pressing it between my Hands, it presently flew open, and discovered a Paper, which having unfolded, I saw with no small Transport the Character of my dear *Melicourt*————that faithful Husband, expressed himself in these terms:

To my ever charming, ever dear MI-NETTA.

TO what Stratagems am I oblig'd to have Recourse, to let you know, that you have a Husband, who in spite of all the Difficulties that surround him, still lives to adore you.————*Who thinks of nothing but you*————*wishes for nothing but you*————*and fears nothing but that the many Disappointments our Affairs have met with, should press too hard upon your tender Nature ;*————*but be comforted, my Angel, be comforted*————*I have obtain'd a Letter from the Duke De* E————*to the Nuncio, which I flatter myself will have more Weight than all the Interest your inhuman Parents can make against us.*———— *That Prelate gave me a favourable hearing, and seem'd full of Commiseration.*————*I have his Commands to attend him in eight Days, and bring what Witnesses I can to attest both the Time and Place of our Marriage*———— *if this comes safe to your Hand, as I hope it will, the Bearer who was my Nurse, and who I have placed near the Monastery, will from time to time bring you an Account of my Proceedings, and also let me know how you support yourself under our mutual Afflictions.*————*Farewel, my only dear, belive me to be what I am, and never can cease to be*

Your everlasting Admirer, and

most tenderly affectionate Husband,

MELICOURT.

Judge, beautiful *Jeanetta,* continued *Saint Agnes,* how great a Consolation these few Lines afforded me ; I presently wrote an Answer, wherein I laid open all my Soul to this worthy Husband, and the Orange-Woman coming as I expected the next Day to the Grate, I easily found means to slip it into her Hand. ————This Communication pass'd undiscovered, and

I

I received and sent several Letters, all confirming that Affection we had vowed to each other————the time now past more agreeably with me than it had done, and Absence lost the greatest Part of its Irksomeness, by the Imagination that it was very near drawing to Period ; but, alas! when I most flatter'd myself with my Wishes being accomplish'd, I received News of all *Melicourt*'s Endeavours being utterly defeated.————I will not repeat the Letter he wrote to me on that Occasion———— it was full of Despair, which even now I shudder but to think upon————the Business of it was to acquaint me, that the Prince *De*————whose Father had received some signal Services from mine, had in Return, took such Part in the Affair, that the *Nuncio* found himself obliged to yield, and had decided in Favour of my Parents.————By this Decree I was not only to continue in the Monastery for Life ; but also to submit to whatever Penance the Church should think my past Crimes demanded. Ah ! cry'd I out, whatever is inflicted on me can be but of short Duration, Death will soon deliver me from my cruel Persecutors. I had scarce finish'd reading this fatal Letter, when the sweet-temper'd *Lindamine* came into my Cell, with Tears in her Eyes, and confirm'd the Tidings it contain'd :———— She told me an Order was just arrived, that I should not be suffer'd to come near the Grate any more————be retrench'd even in my Food, and the Hours allow'd for Sleep, moderate as they were before ; and, in fine, that whatever might be looked upon either, as a Pleasure or Convenience denied me.——In fine, the Severity with which I was treated, had certainly no Precedent nor Parallel, and must in good earnest have put an End to my Days had it continued but a very little longer.

But it is the Will of Heaven, the more to shew us on what we should alone depend, to raise or to abase us when we least expect it.————I was now past all Hope, abandon'd to Despair, worn out with Grief and Hardship, my Mind as well as Body weakned and deprest, and waiting, nay, wishing for the Moment of my Dissolution ; when a Chariot with my Mother's Woman in

it,

it, and attended by two Servants on Horseback, came to the Monastery, and having acquainted the Superior, that my Father lay at the Point of Death, and could not expire till he had seen me, I was order'd to obey his Commands, and accordingly went into the Chariot.——— So strange a Turn could not but astonish me.———I durst not hope, yet had nothing to fear from it.——— Mademoiselle *Bretigny*, now cured of her foolish Passion for the Pilgrim, since she knew he was *Melicourt* and my Husband, assured me that my Father was sincerely grieved at his Usage of me, and resolved to re-unite me to *Melicourt* before his Death.———This she protested to me she had heard him say, and that in the midst of his Agonies, he continually repeating my Name.

Relays being order'd on the Road we soon arrived at the Castle, my Mother met me on the Stair-Case, and after affectionately embracing me, come, my dear *Minetta*, said she, you are at the End of all your Troubles ; but mine are beginning———you are going to receive a dying Father's Blessing, I to lose a Husband ———in speaking those Words she led me into the Chamber where my Father lay ; I threw myself on my Knees by his Bedside———the Condition I found him in made me forget all his Cruelty.———I shed Tears of unfeign'd Sorrow, and entreated his Forgiveness for any Action that had occasion'd his Disquiet. You are too good, *Minetta*, replied he, with a feeble Voice, and ask that of me which I deserve not to obtain from you——— I am now sensible I have greatly wrong'd you, and cannot resign my Soul in Peace, till I have made Attonement. Then turning to his Valet de Chamber, who attended at the Feet of the Bed, call in the Company, said he, that they may be Witness of what I would have done.

Immediately enter'd Father *F*———his Confessor, two Physicians who attended him, a Surgeon and a Notary Publick ; and when they approach'd near enough to hear his Words, before you all, said, my Father, I acknowledge *Minetta* for my lawful Daughter, and Co-heiress with her Sister Madam *De S*———*B*———of

my

my whole Eftate————next I abfolve her, and hope the Church will do the fame, of the Vows I wickedly compelled her to take ; knowing her to be at that fame Time the lawful Wife of Monfieur *Melicourt* ; and laftly, I entreat and require of you all who hear this my Acknowledgment, to publifh it to the World ; fo as that fhe may be at Liberty to purfue her Duty in her firft and voluntary Engagements, and neither fhe nor her Hufband fuffer any longer in being feparated from each other.———— Would Heaven have prolonged my Life to have feen all this performed, I fhould have died content ;————but fince that Bleffing is denied me, permit me, however, to depart with the Affurance of your fulfilling in every Article of this my laft Will.

My Mother knelt down firft, then all the others, and laying their Hands on the holy Ritual, fwore to fee all he had defired accomplifhed. I was all this time fo confounded between Grief for my Father, and Gratitude for this unlook'd for Tendernefs, that I had not the power of Speech————I could only teftify the Senfe I had of it by my Actions. I took his Hand which he held out to blefs me, kiffed it, and bath'd it in a Flood of Tears ; but as foon as I was able to fpeak, I poured out my whole Soul in the moft ardent Prayer to Heaven, that he might be reftored to Health, and live to fee what now he was fo good as to permit.

Whether it were that the Force he had put upon himfelf in fpeaking fo much, or that my Prayers had really any Efficacy, I know not, though I fcarce dare flatter myfelf with the latter ; but in that Moment he fell into a Sweat, which before, not all the Recipes given him could procure.————The Phyficians obferving it, prefently pronounced he would recover, which, indeed, he did in a miraculous Manner, being in three Days judged entirely out of Danger.

He imputed his Prefervation to my Prayers, and his own Repentance of his late Cruelty to me, and expreffed the utmoft Impatience to make me as happy as I had been the reverfe.————He wrote a Recantation to the *Nuncio* of all he had alledged ; acquainted every

bod

body with this Change in his Sentiments, and gave my patient enduring what he had inflicted on me such Encomiums, as I am in reality far from meriting.

Having some Affairs to finish at Court, before the Ceremony of being re-united to *Melicourt* can be compleated, he would needs take me with him; and we are now going to *Versailles*, where by a Letter being apprized of all that has passed, my Husband is to meet us. Thus, my dear Friend, has Heaven at last granted my Prayers, and render'd me more happy by the Addition of my Parents Love, than ever I could have hoped to be.

Here the beautiful *Saint Agnes* gave over speaking, and after having sincerely congratulated her on her good Fortune, I asked where her Father was, that I had not the Honour of seeing him: She told me that he was oblig'd to stop at the House of an old Friend, about half a League distant from the Village; and that she had asked his leave to take this Opportunity of seeing me more at leisure; and also that *Melicourt*, having acquainted her with my late Adventures, and where I was retired, she had prevailed on her Father to pass through the Village of *D*————; though it was somewhat out of their way to *Versailles*, that she might have the Pleasure of communicating to me her good Fortune, in which she knew I took so much Interest.

I expressed my Acknowledgments to her in the tenderest Manner, and having at her own Request, entertained her with all the Particulars of what had befallen me, since we last saw each other, of which, she said, *Melicourt* had given her but an imperfect Account, is it possible, cry'd she, that at your tender Years, you have had Fortitude enough to support under so many Disappointments? You have reason to hope you are now near the End of your Troubles, and that you will one Day be as happy, as you have hitherto been unfortunate. ————My Example may serve to convince you, that Patience and a due Confidence in Heaven surmounts the greatest Difficulties.

As

As much, however, as we were taken up with our own Affairs, neither of us forgot the beautiful *Linda-mine*; my lovely Friend gave me such an Account of her Piety, as perfectly charm'd me, and made me wish I cou'd bring n yself to the same happy way of thinking; and at once resolve to quit a busy bustling World, where nothing but Vexations seem'd to spring one out of another, and continually distract the Mind attach'd to it. She told me also that *Belizay*, by the Divine Assistance, had truly repented his former Extravagancies, and following the Example of his Mistress, was become a *Carthusian*; since that time, added *Saint Agnes*, *Lindamine* has been perfectly happy; her Days have past over with an uninterrupted Tranquility, and never did Spirit of Devotion, appear in any one with greater Beauty and Sweetness.———Every one in the Monastery admires her, and fortunate do those account themselves, who can boast of being among the Number of those she favours with her Friendship.———I own that the loss of her Society will be always regretted by me, even in the midst of that Happiness I am going to enjoy, nor shall *Melicourt* refuse me the Pleasure of taking a Journey sometimes to visit her.

I joined with her in testifying my Regard for that worthy Nun; but, added I, smiling, I fancy Mademoi.lle *De Renneville* is not among the Number of those who are edified by her Example; if I mistake not, you promised, that if ever we were happy enough to meet, you would inform me something of that wild giddy Creature.

I protest, replied, *Saint Agnes*, the thought of her was wholly swallowed up in more deserving Contemplations; but what I have come to the knowledge of concerning her, you shall not be a Stranger to.

The History of Mademoiselle DE REN-
NEVILLE.

YOU remember, my dear, said my lovely Friend,
that this young Lady being defcended of a Family
which had lefs Wealth than Titles to boaft of, fhe was
condemn'd to a Monaftick Life, to prevent her marrying beneath the Dignity of her Birth. You know alfo
that feigning herfelf contented with her Lot, and appearing always chearful, fhe had greater Liberties allowed her,
than was confiftent with the Policy of the Place to permit to thofe, whofe Melancholy render'd them more liable to Sufpicion————gay and thoughtlefs as fhe feem'd,
however, all her Thoughts were bent on making her
Efcape ; it was not that fhe was in love with any one particular Man, that made a Convent fo difagreeable ; but
fh ated Confinement, and whoever had made his Ad-
drefies to her on the Score of Marriage, would have
been well received, becaufe fhe wifh'd for nothing but
to live in the World.————As fhe aim'd, therefore,
to attract fome Admirer, whenever fhe was at the Grate,
and any Gentlemen in the Parlour, as you know there
f.equently are, to vifit the Nuns, fhe exerted all
her Wit, and made vifible every Charm that fhe thought
might gain a Conqueft————her Defires at laft were
crowned with Succefs ; a young *Navarrinan,* who had a
Sifter in the Convent, was captivated ; he made his Ad-
drefies, his Sifter knowing the Family of Mademoifelle
De Renneville, imagined that if fhe were once married,
they could not refufe giving her a Dowry ; and as fhe
was not a profeft Nun, thought fhe committed no Sacrilege, in forwarding her Efcape.

De

De Renneville having confeſt to this young Lady, that ſhe did not diſapprove the Paſſion Monſieur *De Bonville,* for ſo he was call'd, had for her, they contrived a Scheme between them, which had its deſired Effect

One Morning as we were altogether in the Chapel, Mademoiſelle *De Renneville* pretended to be ſeized with a ſudden Diſorder in her Head———ſhe affected a kind of Delirium at firſt, and then fell into ſuch violent Fits as frighted all the Convent ——— proper Remedies were applied, but to no Purpoſe ; and, indeed, ſhe ſo admirably counterfeited, that it was impoſſible for any one who ſaw her, not to believe real what ſhe ſeemed to ſuffer———for my Part, though I never had what might be juſtly termed a Friendſhip for her, on the Account of the vaſt Difference of our Humours, yet I ſincerely pitied her, and prayed for her Recovery ; as did alſo the pious *Lindamine,* who, though ſo well ſkill'd In Phyſick, was as much deceived as myſelf.

Her Diſorders ſtill encreaſing according to all Appearance, Madam the Superior thought proper to acquaint her Parents with it ; a Phyſician who had attended the Family, and was perfectly acquainted with the young Lady's Conſtitution, was ſent to viſit her ; far from finding out the Fallacy, he pronounced her Condition to be extremely bad, and returned to acquaint Monſieur *De Renneville* her Father, that there muſt be a Conſultation, for in a Diſorder ſuch as hers was, he would not preſume to preſcribe any thing of himſelf.

This was all our young Projectors wanted : Monſieur *De Bonville* aſſumed the Phyſician, and being habited as ſuch, and accompanied by a grave old Matron, who he told the Abbeſs had been *De Renneville*'s Nurſe, and was deſired now by her Mother to remain with her till the Danger was over, they both had Admittance to the ſuppoſed ſick Perſon. The pretended Doctor brought Letters of Credence with him, which were forged for that Purpoſe, and ſign'd by the Names of both *De Renneville*'s Parents, ſo that there was not the leaſt Suſpicion of any Deceit in the Affair.

He

He visited her twice a Day to give every thing the better Glofs, and the old W man ftaid in the Convent, waiting a fit Time to put their Defign in Execution. One Evening when we were all at Vefpers, except the Portrefs and one Lay-Sifter, *De Renneville* changed Cloaths with the Nurfe, and taking a Bafket in her Hands, as if going to bring in fomething neceffary for the fick Perfon, paffed the Gates without Sufpicion, and got fafely to her Lover's Arms, who waited at the End of the Village with a Chaife and Six ready to receive her; as for the fuppofed Nurfe, who had been a Dependant on the Sifter of *Bonville*, fhe quitted the Convent with the fame Facility foon after; for being accuftomed to go often in and out, the Portrefs had forgot that the Perfon fhe before let pafs had not return'd. In fine, nothing of this Matter was difcovered till next Morning, when fome of the Nuns going in to vifit *De Renneville*, and finding the Bed empty, immediately fill'd the Convent with their Cries.

The Superior was no fooner inform'd, than fhe fent to the Magiftrates that diligent Search might be made after the Fugitive; but all who were employed in it return'd without Succefs, and as we afterwards heard, thofe they fought for were married at a Neighbouring Town, fome Hours before *De Renneville* was miffing. Before her Departure fhe left a Letter for the Abbefs upon a Table: It contained, as near as I can remember, thefe Lines.

To Madam———*Abbefs of the Convent of* Auguftine's *at*———

Madam,

*A*S *I was only compell'd to conform myfelf to Rules, no way agreeable to my Inclination, I do not think my breaking through them the firft Opportunity that offered, ftands in any need of an Apology, and, therefore, give you the trouble of this, for no other Reafon than to fpare you the Pains of any fruitlefs Search after me: I fhall very*

foon

soon dispose of myself, so as to transfer all power over me, to one who will know how to defend his Right; and think that I less offend Heaven, by answering the End of my Creation, than by continuing in a Life, to which I have no manner of Vocation.

I am not insensible of the Lenity with which I have been treated, while I was under your Care, nor the many kind Offices I have received from the good Sisters I leave behind me.———May you, and them be ever happy in the Lot you chuse, and according to the Charity you profess, pardon the Errors of,

Your most obliged Servant,

DE RENNEVILLE.

It was some Weeks before the Parents of this Lady could be brought to hear of a Reconciliation, nor, perhaps, had so soon consented, had not one of her Sisters died; to whose Dowry, there being no Exceptions to the Husband she had made Choice of, she was at last permitted to succeed. Thus, added *Saint Agnes*, she has fulfilled what she used to tell us her Dreams foretold; and may, perhaps, be more happy than those of a more delicate manner of thinking, a refined Passion being not always the surest Road to Tranquility.

We were moralizing a little on the Temper and Behaviour of the Person, whose Story *Saint Agnes* had been relating, when her Father arrived; I received him in a manner becoming his Rank, and the Friendship I had for his charming Daughter, nor was he less polite in the Compliments he made me.————*Minetta*, said he, has less reason than I imagin'd to regret her Confinement in the Monastery, since by it she obtain'd the Friendship of so amiable a Person as Mademoiselle *Jeanetta*; and as I then intended only to punish her, ought first to have inform'd myself, if there was not a Lady whose Society would render any Place agreeable;————but

Heaven,

Heaven, continued he, was of her fide, and turn'd every thing I defign'd for Chaftifement into Bleffings.

He faid many other gallant things, and in the fhort time he ftaid, which did not exceed half an Hour, difcovered enough for me to fee, he was not only one of the beft bred Men, but alfo one of the moft Senfe and Penetration, except the old Marquis *De L——V——*, I had ever feen.

I lamented my want of Convenience to entertain him as I wifh'd ; but he affured me, that were there never fo good Accommodations in the Village for his Retinue, he could not poffibly continue there ; Bufinefs of the moft urgent Nature calling him with all Expedition to Court, which till I have concluded, faid he, my Daughter's Happinefs cannot be compleated.

This was a fufficient Reafon for me not to prefs him to ftay————the Lady and I parted with mutual Proteftations of an eternal Friendfhip, and Promifes of communicating all that befel either of us, worthy the Knowledge of the other.————Monfieur *De*————afked me if I had any Commands for *Verfailles* ; but I entreated he would not mention me there on any Account ; and told him it was of the utmoft Confequence to my Peace, not to be remembred there : On which both he and his Daughter affured me I might depend upon their Secrecy.

They had left me but a few Moments before the Marquis came ; he had now thrown off his Courier's Habit, and would have appeared perfectly amiable, but for the Patch on his Forehead, which he wore to prevent being known, much larger than he need to have done on the Account of his Wound. He exprefs'd the Tendernefs he had for me, in the moft paffionate Terms that the Heart could dictate or the Tongue pronounce, and difcovered an Impatience of being united to me forever, with greater Ardency than I had ever obferved in him before.————My Father's Paffion for you, faid he, is a Difficulty that feems almoft invincible————which way, O ! moft adorable *Jeanetta*, fhall we attempt to conquer it————I could almoft wifh you were lefs beautiful, fince your Charms have had fo unhappy an Influ-

ence

ence on him.———How shall I mention you to him, and entreat a Completion of a Felicity for myself, which must involve him in endless Despair.———Before he loved you, he could only blame my Indiscretion as he term'd it; but now he is become my Rival, will he not expect as his Son, I should recede to him?———Ah! *Jeanetta!*———*Jeanetta!* there is no way to shun the Dangers I apprehend, and save our mutual Tenderness, now on the Brink of being everlastingly overwhelm'd by unrelenting Power.

Though I easily guess'd what way it was he hinted at, and was far from approving it, I made no Reply, because, indeed, I could find no Words immediately which I thought proper to form a Denial to a Lover who deserv'd so greatly of me; I was studying what to say, when he taking my Silence as a favourable Omen to what he had to propose; yes, charming *Jeanetta*, resumed he, the only Expedient that can cut off at once all my Father's Hopes and Expectations is for us to be privately married.———Women, continued he, of the first Rank have had Recourse to it, and we may be above all others excused when so strong a Necessity leaves us no other means to avoid the sure Destruction, of all we would preserve in Life.———I will, therefore, contrive it so as———hold, my dear Marquis, cry'd I, interrupting him, as we have begun, and for so long a course of Time, had the strictest Rules of Honour and Decency as Guides to Youth and Passion, let us not now swerve from those faithful Directors; nor by one rash Action tarnish the Glory of our former Conduct.———Clandestine Marriages can never be approved either by Heaven or Earth.———

Doubt you my Honour then, cry'd the Marquis with some Vehemence?———do you believe me capable of deceiving you, or that the Vows I should make to you in the Presence of one Priest, would be less binding than before a thousand Witnesses?———Are you so little acquainted with me, as to suspect I ever can abjure what now I so ardently desire?

No

No, my Lord, anfwer'd I, my Heart needs no
Vouchers for your Sincerity, your Love, your Conflan-
cy ;————but yet to agree to the Propofal you do me
the Honour to make, would deprive me of that interior
Peace, I have ever enjoy'd in the greateft of my Mif-
fortunes————what cannot the Authority of a Father,
fuch as the Marquis *De L————V————*effect ?————
might we not, when moft we thought ourfelves fecure,
be torn from each other's Arms like *Melicourt* and *Minetta*, or if it fhould not happen fo, muft I not live in the
continual dread of it ?————The Happinefs of being
yours, is too precious to be blended with Tears, frightful Apprehenfions, and Uncertainty of preferving it.
————What ever happens, added I, preffing his Hand,
you will be ever dear to me; and if I am fo unfortunate as to be feparated from you, I fhall at leaft have
the Confolation of having contributed nothing to my
own Wretchednefs.

The Marquis fetch'd feveral deep Sighs while I was
fpeaking; but, as his Reafon could not but convince
him I was in the right, he told me he would infift no farther on a thing to which I feem'd fo averfe. I thank'd
him for this Proof of his Complaifance, and fhewed the
Senfe I had of it, by all the innocent Careffes poffible. I
muft have Patience then, cry'd he, charm'd with my
endearing Behaviour. ———— I will wait, my lovely
Jeanetta, provided you referve for me that Heart on
which all my Happinefs depends, and alfo keep your
dear Perfon fo well concealed that it be not forced from
me—'tis poffible that Time and Abfence may abate
my Father's Paffion for you, and he no longer oppofe my
Defires ;————but if thofe Hopes prove vain, I want
but three Months of being at Age, and then the Law
makes me my own Mafter, and I may difpofe of my
Hand as Reafon and Inclination joined in one, commands.

Ah, my Lord! cry'd I, you fay this, but to make
tryal of me————I have too high an Idea of your Virtue,. to believe you will have recourfe to Methods, too
frequently, indeed, made ufe of; but fuch as deftroys all
Duty

Duty and Gratitude to Parents.————Rather let the unhappy *Jeanetta* drag on her lonefome Days in an eternal Banifhment from all that's dear to her, than fuffer the juftly valued Object of her Soul to come to fuch Extremities. ———— No, continued J, never will I yield to any thing that fhould make you become a Criminal————win over a Father, who merits all your Efteem, and who is only cruel in oppofing an Inclination he has many Reafons to difapprove, and by a long and uninterrupted Series of Obedience deferve he fhould at laft confent to your Defires————thefe are the only Means I approve of, for engaging the Compliance of a Parent, all others are highly blameable, and inconfiftent with the Dictates of Nature as well as Religion.

I utter'd this with an uncommon firmnefs of Voice and Deportment, the Marquis look'd at me with Aftonifhment, and when I had ended ; charming Creature ! cry'd he, is it poffible that to the moft Angelick Form, there fhould be joined fuch Wit, fuch Prudence, fuch an Underftanding, and above all fuch a Dignity of Sentiments, which though oppofite to my Defigns, fill me with the extremeft Reverence————you are not to be loved as Woman, but adored as fomething Divine.———— O ! all my Hopes are vain, my Father muft have obferved this in you as well as I, and never can be prevaii'd upon to relinquifh fuch a Treafure, even though it cofts him the Life of an only Son !

This Exclamation foothed my Vanity too much———— I would not fuffer him to proceed, but entreated him to forbear, and protefted to him I had no Ambition, but to acquit myfelf of the Duty I owed to Heaven, and to pleafe him, and deferve the Continuance of his Love.

The Marquis, after kiffing my Hand with a mixture of Paffion and Refpect, was going to make fome Reply, when the Valet de Chamber, whom he had fent to the Camp, came haftily into the Room, his Mafter expreft the utmoft Surprize, at feeing him return, and afked him haftily what had prevented his profecuting the Journey he had ordered him to undertake. What I
have

have to inform your Lordſhip, replied he, will make you ſenſible it was needleſs——happening to call at an Inn about ten Miles diſtant from this Place, I ſaw the Servant your Lordſhip ſent me to, talking with the Man of the Houſe: He no ſooner perceived me, than he took immediate Flight, I purſued him, with all imaginable Speed, till he took ſhelter in a Wood, where judging it impoſſible to find him, I returned to the Houſe, hoping to inform myſelf on what Buſineſs he came there ; and was told that he had not arrived above ten Minutes before I came, and had enquired if a Chaiſe attended by three Servants had paſs'd that way. This was enough to make me know, that he is endeavouring to diſcover which way your Lordſhip took, ſo thought I could do no better than to return and acquaint you with it.

The Marquis on hearing this no longer doubted but that he was betrayed, that his Father was in Poſſeſſion of his Letter, and alſo acquainted with his Journey. It was eaſy alſo to ſee, that this Traitor of a Servant was order'd to find out to what Place he was gone, as the ſureſt means of diſcovering where I lay conceal'd.

After ſome Reflections on this perplexing Affair, the Queſtion was how to behave, as it was not to be doubted but the old Marquis would have the Purſuit continued, there was little Probability his Son could long eſcape it ; ſo that we both agreed it was highly neceſſary for him to depart ;————but this, alas, was more eaſily reſolved than executed————we had been too long abſent to endure to be ſeparated again ſo ſuddenly————we talk'd of it that whole Evening————the ſame the next Morning when he came to me again————that whole Day paſs'd over, a ſecond, and a third alſo were taken up in tender Adieus, yet ſtill he did not go.————The Evening before that, in which he was determined to quit the Village, we went to enjoy the Benefit of the Air, after the Heat of the Day was over, in a little Wood about half a Mile from our Houſe: Nature never formed a more delightful Place than this, a fine Stream ran through the midſt of it, near which there were

ſeveral

several Groves so thick, and the Trees so well ranged, that they defended equally from the Sun and Rain, or any other Annoyance from the Firmament————a thousand Nightingales perched upon the Boughs, and regaled the Ear with their melodious Notes———— every thing was ravishing about us, and inspired Love and Tenderness————it was here we gave and received all the Proofs of mutual Love that Virtue could desire, or Innocence bestow————we were in this pleasing Entertainment when we heard the trampling of a Horse pretty near us, and presently after heard a Man enquire the Road to the Village of *D*————, and how far off it was. At first we thought he had been speaking to some Person he had met with on the Road ; but on his calling out, and repeating the same Questions, without any Answer being given him; alas! said the Marquis, this is some some Stranger who has lost his way, and finds no body to direct him——and presently stepp'd forward; and told the Man which way he should go. The Stranger seem'd overjoyed, and having thank'd him, asked him if he were of the Village ? Yes, replied the Marquis in a feign'd Voice, who now had his own Reasons for this Deception. Then, said the other, did not an Officer of Distinction come here three or four Days ago in a Chaise, attended by three Servants ? If you can inform me whether he continues here, or if gone, which Road he took, I will reward you handsomely.————You are very lucky, answered the Marquis, to meet with me, because no-body could have given you so good an Intelligence.————The Person you mean lodges at my House, is he not a tall young Man with black Eyes, wears a large Patch over half his Forehead, and has long curled Hair ?————You are right, said the Man, and pray what does he pretend is his Business here.——Nay, as to that, replied my Lover, it is none of my Business to ask any Questions ; but there is a very pretty young Woman, that they say, has brought him down here.——To tell you the Truth, added he, lowering his Voice, and drawing nearer, they are together now in this Wood —— I have been listening to their Conversation, and if you

have

have any Curiosity, you need only alight, and follow me to be convinced.

I knew very well by all that had been said, that this was no other than the unfaithful Servant, who had given us so much Concern, and was terrified beyond Measure, left the Marquis in the first Emotions of his Rage should dispatch the Wretch; who immediately dismounting on what his Master said, he seized him by the Throat, and no longer disguising his Voice, I have you, Villain, cry'd he, and at the same time drew his Sword, confess or die this Instant. ——I screamed out at these Words, fear nothing, Madam, continued the Marquis, and than turning to the Man, own the Truth, said he, and I, perhaps, may pardon what you have done against me.

The Traitor finding who it was that spoke to him, seem'd quite thunderstruck, and fell at his Feet begging he would spare his Life: Speak then, continued the Marquis, I promise to forgive you if you conceal nothing of what you have done against me; but if you again deceive me expect no Mercy. The Servant who knew very well he might depend upon his Master's Word, inform'd him, that he was drawn in, and corrupted by the old Marquis's Gentlemen.—What *Forfan*, cry'd the Marquis? 'Tis false——my Father has discharged him his Service.—It was in order to make his Peace again, replied the Man, that as soon as he heard Madam *De Roches* had left *Paris*, he bethought him, knowing his Lord's Passion for her, of using all his Endeavours to find out the Place of her Retreat.——He was certain, he said, that there was a Correspondence between your Lordship and the Lady, and could not fail of discovering where she was, provided he could intercept one of your Letters.

On this Project he came to the Camp in a very private manner, and unfortunately pitch'd upon me as his Instrument in the Affair. Not only because I am his Countryman, and was also formerly his Servant; but also because it was through his Recommendations, I obtain'd the Honour of being in my Lord's Family. After calling all this to my Remembrance, he told me

what

what had happened to him, and that if I would affift him in the Execution of a Scheme he had form'd for getting his Pardon, and at the fame time being reveng'd on the Lady, who had occafion'd his Difgrace, he would not only give me an immediate Recompence, but alfo make my future Fortune. He found me, alas! but too much difpofed to come into his Meafures, and acquainted me with his Contrivance; which was to keep always as near your Perfon as poffible, to be more affiduous and diligent about you than any other of the Servants; to the end I might gain fome fhare in your Confidence, and when you wrote any Letters to be entrufted with them, which inftead of delivering according to your Orders, I was to put immediately into his Hands.

I obeyed all the Injunctions he gave me but too well: And when your Lordfhip commanded me to go to *Paris*, went no farther than a fmall Town not five Miles from the Camp, where he lay concealed expecting to hear from me.———He was transported with Joy when he read the Letter you had entrufted me with———this is all I wifh'd, cry'd he, I am now certain of retrieving my Lord's Favour, and, perhaps, a greater Portion of it than ever. He was not deceived in this Hope, we went together to *Verfailles*, where the old Marquis then was, and he had no fooner wrote to him, that he was arrived and had News of Madam *De Roches* to impart, than he had Admittance and was reftored to his Place; it was refolved I fhould return to your Lordfhip with the Anfwer I brought, and continue to intercept your Letters, in order to difcover where the Lady was, which you did not mention in the Packet you fent by me.

But your fudden Departure from the Army difconcerted all the Meafures that had been agreed upon, efpecially, as your Lordfhip did not take me with you; all I could do was to acquaint Monfieur *Forfan* with it, and what Road the Equipage, with which I was left, was to take. The next Day after we fet out, a Footman belonging to the old Marquis met me, with a Letter from Monfieur *Forfan*, ordering me to quit the Baggage, and endeavour by all the Means I could to difcover what

2 Road

Road you had taken; with a Promife that if I could find out Madam *De Roches* by it, he would provide for me in the hardfomeft manner all the Days of my Life.
————This, my Lord, was the Inducement of purfuing you with fo much Diligence, and of my flying when accidentally met by your Valet de Chamber. I doubted not but you had difcovered my Infidelity, and knowing myfelf loft with you, renewed my Enquiries more zealoufly than ever.————I fuffer'd no Town nor Village to efcape me, between the Camp and this, where your Lordfhip has furprized me ;————but Heaven to punifh my Perfidy has render'd all my Hopes fruftrate.
————I am in your Lordfhip's power————difpofe of me as you pleafe ; but I hope you will fhew Mercy to a poor Wretch, who has fuffered himfelf to be corrupted by fine Promifes and Hopes of a Settlement for Life ; and who befides all this, was really informed, that what they wanted me to do was wholly for your good, and to break off an Affair, which Monfieur *Forfan* fwore to me, would fooner or later end in your Deftruction, and which the old Marquis was determined to prevent, if poffible, at any Rate.

The Fellow ended thefe Words, with throwing him-felf a fecond time at his Mafter's Feet, and wept fo bit-terly, that I could not forbear interceding in his Be-half.————I will keep my Word with him, Madam, faid the Marquis, and fpare his Life, with this Provifo, that he never more comes into my Sight.————Pru-dence, however, obliges me to fecure him till I am got Home again, and you are difpofed of in fome other Place, to prevent any farther Effects of his Treachery. Ah, my Lord, cry'd the Man, I fwear by all that is holy, that if your Lordfhip vouchfafes to give me your Pardon, I will make no other Ufe of it, than to repair the Fault I have committed.

There was fomewhat in his Behaviour, that had fo much the Air of a true Penitent, that it moved me very much, and I pleaded for him with all the Earneft-nefs I was able————the Marquis paufed a little after I had done fpeaking ; but when he had well weigh'd the

2   Bufinefs

Bufinefs in his Mind———this, faid he, is the only Re-queft in which I either can, or ought to refuse you———to put it in the Power of a Perfon who has once be-trayed my Confidence, to deceive me a fecond time, is being a worle Enemy to myfelf than he can poflibly be, and is what I have laid down as a Maxim never to be guilty of;—but to fhew you how ready I am to comply as far as is confiftent with Difcretion, though I cannot fuffer him about myfelf, I will be no hindiance to his being provided for with another Mafter. ——— 'Take then my Pardon, continued he, and with it fomething to fupport your Expences, till you get into Service. With thefe Words he gave him four *Lewis D'Ors*; and added, his Thanks were due to me, whom he defign'd fo cruelly to injure. After this the Fellow retired full of Grief, and I believe unfeign'd Repentance ; and we return'd Home making various Reflections on this Ad-venture.

The next Day the Marquis forced himfelf, purfuant to the Refolution he had taken, to quit the Village of D——— ; how difficult both of us found it to part, would be a Tafk for the moft fluent Pen to paint—all the Courage, all the Fortitude I could call to my Affiftance, was fcarce fufficient to enable me to fupport the Grief, with which I was overwhelm'd. ——— Remember, faid I, embracing him with the utmoft Tendernefs, re-member on your Fidelity depends my Fate.——Alas ! replied he, is it poffible for me to live without adoring you !———great as our Difappointments are——— invincible as the Bars between our mutual Wifhes feem, there is a Pleafure even in fuffering for you, beyond what all the World without it could beftow.———While abfent from you I both fee and hear you, your dear Idea is fo ftrong upon my Faculties, that I converfe with you as when prefent.———O ! love me with the fame Fer-vour, and we neither of us can be truly unhappy.

It would be too tedious to repeat the hundredth Part of the foft endearing Expreffions we made ufe of to each other ; fo I fhall only fay, that inftead of going in the Morning as he intended, they took up fo much time that it was near five in the Evening before we feparated ———at laft he threw himfelf into his Chaife, and gave me fo tender an Adieu with his Eyes, that mine gufh'd forth a Flood of Tears in fpite of my Endeavours to reftrain them. The Country People, who were gather'd about the Chaife, as every thing furprizes in a Village, were Witneffes of our Parting, and I could hear them fay, this is being like Brothers and Sifters, indeed ; ———how fond they are of one another.

Had not my Heart been too much oppreft, I fhould not have forborn laughing at the Simplicity of thefe poor People, though at the fame time it fhewed their own want of Guile, not to fufpeft it in others.———They took the Marquis for my Brother, becaufe they were told he was fo, and to be able to penetrate too deeply, is not always the moft laudable Qualification.

My dear Marquis was no fooner gone, than I fhut myfelf up in my Clofet and gave the full Scope to my Tears and Lamentations———when, cry'd I, fhall I fee again this Lover fo truly worthy of all the Affeftion I have for him ?———What will be the Event of fo tender, and fo unfortunate a Paffion ?———Are we never to meet without our Felicity being embittered with the Thoughts of Parting ?———The old Marquis came next into my Head, enraged as he is, at my abfenting myfelf, faid I, how know I but he may compel his Son to reveal to him where I am, or if not fo, fome other means may betray the Place of my Retirement.——— Perhaps, when I leaft expeft him he may appear——— may accoft me with Fury in his Heart and Eyes—may fay, take your Choice, *Jeanetta*, either my Bed or a Cloyfter is your Doom———it is in vain for you to depend upon my Son, he can afford you no Affiftance, nor ever fhall be yours.———You ought to tremble at having fo far incenfed me, as it is in my Power to make you both pay dearly for the Advantage, he has gained of me in your Affeftion.

Thefe Imaginations were fo ftrong and lively that I fell into a Fit of Trembling, as if what my Fears fuggefted were already come.———I believe, my Reader
will

will shortly have Reason to think they were a kind of Prognostick, of what was shortly to happen to me : I check'd myself, however, and endeavoured not to give way to them, but in vain———I went to my Devotions, yet still they mingled with my Prayers.———Heaven, alas ! was deaf to my Entreaties, nor could a Heart attach'd as mine was at that time to worldly Objects, expect Assistance from above. To merit Divine Consolation, one ought to be ashamed of that Weakness I too much indulged ; so that left entirely to myself, Tears and Complainings were all the Relief I could find, in the Oppressions I then labour'd under.

The End of the ELEVENTH PART.

O 2   T H E

THE

VIRTUOUS VILLAGER,

OR,

VIRGIN's VICTORY.

PART. XII.

HREE Days from that of the Marquis's departure, I paſſed in little
elſe than Tears; but then the expectation of receiving a Letter from him,
with an Account of what I had to
hope or fear from his Father, gave
ſome truce to my Melancholy, but
none arriving either by the Poſt,
cr any particular Meſſenger, I relapſed into my former
Sadneſs, with this additional Cauſe, that ſomewhat very
extraordinary muſt have happened, which could occaſion a Delay in what he knew muſt be ſo neceſſary,
not only for my Peace of Mind, but alſo for the regulating my Conduct, as to removing from, or continuing in
the Village where I was.

My

My Father, Mother, and good Aunt were much troubled at the unufual Penfiveneſs they obſerved in me, and omitted nothing which they imagined might divert me,————but all their Attempts were unfucceſsful, even Reading, my favourite Amuſement, had no longer any Charms for me, my Thoughts were too perplexed to ſuffer me to give any Attention to what I had no immediate Concern in, and even thoſe Books of Devotion, in which the pious Souls of the Compoſers were poured out in fervent Ejaculations, failed of inſpiring me with thoſe Sentiments, which in reality could only have afforded me that Serenity I ſtood ſo much in need of.

A whole Week was now elapſed, I had no News, and began to grow impatient, and almoſt wild with the various Perturbations of my Mind————Good God! would I often cry out, what can have happened !———— what Accident ſo dreadful that my Lover ſhould fear to inform me of————I was walking haſtily about my Apartment, the Agitations of my Mind, rendering my Body no leſs reſtleſs, when my Mother came haſtily into the Room, to tell me that a Chaiſe and Six with a Gentleman in it, deſired to ſpeak with me. As my Apprehenſions of the old Marquis were always in my Head, I concluded it was he, and was ready to faint away ; I recovered myſelf, however, and deſired he might be brought in ; but what I endured in that Interval is not to be expreſſed.

But how were my Fears converted into Pleaſure, when I ſaw inſtead of him I imagined, the Valet de Chamber of my Lover, the faithful *Dubois* came into my Chamber, and preſented a Letter to me : Heavens ! cried I, is it poſſible that after the Apprehenſions the Marquis and I were under of your being ſeen here, that he ſhould venture to ſend you ? I have taken a ſure Precaution to prevent being known, ſaid he, ſhewing me a falſe Noſe, which it ſeems he had worn till he came into my Room, this Noſe would diſguiſe me to my own Father ; ſo that there is nothing to be feared on that ſide,————would to Heaven, continued he, I could as eaſily reconcile you to the News I bring——

O, Heavens! cried I, earnestly, what has happened? Read, Madam, rejoined he, and you will then be judge whether my Lord Marquis could properly send any other Person than myself on a Business which will require all your Fortitude to sustain.

So dreadful a Preparation might very well alarm me, Heavens, cried I, what new Disaster!————what Ills has Fate now prepared for the unfortunate *Jeanetta*!——the Seal broke open I found what I cannot even now reflect on, without shivering————Grief sure was never mortal, for if it had I could not have survived the reading this Epistle.

To mine no more, the fatally enchanting JEANETTA.

WHAT shall I say, O, thou too lovely Creature! how express the Situation of my Heart! Grief! Horror! Desparation! Madness are all Words too poor to give you any just Idea of it ———— Fate, exquisite in Cruelty, is not content to render me the most wretched of Mankind, without compelling my own Hand to give the Blow, which forever sinks me from my hopes————yes, Jeanetta, *it is so ordained, that I must use all the Power I have over you, to engage you to think of me no more————to banish me entirely from your Heart————that Heart which to obtain I have done and suffered so much————This I must do, or forfeit all Title to better Fortune————let me than rather be miserable than merit to be so————but, why do I keep you in suspense? the dreadful Riddle must be at last explained————Take it then in few Words————My Father lies at the point of Death, brought to this Extremity by you and me————your Name is ever in his Mouth————he calls for you————and says he shall expire in Peace, if he carries to the Grave the Name of your Husband———— can I be a Son, and not do every thing in my power to preserve so precious a Life, as that of a Parent:————*

if

if I am so unhappy as to lose him, let me not reproach myself, with being the horrid Cause of his Death————the Name of Parricide, is what I cannot bear————if ever therefore I was dear to you, save him who gave me Being————even now his last Agonies seem approaching——haste then, O most excellent of thy Sex ! ————a Minute's delay may make the Succour you would bring too late, and render me the most guilty, as well as most wretched of Mankind————

Yours, as far as I now dare to call myself,

L——V——.

What is it to me, cried I, bursting into Tears, let the cruel Parent die————am I to be punished for the Fury of his Passion, and the Condition to which it has reduced him !————Rigid Heaven ! am I preserved for this————why was I born with these destructive Charms————why endued with a Soul capable of distinguishing what real Happiness is, if I must be plunged into the Depth of Misery ?————as I spoke this, my Grief so overwhelmed me, that had not *Dubois* supported me I must have fainted away.

The Marquis doubtless had forseen to what a Condition his Letter would reduce me, and gave his Valet de Chamber a Phial, whose rich Elixir restored me to myself————alas ! said I to *Dubois*, why would you not suffer me to die————why apply this barbarous Relief————like a Wretch condemned to expire in Torments, you strengthen me only to prolong my Pain.

Tho' *Dubois* by the Knowledge he had of my Love for his Master, might be supposed to be pretty well prepared for such a Scene, yet was he so dejected at it, that he was scarce able to utter any thing for my Consolation————at last, in the Name of all that's dear to you, Madam, said he, endeavour to bear up against this unexpected Blow————think to what a Condition it has reduced my Lord, and how dearly he pays for his Discharge of his Duty————should he see

O 4

your

your Griefs————what would become of him ? O,
it is that which overthrows all my Fortitude, replied I,
did I suffer alone, Death would soon put a Period to my
Sorrows ; but the Considerations of my dear Marquis's
Despair retards my fleeting Life————what would indeed
become of this faithful Lover, if he should be told I was
killed by the Injunction he laid upon me ?————Yes,
cried I, after a short Pause, to comply with his Desires,
to make him easy, in the cruel Sacrifice he makes of
what is dearest to him, I must not only preserve the
Life of his Father, but my own————He shall be
obeyed————

My Sighs for some Time intercepted the Passage of
my Words ; but suppressing them with all my Might,
————let us go, cried I, the Marquis shall know how
extensive his Power is over me————I designed myself
for him, myself was all the Present I had to make him,
and for a long time he has been Master of me————he
may dispose his own————I will not offer to resist————
by acting in this manner I shall at least prove, that tho'
I am infinitely inferior to him in Birth, I am not at
all so in noble Sentiments, and any Example he can set
I shall never want Resolution to imitate.

What a Dignity of Mind do you make known,
Madam, cried *Dubois* with Tears in his Eyes :————
a way of Thinking such as yours is worthy of a Throne,
————none that truly know you can be astonished at
that Excess of Passion you excite————ah ! would to
Heaven you were as fortunate as I am sure you ought to
be !

I was too much overwhelm'd with Affliction to make
any Reply to these Words, nor had even my Vanity, which
I have a thousand times acknowledged was my predominant Foible, any Dominion over me in this dreadful
Crisis. I called for *Barbara,* and ordered her to pack up
my Things immediately for my Journey————Ah,
Heavens ! are we going to leave *D*————then ! cried
she ; perhaps we are, said I, with more Sternness than
I had ever spoke to her before, it's not your Business to
enquire but to obey. The good Creature was silent on
this ;

this ; but went about doing as I had commanded, tho'
I believe with a very akeing Heart.

My Defigns were no fooner known, than every one
was in Tears——what muft we lofe this charming Lady,
cried my Mother ? I hope, rejoyned my Father, who
happened to be at home, it is not through any Fault of
ours ? no, no, anfwered I, on the contrary, I leave you
with a regret, which at prefent you are not able to conceive——an indifpenfible, a cruel Neceffity tears me
from you——I fhould have thought myfelf bleft to have
paft all my Days in this peaceful innocent Obfcurity;
but a Mandate I am bound to obey, leaves me not the
Miftrefs of my Inclinations.——

As I fpoke thefe Words, I took my Mother in my
Arms and tenderly embraced her, my Father out of
Refpect drew back; but I flew to him, and throwing
myfelf upon his Neck, permit me, faid I, to teftify
how dear I am to you——a little Time perhaps will
fhew I do but my Duty.

After this I got into my Chaife, leaving my Parents
very much aftonifhed, efpecially my Father, whofe very
Soul was touched at my endearing Behavior : My Aunt
jumped in after me, as fond as fhe was of her Village,
and cried, fhe would leave all that was dear to her in the
World to follow me ; on which I kiffed her by way of
Acknowledgment ; juft as we were driving away, my
Mother afked me what fhe fhould do with the Goods I
had left behind——keep them, cried I, ftretching
out my Hand to her, whither I ever Return to you or
not, all I have is yours, both through Gratitude and
Duty.

I could not hear what Anfwer fhe made, the Chaife
at that Inftant began to be in Motion, but doubtlefs my
Words were as furprizing as the Hurry in which I went
away. *Dubois*, whofe Orders were to make all poffible
Expedition, haftened the Poftilion, and all the Poft-
Houfes having notice, the Relays were in fuch readinefs,
that we did not lofe a Moment.

I was all the Time buried in the moft profound Melancholy, which *Dubois* perceiving as he rode by the

side

side of the Chaise, begged of me to conquer my Affliction as much as possible, and told me, that if the young Marquis should be sensible of half the Grief he saw me in, he could not answer but that it would be fatal to him.

I loved with too disinterested an Affection not to do every Thing that might contribute to the ease of that dear Man, and assured *Dubois*, I would use my utmost Efforts to stifle my Sighs, my Tears, and all that should denote Distress, which was the utmost could be expected from me.

My poor Aunt, who heard all this without being able to comprehend the Meaning of it any farther, than that something had happened to give me Disquiet, cried every Moment, bless me, I wonder any body can have the Heart to vex so good a Lady ; but I will pray so heartily to God for you, that I am sure you will be rid of every thing that troubles you at last.

How well, thought I, does the Simplicity of this good Creature remind me of my Duty ! it's to Heaven alone, we ought to have recourse in our Calamities—— it's Heaven alone can relieve us.——Vain are our own Endeavours——vain the Consolation that human help affords !

The Relays all the Way were so exact, that the Speed we made was incredible, Day was but just withdrawn when we arrived at *Paris* ; but there are some periods in Life, when every thing goes wrong, and makes it seem as if Misfortunes of every kind combined to our Vexation. *Dubois* was so eager in hastening the Postilion, that in his hurry he drove against a Coach and overturned it, just as we passed by the Opera-House, which breaking one of our Wheels obliged us to stop : The Shrieks of the Women in the Coach drew together a hundred Flambeaux, and a vast Crowd of People, so that every thing that passed was as plainly to be seen as at Noon-Day——*Dubois* had left me sitting in the Chaise, in order to go and bring a Chair——while he was gone, the Footmen belonging to the Coach that had received this Injury, fell upon my Postilion, the Fellow

unable

unable to make his Party good againſt ſo many roared
out for help; his Cries drew ſtill more People about us,
and the Confuſion was ſo great, that *Barbara* and myſelf were terrified to that Degree that we were ready to
faint away; but my Fright ſoon gave way to my Vexation———I was looking earneſtly for *Dubois* to return,
when the Duke *De*———unluckily going to the Opera
knew me from his Coach, and called out to his Servants
to ſtop———make up to that Chaiſe, cried he, and prevent the Lady from coming to any hurt by this Accident———ſhe is my Acquaintance, and a Woman of
Quality.

Not all the Danger I was in, ſeemed half ſo much a
Misfortune as the meeting this Nobleman, and would
much rather have remained in it, than owed my Aſſiſtance to a Perſon, from whoſe Love or Gallantry my
dear Marquis had ſuffered ſo much———beſides, I
knew not what Diſcoveries the real Madam *De Roches*,
might have made after I was gone, nor what I ſhould
reply in caſe, when this Buſtle ſhould be over, any
Queſtions ſhould be aſked me concerning my having
aſſumed that Name.

The Duke's coming up drew the Eyes of the whole
Crowd upon me; but, good Heavens, how was I alarmed,
when the Ladies being by this Time, with much ado
dragged out of the Coach, which lay quite turned over,
I ſaw that one of them was Madam *D'Eſtival*, that
Madamoiſelle *D'Elbieux*, by whoſe Malice I had been
brought into ſo many Troubles———what would I not
have given to have been any where but where I was!
———I pulled my Hood over my Face to prevent her
knowing me; but ſhe had already got a Glimpſe of my
Face, and was no leſs quickſighted than myſelf? what,
ſaid ſhe, to her Servants, and the People about her, is
that the Chaiſe that has offered me this Inſult, and being
anſwered in the affirmative, and has that infamous little
Wretch eſcaped till now the Puniſhment of all the
Miſchiefs her Artifices have occaſion'd———is ſhe ſtill
at Liberty, and has the Impudence to affront a Woman
of Quality?———drag her Headlong from the Chaiſe

into the Kennel, added she, to her Servants————there is no Usage bad enough for her.

'Tis easy to imagine what I felt on this Occasion, and how I looked at the approach of four Footmen with their Flambeaux ; but a Protector was not wanting———— The Duke having quitted his Coach, came running with his Servants, and drew his Sword————let me see who dare come near this Chaise, said he————this Lady is my Acquaintance, and whoever has the Insolence to molest her, shall repent it. These Words, and the Knowledge who it was that spoke them, made the Footmen of Madam *D'Estival* draw back————Here the Affair might possibly have ended, had not the too couragious *Dubois* came that Instant up, and seeing the Danger I was in, began to lay about him with his Whip, on which they all turned upon him with their Flambeaux, the Duke's Men took his Part, and had it not been for the Guards, who some were prudent enough to call, a great deal of Mischief must have ensued—the Duke, who took this Opportunity to give me a Proof of his Passion, had engaged in the Fray himself, but the Officer on Duty appearing, the Tumult abated, and the Duke entreating him in a very polite Manner, to assist in conveying me to his Coach, which he said was waiting for me, he came to offer me his Hand for that Purpose; when Madam *D'Estival*, perceiving I was likely to get away, called out to him, what are you about Monsieur, said this cruel Woman, would you protect, and hinder me from punishing a sawcy Wretch, who out of meer Malice pulls over my Coach, and insults me in the Face of the World !————there are a hundred Witnesses to swear this, 'tis unjust to protect a little mean Creature, after such a Behaviour, and have no regard to the Remonstrances of a Woman of Quality————the Officer surprised at these Reproaches, and knowing she was indeed a Woman of Rank, turned towards her, and told her, that it was not for him to decide the Matter———— that he only did his Duty in preventing Mischief———— that my Chaise was broke down, and it was but just

to

to help me out of it; and that I was a Person of Diftinction too——

How! cried Madam *D'Eftival*, of Diftinction!—— you are impofed upon Monfieur——the Wretch is the Daughter of a poor Wood-Cutter in the Foreft of *Fountainbleau*, and Tenant to the late Count my Father.

The Duke *De*——who was fo perfuaded that I really was what I had pretended to be, that I believe he would have loft his Life in the Defence of his Opinion, cried out, it was very unbecoming to have recourfe to Calumny, in order to gain a Point; that he knew me very well, and that there was not one Word of Truth in all fhe had alledged. Befides, faid he, appealing to the People, why fhould this Lady be blamed for the Careleffnefs of her Poftilion!——'tis eafy to fee fhe is the Perfon moft frighted at the Accident, and inftead of ufing her ill, every body ought in Honour to give her what Affiftance fhe ftands in need of—but I am not much furprized, continued he, in an Air of Ridicule, at the Ill-nature which would fubject her to every kind of Misfortune——you fee fhe is extremely handfome, and that is a Crime never to be pardoned by Ladies of a certain turn of Mind.

This extraordinary Conclufion fet every body into a loud Fit of Laughter——they turned their Eyes firft on me, then on Madam *D'Eftival*, and then on me again——a general Murmur was heard in my favour, ——a hundred Arms inftead of one——a hundred Coaches were offered to receive me——all now went wonderfully for me, but I was deftined to undergo one more Mortification yet before I could get rid of this Adventure.

Publick Entertainments at *Paris*, and I believe every where elfe, bring People together, who otherwife perhaps never would have met. My ill Stars decreed it fo, that the true Countefs *De Roches* was that Night at the Opera——the Stop of Coaches I had fo innocently occafioned, prevented her coming out, and enquiring, as it was natural, the Reafon of this Difturbance, and the

Names

Names of the Ladies, for whofe different Interefts there had been a kind of Parties made, one of the Duke's Servants unfortunately happened to be near her, and anfwered, that as to one of the Ladies he did not know her, but the other was Madam the Countefs *De Roches*.

————How ! faid fhe, to two Ladies who were with her, this Accident is odd enough————this is certainly the Woman, who took my Name upon her, and received that Bounty from the King, which I ought to have had————I'll have her apprehended upon the Spot, if fhe efcapes now, I may make as many fruitlefs Enquires after her as I have done.

While this Confpiracy was forming againft me, and which I heard nothing of ; they were helping me out of the Chaife : the Duke *De*————took hold of my Hand, and would have obliged me to go into his Coach ; but *Dubois* whifpered fomething to his Grace, on which he anfwered, that is very true, and then led me to another, which I faw had the Marquis's Livery, we were juft going to drive away, when a Voice cried out, ftop————ftop the fictitious Countefs *De Roches !*—— *Dubois*, who had heard fomething of this, tho' I had not, had jumped into the Coach with me, and putting his Head out of the Door, bid the Coachman to drive as faft as he could, and regard nothing————this Direction faved me, it was executed with fuch Rapidity ; to the Misfortune of all the Carriages that ftood in our way, the Horfes unufed to the Whip, now feeling it, bore down every thing they met, and whirled me from this Difafter, which otherwife might have proved of very ill Confequence to me.

It was near Eleven however, when I reached the old Marquis's Houfe : all his People ftood ready to receive me as I alighted from the Coach, eager and curious to fee a Perfon fo remarkable by her prefent Circumftances ; the young Marquis himfelf waited for me in a Gallery ; he looked pale, wan, dejected, and as a Man quite born down with Affliction————the Diforder of his Drefs, and even his very Hair befpoke the Trouble of his Soul————with a Sigh, which feemed to rend

his

his Heart, he took me by the Hand, and tenderly pressed it; but had not power to utter one Word, tho' I perceived he more than once attempted it——I was in the same Condition, fain would I have spoke something to convince him of the greatness of the Sacrifice I was going to make him; but I was deprived of Voice, and thus in the most perfect Attitudes of dumb Sorrow, did we pass thro' several large Rooms before we came to the Marquis's own Apartment.

We arrived at length at the fatal Door, it was so dark, that I could distinguish nothing at entring, but two Wax Candles, whose feeble Glimmering, was half obscured by the Shade of a Screen. The Marquis squeez'd my Hand a second Time, sigh'd again, and having led me into the Middle of the Room, left me there, and went to his Father's Bed-side;——my Lord, cried he, in a faultering Voice, the beautiful *Jeanetta* is come to offer herself to you——she will no longer oppose the Honour you defign her——shall she approach?——a low Voice, like that of a Person whose latest Moment was arrived, answered, what say you, Son?——the Marquis attempted to repeat what he had said; but his inward Agonies would not permit him, and all he could do was to make a Sign to *Forfan*, who was waiting, to perform that Office for him.

The old Marquis no sooner seemed to understand what they were saying to him, than he cried out in a Voice somewhat louder than before——Son, I am satisfied——and then remained silent.

My dear Marquis, who had been struggling with his Griefs, had now gathered Courage enough to ask him if he would not see me——I fear, replied he, I have not Strength sufficient to bear it——however let her approach. I did so, trembling and almost dying at every Step, the Marquis took my Hand, and presented it to his Father, who called for a Light, but when one was brought, seemed unable to bear the glare of it, and bad then remove it again——it is enough, said he, I see I am not deceived, it is indeed *Jeanetta* herself;

he

he said no more, but appeared deep in Thought, during which he cast his Eyes sometimes on me, and sometimes on his Son alternately.

We all were in a profound Silence for some time, the young Marquis was the first that broke it, and testifing the Conquest he had gained over himself, well my Lord, said he, in a more intelligible Voice, how do you find yourself?———will not the Sight of a Person so dear to you give some happy turn to your Distemper ? Alas! cried he, it is too much———I have not Spirits to support the Joy———then addressing himself to me, you have spoke nothing to me, O too charming *Jeanetta!*——— I fear your coming hither is an Affliction to you. No, my good Lord, repled I with a Resolution which surprized even myself, and I swear to perform whatever your Son has engaged for me. How generous is this, cried the old Marquis, why cannot I imitate it——— why abuse such Goodness ; but Fate must be obeyed.

When he had spoke these Words, he made a Sign to *Forsan* to come near, after which this Gentleman presented me his Hand, and said, it was the Marquis's Pleasure he should have the Honour of conducting me to the Apartment alloted for me ; would it were my Grave, said I to myself, yet suffer him to lead me, and kept back the Tears which were ready to burst, and give vent to the Anguish of my swollen Heart. He took the Opportunity as we were going to ask my Pardon for all his past Transgressions, and begged me to believe he would attone for them by the Fidelity and Submission of his future Conduct. To all which, I answered very cooly, and if I was capable of feeling any Relief in this dreadful Situation, it was when I was rid of him.

The Apartment in which he left me, was furnished and adorned with a Profusion of Magnificence———the Gildings, Carvings, Glasses shined on all Sides——— my Eyes were struck with the Glare, but my Heart was in such a cruel State of Dejection, that it scarce was sensible of any Thing. I throwed myself into an easy Chair, and the long restrained Tears now I was alone, burst forth, and afforded me some little Ease, else I

verily

verily believe I had been suffocated————but I enjoyed
this poor Relief but a short Time: The House Steward
came in, and with a great deal of Respect, asked me
if I would have Supper served up. I want nothing,
answered I, and the greatest Pleasure you can do me,
is to suffer me to retire to rest; but he replied, that tho'
his Orders were to obey me in every thing, he could
not consent I should be without Refreshment, after the
Fatigue of my Journey. With these Words he left me,
and presently after entered two Footmen, with the Services of the Table, the Cloath was laid, and I was not
a little surprized to see two Plates.

When all was spread: a number of Men in rich
Liveries, brought in the Dishes, and delivered them to
the Steward, who placed them on the Table, I was
not accustomed to these Ceremonies, and in spite of my
Melancholy they amused me.

The Moment the first Course was placed, a Valet
de Chamber appeared at the Door, carrying two Flambeaux, and followed by the young Marquis, he made a
low Bow to me, and after having presented his Hand,
to lead me to the Table, sat down just over against me,
without speaking one Word.

This Sight produced in me an odd kind of Emotion,
and which I am utterly unable to describe————it could
not be called Pleasure, our present Circumstances would
not admit of it, nor was it truly Pain; the Presence of
a Man so much the Lord of all my Faculties could not
be disgustful to me————it was therefore a Mixture of
both, and created a hurry of Spirits greater than in all
the various Accidents of my Life I had ever known before. The Number of Servants in waiting was such
a Restraint upon me, that I scarce durst look upon him.
and when I did it, was but by Stealth: He either did in
reality, or I imagined it, appear under less Affliction than
when I saw him first, and this gave me no small Surprize, for tho' his Grief was Death to me, yet I thought
he ought not to be able to overcome it.

In this Situation of Mind, it could not be expected I
should have any Appetite to eat, tho' the Marquis was
very

very diligent in carving for me, whatever he imagined might be agreeable to me————we drank to each other several Times by a Bow, but spoke not a Word, and this dumb Scene lasted all the Time we were together.

As full of Inquietude as I was, I had not power to rise from Table for a long Time, till recollecting that my Tediousness might be taken Notice of, and the Motive of it suspected, I quitted my Chair, and the Marquis immediately took me by the Hand. The Flambeaux led the Way, and I was conducted into a Bedchamber, where I found two Women waiting on each side a rich Toylet, that very Toylet which had been presented to me, and I had left behind me in my Lodgings at *Paris*; one of them advanced an easy Chair the Moment I came in, and then with the other attended behind it, ready to receive my Commands.

As soon as I was seated the Marquis made me a profound Reverence, and went out of the Room———— as I cast my Eyes on him, that Instant I saw he was in Tears, that Sight melted down all my Resolution, and I burst into an immoderate Fit of Weeping.

On this, one of the Woman drew near, and with a great deal of Sweetness, as well as Humility, begg'd I would not afflict myself, but exert that good Sense the World allowed me to be Mistress of, in surmounting my Distresses, if it were possible I could labour under any, in the splendid Condition I now was. Alas! cried I, with a Sigh, I deserve not these Favours from Fortune— why are they not bestowed on one who would become them better?

I then began to think of my poor Aunt, and enquired if a Woman I had brought with me, and very much loved, were removed from me? They assured me to the contrary, and said that when the young Marquis conducted me to his Father's Apartment, the Comptroller of the House had taken her into a Room, and that she was now at Supper in the Steward's Parlour, where she was treated with all imaginable Kindness in Respect to me, and I should see her instantly.

I

I was highly satisfied with this Answer, and as soon as she came in, I desired to be left alone with her, which Order being obeyed, I began to question her about what she had observed in the House, and in what Manner they behaved to her. Ah! my dear Lady, replied she, with Eyes sparkling with Joy, a thousand Times better than ever I could have expected, I have supped with the young Lord's Nurse, who is extremely kind to me————all the Men, dressed as fine as Counts, waited upon me, and called me Madamoiselle at ever Word— I never was so treated in all my Life——methinks I am in Paradise————I believe indeed it's all upon your Account; but no matter for that————I take the more Pleasure in it for being obliged to you for it.

So great was her Transport, that I believe she would have talked all Night, if I had not interrupted her, by saying I thought it requisite we should both of us go to Bed after our Journey ; with all my Heart, said she, for my Heart's at ease, and I am sure I shall sleep well. I then asked her, if she knew where she was to lie? Yes, indeed, said she, taking a Candle in her Hand, while you were at Supper, the Nurse shewed me all your Apartments, and the Chamber appointed for me————See there, Madam, said she, making me look into a small Room, that opened from my own ; what a fine Field-Bed there is————good God! continued she, laying her Hand on the Bedding, it is almost a Sin to spoil all this————what Sheets are here, our Curates Surplice is not half so white and fine————her Exclamations would have made me laugh at any other time ; but I was now incapable of being diverted with any thing, so made her put me to Bed with all the haste she could, after which she retired.

Weary as I was it was not without great Difficulty I went to Sleep, there was something so astonishing in what had happened to me that Day, that I could scarce believe but it was all a Dream : But these flattering Ideas were of no long Continuance.————Alas! cry'd I to myself, and weeping bitterly, it is but too true————I

lose

lose for ever all I love——marrying the Father, all
Hopes, even the most distant ones in regard to the Son,
are cut entirely off.——Great God! what have I done
——in what Miseries has my Obedience to the Will of
that dear Man plung'd me in——why did I consent to
this shocking Sacrifice?——if it was determined I
should be unhappy in being forever separated from my
Lover, sure I might have allowed myself the Consolation
of never being another's.——I might then have loved
him, and been beloved by him without a Crime——tho'
our Eyes had never met, our Hearts would have sympa-
thized, and bore a Partnership in each others Woe, and
that very Knowledge would have enabled both to support our mutual Misfortune;——but now what Relief
remains——even the Privilege of complaining is denied.
——O! wretched——wretched *Jeanetta*, pursued I,
wringing my Hands, and yielding to the most violent
Despair, till a Heaviness like that of Death came on
me, and I no longer was sensible of any thing. I
cannot call this Interval of Torture true Repose, because when I waked from it, I did not find myself in the
least refresh'd; nevertheless it was broad Day when I
opened my Eyes, and found *Barbara*, who was accustomed to rise early, at my Bedside. She enquired after
my Health, and told me she fear'd I was not well, having heard me groan several Times; I told her that my
Mind suffer'd more than my Body; so much the worse,
cry'd she, the Body will soon feel the Effects of it, and
then both will be bad. These Words were, alas! but,
too prophetic, as it soon after proved.

The Moment I was up the two Woman I had dismiss'd the Night before, came into my Chamber and
begg'd leave to dress me, in order to pass into the Apartment of my Lord Marquis, who entreated the Favour of
seeing me as soon as possible.——I trembled at a Request
I knew to be a Command, and sat down while they prepar'd my Hair, and adorned me a gay glittering
Wretch.

As I cast my Eyes on the Pictures that hung in my Chamber, that of a very beautiful Infant, whose Features methought

thought had some Resemblance with those of my dear Marquis surprized me; and immediately I ask'd for whom it was design'd? For our young Lord, replied she that was dressing me, and that next to it is his Mother's, our first Lady. How! cry'd I, has the Marquis been twice married? No, Madam, answer'd she, but we look upon you as our second Lady. I said no more————these Words, though informing me no more than what I too well knew before, were like so many Daggers to my Heart.————The Thought was dreadful, and Nature avoids as much possible every thing that shocks it.

I was scarce got ready when a Valet de Chamber from the young Marquis, came to enquire how I had pass'd the Night, and if I were disposed to go into his Father's Apartment. I answer'd, that when he pleased I would attend him, and then enquired how the sick Lord did. The Valet de Chamber replied, that he had enjoy'd a very quiet Sleep, and now spoke with more Facility than he had done, which was look'd upon as a good Sign, and gave great Hopes of his Recovery. While he was speaking, Monsieur *Forsan* enter'd, and told me they waited for me with Impatience, to hear the Contract read to me, which was just drawn up, and to have it sign'd.

The very Name of Contract threw me into a cold Sweat, and not able to conceal my Disorder, I thought, said I, they would not have perform'd that Ceremony till the Marquis was perfectly recover'd. He is eager, Madam, answer'd he, to secure his Happiness.———— He has past the greatest Part of the Night in giving Instructions to his Lawyer; and when you hear what he has done for you, you will judge of the true Esteem he has for you, and confess the Advantages that arise from marrying a Man advanced in Years.

I said nothing to all, but suffer'd him to lead me through the Apartments: I knew not how I got to the sick Person's Chamber: My Knees bent under me through Trouble and Weakness, and I stagger'd at every Step I took; on my Entrance I found two Strangers there, the one Writing, and the other seeming to dictate

tate to him at a Defk at the lower End of the Room, I
doubted not but they were proceeding on the cruel Contract, and look'd on them, as a Wretch condemn'd does
on the Executioner.

The old Marquis was fitting up in his Bed, with a
rich Night Gown thrown over him, as there was more
light in the Room than had been the Night before, I
had a fuller View of him, and was furprized to find his
Looks fo little alter'd in an Illnefs fo dangerous, as his
was judg'd to be.———When I drew near, he took me
by the Hand, and preffing it with more Violence than
one could have imagin'd in his Condition, gave Orders
to be left alone with me, which being that Inftant
obeyed, he fpoke to me in thefe Terms.

My prefent Weaknefs, lovely *Jeanxuta*, faid he, will
not permit me to fpeak much, therefore, expect a direct
Anfwer to what I fhall fay.———This it is———the
State to which you fee me reduced is owing to you———
if I recover it is to you I fhall be indebted for my Life
————my Son affures me you are ready to make me
happy.———*Dubois* has inform'd me in what a heroick
manner you confented to this Sacrifice :———Tell me if
you repent it :———It is not yet too late————fay
but the Word, and I fhall leave you at your Liberty,
and facrifice in my Turn the fmall Remnant of Life,
Fate might otherwife have allotted me.

No, my Lord, anfwer'd I refolutely, my Word is
given to your Son, and I will not recall it : Since to
preferve a Father he yields up all he holds dear befide,
I will convince him, that fhe who has been honoured
with his Affection is in fome Meafure worthy of it, by
foregoing all fhe had to hope in Life, in order to gratify
his Wifhes.

I ftifled my Sighs, reftrain'd my Tears, and if I
could would have alfo difguifed that deadlike Palenefs,
which I have fince heard o're-fpread my Lips and
Cheeks while I was fpeaking thefe Words.————I
perceived the Marquis obferved my every Look ; but he
took no Notice of it, and when I had done: It is
enough, faid he, my Son fhall be call'd in, and the
Contract fhall be read.   He

He then rung a Bell which was placed at his Bed's-head, and *Forfan* entring, received his Orders, in the mean time, is not being so near me disagreeable to you *Jeanetta?* said he ; but I was able to answer only with a low Bow : The young Marquis that instant came in, drest with the utmost Magnificence, all the melancholy which had clouded his dear Brows the Evening before, seemed now totally dissipated, and he appear'd like one going to a Party of Pleasure. This second Effort, cry'd his Father, giving him his Hand, moves me as much as the first : The Contentment I see in your Countenance assures me, I am truly dear you ; and that strong as Inclination was, paternal Affection, for I put Duty out of the Question, gets the better.————I wish to God, continued he, turning to me, you could in this too imitate his Example. I bowed again but could not speak. ————Alas ! what Answer had I to make, my Looks would have then given the lye to whatever I had said.

How weak and unstable is a Mind in Love : I wish'd in reality nothing more than the young Marquis's Contentment, yet when he seemed to be possest of it I was disquieted, and reproach'd his Want of Love. I now looked earnestly upon him, having an Opportunity as he was talking with his Father, and observed somewhat in him, which shew'd me that his Air of Satisfaction was but borrowed, and that he suffer'd inwardly, perhaps, equal with myself————this gave me some little Ease. ————He loves me still, thought I, with the same Passion as ever, and like a Victim is adorn'd with Chaplets only to render the Sacrifice more magnificent. I should here have enter'd into a Train of Reflections ; but the Lawyer came in with the Contract, and beginning to read, it put a Stop to them.

The Names and Titles of the Parties were pass'd over, and he came immediately to the Articles which regarded me.————I had a Jointure of seven Thousand Livres :——Jewels to the amount of an hundred Thousand Livres.————A Coach, and Chariot with six Horses each, and four for my Retinue————the Palace,

lace, my intended Husband lived in, with all the Plate and Furniture, in Case he died without Issue ; and if I had any Children by him, to enjoy the whole Estate till they should come of Age ; and then be accountable to them for the Profits of it.

Though I understood little of Business, and less of Law, I was very much surprized to hear no mention made of his Son : I thought he ought to have been the principal Party in this authentick instrument, and that he had behaved himself too well in this Affair not to deserve to be consider'd.————This Idea struck me so strongly that I could not help speaking of it ; which as soon as I had, what an adorable Creature are you, *Jeanetta*, cry'd the Marquis, how just !————how delicate your Sentiments ! but be easy, my Charmer, I have not forgot so valuable a Son————he will be satisfied when he knows what I have done for him, and so will you.

I said no more, but could not conceive what he could have done for him equivalent to the Loss of a great Estate, all settled on me and my Heirs.————Sometimes I imagin'd he had obtain'd an additional Title for him of the King, or some Office at Court, yet neither of these seem'd in my Judgment a sufficient Compensation for his right of Inheritance.

After the Contract was read over they brought it to the old Marquis to sign, it was then presented to his Son who did the same ; but was not able to constrain himself so far, as not to tremble while he wrote his Name, and let fall some Tears, which in spite of him forced their Passage through his Eyes. This Sight moved me to that Degree, that I let the Pen fall from my Fingers two or three Times before I was able to set my Name. — The old Marquis, sick as he was, observed it, and cryed out ; ah, do not force her to it————then turned himself on the other side.

The young Marquis took this Opportunity to throw himself at my Feet,————Ah ! *Jeanetta* ! said he, what are you doing ?————Would you wish me to lose the best of Fathers ?————the Vehemence with which he pronounced these Words, and the Action that accompanied

3

nied them pierced me to the Soul, and calling to my Aid all the little Stock of Spirit I had left, they enabled me to sign my Name.

The young Marquis then acquainted his Father with what I had done, on which he turn'd himself and gave me his Hand: It is enough, lovely *Jeanetta,* said he, I know your Sincerity, and am assured you will never hate the Man, whom you have set your Hand to love. ———The more Difficulty you had in bringing yourself to it, the more you will remember the Obligation. After this he seem'd disposed to sleep, and order'd *Forsan* to conduct me back to my Apartment, and endeavour to amuse me.

We all went out of the Chamber except the young Marquis, who remained with his Father: He waited on me to the Door, and made me Signs of applauding my Behaviour, which gave me a kind of melancholy Satisfaction; how wretched was my Condition any one may judge, when the only Man I ever did or could love, approved of my giving myself forever from him, and the only Comfort I had felt was that he did so.

I was no sooner got into my Apartment, than I found myself extremely indisposed: It cannot, indeed, be thought strange I was so, 'tis rather to be wondered at that the Horrors I endured, had not a greater Effect on me, and that I survived even the first Knowledge of what they expected from me: I resisted as long as I could, several alternate Fits of Heat and Cold; but at length grew so excessive ill, that they were oblig'd to put me to Bed, where after I had lain a Minute, I seem'd more composed, and the Women about me flatter'd themselves I was better.

Neither the old Marquis nor his Son were made acquainted with what had befallen me, the whole Family knew how dear I was to both, and the Violence the one did himself in resigning me to the other; so with Reason apprehended that neither of them would be able to sustain the Knowledge of what I suffer'd.

It was not, however, possible to keep it long a Secret———it seemed as if what I had done work'd a Miracle.

racle in Favour of the old Marquis, he was visibly recovered, and every Body pronounced him entirely out of
Danger : Which he no sooner heard than he declared
his Intentions of concluding the Marriage, to the A-
mazement of the whole Family, to whom it appear'd
strange, as well, indeed, it might; that a Man who
was thought one Day to be on the Brink of Eternity,
should on the very next resolve to become a Bridegroom,
and celebrate his Nuptials on the same Day the Contract
had been sign'd, yet such were his Orders, and who
durst offer any thing in Opposition ! The Priest was sent
for into his Chamber, and having made the young Marquis be call'd, my dear Son, said he, the Proofs you
have given me of your Love and Duty, are, perhaps,
greater than a Father could expect——yet have I one
more to ask, and then all will be fulfill'd;—it is, continued he, that you will take upon you the Office of
conducting *Jeanetta* hither, that I may receive her from
your Hand——though they tell me I am better, I am
not certain I may live to another Day, and could not die
in Peace, without the Consolation of leaving her the Title
of Marchioness *De L—V*—. The young Marquis made no
other Answer than a low Bow in token of Obedience,
nor, indeed, as he has since told me, was it in his power
to have uttered one Word——To conceal his Confusion therefore, as well as to seem ready to do what he
knew there was no avoiding, he left the Room precipitately in Order to fetch me; but how great was his
Surprize, when entring my Chamber, my Women
desired he would tread softly——what's the Matter,
cried he, impatiently ; my Lady is gone to Bed, answered
one of them, and is, we believe a Sleep——he exprest some Surprize, that I should go to Bed at so early
an Hour, and presently suspecting the Truth, would be
informed of the Occasion, on which they were obliged
to tell him the Condition I had been in——Alas,
cried he, in a pretty loud Voice, this is what I always
feared.

I was not asleep, and these Words made me open
my Eyes, and put my Head out between the Curtains

I

I faw who it was, and reaching my Hand, approach, my Lord, faid I, you feem under fome Concern, what is it you require further from me? Dreading to renew my Diforders, he would not relate the Nature of his Meffage, till he had afked me feveral Queftions concerning my Health, and I, cautious of giving him Difquiet, told him I felt no Pain, and was much better; on which he took Courage to inform me on what Bufinefs he came, and entreated me in the moft moving Terms to finifh what I had fo well begun——my Love and Submiffion to his Will, made me refolve to do every Thing he required, tho' at the expence of my Life, and I anfwered him with a greater Calmnefs than I believe he expected, that he fhould have Reafon to be content, and he then went into another Room, while they dreffed me: and as foon as I was ready, tho' I had a Mift before my Eyes, a Death-like Dew upon my Face, Trembling in every Limb, and all the Symptoms of Diffolution on me, I followed him without Murmuring at my Fate, and determined, if Life would laft fo long, to force myfelf to compleat the Sacrifice.

Every thing was ready for the fatal Ceremony; on entering the Chamber I was conducted to the Bedfide, the Prieft advanced, the young Marquis let go my Hand, and retired to a more diftant Part of the Room, I gave up myfelf and him for loft——all the Courage I had affumed forfook me——Refolution yielded to Nature, and after giving a great Shriek, I fell motionlefs to the Ground.

What then was done about me, I was wholly ignorant of, but when I recovered I found myfelf in Bed; and foon after felt I had a Fever——the Diftemper was violent, and brought me to the laft Extremity—— my Life for two Days was defpaired of, but on the third was judged fomewhat better. But how was I furprized, when waking out of my Sleep, and offering to put my Hand out of Bed I found my Arms tied down,—— I called out to know who had done this, and ftrugg'ed to get free, but the Woman who attended me held the Bedcloaths clofe to me, and begged me with Tears in

their

their Eyes to lie still, telling me my Life depended on my being kept warm, and free from the leaft Breath of Air : I then defired to know why my Arms were bound, to which they making only evafive Anfwers I grew impatient, and would needs be informed of the Nature of my Difeafe———— at laft they told me it was the Small-Pox————the Small-Pox! cried I, oh! then I am dead. No, Madam, replied a Prieft, who had been called in, if this favourable Turn continues, your Phyficians fay, you will be entirely out of Danger ————put therefore your Confidence in God, and refign yourfelf to his Difpofal both here and hereafter. Ah! do not flatter me, dear Father, cried I, let me know the real Truth, that I may do what is neceffary for the welfare of my poor Soul.

The good Ecclefiaftic commended my Piety, and tho' he again affured me, that it was the Opinion of the Doctors that I fhould recover, yet he faid I ought not to neglect making the fame Preparations, as tho' I were certain I muft that Inftant be called to appear before the dread Tribunal, whence there is no Appeal. This Reflection indeed terrified me fo much, that I confeft myfelf with great Devotion, and muft avow, tho' fome will call it Superftition, that from the Moment I had done fo, I vifibly mended.

My firft Thoughts as I grew better were, whether the young Marquis were acquainted with the Nature of my Diftemper or not ; I thought it would not be proper to afk that Queftion of thofe who attended me, and *Barbara* I had not feen fince I was taken ill, which I very much wondered at————I enquired for her, but they faid, that finding fhe could do me no Service in my prefent Condition, fhe was gone into the Country on fome Bufinefs fhe had there ; but would foon return ; this feemed odd to me, but as it was not in my Power to come at the Knowledge of any thing but as they pleafed to tell me, I was obliged to reft myfelf contented.

At laft, however, I bethought myfelf of an Expedient : I enquired concerning the old Marquis's Health, on which they anfwered, that the Accident that had hap-

pened

pened to me in his Prefence, had like to have coft him his Life ; but that now he had been two Days out of Danger. And how then, cried I, does his Son fupport the Relapfe of a Father fo dear to him ? He is pretty well, faid one of my Attendants————I was a little ftartled at the Word *pretty well*; does he know the Condition I am in, faid I ? No, Heaven forbid he fhould, replied fhe, no body dare inform him of it, left the Confequences fhould be fatal.

This unwary Anfwer, which fhe that gave as well as the other that ftood by, endeavoured afterwards to give a different turn to, convinced me, that my beloved Admirer was fick ; however, as I thought the beft way to come at the Truth, was to take no Notice I fufpected it, I forbore making any further mention of the young Marquis ; but expreffed the utmoft Impatience for the Sight of *Barbara*, hoping, that to humour me, they would fuffer her to come, for I could not be brought to believe fhe had quitted the Houfe, and left me in the Danger I was apprehended to be.

So much Difquiet of Mind, or the Courfe of the Diftemper, I know not which, brought the Fever again upon me, which my good Aunt hearing, would no longer be kept from coming into my Room ; as I was now given over by the Phyficians, they did not oppofe her, and fhe was at laft admitted : She had no fooner looked upon me, than fhe cried out, that as fhe was my Servant, fhe would have the Management of me, or fhe would tell every Body that they kept her away, only becaufe they had a mind to kill me————this Paffion, and the Belief that whatever was done to me, could now neither make me better or worfe, prevailed on them, to let her do as fhe would, which indeed faved my Life. Indeed the over care which in great Towns is taken of fick People, efpecially of thofe in the Diftemper I was in, I am convinced is very often fatal to them ; my Aunt proceeded with me, in a quite contrary manner than they had done ; fhe took off by degrees fome of the Clothes, with which they had loaded my Bed to keep me in a continual and indeed immoderate

Heat

Heat——— she suffered me to drink a little Wine, and to breathe more Air, which it is certain I stood in need of; and in fine, ordered me so well, that in three Days the Fever quite left me——— every Body wondered at the Change, and my new Nurse gained great Reputation by it——— as contrary as she had acted to the Rules prescribed by the Physicians, they could not but allow she had been miraculously successful, and agreed that I was now entirely out of Danger.

This News being reported to the old Marquis, who had been anxious beyond Expression on my Account, and had sent continually to enquire after my Health, was transported to be told I was likely to recover——— then, said he, I am happy, and immediately dispatched *Dubois* to my Chamber, with this important Message.

I come, Madam, said he, from my Lord Marquis to congratulate the Amendment he hears there is in you, and to assure you from him, that no future Disquiet shall ever arise to you on his score——— he begs you therefore for the sake of all you hold dear in the World, to contribute all you can to your speedy Recovery, by a perfect Ease of Mind——— he bid me also add, continued he, that the Time is now at Hand, in which all the Troubles you have undergone shall be fully recompensed.

How! in what manner, cried I, impatiently? that is not for me to resolve, answered *Dubois*; but if you will take my Opinion, it is in such a way as you will have nothing left to wish.

But the young Marquis, said I, is he well? not perfectly, Madam, replied *Dubois*; but I believe will soon be in a Condition to wait upon you. I durst say no more, my Women were in the Room, nor durst I dismiss them, in order to have any farther Discourse with him, for fear of giving any Cause of Offence, where it so much behoved me to keep well!——— I said no more therefore than to give my Duty to the Marquis, and entreat *Dubois* to make my acknowledgments for all his Favours in the best manner he could.

Barbara

Barbara, after the Success of her Endeavours took so much upon her in my Apartment, and on the old Marquis's being acquainted with the care she had of me, the whole Family had such strict Orders to obey her in every thing, that no body durst approach me without asking her leave, so that now we were very often alone together————I had two great Requests to make her, but was sometime before I could bring them out ; for I no sooner began to open my Lips to ask her any Questions, than she enjoyned me Silence, and told me very peremptorily that I must either be ruled or buried———— the Thoughts of Dying terrified me so much that I was glad to hold my Tongue————so excellent a Means is Fear to render one obedient.

I had now been ill thirteen Days, and still I was not suffered to talk ; but at the end of that Time a little Liberty of Speech was allowed me————ah, my dear *Barbara,* said I, taking her round the Neck, and kissing her, I owe my Life to you————and I will never forget your Goodness————I have done but my Duty, answered she, so deserve no Praise on that Score ————you having nothing to do, but to get well, and then they say you will be as happy as a Queen.———— Well, but my good Friend, resumed I, you must grant me one Thing, and that will compleat my Cure. I wish it does not hinder it, cried she, for I'll lay my Life it is somewhat about the Marquis, the young one I mean, for as to the old one, I do not suppose you are under any Concern about him.————You are much in the right indeed, said I, tell me then, how he is, and what he says to my Illness. You must know then, said she, looking down on her Fingers, as was always her way, when she told an Untruth ; he is gone a Journey into the Country, but he will come back soon I hear. Ah ! *Barbara,* resumed I, how have I deserved that you should impose upon me————I see now you don't love me. When I had spoke this, I turned to the other side of the Bed, and pretended to be very angry————How strange this is, now, said she, if one does not tell you Things you are vexed, and if one

did

did, it may be that you would vex more—there's no humouring People that have such Fancies in their Heads as you have.

There are many People, who by not telling a Thing directly, make it appear rather worse than it is————my poor Aunt was of this Number, she would not give any Answer to my Question for fear of giving me Pain, yet by attempting to conceal what I desired to know, made me imagine all that Terror could suggest. I thought no less, than that my Lover was dead, or in such a Condition that his Life was despaired of; but resolving to continue no longer in suspence, well then, said I, since you will not satisfy me, I'll rise this Instant and go and convince myself————Oh, Heaven forbid, cried *Barbara*, frighted at my Words and the Motion I made, as if determined to do as I had said, lie still, and compose yourself, my dear Lady, and if you'll promise me to put your trust in God, and not torment yourself, I will tell you the whole Truth. I was too impatient not to promise every Thing she desired on that Condition, but how little was I able to fulfil it when she acquainted me with what had happened.

That dear, that amiable Man, she told me, was taken ill the Moment I fainted away; the Constraint he had put upon himself, in giving his Father Proofs of a more than filial Affection, joined to the Grief in which he saw he had involved me, turned all his Blood, and threw him into a burning Fever————in his Ravings, my Name was continually in his Mouth, and he became at length so wild, that for the safety of his Life, they were obliged to bind him; he having in one of his Fits broke from those that attended him and run to my Apartment, crying out he would see me and die.————This it seems happen'd when my Distemper was at the height, and as he had never had the Small-Pox, the Infection seized him, and for eight Days there was little hopes of his Life.

I was obliged to keep my Sighs and Tears during this melancholly Account, restrained for fear of not hearing what succeeded so sad a beginning; but, thank Heaven,

Heaven, the worſt was paſt, my Aunt aſſured me that his Father had ſent him a Meſſage, but what it was ſhe could not learn, that had given a turn to his Diſtemper, and he was now in a fair way of Recovery, tho' every one ſaid he would be very much marked, and not half ſo handſome as he was.

Alas! ſaid I, of what Importance is that, provided his dear Life be ſafe————How unfortunate am I not to be in a Condition to attend him——never would I quit his Chamber————never cloſe my Eyes, till aſſured I ſhould behold him living when I waked. I was running on in this manner, but *Barbara* interrupted me, and charged me to compoſe myſelf. I was for making ſome reply, but ſhe told me if I ſpoke a Word more, I muſt not expect ſhe would ever give me any farther Account of the Marquis ; this Menace prevailed upon me, and my Tongue was huſhed, but my Thoughts continued as anxious and as active as ever.

After having revolved a thouſand Things in my Mind, I began to remember the other Requeſt I had to make, which was to conſult my Looking-Glaſs, that I might judge how far that fatal Enemy to Beauty the Small-Pox had ſpared me————I had often been un-eaſy when I reflected that it was poſſible all the little Charms I had been Miſtreſs of would vaniſh, and I might become diſagreeable, nay even ugly, by the cruel Marks it might leave behind—tho' I had never dared to flatter myſelf that the old Marquis's Meſſage, in which he promiſed to make me Recompenſe for the Troubles I had ſuſtained, would extend ſo far as to conſent to my Union with his Son, yet it ſhocked me to think that the Man who once adored me, ſhould hereafter look on me with Loathing, ſo that tho' I had Vanity enough—Heaven knows too much, yet at this Time I may ſafely ſay my Love, and Deſire of being always loved by the Marquis, was the ſole Cauſe of my Anxiety on the Score of my Face.————Heavens! cried I to my-ſelf, how unhappy ſhall I be, if I become deformed—was it not my Beauty that firſt inſpired the Marquis with ſo violent a Paſſion for me, and will not my loſs of that Beauty, extinguiſh likewiſe all the Deſires it

excited?

excited?———it was in vain that I reflected on his Generosity, the Vows he had made of everlasting Constancy, when once the Cause ceased, I was assured the Effects would do so too.

I heard, however, the next Day a piece of News which was very agreeable to me———it was of the Count *De Saint Far*'s Arrival; I was told also that he was greatly moved at the Recital of what I had gone through, and that he sent his Compliments with an Assurance of waiting on me, as soon as I allowed any one the Liberty of seeing me. Nor was this a meer Piece of Form, he came ten Times in a Day to my Chamber Door, and then past to his Cousin's, divided as it were between us———sure never was so disinterested a Friend, nor so generous a Rival.

I promised myself a great deal of Satisfaction in seeing this amiable Friend, I could depend on his Probity in informing me of all I desired to know; but as the Curiosity of discovering what Effect the Small-Pox had on me, still remained, I took Courage to beg my Aunt to let me have a Looking-Glass; with a good deal of Difficulty she complied, but soon repented it, for I was so much surprized at the hideous Roughness of my Skin, which before had been so delicately smooth, that I screamed out, and let fall the Glass.———I thought what would come on't, said *Barbara*, picking up the Pieces———you are much better for your Curiosity— I warrant now you think your pretty Face is quite spoil'd? but I know that you'll be as handsome as ever———thanks to my care———I was so persuaded she deceived me in this Particular, that I fell into Tears, which made her Murmur at me grievously: in order to make my Peace with her, I promised to be very patient for the future on condition she would let me see myself again———and she brought me another Glass, whether what she said had prejudiced me, or that I really did not appear so frightful, as I since have seen some do, I know not, but I was much better contented than I had been—I found my Features were not swell'd———that my Eyes retained all their

former

former Fire and Sweetneſs, and lifting up one of the dried Pocks, found my Skin was ſmooth underneath——this gave me a new Life as it were——all my Diſquiet vaniſhed ; but it furniſhed me afterward with matter of Reflection on the Weakneſs of Humanity, which ſuffers itſelf to be elated or depreſſed by the meereſt Trifles—in fine, we are but Children at all Ages——Toys are ſtill our Purſuit, and however they differ in their Form, and Name, their eſſential Worth is much the ſame.

The next Day I was agreeably ſurprized with a Billet wrote by the young Marquis's own Hand, which contributed more to my Re-Eſtabliſhment than all the Doctors in the World could have done. The Lines it contained were theſe :

To the adorable *Jeanetta.*

*T*H E *News that you were upon Recovery, has worked a perfect Cure on me ; if your Affection is equal to mine, what I now ſend will have the ſame happy Effect on you*————*were I not bound to Secrecy, I could add ſomewhat I flatter myſelf would haſten it*————*but that is a Pleaſure my Father has reſerved to himſelf, and I muſt leave you to gueſs at it*————*adieu, my Charmer* ————*make me eaſy by knowing you are ſo.*

Yours

L—V——.

What had I not to hope from this Letter—— did it not ſeem to tally with the Meſſage ſent to me by the old Marquis !————could I have been blamed if I had indulged the moſt flattering Ideas !——my Lover bids me gueſs, cried I to myſelf——what can I gueſs ſo fortunate for both, as that his Father, touched with his Piety, will no longer be an Obſtacle to our mutual Wiſhes !——but then the fatal Paſſion he is poſſeſt of for me,——has it not already brought him to the Brink of the Grave——will he in order to reſign me, reſign himſelf to Death ?——or will that dutiful——that tender Son conſent he ſhould do ſo?——the more I

thought,

thought, the more I was confounded——it was an Enigma paſt my Power to explain, and I at laſt, tho' with much Difficulty, reſolved to wait with Patience till Time ſhould produce the Event.

Saint Fal was now permitted to come into my Chamber, and I hoped to learn from him the Truth of what I was ſo nearly concerned in ; and all he could inform me was, that the moſt pleaſing Serenity ſat on the Countenances of both the old, and young Marquis ; that the former had told him, he had never known ſo perfect a Satisfaction as he now enjoyed, and the latter entertained him with nothing but Diſcourſes on me, yet ſuch as were far from ſeeming the Dictates of a diſappointed Love————this ſtill added to my Hopes, yet dared I not too far give way to them : ——I thought proper to anſwer the Marquis's Letter, but was at a loſs for terms to expreſs myſelf in my preſent Situation, ——to write to him as a Lover, would ill become a Woman, who was contracted to his Father, and I had been ſo accuſtomed to treat him as ſuch, that it ſeemed aukward to depart from it. I ſtudied a Medium, however, as much as poſſible, and expreſſed myſelf in this Manner.

To the Marquis *De L——V——*.

IF the Deſire of obeying your Commands could reſtore my Health, I ſhould be able this Moment to tell you in Perſon how much I rejoice in the Recovery of Yours; but we muſt both attend on Time for that, as well as an Explanation of thoſe pleaſing, and at once ambiguous Hopes your Letter contains————Be aſſured of this, however, that all my Wiſhes are centered in your Happineſs, and whatever contributes to that darling Point, will be ever grateful to

Yours

Jeanetta De B——.

P. S.

P. S. As greatly as I wish to see you, I am certain I shall have sufficient Reasons for Mortification, when I do———the few Charms I was once Mistress of, are now no more; but as I valued them only as they secured the Affection of one Person, if by other Motives deprived of him, I shall little regard the loss of Beauty.

I entreated Monsieur *De Saint Fal*, to be the Bearer of this Billet, and to let me know what his Cousin said concerning it: He promised to give me an exact Account, and I knew him too well not to depend entirely on him.

He stayed some time before he returned, and never did any Moments seem more tedious———Alas! cried I to myself, the very Idea of my being less handsome has perhaps done more than all the Obstacles our Love has met with has had power to do———what now avails it, tho' the old Marquis, in consideration of the Sorrows he has occasioned me, should consent to our Marriage, if he himself should grow averse to it——— Yes, I am lost, if Beauty was the sole Attraction— Men, especially of his Age, are guided by meer Outside ———where the Eye is not pleased they give themselves not the trouble of examining whether the Deficiences of the Form are not atoned for by the Riches of the Mind———yet, continued I, my dear Marquis, seems to have more elevated Ideas——he has a thousand Times sworn, that it was my Soul he loved, and that remains the same, tho' it may cease to shine with so much Energy through my Features, as before this cruel Distemper seized me.

In these Meditations, the Count found me, and brought an Answer with him which quieted all my Doubts. These were the Words:

To the ever charming *Jeanetta.*

WHILE I cannot see yourself, to see any Thing from you is the first of my Wishes, and of my Happiness——not a Syllable wrote by that dear Hand, and dictated by that dear Heart; but is a Cordial beyond all can be administred——my Strength and Spirits are encreased to a double Propotion of what they were two Hours ago, and as I design to make your Letter the Entertainment of the whole Night, I doubt not if by To-morrow I should be able to walk as far as your Chamber; if the abominable roughness of my Face did not make me fearful of frighting you, instead of affording that Satisfaction which it's my sole Ambition always to give, to the lovely Jeanetta's

Most truly devoted,

L——V——.

P. S. I ought to chide you for your cruel Postcript—— do you know me so little as to imagine any Alteration in your Person, can abate a Passion, which has Virtue, and the highest Reason for its Foundation?——No, Jeanetta, your Soul will be forever lovely, and requires not the Assistance of any exterior Charms to shew itself to a Heart like mine——I hope you are of the same way of Thinking on my Score——else how shall I appear before you, thus changed, thus deformed as I am in every thing, in which the Eye is concerned.

When I had finished reading this agreeable Billet, the Count *De Saint Fal* fell a laughing very heartily—your Letter to my Cousin, said he, occasioned a diverting Scene, it seems you discovered In it some Apprehensions of being less beautiful than you were, on which he immediately called for a Looking-Glass, and having examined himself, cried out, O, how will the charming *Jeanetta,* be ever able to look upon me again——

it is impoffible fhe can know me———he run on for
half an Hour together I believe in thefe kind of Exclamations, then fat down to write, and I dare anfwer,
that if you confefs the Truth he has attacked you with
your own Weapons.

I laughed at what Monfieur *De Saint Fal* faid, and
after a little Raillery on the Subject of Beauty, we both
concluded that where Love was perfect and fincere, no
alteration of Perfon either by Time, Sicknefs, or any
other Accident, could in the leaft abate the Purity of it,
much lefs render difagreeable what was once the contrary.

After this I paft my Time with as much Tranquillity
as could be expected from my Situation ; the good-
natured *Saint Fal* brought me the News of the Marquis
three Times a Day, and as often reported what
Meffages I chofe to have delivered to him ; and it is
certain this tender Intercourfe greatly contributed to both
our Recoveries.

The old Marquis fent his Valet de Chamber every Day
toenquire after my Health, and bid him defire me from
him to contribute all in my own Power to get well again,
for he has a Prefent to make me, which he was impatient
till I was in poffeffion of———thefe Meffages were
ftill more and more flattering to my Hopes, yet durft
not I build too much upon them for fear of a Difappointment.

The firft Day I fat up, *Dubois* came from the young
Marquis to let me know he had received a Vifit from his
Father, who was perfectly recovered : He confeffed that
this Sight had given him a double Pleafure, as he confidered he owed the Obligation to me, who under Heaven
had reftored him to this new Life, having little appearance of it till I came. He added, that tho' he was
forbid feeing me till further Orders he was not troubled
at it, nor would have me be fo, for there were Reafons
for that Command which would not be difpleafing to
me in the end. The old Marquis, faid *Dubois*, is pofitive in whatever he has a Mind to do, and will be
obeyed,

obeyed, but then he is always juſt————He goes this Afternoon into the Country, and tho' I cannot ſay I am acquainted with the Motives of his going, yet I have ſome ſort of a Gueſs at them, and if I am right, we ſhall hear from him again in leſs than eight and forty Hours————He is a Man who affects to be myſterious to the laſt Moment, but it would be to injure him to ſay he is ever obſtinately in the wrong, or ever to be diſſuaded from what is right.

I then aſked *Dubois* if he thought I ſhould ſee the old Marquis before his Departure————No, anſwered he, it is not to be expected, for he dreads a ſick Perſon like Death itſelf————never did he give ſo great a Proof of his Tenderneſs for my Lord, as in the Viſit he made him this Morning ; but if you had ſeen the Precautions he took before he would venture into the Chamber, you would not have been able to refrain from Laughing.

This faithful Servant alſo acquainted me, that the Count *De Saint Fal* accompanied him out of Town, tho', ſaid he, I believe the young Lord is little ſatisfied with the Journey, tho' his Duty and Complaiſance to his Uncle have made him comply with it.

We were diſcourſing in this Manner, when ſomebody knocked at my Chamber, and my Aunt going to ſee who was there, it was immediately thrown wide open, by one of the old Marquis's Valet de Chambers. Ah ! cried *Dubois*, it is my old Lord himſelf, come to bid you adieu, his Affection muſt indeed be great to ſurmount his Apprehenſions.

It was indeed the Marquis, who ſtopping about five or ſix Paces from the Door, called out, I am come to know how you do, charming *Jeanetta*, and to take my leave. I then turned to him, and congratulated him on his Recovery. I have much to ſay to you on that Head, replied he, and many others at our next Meeting————I am now going into the Country, but we ſhall ſoon ſee each other again————in the mean Time I will ſend a Lady to keep you Company————one who is a dear Friend of yours, and whom you little expect————Farewel, lovely *Jeanetta*, take care of yourſelf, and remember

remember he defires it of you, who has it in his Power
to recompenfe any compliance you make————our
Separation will be but fhort. In fpeaking thefe laft
Words he made a low Bow and retired.

Saint Fal came the Moment after to bid me adieu—
in entring, fo beautiful *Jeanetta*, faid he, my Uncle
has been to vifit you ?————I was amazed to find he
could fo far overcome his Fears. It is a very great
Obligation he lays me under, anfwered I, but can't you
inform me, who this Friend is, that he has promifed to
fend. No, refumed the Count, he has not let me into
the Secret, but I wonder not at it, he loves to furprize
every body. It muft certainly be *Saint Agnes*, cried I,
that he means. That is impoffible, replied he, for fhe
is gone out of Town with her Hufband————I faw them
both fince my return : and they defired I would make
you in their Names, affurances of an everlafting Friendfhip.

As it was impoffible for me, to comprehend who the
Marquis meant, I refolved to think as little as I could of
it, and indeed the manner of *Saint Fal*'s taking his
leave, and his generous Refolution to make Love recede
to Friendfhip was fo moving, that it for a Time banifhed
every thing elfe from my Mind.

I had but juft dined when my Aunt acquainted me
a Lady enquired, whether fhe could fee me without
giving me any uneafinefs. As I did not doubt, but it
was the fame the Marquis had mentioned, my anfwer
was that I was impatient for her Company. I was
fo indeed out of Curiofity, but had I been able to
guefs who fhe was I fhould have looked on every
Minute as an Age, till I had her with me. It is wholly
impoffible to exprefs my Tranfports when fhe appeared,
and I found it was my dear Patronefs and Friend, the
excellent Madam *De G*————I fcreamed out for Joy,
and run upon her with open Arms————we held each
other for fome Moments in the moft ftrict Embrace,
without either of us being able to fpeak. The Pleafure
of meeting after fo long an Abfence was too great for
Words————at laft I broke out————Is it you, Madam?
Nay,

Nay then I shall begin to think Fortune is grown weary of persecuting me, since I have found you again————in all the dreadful Tryals I have undergone since I was torn from you, my Mind has ever preserved your dear Idea————Your precious Picture, the Pledge of your Friendship to me, I have kiss'd a thousand Times, and said as many Prayers for its Original. Poor Thing, cried Madam *De G*————, thou art still the same grateful, kind Creature, nor have I less remembered thee————tho 'till this Day despairing of the Happiness I now enjoy.

Near an Hour was past in mutual Endearments, but as desirous as I was of being informed, how I came to be obliged to the old Marquis, for the Pleasure of seeing her, good Manners rendered it necessary I should, first, enquire after her Daughter, and Monsieur *De G*—; they are both well, answered she, and impatiently expect your Company at our Country-Seat. How! said I, shall I be so happy to be again under your Protection? Yes, my dear *Jeanetta*, replied she, 'tis on that Account I am come, but I shall not enjoy you long————You seem surprized, continued she, but ask no Questions————I have promised Secrecy, and you know I never break my Word.

So many Precautions taken to keep me from the knowledge of what was decreed for me, gave me some little Uneasiness; I confest it to my dear Friend, but she re-assured me by these Words ; you have no Reason to be alarmed, said she, you may be certain I should never have been chose for an Instrument in any thing to your disadvantage. But, Madam, answered I, you know not perhaps that the Situation you find me in is owing to what I have undergone from both the old and young Marquis. Yes, said that worthy Lady, I am acquainted with the minutest Circumstances of every thing————but it was your own Fault———— Your Apprehensions were too precipitate, and threw you into a real ill, instead of an imaginary one.— But I have said too much, continued she, if you have any Esteem for me ask me no farther Questions————

my

my Love for you makes me diffident of myfelf, and I will never forgive you, if you take any Advantage of it to the prejudice of my Honour, which I once more repeat is given to preferve an inviolable Secrecy in this Affair.

I too well knew her to perfevere in my Enquiries, and notwithftanding a Curiofity which might be allow'd me, in a Matter of fuch Moment, I never fpoke one Syllable more, which fhould make her think I fhould be glad if fhe would break through her Engagement. I afked a thoufand Pardons for my Imprudence, and proteſted fhe fhould have no future Reafon to complain of me———She took me in her Arms, and exprefs'd the utmoſt Concern, for being obliged to be fo much on the referve with me, declaring fhe had an entire Confidence in me, of which fhe would foon give me convincing Proofs, and that nothing but rendering herfelf unworthy of my Friendfhip, by forfeiting her Honour, could make her conceal any thing from me.

This dear Friend never quitted my Chamber all the time I was obliged to continue in it ———At length the Strength of my Conftitution, the fweet Society of fo amiable a Companion, and the Meffages I every Day received from my dear Marquis, fully re-eftablifhed me— My very Looks were fo much the fame, that except a little Rednefs, it was fcarce difcernable I had ever had the Small-pox: And I diverted myfelf very much, in reflecting how much I fhould furprize my Lover, when he fhould fee how favourably I had been treated by that terrible Diftemper. I knew very well it was my Mind he moft efteemed, but I alfo knew, that a fine Jewel well-fet is much more to be prized, than when obfcured by the bungling Workmanfhip about it.

Madam *De G*——— now finding me fit to go abroad, afk'd me if I was willing to accompany her to her Caftle, where we were fo much defired : I told her that nothing could be more pleafing to me ; and 'tis not to be doubted but I fpoke the Truth, fince it was there I was made to hope the Myftery of my Fate would be unravelled.

The

The Day before we were to fet out, I begged fhe would permit me to go to Church, and render Heaven thofe Thanks, I ought to do, and give the Charities which my Recovery demanded————it was my Opinion, that when one receives a great Benefit, one ought to confer fuch Benefits on others, as are in our Power, and I could never difpenfe with this Duty————Madam *De G*————applauded my pious Refolution, and told me fhe would accompany me in the Performance, and add to the Alms I intended to give ; for, faid fhe, I look on your Recovery as a Bleffing to myfelf, and therefore ought to give Thanks for it, and alfo make the poor in fome Meafure partakers of it————Perfevere in your Piety, my dear *Jeanetta*, faid fhe, it is that which gives you a title to the protection of all difpofing Providence————it is that which has preferved you amidft fo many Dangers, and it is to that you will undoubtedly owe the happy End of all your Troubles.

Alas, I little thought my truly fincere Defign of paffing this Day in a kind of holy Repofe, would have met with any Interruption, and that of fuch a Nature, as threatned me with ending it in a Prifon.

After having received the Euchariſt, I tarried a little to meditate on the facred Ceremony, when all on a fudden I found myfelf pull'd by the Sleeve, I was fomewhat furprized at the Liberty taken with me, and turning my Head faw a Woman, to whofe Face I was utterly a Stranger.

Very well, Madam, faid fhe, I am glad we have met at laft, now it will be proved who is the true Countefs *De Roches*————my Reader will eafily judge without my making any Defcription the Fright I was in———— I could not fpeak one Word, but rofe and pufh'd from her with all my Strength, till I got to Madam *De G*———— who was at fome Diftance from me————fhe faw me pale and trembling, and as I had related to her, what happened to me before on Account of that unlucky Name, I only faid the Countefs *De Roches*,————and fhe underftood the Caufe of this Change in my Countenance. She bid me not be alarmed, and we both made
what

what hafte we could out of the Church. The Perfon
that had given me this Confufion, did not follow me ;
but as I afterwards found kept her Eye conftantly upon
me, and when we were preffing through the Croud to
reach Madam *De G*————'s Coach, which waited for
us, we heard a Voice cry, ftop————ftop the fictitious
Countefs *De Roches :* She had told her Story to the
People about the Door, and all Eyes were turned
upon me ; but the Equipage of Madam *De G*————
kept us from receiving any Infult, but from one Man
who cryed, I ought to be detain'd till a Commiffary
fhould be brought : How ridiculous a thing would that
be, cryed my dear Friend ! The Woman who makes
this Clamour may, perhaps, be deceived by fome Refemblance between this Lady and the Perfon fhe mentions ; but I will anfwer, that it would be highly dangerous for any who fhall dare to affront us. Thefe Words
fpoke with a refolute and determin'd Air, joined with
the Figure Madam *De G*————and her Attendants
made, filenced the Fellow, but not the Countefs, whofe
Cries purfued us, after we got into the Coach.————
We drove, however, at too great a Rate for any one
to overtake us ; though one of the Footmen told us,
that two Serjeants, who were accidentally paffing by, and
heard the Complaint, followed us a confiderable way.
We arrived fafe at the Marquis's, but I could not prefently get rid of my Fright, and, indeed, the Affair
might have been of very ill Confequence ; fo dangerous
as well as filly a thing it is to affume another Perfon's
Name, though done with no Defign of prejudicing any
one.

The next Day we fet out, and as foon as we were out
of *Paris,* Madam *De G*————faid the Tedioufnefs of
the Journey would require fomething to amufe me : Hitherto, faid fhe, I have had no Opportunity to entertain
you with any thing concerning myfelf, and it is but
juft I fhould put the fame Confidence in you, that
you have always done in me : I will, therefore, continued
this amiable Lady embracing me, give you a little Detail of what I have gone through fince we faw each

other.

other. I made her thofe Acknowledgements her Goodnefs demanded from me, and told her that any thing
relating to her, would be in an inexpreffible manner interefting to me; on which fhe began the little Narrative
fhe had promifed, in thefe Terms.

The Hiftory of Monfieur De G⸺.

YOU are no Stranger, faid fhe, to the Difpofition
of Monfieur *De G*⸺, nor to his amorous
Inclinations, fo will eafily imagine I am going to entertain you with his Gallantries : Heaven only knows how
greatly I have fuffer'd by them; for you are the firft to
whom I ever divulged this Error in his Nature ; and
contented myfelf with fecretly bewailing my Misfortune,
and befeeching Heaven to put an end to it.⸺I muft,
indeed, do him the Juftice to fay, he behaved to me
with the greateft Refpect, and that in part compenfated
for the want of that Tendernefs, which I was fenfible
he beftowed elfewhere ; but at laft even that was withdrawn, I obferved a vifible Change in his Looks, and
manner of fpeaking to me ; he now was not only cold,
but alfo rugged and churlifh, whenever I came into his
Prefence, nothing that I could fay, or do was pleafing to
him ; and I began to tremble, left I fhould lofe all his
Friendfhip as well as Love. I thought he muft now
have an Amour with fome Woman, who had either Merit, or Artifice enough to engage his ferious Affection,
and that I ought to fearch into it, and try all my Efforts to win him from fo formidable a Rival.

But, alas ! how difficult a Tafk this was, I need not
tell you, who knew fo well his Secrecy in Matters of this
kind ; I was, therefore, very much at a Lofs how to
proceed,

proceed, that I might come at the Certainty of what I was fo deeply concern'd in. That he was paffionately in Love all his Actions denoted————he was hardly ever at Home, and when he was fo, fullen, peevifh, and fometimes extremely melancholly.————I had no room to doubt of my Misfortune, but the Author of it was hid in Clouds.—I endeavour'd to gain fome of his Servants, who I knew were in the Secret, but to no Purpofe; they were more in his Intereft than mine, and my Enquiries, which they doubtlefs inform'd him of, ferved only to render him more cautious, and at the fame time encreas'd his Ill-Humour to me; this threw me into very great Agitations, nor could I fee any way to extricate myfelf.

I was one Day extremely melancholy, and had retired to my Clofet, to give a loofe to my Complaints, on Account of fome very unkind Speeches I had that Morning been treated with, by Monfieur *De G*————. *Chriftina*, that trufty Servant who you cannot but remember, fince it was fhe whom I entrufted to bring you from the Convent, came in and found me in this Condition. She prefs'd me fo earneftly to reveal the Occafion, that moved by the Grief fhe fhewed, and convinced of her Fidelity, I difcovered the whole Affair to her, which as foon as I had done. Ah, my dear Lady, cryed fhe, you are too good, and have too long fubmitted to the Caprices of an unworthy Hufband.————Inftead of Tears and Lamentations which may prejudice your Health, you fhould rather think of fome way to put an End to his Irregularities.

Alas, *Chriftina*, replied I, what is it in my Power to do————is it poffible for me to prevent his liking another Woman and flighting me?————Yes, Madam, faid fhe, in my Opinion, Men are juft what we pleafe to make them————haughty when we are fubmiffive, and as meanly cringing when we exert ourfelves———— too much Tendernefs on our fide, is the fure way to deftroy theirs; and Indifference the only way to preferve any fort of Equality with them.

Thou

Thou fpeakeft, anfwer'd I, like one who has never
been a Wife, or rather if thou hadft a Mind rather to
divert my Troubles, than wert able to offer any thing
for their Mitigation. If I cannot do the latter, faid
fhe, indeed it would be fome Pleafure to me to think I
could the former ; but yet I cannot help imagining, that
if it were poffible for me, to be in your Ladyfhip's
Place, I would foon cure Monfieur *De G———*, of
his Paffion for his Miftrefs, and make him more in love
with me than ever. That would be extremely difficult,
replied I, for two Reafons ; the moft important of
which is, I have no longer that blooming Youth fo enchanting to Mankind. ——— Ah ! Madam, cried
Chriftina, interrupting me, you are ftill as beautiful as
an Angel.———The other Reafon, refumed I, without taking any Notice of this Piece of Flattery ; Monfieur *De G*———was always a Lover of Variety, and
this Foible is fo engrafted with his Nature, that I have
the leaft hope he can ever throw it off ; fo that could I
difcover the Object of his prefent Flame, and by any
Stratagem make him become afhamed or weary of
it, the Confequence of my Endeavours would be only to
make him transfer it on fome other, and but the more
eftrange him from me, efpecially if he found out that I
made any Noife of it.

I allow this Obfervation to be juft, Madam, faid
Chriftina, after having paufed a little———though I
have little Experience of Mankind, I know there is a
Pride in them, which renders them impatient of controul.———I would never, therefore, advife a Woman to appear to lay any Reftraint upon her Hufband,
for as they never will acknowledge themfelves guilty
though never fo glaringly fo ; they make an Accufation
an Excufe for their Extravagancies, exclaim in Publick
againft the Ill Humour of the Perfon they injure, and
treat her infupportably in private.———Nay, the Obftacles laid in their way, frequently give frefh Vigour to
Inclination, and give a double Relifh to Enjoyment, fo
that Stratagem, and that alfo very clofely carried, on is
the fafeft way a Woman can proceed.

I

I knew this Girl had been well educated, and had Wit ; but had not expected fo much good Underftanding as I now found her Miftrefs of.————I agreed entirely to her Opinion, but told her as I had obferved the Maxims fhe now mention'd, yet found them without Succefs, I could not fee which way I could proceed to reap any Advantage.   There are fome Occafions, Madam, anfwer'd fhe, when it is right to deviate from the common Ru'es of Prudence ; but the great Art is to find out the fit Time for it

Permit me, Madam, continued fhe, perceiving I was filent and feem'd penfive, before I prefume to offer my little Advice for the reftoring your Tranquility to amufe you with an Adventure, I had fometime ago with Monfieur *De G*————.   I never mention'd it before fearing to difturb your Peace, and thought I ought to be fatisfied with the Confcioufnefs of having behaved as was my Duty without acquainting you with it.————At that time I knew not you had any Sufpicion of his Fidelity, though I knew he gave but too much Reafon for it, and was fearful of creating in you any Difquiet on that Score, though he gave me very cruel Motives of Complaint ; but as I find now your Ladyfhip is no longer deceived by his Pretences, I think it proper you fhould not be ignorant of what is in my Powere to reveal, becaufe it may give you fome Hints what   Courfe will be moft likely to reclaim him. Here fhe ceas'd   attending my Permiffion, which I immediately gave her, and was, indeed, not a little impatient to hear what fhe had to fay.

I was not quite Sixteen, faid fhe, when Monfieur *De G*————happening I fuppofe to have a Vacancy in his Heart,   which any new   Object might fil up, took a Fancy to me.   You may remember, Madam, I had not then the Honour to be fo near your Ladyfhip's Perfon, as I am at prefent : My Bufinefs was to attend your Daughter, and wholly taken up with pleafing her, my Ambition extended no farther, and as I was never much guilty of diving into things in which I had no Concern, I penetrated not into the Affairs of the Family, nor had heard of any of that Talk of Monfieu

De G————Amours, as I since have done, and for that Reason was the more surprized, at what afterwards befell me on his Account.

One Day when my young Lady was gone with you to the Opera, Monsieur *De G*————came into my Chamber, where I was ordering some little things of my own in her Absence. What are you alone, *Christina*, said he ?————How happens it you are not with my Daughter at the Opera ? Are you not fond of Musick, or is my Wife so barbarous, as to deny you that Pleasure ?————I knew not well what I said, I was so much surprized at seeing him in my Chamber ; but the Purport of my Answer was that you were too good to all your Family, to refuse them any convenient Satisfaction : Indeed, Madam, continued she, my Confusion was so great at the Honour he did me in speaking to me, which before that time he had never done, that I believe I look'd silly enough, to make him imagine I should readily yield to any thing he should propose.

I perceived he look'd at me with the utmost Attention, seeming to measure me with his Eyes from Head to Foot, the more Eagerness he exprefs'd in viewing me, the more my Consternation encreased ———— you are very beautiful, *Christina*, said he, taking hold of my Hand.————I think it is an Injustice in Fortune to suffer a Girl of so much Merit to be in the Station you are ; and am determined to make you happier than you could ever expect to be. Your Honour is very generous, said I, blushing, to take any Thought of so insignificant a Creature as I am. I know not, resumed he, how mean an Opinion others may have of you, but I see nothing in all *Paris* so amiable————you have a fine Complection————regular Features————a most delightful Shape, and Eyes full of Spirit and Sweetness.————I wish no greater Pleasure than to gaze upon them at full Liberty————why do you turn your Head away ? continued he, coming nearer to me, I must not be denied a Kiss from those little pretty pouting Lips.————For Heaven's sake, Monsieur, cry'd I, leave me, if my young Lady's Governess should happen to come, and see your Honour here, and inform your Lady, what

would

would become of me,————fear nothing, reply'd he,
I have a Servant that watches on the Stairs, and will
give me Notice of any Interruption. In fpeaking this,
he not only kifs'd me with a Vehemence which I
could not approve; but alfo pull'd my Handkerchief on
one Side, and was about to put his Hand into my Bofom; I thought it was time for me now to be very loud,
in hopes that the fear of being heard would oblige him
to retire; but I was miftaken, he had took the wicked
Precaution to fend moft of the Servants out of the way
on various Pretences, and I found myfelf too much in
his Power; for though I had cry'd out twice no body
appear'd to my Affiftance, and he was proceeding to
Extremities.————I was in the utmoft Terror, but
did not lofe a Prefence of Mind which alone could have
faved me————if you have that Regard for me you pretend, faid I, you will give me firft fome Reafon to be
convinced of it.————Take me out of the Servitude I
am in, and I fhall believe you love me, and will be
yours in the Way you defire. With all my Heart, reply'd he, make your Terms, let me but enjoy your
Love, and all you can demand fhall be fettled on you,
beyond even my own Power of taking it from you.
Well then, faid I, you fhall give me a hundred *Lewis
D'Ors* by way of earneft, and after that prepare a
Houfe for me to live in above Contempt. I agree,
cry'd he, quite tranfported, and taking me in his Arms;
no, faid I, drawing back, no Favours till I have the
Money.————Well, refumed he, a little furprized, I
believe, to find I was fo much more forward than he
had Reafon to expect on firft attacking me, and withal
fo cunning and mercenary, you might have depended
on my Word, loving you as I do; but fince you infift
upon it, I'll run to my Clofet for the Money, and be
with you again in a Moment.

He was no fooner out of my Room, than I flew up
Stairs to one of your Women, who at that time lay ill,
and by Confequence I was fure to find.————He'll not
come after me here, faid I to myfelf, and I'll take care
never to be alone again.

I took, indeed, so much Precaution, and was always so much upon Guard, that for several Months he could not get an Opportunity of speaking one Word to me; though he made many Contrivances, all which I baffled by the Assistance of my Guardian-Angel.

I began at last to flatter myself, that tired with so many fruitless Attempts he had given it over, and thought of me no more; when as I was rising one Morning, I heard him in my young Lady's Room: A Wainscot Partition only dividing the two Chambers, not a Word that pass'd escap'd me. I was not surpriz'd at his being up so early, for I knew he never lay long; but it seem'd a little strange that he came into his Daughter's Apartment at that Hour, and that the Door was open'd without my being call'd.

At first I could not tell what to think, as Mademoiselle *Mignon* was too young and innocent, to apprehend any thing of that kind her Father had in his Head; I knew not but he might make some Pretence or other of coming into my Chamber, my Door was not fastened, so I bolted it, but so softly as not to be heard, and having thus secured myself, I listened to the Conversation, with more Curiosity than I ever knew before, or have since felt.

Why would you have me complain of poor *Christina* to my Mother, said my dear Lady? She never offended me in her Life, or deserved I should say the least unkind Word of her———That's nothing, reply'd Monsieur *De G*———'tis for her good that I put you upon it:———Therefore do as I command you———I have a Husband for her, and while she continues in our Family, she won't think of settling herself in the World——if you knew the Advantage it would be to her, you would do it without my bidding; but I am sorry to see that one of your Age should so little regard what I say.

He added many other things to the same Purpose, which at last put the young Lady into Tears; but still she remain'd averse to accusing me, still protesting that as I never gave her any Cause she knew not how to frame her Words to such an Untruth. A Remonstrance such as this from a Child, one would imagine should have made a Parent ashamed of his Injustice; but how hardened

dened is the Heart inspired with Inclinations, such as those of Monsieur *De G*————at that Time!

Finding he could not prevail on her to become his Agent in this wicked Purpose, he flew into a Passion, and rising hastily from the Chair he was sitting in, well, said he, I have done; but remember, *Mignon*, I will never forget your Disobedience.

You know, Madam, said *Christina*, the uncommon Love and Respect this sweet Lady has for you both, she burst afresh into Tears, and begging Monsieur *De G*——to come back, entreated his Forgiveness, and promised to be directed by him.

If your Repentance be sincere, said he, I shall forget what's past, but 'tis upon Condition you punctually observe what I shall enjoin.————Tell your Mother, continued he, that you perceive *Christina* is in Love——that she has had the Boldness to entertain her Gallant in your Apartment when you have been abroad——and that coming Home one Day unexpectedly, you found them together and saw him————

I was so terrified, and at the same so provoked at the cruel Stratagem contrived against me, that I unbolted my Door and flew out, what, said I, must Innocence itself be rendered guilty to accuse me?————I see now that nothing will be spared for my Undoing; but mean as I am, my Complaints, perhaps, may move Compassion, when I proclaim to all the World, the Motives Monsieur *De G*————has for having Recourse to such infamous Proceedings;————but first, continued I, my Lady shall be acquainted with the whole Affair———— she is too just and generous not to pity, and afford me her Protection.

I was all in Tears, as I spoke these Words, and was, indeed, coming to inform your Ladyship of the cruel Plot against me; but, Monsieur *De G*————stopp'd me, you are a foolish Girl, cry'd he, you don't think sure I was in earnest.————I said all this only to make you come out of the Chamber, in a Rage, and afford some Diversion to my Daughter. I should, indeed, have been very foolish, if I had not seen this was

spoken

spoken with a Design to give a Turn to the Affair, and by making it pass for a Jest, prevent Mademoiselle *Mignon* from thinking of it any more, or mentioning it to you. I paused a little confidering what was best for me to do, and for the Reasons I have already mention'd, being unwilling to trouble you with it, I retired, though not without a Murmur that exprefs'd my Diffatisfaction.

When I reflected on this Affair, after my Paffion was a little abated, I was perfuaded within myself that as he had ventured to go this Length, he would go yet farther, and never reft till he had found fome way to get me difcharged from the Family, in hope that Misfortune would reduce me to accept of his Propofals, or in Cafe of my Refufal be a fufficient Revenge for the Difappointment I had given him. How to proceed I knew not, loth I was to leave my Place, and ftill more loth to give you any Caufe of Complaint, fo refolved to wait the Iffue, but to be fo careful of myfelf, as never to give him any Opportunity of furprizing me.

Near a Year paft over without my receiving any Moleftation of that kind, when accidentally, pardon me Heaven, I ought not to make ufe of that Expreffion, fince 'twas by thy all-directing Providence alone, I made a Difcovery of a fecond Plot againft me, if poffible more cruel, and more dangerous to me than the former.

Maria the Chambermaid under me, had pretended an exceffive Fear of Spirits, and very much prefs'd me to become her Bedfellow, as both of us lay alone : Though I never did any thing but laugh at fuch Apprehenfions, I complied at laft with her Importunities, and after we had agreed upon it————on the very Night I was firft to be her Gueft, going up Stairs I found a Paper, which I perceived had been folded up in the manner of a Billet.————I open'd it, and read to my inexpreffible Surprize thefe Words.

The LETTER.

E Nclofed you will find a Bill for the five hundred Livres I promifed you ;————I rejoice to hear your Project has been fo fuccefsful————I pretend to go out of
Town

Town to-morrow, that I may not be expected by my Wife; but shall return late in the Evening, and be admitted by one of my own Men, who is in the Secret——— I shall then steal softly into your Chamber, and conceal myself in the Closet you mention, till I find Christina *is in Bed———as she will suppose it to be you, she will make no Noise till it is past her Power to prevent my Designs: all you have to do therefore is to get her from my Daughter's Apartment as soon as possible———I had no Opportunity of speaking to you, so took this Means of giving you a Caution———Farewell, know me always for your Friend.*

Tho' there was no Direction to this Letter, nor Name subscribed; it was easy for me to know the Person that wrote it, or for whom it was designed, and the Danger I had so miraculously escaped; I was sometime before I could resolve how to behave in this Affair, and as it was now near the Time of going to Bed, I was ruminating on it, when the wicked *Maria* came into my Chamber, and told me that your Ladyship had ordered her to do something, which would detain her later than the usual Hour, so desired I would not wait for her but go to Bed, as soon as I was dismissed from my Attendance on Madamoiselle. I looked on her while she was speaking, and whether it were owing to her own Sense of the Crime she was about to be guilty of, or my Knowledge of her Intentions, I cannot say, but certain it is, that she that Moment looked with a Countenance that had something in it hideous———I could not bear to turn my Eyes upon her, but as soon as she had done speaking. I have found a Letter, said I, which I believe belongs to you, and then presented her with the shocking Paper ———never was Confusion such as hers at my delivering it to her, she but cast her Eyes upon it, and was Thunder-struck———good Heaven, cried she, as soon as she could speak, how mysterious are all thy Ways!——— Pardon me, good God! and pardon me, *Christina*——— I see and am ashamed of what I have done, and now re-joyce in the midst of my Disgrace, that the horrid Crime I had consented to further is disappointed of

Q 4

being

being perpetrated. With thefe Words fhe burft into a Torrent of Tears, and appeared fo truly penitent that I was very much moved at it. Well, *Maria*, faid I, I will believe you were unwarily drawn into a Partner-fhip in this cruel Defign upon me————I am pre-ferved, and innocent————it is therefore my Bufinefs now to comfort you————depend upon my free For-givenefs, and that I will always pray you may find Pardon from above————I do affure you I will never divulge any Thing to your Prejudice in the Family————all I have to afk, is that you would write a few Words to Monfieur *De G*————in the manner I fhall dictate; the poor Creature was fo much pierced with my good Nature as fhe termed it, and a juft Senfe of her Error that fhe was willing to do any Thing that would appear a Reparation of her Fault; what I defired her to write was in this Manner.

To Monfieur *De G*————

*T*HE *cruel Project you communicated to me, and which I too readily agreed to forward, is miraculoufly pre-vented from taking Effect————I beg for the fake of your own Peace both here, and hereafter, you will no more profecute an Attempt, which I dare believe Heaven will always render fruitlefs————I am convinced that true Virtue is Heaven's peculiar Care, and if fo, it will be in vain for any one to aim at its Deftruction————the Maid whofe Deftruction both of us had confpired, affures me, fhe will pray, that we have better Minds————a juft Confcioufnefs of my Crime has made me a Convert, I hope the Monitor within your own Breaft will have no lefs Weight with you————all will remain a Secret to my Lady, but it muft be on Condition you for the future forego all Defigns, perillous for thofe who engage in them; and in the end fhameful to yourfelf————that you may do fo therefore is the earneft Wifh of*

Your moft dutiful Servant,
Mar

T

To this she would need add a Postcript, the Words or which as near as I can recollect, were these;

P. S. *I return you the five hundred Livres you were pleased to enclose, for as I look upon them as the Wages of Sin, I durst not put them among those I have acquired by honest Labour, and hope you will convert them to uses more pious and more laudable, than that for which they were bestowed on me.*

When she had finished this Letter, she gave it to the Man whom she knew was entrusted with all the Secrets of his Master, and who had brought her the Letter and the Money. She ordered him to deliver it into his Hands as soon as he should arrive from his pretended Journey, and when she had settled every Thing necessary with him, she returned to me, and gave me the whole Detail by what Sollicitations he had prevailed upon her to become accessary to his intended Crime——— I flatter myself her Letter had some Effect on him, for he has never since, tho' near three Years have been elapsed, ever spoke one Word to me, nor much less ever renewed any Attempts of the Nature I have been mentioning———*Maria*, however a true Penitent, and always ashamed to look me in the Face, in spite of all my Endeavours to reassure her, was never entirely easy and having the offer of being entertained in Madam *De L———*'s Service, your Ladyship knows she quitted yours, since which I have never seen her.

Here *Christina* ended, said Madam *De G———*, and I asked her what Inference she had drawn from this Adventure, that would be of any Service to me. That he stands more in Awe of your Ladyship, replied she, than you perhaps imagine, and that proper Methods might put a stop to his Career of Vice.

The first thing in my Opinion, continued she, should be to find out the Woman who misleads him, then to have her informed that if ever you should find out the Intrigue, you have Power enough to have her confined for Life———at the same Time I would have some Friend of Monsieur *De G———*'s talk to him in a very serious manner and after remonstrating to him the Injustice he

was

was guilty of, and that if he did not immediately change his Course of Life, you should be informed of it, and consequently a Rupture would ensue, your Grievances would be laid open, and his Reputation, which hitherto he had seemed so tenacious of, entirely ruin'd.

Tho' *Christina*'s Advice did not suit with my Inclination, it occasioned in me a whimsical Resolution, and such a one as perhaps no Woman beside myself ever thought on, much less put in Practice————you shall judge of it, my dear *Jeanetta*, continued Madam *De G*————I never remember it without laughing, and I care answer when you know it, you will be no less diverted. But I will not tell you at once the Plot, that came into my Head, tho' I did *Christina*, but acquaint you how step by step I carried it into Execution.

I began with going one Morning into my Husband's Closet, and having enquired how he did, the Carnival, said I, is near at hand, and I have an Inclination to pass both that and the Lent in the Country, and not return to *Paris* till after *Easter*, but would not do it without your Permission, so beg to know how you approve of it. The Idea of my Absence was too agreeable for him not to give a ready Consent ; he not only told me I was my own Mistress, and should be ever so ; but also accompanied that Compliment with a Purse of Gold, in order as he said to make the Carnival more pleasing.

The same Day *Christina* and I set out on our supposed Journey ; but instead of going to my Castle, I went to her Mother's House: having made that Woman acquainted with my Design the Night before————a Man's Taylor was immediately sent for, and they having provided me with a Night-Gown, Cap and Slippers to prevent his having any Suspicion I was not of the Sex I pretended, I made him take my Measure, and bespoke two Suits of Cloaths, the one extremely rich, the other less so, and ordered them to be made with all possible speed. My Commands were punctually obeyed, and in less than four Days every Thing was got ready and I was metamorphosed into a fine Monsieur, and you cannot conceive how much this Disguise became me. Both *Christina*, and her Mother protested that I personated

a

a Man ſo naturally, that it was impoſſible for any one to think I was not really ſo.

Now, my dear *Jeanetta*, you will ſoon ſee into my Plot, which hitherto I dare anſwer you have no Notion of ;———I had one Footman who I knew was perfectly in my Intereſt. This Fellow I had ordered to be a conſtant Spy on my Huſband, and watch wherever he went, that he might find out where this Miſtreſs who gave me ſo much Pain was lodged.

As Monſieur *De G*———imagined me out of Town, he was ſomewhat leſs cautious than he had been, ſo that it was no difficult Taſk for my Deſires ſo far to be accompliſhed In three Days the Man brought me News that a Lady whom my Huſband went every Day to viſit, often dined with, and ſeldom ſupped from, was called Madamoiſelle *Julia,* and that ſhe lived in a little Street near *Fauxbourg Saint Honoré.* This Diſcovery I looked upon as half Succeſs, and immediately employed a Perſon *Chriſtina*'s Mother recommended to me, to enquire in the Neighbourhood where this Woman was lodged, what publick Places ſhe frequented, and I ſoon found out that ſhe went very often to the Opera, and Comedy, both of which ſhe was extremely fond of. I hired this Fellow as a Footman, and without entruſting him with my Secret, for he imagined he ſerved a Maſter not a Miſtreſs, I made him get acquainted with *Julia*'s Servant ; and he ſoon proved how fit he was for the Purpoſe I employed him in, for ſuppoſing I had a mind to have an Intrigue with this Woman, he brought me an exact Intelligence of all her Motions.

Being informed ſhe was gone to the Theatre, what Dreſs ſhe had on, and in what Box ſhe was ſeated, I followed her thither, and ſoon diſcovered by the Deſcription, which of the many Ladies there, was ſhe I ſought after. She was tall, well ſhaped, and accompanied by another Woman, ſomewhat elder than herſelf, but very well dreſſed. I went into the next Box to her's, but had not preſently a full View of her Face, it being ſo early that the Candles were not yet lighted, excepting ſome few here and there. The Houſe however was extremely full, as it could not be expected to be otherwiſe, that

being

being the firſt Night of the Repreſentation of one of Monſieur *Voltair*'s Tragedies———you have heard me often ſpeak, continued Madame *De G*———of that admirable Author, and may remember with what Praiſes ; indeed in this, I but concurred with the publick Voice in doing Juſtice to his Merit———the Knowledge of the Author who furniſhed this Night's Entertainment, was ſufficient to draw all the Perſons of Senſe, or who deſired the Reputation of it to be preſent.

When the Candles were lighted, I had a full View of the Face of Madamoiſelle *Julia*, and heard her ſay in a very low Voice to the Perſon who was with her, that ſhe trembled leſt Monſieur *De G*———ſhould come to the Play. By this I found ſhe had not acquainted him with it, and could gather from ſome other Words they ſaid to each other, that he was jealous of her, which pleaſed me extremely, as it forwarded my Contrivance.

Here I could not forbear interrupting Madam *De G*———I am in the utmoſt Impatience, cried I, for Heaven ſake dear Madam do me the favour to tell me what end you propoſed to yourſelf by doing all this ; for I am utterly unable by what you have ſaid to comprehend any Part of your Deſign.

You are in very great haſte, replied Madam *De G*— with a Smile, it would be but juſt to keep you in Suſpence, as they do in Romances, 'till the Incidents that follow, ſhould by Degrees, give you leave to gueſs at the Cataſtrophe ; but I ſhould make a very gracious Queen, I don't love to refuſe any thing in my power to beſtow, without Prejudice to others———know then, that my Deſign was to get if poſſible the Affection of Mademoiſelle *Julia*, make an Aſſignation with her, and contrive it ſo, that my Huſband might ſurpriſe us together, and to be convinced of the Infidelity of thoſe ſort of Creatures.

Had I been a Man, I know not if I had not in good earneſt, become the Rival of Monſieur *De G*——— *Julia* had an enchanting Sprightlineſs in her Countenance———her Complexion was of a dazzling Whiteneſs, and when ever ſhe looked upon you, her Eyes

ſeemed

feemed to fpeak, and command your Admiration——the more I examined her, the lefs I was furprifed at my Hufband's Paffion for her, yet it did not hinder me from profecuting my Defign, and tho' I was far from hating her, I could not bear he fhould continue to love her.

It was no difficult Matter for me to make an Acquaintance with her : Women of her Character, tho' never fo well fupported by one Man, are ready to enter into Converfation, with as many as fhall think it worth their while to endeavour it. I talked a great deal to her, and as I was well drefs'd, and fhe took me for a Perfon of Diftinction, was very much pleafed with the Compliments I made her. I entreated Permiffion to vifit her, and tho' fhe did not immediately grant my Requeft, I eafily perceived fhe would do fo before we parted——when the Play began, I was fo charm'd with it, that I had like to have forgot the Bufinefs which brought me there——raife your Idea to every thing that can be called excellent, yet it will ftill be fhort of what this juftly celebrated Poet prefents us with——a Delicacy of Sentiment could never be carried to a higher Pitch——every thing was majeftic, noble and interefting——the Actors were more the Heroes they perfonated, than themfelves ever were in reality—— Fancy, Energy, Sublimity, Tendernefs were all united in this inftructive Compofition——Happy are they who poffefs Talents fuch as *Voltaire*, they merit to have Monuments erected to their Memory, which fhould continue to the end of Time—in doing Honour to Authors of this Rank, we do Honour to ourfelves, and fhew pofterity we had a Tafte capable of relifhing Perfection.

I was not however quite unmindful of myfelf, and took the Opportunity of attacking *Julia* between the Acts, and had the Satisfaction, to obferve that every time I fpoke to her, fhe feemed more and more difpofed to liften to me, and when at laft I prefs'd her very home, it is not, faid fhe, out of any diflike to your Perfon, or Converfation, that I am at all reluctant to admit your Vifits; on the contrary, you appear in my Eyes a dangerous Man——there is fomething too agreeable both in your Form, and Wit, for a Woman, who would pre-

serve her Heart, to truft herfelf much with————Befides, continued fhe, I have fome other private Reafons,
which deter me from entring into an Acquaintance with
you. Here fhe ceafed, but as I would not take what
fhe faid as a Denial, I renewed my Petition in terms
fo ftrong, that fhe at laft confented, with this Condition, that the Vifits I made her, fhould be between the
Hours of Dinner and Supper, and that I would never
infift on ftaying a Moment longer, than fhe thought
it proper I fhould go. All this I readily agreed to,
and the Preliminaries being fettled, I had leave to vifit her next Day, on which I faid every thing that Men
ufually do on fuch Occafions, and perhaps exceeded moft
of them in my Complaifance, Women knowing beft
what will be moft pleafing to their own Sex. She feemed,
indeed, charmed with the Tranfports I exprefs'd, but
faid, as I was leading her to a Coach, that waited for her,
and the Perfon that accompanied her, You Men are deceitful ; while we are new to you, nothing fo complaifant
and fond ; but when once you have obtained your Wifhes,
nothing more carelefs and indifferent————However,
tho' I know this, there is fomething in my Heart, which
will not fuffer me to be ungrateful to the Efteem you
exprefs for me. She fpoke this with fo engaging an Air,
that had I really been what fhe took me for, I had certainly been in love with her.

I was careful not to omit the appointed hour next Day,
but was very much mortified at being obliged to quit the
Houfe, without feeing her, tho' indeed I learned enough
to make me know my Plot was in as fair a Way of fucceeding, as I could wifh. At my Arrival, I found
ftanding at the Door, the Woman who had been with
her at the Play, and who I foon difcovered was no other
than her Servant and Confidant: She took me into a little
Parlour, and told me, that Madamoifelle *Julia* was extremely concerned, that I fhould have the Trouble
of coming at a Time, when it was impoffible fhe could
admit me, a Perfon whom fhe did not expect being, unluckily with her, and it was wholly improper I fhould be feen.

I thought, at firft, that this Difappointment was a
Piece of Artifice, common enough with fuch Women, to
heighten

heighten the Paffion I had pretended, and to bring me
to explain myfelf, as to the Advantages, fhe might expect from my Acquaintance: in order, therefore, to prevent my labour being loft, when I fhould come again,
it feemed proper I fhould begin by gaining *Gogo*, fo
was this Woman called, fo made her a Prefent of ten
Lewis D'Ors.————She blufhed at receiving them,
but whither through Joy, or Modefty, I leave you to
guefs, the Gold however had its ufual Effect————it
purchafed every Secret I defired————She informed
me that Monfieur *De G*————was paffionately in love
with her Miftrefs, that he was extremely jealous of her,
and that it was no other than himfelf, who was at that time
above with her————he was told, faid fhe, by fome
of his Spies, that you talked to her at the Play laft
Night, and when we came home we found him waiting
for us: he reproached her Ingratitude and ill Conduct,
as he termed it, and has never left the Houfe fince.
What makes us more unhappy, is, that his Wife is now
out of Town, and having no reftraint upon him, we
fhall find it an infinite Difficulty to do any thing without being in Danger of his furprifing us————We ufed
to have fome Hours of the Day to ourfelves, but now
he either fends or comes fo perpetually, that we have a
miferable Time.

I then afked if Monfieur *De G*————made any amends
by his Liberality for the Trouble he gave. To which
fhe replied, that they had no reafon to complain, but that
fhe thought he might do better, for fhe knew him to be
immenfely rich: But, added fhe, Madamoifelle *Julia*,
is not of a mercenary Temper————Complaifance more
endears a Man to her, than all the Riches in the World
————to offer her a Gratuity, for any Favours fhe
beftows, is the fame thing, as ftriking a Ponyard to her
Heart————I have often blamed this Folly in her, but
there is no conquering Nature————I am obliged, continued the cunning *Gogo*, to receive all the Prefents made
to her, and to inftruct her Lovers how to behave if
they would fucceed——if any one was to bring her a
Sum of Money, or even a Ring or Bracelet, fhe would
that Minute forbid him her Houfe.

I took no Notice of what she had said on this Score,
being determined not to pay too dear for my Curiosity,
but asked her, how Monsieur *De G——* behaved,
so as, to get into her good Graces ; why that, Monsieur,
answered she, was all owing to me——he was quite
brutal at the first, he fell in love with her at the O-
pera, had her followed home. and the next Morning
wrote a Letter to acquaint her, that he was very much
charm'd with her, that he knew she was kept by a Counsellor of the Parliament, who did not allow her very handsomely, and if she would break with him, said her I
will give you a hundred *Lewis d'Ors* in hand, and a
thousand Crowns per Month.

A fine way of Courtship indeed, cryed *Gogo*, my Mif-
tress was highly affronted, and I went to him and re-
proved him, for his want of Politeness to a Woman of
her Merit——he swore he had made use of the same
Method to above twenty, who had never resented it,
and to prove the Truth of what he said, shewed me a Letter, which he told me was the Original of what he wrote
to all whom he had any Design upon of that Nature.

I could scarce forbear Laughing, when she spoke this,
in her Account I saw my Husband's Picture drawn to
the Life ; but as I wanted to be informed of all relating
to this Affair, I asked her how she brought it about,
that two such Opposites as she described, should at last
agree. Why, said she, I undertook to reconcile my
Mistress to him, but obliged him to pay down a whole
Years Advance into my Hands, besides the hundred
Lewis d'Ores, and then he had leave to come, and the
Counsellor was dismissed——But, pursued she, you
cannot imagine the difficulty I had to bring him to part
with all that Money at once, and I don't know whither
ever he would have done it, if I had not made him believe the Counsellor was so much in Love, that we
were in hopes of drawing him in to marry her.

I was now sufficiently instructed by this most extraordinary Servant, every Passage relating to my Husband
and his Mistress, and could not help reflecting how
ridiculous Men make themselves by putting it into the
Power of such Wretches to expose them at their Pleasure,

but

but this not being a Place to indulge Meditation, I took my leave after having gained a Promise from her to contrive some means of my seeing her Mistress the next Day either at her own House, or some other Place she would find out.

By all that had passed I had no reason to Despair, and I found *Gogo* punctual to her Promise the next Day—they had on some Pretence or other got rid of Monsieur *De G*— and the beautiful *Julia* received me in a manner, which left me no room to doubt I had made a real Impression on her Heart, a thing not very common with Women of her Stamp————she was alone, and I could easily perceive she had summon'd all her Charms that Day, to compleat a Conquest over me————I say again, that had I been of a different Sex I must have loved her, there was a Modesty and Sweetness in her Conversation, that in spite of the Injury she had done me, made it impossible for me to hate her, and I found some kind of Consolation in my Misfortune, that I was not sacrificed, as I have known some very deserving Women, to a Wretch without any one Allurement, but Vice to justify the Change. I had not forgot the manner in which the Men make their first Advances, and behaved so as to make a very swift Progress in her Favour; all that remained farther for the compleating my Project was to procure an Assignation at Night, and contrive it so that my Husband should surprize us together.

But, my dear *Jeanetta*, continued Madam *De G*— when I was on the Point of entreating this destructive Favour of her, a Tenderness rose in my Heart, and pleaded so strongly in her Favour, that I hesitated a good while before I could speak of it————she seemed to love me so sincerely, had given me so endearing a Reception, and I discovered so much Sense and Good-nature in her, that I thought it an unparallelled Piece of Cruelty to contrive the Ruin of so amiable a Person, and who put so much Confidence in me————in fine, tho' Resentment struggled hard, yet I could not bring myself to a Resolution.

I had visited her four Days together, without coming

to the Point, for which I had taken all this Pains, but on the fifth, she put a Period to my Agitations, by making me of her own accord an Appointment to come the next Day towards Evening, which, said she, I am determined to pass with you, having something to communicate to you in private.

It was then my Business, according to the Scheme I had laid, to order that Servant I before mentioned as in my Interest, to acquaint Monsieur *De G——* that *Julia* had a new Gallant, and that they were together at that Time, that he might have come and detected her in her Perfidy, yet did I not do this, and perhaps my Pity would forever have got the better of my Jealousy, had not Chance done that for me, which I could not prevail on myself to do : But of that hereafter.

I went according to the Time : *Gogo* was ordered to tell my Husband in case he should come, that *Julia* was gone abroad——I know, said that unfortunate Woman, that he will be incensed to the highest Degree, and perhaps run in search of me over half the Town, but where we do not love, we little regard the Pains we give to our Admirers——I know at any Time how to make my Peace with him, a few Tears, or a well counterfeited fainting away, will make him forego even the Testimony of his own Eyes, so, my dear Chevalier, continued she, we will have some Hours to ourselves in Spite of all his jealous Watchfulness.

You must know, pursued Madam *De G——* that as it was necessary I should assume some Name, I took that of the Chevalier *Bellcour* upon me ; but I now began to think I had brought myself into a Perplexity I should not know how to extricate myself from : *Julia's* Advances made me fearful she would expect I should be more the Lover than was in my power to be, and how to excuse a Coldness so out of Nature, and contrary to the Passion I had professed for her, I could not by any means contrive——I was just thinking to pretend a sudden Indisposition had seized me, and take my leave ; and was preparing my Countenance to agree with what I designed to affect, when the charming *Julia* eased me of my Apprehensions, by these Words.   I

I love you, my dear *Belicour*, said she, and it is my Opinion of your Honour that engages me to do so, and also to make you the Confidant of the most secret Passages of my Life———tho' you are a Man, I imagine I see something in you directly opposite to the common Artifices, Deceptions, and Vices of your Sex, and therefore I will venture to lay open all my Soul, and implore your Assistance, as a Man of Virtue, and a Friend ; for believe me that notwithstanding the Life I lead, I often waste whole Days in Tears and bitter Reflections. On what, beautiful *Julia*, interrupted I, you much amaze me———such Discourses are indeed what I little expected, but I beseech you let me know in what I can be able to serve you. What she had said had indeed very much moved me, and at that Instant I felt for her all that could be expected from a Friend, such as she seemed to want.

Yes, my dear Chevalier, resumed the weeping *Julia*, you are the only Person I ever saw who seems qualified both by Power and Inclination to put an end to my Distresses, and restore to me that Peace of Mind, which has long alas been a Stranger to me, but you shall be judge yourself, if you will will permit me to reveal my unhappy Story, it will not be tedious and perhaps may let you more into the Deceit and Hypocrisy of some Sort of People than yet you have any Notion of.

I told her she would do me a Pleasure in reposing such a Confidence in me, which I gave her my solemn Promise never to abuse, on which she began her little Narrative in this Manner.

The HISTORY of *Julia.*

I OWE my Birth, said she, to the Amour of Monsieur the Marquis *De*———a general Officer, and Mademoiselle *De R*———the late celebrated Comedian——— I was privately brought up by a Woman, who had lived with

with my Mother, but falling into very bad Circumstances, I was left without Support————accustomed to Ease I knew not how to get my Bread by Labour———— Necessity, not Inclination, made me enter into the way of Life you find me in————the first I yielded to, made me hope a Provision for my whole Days, but all his Promises were vain————he quitted me for a new Object, I was obliged to listen to the Temptations of a new Lover————he deceived me like the other————a third————a fourth————a fifth did all the same, and tho' so oft a Mistress, found myself without a Friend—— it has not been in my Power to quit a Life which I so much detest, that the Approaches of a Man on that Score, is dreadful to me, and I shudder at the Apprehensions of what some of my Sex as well as yours, are but too well pleased with————I am every Day doing Penance, even while I am going the Road to Perdition, and I hazard the Salvation of my Soul elsewhere for doing what I would give any thing but my Soul to avoid———— miserable here, and desponding for hereafter, I shall be reduced to the most frightful Extremity if not speedily relieved.

You seem surprized, continued she, and indeed have Reason to be so————I know my Words carry an Enigma in them which nothing can solve but entring into a serious Consideration on the Circumstances I am in—— I am sensible that most People would tell me it was easy for me to quit a Course of Life so infamous to the whole World, and which I myself pretend to have an Aversion for————they would say all is but Artifice in me, that if I really repented I should reform, and that there were many ways by which I might subsist, if my Inclinations to live virtuous, were sincere.

But *Chevalier*, pursued she, I think, or I am much deceived, yet have a fund of Compassion in your Heart, that will not suffer you to judge of me with so little Charity, you will reflect how hard it is for a Woman educated in a genteel, tho' not a grand Manner, to descend to servile Offices for her Support————you will also think that even were all remembrances of former

Plenty to be forgot by me, the Vices I have been guilty of, would not be so far forgot, as to suffer me to be received into any Family of Reputation————you will rather pity than condemn me, but to shew you how much I have been disappointed hitherto in all my Attempts to change my Situation, I shall relate what I believe will seem very strange, but yet what Heaven knows to be true.

About a Year ago, being as now extremely alarmed at the State I was in, I made a firm Resolution to quit it, and of doing every thing in my Power to lose myself from these scandalous and wicked Bonds, which so long had fettered me————for this Purpose I sent for a Priest, I entreated he would take upon him the Direction of my future Actions, acknowledged to him my past Faults, lamented the Misery of my present Situation, and conjured him by his sacred Function to take Compassion on me, and find some charitable Means of extricating me from the Labyrinth of Guilt and Shame, I was involved in.

He listened to me with all imaginable Attention, exacted as the first Proof of my Sincerity, that I should make a general Confession, and while I was preparing for it refrain any Repetition of my former Irregularites, and concluded with assuring me, that if he found me a true Penitent he would exert the utmost of his Power to procure me an honest Subsistance.

This gave me some Consolation, and resolved to be guided entirely by his Advice, I discharged my Servants; sold the best Part of my Furniture, and all the superfluous Ornaments of Dress; broke off with a Lover who had provided for me, and retired to a little Lodging some distance from Town, where I lived concealed from all my former Acquaintance, past my Time in bewailing my Errors and beseeching Heaven to enable me to abandon the World for ever and its deceitful Pleasures.

My Director came frequently to visit me, and examine what Progress I made in my pious Resolution———— I hid from him nothing of the Truth, omitted no Part of the Penances he enjoyned me, and prayed twice as often as he had told me was necessary————no Acts of Mortification but what I chearfully went through, yet

in

in fpite of this State of Humiliation, Tears, Fafting, and all that can denote a Convert, I was three whole Months without being able to prevail on him to give me Abfolution. He told me he durft not pronounce the facred Benediction, till he was fully convinced, that what I called a Converfion, was not rather a Difguft, which might perhaps wear off, and I return to my former Vices——I then afked what I could do farther to render myfelf worthy of what I defired with fo much Ardency ; and he anfwered that I muft perfevere, and time alone could prove the Sincerity of my Intentions. I often bemoaned myfelf to him, that I was fo long delayed the Seal of my Tranquility, he remained inflexible, and nothing I could urge had the leaft Efficacy.

All this Time I was diminifhing the little Money I had received for the Goods I had difpofed of, and at length I had nothing left for the common Neceffaries of Life——I then fell into a Melancholly, which was bordering on Defpair, and rendered me guilty of frefh Sins——this I communicated alfo to my Confeffor, and than it was I found the true Motive of his behaving to me in that manner——.

O my dear Chevalier, continued the forrowful *Julia*, this Wretch, for I can call him by no other Name, fince he prophaned the facred Order he had affumed, made Religion a Cover for the moft deteftable Purpofes, and inftead of leading his Penitents the way to Heaven, aimed to plunge them headlong into Perdition——this Man, this Monfter, was become enamoured of me, and knowing by my Confeffions, that my Soul was averfe to any fuch Crime, tho' I had fo oft been guilty of it, contrived thefe Delays to the end my Subftance being gone, he might ftarve me to Compliance.——
When he found me reduced to the laft Extremity, he made his impious Propofals to me, and in fuch daring, fuch blafphemous Terms as I tremble to remember——enraged, and fhocked I drove him from my Chamber, told him that if he ever prefumed to come into my Sight again, I would make my Complaint to his Superiors, that he might be punifhed according to his Deferts.

I

But

But alas! what was I preparing for myself? I might have thought he that could proceed so far would scruple nothing————my Refusal of his horrid Offers, turned the Love he had for me into the extremest Hate: He swore he would be revenged, and he kept his Word.

I fell into a violent Passion of mingled Grief and Horror after he was gone, and when I had a little vented it in Tears, prayed Heaven that the Baseness and Cruelty of this true Wolf in Sheep's Cloathing, might not stagger my Resolution, and I do assure you, that after having paid this Duty, I found my Heart more at Ease, and I determin'd the next Day to seek for some other more worthy Pastor; but here again my Designs were frustrated, about the Close of Day came an Exempt and four Soldiers, and hurry'd me to Prison without acquainting me with my Offence, or assigning any Reason for doing so, but the Execution of their Commission.

O! what an exorbitant Power has the Church, and how careful ought they who are the Heads of it, to be in strictly examining the Morals of those received into Holy Orders!————This cruel Priest, I afterwards heard had accused me of having spoke contemptuously of the Priesthood, and this was enough for being confined, till I should make my publick Submissions, or rather a private one to this Seducer; who frequently sent me Word, that if I would comply with what he had proposed, I should not only be enlarg'd, but maintain'd in a handsome manner, out of the Charities given to the Church; but I chose to perish sooner than ever yield, to what I always look'd upon, and still do, as the worst kind of Sacrilege. It was to no Purpose, I told my Story to all that came near me————it was in vain I wrote and petition'd—all I alledged was look'd upon as an Invention, and an Aggravation of my Crimes————some would not report it, and those that did, had no other Effect than to occasion my being more severely treated.

Near three Months did I languish in this miserable Situation, and I began to despair of ever being released, when Providence ordain'd it so, that the Author of my Misfortune should also, though much against his Design, be the means of delivering me.—He had the Bold-

neſs to make the ſame Overtures he had done to me, to
the Wife of a Commiſſary———ſhe had Preſence enough
of Mind to ſeem yielding to his Deſires, appointed him
a Time to viſit her, acquainted her Huſband with it,
who with ſeveral Friends and two Prieſts, who without
knowing why they were invited, were placed in the
next Room, and wereWitneſſes of his Prophaneneſs———
He was immediately ſeized, the Order was ſcandalized
by it, and a long Series of Crimes of the like Nature
being afterwards proved upon him, my Complaint came
under Conſideration, and I was ſet at Liberty———what
became of him I know not, but it is thought he was
privately made away with, to prevent farther Noiſe.

The firſt Uſe I made of my Enlargment was to go to
Church, and return Thanks to Heaven. I had heard
from the Woman with whom I lodg'd, of a Man who
had an excellent Character, both for his Piety and Learning———to him I applied, and acquainted him with my
whole Hiſtory : He ſeem'd ſtruck with Horror at the
Proceedings of my former Confeſſor, and took three
Days to conſider what could be done for me ; at the
End of which he came to me, and told me he had now
thought of ſomething to enable me to paſs the Remainder
of my Days in Peace.

I had not Patience to aſk him what it was, ſo tranſported was I at the hope of being reſcued from Want,
which I now felt ſeverely.———I threw myſelf at his
Feet, aſſuring him I ſhould be eternally oblig'd to him,
and that I would pray inceſſantly to Heaven for his Preſervation.

But, O ! *Belcour*, what had he done for me !———
is it thus good Heaven, that the Stewards of Charity di-
ſtribute the Sums that are raiſed in pious Contributions !
———He had ordered I ſhould be received into the
Convent of *les Filles du bon Paſteur*, and order'd me to
be there next Day, where he would meet, and introduce me.

I knew very well what ſort of a religious Houſe this
was, and that in order to be admitted, I muſt own myſelf to have been a common Proſtitute; as I had never
been what can juſtly be called ſo, though render'd too

guilty

guilty by my Neceffities, that Thought was infupportable: Neither, indeed, did a Convent, though of the moft reputable kind, at all fuit me ——I ftifled my Grief and Difappointment, however, as well as I was able ; knowing by Experience how dangerous it is to irritate the Church, and promifed to be there at the Time he mention'd; though, indeed, I never intended to keep my Word, nor feek Confolation from fuch People, where fo much is wanting to render them either compaffionate or charitable, and who think all Virtue confifts in a blind and rigid Zeal.

I was now oppreft with Sorrow, and in the moft deftitute and forlorn Condition imaginable, after a thoufand cruel Reflections, I bethought me of a Servant who had formerly had lived with me, and received fome Profit by her Service.——I wrote to her to come to me, and fhe immediately obey'd my Summons ; fhe had always a tender Regard for me, and fhe gave me Proofs of it, after I had with Tears related all that had happened to me——inftead of making me any Anfwer, fhe left my Chamber with as much hafte as fhe had entered it; and I began to think that fhe had deferted me on the Account of my Diftrefs ; but I was foon convinced to the contrary, in about a quarter of an Hour fhe returned, and brought with her all fhe was Miftrefs of in the World, defiring I would make ufe of it as my own, and that fhe fhould think herfelf happy to be again my Servant, and to fpend all her Days with me.——I embraced her with Gratitude and Tendernefs, accepted her Offer, and gave her my Promife that whatever happened, I would never more part from her.——It is this *Gogo* who you now fee with me, and to whom I have been fo much obliged, that I love her with the Affection of a Sifter.

Thus was I compell'd again by my cruel Deftiny to return to what I had taken fo much Pains to avoid — a Counfellor of the Parliament for fome time fupported me ; but as I found he was on the Point of withdrawing his Allowance, I broke off with him in Favour of Monfieur *De G————*, from whom I at prefent receive a handfome Maintainance. This, dear *Belcour*, is my real

History, from which you may easily comprehend, how much I abhor the Life I lead, and how infinitely I should rejoice in having an Opportunity of quitting it.

I was moved even to Tears, continued the excellent Madam *De G*———at this melancholy Relation; but had the utmost Impatience to know what Designs she could have on me, and why she had made Choice of one so much a Stranger to her, for her Adviser and Confident. I was going to ask in what she would command me, when she prevented me by saying; you are the only Man in the World that I depend on to draw me from the Precipice in which I am fallen.———You have often assured me that you love me, and as you have never approach'd me with those Freedoms which render your Sex so disagreeable to me, I am apt to flatter myself it is rather a solid Friendship, than a vague and wanton Passion you are inspired with in my Favour.———I hope I do not deceive myself in this Conjecture; but to make Tryal of it, assist me I conjure you in taking the only Step I wish.———I only ask your Protection———the Money Monsieur *De G*———has bestowed on me, is sufficient to set me up in some honest Trade; I would change my Name, and Place of Abode, as well as my Conduct; and as a Person cannot go to any strange Place without some Recommendation, 'tis that I would entreat of you, depending on your Secrecy and Readiness to promote my Interest, when you shall find my Industry entitles me to it.

I was opening my Mouth to answer her Requests, and to encourage her in a Design I so much approved, when we heard *Gogo*'s Voice screaming at the Door, and using her utmost Efforts from hindering Monsieur *De G*——— from coming in.———He had been inform'd that *Julia* was not gone out, and that a Gentleman had been seen to enter———half frantick with Rage and Jealousy, and determin'd to be convinced, it was in vain she attempted to obstruct his Passage, he rushed in with two of his Servants, flew up Stairs, and seeing the Door shut where we were, order'd them to break it open immediately.

Julia was terrified lest Murder should ensue, if I were found with her, I told her that I had infallible Means to pacify him, yet to make her easy I would conceal myself——she entreated I would, and I went into a Closet while she unlock'd the Door. The Scene was very pleasant, my Husband began to storm, on which she affected to be as much in a Passion.——He asked what she had done with her Gallant, she protested none had been with her ; but that being indisposed, she had order'd *Gogo* to deny her to him.——In fine, after a great many Reproaches on both sides, they quarrelled themselves Friends ; and *Julia* desired he would go with her into the next Room, pretending she had something to shew him, imagining no doubt, but that I would take that Opportunity of escaping ; but that was not my Business.——No time could be so fit as this for the Execution of my Design, and just as my Husband passed by the Closet, I stirr'd myself so as to make him hear somebody was there——he started, and then cry'd out, infamous Woman ! is it thus you have deceived me ? these Words were accompanied with several Blows, which made her cry out.——I flew from my Concealment and, laying one Hand upon my Sword, and with the other, taking him by the Shoulder, fye, Monsieur, said I, how dare you treat a young Lady with such unmanly Insolence ?——Monsieur *De G*——was never very fond of Rencounters, such as my Behaviour threatned ; he grew pale, and stepping back, cry'd he had paid too dear for that unworthy Woman, not to have her all to himself ——that might have been proper enough some Years ago, said I ; but Men of your Age are fit only to maintain Mistresses for those who are younger.——I could, not speak this without bursting into a Fit of Laughter which spoiled all. Monsieur *De G*—— presently knew me ; but was, perhaps, more alarmed at doing so, than he had been before.——My Wife, said he, and was so disconcerted that he fell back into an easy Chair ; as I was fearful of the Effects of such a Surprize, I threw myself upon him, and instead of reproaching his Infidelity, rally'd him in a fond manner, for his tyrannical Treatment of so lovely a Creature as *Julia*.

His Astonishment and Confusion being a little over. he begg'd to know the meaning of this whimsical Adventure,

venture, I gave him the whole Detail of it without Difguise, and concluded by saying, that so far from disapproving the Esteem he had for my charming Rival, I would be the first to entreat he never would withdraw it.

If seeing me in her Apartment, and in a Habit he could little have imagin'd I should ever assume, had surprized him, it was far inferior to what this Request occasion'd in him——he look'd on me, and then on *Julia* ——lifted his Eyes one Moment to Heaven, the next fixed them on the Ground, and appear'd in such Perplexity, that I thought it necessary to ease him of it, which I did by obliging *Julia* to repeat her Story. Not all the Terror and Confusion, the Discovery who I was had given her, could hinder her from discanting on her Misfortunes with a peculiar Grace.———She concluded with the most earnest Entreaty, to be taken from her present way of Life, and interwove her Supplications with such pious Reflections, on the Article of Salvation, that Monsieur *De G*———could not help being moved. ——We all wept in Concert, and on my desire my Husband settled a Pension on her, sufficient to maintain her above Want.

Thus, my dear *Jeanetta*, continued Madam *De C*———ended an Adventure, on the Success of which I do not a little value myself.———*Julia* remains in *Paris*, and lives in a manner conformable to the good Inclinations, which won me to take pity of her.———I visit her as often as I come to Town, and have a great deal of Pleasure in her Conversation; but my greatest Happiness is, that Monsieur *De G*———is entirely reclaimed, and leads a Life of the utmost Regularity, for which he is so complaisant as to tell me, I may thank my own good Conduct and Sweetness of Disposition.

We enter'd the Town where we were to dine, just as Madam *De G*———had finish'd her Story.——I thought it no less agreeable than interesting, and it gave Occasion to many Reflections on the Temptations of Poverty, and the Duty incumbent on Parents to provide for their Children a Refuge from it, as far as is in their Power.

The Evening of the fame Day we arrived at the Caftle————Monfieur *De G*————received me with the greateft Refpect, and the young Mademoifelle *Mignon* with an equal fhare of Tendernefs.————I teftified my Gratitude by all the Acknowledgments that Words could form, and as all the Civilities that pafs'd between me and this amiable Family were perfectly fincere, the Pleafure was fo too.

After the firft Compliments were over, I afk'd for *Chriftina,* fhe was in the Room, but fo alter'd by a late Fit of Sicknefs, that I did not know her; but on hearing me mention her Name fhe flew to me, took me in her Arms, and thanked me for remembring her. Indeed, I always loved her, but the Inftance her Lady had given me of her Virtue, render'd her much dearer to me than ever.

Madam *De G*————conducted me to the Apartment defign'd for me, and I had fcarce put off my Travelling Habit, when her Hufband, who had left us alone together, came in and afk'd if I was ready to fee fome Company who were juft arrived? I had no time to reply, that Moment the old Marquis enter'd follow'd by his Son, and the Count *De Saint Fal.* I was all in Confufion at the fight of them, for though by all Circumftances I concluded I was to meet them there, and that in this Houfe I fhould receive the Decifion of my Fate, yet I could not help feeling at their Prefence, fome Emotions to which I knew not well how to give a Name.

The old Marquis complimented me on my Recovery, but neither of the young Noblemen fpoke a Syllable, nor offer'd to approach me; I followed their Example, and directed my Difcourfe wholly to him who had fpoken to me;————after I had wifh'd him Joy on his looking fo well, he told me that the Small-Pox in his Opinion had rather improved than any way diminifh'd my Beauty ; but as to my Son, faid he, it is quite otherwife, if ever he was happy in the Affections of the fair Sex, he muft not now expect a Continuance of it; that rugged Face of his will entirely lofe him among the Ladies. This little Piece of Raillery I thought touch'd me, and I could not keep myfelf from anfwering, that the Love of a Woman, who regarded only the Perfon of

a Man was little to be valued; but put the Cafe my
Sex were all fo weak, the young Marquis had no Reafon to be alarm'd fince he feem'd the fame as ever in
my Eyes. I took this Opportunity of giving him a
Glance, which convey'd much more of my Soul than
was proper for me to reveal in Words   You are very
good, *Jeanetta*, faid the old Marquis, but partial Eyes
fpy no Defects, fo I am not furprized at it.

I made no reply to thefe Words, but blufh'd and hung
down my Head, as fearing I had already fpoke too
much.————The old Marquis feem'd all collected in
himfelf, and ruminating on fomething very material——
in Complaifance to him the whole Company were mute,
and there was a general Silence, for I believe the Space
of Three Minutes.————I knew not what to think
————Hope and Fear by Turns poffefs'd me, and Suf-
pence gave a hurry to my Spirits, which had it continued much longer, might have had a bad Effect on me.
————I trembled inwardly, and it was with Difficulty
I kept my Countenance from changing, when the Father
of my Lover afk'd Monfieur *De G*————if he had
given Orders we fhou'd not be interrupted, to which the
other anfwering that he had, it is well purfued he, then
turning to me, fpoke in the following Terms.

The Time is now come, my dear *Jeanetta*, faid he,
to put an End to all your Troubles, and to crown your
Virtue.————I muft acknowledge that your Beauty,
and your Wit merit a Fortune fuperior, to that which you
are going to enjoy; but yet thefe Qualities would never
have gain'd upon me to decide in your Favour ; it is
the Proofs you have given me of your Virtue, and a certain Majefty of Sentiment, which I could never have
imagin'd in you, without the Tryals you have been put
to————fevere in the enduring, I confefs, but glorious in
the End ————What thefe Proofs, or thefe Tryals were
are yet a Secret to you; but I will now explain all.————I
knew the Paffion you had for my Son, as well as the Excefs of his for you;————but I knew not whether you
were worthy of the one or the other, or whether either
of you were worthy of my Approbation, of your
mutual Defires, to prove you firft, I therefore affumed
the Lover, omitted nothing that I thought might gain
your

your Favour, I went so far as to offer to marry you, in order to discover whether a certain present Establishment, might not tempt you to forego one altogether uncertain, and which according to the Sentiments I seem'd possest of, you had little Reason to hope would ever be your Io:.———I could not suffer a Son for whom I had so great Affection, should run the Risque of marrying a Woman, who had only Grandeur for her Aim, in engaging his Heart, and this was the Method I took to penetrate into the inmost Recesses of yours.———My Search discover'd even more than I could conceive of Fidelity, Tenderness, and Sincerity, and from that, I set you down as worthy of him, as his considering your intrinsic Merit, without any Regard to Birth or Fortune, render'd him worthy of you.

All that now remain'd, continued he, was to discover if this Son, so much beloved by me, deserv'd I should sacrifice for his Contentment, all Memory of my Rank, and all Regard for public Censure, in consenting to a Match of such Disparity in Point of Blood, and this I thought could be done by nothing, but his being willing to resign all that was dear to him in Life, for my sake. ———Had *Forsan* succeeded in his Endeavours of finding where you were conceal'd, I should have begun this Tryal by obliging my Son to confess the Truth, and deliver you into my Hands, and this would have saved both of you the many Dangers you have run; but Heaven, that has punish'd my Presumption in attempting to fathom like itself the Hearts of Men, after threatning to deprive me of my Son, has been pleased to restore him to me, and also preserve a Treasure for him, with which his very Life was wound up, and which was ever destin'd to be his.

My next Stratagem, dear *Jeanetta*, was that pretended Fit of Sickness, which every one imagin'd to be real ————How, my Lord, cry'd the young Marquis, kissing his Father's Hand, is it possible the cruel Condition in which you seem'd, should be no more than counterfeited? No more, indeed, reply'd the Marquis, but let me proceed, and every thing shall be made clear.

I think, pursued he, I acted the part of a sick Man naturally enough, nor was it difficult for me to make it believed, as I would have it; *Forsan*, whom I had taken

into

into Favour again, on the Service he had done me, in getting your Letter intercepted, was let into the Secret, as was also my Physician, and two Valets-de-Chamber, as these were the only People who came much about me, it was easy with their Assistance to impose on the rest of the Family——The Event answered my most sanguine Wishes; and by sacrificing your Love to me, have prov'd, you merit that I should sacrifice all the Scruples that might oppose your Happiness——Nor, added this excellent Nobleman, addressing himself to me, was I less satisfied with your complying with my Son's Request, in so tender and trying a particular——Immediately had both your Virtues been rewarded——you were just going to be united, when Nature too powerful for your generous Resolution, retarded your Happiness——one Moment more, and my Son had been in Possession of that Hand, you thought yourself about bestowing upon me——your fainting away, the Sickness which ensued, prevented the pleasing Surprise I had prepar'd for you. Oh! how severely did I then repent, my not discovering myself sooner.

But Heaven, whom I never ceased imploring, in Mercy has restored you to me, and gives me the Power to finish what I have begun——Approach, my dear Son, continued he, taking me by the Hand, receive from me that *Jeanetta*, for whom you so long have sighed ——by yielding you have gained her, and in her a Jewel, you can never set too great a Value on.

Never were Agitations equal to mine at that Instant ——my Joy was so great it even became painful—— My Heart was full, and my Eyes poured out my Transport——the old Marquis himself dropt a Tear, Monsieur and Madam *De G*—— with generous *Saint Fal*, joyned in this affecting Scene ——my Lover could not speak, but we both fell at the Feet of him, whom we now look'd upon as more than a Father.

Rise, my dear Children, said he, I am truly happy in what I have done——but yet this is not all that Prudence requires, every one ought to have some regard to the World——I have concerted Measures so, as to keep the Extraction of *Jeanetta* a Secret——we that know her, know her to be greater in her Qualifications than any Birth could make her, but considering what Slaves we are

are

are to Prejudice, I think it Policy to impose on those of my own Rank, and pretend her descended of a Race, which has no Existence, but in my own Invention.

In fine, I have made every thing ready for the Celebration of your Nuptials—The Contract you both sign'd, and has cost so many Tears, is drawn in your Names ————so, my dear Child, said he to me smiling, you see I did not forget my Son, the Uneasiness you exprest on the Account of a Provision for him, was without foundation, but you may remember, I then told you we should all be satisfied, and I think I have kept my Word. ————I have nothing now more to inform you of, than that as soon as I found you were recovered, I came to these worthy Friends, and related to them the whole Affair; but I enjoyned Secrecy, because I was willing to be the first, from whom you should receive the News of your Happiness.

Thus ended the Marquis his obliging Speech, fain would I have given Vent to the Extacy of my Soul, in the most tender and grateful Acknowledgements, but Modesty restrained my Tongue ———— not so my Lover, he threw himself twenty times at his Father's Feet, kiss'd his Hands as often, and seemed even wild, with Gratitude and Joy——After some time spent in Acknowledgements on our Parts, and Congratulations on the other, the Marquis told me, that my Father and Mother were in the House, he having desired Monsieur *De G—* to send for them, in order to be Witnesses of my Marriage, tho' as yet they knew not on what Occasion they were invited ; but gave me to understand, they must return no more to their Cottage, it being not consistent with the Measures he had taken of concealing who I really was ————they shall not be Losers by it, said he with a Smile, I will give you my Estate *De F————A————,* which is an hundred Miles off, and will bring you in twenty thousand Livres a Year————you shall live there with them, and your Husband, 'till I find a proper time to have you nearer me ; but your Parents shall remain there, and enjoy it for their whole Lives, and that will be an Attonement for quitting their native Place————you'll have time enough to instruct them, in
your

your Journey, how to behave : it is not very difficult to assume an Air of Eafe, when one is really at eafe.

How excellently good was this !——how greatly did this worthy Nooleman requite all my Sufferings on his Account ! but if I should attempt to speak my Gratitude, it would be impofing a Tafk upon myfelf, which I should never be able to perform, and I have often thought, that it is on fuch Occafions, that we are truly fenfible, how infufficient the Organs of the Body, are to reprefent the Ideas of the Soul.

Hitherto I never had Courage to own to the old Marquis that *Barbara* was my Aunt, but the Profufion of Kindnefs he now treated me with, emboldened me to it ; on which he faid, I am glad of it, we fhall make one more Perfon happy.

This dear and worthy Father of myLover, informed us alfo, for before he had not Time to do it, for Subjects more interefting, that he had retained in his Service, only thofe who attended him in his pretended Sicknefs, and difcarded the others to prevent Difcovery——I have difmiffed *Forfan* too, faid he, becaufe he once was impertinent, and exceeded his Commiffion, but have provided fo well for him, that he has no Reafon to complain.

My Happinefs was too perfect to admit of Refentment, and I interceeded with fo much Eagernefs, that he might be admitted to partake of the common Joy, that he was again received into the Family, and as I have fpoke of his ill Behaviour,'tis but juft in me to fay,that after hewas fo, he never gave any Caufe for Difcontent.

Madam *De G*—— perceivingevery thing was fettled, reminded us of going to Supper : every one feem'd ready to agree to her Propofal, the Satisfaction of the Heart generally gives a good Appetite——'tho I dare anfwer, that till fhe fpoke, the young Marquis, any more than myfelf, never once thought of it————as we fat at Table, I could read Impatience in his Eyes, perhaps too mine fpoke the fame Language. I have in the beginning of thefe Memoirs promifed Sincerity, and have always maintained it, I will not therefore in the Con-
                                                          clufion

clufion deviate : 'tis certain I longed to have my Happinefs compleated, nor is it to be wondered at, fince I had experienced too many Difappointments to be fecure of any thing till I had it in poffeffion ; but bleffed be Heaven they were now all over, and all ill Fortune quite forfook me.

When Supper was ended, I flew to my Apartment, where my Father, Mother, and Aunt attended to fpeak with me, tho' they little thought on what Bufinefs,——I prefently difcovered myfelf to them, fell at their Feet, entreated their Forgivenefs that I had deceived them by a fictitious Name, acquainted them with my Reafons for fo doing, and the Honour I was at laft raifed to—Tears and Embraces could alone exprefs their Joy,—my Mother, preffing my Cheeks clofe to hers, cryed, Heaven be praifed—I told them in two Words what was intended for them, and then propofed to my dear Aunt, who could hardly be perfuaded I was her Neice, either to accompany us, or return to her beloved Village, offering her my Father's Houfe, and Money to buy a Piece of Land to it———No, no, my dear Neice, cryed fhe, fince Providence has ordained it to be fo, I am for no Village, when you are not there———you faw I quitted it to follow you, when I little thought the fame Blood ran in both our Veins, and do you think I'll ever leave you now———Befides your Affairs are to be a Secret, and I wont fo far deceive you as to fay, I could keep myfelf from telling the whole Story to every Body, at leaft to the Curate, and then I am fure it would foon go through the Parifh. I could not forbear fmiling at her honeft Simplicity ; but begged fhe would neverthelefs be on her Guard for my fake ; her Reply was, that I had nothing to fear, provided fhe kept out of her Village, as I had experienced in the Time fhe had lived with me.

It cannot be fuppofed, that any of us, efpecially myfelf, flept much that Night———Excefs of Joy is as great an Enemy to Repofe, as Excefs of Grief—all my paft Sufferings occurred to my Remembrance, and heightened the Idea of that Happinefs, I was going to enjoy———the whole Family to whom I had been always

ways

ways dear, partook in my Felicity, and were up much before the ufual Hour————*Chriſtina* came into my Chamber, to affiſt me in dreſſing for the ſacred Ceremony ——my Mother and Aunt followed her, but I had ſcarce got my Cloaths on, when the impatient Marquis ran up Stairs, and cryed, through the Key-Hole, every thing is ready my Angel——they wait for you. The Door being opened to him, he flew to me and taking me in his Arms, kiſs'd me with ſuch an eagerneſs, as made me bluſh to Death, after this he ſaluted my Mother and Aunt with great Tenderneſs, calling them by thoſe affectionate Names, and then turning to me, cried, what is it we ſtay for now ? his abrupt Eagerneſs made me ſmile, and giving him my Hand, he led me to the great Drawing-Room. The old Marquis, Monſieur and Madam *De G—*, with the Count *De Saint Fal*, and my Father received us, and conducted us to the Chappel, where before the holy Altar thoſe Vows were made, which are never to be broke, and which my dear Marquis continues to aſſure me, he no more than myſelf, ever once repented of, that charming Ceremony, authorizing the moſt paſſionate Endearments, they are laſting as they are great.

The old Marquis's Scheme for concealing my Extraction was punctually put in Execution, and tho' there were many inquiſitive, and buſy Tongues, employed concerning our Marriage, their Diſcourſe made no Impreſſion to diſturb our Peace——Entirely taken up with our own Happineſs, all foreign Objects are unworthy our Attention ————Two Sons and a Daughter, are the Fruits of our mutual Loves ; amidſt the great World, 'tis in my own Family I find my Pride and Pleaſure, my dear Marquis even more, if poſſible, my *Lover*, ſince he became my *Huſband*, joins with me in paternal Fondneſs, and altogether we enjoy that true Felicity, which only Virtue can beſtow, and only virtuous Minds be capable of receiving.————O, may our Example have many Imitators, and all who purſue the ſame Methods, be attended with the ſame Bleſſings !

FINIS.